# A CHANGE OF SEASON

# A CHANGE OF SEASON

## SUZANNE GOODWIN

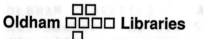

Michael Joseph
LONDON

## MICHAEL JOSEPH LTD

Published by the Penguin Group
27 Wrights Lane, London W8 5TZ, England
Viking Penguin Inc., 375 Hudson Street, New York, New York 10014, USA
Penguin Books Australia Ltd, Ringwood, Victoria, Australia
Penguin Books Canada Ltd, 2801 John Street, Markham, Ontario, Canada L3R 1B4
Penguin Books (NZ) Ltd, 182–190 Wairau Road, Auckland 10, New Zealand

Penguin Books Ltd, Registered Offices: Harmondsworth, Middlesex, England

First published 1991

Copyright © Suzanne Goodwin, 1991

Typeset in Monophoto Lasercomp $11/12\frac{1}{2}$ pt Ehrhardt
Printed in England by Clays Ltd, St Ives plc

A CIP catalogue record for this book
is available from the British Library
ISBN 0 7181 3354 4

# PART ONE

# 1

It was an odd place to land up. But as Lisa's brother Charles remarked, it was tremendous luck to have the flat at all. One of his friends who had been in the same regiment with the Fourteenth Army in Burma, a pleasant young Scot, was on their ship. He was returning home too. 'A generous chap, always was,' said Charles when Andrew McAllister suggested they should borrow his London flat for a spell.

'Now I'm demobbed I'm going up to see my parents in Newcastle. I'll probably stay at least three months, they're hankering to see their only son,' said McAllister. 'Do have the flat, both of you. I'd be glad to think somebody is living there.' He gave Lisa a friendly grin. He was attracted to her and at the party on their last night on board said, 'How about a kiss as rent in advance?'

The flat in the Cromwell Road turned out to be a cheerless high-ceilinged apartment, shabby and cold. During the war it had been let sometimes, sub-let now and again, and often left empty. Lisa found traces of previous occupants. Bills. A Royal Engineer's button. A cardboard box crammed with little packets of pre-war book matches from Mayfair hotels: Claridge's, the Carlton Club, The Ritz. Whoever had collected them had spent money in expensive places. There was also a fragrant, empty cigar-box. And a bottle of Chanel No. 5 with a few drops of scent left.

Charles was in good spirits during the long sea voyage back to England, amused by the novelty of their return. But

Lisa was dubious. They were as rootless as refugees. And when they arrived, London was filthy and battered and a shock.

That evening the weather forecast on the wireless said there would be snow, and by four on the dark January afternoon the flakes were floating down from skies which seemed to be resting on the chimney-pots. Lisa had been shopping. Her recently acquired ration books were a second shock: there seemed nothing to buy now at the start of 1948. She and her brother had come from the Far East where if you were ingenious and British you could sometimes get luxuries for little. Scented tea. Fruit. Whisky. Everything in England was rationed: milk and soap, sugar and butter, tea, bacon, and clothes. The meat allowed to each person was exactly eight pennies' worth a week. Lisa walked back from the Earl's Court Road in the sharp cold with a frugal basket of food over her arm.

At least we're *home*, she thought, using the word thousands upon thousands of British people scattered across the Empire had used for two hundred years. Charles is alive, not dead in the Burmese jungle. I'm alive, not buried in a Calcutta cemetery. We have each other.

She worried just the same because her brother did not.

Where does Charles get his carefree attitudes from, she thought, especially about money? Not from our father, that's for sure. She recalled her dead father's pursed face and the dry kiss he gave her when they said goodbye ten years ago. When she thought of him, which was rarely, she still had a sensation which was half resentment and half an unwilling affection. There was no answer to questions about him, and there never could be.

Trailing up the dim-lit stairs of a house built for the glory and prosperity of 1851, Lisa opened the flat's front door. She went into the drawing-room. A hundred years ago it had been filled with people, with bulkily dressed, frock-coated men, billowing, crinolined women, maiden aunts, stout children. There had been tables loaded with albums, vases of pampas grasses, oil or gas lamps glowing and sputtering, a coal fire so huge that ladies used fans to protect their complexions. Now across an acre of stained oak boards one threadbare Persian mat floated and a one-bar electric fire was doing its best.

Charles was sprawling in the only comfortable chair. He stood up as she came in.

'There you are,' he said, taking her basket. 'You'll be surprised to hear I've made the tea.'

When she picked up the pot it was cold and she knew he must have made it half an hour ago. She said tactfully that she'd get some hot water and carried the tray out to the kitchen. She never discouraged her brother's fantasies. While she was making fresh tea, he switched on the wireless and a voice began encouragingly singing about Blue Birds Over the White Cliffs of Dover.

Charles looked delighted when she came back with tea and toast. He waited to be served, remarking 'What a little mother you are.'

Brother and sister had only a slight resemblance. Both had thick, dark hair, not well cut or cared for. Lisa wore hers longer than was fashionable. It framed a small, sallow face, large-eyed, with a chin like a kitten's. She looked interesting and at times nervous and when she laughed there was a look of Charles. He was the more remarkable, more noticeable, more everything. He was lean rather than thin, his face lined for a man only just past thirty. Tall, six foot two, he had a graceful ease about him, an ironic, pleasure-loving air. Lisa spoiled him. So did most women.

'I've got some news,' he said.

'Good?'

'I think so. An old mate from Burma rang me just now, name of Jeff Ingoldsby. Apparently he found our number from Andrew McAllister who popped into the United Services Club before he went to Newcastle. Jeff asked if he could come round for a drink this evening. I said alas, not a drop of alcohol in the house. So he said he'd bring some sherry.'

'I'm glad about the sherry.'

5

'You'll be glad about Jeff too, he'll make you laugh. A bit facetious, but no harm in that. One of those cheerful souls.'

'What does he look like?' She was faintly interested.

'Thin. His bones stick out. The last time I saw him when we were in Rangoon after VJ Day, I remember thinking he looked like a walking skeleton. Dysentery does that.'

'Poor Jeff Ingoldsby.'

'Not really. He happens to be rather rich. Used to tell us so, which some of the chaps thought a bore. But a cheerful soul and ate like a horse.'

Lisa was pleased that somebody was calling to see them; it meant Charles would stay at home this evening. They had been here in London for two weeks now and Charles was out so much she knew he had begun to gamble. Her brother's gambling was part of him, like his thin, haggard face and brown eyes. He was clever at cards – poker was his game and he played it with skill. He sometimes won a great deal, and often lost more than he admitted. Lisa did not understand – she never had – the gambling passion. One of her friends in Calcutta had called it 'the adventurer in every man'.

That was all very well, but suppose you couldn't control it? Charles laughed when she said that, and assured her that he always could.

At present she was in no position to lecture him about anything. It was one of Charles's friends, from past poker games in the Army, who had lent them the flat without which they would be homeless. It was Charles, using what he had saved from his pay, from poker and the remainder of a small inheritance from their uncle, who was keeping them both. He had paid McAllister the rent in advance, and he now doled out – he disliked paying money for food – Lisa's meagre housekeeping. As for Lisa's own finances, all she had in the world was ten pounds hidden in her underclothes. She kept the money for an emergency – whatever that might be – and never took it into any calculations. The ten one-pound notes, much creased, remained in an envelope among her French knickers.

As soon as they had settled into the flat, Charles began to

go out to some club or other. He was a stranger in London – she couldn't imagine how he discovered these places – but he had a knack of getting whatever he wanted. He often returned home late in the evening, sometimes wearing a certain expression which she recognized. A lazy look, mostly about his eyelids. That was when she knew he'd been winning.

'Not such a bad old place, is it, Lou?' he would say, regarding the vast drawing-room, the minute electric fire, his sister on the floor beside it, and the wireless playing. 'Buy us something decent for supper tomorrow.' He would give her a pound note.

I don't see how I can go on at him when his money is all we have, she thought. Until we can get work of some sort – but doing what?

It was dark and everywhere outside the radius of the fire was penetratingly cold. Charles was reading the evening paper. Determinedly optimistic dance music thumped through the flat. Lisa had a moment of longing. To go somewhere expensive, to one of the hotels named on the book matches perhaps, wearing clothes like those on the cover of *Vogue*. To flirt with a man who thought her fascinating. She felt like a plant thirsting for water. What about Jeff Ingoldsby? Perhaps he would be nice and become a friend, she thought. She went into yet another enormous, high-ceilinged room – her bedroom – to do her hair. It was six o'clock and she could hear the news from Charles's wireless. Once again, it was about the partition of India, divisions of great bitterness between Pandit Nehru and Sarar Patel, the massacre of tens of thousands of people, Hindus and Moslems alike.

She shuddered. She'd lived for six years in India, it had become *her* country, she had loved it and broken her heart there. Now the news was drenched in blood . . .

The front doorbell rang. Charles sprang up. 'Good, that's Jeff.'

Her door was ajar. She heard her brother greeting the visitor, and an unfamiliar voice replying. There were

7

exclamations, 'My dear chap!' and 'It's been an age!' and, after mutters, a burst of masculine laughter. She gave herself a hopeful glance in the looking-glass on the wall, and saw a girl in a navy-blue sweater with a line of dull pink stars across the shoulders, a skirt which had seen better days and scuffed shoes.

When she walked into the drawing-room, the two men stood up and Charles introduced her. 'Jeff. Here's my little sister.'

'Delighted,' boomed the visitor, energetically shaking her hand.

Where was the skeleton from Rangoon? He had plump, ruddy cheeks, the beginnings of a double chin, a Dickensian curve to his stomach. His face was freckled and radiated cheerfulness. He seemed the right size for the enormous room and with a merry 'look what the doctor ordered', began to unwrap a bottle from a twist of paper and set it on the table. There was much fetching of glasses, pouring out, sipping and compliments. The sherry tasted good.

'I remember Charles talking about you at Tamu,' said Jeff to Lisa. 'We'd found a camp site, not half bad. Next day we swam in the river, and some Burmese kids gave us fresh limes to eat with the fish we'd caught. Charles talked about your letters. He quite looked forward to them.'

'I'm glad to hear it,' said Lisa.

He missed her tone of voice but Charles didn't. 'They were wonderful. I used to read out the amusing bits, didn't I, Jeff?'

'Extraordinarily good value,' agreed the visitor.

From the moment he entered the room, Lisa had given up any idea that he would ask her out. The sherry was warming her like central heating; she settled down to listen while the men dived into shop talk. She did not dislike the role of onlooker. Charles's friends accepted her and she often stayed silent. She didn't interrupt, exclaim, try to make her mark and have an effect as many women did. Lisa never said without saying it, 'Look at me. I'm attractive, am I not? Pay attention.' She was content to be with her brother and listen to him talking to his friends.

She didn't know why, but this evening she was not as comfortable as usual. She wasn't quite sure what she thought about the one-time skeleton, now fat as butter, dispensing the sherry. He was very nice to Charles and somewhat facetiously attentive to herself but something seemed to have arrived with Ingoldsby which bothered her. Was it that for all his loud laugh and old jokes he was unhappy? Many people were nowadays. Peace had not brought plenty, but only different kinds of anxiety. The future was no longer a rising sun on a Ministry of Information poster. Whatever it was that she sensed about Jeff Ingoldsby she began to wish inhospitably that he would go.

'I saw Bill Dunkley at the club a couple of nights ago,' Ingoldsby remarked. 'He tells me he's going into farming.'

Charles looked dubious. 'Will that be a success? If I remember rightly, Dunkley's speciality was filling in forms and droning about Army regulations. A born desk clerk. I can't imagine him up in the morning at four, busy in the cow-shed.'

Ingoldsby laughed but Lisa saw that her brother's unwillingness to exclaim 'Good show' at anything and everything was an embarrassment.

'We all have to change gear, my dear chap. Socialists in power and all that. You must be finding one or two changes yourself.'

'Oh sure,' said Charles, who had begun to think the visitor a bore.

Ingoldsby continued to be jovial. 'Talking of changing gear, my news will surprise you. Where do you think I'm going next week? To Bristol University. Yes, all set to become an undergraduate, ha ha!'

Charles brightened at a chance to tease. 'I hope you've bought yourself some bicycle clips. Otherwise you'll get those smart trousers covered in oil. Only one means of transport at university, you know. You're going to need a lot of practice.' Charles gave his visitor's bulky figure an unmistakable up-and-down look.

Ingoldsby, either impervious or unobservant, agreed; he

9

would buy a good bicycle directly upon arrival in Bristol. 'I shall enjoy spinning along.'

'Spinning down and toiling up. Bristol's built on steep hills. What subjects are you reading?'

'My favourites: modern languages.'

'Really, Jeff? You're as full of surprises as Bill Dunkley. *Tu, aap bohut zaban bolte ho, sahib*?'

'What on earth are you talking about?'

'I merely said "so, you speak many languages, sir' in Hindi. Tut, tut, Jeff.'

'No, no, European languages – French and German,' corrected Ingoldsby with a hearty laugh.

Lisa glanced at her brother, wondering when he was going to notice the growing tension. Charles looked his usual teasing self.

Ingoldsby continued to talk. Did they know about the special arrangements for returning officers to go to university? His parents were delighted. Just what they'd dreamed for him, particularly his father. 'Naturally they'll have to pull in their horns. Scrape about for the wherewithal while I'm a student.' His tone grew heartier. 'So – just one little thing to clear up. The matter of a certain sum you owe me, my dear chap.'

Charles was surprised. 'Do I? I don't remember that.'

'I'm sure you don't. Jove, it's nearly three years ago, I feel quite guilty for reminding you. But do you recall some poker we played at Tamu? Quite a session. Lisa, we went on into the wee small hours and I was on a winning streak. Didn't seem able to play a bad card. But then your brother –'

Charles slapped his forehead with the back of his hand. 'Good grief, I remember! You'd been winning all evening but then I really thought I had you at last with my three queens . . . no, wasn't it a full house and nines and sixes?'

'Sevens.'

'Well, whatever it was. I just couldn't believe it when you produced four threes. That was six months of my pay up the spout.'

'Hard luck, it was certainly hard luck,' agreed Jeff, taking out his wallet. It was made of pigskin with gold clasps and looked as if it had been bought yesterday. 'Here's a relic from our good old Army days.' He passed Charles a scrap of paper.

Charles unfolded it and whistled. 'I did go a bundle, didn't I? Would you prefer cash?'

'My dear fellow, a cheque will do perfectly well. You don't suppose I don't trust you, for heaven's sake.'

'Oh, cash is simpler,' said Charles, going out of the room.

Ingoldsby turned to Lisa. 'You can always tell the real sporting man, you know. He loses so well.'

She smiled and said nothing.

Charles came back carrying a worn-out wallet, sat down and counted the money out on to the table. The five-pound notes, thin as tissue paper, rustled as Charles placed them one on top of the other. Forty of them. Lisa guessed that they must be his recent winnings. What an enormous sum of money . . .

Ingoldsby picked them up in a bundle and thrust them untidily into his trouser pocket. 'Thanks, old boy. Any time you want your revenge, let me know.'

'I'll keep you to that,' said Charles with a smile.

'Well, well, I'm afraid I must love you and leave you. The parents are buying me a slap-up dinner in Soho before I turn into a schoolboy again.' He stood up, the fatter, thought Lisa, for her brother's money. He said goodbye to them both and Charles walked with him to the front door, talking pleasantly. The door shut with a slight slam.

Charles returned, rubbing his nose.

'Of all the pigs!' Lisa burst out. 'Calmly appearing here when you haven't seen him for ages –'

'Three years, actually.'

'Three years! And coolly asks you for that colossal sum!' She was so furious with Ingoldsby that she forgot Charles's own part in the fiasco. She was alarmed, and anger was a release. She was practically spitting. 'He didn't even ask if you could afford it, or suggest you could pay it back in instalments. *A pig*. That suit he was wearing must have cost

11

a fortune, it looked brand new to me, and what does he *mean*, his parents would have to scrape together to help him at University? I thought you said he was rich. I bet he's rolling. Oh, how could he! How could he! It's awful,' she wailed.

Charles listened with mixed feelings. She touched him. She often did and there were times when the satisfactions of sex or the intense emotion and thrill of gambling faded, and his love for this small, angry sister seemed the only real thing in his life.

'Don't get so upset, Lou. Of course he wanted to be paid. He must have been pretty chuffed when he managed to find out where I was living. It was fair enough to turn up and ask for the cash. I'd have done the same thing.'

'Of course you wouldn't.'

'Poker games aren't exactly your subject, are they?'

Her blow-torch of anger turned on him. 'Gambling's horrible. I hate it.'

'My dear woman, I played poker with Ingoldsby in 1945, for God's sake! I told you recently I now play for lower stakes, and that's true. But don't start rampaging because he appeared and scooped the pool with an IOU that's three years old. I must say it was a surprise he'd kept it so long. Most people chuck them away after a while.'

'Have *you* got any?'

'Any what?'

'IOUs.'

'Probably. Somewhere or other. Not three-year-old ones, though.'

She looked sallower because she was upset. 'What do you mean, "probably"? So people owe *you* money, then?'

'Sometimes. It's the luck of the thing.'

'Do they pay?'

'Of course they do. Lord, girl, we've been through this boring subject before. I know I shouldn't play too high, but neither should you behave like a lass in the Salvation Army. As it happens, I haven't actually seen anyone put down more than a fiver in a game since I came home. And as for me . . . there, does that put your mind at rest?'

12

He gave her a grin. He was relieved that his sister hadn't yet demanded to know the state of their finances now that Ingoldsby had gone off with so much cash. Fortunately, Lisa was at a tangent.

'If men owe you money, I don't see why you don't march into their houses and get it,' she said.

Charles sighed, and at that moment the electric fire, which worked on a meter, gave a loud click and went out. In the way of lofty Victorian salons meant for coal fires lit by servants at seven in the morning and piled high all day long, the room at once grew freezing cold. Lisa went to look for sixpences and came back with two. She knelt down, put them into the meter slot and switched down the handle. The fire obligingly glowed orange, lighting her face and the dark curtain of her hair. Looking at his sister Charles felt a stab of pity. He was never sorry for himself.

'You didn't answer my question, Charles.'

'About not claiming old IOUs, supposing I had any? No, I wouldn't. The games were then, not now. Some of the chaps are dead, now I come to think about it. Quite a lot of them . . .' That shut her up for the time being. He sat watching her as she knelt by the fire. 'You mustn't be so tragic because he waltzed off with some booty. Plenty more where –'

'*Don't say that, I can't bear it!*'

'My dear girl! It's not desperate. It's never as bad as you imagine.'

'Isn't it? Isn't it?' She sprang up, went to the sofa and crouched down like an animal in hiding. 'Charles.'

'What is it now?'

'How much have we got left?'

Ah, he thought. Here it comes. 'I haven't counted since the departure of my fellow officer.'

'Tell me the truth.'

He grimaced, took out his wallet and produced two pound notes.

'And what's in the bank?'

'Not much more than a tenner, I fear,' he said casually.

Lisa was too appalled to speak. She thought: what's to become of us? We're untrained and penniless, landed in this freezing country everybody calls home. And the only person I have in the world is a brother who gambles away our future.

She climbed off the sofa and ran out of the room, slamming her bedroom door and locking it. Charles went after her. He knocked, laughing, and knocked again, saying comforting things. She shouted, 'Go away. I won't talk to you. *Leave me alone.*'

Silence followed.

Lying in bed, shivering more with anger than cold, she hated her brother just then. That's how our father felt about him, she thought. She had never understood it until now. She knew perfectly well she was being unjust to feel angry with him over a disaster which dated back to the war, to the years when they were parted, to long before she had dragged promises from him. She was furious because she was afraid. It was an inescapable fact that he wasted money, had always wasted it because he loved cards at which, people had told her, he was a brilliant if erratic player. She had once read a poem which described Charles:

> He either fears his fate too much
> Or his deserts are small,
> That dares not put it to the touch
> To win or lose it all.

That trait, that vice, had been with him since he was a child. Once she had heard her father talking to her mother. He had said in his prissy voice, 'The boy's a throwback to your uncle. It's his Irish blood.'

Her mother had burst out laughing, and answered that he was exaggerating. Why, all Charles did was to play bridge at school, 'and don't all the boys love a good game and a bit of a shout at each other? Anyway, Charles always wins.'

It was their mother's excuses which sustained Charles during his boyhood. Lisa used to hear them laughing together about his winnings, and laughing more when he lost.

14

Their mother had died suddenly of a burst appendix, when Lisa was scarcely fourteen. Her loss was impossible to grasp. During one week there she was, laughing and talking in her pretty, lilting voice, making plans, kissing Lisa; then – she was gone. After the first stunned weeks of grief, all Lisa's life began to centre on her brother. She adored him. He was five years older than she was, but he always treated her as an equal. He was so tall – she was little. He began to take her about and introduced her to his friends who dazzled her with their camaraderie; in a way they made a pet of her. It was a golden time for a motherless girl.

The family lived just outside Stratford-on-Avon. Alec Whitfield was county born and bred; he would at one time have been called petty gentry. He was a reserved man with none of his son's masculine beauty and dash. His wife had been Irish and pretty, and had come from a family made poor through waywardness – love of horses, love of drink. She bequeathed her good looks to her children and perhaps his vice to Charles. It was a convenient theory but Lisa did not accept it. Surely what you inherited from your parents, your ancestors, was a propensity, a bent, a leaning towards this taste or that. If there was a flaw in your character you didn't have to let it rip. Lisa herself liked extravagance, enjoyed splashing money about, giving presents and – a bad habit – promising to do things for people. That could have turned out to be as much of a vice as Charles's gambling if the promises were later forgotten. Why be so keen to appear generous? She asked herself if it was plain vanity. But it wasn't until she had been sent to Calcutta to live and work that she was forced to control her desire to waste money showily, learning at the same time to hold her tongue when wanting to promise somebody the more flamboyant gift of her time.

The cavernous room stretched above her. Outside the windows was the old, cruel city, with bombed squares and blackened ruins, shortages and rationing and food queues, and faces pale with weariness. She felt beleaguered. She guessed her brother was still in the sitting-room, reading by

15

what was left of the shillingsworth of electricity, relaxed and absorbed. Later he would put down his book and simply stare at nothing; how could he be so unphased, as the Americans would say?

Her anger faded into helplessness; she could rarely hold out against Charles for long. She loved him, and she owed him something which had been more important than anything else that had happened in her life. Something vast which had brought her sorrow but which she wouldn't be without and could never forget.

After their mother died, things never went well between father and son. There was no bright face, no coaxing voice speaking to Alec Whitfield with the confidence of beauty.

'Will you be after listening to me, dear man?' Or to her son, 'If you don't swear by Our Lady to do what I say, Charles, won't I cut off your head?'

Bernadette had been an Irish Catholic. Her religion was the strongest part of her; she took it for granted, leaned on it and made jokes about it. It was round her, like scent. Yet the paradox was that she brought up neither of her children in her own faith. Alec Whitfield persuaded her somehow, when they first fell in love and she was at her most vulnerable, that his children must be reared in *his* church, the Church of England. Convinced of sin, Bernadette wept a good deal. But her nature had no Irish fight, only Irish kindness and she gave in. When she was alone with the children, she made inefficient allusions to their becoming Catholics. 'You'll both come into the True Faith in the end,' she would say. Hopefully.

With Bernadette gone, with no dashing off noisily to Mass on Sundays, no rosary hung round a picture or a doorknob, the house was hideously quiet. Lisa, slowly mending, was sent to boarding school near Warwick. Her sad face upset her father, who disliked her arriving home every day with no mother to wait for and run out into the drive, help with her homework and shout with ignorant laughter. Lisa was alarmed at the idea of boarding school, and was soon plunged into an ordered and entertaining life of close friendships and

16

small wars, of fierce tennis matches and boring lacrosse, of history, English, the lure of poetry, the puzzle of mathematics. The book of learning opened and the book of childhood slammed shut.

But the holidays were very bad. Charles and his father avoided each other as much as possible, or there were bitter arguments. When Charles wasn't out with his friends and Lisa, he was bored, falling into fits of idleness which Lisa grew to fear. Then he wouldn't read or ride, but simply sit in the garden in summer or by the fire in winter, staring into nothing. In a day or two he would suddenly rouse himself, telephone his friends and drive off to parties in a borrowed car.

Alec Whitfield refused to buy his son even a cheap, second-hand car. He begrudged him his allowance at Oxford, suspecting that Charles was gambling. Of course he was, he always had. As a child with conkers on pieces of string and the jeering challenge 'bet yours isn't as tough as mine'. At prep school playing loud-voiced snap. Bridge and billiards at public school. Then at Oxford play became serious. It was in his third year, when Charles was twenty-two, that the worst happened.

It was early February. There was a cool sun on some days, warm rain on others, and the snowdrops in the orchard were in thick clumps. Charles came up to the old playroom which Lisa now used as a place to tackle her none-too-brilliant homework. She was trying for Higher Certificate without much enthusiasm, mostly because her friend Polly Holt looked as if she would pass with flying colours. Charles put his face around the playroom door.

'Busy?'

'I'm trying to write my essay on Cardinal Newman.'

'Then you aren't busy.'

He lounged across the room and sat down on a window-seat which had a hinged lid, covering the toy cupboard where Lisa used to keep her animals, games, toyshops, ludo. Now it held chipped croquet mallets and balls which had lost most of their reds and blues and yellows.

17

Putting down her pen, Lisa looked at him expectantly. Charles coming to look for her invariably meant some kind of invitation. He was staring thoughtfully at Rory, the old rocking-horse who stood in his place in the corner of the room. Rory had been bought for Charles by his mother. The horse had been passed on to Lisa in due course, and she had proudly ridden him for years. Now Rory stood motionless . . . waiting for other children to creak him into life. His mane fell on his forehead but no small hands combed it. His tail was getting rather thin. Lisa saw that her brother was looking at the rocking-horse and estimating the strength of the wooden back.

'Do you still ride him, Lou?'

'Don't be an idiot.'

'You once told me when you were on Rory you could rock yourself into a better mood.'

'Did I? Well, not necessary now. I'm fine.'

He gave her an odd look. 'Why have you gone all red?'

'Have I?' She put her hands to her cheeks. 'I don't know. You scare me sometimes. You're –'

'What am I?'

'Enigmatic.'

He gave a hoot of laughter. He enjoyed her admiration, although his friends told him it was bad to have an adoring younger sister.

'I believe I do alarm you. That's nice.'

'Only if I think there'll be ructions with Dad.'

'You're not scared of *him*, surely?'

She frowned. 'I loathe the rows. You get so sarcastic and he goes all thin in the face. And then I keep wishing and wishing Mother was alive.'

'Only then?' He had loved their mother.

Lisa didn't answer and didn't want to.

'Fathers and sons mostly do row,' he remarked, examining his well-kept hands. The negligent voice soothed her, her cheeks returned to their natural pallor. She sat looking at him, wondering as she always did why there were lines on his young face, and if they were an accident of birth, and why they were attractive. How full-lipped his mouth was.

18

Stretching out his hand, he set Rory rocking to and fro. 'You mentioned ructions. That's what I came to tell you. We've just had an almighty one. The worst, one might say, to date.'

His sister's face spoke, though she said nothing.

'Poor Lou, I'm a beast to worry you. I don't mean to, but you have to know sooner or later. Father's just heard about my beastly debts. Thirty quid. More, actually. Jack Seward's father wrote and told him, can you beat it? Demanding that the money be paid pronto, and adding some cock-and-bull story about Jack having had to pawn his overcoat. To my certain knowledge Jack doesn't know the way to the pop shop, and what's more he's got a fat account at the post office, lucky beggar. I can't tell you how Father went on. You'd have thought I'd murdered somebody. It was all very stupid.' He did not look as if it had been.

'Oh Charles.'

'I know, I know, I shouldn't play, should I? What people mean by that is you shouldn't play unless you win. They're always very pleased if you're in the money. But the fact is I do play and it's been good lately, but then I went on too long because I felt depressed and Jack had a sudden run of the cards, and I didn't call it a day. However, I'm not here to bore you with stories about games of poker. I came to say our father has made up his own mind I must go down.'

'Leave Oxford!'

'That's about the size of it.'

'But you can't! You only have two more terms and –'

'It isn't all that important,' he broke in. 'I wouldn't have got my degree, you know. Only swots do and I scarcely open a book. I was under the impression,' he sounded older than his age, 'that one was sent to university for other reasons than to get a piece of paper at the end of the three years. One makes the odd friend, circulates, if you see what I mean. You're supposed to acquire a sort of polish, get an interest in all kinds of things, sport, theatre, the classics if you happen to like them. Not according to Father. One's there solely to study and not waste his bloody money. Lou, the party's

19

over. He's written to the Principal of Lincoln and what's more he's posted the letter. I saw him give it to the postman at tea-time.'

'But you could persuade –'

'No, darling, I could not. And don't want to. After we'd both stopped shouting – well, I did the shouting and he got quieter, poor old thing – we finally agreed that it may all be for the best. He suggests I might try my hand with Uncle Rod.'

'*But he's in Burma!*'

'So he is,' said Charles rather tenderly.

He was in a quandary. He liked what was new, what was dramatic. By nature idle and pleasure-loving, he welcomed change which gave salt to life, and his already seemed to him very dull. He chased girls at Oxford and caught some of them. He ran after girls here in Warwickshire, but they were young upper-middle-class virgins, and kisses in the backs of borrowed cars were as far as they would go. His sexual experiences so far had been with girls who worked in biscuit factories or shops, sexually-aware, laughing, predatory girls who, unlike the débutantes, were skilled at sex. Often more skilled, so far, than he was. Charles needed sex – lots of sex – all the time. The prospect of leaving England, of sailing off God knew where to lands of great heat and wonderful Eastern women, was alluring. Except that he must leave Lisa who looked so doleful that he could scarcely bear it.

'Uncle Rod might give me a job, Father says. He's in rubber or something.'

'No he isn't. He's in timber.'

'How on earth do you know that?'

'Because he writes to me occasionally. He's my godfather, in case you've forgotten,' she said, crossly because she was in pain.

'So he is,' agreed Charles. And then – he hated to see women unhappy – he suddenly said, 'Why don't you come too?'

Alec Whitfield was in his study, reading comfortably, when

his daughter tapped on the door. He called 'Come in,' but as she entered he put down his book ostentatiously, saying 'Yes?' with a martyred air.

He was a thin, bearded, donnish man, who seemed as if the physical life enjoyed by other human beings – food and drink, jokes and laughter, even sex – were things he had nothing to do with. When not avoiding his children by shutting himself in his study, he was out a good deal. He went to Birmingham to see – often to change – his solicitors. He visited his only close friend, Guy Bowden. He conferred with the gardener, to whom he was pleasanter than he was to either Charles or Lisa. He also went for long walks with his short-legged, short-tempered Sealyham. Occasionally, always to do with his muddled finances, he went to London where he stayed at an expensive club in St James's to which he belonged; there he met old friends who wanted nothing from him. He was only easy in masculine company, and it had been entirely due to his wife's Irish vitality that he had married. She had been his first and last woman.

Faced with his daughter, who was standing in a manner which got on his nerves, her arms hanging as if on strings, he accurately read the expression on her face. Charles had told her. But he was surprised when she said, 'You'd never let me go out East with Charles, I suppose?'

'So your brother has informed you of his decision?'

It was like him, thought Lisa, not to answer her question. 'He said it was you who decided he's got to go.'

'Your brother has been a source of great anxiety to me,' said Alec Whitfield resentfully. He might have been speaking to somebody of his own age. 'To serve the Empire may prove his salvation.'

Lisa thought her father sounded like a preacher planning to save a sinner from perdition. She trod carefully. 'Perhaps he'll do marvellously with Uncle Rod.'

She had an impression, something in his face and voice told her, that he wasn't going to turn her down flat. She couldn't believe her luck and remained with the respectful expression of a servant waiting for orders.

He regarded her with indecision. He had never understood his only daughter and rarely had a conversation alone with her since she had been born. Her sex literally embarrassed him. He thinned his lips for a moment.

'Do you in actual fact realize what you are asking, Lisa? I fear I could not possible afford for you to come home from Burma for a considerable period. The fare costs a great deal of money.'

'Oh, I wouldn't expect to come *home!*' she exclaimed, her voice joyful. He winced and she got the point too late, hastily adding that of course she would want to come back to England to see him but only when he could afford it. And Charles would simply long to come too when he had leave or whatever they called it.

Alec Whitfield stopped looking as if she had given him a glass of neat lemon juice. He accepted the gabbled filial respect and said he would think about it and discuss the matter with Mr Bowden. He never called his friend by his first name to Charles or Lisa. 'I will let you know later,' he said and she left the room starry-eyed.

Alec needed Guy Bowden's opinion on anything and everything. He discussed all his problems with him, listened in silent attention and often – Alec had never been clever – ignored Bowden's good advice. The two men had been at Eton together and had the curious similarity of both having survived the murderous 1914–18 war and lost their wives. Alec's had died too soon. Guy's had deserted him. They were both fathers to motherless children. Alec's were adults now; Guy had a small daughter of seven years old.

After the divorce, Guy Bowden's wife had married her lover, a rich and vulgar industrialist who took her to live in Panama. Possibly because of the second husband, she never asked to see the child. Guy had sole custody of his daughter whom he spoiled. Lisa and Charles thought her a pert little show-off and couldn't bear her.

The two men liked each other for different reasons. Guy was fond of people he'd known since his youth. He was self-sufficient but once he took you into his life, he was a loyal friend. Hard-centred, very practical, and wealthy, he enjoyed Alec's erudition and disapproved of his financial messes.

When Alec told him of Charles's disastrous behaviour at Oxford, it was Bowden who suggested sending him abroad. He had an Edwardian idea that packing off a scapegrace son to some far-off place in the Empire was a wise move. Hard work would put the boy on the right lines and the smaller the allowance given to the emigrant, the better for his soul. It was Guy who helped Alec Whitfield draft a letter to Alec's brother in Burma. But when, the day after Lisa had seen her father, Alec told him what she had asked, Guy was astounded. He attempted to dissuade him. After all, she was a girl! They talked long and late and Guy soon realized that while Alec paid lip-service to his opinions, nodding and saying 'So. So', he actually *wanted* his two children to leave England. Guy continued to try and get him to see things differently. Without success.

While she waited and longed to know her fate, Lisa grew more and more passionate about following Charles. She wanted nothing else but to be with Charles. To travel with him. To share what she hazily imagined would be the life read about in a Kipling short story. She saw herself dressed in white surrounded by Charles's handsome friends, fanning herself lazily and stepping into a rickshaw. She imagined a huge Eastern moon and the twang of strange instruments, then a regimental band playing polkas and herself whirling in the arms of the subaltern who had won her heart. The idea of staying here at home rattling about like a pea in a box, facing her father for near-silent meals, filled her with misery. It was true she had many local friends, but what did they matter if Charles was gone? She had recently been courted by her first real admirer, who had been to Oxford with Charles. But Michael's chaste kisses, his swarthy looks, the low-slung car envied by her girlfriends, faded into nothing when she tried to visualize her life in Burma. It was Charles she loved. He created the fun, the uncertainty, the excitement, the promise. She knew his faults and couldn't bear to live without him.

After her interview with her father she went to look for Charles and found him in the conservatory playing patience on a rickety card-table. She reported her conversation and he listened to her without comment.

'So he's going to chew it all over with Mr Bowden,' she finished, 'who'll say I can't go. Mr B. has never liked me.'

'I agree. He will say you shouldn't go because *he* couldn't bear to be parted from Jenny-Penny.'

It was the name Guy called his child when he was alone with her; he wasn't aware he'd ever used it in public but it had slipped out once when he and the little girl had come to tea. Charles and Lisa had seized on it like sharks.

'You mean just because he keeps little Jenny-Penny glued to his side, *I'm* to be stuck here too!' She sounded desperate. 'That's what he'll think and that's what he'll advise Father.'

Charles rubbed his chin. There were times when he was delicate with his sister's feelings. He felt in his bones that his father was going to agree to her coming East and that getting rid of both of them in one clean sweep would suit him just fine. Charles didn't say that to Lisa.

'I have a feeling it's going to be okay. I don't know why,' was all he said.

Of course, he was right. To the deep disapproval of Guy Bowden who found it difficult not to say what he thought now the die was cast, Alec gave his daughter permission to go to Burma. He also presented her with fifty pounds for her clothes.

Roundwood, the big unremarkable house where the Whit-fields had lived since Alec and Bernadette had married, suddenly became a hive of telephone calls, steamer trunks and deliveries from the Army & Navy Stores. Visits were made to London. Farewell suppers were given in Stratford. The house was comfortable and had room to spare. So trunks in passages were no trouble, nor were friends clatter-ing up and down the stairs, nor the general bustle and flurry of preparations. The house had been built in the 1920s; it was panelled, spacious and could be seen in every West End play which began with a maid bringing in a vase of calico

24

delphiniums. Lisa never spared the place a thought. She was too excited to bid it any sentimental goodbye. When the country had started to settle into a November sleep, when the trees had blown their leaves across soggy lawns, rooks wheeled like pieces of black paper in the sky and raindrops on gate bars hung in a row, Charles and Lisa took a train to London, a train to Southampton, and boarded the S.S. *Eastern Star* bound for Rangoon.

It was that voyage ten years ago which Lisa remembered, lying in a cold room in the Cromwell Road on a London night in 1948. The ship had sailed through the Mediterranean, which showed its teeth in great rough waves for a while. But then it changed; the sun smiled and Lisa and Charles grew brown as berries. They sailed with a company of dolphins frolicking ahead as if showing the way. The *Eastern Star* sailed down the Suez Canal into a sea of blinding blue, then on to the vastness of the Indian Ocean where at night the now emerald water shone strangely as if on fire. They spent the weeks in a kind of unending party. They drank cocktails and played deck games. They flirted. In Lisa's case there was a moment when she thought she was in love. The man was in his late forties, had a low quiet voice, a wry manner and – what fascinated her most – seemed tired all the time. 'Weary man I love,' wrote Lisa in her diary.

The ship sailed to Colombo and she and Charles stood on deck watching snakes swimming in the water. Then at last, with Stratford vanished as if it had never been, they came to a country smelling of sandalwood. At night fireflies winked in the casuarina trees. They saw dark jungles, heard the screams of birds whose plumage was no more vivid than the crimsons and yellows worn by small, beautiful Burmese girls, their necks entwined with silver, amber and jade.

It was Charles to whom she owed all that. Owed two whole years in Burma before war came. If it had not been for him she would never have seen the East. She would have stayed at home in dreary England, would never have loved the man who still, though lost, grasped her heart. There

25

were times when she could not bear to remember the violence and bliss of that love. Yet she was glad of everything she had known and suffered and become. She wouldn't have changed a day – and it was all because of Charles.

She fell asleep because she was no longer angry with him.

# 2

_____

Snow fell heavily in the night, muffling the sounds of the city. It stopped before dawn, but when Lisa went into the kitchen to make breakfast, there were nearly two inches of freezing snow outside on the window ledge. She shivered and lit a ring of the inadequate gas cooker.

She was slicing bread when Charles came in, wrapped in a thin cotton dressing-gown of the kind worn by everybody in the East, patterned with grey bamboo leaves. Lisa wore the same. Their clothes were pitifully thin, no protection against the sharp knives of English weather.

Charles's hair was on end, the stubble blueish on his dark face. When he was unshaven he looked, she thought, like a pirate out of *Treasure Island*.

'Sorry I yelled at you,' she said. 'It isn't as if what happened was recent. Poor Charles – having to pay that ages-old debt.'

'It was still my fault.' He always disagreed when she said things were not his fault. 'Any marmalade?' he added, sitting down.

'Scrape the pot. It's the end of our ration.'

'Rations! Who'd have imagined that when we got home everything would be worse than India?'

They ate their breakfast in thoughtful silence. Nothing in England was what they had expected – how could it be after six years of war? They had persuaded and begged and paid through the nose to get back here. The ship had been

27

crowded with civil servants leaving Burma for ever. The seventy years of British rule, in which Burma was an outlying part of British India, had actually come to an end in 1942 with the Japanese invasion. It was true the Burmese had welcomed the large victorious British army at the end of the war, but that was a form of farewell. Nationalist Burma wasn't going to tolerate being behind India in declaring her independence. The old Empire days were gone.

Men and women travelling back to England were sad for a way of life that was lost to them. Lisa and Charles had known that life too. They had lived in Taunggyi before the war, played tennis and polo and been waited upon like youthful royalty. But all that was over and now nostalgia bored them. They were sorry for the ex-civil servants and avoided their company. They themselves were sanguine, despite the knowledge that they would have no home. Their father had sold their family house in 1939, two years after they'd both left for Burma. But this didn't worry them. They were returning to a new age, weren't they? The war was won, victory achieved, the horizon bright and when Charles did gamble on board ship he usually won. It was symptomatic of their carefree feelings that his sister quite encouraged him.

They had not been prepared for post-war England. Of course they had read about it, but it was different, thought Charles, warming his hands on his cup, when you actually *saw* it. I suppose we were idiots to be so optimistic and not realize it would turn out to be a dirty wreck. However much people tell you about what has happened to a country and a people, he thought, you can never imagine the way it really is. Like every other member of the Forces overseas, Charles knew about gallant little Britain. He and Lisa had separately been proud of their country's courage during the Blitz: bombs whistling down, friendship and brave faces and people in the Underground laughing and singing 'Roll Out the Barrel'. In their minds he and Lisa saw a cocky little island which had rightly earned the admiration of the world.

They themselves had grown accustomed to the aftermath

of war in the East. To night-long queues for transport, to huddling on railway stations, to begging air lifts across a huge land of shifting and trekking peoples, displaced and ruined – but alive. When Charles had managed to find Lisa in Calcutta and they decided to return to Burma, they'd encountered appalling difficulties. But they had not needed to walk with bundles on their heads or travel in bullock carts filled with mattresses. There were always the British to help them and Charles was still in uniform. Brother and sister journeyed – how they journeyed! And at last, after months, they managed to get to Taunggyi – to find that their uncle's bungalow had, quite literally, vanished. It had been the most eerie experience of their lives. The garden where Uncle Rodney had grown nasturtiums and sweet peas, the spacious comfortable house, the verandah where they'd sat in the evenings – all had been obliterated. There was nothing now but the voracious, verbena-scented lantana.

They had walked to the village. Much of that had also been burnt, but had been rebuilt in the way of Burmese houses, put up in a few days, walled with matting of plaited bamboo and standing on stilts. Underneath were the usual chickens and a few pigs. The compounds were clean, and somebody had planted jasmine in an empty petrol tin.

Charles spoke to the first villager, an old man with a bald, brown head, sitting on his haunches smoking a green cheroot, a Buddhist rosary round his wrist; he asked in Burmese for Rodney. The man's wizened face brightened at hearing his own language spoken by a *Thakin*, as they called the British. Yes, he said, he had been there 'at the time of the death'. Their uncle, it seemed, had waited until the Japanese troops emerged from the jungle and then charged, firing with his rifle.

'He was a man crazed,' said the old man. 'They killed him quickly. His ghost still comes to the great tree in the place where he lived.'

Yet it had not been the enemy who had destroyed the bungalow . . . Charles and Lisa were taken in a jeep by some good-natured English journalists into the jungle to look for

29

Uncle Rodney's plantations. All had been destroyed by British bombardments.

'Apparently they got it wrong,' Charles and Lisa were told later by officials in Rangoon. 'The RAF were supposed to bomb Meiktila. But the best laid plans . . .'

It was history now.

They had travelled for long, agonizing weeks to find their uncle. They'd had the idea, a wild one but cherished, that they could be with him again. But even supposing he'd survived, nothing belonged to the British any more. The only thing for Charles and Lisa to do was to turn round and go back to England.

Yes, thought Charles. The journeys had been hard, the end was a tragedy. He looked with distaste out of the window. On the sill the snow was already freckled with smuts. Burma had been clean, he thought. People swam every day and caught fresh fish and washed their clothes in the river. The girls still wore flowers in their hair . . .

'Charles,' said Lisa, who was feeling better. The air in the kitchen was quite warm.

'Mm?'

'I've had an idea. Why don't we go to Stratford?' She had suggested it to him two or three times since they had come to London. He always refused, saying it was pointless since they had no home there any more. 'I'd like to see Stratford again. And there's something else. Do you remember that letter from Drury & Sons, the depository on the Bicester Road?'

'God knows what happened to *that*.'

'You don't need the deity, *I* know what happened to it because I've still got it. They wrote and told us Father had stored some of his boxes with them. We got the letter before we left Calcutta. Do you think our stuff is still there? Or do firms sell things if you don't pay for the storage?'

'I haven't the foggiest. What are you burbling about? You know Father died broke.'

'Sure. Everything was sold, except whatever was in the boxes at Drury's.' He was being very slow this morning.

'How do we know there isn't something there which is worth having, Charles? I mean worth selling. We don't know what he decided to keep, do we? He didn't leave *nothing*,' declared Lisa, optimism producing a double negative. 'I think we ought to find out.'

Charles had been thinking about other journeys; together they had travelled across countries where danger or death might appear at any time like evil gods. He and his sister had been united then with a single determination. To get to Taunggyi. To find out what had happened to Uncle Rodney. To pick up – a vain hope – some shreds of their former life.

Returning to Stratford would not be like that. It wasn't a quest, it was a small, mean idea and he disliked it. He and Lisa had nothing of their own any more; former friends, supposing any still lived in Warwickshire, would merely be sorry for them. But Jeff Ingoldsby had taken away more than Charles's money last night. He had destroyed Charles's insurance against having to seek out their English past.

Wearing four layers of thin Eastern clothes, brother and sister came into the Cromwell Road and crunched over thin layers of snow already trodden down by passers-by. A small pre-war Austin, also a loan from Andrew McAllister, was parked by the kerb. Petrol was virtually unobtainable but Charles had managed (Lisa did not ask how) to get hold of some petrol coupons. The camaraderie of loans, of large empty flats and small, tinny cars was not going to last, thought Charles; we may as well make the best of it while it does.

Lisa had found a man's Rugby scarf in her wardrobe, red, white and blue, and smelling of cigarettes. She muffled it round her neck and over her hair. She was feeling considerably more cheerful than last night. Despair was gone because of action. Once or twice she did remember Ingoldsby with a spasm of vicious dislike, but then she forgot him and returned to wondering what was waiting at the end of the hundred-mile drive. Fortunately Charles had filled the car with petrol the previous day while he still had money in his wallet.

31

It was icy inside the car and Lisa was soon banging her hands, in knitted Army issue gloves, to make the circulation work. Charles was glad to be driving and indifferent to the worsening weather. His sister looked better; he hated it when her face blanched the way it had done when that sod took all their cash. Lisa's pallor sometimes had the drained look he remembered when soldiers were going into action. How sallow she is, poor little love. Of course he was too. He saw his own curiously olive-tinged yet pale face every morning when he was shaving. But he liked Lisa pretty, not pinched. And she was thin as a bird.

They drove in silence broken by the squeak of the windscreen wiper battling to remove little wedges of the fine snow which had begun to fall. As they approached the outskirts of Oxford, the snow blew in flurries. This car is just the kind to break down at the other end of nowhere, thought Lisa. But the prospect of being stranded somewhere in this small country did not alarm her. Like Charles, her mind was on their past travels together. Of the trains, fuelled by wood and travelling at ten miles an hour, which sighed to a halt in the midst of vast dried up yellow plains looking as if they were turning into deserts while you watched. Of nights spent on station platforms swarming with troops, the rain drumming down as they sat not bothering to avoid the piercing downpours, while steam rose from the crowds as it did from cattle in wintertime. Lisa and Charles had travelled in trucks shuddering over tracks scattered with rocks or pitted with shells. They had gone without food, they'd drunk filthy tea and eaten sweet cakes and unleavened bread and slept on wooden boards. They'd made friends parted with in a day. They'd seen country so beautiful that they had gasped, and been battered by monsoons which threatened to drown them. The empty road beside the walls of an Oxfordshire manor seemed the height of civilization compared with what she and Charles had known. She looked indifferently at the snow, wondering what was in those boxes her father had decided to keep . . .

He had written to Charles before the war while they had

32

been living in Taunggyi with Uncle Rodney, saying he had decided to sell Roundwood.

'I plan to buy something smaller and more suitable, nearer to Mr Bowden. I will send you my new address when things are settled.'

Rodney Whitfield, as fat and practical as his brother was thin and muddled, had sniffed. If he did sell Roundwood, Rodney remarked, he would get a bad price. If he bought another house, he would pay over the odds. But when their father wrote again he gave Guy Bowden's address, explaining that he was having trouble finding 'the right place which suits my needs'. He was at present staying with Mr Bowden, 'who is most hospitable'.

Alec Whitfield's alibis came to light when he died of pneumonia in 1943. He had never even tried to buy another house. He was deep in debt from many ill-judged investments, and the sale of the house had gone to pay off most of what he owed. He left his affairs in a financial mess which neither Charles nor Lisa grasped. Solicitors' letters came when Charles was fighting in the jungle and Lisa working in Calcutta. Both Alec's children were swallowed up by the war, and what happened in far-distant Stratford-on-Avon seemed of utter unimportance.

Lisa looked out of the car window which was misted with steam. Ploughed land stretching away into the distance was now frozen hard. Hedges were beginning to whiten. Empty, silent, whirled about with snow and set with tall trees, the scene moved her. Ten whole years had gone by since she and Charles, with trunkfuls of tropical clothes, had taken the London train and left this countryside behind them. The East had been waiting then, dawning in their thoughts, cloudless, interminable, as mysterious as it had been for travellers hundreds of years ago.

'Blow, blow, thou winter wind,' sang Charles. 'I say, darling, it looks as if it's getting worse.'

'It *is* worse.'

'The Ruby Saloon is a valiant animal.'

'Suppose we break down.'

33

He glanced sideways at her. 'Cassandra is your second name. Why should Ruby let us down? She never has.'

He slowed down. The road was glassy from the freezing frost of the previous night. A farm cart appeared in the distance, moving slowly and drawn by an enormous white farmhorse whose coat looked brown against the dazzling brightness.

Lisa began to recognize landmarks. A crossroad beside which was a cottage with thick yew hedges and a lopsided gate; the hedges had grown twice as high, the gate remained unmended. There was a manor-house with a formal Palladian front, and there a certain church-gate oddly thatched. They drove through Shipston, past its Georgian houses and on to further deserted country roads. Memory hides things but doesn't destroy them, thought Lisa. All the time that she and Charles had been under glaring blue skies, in peace, in war, in peace again, these places had remained. That tree had budded, flowered, fruited and slept under the snow. It was people who changed.

They were getting close to Stratford now. She knew the curve of the road, a stretch of rolling fields where she'd once seen a herd of deer. They passed the Victorian Gothic shape of Alveston Manor, its turrets and cupolas rising against a dun-coloured sky.

'Shall we go to the furniture depository right away?' asked Lisa. The old familiar sights had begun to oppress her. She wished every single thing had not shrunk.

'No, ten to one the place will be locked. Probably stays like that for months. We'll have to get hold of somebody to open up for us. You haven't forgotten the papers from Drury's, by any ghastly chance?'

'Of course. I left them in the flat. Don't be a fool.'

'Good, good,' said Charles heartily, 'I tell you what. We'll pop into The Shakespeare for a drink. We can telephone Drury's from there.'

Lisa didn't ask how he could afford The Shakespeare. He looked in such a good mood.

Stratford was almost empty except for a few figures hurrying by under umbrellas. The shop windows shone out into the dark morning; scarcely a footprint showed on the whitened pavements.

Lisa was slightly touched and slightly amused that Charles should suggest they go to the place which had been a favourite haunt of his in the thirties. She wondered if The Shakespeare was still open. Had anybody the money to stay in good hotels now? But when he turned the car into Chapel Street, there was the hotel's picturesque front, gabled and crooked, curiously welcoming and as handsome and ancient as she remembered. Yes, it was open. There were lights, and she saw a man going through the front door.

Charles drove round to the back of the hotel to park the car. Four other cars were already parked there. So someone, thought Lisa, can afford it.

Inside, the timbered and panelled rooms smelled of wood-smoke. The scent reminded her of wood fires in her uncle's bungalow when it was bitter cold and the jungle outside was lashed into hectic green by the monsoon. But here they were in the heart of England. They walked through rooms they remembered, to a front lounge and a log fire. Charles went to look for a waiter.

Lisa sat down gratefully. She felt comforted simply because the hotel had remained the same. Austerity and shabbiness had little effect on things three hundred years old. Sixteenth-century furniture was blackened and scarred by the years. It had a patina of time; and somebody had put laurel leaves in a brass water-jug.

Charles returned, looking pleased. 'Chicken sandwiches and sherry.'

'It sounds too good to be true.'

'I had to do a bit of persuading, but at least they didn't say there had been a war on. I mentioned that we were valued pre-war clients just returned to Stratford and Father had given your twenty-first birthday party here.'

'Charles, what a lie! I was in Calcutta.'

'You don't imagine they'll check up, do you? I was most complimentary about the hotel and anyway your party would have been here if we'd been around. I tried out something else rather nifty. I enquired after Guy Bowden.'

'What on earth for?'

'You are not being your bright self. To discover if he's still in the land of the living, of course. Well, he is. The waiter knows him. "Mr Bowden and his daughter Miss Jennifer. Such a pleasure to see them dining here."'

'Jenny-Penny. Ugh.'

'I know. I should think she's worse than ever, wouldn't you? However, Bowden could be useful. He may know more about our pathetic affairs than we do. Here we are. Food.'

The waiter was very old and very thin and Lisa would have liked to help with the heavy tray, but knew it would never do. His black tail-coat was too big; perhaps he had grown smaller. He painstakingly laid a white cloth, white napkins, glasses, and produced a dish with a silver cover. He unsteadily poured the sherry. When Charles thanked him he gave a dim smile, having already succumbed to the charm that almost nobody resisted. As proof of service, the old man shuffled over to put a fresh log on the fire.

He bowed and left them. Charles lifted his glass.

'Cheers.'

Lisa lifted hers in return. Her brother had brought her to the best hotel and ordered her a delicate lunch – it was just like him. Sometimes his gestures resembled filling her lap with flowers. He gave her style and warmth and food and drink. All this was not going to last, of course.

They ate and drank, and the old waiter appeared with coffee. Afterwards Charles telephoned Drury & Sons, returning for a second time with a look of satisfaction. After last night's trouncing, he was having a better day. His luck was running with him. He had arranged for them to meet a Mr Prynne outside the depository.

'He's going to unlock for us,' said Charles.

Lisa did not reply. It was as if she'd been holding in her hand a paper fan called hope. Now the time had come for it to be destroyed. The fire no longer warmed her and the sherry and food did not give her comfort. Already she felt diminished by the bony hand of poverty. She knew with certainty that their father had sold anything worth having; this expedition was pitiful. She did not look at her brother, sitting relaxed and content. All her fears were selfish.

He went over to the fire and kicked the log, making it shower sparks and spring into small, licking flames.

'Time we were off, Lou. Prynne sounded like a man who is punctual to the minute. Don't want to let him freeze outside the place, do we?' He looked at her observantly. 'How do you feel?'

'Fine,' said Lisa, and at her hollow voice he burst out laughing.

Drury's Depository was at the end of a street of houses built for tradesmen and workers in the 1900s. The tiny houses, which looked too small for the large families of the past, had been the homes of clock-menders, carpenters, painters, sweeps. There had even been a private pawnbroker known for his discretion. People were ashamed to borrow at a big jewellery shop whose three golden balls hanging outside were a loud announcement of penury.

Somebody during the war – in a fit of the same patriotism which encouraged women to give up their saucepans – had removed every railing in the street. The little front gardens where roses and hollyhocks grew in summer were now edged with fragments of broken wooden fencing. Many had nothing at all to protect the snow-covered patches; they were unenclosed, uncared-for and forlorn.

The depository itself was a large building roofed with snow; outside its double doors a short, stout man in a red muffler was walking up and down to keep warm. He looked like a winter robin. Charles parked the car and went over to introduce himself.

Lisa followed more slowly. As in the case of the old waiter at The Shakespeare, Mr Prynne immediately became her brother's servant. He nodded to everything Charles said. When Prynne tried to unlock the padlocked doors and couldn't manage them, he surrendered the keys and Charles opened the doors. Mr Prynne was very complimentary.

'This is my sister, Mr Prynne,' said Charles.

'How do you do, Miss Whitfield.' Prynne shook her hand. The trio then entered an icy cavern which smelled strongly of damp.

Neither Charles nor Lisa had been into a furniture depository before and Charles thought it was like a kind of cemetery. The place was full of furniture muffled in dust sheets and tied into curious shapes not unlike crosses or angels. There were mouldy cabin trunks and wooden boxes which, although the wrong shape, were large enough to be coffins. Names were chalked or painted, written on labels or in brass nail-head lettering.

'It looks to me,' said Charles to Prynne, 'as if some of all this has been here since the year dot.'

'A decade or two certainly, Sir.'

'How long do you actually keep it?' Charles presumed his father had paid for the storage in advance, although it would not have been like him.

'We store people's possessions as long as they wish us to take care of them, Mr Whitfield,' said Prynne, as if the sheeted and locked, dust-covered and mouldy objects crowding about were regularly cleaned and watched over.

'And as long as he pays, I suppose?'

'Well, naturally. You know, Sir,' said Prynne, who took pleasure in talking about his work, 'it surprises me how customers will continue to pay for such long periods. The years go by and they don't even return to look at their property. We've trunks here dating from the 1920s. Those cabin trunks in the corner – the family pays us regularly every quarter. Have done for twenty-five years. It is most curious.'

'I would have said incurious.'

Mr Prynne laughed as if Charles had made a remarkable witticism. Lisa was getting impatient. They had driven a hundred miles, were half frozen and had spent money they couldn't afford, and here stood two men exchanging ridiculous remarks. She asked coldly if Mr Prynne could show her where their boxes were.

'Of course, of course, thoughtless of me to keep a lady waiting. Aisle Seven. Down on the right, second section.'

Lisa walked ahead across a floor strewn with straw and gritty with ancient dirt. She saw the packing cases. There were four – three smallish, one larger – neatly stacked two upon two. When she came to them she felt a stab of recognition. The labels were in her father's small, slanting hand.

'You'll need this, Mr Whitfield,' said Prynne, and took a workmanlike wrench from his pocket. 'The nails are such a nuisance.' He and Charles tugged the cases out into the aisle which ran between the shrouded furniture and trunks. 'Would half an hour suffice you? You could then give me an idea of what you wish to take away and whether anything is to remain. I must leave you, I have another client to see. I'll be back punctually.'

'Half an hour is fine, Mr Prynne,' said Charles.

Switching on more lights, bare bulbs suspended from the ceiling on wires hairy with cobwebs, Prynne left them, shutting the two doors.

Charles flourished the wrench. 'Well, Lou? Shall we see what's in the bran tubs?' He began to lever rusty nails from the first box.

Inside, packed close and enveloped in many sheets of yellowing newspaper, were numerous parcels which looked promising until Charles and Lisa discovered what they contained: a complete set of plates and dishes – a Victorian dinner service. Forty-eight plates, four dishes for nuts to be served with port, fruit dishes on stands. The service was elaborate, patterned with yellow poppies, and the edges of the plates curved and gilded. Neither Lisa nor Charles had ever seen it before; Lisa supposed it had been a wedding present belonging to her parents, stacked in some cupboard at Roundwood 'for best' and never used.

Below the china were half a dozen cardboard boxes filled with photographs backed with faded red velvet and framed in silver. There was their father in his university gown. Their mother on a tennis court, laughing, with a frilled baby in her arms – Charles. In other boxes they found scores of cut-glass vases which had once held flowers dead a quarter of a century ago, wine glasses, tumblers, liqueur glasses small enough for a doll's house. They arranged their possessions on the top of a flat trunk, commenting and making grimaces. 'This is just what we need.' 'Oh, do look at *this*!'

In the base of the second case, Charles discovered a large box. 'Now, this *is* promising.'

It was a fifty-year-old, hand-operated sewing machine once used by the Whitfield maids to repair torn sheets. Charles and Lisa made jokes as they regarded their booty. What was it all worth? Nowadays very little. Who would want a dinner service for twelve people and five courses?

Lisa was neither disappointed nor surprised. Her previous optimism had been assumed to cheer herself up after the shock of Jeff Ingoldsby. What she hadn't known until she looked at a poppy-patterned dish or the sewing machine with its cast-iron base decorated with wreaths of roses was the power of inanimate objects. Packed in their cases, hidden in their newspapers, they had the past sticking to them. Dead hands, once warm, had touched and used them. All the summers of being young lay among the chipped croquet mallets and all the embraces of their mother in a cardboard box. The photographs were the worst because the moment was there, captured, eternal, showing such mortal human beings.

'Don't say it,' said Charles, picking up a mallet and hitting an imaginary shot. 'Why the blazes did he keep this rubbish?'

'For us, I suppose.'

'Or because in wartime he wouldn't get a cent for it.' Charles unwrapped a large gold-framed picture of sheep returning to the farm at sunset. He began to read the newspaper round it. 'Here's a good paragraph. "The Japanese Army use many types of grenade, all of which are much inferior to those used by the Allied Forces." Oh, they were, were they? What about the fact that with Jap grenades you didn't need to pull the pin out just before you threw it? You pulled out half a dozen, lined them up like mud pies and threw 'em when you needed 'em.'

'You've left the largest case to the last,' said Lisa, who was sure her brother was going to settle down with the newspapers, and that Prynne would soon be back. 'Perhaps it is the one which actually has got something valuable in it. Father's gesture to us both.'

'Do you believe that?'

'Not really.'

'Here we go, then. Now for the *pièce de résistance*. A kitchen cupboard or a scullery chest of drawers.'

He began to lever out the nails. Together they lifted the lid and scrabbled among newspapers. Emerging under their eager hands was a mottled grey head and a wisp of coarse hair. They shouted in unison.

'Rory!'

Lisa plunged her hands into the paper to clear the mournful face of the rocking-horse. He was sadly knocked about, his paint as chipped as the croquet mallets. But it was the face of a friend.

'We'll keep *him*,' she said, more to the horse than to her brother.

He agreed in the manner of a man with a child, and sitting among war news four to five years old, surrounded by dinner plates and gravy boats, they discussed ways and means. Charles was for selling the lot. Lisa disagreed and suggested the things should remain 'until we've decided where to live'.

'The only snag is the little matter of who's paying for storage.'

'I thought of that. Perhaps Father paid in advance.'

'Oh, funny joke. Well, perhaps he did . . .'

With nothing settled they repacked the past and nailed down the lids of the packing cases. They shoved them back in the dusty corner and Lisa began to walk slowly down the aisle. She was frowning. Suddenly she exclaimed, 'Got it! I knew something was missing. Our silver isn't here.'

'What silver?'

'Charles, do stop reading those blasted newspapers. I'm talking about the silver which belongs to you and me. Father couldn't have sold that.'

He looked amused, remarking that she was a little mine of information. First she produced the depository letter – now this. He'd never heard about the silver. How did she know?

'Because Mother told me. We were having tea once, and she was pouring out – remember how carelessly she did it? And she said, "Just look at this teapot, that's good Irish silver. Would you imagine it came across the sea, and was once used by a baronet with his own green acres and lakes and a castle or two?" She said you and I would have her silver one day. She'd brought it with her when she got married. "I didn't have a dowry" she said – Charles, what funny words people used – "I didn't have a dowry, but I did have a teapot and a milk jug." Then she laughed, you know, in the way she had.'

Before he could reply, the double doors at the far end of the building opened, letting in a little cascade of snow and, shoulders whitened, Mr Prynne came trotting up.

'Everything ship-shape, I trust? You checked with your own copy of the inventory?'

'We haven't got one,' said Lisa.

The man couldn't believe his ears. No inventory! He'd never heard of such a thing. No inventory! Why, how could they know that Drury's Depository had kept their valuables safe for the duration if they had no list to check through? He himself had called on their late father; he remembered the day well: it was the morning after the Dieppe raid.

'We were all very anxious at that time. I remember discussing it with your late father. I gave him the inventory to sign, of course, and he retained a copy. After the sad event, Sir, a second copy was mailed to you through the British Forces Post Office.'

'I'm sure it was,' said Charles, adding, his mind still running on the old newspapers, 'Perhaps your letter was torpedoed.'

Lisa giggled but Mr Prynne was upset. Scrabbling in a version of a school satchel which he carried, he fished out some documents and handed them to Charles.

'You'll find the complete list there, Mr Whitfield.'

Charles handed back the list politely without looking at it, saying that for the present they'd decided to leave the things in the depository.

Lisa could see in Prynne's face that he considered Charles's exhibition of trust despicable and his opinion of Charles had gone down a peg or two. They walked out of the building and padlocked the door. It was dark now yet pale with snow.

Charles murmured their thanks, and was just leaving when Lisa spoke out. She had none of her brother's ingrained courtesy; she was thinking that the flat in Cromwell Road would be freezing on their return.

'You don't happen to know anything about our family silver, do you, Mr Prynne? It wasn't in the packing cases.'

She avoided her brother's eyes. He disliked crudeness and never went to the point if it meant hurting anybody. The unfortunate man might take Lisa's question as an accusation.

Lisa waited for the shocked disclaimer.

'The silver, Miss Whitfield? Surely Mr Bowden –'

'What has he to do with it?' interrupted Charles, struck and curious.

'Mr Bowden has paid the storage bills since your father's decease,' said Mr Prynne stiffly. 'It was at Mr Whitfield's particular request that our men packed the silver separately. The case was sealed, I remember. We delivered it to White-friars.'

# 3

They sat watching Prynne's tail-light vanish into the night mist.

'To Whitefriars?' said Lisa.

'I suppose so.'

'We might just as well, Charles. They say silver doesn't lose its value.'

Charles shrugged. He began to drive with great care, for the intensifying cold had made the road glassy. Soon they left Stratford behind, and were on a road of white icing sugar, marked here and there with a single track of tyres. Lisa felt pleased with herself for remembering their mother's silver. She knew Charles didn't want to call on Guy Bowden – old dislikes never die. But they couldn't afford pride any more. Her brother had fallen into one of his silences; she decided to let him stew.

He drove slowly and Lisa leaned forward staring through the breath-blurred windscreen to try and help him if it were possible. At last they recognized, in a road which the snow had disguised, a row of thatched cottages. The last cottage in the row had been the home of the chimney sweep; his card used to hang in a front window. Next to the sweep had lived the man who came to Roundwood, the Whitfields' old home, as well as to Whitefriars, every Saturday morning to wind the clocks.

Charles slowed almost to walking pace as they descended a steep gradient towards a place called the Sloop which tradition said had been a plague pit in medieval times. Beyond the Sloop was a low bridge spanning a muddy tributary of the Avon. The house lay in a natural hollow at the end of a curving drive of unmarked snow. Squares of blurred golden light shone here and there in the dark. The gates were open, and Charles turned the car through them and almost slid down the slope. He drew the car to a stop and switched off the engine.

Brother and sister sat for a moment.

Whitefriars, built between 1570 and 1590, was one of the loveliest timber-framed buildings in the country. The master carpenters and joiners who had created it had not been content with mere plain oak beams. The timbering was in herring-bone patterns, in Gothic quatrefoils, in diamonds and circles. The frontage of Whitefriars was as intricate as an Elizabethan knot garden. The upper floors of the house projected, as if they had been added at a later date. They thrust forward like the prows of ships which had fought in the Armada.

This black and white jewel of which Warwickshire was so proud was scarcely two and a half miles from Stratford and had been a walk of ten minutes from Roundwood. Charles and Lisa had known the Bowdens since they were born. Ten years lay between the last time they had come here and this moment. The invitations to Whitefriars for tea and tennis seemed as unreal as celebrations in ancient Rome.

'It looks as if somebody's in,' Lisa said.

'I'm afraid you're right.'

'Cheer up, Charles. Think. Lovely silver to sell. And perhaps Jenny-Penny will be more awful than before.'

Charles did not reply. Seeing the house again he remembered just how much he'd been certain Bowden had disliked him. He had always suspected when his father had been at his most unpleasant that Bowden egged him on. He was sure it had been Bowden's idea to send him to Burma. He didn't bear him malice for that, but he recoiled from turning up cap in hand. There was a farcical sort of similarity between his present situation and his last term at Oxford. Broke both times.

45

When he rang the bell, a volley of barks burst out.

'He always had a pack of dogs,' remarked Lisa. The barks on the other side of the front door had become high-pitched yelps. It sounded as if slavering hounds were poised to leap out with bared fangs. Lisa almost expected to hear thuds as they threw themselves against the door.

The noise went on. Nobody answered the bell.

'Oh, do ring again, Charles. My feet have gone dead.'

Charles pressed it two or three times, and they finally heard a voice shouting at the dogs. The door opened and light and warmth streamed out. A girl stood framed in the glow.

'Yes?'

'Is this Mr Bowden's residence?' inquired Charles, sounding, thought Lisa, like a butler.

'Yes,' replied the girl shortly. 'Have you broken down or something?'

Good heavens, could it actually be Jenny-Penny? The girl was slim, ash-blonde, with the radiance of very fair people.

'No, our car hasn't broken down,' said Charles, and Lisa knew that voice of old. It had a particular winning tone used for pretty women. 'We've come to see Mr Bowden if he is available.'

What language, thought Lisa.

'Whom shall I say?' asked the girl suspiciously.

Lisa was thoroughly annoyed and freezing cold. It was outrageous of this girl to leave them on the doorstep like Victorian beggars when they'd visited this place so often as guests and all *she'd* been was a fat-faced little prig of seven years old.

'Our name is Whitfield and do you suppose we might come in or I shall definitely die of frostbite,' snapped Lisa.

The girl was non-plussed and stepped aside without replying. Charles and Lisa walked into the house in some relief.

'Surely you can't be Jenny?' said Charles, charmingly at ease with the rude teenager.

'Yes. I'm Jenny Bowden. Sorry I didn't recognize you.'

She spoke in the clipped upper-class tones Lisa hadn't

heard for years. That way of speaking was not used in the Forces. With the words both shortened and exaggerated Jenny Bowden sounded like the heroine of an old 1930s film. She did not look directly at either Charles or Lisa but beyond them as if avoiding their eyes. She was relieved when all the dogs surged forward, some wagging their tails and all waiting for orders. There was a red setter, a tall wolfhound, and some indeterminate mongrels. Jenny Bowden ordered them out of the way with authority and they disappeared in a mass, satisfied they had done their duty.

'Might we have a word with your father?' asked Charles.

She said she would go and see.

'Kind of you,' replied Charles and smiled down at her. When she finally looked at him, somewhat unwillingly, she blushed; Charles, as usual, was having an effect.

When she'd gone Charles turned and winked. 'Rather attractive, wouldn't you say?'

'I suppose so.'

'I like those boyish English girls. Wonder what her father's like. Still drooling over her, I'll bet.'

'Sh. She might hear you.'

'Don't be so jumpy. I heard the drawing-room door close. She must be asking if he'll see us. And why should he not, pray?'

'Perhaps he's got visitors.'

'Oh tripe,' said Charles. Despite the charm that he'd conjured up to use on the girl, he found the old house oppressive. He seemed to recognize every stick and stone. A dark oil painting of a castle over the empty fireplace. An umbrella stand filled with walking sticks. The Persian mats thrown on the stone floors, the fringes straight as if they had been combed. Bowden had servants, apparently. Hadn't the war touched him at all? The very air was wealthy and told on Charles's nerves.

Jenny Bowden reappeared and said her father would be glad to see them and was 'abs'l't'ly' bowled over at the news that they had come. She had distinctly thawed and said

47

would they come to the drawing-room and have some tea. They followed her in silence down a panelled passage hung with small, ugly, seventeenth-century portraits of pinched or angry men. Not a woman in sight.

Jenny lifted a heavy curtain which hung on a pole outside the door to keep out draughts and led the way into the drawing-room. Like the house itself this Whitefriars room was quite famous, a perfect Tudor room, panelled, flagstone-floored, with an elaborate stone fireplace and a long row of wooden shields, the arms of sixteenth- and seventeenth-century owners fixed above a shelf just below the ceiling.

Standing by the fire was their father's old friend. He strode over and shook them both by the hand.

Bowden was the sort of Englishman who does not age but simply grows grey. His hair, which was once barley-coloured, had silvered but was thick and bushy, worn short on his rather bullet-shaped head. The face was strong, chunky, a sportsman's face, toughened by physical exertion but no stronger – it did not need to be – than when he had been thirty years old. He had bright blue eyes. He wore the sporting clothes of the shires, a tweed jacket, fine twill trousers, highly polished brogues, and matched his setting so exactly that he was almost a caricature.

'Sit down, sit down. Jenny, ask Mrs Dickens to bring tea, would you?'

Jenny disappeared, shutting the door quietly.

'Well?' said Guy Bowden, looking from one to the other and giving a somewhat strained smile – he wasn't a man who smiled much except at his daughter. 'It's been a long time. I don't think I would have known either of you.'

'*You* haven't changed, Sir,' said Charles.

Guy Bowden made a dismissive gesture. He was thinking that these strangers who had appeared out of the filthy weather like revenants were totally unrecognizable. Charles took him aback. Alec Whitfield's son had been a self-indulgent youth at university, a womanizer and a wastrel, selfish, and none too pleasant when he'd visited Whitefriars.

He had been a cause of deep anxiety to his father. This dark man with the lined face, older than his years, appeared to have nothing in common with the young man Guy remembered. His expression was sardonic, his manner too easy. He looked lazy but curiously alert. Even Bowden, not given to such ideas, saw that he must be sexually attractive. He had discerned it in Jenny's face before she left the room just now. As for Lisa Whitfield, in the past Bowden had paid no attention to Alec's daughter, he'd been and still was too wrapped up in his own. But when Jenny had introduced them, Lisa Whitfield had been standing next to her and Bowden was shocked by the contrast between the two young women. Lisa Whitfield had the sallow skin of somebody who has lived for years in the East. She was scrawny, too, and looked older than her age, which was somewhat younger, he recalled, than her brother. Next to Jenny, she was a thorn bush by a branch of apple blossom.

He asked his guests to sit down and began to talk politely, making the usual meaningless enquiries. He had his daughter's abrupt upper-class manner and voice, the same way of swallowing consonants. He directed all his remarks to Charles, only glancing at Lisa occasionally. He was a man, she thought, who would always talk to another man in a room and avoid a direct remark to a woman. Whether women didn't interest him or even embarrassed him she couldn't guess. She thought him formidable. She remembered, studying his face, that she had always thought he looked as if he had been in a fight. His features were uneven, his nose was oddly shaped as if it had been broken. His mouth was thin and his chin had a lump on it as if stuck on with putty. His manner was authoritative and collected.

In a boring fashion he and Charles were discussing the war, and at the end of his recitation Charles explained that he and Lisa had only fetched up in England in the last three months.

'Great Scott. That's two years or more since VE Day . . .'

'Yes, Sir. It was quite a mess out there.'

'Of course, of course. You nursed in Burma, then, did you?' he enquired, finally addressing a remark to Lisa.

Doesn't he know anything, thought Lisa? Didn't Daddy tell him I was packed off in the last plane to Calcutta? She muttered that she had been evacuated to India and had worked in the Ministry of Munitions.

'Charles and I finally managed to get together,' she said.

'We travelled back to Burma, Sir,' said Charles.

'Why was that?'

He's simply going through the motions, thought Lisa. He doesn't give fourpence what happened to us. Charles, on the other hand, did not seem daunted by the automatic response. He was used to men of this kind, having met scores of them in the Army. In a few words he described the death of Rodney Whitfield and the destruction 'by our own planes' of the timber plantations . . .

'Good lord,' said Guy Bowden. 'How appalling.'

The door opened and Jenny came in followed by a hard-faced woman carrying a tray. Guy Bowden sprang up at the sight of his daughter. His expression changed.

'So you've been helping Mrs Dickens with the toast,' he said tenderly.

'She likes to do it, Sir,' said Mrs Dickens.

'Because I use the toasting fork, don't I, Mrs D?' said Jenny. There was a joke from Guy Bowden. The woman set down the tea-tray, gave a curious look at the visitors and left the room.

Hot food, hot tea and the presence of Jenny Bowden improved the atmosphere. Jenny had taken a shine to Charles and smiled when she passed him the silver dish of buttered toast. She poured tea and parried her father's teasing remarks as if talking to somebody of her own age. The dogs padded into the room and lay down, a mass of brown and russet and black and white in front of the fire.

'They grab all the warmth,' said Jenny, pushing them aside.

'What brings you both to Stratford? Have you come to look up old friends?' inquired Guy Bowden. Implicit in the sentence was the fact that they had no home here any more.

'One or two business matters, Sir,' said Charles. 'By the

50

way, I do apologize for turning up without telephoning you first. We were actually returning to London but then we felt we couldn't leave Stratford without calling at Whitefriars.'

Oh neat, thought Lisa. Not so neat when we mention the silver, though.

'Quite right, glad to see you,' said Guy Bowden. His tone became businesslike. 'I daresay you'll want to collect your property, hm? It's been in my attic since your father asked me to look after it. I've often thought I should get in touch with you but frankly, Charles, I wasn't too sure of your whereabouts. I did know through the Army lists that you were still in the land of the living, so I presumed you'd turn up here eventually. Of course I wrote, a considerable time ago.'

'I never heard from you, Sir.'

'Not after Alec died? Good God!'

His reaction was just like Prynne's; he was astounded at the vagaries of wartime mail. It was as if neither man had taken into their calculations that ships were lost.

'I naturally wrote when your father was taken ill, and again when he died.' Bowden was frowning. 'What must you have thought. This is dreadful. Quite dreadful.' He glared at the carpet.

The three young people sat looking at the man of an older generation shattered at the omission of essential proprieties. They said nothing.

Bowden looked up again. 'If you didn't receive my letter how did you happen to know that some of your property is here?'

'The man at Drury's mentioned it.'

Guy Bowden seemed faintly disgusted at the idea of employees discussing private matters.

'Would you like the packing case to be brought down from the attic right away?'

He made it clear that this would be inconvenient at present. Charles replied that any time that suited Bowden would do. They would call again, having telephoned in advance.

51

The air cleared and Bowden, who had cheered up, remarked that it was a pity it was dark and the weather so bad, or they could have seen their old home.

'Roundwood's been bought by some Birmingham people. They keep it quite shipshape,' he added with a note of patronage.

'I'm not sure I want to see it again,' said Lisa, speaking for the first time in a quarter of an hour.

Guy Bowden did look at her then. He gave a dismissive laugh.

Jenny said, 'I abs'l't'ly agree. It's hideous going back. I try to avoid going to St Catherine's. Frightful.'

'But you were happy there,' said her father.

'Daddy, that's the *point*.'

Charles and Lisa did not leave for a while. Politeness kept them in the warm, beautiful room with people who cared for them as little as they did in return. They spoke of old friends. Of this family and that. The tedious facts which people pay out like money on a counter were given and received. The Milne family had lost their son, a submariner. The Polglaze girl was killed in an air raid. She had been heroic; did they know she'd been awarded a George Medal? Oh yes, Polly Holt and her family were still about.

'She's by way of being an actress now,' said Guy.

The theatre itself at Stratford came into the conversation. Guy said his daughter insisted on him going to see a good deal of Shakespeare.

'You're a governor so you have to go and anyway you enjoy it,' said Jenny in the tone she kept for her father.

'How do you know that?' he said, smiling.

It seemed the moment for the Whitfields to get to their feet and make their adieus. Lisa wanted to add their thanks to Guy for paying the storage bills but she knew he would think it vulgar. As they walked to the front door, Lisa saw Jenny steal a look at Charles from under her eyelashes.

Guy Bowden switched on the light at the entrance. He and Jenny and the inevitable dogs stood there like a group on the front page of *The Sketch* magazine: 'Mr Guy Bowden

52

of Whitefriars with his daughter Jennifer Mary, one of this year's most beautiful débutantes.'

The car bumped away into the snow.

The next day Lisa could scarcely afford to buy some chops – half the week's ration – flour, milk and bruised-looking apples for supper. It was not yet thawing and snow lay in the streets, frozen into rocky furrows. People had to pick their way over it as if crossing a ploughed field. Londoners wore their thickest clothes and Wellington boots and Lisa, shivering in a raincoat, put on three pairs of Charles's tropical Army socks.

When she returned to the Cromwell Road flat the first thing she saw was a note on the drawing-room table – a sheet of her writing-pad on which Charles had scrawled:

> Gone to the club for a spell. Hope to be home sevenish but could be later. You keep warm!
>
> C.

How much money was left after he paid for the meal at The Shakespeare? she wondered. Does he play for IOUs? She didn't know and wouldn't ask; her ignorance of Charles's gambling was deliberate. She had no intention of behaving to him like the sister of a drunkard, hiding the bottles or pouring their contents down the sink. Provided that he did not ruin himself and drag her down with him, she left him alone. She loved him.

She was eating a solitary and frugal lunch when the telephone rang. Another Jeff Ingoldsby with another bloody IOU, she thought. I shall say he's gone away.

'Miss Whitfield. Sorry to bother. Is your brother around?' The clipped voice was instantly recognizable. Jenny Bowden.

Lisa said Charles was out and wouldn't be back until this evening. She waited for the girl, disappointed, to ring off. Lisa had had this kind of conversation before.

'Your packing case was brought down from the attic this

morning,' said Jenny Bowden. 'My father thought p'r'aps you'd want the things. We wondered when . . .' Her quick flat voice trailed.

Lisa wasn't deceived. Since he had been sixteen years old, Charles had been telephoned just like this. Girls with names like Pixie and Topsy had rung Roundwood with weak excuses. Married women, too, with drawled invitations to dances and balls. In Burma there had been the girls who had come out to the East with parents, whose brothers Charles knew. Even yesterday, here at the flat, a woman who said 'Just tell him Claire' had telephoned. Lisa wondered who *she* was.

'It's kind of you to let us know. Is it okay if Charles rings you later today?'

Jenny Bowden said it was 'abs'l't'ly' fine and if her father was out and Charles wanted to make a date to come to Whitefriars, she would arrange it.

I'll bet, thought Lisa when she said goodbye.

Returning to the fire, she sat with her arms round her knees, thinking what should be done. She visualized another Stratford journey, but the impossible problem of petrol coupons might stop the chance of that. As for money, perhaps Charles would win at poker today . . . Lord, she thought, what a thing to depend on. She knew that they must both somehow put their minds to getting work. But doing what?

Men of Charles's age returning from the Services took up the training they had relinquished when they went into uniform, or went back to jobs that had been kept for them, or had the chance of going to university like Jeff Ingoldsby. Girls, too, were not the tenderly protected creatures of the past. Leaving the Services, they had trades. They could drive or had learned photography, or worked in electronics or had been highly efficient secretaries. I wasn't too bad at the Ministry, thought Lisa, my bosses quite approved of me. I suppose I could get some kind of work as a clerk. Somehow she could not visualize Charles working at all, nor see herself in an office as dark as this room in inhospitable London.

One thing shone in her thoughts just then, her own and her brother's single asset. Silver. Blueish and gleaming, reflecting and distorting the tables on which it stood, marked by fingers and then polished with care, her mother's silver occupied her. She remembered a Roundwood maid called Minnie who had cleaned it every Friday morning. Bernadette Whitfield had three maids who came from the same orphanage and were paid £15 a year and their uniforms. Minnie used to sit at the kitchen table spread with newspapers, and smear pink powder dampened with methylated spirits on to the tea-pot, milk jug, a line of Apostle spoons. She rather liked the task although it made her hands filthy.

Then, because silver was in her thoughts, Lisa remembered a bracelet. It was broad and heavy, closing with a snap, and across the front was a Maltese cross worked in brass. Tom Westbury had given it to her. They'd talked about the King awarding the island of Malta the George Cross for withstanding enemy air attacks so bravely. Tom said the bracelet was 'for gallantry'.

Lisa had put out her wrist for him to clasp on the bracelet, wondering what was gallant about behaving well when there was no choice to do anything else?

It was the only present her lover ever gave her. One night in India when their affair had been the most intense and secret part of their lives, they had gone to a flat borrowed from an acquaintance of Tom's. People were kind before they forgot you, and to be alone meant she and Tom could make love. The windows of the flat were wide open to the purple sky crammed with stars. The moon was a crescent out of Arabian nights. In the heavy breathless heat they made love hungrily, the sweat running off their fused bodies, love and sweat glueing them. How they'd loved in those hot nights! How delirious and then exhausted they had been. At last they had come and he had walked naked to where his uniform lay and returned to Lisa, washed in after-bliss. He had put the bracelet around her wrist. She had lazily raised her arm and turned it to and fro, to see the dull gleam of the silver and feel with her finger the bump of the brass-inlaid cross.

55

'It was the badge of the Knights of Malta,' Tom said. 'Those are four barbed arrow-heads, the points meeting in the centre.'

'How suitable,' she said.

'Yes, my dear love. Wear it for me. It's for gallantry.'

When she pulled him close and they embraced he laughed and said the bracelet had scratched his back.

'Good. I want to scar you for life,' Lisa replied.

But the bracelet was lost as Tom was lost. After the war when she and Charles were trying to get to Burma, they had spent a long frustrating day at Army headquarters and returned to a seedy Calcutta hotel tired and dispirited. Sometimes when Lisa slept wearing the bracelet, she woke the next morning to find she'd leaned on her arm and there was a crimson weal round her wrist, for the bracelet's edge was sharp. That night she unsnapped it, put it on the table beside her and fell at once into a deep weary sleep.

Some phantom, light-footed, with long quick hands, had snatched it away. When she awoke the badge of gallantry was gone. She cried for hours and Charles took her in his arms and hugged her and said nothing.

Charles was spending a far more enjoyable winter afternoon than his sister. He was making love to a woman he had known only three days.

Her name was Claire Thompson. She was older than he was, in her late thirties, a slim blonde with a large, promising mouth and that fine skin which shows blue veins, as in marble, on the inside of her arms. When he rang the bell of the flat Claire received him with a grin. She was alone, she said, 'for simply hours'.

The flat in Mayfair was luxurious and before the war had been lavishly decorated by Syrie Maugham. The furniture was creamy white and so were the carpets. There was a slightly chipped elegance about Claire's home which suited a young woman who went in for white dresses and white fox fur coats. Vases of lilies stood about.

Claire had a virginal air, which she retained with her legs

spread wide apart and her clothes thrown on the floor. She and Charles made love like professionals of the art. He slipped inside her slowly, savouring the delight of sex with a stranger – it was exciting to know so little about the woman whose body was penetrated by his own. She was hungry for sex; he liked that too. They made love without a word, panting, breathless, twined into knots or rolling over and over on the outsized double bed. Once they almost fell off. When they finished, their timing in perfect unison, they untwined and separated with the same half smile. Neither of them went to sleep; they lay against the pillows, smoking Claire's cigarettes.

'When's your husband due back?'

'Not till seven. Want a bath?'

'What a good idea,' said Charles, remembering the tepid water at Cromwell Road. He bathed and dressed, kissed her hand heavy with diamond rings and said, yawning, that he ought to go. He was due at the club at half past four.

Claire looked at him through the cigarette smoke. She wanted Charles Whitfield as a regular lover. He was the best she'd ever had; he relaxed her as no other man managed to do. And Lewis was rotten in bed. A good many men hung round Claire. She slept with some of them, but this man was no pet dog. Since her husband played cards with Charles she felt confident that she would manage to see him now and then. Would it be enough? Her instinct told her not to show how strong had been the effect of sex with him. Sex shouldn't make you feel uneasy, thought Claire, and waved to him care-lessly.

'Shall I tell Lewis you'll be at the club tonight?'

'Well . . .' said Charles, remembering his sister somewhat guiltily. 'I'm not sure. 'Bye, Claire.'

He left the scented flat, walked down the staircase which had the particular hush that money buys and went out into Hill Street. He was in excellent spirits after having Claire. Tonight he would win . . .

The game of sex. The game of chance. They were Charles's occupations. War had interrupted them. He'd fought in the Fourteenth Army in the jungle, danger alternating as it always did in war with discomfort or illness or plain boredom. The monsoon fever made soldiers' teeth chatter in their heads, there was the agonizing lack of sleep, the staring-eyed watch relieved by hot, sweet tea brewed in petrol tins. They lived in the jungle with the snakes, the bitter cloying smell of teak, the awesome sight of swollen rivers, the hidden enemy. All that was ended and he was back with games of peace.

He liked the cards. Poker suited him; you needed to use your head. He thought roulette uninteresting. You did nothing but hang over the table to watch a ball bounce with its metal clicks, until it landed on any number out of thirty-six which took its haphazard fancy. Cards were a different matter. They had their own thrill, as sex did.

He had met Claire through his gambling. Like all the men who had come out of the Services after years of war, he had a large number of acquaintances, some of whom – by the coincidences of post-war London – he now met again. There were regimental friends, RAF drinking companions, lieutenants he had played poker with behind the front line during long nights of the monsoon. One acquaintance led to another, and after an evening spent at the United States club, he had called on Lewis Thompson, cousin to his Colonel in Burma.

Thompson was out. Claire, his wife, at home. She perfectly conveyed without a word as she poured Charles a cocktail that she was interested in a little sex on the side.

Charles had no conscience about taking a married woman to bed – in this case her own bed – if she indicated that was what she wanted. In matters of sex he worked on a simple rule. If a girl was married, then she must make the first move. He had no intention of breaking up a marriage which, until he appeared, had possibly been happy. But if the girl was single, he did the hunting. His rule worked wonders. He had long since stopped trying to remember how many women he had pleasured, as the rakes of the eighteenth century called the act of making love.

When he let himself into the Cromwell Road flat he

sniffed. There was an aroma, not of French scent but of fish. Lisa was in the kitchen at the cooker with her back to him. He went in softly, as children do to surprise people, crept up behind her and kissed the nape of her neck. The afternoon had put him in a good mood.

'Have we bought a cat?'

Lisa twisted round. 'I'm trying to make kedgeree.'

Charles felt a stab of discomfort at the contrast between Claire, naked, big-bosomed and creamy, and his sallow, cross little sister.

'I'm sure it'll be very appetizing, Lou, but alas I'm going to be out.'

'You said you'd be home. You went out this afternoon.'

'Dear me. So I did. I called on some guys. Quite amusing. I'm popping round to the club now. I'll have a sandwich there. Sorry about the meal, Lou.'

'What are you going to use for money?'

He made a tut-tut sound and shook his head. 'I trust you're not turning into a private detective. The part doesn't suit you. Life isn't so bad, is it? Think of Mother's silver stashed away at Whitefriars. No, Lou –' he stopped her from speaking and held up his hand. A stranger looked out of his eyes. 'It's no good going on at me. I'm off to the club, and tomorrow we'll talk about the future since clearly that's what you have in mind.'

'Jenny Bowden rang. Her father's got the packing case out for us.'

'Good. Good. We'll drive down to Stratford again.'

He was perfectly obliging now; leaning against the kitchen wall, a temporary prisoner of affection.

'Shall we go tomorrow?' asked Lisa, pressing her advantage.

'Hardly. A little matter of petrol coupons,' said Charles, actually thinking about Claire. 'There's no desperate hurry. At least we know we are going to have something to flog. Look, don't spend the evening alone. Why don't you ring up those nice Rogersons, the ones we met on the boat? They liked you a lot, they kept asking you to go and see them.'

'I might,' said Lisa.

59

It was true. The Rogersons had been lively and funny and had made a fuss of her. But Charles was fobbing her off.

She read every thought in his head except those about sex. She knew that for the moment she had lost him, that he was occupied with plans to waste their money when he eventually got his hands on it and in the meantime was perfectly content to live on credit.

'Good. I like you to enjoy yourself,' he said, with a patronizing touch on her hair.

She waited until he had left the flat, listened until his steps receded down the staircase. She was filled not with resentment but energy. She had lived a whole life without him during the war. She had better start again. She went to the telephone, and later to her underclothes drawer where she took out the ten grubby pound notes from under her knickers. This was the emergency she had been saving for.

The train from Paddington the next morning did not go direct to Stratford but steamed its way in clouds of smutty smoke as far as Leamington Spa, where anybody visiting Stratford had to descend. Lisa got out and sat in the waiting-room drinking Bovril and hot water while she waited for the connection. The journey, made often during her girlhood, hadn't changed. She had always travelled to London and back by train when she had been invited to dances; her father never offered to drive her in his expensive Buick car.

The local train for Stratford finally drew into the station, smelling strongly of diesel oil. The long compartment was open, with wooden seats like those in an old-fashioned tram. There were no corridors. From London the journey had taken less than an hour and a half. To Stratford, ten miles further on, it would take almost another hour.

The diesel made its slow, smelly way through deep country, stopping at stations whose names Lisa thought she'd forgotten but now recalled like a litany. Hatton. Claverdon. Bearley. At each tiny station a few people left or boarded the train. The platforms, slippery with ice, were scattered with gravel. Everywhere – apart from the monotonous chant of the guard at each station – was very quiet.

This journey was not only an impulsive action of Lisa's. She knew, more in her stomach than her heart, that she must do something at once. It wasn't safe to leave anything to Charles any more. Perhaps it never had been. The message from fate had been delivered by the fat hands of Ingoldsby and Lisa had read it correctly. When she had crept from the house at half past eight in the morning, Charles had been asleep. She had left a laconic note on the kitchen table:

> Gone to S/Avon. Thought we'd better get started. Home tonight.
>
> L.

Now she stared from the window at the bare trees and dull-coloured winter grass, at a muddy lane leading nowhere, at the colourless scene in which browns and faint reds and greens without light were spread on either side of the railway line, denying there would ever be a summer.

The lightless white sky, the bare bones of trees affected her. She was homesick for this country. She had had no time for emotion during her last visit to Stratford with Charles; you needed to be alone to sense invisible things, the worst or best of the past. Perhaps we could live here again, she thought. Her girlhood had been a country idyll, a time of kingcups. The East with its sudden gigantic flowers, un-earthly in colour and withered in half a day, was dying in her as love itself had been made to die. She wanted to come home. Were any of her friends still living here? Boys and girls who had played tennis with her, middle-aged couples at whose houses she and her father and brother had sat at pretentious 1930s dinners, waited upon by maids in lace caps. There's the rub, she thought: I'm Rip van Winkle returning home after all those years. Everybody will be married or dead.

The diesel drew up at last with a sigh at Stratford station, the end of its journey, and Lisa climbed from the train with a group of other passengers who were more warmly clad than she was, a small figure in a thin black coat, hatless in an icy wind. She came out of the station, glancing to where the taxis used to stand. There stood an ancient, mud–splashed Ford, waiting hopefully. Longing to climb into it, she turned her face towards the town. She must find a bus or be forced to walk the three and a half miles to Whitefriars.

The idea of walking did not oppress her once she had stopped yearning for the cab. Putting her hands in her pockets, she swung along fast, her steps crunching, passing the cattle market with its network of railings and enclosures, its scattered muddy straw. That hasn't changed, she thought. Nor had the curve of Meer Street, a line of shops, a familiar pub on a corner. Even the scent of the town was the same.

Just as she reached Bridge Street a car went by. It was driving quite slowly and Lisa glanced at the driver without curiosity. A knife of recognition pierced right through her. Of course the man in the car wasn't Tom. She hadn't set eyes on him since the terrible night in India when they had parted. He could be anywhere. He could be dead. Was the shape of a man's head, the set of his shoulders, going to continue haunting her? She had thought she was free of ghosts. She shivered, loathing the moment of hallucination.

She began to walk faster, as if to escape it.

# 4

In January the Calcutta nights were cold and Lisa pinned eiderdowns up at the windows. The flat where she and two girlfriends lived was part of an enormous house in the Chowringhee, a spacious road once the height of fashion in British India. Flat-topped classical mansions in the style of the great London houses had been built along the road, facing stretches of grass where bullocks grazed. The mansions had high walls, there had been gardens with trees and fountains, and the rooms were marble-floored and jewelled with stained glass.

The Chowringhee was no longer the Park Lane of Calcutta; it was now littered and filthy. Offices and shops had replaced many demolished houses, and those still standing were now ramshackle flats. In the wide thoroughfare where once the carriages had bowled along bearing girls under silk parasols were tanks and Army cars, bicycles, urchins with tin whistles and refugees with hand-carts. Lisa and her friends lived like gypsies in three huge, dilapidated rooms in which they entertained the world.

She was standing on a chair, struggling with safety pins and holding up a Persian-patterned quilt, when there was a loud knock at the front door.

'Your turn,' shouted Marguerite from the bathroom.

'Why can't Peggy answer it?' yelled Lisa, still trying ineffectually to fasten the heavy quilt. The flat was in its usual chaos.

63

'She's not back from hospital. Oh Lisa, for Pete's sake, answer the door or whoever it is will think we aren't here, poor thing.'

Lisa unwillingly let go of the quilt and picked her way across piles of blankets, kit bags, rolls of bedding and suitcases. At the front door, inevitably, she found a British officer.

'Do come in.'

'How kind of you. My name's Westbury. Tom. I'm a friend of Bob Shaw, he's in my squadron. He was here with you last month and did mention . . .' said the young man.

They always introduced themselves like that. Being a guest at the girls' flat was like participating in a chain letter. One officer meant six more, and those six another six. Marguerite once counted the visitors and stopped at a hundred and seventy-two.

'I'm afraid everything's a bit –' said Lisa, gesturing around her. There had been ten officers sleeping the previous night and although the Punjabi cook and her husband did their best, they fought against the tide.

The new visitor was in RAF uniform, a pilot's wings on his blue tunic. He was tall, broad-shouldered, with black hair cut very short and curling all over his head. His face was amusing and tired. He looked self-assured. Many of the visitors were shy; Lisa preferred that.

'Keeping out the cold? Good idea,' he said, seeing the fallen quilt, in the corner of which Lisa had fixed her only large safety pin. 'Can I help?'

In a matter of minutes he had fixed three quilts to three windows. He was neat-handed and when Lisa complimented him he said he had been good at carpentry when he was a kid. 'Makes you a wizard with pins.'

During the evening Peggy returned from the big hospital where she nursed, and she, Marguerite and Lisa entertained the usual eight or ten officers who were grateful and talkative, eager to help, instantly friendly and arriving with offerings. There might be a bottle of Scotch or a sweet Indian cake. Flowers (orchids), playing cards (dog-eared), liar dice (the

64

kings and jacks almost defaced). Tom Westbury stayed at Lisa's side all the evening. They went out into the kitchen, where the cook had worked miracles – a very large curry had been prepared and was bubbling gently on the stove. But the numbers for supper had risen to twelve.

'What do you think?' asked Lisa, stirring the rich yellow mess.

'It looks luscious.'

'There isn't enough to go round, though.'

'You – are – quite – wrong,' said Tom, bending to kiss her cheek. Lisa quite liked the embrace which was no more than the usual salutation that all the officers gave the girls who had been good enough to welcome them.

'Why am I wrong, as a matter of interest?'

'Because I shall serve out. Ah, there's the rice, and isn't that dhal? My favourite. And some aloo and puris. I shall make it go round miraculously. I have a mathematical eye.'

'Is that useful?'

'Of course, it is! Distances. Weights. Measurements. Girls.' He put a large hand around her waist. 'I calculate your waist is twenty-two and a half inches. Perhaps less. Am I right?'

They began to ladle out fresh coriander chutney. She laughed and said he was, to within a quarter of an inch, but she didn't see why knowing her waist measurement was useful.

'It will be. I didn't bring you anything tonight, to my shame. Actually I couldn't believe you girls were going to allow me to stay at all. Tomorrow I shall buy you the most beautiful belt in Calcutta.'

Lisa lived in the flat off the Chowringhee for a year. She had been forced to leave Burma, feeling her heart would break. In December 1941 the Japanese had bombed Rangoon. Huge clouds of war were coming towards Taunggyi, yet the English colony at the club were perfectly unruffled. They gave parties. Life went on despite the refugees crowding in from Rangoon. Nobody treated the danger seriously.

Uncle Rodney had his own ideas and told her one morning,

out of the blue, that he intended to get her out while it was still possible. He had friends in Calcutta and had arranged a seat for her in a plane bound there the next day. Lisa saw, by her uncle's face, that arguing was no good. She packed a few possessions – 'the plane's small, the less you take the better,' he had said. He gave her four judicious letters of introduction.

'Now listen to me, my dear. You must see these people personally. They're all old friends of mine, and one or other of them will give you a hand, sure as a gun. I've also arranged for some money in our Calcutta bank to keep you going.'

Her uncle and her brother saw her off to the plane: one small figure bound for enormous India.

When the plane was airborne Lisa cried. For Charles, in unfamiliar Army uniform, making a joke as he kissed her goodbye. For her uncle, whom she loved far more than she'd ever loved her father. For the bungalow which had become home, where in the short winter the wild flowers sprang up like in an English June – wild roses, enormous violets – and where across the thick, massed trees the golden pagoda glittered. She looked out at the relentless sky and tears ran down her cheeks.

The wife of a major, whom Uncle Rod had telephoned, met her and received her kindly. Lisa was grateful. But she set off within a day in the sweaty heat to do as her uncle had instructed, to deliver his letters. Two of the important friends had left Calcutta, one was too grand to bother with a young refugee, but the fourth was a colonel who had a daughter of Lisa's age in England. He talked to her, gave her tea at the country club and found her a job. Lisa became a clerk in the Ministry of Munitions. The work was detailed, dealing with the despatch of trains loaded with munitions, tanks and machine guns. It was monotonous but Lisa was fortunate in her boss, a Captain Entwistle from Lancashire, permanently tired and a chain-smoker, who called her 'lass'. It was he who heard about the flat in the Chowringhee.

Now over a year later in 1943, the flat was her home and her life.

Calcutta was a huge Oriental city swarming with the poor, and filling, week by week, with refugees driven to it by a recent famine in Bengal. The people spoke many different languages, they worshipped hundreds of different, often cruel gods. Sometimes there were air-raid warnings, and crowds streamed out of the city like a great white river.

But for Lisa and her friends the place was enjoyable, familiar, the city where they worked and where they looked after any and every visiting soldier. During the day camp beds, made of string stretched on folding frames, were propped up in the kitchen and in the passages. Every night new young men appeared, some already known, some total strangers. They came off the trains or from planes, were mostly British but sometimes American and Australian. Every man was glad of a bath, of a chance to talk to three pretty girls who welcomed him like a brother. The atmosphere in the flat, hot, disorganized, noisy, was that of a continuous party.

The other girls were Marguerite and Peggy. Marguerite was quiet, dark and melting. She worked with Lisa at the Ministry and was permanently in love. When the officer, whoever he was, had to leave, Marguerite wept. She vanished into the bedroom she shared with her two friends and wrote a burning letter ten minutes after the young man had gone. By the next day her tears were dry and only too soon she was falling for another temporary visitor.

'Your trouble,' said Peggy in diagnosis, 'is being in love with love. I pity any guy dotty enough to marry you.' Marguerite liked insults on those lines.

Peggy was married to a doctor who'd been taken prisoner in the 1940 débâcle in France. When she knew he was alive, but in Germany, Peggy put in for work overseas. She was thin, fair, and what Marguerite termed 'hideously practical'. Friend to everybody and lover to none. She knew when the Red Cross parcels arrived at her husband's camp, what date he received her letters and how his health was – he described it as 'not too bad'. That was a phrase he often used; the life of a prisoner was 'not too bad' either.

67

She didn't believe either of those things. She rarely talked about him and behaved as if she were going to see him again tomorrow.

Lisa herself had flirtations and went to bed with nobody. She was twenty-one and in a world of men it seemed wise.

This way of life – in which strangers were friends from the moment they rang the front doorbell – could not fail to suit the three girls. They flowered in masculine company.

There were the two Punjabi servants – fat, motherly Taro and her husband, thin and bearded Jeeta – who looked after them. Taro was a magnificent cook, wore flowers in her hair, and taught the girls the mysteries of curry. Jeeta did the marketing, some of the housework and vanished every day with a basket full of laundry. When the Punjabi couple finished their work – Taro always left a hot meal ready for them all – she made the girls promise not to wash up. Next morning she always discovered that the officers had done it.

The Punjabi couple called the many visitors 'the Angresi', and liked them. Living with an enormous family of half a dozen children, aunts, cousins and elderly parents, they were at home with noise and laughter, raised voices and too many people crowding into rooms and overflowing on to balconies. What they told their relatives about the Chowringhee flat Lisa often wondered. She was sure Taro and Jeeta imagined orgies.

The odd thing was there were none. The men arriving were exhausted and dirty and Jeeta took away their uniforms, returning them – spotless – in a matter of hours. The visitors came from endless journeys, isolated outposts in the battle zone, airstrips. Here, miraculously, they found a small patch of civilization, pretty girls who behaved like sisters or cousins or friends met in peacetime. Sex reverberated like music, but you couldn't make love in a flat packed with people.

Lisa did not resemble the susceptible Marguerite. She had met men of every kind from fatherly, well-set up officers in their fifties with daughters of her age, to angry, demanding young men who wanted to leap on her and were only

68

prevented by the crowds in the flat. She did not fall in love with anybody. She had been in love only once before Tom came on the scene. It had been an experience she remembered with disbelief. Philip had been a friend of her brother's in Burma, a handsome, olive-skinned, confident man who had singled her out at dances, partnered her at tennis, bought her champagne and paid her compliments. He was attractive and Lisa loved him with the adoration of a first sexual awakening. A day with Philip was 'bliss', she wrote in her diary. A day without him 'despair'. When he kissed her she was so excited she scarcely knew what was happening. Once he opened the bosom of her dress and kissed her breast and Lisa thought she would faint.

Unexpectedly he told her he was leaving. The next day he went back to Rangoon. She was devastated.

Charles did not give her an ounce of sympathy. 'All this misery and not a bit of commonsense. Phil is rich. You knew that, didn't you?'

'What do you mean?'

'My good girl, people with money marry money. It's a law of nature.'

'I didn't know,' said Lisa looking bleak.

He sighed. 'You're quite pretty in a way. But don't be so keen. Men prefer to do the hunting. You did run after Phil. Don't do it again with the next man.'

Charles was annoyed because he was sorry for her. He liked hearing her laugh, seeing her in a new dress, watching her tease Uncle Rod, knowing that at parties she would be surrounded by admirers. He was pleased when she danced her shoes shabby. Of course Phil wouldn't have looked at Lisa as a wife – she hadn't a farthing.

Two or three months later, exactly as prophesied, Phil married a girl with money who also happened to be an Honourable.

That had been five years ago and Lisa remembered nothing about Phil but his swarthy good looks and her own foolish misery. It made her smile. Falling in love was lunacy. She didn't fancy it . . .

69

Certainly she liked Tom Westbury's appearance. He was a big, commanding, yet rather graceful man. She liked his resonant voice, his short, curling black hair. Having a brother who had towered over her from her childhood, she felt at home with Tom's height as she did with his conversation. She liked the laughter lines at the corner of his eyes. He was old to Lisa – twenty-eight – and she liked the fact that he took nothing seriously. He understood inferences, challenged her opinions, criticized what she said. She was used to men who agreed with her because she was pretty.

She knew very well he found her attractive, after the first night that he spent on the floor at the Chowringhee flat, and she was pleased and not a bit surprised when, emerging into the baking heat rising shimmering from the pavements at the end of her day at the Ministry, she found him waiting.

'Tom. How – how nice.'

'Did you expect me?'

'Well . . .'

'Yes you did, conceited woman. Shall we go to the club?' He saved her from instant death as an Army-requisitioned Ford practically skidded on to the pavement. Lisa was wheeling her bicycle.

'I can promise your bicycle will be quite safe at the club,' he said. 'I checked. They'll keep it for you in the cloakroom. I was talking to Marguerite this morning – she told me she's had one of her wheels stolen three times "so far". I thought it ominous.'

'Marguerite tends to forget where she's put her bike.'

'Ah,' he said, smiling. 'One wonders why.' Again steered her out of harm's way. The pavements were thickly crowded and she was small and easily jostled.

'What do you say to ice-cold champagne?'

'It sounds unbelievable, but I ought to change.' She was conscious of her dull cotton dress crushed after the day's heat in the stifling Ministry offices.

'Nonsense, you look lovely. I remember when I first saw you I thought that. Now you're even more so.'

'You mean when we first met last night?' answered Lisa, quite willing to flirt.

70

'Aha. I thought so. You don't remember me.'

Lisa came to a surprised halt, to the annoyance of a naval officer walking behind them.

'Steady on there,' exclaimed the officer. He looked down with indignation to discover that her bicycle wheel had made a long dusty mark on his immaculate white uniform trousers.

'I am so sorry. My friend is an appalling driver,' apologized Tom. Far from mollified, the unfortunate man walked gloomily away. 'The poor beggar will have to go home and change,' remarked Tom, watching him.

Lisa was selfishly paying no attention. 'I'm certain we haven't met. You've never been to the flat before.'

'True. I haven't been to the Chowringhee.'

'Then were you in Burma? At Taunggyi? Surely I would remember —'

'So I should hope. Further back still.'

'Oh, do stop looking as if you'd swallowed a jug of cream! Where have we met before?'

'Try Lincoln . . .'

'I have never been to Lincolnshire,' said Lisa who thought him very silly.

'Nor have I.'

'I come from Warwickshire.'

'Same here. Try Lincoln College, Oxford. Ah, now you remember. I met you there with Charles at a party during Eights Week. You danced with me once or twice.'

She was for a moment overwhelmed. It wasn't a very exciting coincidence. It happened often when people met who came from the four corners of the earth. Yet it affected her. It seemed oddly valuable, something different from the casual bond as short-lived as a bunch of flowers which withered in less than a day in the Calcutta heat. This man wasn't a one-night or two-nights visitor, grateful, hot, tired and passing through as if the Chowringhee flat were a sort of railway station. He came from her part of England. They'd danced in a college in Oxford, and he had known Charles, which made him precious. Perhaps they had sat in the

71

quadrangle on the rim of the fountain. They had breathed the same English air long ago.

'We're old friends, you see,' said Tom Westbury, leading her into the huge white building constructed in the last century as a hymn to English glory. The palace was meant for stately receptions, balls when the girls wore kid gloves to their armpits. The music of the polka. Durbars, even. Tom pushed the bicycle expertly to a cloakroom, while Lisa stood adrift in an entrance hall large enough for a cathedral. He returned smiling.

'The cloakroom attendant has a varied life. A monkey on a chain. Enormous bunches of roses in a bucket. A ring-necked parakeet with a bright blue tail, who's trying to talk and letting out wild shrieks. And two hundred Army caps. The RAF seem in short supply this evening. Come along, we'll track down some champagne.'

They sat in a window-seat overlooking the parched garden. The sun was swiftly setting and the shadows were blackened fingers.

'Shall we drink to getting back home in one piece?' he said, lifting his glass. Lisa did the same.

'I'm a cheat, really,' she said, after a moment. 'I mean, I pretend to be like everybody else, homesick for England, but it's five years since I came out. This is what is real. Charles and I left for Burma in '38, you know.'

'I remember asking somebody where Charles had got to and being told he'd left at the end of his second year. Was he bored with university? Some of us were.'

'No.'

His expression was rather satirical, but since he asked no more questions about her brother, it would have been easy for Lisa to change the subject – which was why she continued.

'Charles had to go down because my father was fed up with him gambling.'

'He was quite a star at poker.'

'Not starry enough. Debts and things. We have an uncle in Burma, in forestry, and he said Charles could go there.

Charles worked for Uncle Rod in the jungle, as a forest man. He'd never done anything but enjoy himself at home and suddenly there he was, learning to be in charge of a hundred elephants,' she said. 'They used to fell the teak and float it down the river. Some of the teak log-rafts literally took years to reach Rangoon. Charles enjoyed it. It was tough and he made good friends. He enjoyed his leaves too. Dances and full-speed polo.'

'What about you?'

'I went to Burma for the fun of the thing.'

'And was it fun?'

Lisa paused, remembering rides in the fresh mornings, frangipanis with thick, creamy petals, a pagoda huge and golden floating over the trees.

'Oh yes.'

They sat in the filtered light of the vast old-fashioned room while figures moved about – waiters with trays or silver buckets of ice, men in uniform arriving or leaving. There was a continuous hum of conversation, sudden bursts of laughter. While she and Tom Westbury talked of the present and the past there came from him a warmth which was the antithesis of the cruel heat of the tropics. Something about him embraced her. She liked many though not all of the scores of young men who came to the Chowringhee flat to sleep on the floor and be looked after for a little while. One evening she had spent an hour fending off the sexual supplications of a sad young Welshman with brown eyes, who'd begged and begged her to make love with him. They'd go to his club! To a hotel! Oh, he couldn't express how he felt about her! His Welsh voice was full of poetry, and his face moved her. But though she found him attractive, perhaps because of his desperation and a sense of sorrow, she never for a moment considered accepting his earnest pleas. She discussed what had happened with Marguerite, who opened her eyes wide and said 'Of course you said no. You didn't love him.'

There were times when Lisa was a little fretful, sharing a flat with a helpless romantic and a rigorously faithful wife. Two extremes and she did not feel in accord with either.

Tonight as she sat and talked to Tom Westbury she did not understand her sensation of happiness. It must be because this pleasant man knew her brother. It made Charles, whom she sorely missed and rarely heard from, seem more real because Tom actually knew him.

They walked back after a long, idle meal through Calcutta streets smelling both of flowers and refuse. The city was never deserted; muffled white figures slept in the shadows of buildings, under archways, by walls, wrapped like figures of the dead. There wasn't a sound. Tom wheeled the bicycle and they talked as if they were old friends although, in reality, all they had spent was a few hours together.

The moment they entered the flat, they were welcomed and engulfed in company. An Australian pilot had arrived that evening. His offering to the company was half a dozen Christmas puddings which he was now frying, to the disbelieving shrieks of Marguerite and Peggy. An Australian voice could be heard exclaiming plaintively, 'But I tell you, kids, they're going to taste good!'

Tom had four days' leave before returning to active service. He'd come from an advanced airstrip very close to the fighting. In the way of men in uniform, he told Lisa little; all he said was that he was flying supplies over the Japanese lines to troops in the jungle. His main job was to evacuate the wounded.

'Do you do that every day?' asked Lisa.

'Well . . . twelve trips is a good average.'

'But how many men can you fit into your plane?'

'A total of fifty or sixty in the day.' He said it was all pretty well organized. The wounded lay about on the airstrip while the pilots drank tea and waited their turn to fly. 'Some of the soldiers have come straight out of action. They're so quiet. Wounded men always are when they're waiting to be moved.' In the plane the badly wounded lay on a bench, the less wounded crouched on a seat or the floor. Four men meant a lot of extra weight and the trouble was getting airborne. 'Sometimes we only just about make it. Once we built a damned great pile of sandbags, flew the crate straight into it and that made it jump into the air. I wish you'd stop looking at me like that. Admiration's bad for a man.'

The following evening Tom took her out for a meal again, rather than sharing with a dozen people the noisy scramble at the flat. Both Marguerite and Peggy noticed Lisa's changed manner when she was getting dressed. They winked at each other. Lisa, who never took long to get ready, took an hour. She put on a salmon pink silk dress made from a Burmese *longyi* – one of the treasures she'd shoved into an old Gladstone bag of her uncle's when she had taken the plane for Calcutta. She stared at her face in the mirror, wishing she wasn't so pallid. And thin as a rake. After some thought she pinned a flat white orchid in her hair; she'd bought it on the way back from the Ministry. It had cost the equivalent of threepence.

Tom took her to The Great Eastern Hotel. They ordered Burmese food, of which these Warwickshire-born creatures were fond. A dozen plates shaped like white flowers were placed in front of them; there were sesame seeds, dried shrimps, pickled tea-leaves, roasted peas, salted ginger, mounds of white rice, cinnamon chicken and brightly coloured vegetables.

Lisa was happy. A drenching sweetness came over her; she knew she wouldn't be anywhere else in the entire world. The world was here. She scarcely bothered to talk, leaning her chin on her hand. She scarcely bothered to eat either, but sat pushing small grains of rice round the edge of the plate piled with spiced food. Most of the flower-shaped dishes were still full despite their first interest in them.

'Lisa,' he said.

She roused herself and gave him a slow smile. 'Mm?'

'Shall we make love?'

She felt as if she were falling. 'Could we?'

He didn't even stretch out his hand. 'I think I'll go mad if we don't. I want you all the time.'

'Me too.'

He sighed, as if her confession was sad.

75

Lisa looked at him with heavy eyes. 'We can't go back to the flat.'

He smiled, but only just. 'No, we can't go back to the flat. I can't exactly lay you down on the floor among my fellow officers, can I? But I've thought of something.'

They lingered at the table, but neither of them could eat after all. In the end Tom paid the bill and was salaamed by the head waiter who knew all about untouched meals. The couple, of course, were mad. He had plans for the excellent meal they'd abandoned. There would be a kitchen feast.

Tom and Lisa walked out into the chill of the streets. There had been an air-raid warning earlier that evening and the usual exodus of crowds fleeing from the city. Now only stragglers came sloping back in twos or threes. There were still the ragged figures lying by walls and under archways, too ill or too poor to run to safety.

Tom and Lisa walked in a silence she longed for him to break. She felt unlike herself, tense and excited, as if she were entirely made of nerves.

He had spent his leaves in Calcutta many times before and seemed to know his way through the huge city far better than she did. They passed by a temple dedicated to the goddess Kali. She was worshipped as the queen of war and bloodshed and murder, the incarnation of smallpox and cholera. Lisa was frightened of Kali, a goggle-eyed deity who wore a serpent as a necklace and held a cord for strangling sinners. It was a relief to leave the temple behind and walk beside the river. They came at last to a huge, overgrown garden which had once belonged to a palace now fallen into ruins. She had come here once in the autumn with Marguerite; they had picnicked and then bravely ventured into what was left of the palace to see where rajahs had once lived in splendour. Nothing was left but roofless carved walls, twining creepers, fallen headless images. Marguerite had heard the angry hissing of a little black snake.

The strong moonlight made the gardens unearthly. It coated the leaves of the trees, flooded the dry ground and the broken parched basin of a fountain. Tom and Lisa walked, still in silence, until they reached the base of an enormous tree; it was in full white flower, the blossoms dropping and sending out waves of scent so strong that it felt to Lisa as if she were swimming in perfumed water.

She turned to him and he took her in his arms. They lay down on the iron-hard ground which was covered with dying petals, and then, for the first time, she was heavy with the weight of a man.

He began kissing her, kissing her over and over, and when he came up for air, taking a long breath of the scent, she managed to say, 'I never have before.'

'Do you want to, my darling? Are you sure?'

'Oh, yes, yes, yes.'

They did not undress but somehow undid their clothes, Lisa pulling down her satin knickers, Tom undoing buttons. When he entered her the only part of him which was naked was the loving part; he was still fully clothed and somehow that made it more exciting, as if what they were doing was hidden and wrong.

When love-making was over, they stood up, brushing away the petals, and walked slowly home without saying a word. Tom had his arm looped around her waist and now and then pressed her so close that she felt bruised.

The flat was in utter darkness with the unmistakeable sense of humans sleeping. When their eyes became accustomed to the gloom they picked their way over figures as shrouded as those in the streets. Somebody grunted. Lisa took Tom's hand; she was leading him to the corner where she had arranged a pallet bed.

'Damn, damn,' she whispered, feeling a body where flat blankets should be. 'Somebody's taken it.'

'Don't worry. I'll kip on the floor.'

'I hate you to be uncomfortable,' she whispered, longing to embrace him.

'How could I be. *Now*?'

He did not kiss her but pressed her hand. She reeled into her bedroom in the dark and fell into a sleep so deep it was like diving to the bottom of the sea.

*

77

Why am I thinking of all that? Lisa asked herself, leaving the bus at the crossroads and setting out for the last icy mile to Whitefriars. The dying petals, the almost tangible moonlight, the long lost love were in such cruel contrast to the present. Tall English trees without a leaf. Fading snow and the air so sharp that it pierced into her. The past had come back merely because a man had faintly resembled Tom.

She wished she'd never let herself remember.

It was so cold that as she walked down the drive to the house, her teeth chattered. She began to wish she had waited for Charles to find some petrol somehow and come with him, instead of on this impulsive, miserable expedition of her own.

When Mrs Dickens the housekeeper opened the door she was wearing the same expression of unconcealed curiosity Lisa had noticed on the previous visit. The woman was handsome, white-haired; she looked energetic and self-possessed and Lisa knew perfectly well that *she* knew Lisa had no money.

'Miss Jenny is expecting you, Miss.'

She took her to the drawing-room. Jenny Bowden was sitting by the fire with a positive carpet of dogs at her feet. She wore a blue sweater the colour of hyacinths and when she stood up was immediately busy with the usual country drama of barking, rushing, wagging or growling animals.

'Hello,' said Jenny in brusque fashion. 'Mrs D., do remove Fred. He's decided to show all those yellow teeth.'

Mrs Dickens left the room, her hand on the collar of a snarling mongrel.

'Is your brother with you?' asked the girl.

Lisa had already decided upon her reply and untruthfully explained that Charles had had an appointment 'in the City' which he had tried unsuccessfully to cancel. Jenny looked totally blank, which Lisa took to be the upper-class form of disappointment.

'Oh. I see. Do sit down.'

Lisa did so, her feet and hands beginning to thaw and tingle.

78

'As Charles couldn't come – he was very disappointed –' she said, and relayed an invented message. Jennifer thawed slightly too. There was a pause.

'My father had the packing case brought in here; he thought you and Ch – you'd be more comfortable unpacking in the warm. The seals haven't been broken. It's just the way Mr Whitfield left it,' said Jenny. She went over to a grand piano standing at the end of the room by a wall lined with books. Lisa followed. The case was smallish, of the same kind as those at Drury's, and with Alec Whitfield's handwriting on the nailed label. It was tied with rope and there were red blobs of sealing wax here and there. It looked like a parcel on a Christmas card.

'The seals were my father's idea,' remarked Jenny. 'Are you going to open it? Would you rather be alone?'

'Of course not. Look, could you find a knife to cut the ropes? And we need something to lever out the nails.'

Jenny disappeared, returning with a much smarter wrench than Mr Prynne's and a stout pair of scissors. The two girls were more cordial to each other as they began a task which has been fascinating since the days of ancient Egypt. They cut the strings and levered open the box. They peered in to discover the box was filled with wood shavings, packages concealed among them like prizes in a bran tub. Jenny became quite human when – having first hesitated before being asked by Lisa 'please do help!' – she plunged her hand into the shavings and unwrapped the first package.

'Look! What a pretty cream jug.'

'I've found the coffee-pot. I remember it. Golly, it still smells of coffee.'

'What a dear little silver mouse.'

'I'm sure I remember this cigarette-box.'

They placed each piece of silver on top of the grand piano, which Lisa covered with newspapers – Jenny wouldn't have bothered. When they had finished scrabbling almost headlong to make sure nothing remained, they surveyed the booty.

A silver teapot with a cracked ivory handle. A coffee-pot

of 1920s design with an attached lid. Four cream jugs. A double-handled christening mug engraved with Lisa's grand-father's Irish name and birth date. The silver mouse. A silver cigar-case, and a tiny engraved and initialled box which had contained matches. Only one item of Bernadette Whitfield's had a particular value: a large round eighteenth-century salver which Lisa's mother had called a tazza.

'It's an heirloom, that's what it is,' Bernadette used to say, bringing out the great silver dish with its single trumpet foot in the centre like a little pedestal. The tazza was only used at dinner parties, to serve glass dishes of egg custard.

Beside it sat the mouse with its long curved tail.

'That big dish is pretty,' said Jenny.

'Yes,' said Lisa, busy with its own thoughts.

Hearing in the tone that her visitor was uninterested in her, Jenny had a feminine desire to change Lisa's mind. For the first time since she had opened the door and found the Whitfields sheltering from the snow, Jenny actually looked at Lisa and saw her. Up until now Lisa hadn't affected her one way or the other and had not figured much in the girl's thoughts. Jenny was an excluding young woman; either people were friends or they were nothing. She had felt that Charles Whitfield might become the first kind, and now she even found herself regarding his sister with interest. Jenny had not recovered from the disappointment of not meeting him again; perhaps Lisa Whitfield might be useful. She was very different from any of Jenny's girlfriends: she looked poor and strong. Jenny recognized strength; she had lived with it all her life.

They returned to the fire. The dogs looked up, hoping for action, and then went to sleep again.

'Some of the things are nice,' she ventured. 'Specially that mouse.'

Lisa stirred herself and said on an impulse, 'Do have it.'

Jenny blushed red and scowled. 'Abs'l't'ly sweet of you. Couldn't possibly.'

That, thought Lisa, was a *faux pas* of mine, damn it. By luck, Jenny's father came into the room just then, shook

80

Lisa's hand and enquired if Jenny was looking after her. Lisa made polite replies and Jenny said, 'Charles Whitfield couldn't come.'

'He was so disappointed,' said Lisa for the second time, adding explanations which Guy was not interested in hearing. With no man about, he gave his visitor some attention. He found the spectacle of this young woman in his drawing-room very curious; he'd known her since her birth, yet she was a total stranger and now here she was, with wood shavings and newspapers all over the place, and a load of tarnished silver on his piano.

'I see you've been finding what's what,' he said. 'I fear it will have to be packed up again when you take it to London.' He gave her an enquiring look, indicating that he would help her make arrangements.

'Just what I thought,' said Jenny.

The Bowden manner and speech, their abrupt arrival at the point, was catching. Lisa, unconscious of using their vernacular, said, 'No point in taking it if I can sell it here.'

'Sell it? Some of it, you mean.'

'No, Mr Bowden. The lot.'

He did not reply, but asked Jenny if she'd forgotten to offer her guest any coffee. She had? Then would she go and see Mrs Dickens, please. Jenny left as if she would like to slam the door.

Bowden sat down in a high-backed chair, and looked at Lisa for a moment. Somewhere in her sallow face his old friend looked back at him. Bowden rubbed his chin; he detested messes, there were none in his well-organized life, and Lisa Whitfield and her dirty silver represented the tail-end of the worst mess he'd had the ill fortune to witness. Without the brother present, he found that he did not exactly dislike the sister. She had poise and reserve. But she was still a nuisance.

'It seems unfortunate that you should sell the only things remaining of your old home. Apart from whatever is at Drury's.'

Lisa still spoke in his own tongue. 'There's nothing there

81

worth selling, and Charles and I haven't a bean. Just about scraped together enough to get home. Until we get work, that' – nodding at the silver – 'will tide us over.'

Bowden received this in silence.

'I have no idea how one sells things. Can you advise me?' she asked bluntly.

'What about your brother? He may prefer to keep your silver.'

'Oh no. He leaves things to me.'

'I see. But what you have just said about your circumstances surprises me. Your father assured me when he came to live here after Roundwood was sold that you and your brother were well provided for.'

Lisa did not realize that she made a face. She was not heartless, but her father's ghost never haunted her. He had not loved her. When he had died, she had been sad because he had symbolized her youth and girlhood and had been the husband of her laughing, lost Irish mother. Losing her lover had struck her to the core – but not her father's death.

Faced with his pitiful duplicity she repeated, 'We haven't a bean.' Bowden did not reply, and she added with what he considered unnecessary brutality, 'In any case, the silver was my mother's.'

He said nothing more for a while. He was thinking of Alec Whitfield more kindly than Alec's daughter had done. He recalled his friend's precise manner, the occasional smile which lit the care-worn, bearded face. His nervous voice had a touch of music; he was pigheaded and had a cultured charm. Above all, the essence of the man was his absolute talent for disastrous decisions. Alec had never been so real as he was at this moment years after he was dead.

Bowden's affection finally spoke. 'I believe I know somebody who might be of use to you. She owns an antique shop in Stratford. I'm sure she could advise you about selling your silver.'

Before Lisa could thank him, Jenny put her head round the door. 'May I come in? Hot steaming coffee arriving.'

Coffee was followed later by an excellent lunch. The

Bowdens were pleasant to Lisa, asked her questions about Burma and India and looked interested in her replies. Jenny was impressed by a young woman who'd travelled so far – she herself had never set foot outside England.

Guy Bowden wanted to hear about the years that Lisa and her brother had spent with their uncle. He already knew that Rodney Whitfield had died during the Japanese invasion; he had known Alec's brother well when they were boys, and Lisa saw that he must have liked him. But who couldn't have liked Rodney?

'Such an excellent chap,' said Bowden, 'Pure gold right through. You had a good life with him, I am sure.'

Lisa said her uncle had been so kind, had given Charles his job and had looked after her – her face lit up when she spoke about him. He'd been wonderful. She had often wished that Uncle Rod had been married – he was a real father! She didn't notice what she was saying.

'I used to say to Charles that our uncle stayed single because he liked everything perfectly organized. He was a dear man, but things had to be *his* way. Very autocratic,' she said and smiled.

She was talking to somebody who shared her dead uncle's tastes. Guy Bowden also perfectly organized his life. He was incapable of doing things badly or carelessly. He had served in the War Office during the recent war where his efficiency and a certain ruthlessness had won him praise. He ran his financial affairs, his interest in the arts, his home, his horses, with supreme skill. Nothing escaped his sharp eye. Even his love for his daughter was channelled into the right lines for her welfare, her happiness and her control.

'And where did you live when you were working in Calcutta?' he asked Lisa, remembering that Rodney Whitfield had found it necessary to send this young woman unaccompanied to India. And that had been entirely the result of Alec Whitfield's dire shrugging-off of his children.

'There were three of us who shared a flat. A girl working in the Ministry with me, and a nurse at the Military hospital.'

83

'Yes, I remember now. You wrote to your father to say where you'd fetched up; wasn't it in the Chowringhee?' Lisa was impressed that he should recall the name of that once famous street. 'I'm afraid I never considered you should have been packed off either to Burma or to Calcutta by yourself,' he added.

Lisa answered that her uncle had only just got her out of Burma in time; she'd been on one of the last planes. He had been determined for her to be evacuated.

'Awful, being evacuated,' remarked Jenny with some feeling. 'For the person having to leave, *and* for the people who put them up.' Whitefriars had been full of London children during the war; she had detested every minute of it. Her father thinned his lips. He disliked it when she complained.

The talk changed. They no longer discussed the man whom Guy Bowden had liked and Lisa had loved as her surrogate parent. They spoke about Stratford and the theatre; there had been a brilliant season last year, and there were plans for another to come.

Guy Bowden left the room, and when he came back Jenny was still chattering, with more vivacity than she'd shown until now, about Shakespeare.

'I *howl* at the tragedies.'

'I am sorry to interrupt the theatrical saga,' said her father, 'but I telephoned Mrs Smith who is in her shop this afternoon. She says she could see you and may be able to help with the sale of your silver.'

'It's very good of you, Mr Bowden.'

'Not at all, not at all. In the meantime, you can leave it with me. Telephone when you've made your decision. I shall need to get your silver insured before it is put up for sale.'

'I really am very grateful,' said Lisa, meaning it and adding far too late, 'We never thanked you for paying the storage on my father's things at Drury's.'

Guy Bowden gave a cold smile. He instructed Jenny to drive the visitor into Stratford, then shook hands with her as if with a stranger and disappeared more quickly than was necessary.

It was already dark when Jenny backed an elderly car into the drive and the girls drove off into a countryside still covered with patches of unmelted snow.

'Mrs Smith is an abs'l'te hoot,' remarked Jenny. 'My father's known her ages. She bid for him at a sale the other day for a picture he liked.' She pronounced it 'piksher' and added that her father often brought paintings and went to London to galleries sometimes. 'He bought a Dante Gabriel Rossetti drawing for seven and six.'

When they reached the town, Jenny drove down Bridge Street towards Greenhill Street. There was a long row of prosperous-looking shops, well lit with big windows, and in the middle of these, looking as if it had survived by chance for a couple of hundred years, one ancient, crooked-roofed house. A dull light shone in its little window which was filled with what looked like dusty junk. In Gothic script over the shop were the words 'The Treasure Box'.

'Mrs Smith's domain,' announced Jenny, opening the car door for Lisa. 'You know the way to the station from here, don't you?' She had apparently forgotten that Lisa used to live in Stratford. 'There's the 5.10 and the 6.10,' she added with her father's exactness. 'Good luck.'

She drove away faster than was wise on the icy road.

When Lisa opened the shop door there was a musical peal of bells, the sound of which she instantly recognized. Bells like these hung outside little Burmese pagodas; they were attached to long chains, were made of chased silver and brought good fortune.

Seeing the woman at the counter, Lisa decided the bells had got it wrong this time.

'Miss Whitfield, I take it? Guy Bowden just rang,' said the woman who looked at her ruminatively, as if deciding what price she was willing to pay for her.

Perdita Smith had been pretty as a girl fifty years ago. Now she was in her seventies, with a lined, ruddy complexion and coarse, grizzled hair worn in a fringe and two curtains, one on either side of her face. Her dark red dress swept to the ground and on her bosom was a gold brooch in which three different colours of hair were worked into the pattern of the Prince of Wales's feathers. Her voice, resonant and melancholy, resembled that of an actress of the Edwardian era. She pronounced every syllable.

'Guy Bowden said you want to sell some silver,' she said. 'Do sit down, please. That stool's quite comfortable. Your father left you the silver, did he?'

'My mother, actually. She brought it over from Ireland when she married.'

'Irish silver's not as valuable as English. The workmanship is slightly inferior. Were you aware of that?'

The conversation took the form of playing snap. Down went Lisa's cards, and slammed down on top went Perdita Smith's. Lisa rather liked her and liked her shop more. It was crammed with enticing things . . . sewing-boxes, glove-boxes, chess-sets, teapots, carved wooden spoons, decanter labels, jugs patterned with pansies. It had the lying air of being a place where you picked up a bargain. But Perdita Smith's eyes were expensive.

She was not unhelpful. Since Bowden's telephone call, she had been through some catalogues and found a forth-coming sale which would be just right for Lisa's silver. There was time, she said, to get the property into an additional sales list. She could drive to Whitefriars to collect the stuff.

'You'll have to come with me. We can't have a drama when you discover the best piece is missing,' she chuckled.

She questioned Lisa about the various pieces to be sold. Did Lisa remember where her mother had bought them. Oh, inherited, were they? Where had her mother been born? Lisa replied County Galway and Perdita was unimpressed.

'Crests on them?'

'Initials.'

'Anything you particularly like?'

'The tazza.'

At this Perdita stiffened like a hunting dog pointing at a shot pheasant. Lisa described the tazza and Perdita continued to look very sharp and pointed. 'Well, well, a tazza. That's something. Like some tea?' She went to a cubby-hole behind a curtain. Lisa heard a kettle being filled and a gas ring lit with a pop. 'What train are you taking? There's the 5.10 and the 6.10 but the 6.50 is best – it doesn't stop at Hatton and there's a good connection at Leamington. Sugar?'

Lisa and Perdita drank strong tea and the shop-owner remarked that it was strange she hadn't met Lisa before, since The Treasure Box had been here since the year dot. Well, 1938 actually. Lisa explained that she and her brother had left in 1937.

'India and Burma, eh? Marvellous stuff from India. People used to bring it home by the trunkful when they retired from the ICS. Ivory. Silver, of course. Gold sometimes, let alone carved teak. Inlaid furniture with elephants and so on . . . nobody wants it now. But prices will rise, mark my words. At present you can buy ivory for a song. Buy much in Burma, did you?'

Lisa had a vision of herself at seventeen, filling her uncle's bungalow with gilt umbrellas and brass Buddhas. She said no, she hadn't. Not really. Perdita looked down her nose, indicating that Lisa had wasted her time. By a quarter to five the talk had turned to toy theatres. 'Now, they don't lose their value, particularly in Stratford,' said Perdita Smith. And offered her a job. '£6 a week and every other Saturday morning off unless I happen to need you.'

Lisa accepted.

The journey home took a long time. It was after ten when she let herself into the flat, tired and triumphant. She found Charles in the sitting-room by the electric fire again; if he'd been gambling, he must have come home early.

'There you are at last. I was beginning to worry,' he said. He always stood up when she came into a room. 'You look chilled.'

'Freezing.'

'Hungry?'

'I had a sandwich in the buffet at Paddington. Spam.' She had guessed there would be nothing to eat in the flat.

'I don't know why you dashed off like that, Lou. I could have driven you to Stratford after I'd sniffed out where to get hold of some petrol.'

'I wanted to see the silver. It's all there in good nick.'

'Fine.' He didn't ask for details and was strangely incurious. He offered her a cigarette which she refused. Smoking for a moment or two, he said, 'McAllister rang.'

'How nice of him. I bet it's freezing in Northumberland.'

'He wasn't in Northumberland, he was in Shepherd Market, in that pub on the corner. He's coming home tonight.'

'Tonight? You mean he's popping back for a visit?'

'No, Lou. Back for good.'

'*Charles!*'

'Yes. Bloody, isn't it?'

Charles was a gambler who knew about good and bad odds; if he'd been asked to give them on the owner returning to the flat, he would have said a hundred to five. When you borrowed a place for a song, and Charles was paying ten shillings a week, you could bet your bottom dollar the owner would turn up too soon. Andrew McAllister had hospitably lent them the flat, assuring them that he'd be away for months with his parents. Charles and Lisa would be doing him a favour to live here – it would keep the place warm.

McAllister's months had turned out to be precisely two weeks. Breezy as ever, he had telephoned Charles to say he'd be home around midnight. 'Going to a party first. Don't wait up for me, old chap, I can look after myself.'

As it happened Andrew McAllister was returning to London as a fugitive from Newcastle; he hadn't enjoyed his Northern visit at all. Life was more austere than he could have imagined. His parents had recently left their eighteenth-century house in Jesmond and moved to a small country hotel near Hexham. Life was smaller, duller, colder and poorer than Andrew remembered. The coal shortage had cut so many trains that it had been difficult to get to Newcastle and rather worse to get back to London. But at least he'd now escaped his parents' endless talk about bread rationing. 'We're better off in a hotel, Andrew. Imagine – rationing *bread*! It never happened during the war.'

Andrew couldn't wait for London and the black market.

He said gaily to Charles, 'Don't think I want you and your sister to clear out. I'd love you to stay. You can shack up on the sofa, can't you? Give Lisa my love . . .'

'McAllister suggested we could stay on,' remarked Charles now to Lisa. 'I'm to sleep on the sofa.'

'You can't.'

'Why not?'

'One night on that thing and you'll be the Hunchback of Notre-Dame. Sleep in my bed. I'm short, I can have the sofa.'

'Don't be bloody silly and stop buzzing around like a blue-bottle.'

'You haven't asked how I got on at Stratford.'

'So I haven't. I'm a selfish bastard.'

He was. But his new affair with Claire, which had seemed set for many exciting months, had come to an abrupt halt hours before McAllister telephoned with a second bomb-shell.

Charles had called to see Claire, and found her packing suit-cases.

'Hello, Charles. I hoped you'd hove into view. We've just been invited to Llangellen Castle, what do you think of that? Lord Curig is giving a big shindig for his son, and we've been asked. Lewis and the son met in the Army. There'll be lovely food and drink and a bit of glamour. Isn't it a thrill?'

Although Claire and Charles then made love among the tissue paper and the underclothes on the bed, and although a sated Claire swore she would be back in town 'soon, soon, soon', he had left Mayfair thoroughly disgruntled. Even cards had not worked. Usually playing poker made him feel brighter and more alert; sexier too. Not today. And now, McAllister's call put the kibosh on things.

He roused himself to listen to Lisa describing her visit to Whitefriars. She finished with startling news. She'd got a job. And her new employer was arranging to sell the silver.

'So at least we'll have some cash to tide us over.' She looked at him expectantly, waiting for a compliment.

She put him to shame. She was active and he was passive, she was busy and he had done nothing. Even making love to

Claire and sitting at cards meant nothing. He was suddenly sick of London. People were dingy and so was the town itself. The flat was so dark that you had to have the lights on all day long. There were food queues and chocolate queues and cigarette queues. This wasn't the world he'd expected when he and Lisa had docked at Southampton. He thought of the cold, clean mists of Warwickshire, where people didn't wear scarves across their mouths in case the filthy fog choked them. Of a little town both old to him and new. And the search for luck and love . . .

'What do you say to us going back to live in Stratford, Charles?'

'It sounds okay. This place is a bit of a hole, isn't it?'

It was not a graceful tribute to McAllister's generosity. But Charles had just measured the sofa with his eye. He was six foot two and it was less then five foot nine.

# 5

In February Stratford smelled of woodsmoke. On still days it hung about, coming from the low-roofed cottages along the Bankcroft and the huddled houses in the High Street. There was a quiet air except on market days, when the town filled up and the pubs and the Farmers' Union were noisily packed. World-famous places using capital letters – the Birthplace, Anne Hathaway's Cottage – were unvisited in winter and sometimes closed. A rare American might wander through the town like a bird who had forgotten to migrate. The posters outside the theatre would surprise him, for they announced the D'Oyly Carte or the Stratford-upon-Avon Operatic Company. Where was Shakespeare? Gazing laconically down from his niche in Holy Trinity and telling people to keep away from his bones.

Charles and Lisa arrived after they had been paid for the sale of their mother's silver. Nothing fetched much except for the princely £600 paid for the tazza. Charles was delighted and Lisa wished they could have kept the heirloom. They divided the money in half, knowing it would have to last, and settled into digs which were all they could afford.

Returning to the town they used to know so well gave brother and sister a good deal to talk about at first. Charles took Lisa to The Falcon for a celebration drink, and later they visited the knot gardens of New Place. The yews were as thick as Lisa remembered, and they found the arbour where she had hidden from Charles when she was ten years old.

She began her new job and saw that she was going to enjoy it and Charles, typically, discovered a club where he could play poker. The Wilton was on the first floor of an old house near Scholar's Lane. It wasn't, he said, 'half bad'.

Having settled into their digs they started to look for old friends. But people had moved away or died or, in the case of two girls Lisa had known at school, triumphantly left for the States in 1946 as GI Brides. News of people with whom they'd played tennis, or ridden or gone to parties came filtering through old acquaintances, sometimes through strangers. It was filled with death. Young men killed in Germany, lost at sea, dead in Japanese prison camps. A boy with whom Lisa used to go to the cinema had been in Bomb Disposal, blown to bits three months after he was called up. Apart from one or two elderly people, friends of their father's and not particularly close ones at that, neither Charles nor Lisa discovered a single person whom they looked for. If death hadn't stolen them away, then time had done so. They had sold up and gone to live in Cornwall. They were divorced and had left Stratford. Older friends lived, like McAllister's parents, in hotels. They had emigrated to places like Angmering-on-Sea where they kept small dogs and walked on the beach.

'I vote we give the whole thing up,' said Charles, after telephoning for the seventh time to be told that an old Oxford friend hadn't been heard of for years. 'It's getting eerie.'

But Lisa couldn't bring herself to abandon yesterday. On a frosty night when Charles was out at his club, she decided on one last try. She would spend part of her week's salary on a taxi, and call on three people she hadn't yet managed to talk to. Telephone calls had not been answered. Perhaps her friends were out during the day?

At the station she hired an ancient vehicle driven by a grey-haired, crotchety driver. She described the three calls she planned to make and asked him to set a price. He gloomily agreed to two pounds. Lisa said she would go first to Goring Road.

This first call was on the outskirts of Stratford and too far to walk when she had the other visits to make. Her friend Zoë Silver lived there. Lisa and Zoë had been schoolfriends. They had been in the same lacrosse team, whispered jokes to each other during their sewing class and had long talks during Break on the subject of religion.

'The Holy Trinity is a worry to me,' confessed Zoë. 'God the Father is much too old, and after all the Holy Ghost is only a bird.'

They had shared their sweets, discussed love and lessons and agreed that they adored Maurice Chevalier. They knew the words of all his songs.

Arriving at the big house in Goring Road, Lisa felt optimistic. The house looked prosperous and when she went up the brick path to the front door she saw that the garden was as well-kept as ever. Not a dead leaf on the icy grass. She thought of the fun she had had here with her friend.

She rang the bell. Zoë's mother opened the door.

'If it isn't Lisa Whitfield!'

She was very surprised and pleased and kind; of course she remembered her well and had often wondered where Lisa was and how she'd fared during the war.

'Come in, my dear, come in. How very nice of you to call.'

They went into the Silvers' large drawing-room. It, too, hadn't changed at all – it was exactly as it had been in 1937. There was the same comfort, the same overlarge piano, the same ugly and costly vase on which Neptune and his fishy relatives writhed. The only addition was a misty-eyed, glamorous photograph of Zoë in a silver frame on the piano.

'I'm sorry to appear out of the blue,' said Lisa, using the words she had used to Guy Bowden. 'I did ring but wasn't lucky enough to catch you. I came for news of Zoë. How *is* she? My brother and I have only just arrived back at Stratford and it would be such fun to see her again. Is she around? Or is she away by any unlucky chance?'

Mrs Silver had been standing by the fire. She sat down rather suddenly.

'My dear child, how long have you been away?'

'It's an age. Charles and I went to the East in 1938. Zoë and I did write now and again, but only before the war.'

'Lisa, my daughter died in 1941.'

'Oh, how terrible! Was it in the Blitz –'

'No, no, it was nothing to do with the war,' interrupted the older woman, sorry for the visitor's shock and embarrassment. 'Zoë died in hospital. She was taken very ill and . . . well . . . it was too late to save her.'

Lisa exclaimed, managing words of sympathy years out of date. She said everything that was kind about the lost girl, speaking of how fond she'd been of Zoë, what a sweet girl and such a good friend. Mrs Silver said quietly, 'It's nice to hear you speak of her like that, Lisa. It's always such a pleasure, talking about Zoë, you know. I just wish my husband had been here tonight, but unfortunately he's at the Masons.'

She, too, spoke of her daughter. Lisa did not recognize Zoë in anything her mother said about her. Zoë had been an affectionate, sentimental girl, prettyish and unpunctual and a great giggler. She had been very bad at her lessons and good at making friends. Everybody had been fond of her; she had an endearing personality, wistful yet eager. In Mrs Silver's book she had become a paragon and a star. She had been a brilliant beauty who 'could have done anything'. Zoë's mother talked about her with unselfconscious adoration. When Lisa said goodbye, she was pressed to come again, but knew she never would.

Feeling subdued, she gave the driver the next address. Larry Phillips lived in a far more modest way than the Silvers, in a suburban house in a row of identical houses with an elderly mother who rather bored him. He had a sister, too, but she worked in Birmingham and Lisa had never met her. Larry was an ugly, bustling young man who'd worked in an insurance office and whose passionate kisses Lisa usually managed to avoid. She liked him and was flattered by his admiration, but that was all. As she walked up the garden path of his house, she wondered what he would be like after so long.

94

A tall, thin woman of about thirty-five answered the door. She had an ugly mouth but large, beautiful grey eyes. When Lisa asked for Larry she started violently.

'Didn't you know he was killed? In action in Singapore.'

Lisa gave a long, miserable sigh.

'You'd better come in,' the woman said, and took Lisa into an uncomfortable room where a ceiling light glared down accusingly.

'Do sit down. I'm Joan Phillips – Larry always called me Big Sister. I know he must have told you all about me.'

'Yes, of course,' said Lisa. Larry never had.

Joan Phillips offered to make some coffee but Lisa, who was feeling craven, explained that she had a taxi waiting for her.

'Oh, I see. Then you can't stay. Taxis have got so expensive,' said Joan Phillips going to the window and looking around the curtain. 'He will wait, will he? I don't expect you've paid him yet so he'll have to.'

She returned to Lisa and sat down.

'You'll want to know what happened,' she said, lighting a cigarette. Lisa saw that she was nervous. She said her brother had been in the Army and posted to Singapore very early in the war. When the Japanese invaded, he had been killed by a direct hit from a shell; it had completely destroyed his tank.

'He was right in the thick of it. They should have given him a decoration.'

Joan went to the mantelpiece and handed Lisa a number of curled photographs which had been propped up by a clock. There was Larry grinning under a palm tree and wearing Army shorts. Larry in uniform at the wheel of an open Army car. Larry in civilian clothes, his arm around a Malaysian girl with long hair.

'My mother died soon after the news came.' The hand holding the cigarette shook. 'My fiancé in the RAF was killed the same year.'

When Lisa left, Joan Phillips stood at the open door and waved.

The driver of the taxi clearly hoped Lisa would make no

more calls and it took courage to ask him to drive her to Winchester Road. He was tetchy and wanted to go home. But Lisa was polite and somehow persuaded him, promising she would not keep him waiting.

The old car ground off towards the road where the Maynards used to live. Leaning out, Lisa recognized the house. Up the brick front was the skeleton stem of a thick creeper which covered it in summer with a close coating of leaves. She knocked at the communicating window and shouted, 'That's the one.'

The old man stopped the car, muttering, but Lisa had already sprung out and was hurrying up the path.

There was no point.

The place was clearly deserted. The phantom or village lad, who in every country on earth knows an empty house when he sees one, had broken two of the front windows. The doorstep was covered in piles of dead leaves which crumbled to dust when Lisa walked up to the door and looked through the letter-box. She saw a vista of tiles and darkness and the dim shapes of many letters scattered all over the floor.

She walked back to the waiting taxi.

'No blessed use trying to call on *them*,' said the old man. 'That lot shot the moon months ago.'

'I'm sorry. I don't understand.'

'Shot the moon, Miss. Made off in the middle of the night so's not to pay their bills. Them Maynards never were any good, especially the son. I heard he deserted from the Army.'

When she arrived back at Crocker Road and paid the driver she added a tip she was uncomfortably aware was too small. It was all she could afford. Pocketing the money, the old man shook his head at the dishonesty of the world.

Charles was home. When Lisa, still wearing her coat, blurted out all that had happened he had difficulty in keeping a straight face.

'Sorry, Lou, sorry. It is extremely sad, but you must admit it's funny in an awful kind of a way. You turning up so chirpy asking for people who've been dead for years.

96

You'll have to stop going on like Marcel Proust. As from now.'

The morning after the ill-fated taxi ride, Perdita Smith asked Lisa to fetch a book she'd ordered from W. H. Smith's.

'I need it before I see that dealer in Broadway. Emrys Humphreys is too smart by half. Don't dawdle, now, I don't pay you to waste your time.'

Lisa said she'd be back as soon as possible.

'Well, well, you don't have to run both ways,' said Perdita who had caught sight of a wealthy customer through the window.

Lisa walked down Wood Street in the rain. Smith's was distinctly Shakespearean, with displays of biographies, fresh new paperbacks of the plays and a complete edition illustrated with line drawings of ogling sentimentality. There were commentaries by Shakespeare experts, English and American, and the usual long row of small red volumes – the Temple edition – each containing a single play. Culture for the pocket.

While she was enquiring at the counter and a fussed young man was looking through his order book, a girl with short blonde hair came up behind her.

'I'd best write it all down again, Miss. Can't think where the first order got to. What did you say the book was called?'

The girl behind Lisa had picked up four Temple Shakespeares. She leaned forward to see what he was writing.

'She said "The History of Poole Pottery" and Poole is spelt with an 'e' at its end. I can read upside down,' she announced.

She had a clear, ringing voice. Lisa wheeled round.

'Polly!'

'Snakes alive, it's Lisa!'

There followed exclamations: 'How long is it?' from Lisa, and 'Don't let's work it out!' from Polly, who paid for her books and dragged Lisa out of the shop saying they must have a coffee at The Cobweb. 'Everybody goes there.'

After last night's expedition, poor Zoë's apotheosis into

sainthood, Larry's doleful sister and Pat shooting the moon, Lisa was overjoyed to see a friend from the past.

'Polly, I'd love to but I have to get back to work.'

'Are you working? What at? Look, we'll only be ten minutes, your job won't fold as quickly as that, will it? I get served really fast when I'm in a hurry. Lisa, you cannot refuse me when we haven't seen each other for ever.'

Lisa agreed. Perdita, after all, had said she need not run.

'I do call this a treat,' said Polly, swinging beside Lisa down the street. She was as surprised at their reunion as Lisa, and as pleased.

The two girls had known each other since they were children. They had attended the same snobbish dancing class, the same day-school in the Warwick Road, and had been sent for the last four years of their education to the same boarding-school. In the holidays Polly, when she reached her teens, became quite a star. She played good tennis, she swam stylishly, she danced like a leaf. She was odd-looking, her nose too snub, her face too sharp for beauty. She was small and neat, a *belle laide*, the only child of adoring parents from whom she wheedled money to spend on her spoiled self.

'After all, I'm not pretty. I must have something.'

Polly steered them to the tea-shop which Lisa had not revisited since coming back to Stratford. It was pleasantly crowded and smelled of coffee.

A waitress who apparently knew Polly trotted up.

'Hello, Annie, how's everything?' said Polly with charm. 'Can we have coffee and some of your special biscuits? Could you be angelic?'

It seemed that the waitress could.

'She saw me in the Birmingham Rep once,' said Polly. 'Well, Lisa. So *you're* back!'

'And you're still here,' said Lisa, pleased.

Polly turned her blue eyes on her friend and laughed. 'You don't imagine I live in Stratford, do you? I came from London last night. I'm in the Shakespeare Memorial Company this year, darling. For the first time. I'm by way of being an actress, *quite* experienced though I haven't played here before. Do stop looking surprised. I was a brilliant St Joan.'

During their last term at school, Polly had starred in the school play, a shortened version of Shaw's *St Joan*. She had had her hair specially cut in a medieval bob, had worn chain-mail of knitted silver string and given a pious if somewhat metallic performance. Her voice couldn't manage the lyrical bits but she was good at Shaw's jokes. In one Act she had ridden a real horse on to the stage.

'I still have a photograph of you mounted on Clover,' said Lisa, 'looking up to heaven with a holy expression.'

'Hearing my Voices. I remember that pic. The horse was a rotten idea – everybody knows you can't have a live animal on stage or no one looks at the actors.'

Lisa thought Polly had come on a good deal. Her blonde hair was exquisitely cut, her clothes original, her manner exaggerated and funny and warm. Sitting in the tea-shop, which was busy and buzzing with voices, the girls exchanged news.

'Until I met you just now I thought everybody we used to know had gone away or died,' said Lisa and told the story of her taxi ride. Polly blew out her cheeks.

'You didn't know about Zoë? Poor Zoë, she's not a person to be dead, is she? It doesn't suit her. I don't remember your Larry or Pat though . . .'

She knew nothing of what had happened to the Whitfields. She had 'vaguely heard' that Charles and Lisa had gone to the East.

'If you remember, darling, I was away, alas, when you left Stratford, and we hadn't seen each other since our last term. During the war I was a VAD, by the way. Very attractive uniform, sexy doctors, and loads of men to look after. Florence Nightingale stuff. I did manage to do *some* acting, thank heaven. I was let off nursing to be in a patriotic movie – did you see it? It was called *War Zone*. I played a nurse, of course. The moment peace broke out I got a small part in Birmingham. It was awful, nursing. One thought one would burst, not being able to work.'

'But you *were* working.'

'Don't be pathetic, I mean acting, not carrying bedpans. Nursing isn't work the way we mean.'

'Did you come back to Stratford quite often during the war?'

'Not really. I was at Bart's in London, lots going on there, but I did manage to come and see the old folks occasionally. There were terrific local rumours,' said Polly, eyes gleaming. 'The one I liked best was that if London was bombed to the ground, Parliament was going to assemble at the Shakespeare Memorial Theatre. Wouldn't that have been a lark? However, it didn't happen, of course, and the theatre managed to put on some Shakespeare. The Yanks positively flooded in but the productions weren't too hot. Not like these marvellous seasons now. Where did I get in my career? Ah yes. I played a whore in *Bartholomew Fair*, then a bigger part at the New and behold – here I am. All set for a whole season. Now about you. Are you back at Roundwood?'

Lisa hadn't yet become accustomed to her friend's total ignorance of everything but the faery world turned upside down. She explained that Roundwood had been sold years ago.

'Who bought it? Don't bother to answer, just a silly question. Where are you living, Lisa? Is the sexy Charles with you – surely he's married by now. I say, I hope he wasn't killed.' Polly looked bothered. 'So many of one's men friends . . .'

'No, no, Charles is okay and is with me in Stratford. We're in digs. You must come round,' said Lisa, hoping she wouldn't. 'And I have a job.'

When she described it, Polly gave a little shriek.

'Mick Gould, a pal of mine in the Company who was here last year told me about Perdita Smith. Did you know she played in Shakespeare at the old Stratford theatre in *1908*! He's seen pictures of her, pulling those Shakespearean faces they went in for, hair to her waist – Cordelia apparently, but much too fat. How did Lear pick her up and carry her in the last Act? Mick says The Treasure Box is full of good stuff and the actors last season practically kept the place going –

birthdays and so on. Actors are fools with their money, not that we get paid much.'

Lisa said that runarounds for Perdita Smith weren't too flush either. Polly looked falsely sympathetic. Then genuinely so – a sort of change of mask.

'I'm a pig, I've just remembered my parents told me your father died. I liked your father. I once told him when we were at your house for tennis that he looked like Charles I by Van Dyck. He was half pleased and half stuffy. If I were a man, I'd base a performance on him. I was sorry to hear he'd died. Imagine Roundwood sold as well. Poor you.'

She continued to chat, now and again her blue eyes glancing over Lisa's shoulders to see who had arrived or was leaving. 'This place,' she said, 'is packed with pros.'

A young man with the face of a clown stopped at their table to kiss her. Polly introduced Lisa.

'Mick, this is Lisa. We were at school together where she was brilliant and I was hopeless. Lisa, meet Michael Gould, my favourite member of the Company.'

'So I should think,' said the actor. He shook hands with Lisa and gave her an enchanting but melancholy smile before hurrying away. He walked as lightly as a dancer.

'You and I must meet all the time,' said Polly, refusing to allow Lisa to pay her share of the bill. 'I'll barge into The Treasure Box when things are less hectic and we'll make a date. Don't let Perdita Smith bite off your head – I hear she's a gorgon. Tell her you were with an actress and we all intend to spend far too much in her shop. See you, darling. Oh, if you need me specially, leave a note at the Stage Door.'

Lisa walked thoughtfully back down Wood Street. She was glad to have found Polly again, and like everybody else in Stratford was fascinated at the idea of the actors working in the Shakespeare Memorial Theatre, moored like a great liner on the banks of the Avon.

When she arrived at the shop the door was locked and a grubby card in the window read 'Closed'. Fortunately Lisa had her key. There was a note scrawled on the back of an old sales catalogue secured by a lump of uncut amethyst:

Gone about a sale. May not be back. Trust *you* are!

P. Smith.

Lisa hung up her coat and sat down at the counter. There was nothing to do but be here if needed. She thought about Polly for a while, and then her eyes roamed round the shop; she still felt a mild surprise at having landed in this curious place. She had been searching for *her* past, and the yesterdays of other people were here all round her. But the many many things, each one of which might have been evocative, could not speak; they were silenced by the jumble and the variety, the quantity and the disorder. There was scarcely room to move in The Treasure Box. Porcelain and brass, dirty silver and painted wood, tiny leather books and enamel teapots. Things jostled each other, were thrust under the counter or into corners, lay in crumbling cardboard boxes in the cubby-hole where Lisa made the tea. The comedies and tragedies of ancient things were too disparate, too crammed close to be heard. They had no voices and simply became junk.

There was little work for Lisa when she was alone. When Perdita was there she was given jobs all the time, but Lisa was not allowed to begin anything new on her own. Nothing must be moved unless Perdita was present, when Lisa was given silver to clean and vases and china to dust with a balding feather duster. Charles had called one morning, seen his sister at work flicking off the dust and roared with laughter.

'She ought to wear frilly knickers and suspenders. She looks like a French maid.'

Perdita laughed too; she liked Charles.

Now Lisa had nothing to do but keep shop. Bored with idleness, she went to the window in which Perdita had shoved a basket full of broken necklaces, part of a Lot which had included a case of medals from the last century which Perdita had wanted. She had dumped the necklaces in the window, saying 'They make a spot of colour.'

Lisa took the basket to the counter. The necklaces were so inextricably tangled that the only way to handle them was in

102

a fistful. Impossible to imagine one could ever extricate a single necklace from the mess. Impossible to imagine that any of these knotted, lumpy beads had once hung round a woman's neck. She threaded her fingers into them and managed to unhook the blackened chain from a necklace of green glass. The job would need hours of patience, she thought, pleased.

Bending over the coloured mess, she thought it resembled the England to which she and Charles had returned. Beautiful once, now tangled and shabby and broken and looking as if nobody would ever mend it again. The images in her mind changed, and she thought the green of the beads reminded her of a certain kind of Burmese beetle she used to see in Uncle Rod's garden; there was the same brilliant, yellowish shine. Then a string of dark red beads made her think of the seeds of a pomegranate.

She sat for a moment, remembering that Tom had once bought her a basket of the fruit, which they'd eaten after making love. The juice had run down Lisa's chin and he had kissed her, licking the inside of her mouth and declaring it was a new kind of liqueur.

Sex. Two whole years, a desert, a century since she had known the fever and the after-sleep of sex. Why did she only call it that? What she meant was love. She and Tom had been in love and when they saw each other at a distance had rushed, laughing, arms outflung, to embrace. They couldn't stay apart.

'I've had an idea,' he once told her. 'When we fix to meet shall we try always to be five minutes early? If it's impossible for one or other of us, that's okay. But if we both make it there'll be five more minutes together.'

You couldn't say such a thing unless you were in love.

They had never meant to fall into that crazy state. As she tried to unknot a string of artificial pearls, Lisa recognized that their love affair was a series of 'never meants'. They had never meant to become close friends when they greeted each other in the insouciant way used in the Chowringhee flat. Tom had been exactly like all the other visitors who appeared, to be friendly, eat curry, and sleep on a string bed. And Tom had never meant to tell her he'd met her when Charles had been at Oxford.

'But why shouldn't you tell me that?'

'Perhaps I guessed it would be dangerous.'

He was right. Tenuous links with a life which happened before the war, connection with a peacetime which seemed a dream of happiness and simplicity, drew people to one another. Tom hadn't meant to do that and Lisa had not meant to respond.

She and her two friends met so many men. Single men, engaged men, married men. Almost everyone who came to the flat must have somebody who loved them, back in Britain. Were the girls on the other side of the world faithful? The war was a graveyard of broken vows.

After the first night that they made love, Tom was subdued when he returned to the flat and its usual cheerful chaos – shouts from the bathroom, kit bags hurled down in the hall. He found her on the balcony. A sun the colour of a blood orange was sinking fast over the roofs. Against a greenish sky were all the mosques and temples to so many different gods. The air was cold, and Lisa was lying at full length in a kind of deck-chair, a cardigan on her lap. Her eyes were shut. The only other people on the roof were two officers at a distance, sitting on the parapet.

'Lisa.'

She opened her eyes and said nothing.

He drew up a chair and sat beside her. She had thought about him during every moment of the day that hadn't been absorbed by work. Yet seeing him now, she wasn't ready for his effect upon her. Do you forget in a few hours exactly how a person is? His voice reached to the pit of her stomach. There were two lines across his forehead below that short, curling hair. His ears were beautifully shaped and his neck was thick and powerful. She looked down at his hands. She had not seen him naked and perhaps she never would.

'You're very quiet,' he said.

'I suppose I haven't anything to say.'

'I have. Supper with me? Not here, of course.'

'Yes, please.'

'My leave lasts until Thursday.'

'I remember.'

He paused for a moment, and his eyes continued to search hers.

'What are you doing every night until Thursday?'

That was their love affair in eight words.

Lisa picked at the chains and strings of the necklaces. She used a hatpin – Perdita had a dish of the outmoded things – and pushed it through the knots. While she worked she tried to recapture the very sensation of love-making. How had it felt to be possessed by Tom, so violently and so often? But try as she could, her imagination could not give her back that rapture. She couldn't remember. I've lost him, she thought. Why can't one keep sexual joy in one's memory? Why does it go? Is it the same with everybody, does the sex of the past evaporate so fast, like scent when you drop a bottle on a stone floor?

To make love had become an obsession with Tom and herself. When they met, when they embraced, when they lay spent, they always asked themselves and each other, when can we again? Where can we?

During the two and a half years she and Tom knew each other while she was living in Calcutta, he returned on leave at irregular intervals of about six weeks. The RAF were strict about the number of hours, the number of missions on which the pilots were sent. They could not afford to lose more men. Pilots were lost in action, in fighters and bombers, from Japanese snipers, from sudden sicknesses caught in the tropics, from pushes into enemy territory. They must not be lost because the pilots were merely exhausted.

'They worry that we will fly badly and crash the planes. Which are a good deal more valuable than we are.'

'Tom!'

'It's true, darling. There are more pilots than there are planes. And we're cheaper.'

Tom returned for four or five days of leave, and after they

105

had rushed into an embrace they murmured the same questions. When and where?

When he was gone and the leave was over Lisa was constantly expecting the fateful news that he was lost. Six of the young men Marguerite had loved were dead. The girls in the Chowringhee flat dreaded telegrams and telephone calls. Tom told Lisa that 'if anything happened' – the wartime phrase for being killed or taken prisoner – he had extracted a promise from the CO of his squadron that she would be told.

'It's against regulations. Only next of kin. But he's a mate of mine.'

He survived. He returned to her again and again. He grew thin and colourless, he admitted that he slept badly, he was less solid, more finely drawn. But he was *there*, sitting on the roof with her out of earshot of chattering friends. Racking his brains as to where they could lie down together tonight.

All the different places. They usually returned at night to the palace gardens except when the heat was unbearable or during the rainy season when, desperate to make love, they lay in the back of a car with the rain hammering on the roof like great falling shoals of stones. Once they borrowed a flat from a man Tom knew in the Air Ministry. Once they went into an empty office somewhere – it was always Tom who found places for them to go – and lay down on the floor. Lisa had no other man to compare him with. He was her first and only lover. She had no idea if sex with other men was as unbearably exciting as theirs. She could imagine no other love, no other kind of sex but his. When they had not seen each other for weeks, they came so fast that love was over in a few moments. All to be done again.

In her thoughts, sex was associated with the smell and heat of India. With coconut oil and jasmine, necklaces of dying marigolds and bodies bathing in sacred water. With crumbling palaces on which writhing figures made love immortally in stone, where steps led down to the water and half-burned corpses bobbed past, and the sun scorched you through your thin clothes . . .

106

How curious is desire or lust or want or sexual hunger or whatever you call love of our kind, thought Lisa, delving into the thickest tangles of beads. With Tom and herself the sensation had been instantaneous. Once, late and alone with him in a car in some moonlit waste of ruins – they could not lie on the ground as the place was known as the haunt of snakes – he'd said, turning her face to his in the moonlight, 'I've been told a girl never wants a man at once. I mean, when they meet again after an interval. It's only when love-making begins that she feels like that. Is it true?'

'No.'

'Go on.'

Moist with sex, every barrier between them gone, she described how she felt when she saw him, how stirred and hot, how she thought of nothing but having him inside her. It excited them to talk of that.

During the 1944 offensive in Burma, the mighty assaults by land and sea, with mile upon mile of exhausted land recaptured, there came a day when Tom's squadron was no longer needed to cross the swiftly receding enemy lines. The whole world was on the move. Pouring into ships and trains, flooding across the maps of Europe, roaring through victorious skies.

In the Chowringhee flat Taro cooked meals large enough for a regiment; it wasn't a question now of six young men on the floor. One night in 1944 Marguerite counted fourteen. They slept in corners, on beds made of towels, in chairs, on the roof; one Australian slept 'like a top' in the bath. The flat epitomized the times. Men crowding into it, vanishing daily and nightly, to be replaced by more and more men haggard with travel, recovering from fevers, their uniforms stained and dusty, exclaiming over the luck of being there. Peggy dosed the more exhausted with glucose smuggled from her ward in the hospital. Marguerite sat on laps.

'Come on, Beautiful,' someone always said. 'A big kiss. Haven't I deserved it?'

And Tom came and went. Lisa never knew when it would be, in the war's ebb and flow. But then one night or one early morning, there he would be and Lisa would run into his arms like a poor, nesting bird.

It was into this din, with its smell of alcohol and humanity, stepping over outstretched uniformed or hairy legs, that Lisa saw Tom one spring night in 1945.

'Lisa. Look who's here!' shouted Peggy.

Lisa had the awful feeling that she couldn't move. She watched him coming into the room, noisily greeted by other visitors, picking his way towards her, refusing drinks and answering banter for banter. How had she known what was going to happen? Love gives you an extra sense as it gives you extra pain.

He finally reached her and bent to kiss her and she was sure.

'Tom.'

'Lisa.'

'Come and sit on my bed. Unless someone's already nabbed it.'

'If they have, we'll shove them on to the floor,' he said, as casually as she.

There were four young men sitting on Lisa's bed playing liar dice on an upturned tray, drinking iced beer provided by an approving Jeeta.

Tom exchanged a look with her. When they went out on to the roof, that was crowded too. They walked away from people gossiping and playing a wheezy gramophone to the far end of the roof. There a little fig tree had once grown in a crack. Lisa had watered it sometimes, but now it was dead. The roof was so hot that although it was eight at night she felt it through the soles of her shoes.

They sat down on the parapet. Below them was the great broad road, the principal thoroughfare of British Calcutta, with its border of dead yellow grass stretching as far as they could see. Turbaned figures went by, and women with babies on their backs, and Army jeeps and buffalo carts. Then a regiment, khaki clad, marching with no spring or style.

'I have an hour,' Tom said.

'I know.'

'You do, don't you? We're only passing through, my darling. I said I was going to the club for my mail. I'm due at the depot in' – he looked at his watch – 'fifty-five minutes.'

They couldn't drag their eyes away from each other.

She said the first thing that came into her mind. 'We can't make love.'

'No, my dear love.'

He sat looking at her. 'You know this is goodbye.'

'Oh yes.'

'I love you,' he suddenly said. 'I love everything about you. Your face. Your smell. Your hair and that funny, breathless voice. Those large eyes looking at me so solemnly. You're such a girl. Such a gutsy, brave, beautiful girl.'

'You mean I'm not crying.'

'Oh, crying. I could easily. We are going to find each other again, you know.' She nodded and he said, 'You don't believe me.'

'Of course I believe you.'

'No, you don't. If I'm killed, of course, then you'll be right.'

'Don't say that. I hate it. I was only – only thinking that we don't know where we'll be or what will happen to us.'

'Lisa. If you want us to spend the next' – he looked at his watch – 'forty-five minutes in noble goodbyes, put it out of your mind. And don't come trotting out with stuff about destiny. Don't bite your lips either – your face is sweet, I won't have it ruined. If I'm killed I shan't be able to get to you unless I can fix it to haunt you. I might quite like that. But *if* I make it, I'll find you. I've got to. Okay?'

'Okay.'

'I'll write first, my love, and give you the number of our mail via the British Forces Post Office. Write there until I tell you it changes, which it may do if we get posted somewhere else. I've got this address and, oh yes, give me your uncle's in Taunggyi.'

'Why do you want that?'

109

'I might be at the other end of nowhere when peace breaks out and perhaps *you'll* decide to go back to him.'

'He may be dead.'

'So he may, my darling, that's one of the things we can't know. Anyway, give me the address. Then I can find you whatever happens. We'll write. All the time. Do you swear?'

She nodded again.

He spoke with a different gravity. 'You've known me nearly three years, Lisa. In war that's a lifetime. Do you wish you had never met me?'

She did not reply. All during the waning time while they sat on the parapet, and at last when he had to say goodbye and give his thanks to Peggy and Marguerite, and when Lisa went down the stairs with him out into the wavering heat and they stood in the street, she never answered the question. He took her in his arms.

'I hate to say goodbye. So I won't,' he said, and walked rapidly away.

Lisa went indoors, climbing the stairs and hearing as it came closer the noisy laughter in the flat. I don't wish I had never met you, she thought. I do wish that I were dead.

Her hands filled with beads, she looked up and knew she was crying. Outside the shop was the darkening Stratford winter afternoon. There was no smell of jasmine, no mirage on distant pavements wavering like pools of water. There was no sound of Indian voices or the click of wooden wheels.

The afternoon crawled by. She served only one customer in an hour, a woman who wanted a pewter teapot, took it to the window, opened and shut its lid, waved it in the air and poured ghostly tea from its spout, finally deciding against it.

The afternoon continued to drag by and in the end Lisa relinquished her self-appointed task with the necklaces; it had begun to bore her. She wished Perdita Smith would come back to make sharp remarks and invent jobs for her. Perdita did hate to pay a salary for somebody just to sit about . . .

The bells at the door jangled and Lisa looked up to see a fair-haired young man, who came in with an enquiring look.

'Busy?'

'As a bee. Can't move for customers. Don't be ridiculous, Peter. Shall I make you tea?'

'That is what I was hoping.'

Peter Lang sat down on the stool facing the counter. He was very fair, pale-skinned, wore spectacles and was dressed in clothes which looked aggressively clean and neat, as if brushed morning and night and pressed whenever their owner could get the time. The spotless style was part of him; Lisa had never seen a hair out of place. Until Polly's appearance this morning at W. H. Smith's, Peter Lang was the only friend Lisa had made since her arrival. She had met him at the shop when he called round to see Perdita.

Lang was on a weekly newspaper based in Warwick but much read all over the county and popular in Stratford. His editor was interested in the Shakespeare Memorial Theatre and when Peter had worked for him for six months, agreed to give him a column on the arts. That was one of the plums, however. He also had the job of reporting Council meetings, cattle sales, weddings and, in summer, village cricket which he confided in Lisa he found almost too monotonous to write about. 'But there's so little paper allowed us that I get away with a hundred words. All the readers look for are their own names.' As for his theatre column, he knew something about drama, which pleased his shrewd editor. Peter Lang was pretty shrewd himself, and had found Perdita Smith a useful source of Stratford information.

Lisa liked her new admirer, and thought him a solemn owl. A serious boots. After spending an evening in Charles's company, being with Peter was like entering a nonconformist chapel. But he made it plain that he thought her attractive, and in her new, diminished life she welcomed that.

When she emerged from Perdita's cubby-hole with the tray, Peter said, 'I have news. The actors are arriving.' He spoke as if he had spied a herd of antelope on the horizon, the dust kicked up by the animals rising in clouds. 'They're early, of course, but they like to settle in before they begin rehearsals.' He had his usual air of omniscience.

111

'Yes, I know. I met Polly Holt,' said Lisa.

He was immediately interested. 'I had no idea she was an acquaintance of yours. I have seen her too. She's very good.'

'As an actress, you mean?' said Lisa flippantly. 'I was at school with her and she was in the school play. Pretty dire.'

'Indeed? Wait until you see her now. You'll be impressed. That's why I've come to see you, Lisa. Not about Polly Holt but concerning the new season. You know about the Mayor's sherry party?'

'It sounds extraordinary.'

Her teasing had no effect. He told her that the Mayor of Stratford gave a sherry party of welcome when the new batch of actors arrived. This year Anthony Quayle was going to speak.

'I am covering it for my paper, of course, but also doing some lineage for the *Mail*.'

She liked the painstaking way he described his work.

'So,' continued Peter Lang, 'would you come with me? It's at seven at the Town Hall. Where Garrick made his address and read his own poems about Shakespeare.'

His habit of giving her information amused her. He took everything so seriously and it always made her flippant.

'Yes, I remember. After Garrick went pomping on, it pelted with rain and ruined the fireworks. Coaches had their wheels in two feet of water and the Avon flooded. What a do.'

'You're very well informed.'

'Dear Peter, I only know the stupidest things and I'd like to come with you very much.'

He looked pleased. He then asked, as he often did, how her brother was getting on. He admired Charles for being what he was too polite to call him to Lisa: a lazy bastard. It was a source of wonder to Peter Lang that any man could be like that.

'Still at a loose end.'

'He'll find something sooner or later.'

Lisa looked at him charmingly just then. 'Oh Peter, I suppose *you* couldn't help?'

112

Returning her look, Peter Lang wanted intensely to help her. To have her. 'I'll try.' It was rash but he wasn't his usual practical self when Lisa was about.

Since he had come to live and work in Warwickshire he had met a number of girls, all younger than himself, giggling, cinema-fed young creatures who flirted daringly, wore cheap make-up and tossed their heads when he paid them a compliment. Many were the ex-lovers of the now vanished Americans. One or two of these young women had consented – a word they would have used – to go to bed with him. Peter enjoyed them and then inwardly sighed because, if he was to get enough sex, it meant courting silly women who demanded slavish attention.

Lisa Whitfield was as unlike them as if she were a different species of flower. She was a girl who he was sure had a past. It gave her a mystery. An allure. Sometimes he tried to get her to tell him about the East, but she hadn't the gift of description. His own thoughts were brighter than her lame words. He saw her romantically, standing against a backdrop of golden pagodas.

'You're sweet,' he muttered, leaning forward hoping to kiss her. The temple bells jangled and Perdita swept in.

'You here again, wasting my assistant's time?' she said cordially. 'Off you go, to the work which must be waiting for you in your office. Stop cluttering up my shop when we're busy. Goodbye, goodbye,' with a wave of her hand.

Peter smiled somewhat constrainedly; he disliked the indignity of his exit. He mouthed 'seven o'clock' to Lisa and left to the accompaniment of more bells.

Perdita undid herself from the bulging version of a kit bag slung across her bosom. 'Wait until you see what *I've* pulled off this afternoon while young Mr Lang was getting in your way.' She loosened the strings of her bag.

Lisa had heard an acquaintance of Charles's with whom she and her brother recently had a drink describe her employer as slightly mad. 'Do you think your sister ought to be with her, Charles? Perdita's quite unhinged; I'm not sure I'd want a relative of mine working for her.'

113

Perdita Smith's madness consisted of wearing the kit bag and ankle-length skirts, speaking the bald truth and possessing a catlike quickness over money.

'You should have seen her at an auction I went to in Tiddington,' continued Charles's new friend, who was fiftyish and a good poker player. 'She was sitting on a damned great basket of knives and forks. I said "My dear Mrs Smith, let me get you a comfortable chair. Surely those forks must be painful on the – er – seat?" Do you know what she replied? "Yes," she said, "they are. That's what I like."' Lisa knew about that cutlery: real silver which Perdita had bought as plate.

In the month during which Lisa had worked at The Treasure Box she had sized up her mad employer. A woman of whim. Perdita knew what was valuable and what was rubbish and purchased both if that was what she liked. She was keen as mustard to sell profitably, but sometimes the fancy took her and she wouldn't part with this or that. 'It's resting,' she said when a customer enquired after a Staffordshire greyhound previously seen in the window. Later, to Lisa, Perdita said, '*She* wouldn't give it a good home.'

When certain dealers arrived from Coventry, Warwick or Broadway, Perdita always asked Lisa to make the tea and then sent her out on some footling and time-consuming errand with instructions not to hurry back. With the shop satisfactorily empty, Perdita could sit down to a game played in the market-places of Ancient Greece.

'Give you ten.'

'Sorry, won't take a farthing less than twelve fifteen.'

'How does eleven quid sound?'

'Horrible.'

She was brisk with Lisa and not averse to calling on the saints – she was a good, practising Catholic – if Lisa was ignorant about something in the shop. 'Holy St Francis! St Anselm, give me patience. It is a card-case, my child. A *card-case*. Your mother must have used one before the war – we all did. One left three visiting cards, two with the corners turned down, remember? Didn't that school of yours teach you anything?'

She expected her employee to be an encyclopedia of knowledge on Rockingham teapots, Bristol glass scent-bottles, mother-of-pearl fan-sticks, Derby inkstands, Victorian jewellery, from filigree to cameos, japanned picture trays, silhouettes and candlesticks. She also wished her to be energetic with a duster and to make tea from morning until night.

She used Lisa in all kinds of ways. Lisa went with her to house sales where Perdita soon taught her what to look for and what was beyond The Treasure Box's low budget. When Perdita was confident that her employee was to be trusted to buy small, inexpensive objects, she sent her to junk-shops in towns and villages at a distance from Stratford, allowing her to drive the battered van for which the shop was given a small petrol allowance. Perdita's allowance, however, like the gold in a magical bag given by a goblin, never seemed to run out. 'My van is essential to my livelihood,' proclaimed Perdita to Lisa. 'Supposing I buy a spinning-wheel or a milk churn?'

She was soon giving Lisa greater responsibility – but not if both women happened to be in the shop when a customer appeared. Then she grabbed the customer's attention, wrapping it round herself like a woman using a shawl when she has earache.

As a saleswoman Perdita was a dab hand. 'Take it home,' she would say, turning a little porcelain figure, a box, a clock, round and round to show it off at every angle. 'See how it fits in your house. Keep it for a few days. Then bring it back if you decide against it.' They never did.

Perdita had mentioned to Lisa in an offhand manner that she had once been an actress; she had clearly been in no mood to say more at the time and Lisa hoped to question her later. Peter Lang, however, told Lisa one evening that he'd heard a rumour that Perdita had been an expensive whore who kept a bawdy house in the Oxford Road. An elderly man, retired Army, had said he remembered her driving through the town in a horse-drawn cab wearing a sable coat.

Lisa was enchanted with the story and wanted to believe

it. 'Perhaps that's why she's rather religious now,' she suggested, for Perdita went regularly to Sunday Mass at the small Catholic church in Stratford, and always snapped up Catholic prayer-books at book sales.

'You think she is repenting, like Mary Magdalene?' said Peter and was slightly shocked when Lisa roared with laughter.

This afternoon Perdita began to take out the booty from her canvas bag. She placed it item by item upon the counter for Lisa's inspection. There was a glass paperweight with a pattern like a red dahlia. Two or three quill pens somewhat the worse for wear. A perfect clay pipe with a long stem. A decanter which needed a good clean with soap and water. And a curious arch made of wood, trimmed with ivory inlay which Perdita placed in front of Lisa, looking at it with her head on one side. She waited for Lisa's reaction.

'Well?'

'I'm afraid I don't know what it is, Mrs Smith.'

'My poor child, such ignorance. It is a watch-stand, dear. A very nice watch-stand for a gentleman's watch.'

'It's rather pretty.'

There was a sarcastic sniff. Perdita scrabbled in a drawer and produced an engraved silver pocket-watch. She drew the wooden arch towards her – there was an ivory hook at its top – and hung the watch on the hook. The watch-chain was coiled in a little hollow covered in velvet at the base of the stand.

'You see? At night the gentleman takes off his cuff links and places them on his dressing table. And hangs his watch up like this.' She stood admiring her purchase. 'A perfect specimen. A little gem. Date about 1860. You can get watch-stands of many different kinds. Ebony. Ivory. Carved ivory. Mine is of mulberry wood, a happy coincidence since mulberry is a magical word here in Stratford. Who knows? It may have been carved from a tree in the gardens of New Place. I shall ask a hundred pounds for it.'

'Mrs Smith!'

'A hundred pounds,' repeated Perdita, rolling the sum in

116

her mouth. 'I know an Oxford don who'll willingly pay that. Particularly when I make my point about New Place. He would pay more, I am certain, but I don't think we should take advantage of him.'

Lisa poured her some tea which Perdita accepted with a smile, remarking that she had earned it.

'How much did the watch-stand cost us?' asked Lisa, who was encouraged to think in the plural and also encouraged to ask such questions.

'Well. I'll tell you. Five quid and a glass of Guinness.'

When Lisa arrived back at the Crocker Road lodgings, there was no sign of her brother, and no note from him either, although he usually left a slip of paper saying where he had gone out – invariably to 'the club'. He was not bothering to lie to her. She hadn't the heart to ask him how much of his share of the silver sale he had already lost. Looking at the handsome, haggard face sometimes, she was sorry for him.

She changed out of her dusty Treasure Box clothes into an embroidered black dress that had been made for her in Taunggyi from Burmese satin. She hadn't worn it since she went out one night with Tom in Calcutta. Was it hopelessly unsuitable for this evening? At least it was black.

Leaving Crocker Road, she walked slowly through the town in the direction of the Town Hall. The rain had stopped. There had been watery sunshine this afternoon and now the evening sky was pale. Looking at her watch she realized she was too early and walked down Chapel Lane to look at the green lawns, humped and bumped from years-ago excavations, which were all that was left of Shakespeare's pretty house of brick and timber.

New Place. Shakespeare had built it from the fortune he'd made in London, had lived in it with his wife and daughters, and fourteen years later had died there, after a sociable supper with his friends. It had been the second largest mansion in Stratford, with two gardens, two orchards and 'ten fireplaces'. Lisa remembered that because it was funny. Looking at the site now, she tried to recreate the Tudor house. Without success.

Peter was punctual, and was already standing at the entrance of the Town Hall looking pleased when he saw her. He gave his invitation to a porter at the door, and took her up the handsome oak staircase towards the sound of voices. Lisa was fascinated when they went into the Mayor's Parlour, a long, wide room hung with paintings.

Despite being born and reared three miles from the heart of Stratford, she had only met two real actors in her life, both of them recently. Polly, and her friend Michael Gould. She was interested when she saw the crowds of people drinking sherry and talking. They looked very ordinary. Their faces were lively and somehow worn, their voices spirited, their laughter seemed more intense, their attention focused on each other with an air of concentration. No, they were not ordinary, after all.

Peter took her over to introduce her to some of the players he had known from last year's season. Glancing round, Lisa saw Polly in stiff white taffeta, her waist tied with a flame-coloured sash. Lisa hadn't needed to worry: her dress was positively subfusc compared with her friend's. Polly caught Lisa's eye, waved and didn't budge. She was talking to a tall actor with a mole on his face like an eighteenth-century beauty patch. Polly wasn't a girl to waste her time on her own sex.

A little creature with upswept hair rustled over to Peter, who introduced her as 'Jean Chatto. She's going to play Cordelia.'

'Oh, not yet, not yet!' cried the girl too eagerly, clasping minute hands upon very small breasts. She was, she told Peter rather than Lisa, already shaking in her shoes. Peter listened gravely; Lisa was sure he was making mental notes for his column.

There was a little burst of applause and somebody announced: 'Ladies and Gentlemen. This year's director of the first plays of the Season. *Henry IV Parts One and Two*. Mr Anthony Quayle.'

A tall, good-looking man, as broad-shouldered as Tom had been, took his place beside the Mayor on a dais at the far end of the room. All the Company involuntarily moved

118

closer. He slightly raised his eyebrows as if in affectionate amusement and began to speak.

His voice was resonant, it slightly lilted; it caught at you and made you listen. Shakespeare, Quayle said, in three hundred years had made his fortune and his reputation both in the great world and here in this very market town where he was born and where he had died. His reputation had gone through many changes. Shakespeare had been admired and ignored. Extolled at the very time his plays were being mutilated. 'His birth,' said Quayle, 'has been celebrated with poetry and fireworks yet there was a time when nobody performed his plays. He's been translated and annotated, compiled, interpolated, even repudiated.' Quayle paused and looked at the sea of faces, some young as flowers, some old and worn, mirrors held to nature. 'And all the while his potency, like a great wine, has continued to mature.'

The speech did not last long, perhaps less than ten minutes, but his actors listened in a magic silence. The Shakespeare Memorial Theatre, he said, existed for two things. For the experienced actor to pit himself against the most exacting arts in our English tongue. And for the young actor to take his first uncertain steps towards becoming a fine classical player. What lay at the heart of it all? The playwright.

'Isn't he wonderful?' whispered a voice in Lisa's ear. Polly had wriggled her way through the press of people during the applause. 'I feel,' said Polly, enlarging her eyes, 'inspired.'

Peter Lang seemed similarly affected, for when he and Lisa walked home in the deserted evening after some eggs on toast and tinned fruit at a cheap restaurant in Bridge Street, he talked a good deal about Anthony Quayle.

'I've heard strong rumours that next year he's to be the new director. A new hand at the helm. He's very fine.'

'And you're going to write a piece about him.'

'Naturally.'

She saw he was already thinking about the article, forming sentences in his mind. She said suddenly, 'Why don't you try to get a bigger job, Peter? You write so well and know so much. I can't imagine why you're satisfied to stay here.'

'It is good here.' He didn't sound particularly pleased by her compliment and Lisa, who thought it rather touching that he was clever yet lacked ambition, pressed his arm.

'You're a puzzle.'

'What do you mean?'

She laughed, because she enjoyed teasing him, he was so different from Charles. 'You're odd, Peter. When I tell you you're clever, and I know you could do much better, you look as if you'd rather not hear it. You ignore my compliments about your work.'

They were nearing Crocker Road. The streets were empty, there wasn't a soul in sight. He stopped and turned round to her.

'I don't ignore *you*. You're beautiful.' Taking her in his arms, he gave her an unexpected and passionate embrace.

Lisa responded. Reacted. Put her arms around his neck. His kiss tasted as fresh and clean as he was. She was surprised to find that her body began to melt.

# 6

It took Charles an effort not to show Lisa how much he detested their new life. He had been glad enough to leave London and for an hour or two while they were in the train – they had returned the Ruby Saloon – he had thought with pleasure of living in his home town. It would be pleasant to walk in its ancient streets and be part of Stratford again.

That emotion had not lasted twenty-four hours.

The life he and his sister were forced to lead humiliated him. His clothes were shabby. There were times when he was actually hungry, and the lodgings Lisa had found were three dreary rooms which he left as soon as possible every morning because he could not bear to sit in them. They were on the first floor of a dilapidated house near the station in a terrace built late in the nineteenth century for the workers at the local brewery. It was not until Charles came to live at No. 12 Crocker Road that he understood poverty.

Their landlady, Mrs Ellerton, was a widow. Charles thought she resembled a dog who has been shaved; she was all anxious eyes and teeth. He was charming to her because Charles was that sort of man. If he paid her the smallest compliment she went puce, the flush starting at the base of her neck. Charles was sorry for her and wished he'd never set eyes on Crocker Road.

At Lisa's suggestion, ashamed not to do as she asked, Charles began to write letters. He wrote to the friends they had managed to trace and who no longer lived locally, to

121

friends of their father's in London, to Charles's old head-master, even to a tutor at Oxford who must surely have put Charles right out of his thoughts when Charles left before he took his degree. In his letters he asked in a roundabout way if they could offer any suggestions as to where and how to find a job. Some of the letters vanished into nowhere. Some returned with a ghostly 'Gone Away' scrawled upon them. He did receive a few replies and Charles soon learned that when people are going to say no they take their time about it. The longer the letter was, the less help he was offered.

He admired Lisa for taking a job and actually applying herself to it, leaving punctually every morning and returning, sometimes very tired, at night. She seemed cheerful, so he supposed she didn't dislike her work. But he did not ask in case she told him the contrary. He felt he couldn't cope if Lisa were not happy. He was too busy being miserable himself. What could he himself do, except play cards?

Among Lisa's many suggestions was one he absolutely refused. She tried to persuade him that Guy Bowden would be a good person to approach. After all, they'd recently met him and he had helped *her*.

'Positively no. I'm damned if I'm going to him cap in hand. He's found out we're broke –'

'Of course he has! I told him.'

'I would have very much preferred you to do no such thing.'

Charles had not been present at Whitefriars at any of her meetings with her father's old friend. He hadn't come to the sale of the silver, nor thanked Guy Bowden for his part in arranging it with Perdita Smith. When the sale was done and the cheque arrived – it was their last night in Cromwell Road and Andrew McAllister was out – Charles had scarcely asked her a thing about the silver. All he'd done was agree that the sum should be halved.

She thoroughly disapproved of his attitude to Guy Bowden now and said so.

'I simply don't understand you. Mr Bowden was Father's great friend, practically his only friend. I bet he knows a damned sight more about all the money poor Father lost than we'll ever know. How could I possibly put up a show and pretend things were all right? I told him we were stony-broke and he helped me. He was extremely useful.'

'I'm not going to see him, Lou, so you can forget it. I detest going to that house. I'm surprised *you* could bear to.' He looked down his long aristocratic nose.

Lisa might have replied that she would go anywhere for help, but she did not. She saw that he was sad and knew Whitefriars reminded him that he, too, might have been a man with property, a home, an assured future. That single visit to the Bowdens, it seemed, had upset him and in some way he saw Guy Bowden as the villain of the piece. That was absurd. Furthermore, she was sure it was Bowden who had suggested that Perdita Smith might offer her some work. Once he had called in at the shop to ask how she was getting on; he'd said she must telephone to come and dine and 'bring your brother along'. But she knew Charles would never go.

Scratching around for money, unable to get any form of work he could bear to accept, with an Etonian education that hobbled him and the cliché of champagne tastes and a beer income – in Charles's case no income at all – he went for long walks, drank in country pubs, spoke to nobody, and found – with an instinct as sharp as a retriever's – the small club where he could play poker, use his wits to do what he did well. It lifted the pall of boredom. And, to a certain degree, of shame.

Walking down the High Street on the day after Lisa had gone to the Mayor's party, Charles was thinking about cards. He was reflecting that there was no such thing, in playing and probably in life, as luck. There were simply three kinds of cards: the bad, the not-so-bad, and the first-rate. You must play with whatever came into your hand. As he walked, scarcely conscious of where he was, a girl ambled by mounted on the broad back of a pony. He heard the clip of the hoofs and glanced up. It was Jenny Bowden, wearing a jersey the colour of winter jasmine, her riding hat pushed back on her blonde head. Seeing him, she blushed.

123

'Hello. I've been wondering when we would meet,' he said untruthfully.

She reined in and sat looking down at him from her extra height. She was patently shy.

'I didn't realize you were in Stratford too.'

'You know my sister's at The Treasure Box? Apparently your father kindly gave her the introduction,' said Charles. A second lie. He had thought it patronizing and not kind at all. 'Yes, I'm living in Stratford. Looking about for a job.'

'You must not take just anything. One has to pick and choose,' said Jenny Bowden knowing nothing about it.

They continued to talk. Apparently liking his company, she slid down from her horse and, leading it, walked with him as far as the Guild Chapel. The short winter day was almost over, dusk had begun to fall and the air smelled frosty and sharp.

'I'm keeping you from getting home.' He paused for just the right amount of time. 'Incidentally, may I call you Jenny?'

'Please do.' Awkwardly.

'It's a nice name. I like it very much,' said Charles who'd never thought about it.

'Do you really? I don't. Actually I was christened Jennifer. Even worse – Cornish for Guinevere. Torture!'

They both laughed.

For the first time since he'd arrived in Stratford, apart from an afternoon when he'd won at poker, Charles's spirits rose. Gambling kept him in the company of men, but he was at his best with women. He hadn't seen Claire for weeks. Now on this dark winter afternoon, his sensual self stirred again, a giant waking. The girl was abrupt and shy and when she smiled her teeth were beautiful; he remembered the old-fashioned description 'like peeled almonds'. He wondered how it would taste to kiss her.

'It's quite a way to ride back to Whitefriars,' he said.

'Oh, Midge isn't mine, she's from the stables. I come in by car and now I'm taking Midge back. Daddy doesn't like me to ride his horses, the old meany.'

124

'Could I walk with you to the stables? We might have a drink at The Shakespeare afterwards?'

She accepted nervously. How her eyelashes curled. Charles was willing to bet she didn't use a little curling iron similar to the one he had seen Claire press on her lashes.

They walked slowly back to the stables and then to The Shakespeare in the dusk and sat for half an hour in an empty lounge by a log fire, talking quietly, afterwards making their way to her car outside the theatre which, being closed for rehearsal, glowed only dimly here and there.

All the time he was with her, Charles was almost unconsciously using his considerable gifts, making her interested, flattered and at ease. He was like an animal tamer who speaks in a soothing voice and stands immobile to coax a creature to lose its fear. He was quite taken with the girl but more taken still with the game of sex, at which he was as adept at playing as he was with cards. Even his way of talking was a courtship. His sister would have groaned to see how little resistance he met from the innocent creature already, so to speak, in his grasp.

Jenny Bowden was enthralled by him. She'd never met a man like Charles and determined not to breathe a word of their meeting to her father. Until now she had told him everything that happened to her. But she was sure her father did not like Charles Whitfield, although he hadn't said so. The only male escorts he approved for her were the sons of friends, boys she had known for years, often as young as she was. It was true they could ride and they could dance. But conversation with them was a series of weak jokes. Her boyfriends, personable, polite, were never more than twenty-one.

Charles Whitfield was fascinating. He was also so *old*. Thirty at least. He had been in the war and there was something about his looks which was sorrowful. As a subject of conversation by ex-soldiers, the war was the biggest bore Jenny could think of. When brigadiers, an occasional General, came to dine at Whitefriars, Jenny couldn't wait for the meal to end so that she could slip from the room, leaving them to drink port with her father and talk about either of the two wars. Up in her room alone, she liked to play dance music on her gramophone, the most romantic records she owned, and dance alone in the arms of a dream lover.

Here, thought Jenny, he was.

She wondered what had happened to Charles during that tedious war. Reared on Hollywood films which she enjoyed as a child sucks toffee, Jenny wondered if he had taken part in hand-to-hand battles, been cut off from his men or led some charge or other through the jungle. She wished she had been grown-up when Charles was in uniform. She imagined hectic leaves. The idea of Charles as a soldier was sexually exciting.

Being near him now excited her too. She couldn't meet his eyes.

'Shall we see each other again?' he asked in his indolent voice, standing by her car outside the hotel.

'Okay.' It had the right offhand débutante sound.

'What about tomorrow?' Charles heard himself say.

Jenny agreed to meet him at The Shakespeare at four in the afternoon.

She sang all the way home. But Charles walked very thoughtfully back to Crocker Road.

The new friendship flourished. It blossomed from day to day in a series of walks, drinks, telephone calls when her father was safely out of the house, and drives in the winter countryside. Jenny did not mention him to her father. But at home she was more talkative and laughed more often and Guy Bowden noticed the change with pleasure. He loved to see her giggling and when they played childish card games at night together after dinner, loved her because she was determined to win and crowed when she did.

'Goodnight, my sweetheart,' he said at the top of the stairs.

Jenny gave his weathered cheek a peck, whisked down the corridor to her room, and danced to the wireless.

The meetings with Charles were companionable and they were chaste. Charles had never rushed at a woman in his life

126

and when he kissed her sometimes in her car parked in a quiet chestnut-lined avenue, his kisses were with his lips closed. But one night, when they had been seeing each other for nearly two weeks, he opened her mouth gently with his tongue. Nobody had ever done that to her before and she did not like it, shutting her lips fiercely as he tried to force them open. She felt him shaking with laughter. Later he taught her how it was done and, alarmed at first and understanding nothing of its pleasure, she did as she was told and let his thick tongue explore inside her mouth. Then she began to use her own tongue too and felt a tingling in the lower part of her body and clutched him tightly when he stopped. She felt confused.

Charles wanted her far more than she wanted him. He wasn't used to any form of sexual exchange that didn't end with a climax. His body ached after he'd left Jenny, and it stayed aching for some time while he walked home to Crocker Road. What am I doing with this little virgin? he thought. She's not in my league. Why don't I forget the whole thing?

One evening when he felt more restless and unsettled than usual he telephoned Claire. It was a call on the offchance and – with Charles's luck – she happened to be at home and alone.

'Charles, of all people,' said her purring voice. 'Where are you? Forgetting me quite, of course.'

'How could I do that?'

'Very easily. Instant amnesia.'

'Don't fish, Claire.' His voice was as promising as hers.

'I don't see why not.'

'I've been thinking about you. I want to see you.'

'Do you, Charles?'

He telephoned Jenny the next morning, at a time when he knew her father was out riding, and said he had to go to London on business. That's true, he thought. In a way.

'I'm afraid I'll be back too late to see you. I expect I'll have to take the last train.'

Jenny wailed in disappointment.

Briefly saying to his sister that he couldn't stand another

127

five minutes of Stratford without a breath of London air, he took the train and was in Mayfair by midday.

Like Charles, Claire was hungry. Lewis was getting worse. He seemed to have given up sex altogether, and last night had had the gall to tell her when she indicated what she would like that she ought to 'control herself'. No man had said that to her in her life, not even her father when she'd lain kicking and screaming with temper on the nursery floor at the age of six. She refused to speak to him this morning and having got rid of her daily maid earlier than usual, was waiting for Charles in a long silk housecoat the colour of her eyes when she heard the front doorbell.

He walked in, in his usual rangy way, as if in no hurry. But this time he was.

'Hello, darling Charles,' said Claire, standing at the open door of her bedroom.

'Claire.'

He walked straight over to her, undoing his jacket, unbuttoning his trousers and dropping his clothes as he advanced. Claire merely stood – she liked to make a picture – her housecoat undone and her naked self revealed. Charles stepped out of his final clothes, a pair of shabby pants, left his socks on and – ready for her – thrust straight into her so that she had to open her legs while she was still standing. He thrust upward, held her by the buttocks, and locked together in heat they tumbled on to the bed and made love for an hour. Halfway through they stopped.

Claire gasped, 'Oh, oh, don't let me wait . . .'

'You've got to. Because I shall too.'

Savouring the pain of separation, he went into the kitchen to get them some wine. They had not finished the glass they shared when he went into her again and this time, at long last, they came together, and Claire's groans of pleasure were loud. They rolled apart and slept.

Charles returned to Stratford that night, on the last slow and deserted train.

The next day he resumed his pursuit of Jenny Bowden.

He wasn't at all sure what he was doing and why. Jenny

128

was a fresh, protected young girl, one of the new crop grown up since the peace, for whom the old taboos were back. The war and its sexual excesses were over; virginity was in fashion.

Girls like Jenny were courted as formally as the young women of fifty years ago. They lived in a world where 'abs'l't'ly fine' meant a state of bliss. It was a place of shy meetings and half-compliments and under-statements and chaste kisses. Charles couldn't count the number of women he'd had since puberty, from the shop girls, as they used to be called, in Oxford, the Burmese girls with their polished hair, the American VADs and, on his return to England, the voracious Claire.

But Jenny's virginity was the pearl of great price.

And the plain fact was he liked her.

# 7

The arrival of the Company for the new Stratford season coincided with the first buds on trees near the theatre. The town changed. Lisa noticed it and spoke about it to Peter Lang. Charles was aware of it, and as for Jenny, she was stage-struck. She knew the dates of the first rehearsals, the names of most of the actors, the six plays and their opening nights. She asked Charles to walk with her down Chapel Lane, past the theatre and up Sheep Street. She hoped to spot one of the Company, and when she recognized a player from last year, pinched Charles's arm. He teased her.

'Do you line up at the Stage Door for autographs?'

'Only when I can get away from Daddy. He gets very sniffy if he sees me hanging round. Ooh, look over there at that girl in brown. I'm sure it's Polly Holt. Her picture was in the *Echo*.'

The neat figure of Lisa's friend was walking on the other side of the street in the company of a tall man who must, by his handsome looks, be an actor. Charles didn't say he'd known Polly as a schoolgirl. He preferred Jenny to concentrate on him and not behave like a film fan.

Stratford's theatre had been somewhat provincial before the war; few critics came to see the plays and some of the seasons were dull and slogging. But now it had become the height of fashion. Barry Jackson's seasons shone and there were rumours that one of the London stars, Anthony Quayle, was his heir apparent.

The actors who invaded the market town were like the Players in *Hamlet*, or a flock of birds from foreign climes. They strode about, congregated in a famous pub on the river, could be seen having drinks in the best hotels or eating eggs on toast in tea-shops. They never stayed anywhere for long, were always glancing at their watches and hurrying to the theatre.

The townspeople's attitude to the new arrivals was ambivalent. Stratford was making the headlines now in the national newspapers. There were exciting pictures of stars and productions. Shopkeepers noticed their profits rising and the hotels were often crammed. Local people were proud of this success, yet somehow they resented the strangers who had brought it to them. They felt possessive about Shakespeare, whose awesome power had suddenly engulfed them all like a huge tidal wave. Many of them remembered with regret the days of Frank Benson, or later of Donald Wolfit. Who were these new young men springing up on *their* stage?

They were not exactly disapproved of. There was nothing actorish about the way they dressed; most of the men had been in the Services and wore duffle coats which had been Naval issue, or khaki overcoats with indentations on the shoulders where the marks of rank had been fixed. Sometimes an actor striding down Chapel Street turned up the collar of his coat, or draped a scarf over one shoulder in a rakish way. But their clothes were perfectly respectable. The only thing was that the male actors went about without hats.

People in the streets looked at them with critical eyes. A funny lot. Unpractical dreamy chaps busy with all that make-believe nonsense. What a curious way, after all, to earn your living. There wasn't a Stratfordian who would believe that these creatures who put paint upon their faces were punctual, gifted, quick as lightning and worked like dogs.

Polly Holt differed from the other actors in one way – she had been born and brought up in Stratford. As a schoolgirl she had been taken to the Shakespeare Memorial Theatre with fifteen other girls to see the inevitable *Julius Caesar*. In the following year it had been *Much Ado About Nothing*. She had been filled with pure envy, and certain she could play Beatrice.

To her parents' disapproval she refused to go to RADA, but began her career in a very small repertory theatre in the Midlands where her first part was as a maid in Act One of an Agatha Christie thriller, in which she was murdered before she said a word. Her career improved. She moved to bigger parts; audiences liked her and she knew it.

Unwillingly called up and forced into VAD uniform and the life of hospitals, she remained an actress in her soul. She managed to get special leave when she was given a part in a stirring wartime movie made at Elstree. After the war, on the strength of that film, Polly obtained small rôles in London. She was beginning to do well.

Like every other actor in Britain, Polly was well aware of what was happening in her home town. Sir Barry Jackson had put on two brilliant seasons after the war and when, on the hunt again for work, she heard that Anthony Quayle was auditioning for a new production for the 1948 season, she was excited. She had an actor's arrogance and managed to get on the audition-list.

After much thought, Polly decided on a verse from Auden's 'Lullaby', because she'd read it once on a bus and it had made her cry:

> Lay your sleeping head, my love,
> Human on my faithless arm.

Her other choice was an extract from Daniel Defoe's *Moll Flanders* which had, she hoped, the power to shock.

The audition, called for ten in the morning, was held in a gloomily empty theatre in Shaftesbury Avenue to half a dozen people sitting in the wastes of deserted stalls. Polly had no idea if she was any good and decided she probably wasn't. To her joy Anthony Quayle sent a message later asking her to see him at his house in Pelham Place.

He offered her Doll Tearsheet, mistress to Falstaff in *Henry IV Part Two*. Polly found herself blessing Moll Flan-

132

ders. Quayle also asked her to play a waiting woman in *King Lear*, a lady-in-waiting in *Twelfth Night*, and 'some walk-ons and understudies'.

Polly caught the Stratford train one winter's afternoon and spent the journey with Maggie Nelson, a fat, clever actress up-to-the-moment in useful theatre gossip. She had already warned her parents that she didn't plan to live at Broadoaks, the family home. She telephoned them before her arrival so that the poor old things would have time to get over their disappointment. Her attitude to her parents resembled an actor's feelings about admirers queuing on a wet night at the stage door to have their programmes signed. She would have been bereft and diminished without their love, but at the same time rather pitied them for being so fond of her.

Polly intended to live the life of a pro, mix with others of her kind and learn from them. She needed the infuriating company of her equals and the exhilarating company of her peers. She needed freedom and endless talk and some sex. She had no débutante's 1948 ideas about that; she was sure sex helped her art.

She took a taxi to her parents and hugged them fondly, embarrassing her mother who was shy and making a big fuss of her father who wasn't fooled. She was their disapproved-of star, their heroine. Why she had become an actress, heaven knew. They were very proud of her.

The surge of forty-eight men and women, young, not-so-young, and including one or two distinguished actors with grey heads, meant a great deal of organization at the theatre. There was the annual problem of finding the actors homes for the season. The theatre had lists of furnished houses, cottages, flats, bungalows and lodgings. All of these filled up too fast. More had to be found.

When Polly went to see the girl who had this worrying task she was told that she had been allotted a room at Avoncliffe.

'What's Avoncliffe? Theatrical digs?' said Polly, adding in her easy way, 'I'll be able to find it quite easily – I was born and brought up here.'

'Then I'm surprised you don't know Avoncliffe,' said the girl who was thin and overworked.

Polly sensed she'd made a *faux pas*. 'I daresay I'm mad. It's obviously very special.'

'It used to be Randall Ayrton's house.'

'Oh, of course! I remember now. Big place, rather elegant,' lied Polly.

'That's the one. It belongs to the Trust now and has been divided into flats. There's a huge garden,' said the girl, who had forgiven Polly and liked actors.

'Spiffing,' said Polly. She walked off to the station and took the ancient taxi.

She wasn't sure what she expected, but it certainly wasn't the sight that met her eyes as the taxi ground its way up a drive between stately trees. At the end of the drive was a long, low house with a Regency look to it. It might have been a baronet's domain to which Jane Austen heroines, penniless and proud, were driven in a carriage, longing to be back in a small, unpretentious vicarage. Not Polly. Size – particularly stylish size – was what she liked. She sprang out of the taxi, over-tipped the old driver, refused his help – she was stronger than he was – and marched up to the large double-front of the house and a pair of glass doors which led into a kind of enclosed verandah.

She tugged at an old-fashioned bell. Nobody came.

She tugged again. The taxi drove away and the silences of the country ebbed back. Birds whistled. It was frosty under the trees but a thin sunlight shone.

Bored and rather put out, Polly opened the door. In front of her a curved flight of stairs, carpeted in red, led upwards. Polly thought everything very smart. There were oil paintings on the walls – portraits, landscapes. A grandfather clock was ticking – a sign, thought Polly, of human beings. Putting down her heavy case at the base of the stairs she took one of the many closed doors, this one to the right, and found herself out of the luxury and the stately ticking of the clock in a stone passageway with another staircase, no carpet this time.

A young man came clattering down and stopped when he saw her.

'Polly. You didn't say you were moving in here.'

'Mick. You didn't say *you* were.'

'I'm not. Just visiting.'

Gould's amusing face could look heartrending almost before he'd stopped being funny. It was a quality in his acting but not in his personality. What he liked was to make everybody laugh onstage and off. Polly had known him in a casual way for over a year.

'You look a bit lost, darling, can I help? I had digs here last year, so I'm not half bad as a pathfinder.'

He took her up some stairs, enquired of a passing actor, and was directed to a door on which a card was pinned as if indicating a dressing-room. It had a list of three names.

'Here we are,' said Mick Gould. 'Let's see who you've been landed with. Maggie and Jean. A couple of chatterers, you'll enjoy that. Now, are you okay?'

'I'm fine. Thanks, Mick.'

'Then I'll leave you and go and learn my lines for the *Henrys*. See you later.'

Polly cautiously looked round the flat. It was unoccupied but the other two girls had arrived. Their bedrooms were littered with clothes and books. In the third bedroom, the smallest but with a view of the gardens, Polly dumped a case, opened drawers and cupboards, and then cursed herself for not asking Gould to help her with the other suitcase which weighed a ton.

Sighing loudly, she returned down the stairs again. She was about to go out into the courtyard when she noticed the baize-covered, brass-studded door clearly leading to the main house.

The warmth from the other side of the door struck her like heavy velvet against her face, and she heard a sound which made her smile. Somebody was playing Chopin. She went over to pick up her case which was heavier than ever and stood listening; then, following the sound, she went to yet another door.

135

She entered the sort of anteroom which used to be an important part of eighteenth-century houses. Guests were left there to wait for the nobility. Nowadays it was not a useful room: who hung about to be received by the great? It was small, rather intimate, panelled; a little fire flickered and there was a French clock on the marble chimney-piece. Somebody had made the room his own. He was sitting at the piano filling the air with Chopin's chords – it was the coming season's most famous actor, Lewis Lockton. Hearing the door open he turned round and looked at her.

He was older than the romanticized photographs Polly had seen many times outside Shaftesbury Avenue theatres. Older and cleverer, his face was hard and humorous. When he spoke, his voice came from somewhere deep inside him.

'Good afternoon.' He was very dry.

'Oh, I'm sorry, I took the wrong door.'

'Did you, now?'

This was no hospitable actor of her own age showing her her room and telling her she must share the bath. She was doing her first-ever entrance into a lion's cage.

'And what is your name?' he enquired, looking at her over his spectacles.

'Polly Holt.'

'Stop standing in the doorway like a draught, Miss Holt. Come in, since that is what you had in mind.'

'Oh – sorry – I didn't mean –'

'Of course you did. What is that you are dragging along the ground? A suitcase. It looks to me as if it weighs half a hundredweight. Why do actors always travel like Lord Byron – did you know he took ninety-three trunks to Italy? Leave it in the hall, child, nobody will touch it. Come in. Apparently you are going to live here, are you?'

'You too, Mr Lockton?'

'No, no,' he said, smiling, 'I am living at The Spread Eagle.'

'Do you like hotels?' enquired Polly who could see he was amused by her.

'Indeed I do. I like,' said Lewis Lockton, 'to ring bells.'

Polly spent half an hour with Lewis Lockton, chatting to him and making him laugh. She was a show-off, and the worldly, elderly man liked that. She was piquante, bubbling, even slightly boring in her self-confidence; she made him smile. He had never known, as friends, girls considerably younger than himself. Polly was as taken with Lockton as he was with her. He was world-famous but you'd never think so, thought Polly, and he had an air which was as thrilling as his powerful voice. Polly was delighted with him and with herself. She had all the young actor's reverence for the star. Any star.

After a while she sensed that he'd had enough of her company and stood up. He followed suit.

'You are coming to my party on Sunday, of course?'

'I didn't know –'

'That I was giving one? Why should you, Miss Holt, when you have only just arrived? Dot and Tony Quayle have very hospitably said I may give my party here. It's a good idea, you know, to have a get-together at the start of a season like this one. Most of us are strangers to each other; it will warm us up. Of course there'll be the usual first-night parties but I'm none too keen on those. I'm rather a coward about those shindigs; I never believe a word anybody says. Well, now. You're to be one of my guests at Avoncliffe. What a very long way,' he added, 'you will have to walk.'

Polly settled into Avoncliffe as if she'd lived in the big house all her life. It was a Regency mansion which had been ingeniously adapted and altered; the Memorial Theatre had reason to bless its existence. In the main house, handsomely proportioned, were a large drawing-room, dining-room, the little anteroom and the verandah along the length of the house which overlooked lawns and gardens. This part of Avoncliffe was for the grandees, and Anthony Quayle and his family had made it their home.

But mansions built long ago also included valuable unused spaces which were hospitable for visiting actors. There were stables. Servants' quarters. Cottages. Every possible care was taken to turn these into flats, large and small. In the last century Avoncliffe had buzzed with life and it did so now. Not with housekeepers and butlers, cooks, maids, nurse-maids, governesses – now it housed actors and their wives and children, stage directors or stage managers, wardrobe workers and a brilliant electrician.

Early on any frosty morning a group of cyclists would set off down the drive. There were very few pre-war cars. The inhabitants of Avoncliffe bicycled to the theatre, a distance of two and a half miles or so, and arrived with cheeks tingling from the cold and eyes sparkling from the exercise.

Polly shared her flat with two pros. One was the catty, fat actress, Maggie Nelson, with whom she'd travelled to Strat-ford: experienced in rep, capable, well aware that her bulk was a valuable acting asset. Maggie was always in work. The other flat-sharer was a very pale girl suitably called Jean White, an ASM whose passion for theatre meant a life of little sleep, heavy worries and a head full of gossip. Polly learned of rivalries, jealousies, ambitions, scandals and likely disasters. Maggie and Jean never stopped talking and Polly sat up late drinking Nescafé, constantly enthralled.

She was told a great deal about 'Sir Lew', as everybody in the company called him. Lewis Lockton had been married three times. To a titled woman in English society years ago. To an American heiress, also in the dim distance. And most recently to an English actress from whom he was now separated but not divorced. Maggie swore he'd left her because she talked too much. 'I must say,' said Maggie, who did not stop, 'I don't blame him.' After the marriage broke up, he had gone to Hollywood to make two not very remark-able films. He was now part of the Stratford company, 'staying at The Spread Eagle,' said Maggie, 'living the life of Riley.'

Everybody approved of Sir Lew. Actors did not envy wealth, but the size of billing and the length of rôles. Maggie and Jean admired Sir Lew's way of life, his Rolls, his open sports car, his suite at The Spread Eagle. He had paid for the hotel to clean and fill the swimming-pool – in February. He was very fit and swam early each morning. 'I had to deliver a book to him the other day,' said Jean. 'He was in the pool. There was steam rising out of it and he was swimming up and down like a creature in the Amazon. I could only just see his head.'

Lockton did not spend all his time in Stratford. When he was not called for rehearsals, his chauffeur drove him up to London for the night. He'd been seen in the back of his Rolls, enveloped in a mink-covered rug.

By one of those caprices of Nature, who usually arranges for English garden parties to be drenched in rain and children's picnics to be knee-deep in mud, the night of Lewis Lockton's party was clear, cold and starlit. A bright sun had shone on Stratford all day long, turning the Avon steely blue, with reflections of small clouds. At Avoncliffe the vans arrived from Fortnum's; there was much unpacking, unfolding of starched cloths. Austerity appeared to be a word nobody had heard about, nor rationing either. The girls living in Avoncliffe were having baths, ironing dresses, setting their hair and doing their faces like artists at easels. Lockton, gloriously free of any responsibility but signing the cheque, was drinking a quiet glass of champagne at his hotel and reading the poems of Herrick. It was nice to think people were so busy, bless them, he thought, turning the page.

Peter Lang, with his theatre connections, had been given an invitation to the party and had asked Lisa to go with him. He was delighted to be able to go to Avoncliffe where the bigwigs would be assembled; he hoped to talk to some of the actors, and to use their news in his column. He had seen a production of Anthony Quayle's in London, and heard the rumours that he was to inherit the crown as director of the theatre. Perhaps, thought Peter, I might be lucky and get a word from him.

While Peter dressed, and shaved for the second time that day, he stopped thinking about the party and began to think about Lisa. He was a man who liked to be in control. His life in the past had been disciplined; he was comfortable with rigid rules. The only passion he'd known had been for music and his taste at present was little pleased, for England was in the midst of an orgy of romance. Tchaikovsky and Rachmaninov, full-blown throbbing chords which poured from the wireless and made the ceilings of the Albert Hall ring. Passionate, romantic, yearning, aphrodisiac music thundered in the movies too. Peter couldn't bear it.

Lisa's taste in music was abysmal, yet he even took pleasure in her musical raptures. Everything about her bewitched him: her looks, the little he knew of her past, her air at times as melancholy as the Russian symphonies she loved, her thin figure and sallow skin. He was obsessed with her, odd girl that she was. She and her idle brother had become central to his life. She intrigued him. Her past, it seemed, had been wealthy but her present was comparatively poor. Yet she behaved as if she still had money. She would buy an expensive trifle, a handkerchief edged with real lace for instance. She was always offering to pay her share when he took her for a drink. That upset him. When he told her so she laughed.

'I do not like it when you offer to pay, Lisa.'

'But *I* do.'

'I am sorry. We will not have it,' he said. Lisa looked at him affectionately. She scolded Charles for gambling, but – usually sensible – she, too, had fits of extravagance of which Peter did not approve. She spent a whole week's pay from The Treasure Box, after she'd allowed for her share of the rent, on champagne which she shared with her brother and himself.

As for Charles, Peter rather admired him for being bone idle. It was a state which Peter himself would not have borne for five minute. Like a horse trained in the shafts, Peter wanted to pull a heavy weight. He would have worked if he'd been paid nothing.

When he drove Lisa to Avoncliffe, both of them were interested and excited and as he turned into the gate, Lisa leaned forward to exclaim. The sight was pretty indeed.

Somebody had edged the long drive with glass lamps inside which were night-lights. The effect was one of long, twinkling necklaces.

'How lovely!' exclaimed Lisa.

'They won't last long,' Peter said, as they climbed out into the dark.

'Don't be so practical.'

'I prefer it. I am practical about *you*.' He put an arm around her waist.

The front door was wide open to the cold night, the hall crowded, and the first person Lisa saw was Polly, in a New Look dress with enormous skirts the colour of a pink peony.

'Hello, Lisa! I'd no idea you were coming to the party. You do look spiffing – did you get that in India?'

Lisa, who was wearing yet another of her Burmese satins, this one of turquoise and black, knew the dress was old-fashioned. But Polly had ceased to look at it and was fixing her eyes on Peter.

'Do introduce me to your friend,' she said, putting out her hand and giving a dazzling smile. 'I'm Polly Holt.'

'Of course. I recognize you.'

Peter took her hand and bowed his head. His manners were slightly foreign, Lisa often thought. Like a Frenchman. Polly, looking pleased, accompanied them into the drawing-room with the hospitable air of being their hostess. Over by the fire was Lewis Lockton, tall and thin in a dinner-jacket, greeting his guests.

'We must get into line,' said Polly, joining the queue waiting to speak to the star. Lisa, inwardly amused at the formality, turned to exchange a look with Peter. His face was serious; he might have been waiting to be presented at Court.

Their turn came eventually.

'Sir Lewis, this is my great friend Lisa Whitfield. We were at school together and she was my page when I was Joan of Arc,' announced Polly, switching the emphasis on to herself.

The actor took Lisa's hand and looked at her with a very

pleasant smile. 'I wish you could be *my* page in *Lear*. Will you take the part?'

'Oh yes, please,' said Lisa, laughing.

When Peter was introduced he bowed as he'd done to Polly. He looked very respectful.

Avoncliffe was crowded. The chains of elaborate rooms, the verandah which ran the length of the house, glassed in against the cold, the little anteroom where Polly had found Lewis Lockton playing the piano, everywhere was full of people chattering, laughing, greeting each other with kisses, accepting champagne with delighted smiles. Peter and Lisa took their buffet supper on to the verandah and sat by a mass of broad-leaved plants as if in a bower.

'They talk too much,' Peter remarked.

'Aren't you enjoying yourself?' Lisa was eating tiny squares of smoked salmon, something she had not tasted for years.

'I always am when I am with you.'

She did wish he was not quite so earnest. He never sparkled or teased and even his smile was from good nature and not from amusement. He was ten years or more older than she was, yet Lisa often felt his seriousness resembled the wondering gravity of the very young.

Peter had an old-fashioned look about him; it was something to do with the way he did his fair hair. His features were regular, a straight nose, bright blue eyes. His looks were Edwardian; you could imagine him as a man painted by Sargent. Lisa liked him very much, and enjoyed the occasional triumph of making him laugh. She also liked him physically. He was so clean, his hands always spotless as if he'd just scrubbed them. For all their aristocratic shape, her brother's were sometimes dirty. Lisa liked, most of all, her effect on Peter Lang, the way he looked at her, the way he reacted when he saw her. She felt at ease with him. But she did not love him.

'It's sweet of you to bring me to this glamorous party', she said, looking through the verandah's doors at the shifting crowds, listening to the buzz of talk. 'But don't you think

142

you ought to circulate a bit? I'm sure you ought to talk to some of the Company, and unearth interesting things for your column.'

Peter hesitated. Time was going by and it was already late. People wandered about or danced in a haphazard way; many were sitting in a circle on the floor by Lewis Lockton, listening to him in the devoted silence people give to the famous.

'Go on, Peter. See who you can find. I'll eat my ice and listen to the music. Come and get me later.'

'Are you quite sure? I hate to leave you –'

'Don't be ridiculous. Off you go.'

He touched her hand, and then walked away into the drawing-room with a purposeful step. Lisa wondered who it was he was going to buttonhole. He was good with actors; he made it so obvious that their work interested him. She began to eat the ice, which was delicious. I'll make it last as long as possible, she thought, and remembered that Peggy, her friend in Calcutta, said that was what prisoners of war used to do with the food from their Red Cross parcels . . .

'There you are.' It was Polly who dropped down beside her, fanning herself with her hand. 'I've been dancing with Mick Gould and he's much too good. Makes me feel I have three feet, so I've left him. He's the one doing that be-bop stuff over there. You met him at The Cobweb, remember? He's got real parts in all the plays except *Caesar*, the lucky pig.'

'I thought you said you were relieved at only having Doll Tearsheet and walk-ons.'

'I said no such thing!' exclaimed Polly sharply. She had made the remark to Lisa while getting over her disappointment at not being offered Cordelia. The young actress cast for the part had been taken ill. Another, equally celebrated, was brought from London. Polly had gnashed her teeth. She was doing it again when reminded of her own lie. She took off one of her satin shoes and wriggled her toes.

'Aren't you going to ask what's upset me?'

'I don't expect so.'

'You're infuriating. You were just the same at school, I

143

remember everybody said it about you. Bloody self-possessed. If I bore you, I'll go.'

Lisa snorted with laughter and Polly immediately did the same.

'It's Sir Lew,' murmured Polly, indicating by her eyes the star with his circle of fans.

'What's wrong with him? He seems nice.'

'Nice? He's wonderful. But we were doing a scene from *Lear* yesterday – I'm only Regan's waiting-woman – but I could see him looking at me. He was thinking I can't do it.'

'Polly, I know nothing about acting –'

'True. You don't.'

'Do shut up,' said Lisa good-naturedly, 'I was going to say that even a dimwit like me can see a person improves in any rôle as rehearsals go on.'

'I was giving my all,' said Polly satirically.

She lingered with Lisa, hoping for the sort of sympathy fellow actors would dish out. She knew, they knew, it didn't mean a thing, but she needed it like sugar in her coffee. Lisa wasn't giving her a spoonful and Polly sprang up quickly when Peter Lang reappeared. He had talked to half a dozen members of the Company, and had some excellent stuff for his column.

Giving Peter a melting smile – Lisa was suddenly reminded of Marguerite in the Chowringhee – Polly hurried away. She went and fetched herself an ice. People who don't act, Polly thought sulkily of her old schoolfriend, have no idea of the agony of being no good. *And* of the star saying so, not in words but unmistakeably with his eyes.

She'd fallen for the idea of Lewis Lockton like a ton of bricks. Ambition and egoism filled her. He seemed to Polly to be bathed in glory. She had seen him on the lawns of the Bancroft outside the theatre, walking up and down on the wet grass, rehearsing his lines. How gracefully he moved. Like a panther, thought Polly. She hadn't thought of speaking to him, but had just stood and looked her fill. Then an hour later her own inadequacy as an actress had become horridly evident.

144

Who'd be an actor? thought Polly. Lewis Lockton ended his story to a roar of laughter, glanced up and saw a wistful pink-clad figure. Polly knew her stance was doleful.

He lifted his hand and beckoned, squeezing sideways in his chair to make room for her. She came across the room like a swallow.

# 8

---

Guy Bowden had never felt the need for intimate friends, although he had many people in the county of whom he was reservedly fond. It was an accident that he had become close to Lisa and Charles's father; part of the bond between the two men had been concern on Guy's part and dependency on Alec Whitfield's. Since Alec's death he had never replaced him and the only person whose company he literally needed was that of his daughter.

He came from old Army stock, had served in the Great War with courage, been awarded the DSO and was twice wounded, miraculously with no more serious consequences than a somewhat stiff right arm and occasional shoulder pain in cold weather. When the 1939 war broke out, and the Government passed the National Service Act which extended the call-up from men aged eighteen up to forty-eight, Guy knew he would never be accepted for active service. While young men all over the country waited for their papers, Guy took the train to London to see one or two influential friends. He returned having been given what he described as a 'not very particular' job in the War Office. He said little about his work.

During the war, friends in the county were curious about what Guy actually *did*. He was adept at not answering questions and rumour went round, growing more colourful with the telling. He was hand in glove with Churchill. He was a secret agent. Guy went to London a great deal, sometimes remaining in the bombed city for days. When he returned he was as unruffled as if he had been visiting his tailor.

Abrupt in speech, pleasant in manner, he was somebody whom nobody solved. He was attractive to women, yet appeared to live without sexual adventures. Women friends said heaven knew what he got up to in London. A discreet job of the kind he did was typical of Guy. When peace came the unspecified job apparently ended, and Guy said, when asked, 'Only a desk job. Not needed any more.' He returned to his work in Whitefriars in what had been the library and he had rechristened his office.

His finances kept him busy, and so did managing his land. On the face of it he was a stereotype: the Galsworthian country squire keeping up traditions that war, in less than a quarter of a century, had twice blown into fragments.

A Stratford man born and bred, he revered the arts. Paintings interested him, and he bought English water-colours and one or two landscapes – but not the grotesques – of Rowlandson. He knew the Flower family, reigning Stratford aristocrats, descendants of the famous Charles Flower, head of the Stratford brewery, whose inspiration and money had created the first theatre on the banks of the Avon.

Not long after the 1914–18 war Guy had accepted a place on the theatre's board. When he spoke at meetings, which was rarely, he was listened to. He went to the plays now and then and took part in fund-raising for the new theatre after the fire. But he thought the productions in the 1930s distinctly dull. Now, with the burgeoning of new ideas, the arrival of new young directors and new young stars, he went to all the plays during the Season in the company of his daughter.

'Wasn't it marvellous!' was Jenny's usual reaction when he drove her home after a play.

She liked everything. The aura, the sound of poetry, the elaborate costumes now in fashion after dingy wartime years, the comedies, the tragedies. She laughed and cried at Shakespeare and her father was pleased in his reserved, monosyllabic way.

Among the things Guy did not talk about, the subject upon which he never uttered a word was that of Frances, his divorced wife and Jenny's mother. She had left him when Jenny was scarcely four years old, to live in Italy with a man younger than herself.

It would not have occurred to Frances, who had enough courage to make the break, to leave only a cowardly letter; she told her husband in person. He came home one winter's evening from hunting to find that her trunks were packed. She was in their bedroom, dressed in travelling clothes, locking her little jewel-case. She turned and faced him with hard eyes.

'I'm leaving you, Guy. Don't bother to shout or call me names, it would do no good. I am going to Siena with Rowley.' Later in the conversation she cruelly said, 'He's wonderful in bed. I never knew sex could be –'

Guy gave her no time to finish the insult but walked out of the room and the house. He did not come back until midnight. Frances, her possessions and his car had gone.

Frances was a fair-haired, well-born, tough-minded, arrogant young woman, with the English beauty which is so moving and does not last. She sparkled. She danced. She rode well. Guy had fallen passionately in love with her, she had seemed to return his love, and their marriage had been one of those early 1930s society weddings at St Margaret's with a trail of bridesmaids weighed down with flowers. Jenny was born a year after the marriage; Guy had wanted children and Frances was perfectly willing to comply. But motherhood and Guy began to bore her and in any case Frances was highly-sexed and Guy wasn't. When a different kind of man appeared Frances did not resist.

She vanished from Whitefriars, from her husband's strong presence, her marriage, her position in the county and her small daughter. Later she and Rowley parted and despite receiving letters from her, Guy would not allow her to see the child. Later still, just before the war, Frances went to America where she remarried. Good, thought Guy, and slammed a door in his mind. If anybody had asked him –

148

and nobody would have dared – if he had forgiven his wife, he would have been surprised. He hadn't forgiven Frances – he had killed her off.

At fifty-five Guy no longer went in for the occasional sexual adventures of which women friends in the county used to suspect him. He didn't need sex; it had stopped for him. He was interested in his money and was clever with it, was proud of his house and the land which flowered and fruited round it. He had no worries on that score. He had let most of it to tenant farmers who paid a good price. He loved one person – his daughter – and was absorbed in one duty: his care of her.

In the early spring of 1948 Guy was anxious about Jenny. She wasn't yet eighteen, had left boarding-school the previous July and behaved as if the walls of St Catherine's had been a detested prison. She flew out of the cage which she had in actual fact enjoyed. Entranced with her wings, she scarcely bothered to land occasionally on his outstretched hand.

He suggested she should try for university, but she laughed. Did he imagine she wanted to *study* any more! After making some tentative inquiries in Stratford, he asked her if she liked the idea of training to work in a florist. He was very out of date; he forgot that girls of her class had driven lorries and repaired tanks. In his mind his daughter could just about manage to twist silver paper round the stalks of carnations. This second idea was greeted with a teasing grin and a hug. Dear Daddy. He couldn't get things right, could he? What Jenny wanted was some fun.

She invited her girlfriends home. She went to stay with them and attended parties and dances. The girls tried on each other's New Look finery and experimented with new make-up. They bought black-market clothing coupons from nannies and daily helps, were thoroughly unpatriotic and merry as grigs.

Guy became fretful when people asked him for the umpteenth time, 'And what is Jenny going to do?' 'She'll be presented next season,' he replied as if that settled the

149

matter. The government in power might be Labour, with ideals of equality and classlessness, but well-bred young girls still went to Court as the beginning of being grown-up. Guy considered this essential for his only daughter. He had sent her name up to the Lord Chamberlain and had enquired among married women friends. They suggested a famous school of dancing in London, where Jenny would be given lessons on the art of a débutante's deep, knee-locked curtsey to the King and Queen.

It was one of Guy's meannesses – he had a few – that he refused to buy his daughter a horse of her own. He had two hunters, purchased the previous year; he himself hunted and enjoyed it. He had no intention of spending good money on a horse for a girl who wasn't a brilliant rider and who, as a schoolgirl, had never lifted a finger to look after her pony. He bought her an inexpensive little car instead, and gave her a few of the petrol coupons allowed him by the Government for necessary miles on business. But not a horse. If Jenny wanted to ride, she must hire a horse from Miss Corbett's stables in Stratford. 'Give her a good mount and see she sits properly,' he said to Gwen Corbett, an old friend who admired him.

In February there was a string of sunny days, freezing out of doors and too cold to melt the frost, but invigorating if you went riding. Jenny had spent a thoroughly enjoyable morning in the dazzling weather and came into her father's office bringing with her the scent of the winter. She wore jodhpurs and a pale blue sweater which was the colour of her eyes. Her cheeks were bright pink.

She ranged about the room, picking up books and putting them down, remarking that she'd had a splendid time and her pony, Midge, had been in fine fettle.

'I'm glad to hear it,' said her father absently.

'I saw some snowdrops.'

He gave up trying to work. 'Did you? Where?'

'On the edge of the wood in little clumps. And lots in the Wortleys' orchard.'

She plumped herself down on a chair piled with box files.

He swivelled round to face her. It did not occur to her to apologize for disturbing him. His desk was covered with letters, documents, catalogues from art shows, invitations, theatre schedules and a clip of bills, mostly her own. If you have interrupted a man at his work and been given a smile of love all your life, you know you're welcome. Jenny called the tune.

'Daddy –' She ran her fingers up and down her riding-crop. It was a present from him, the handle of ivory and gold.

'What is it now?' enquired Guy who knew the tone.

The sun came spearing through the window and temporarily blinded her. She came close to him.

'The Hunt Ball at Alcester.'

'Yes?' said Guy, looking at his papers.

'You haven't been and gone and done it, have you?'

He put down a letter he was reading and said, but scarcely with impatience, 'Jenny, what are you talking about?'

'Have you asked Howard Bonville as my partner?'

'Of course. You and I talked about it last week.'

'Did we? I forgot. Botheration.'

Looking at the glowing girl, he was not pleased. He noticed, not for the first time, that Jenny lacked grace. His own abrupt manner was never rude. Hers was. He replied without a smile that it was a pity if she'd made a mistake, but Howard Bonville and his family had been invited and were making up their party. Jenny had known this perfectly well.

She bit her lip. She'd been riding with Charles. Never in her dreams had she imagined a simple woodland ride could be so glorious. All she'd thought about was the chance to spend more time with him – and on an impulse had invited him to be her partner at the Hunt Ball. She had looked so eager and beguiling that Charles was taken with the idea. He recalled hunt balls from the years before the war. Red faces, pink coats, the air zinging with sex.

'I can't tell this man not to come with me now that I've asked him,' she said, with annoyance.

Guy regarded her thoughtfully. 'Whom have you invited?'

151

'I knew you'd ask that.'

'Don't be tiresome. Of course I am asking. I presume it is somebody I know. Who is it?'

Why had she imagined that this was going to be easy? She was so accustomed to being indulged that her father's expression, disapproving, even stern, unnerved her. She was like a girl who had lived all her life in the company of a savage animal she alone could tame. Suddenly she realized her danger, and her confidence oozed away. Her father was actually making her nervous. *Why* had he invited the Bonvilles? They were stupid. Howard was a bore. Poor Howard, young and innocuous, devoted and a good dancer, became the enemy. She fiddled with her riding-crop, her thoughts racing as she wondered what move to make next.

When she looked up she met her father's eyes. An opponent she hadn't faced until now.

'Oh, you make everything so difficult!' she exclaimed, disappointment filling her eyes with tears. 'It's horrible going with Howard, he's a *blimp*!'

She rushed out, slamming the door. Up in her bedroom, a large chamber of chintz, painted furniture and silver-framed photographs, she burst into angry tears.

In the way of women who know they are prized, she waited for her father to make the first move. When they had fallen out in the past, she had only to bide her time and he always made it up. It was as if he couldn't stand being at odds with her. Even when he had been seriously angry over her bad school reports – Jenny disliked hard work – he usually finished by laughing. She was a spoiled little monster and she amused him.

She took a deliberately long time to have her bath after riding. She changed carefully for luncheon, studying herself in the glass with the wrapt earnestness of a seventeen-year-old. Downstairs there were the usual household noises. One of the dogs began to bark. She heard her father talking to Mrs Dickens.

When she finally came downstairs and walked into the drawing-room she had made up her mind to be as sweet as pie. I know I can persuade him if I am really nice, she thought. I was stupid to show I minded and to be so cross. He'll see if I explain how awful Howard Bonville is, going on like a sick calf, and he'll realize I simply can't tell Charles now that the invitation's off.

The housekeeper came into the drawing-room to plump up the cushions. She had a smug look. Jenny did not trust Mrs Dickens and often thought the woman was a spy who reported her doings to her father. But wasn't everybody over thirty a spy for somebody?

'Where's my father?' said Jenny in her short way.

'The Master said to tell you he won't be back till all hours. Very late, he said. He's gone to London to one of those picture shows,' said Mrs Dickens, who considered that money spent on paintings might as well be poured down the sink.

'Oh,' said Jenny blankly. 'How late does he mean?'

'Ten. Eleven. Didn't say, Miss Jenny. I'm to do your supper. And you've got the dogs for company,' said Mrs Dickens, who didn't like her either.

Damn, damn, damn, thought Jenny. Her plans had gone awry. She knew perfectly well her father had left without saying goodbye because he was displeased. She was not upset that he was still annoyed. He was in the wrong. Old people usually were. But until now she had always thought him superior to the stuffy parents whose crimes she discussed with her girlfriends. The new generation of young girls emerging into the new peacetime were willing to toe the line of strict morality, but they were secretly and passionately critical of their antiquated parents.

Sulkily eating the meal which Mrs Dickens served her in solitary splendour in the dining-room, a thought came into Jenny's head. She waited until the housekeeper was safely back in the kitchen, then went softly into her father's office and picked up the telephone. She dialled the number Charles had given her 'in case of emergencies'. It was a telephone in the passage at Crocker Road. A woman's Warwickshire voice answered and Jenny asked for Mr Whitfield.

'It's me,' she said when Charles came to the telephone.

'Hello! This is nice. I thought we weren't going to meet until tomorrow. You don't usually –'

'Ring you. I know. I don't get the chance. But I've got the house to myself at present. Look' – the words came tumbling out – 'Mrs D. goes at five and she's been told to leave me some supper. Why don't you come and we can share it? We could play my new records. My father's gone to London and won't be back until late. Do say yes . . . We could have some wine,' said Jenny who did not drink. 'It would be heaven,' she added.

Charles was intrigued. There was a hint of Don Juan's adventures about secretly visiting a young girl in a manor-house while her father was away. Charles enjoyed adventures, but was becoming more and more aware that there was danger in his friendship with Jenny Bowden. Her nervous laugh told him she was probably falling in love. But didn't he feel the same – in a way? And besides, in matters of love who could predict the future?

'I'd like to spend the evening with you very much, Jenny.'

'Oh, good! Shall I pick you up at your flat?'

'That's kind,' said Charles, inwardly shuddering and quickly improvising, 'but I'll be at The Shakespeare at half past five having a drink with one of the Company.'

'An actor. How exciting.'

'Isn't it?' he teased her. 'It's Michael Gould. I'll introduce you but only if you promise not to pay too much attention to him.'

Jenny was entranced and agreed to come to The Shakespeare before six.

Any hour, minute, moment suited her. The whole day until she saw him immediately became interminable, and when she rang off she called the dogs. They were overcome with gratitude at being noticed; four dogs and one girl set off for a very long walk. It ended with four sets of paws, four hairy stomachs and a good many flopping ears, not counting Jenny's best riding-boots, caked with mud.

It had been one more narrow escape for Charles when

Jenny suggested calling for him at Crocker Road. He was determined to avoid her seeing the horror of where he lived. It didn't matter that he had no car – nobody had a car. People took trains or buses, they cycled or walked. But the poverty of Crocker Road ground into his soul. It made him ashamed.

Charles still had no plans for getting work, had received no helpful letters from old friends, had no prospects apart from gambling. Lisa had drawn up the list of friends and was more disappointed than he when there wasn't the slightest offer of help, not even a useful introduction. When she read the letters, padded out with enquiries about herself and Charles and comments on their return 'to your old haunts', Lisa said crossly that it sounded as if they were both ghosts.

'People are as mean as muck,' she declared.

'No, Lou. They're realists and we are no longer useful.'

'You don't sound as if you mind.'

'I don't.'

With the rest of the day to waste until he met Jenny, Charles put on his only respectable clothes, noticing that the elbows of his tweed jacket were growing worryingly thin, and went out to have a sandwich in a pub in the High Street where, unconscious of the interested eyes of a red-headed barmaid, he sat in a window-seat and thought about Jenny Bowden, his sister and his life. Then he walked slowly to the Wilton Club.

In the Smoking Room, aptly named, a game was already in progress and Mick Gould, with a cheroot between his teeth, said, 'Do you want in?'

Charles pulled up a chair to join the players and was dealt a hand. 'What are we playing for?'

'Small stuff. Put in a fiver for a start,' Charles was told.

They played poker for three hours in silence, broken now and again by grunts or an occasional joke from Mick Gould. The actor was not needed for rehearsals at present, and nothing pleased him more than a good concentrated game. He'd played in India. He played backstage with other actors, at home with his sisters who were no good, and at the club

155

with Charles Whitfield who was very good. But for all that, he hadn't Charles's passion. He enjoyed cards as he enjoyed skating, tennis, things he did well. He never played very high, and when he'd lost as much as he could afford, he threw in the towel. Caution, Charles once remarked to him, was an unexpected quality in an actor.

The game went well for Charles this afternoon. He won seven pounds. One must have money in one's pocket when meeting a girl, thought Charles, who until that moment had had less than a fiver and a clean pocket handkerchief.

He finally stood up, saying he must go. The other players in the room, barred with smoke and warm from the fire, were uninterested.

Mick Gould also stood up. 'I'd better get back. Got to learn my lines for the Fool. *Lear*'s not exactly the easiest play to memorize. See you folks in a day or so. Cheerio.'

The two young men walked down the street together.

'Can I buy you a drink?' said Charles, serenely conscious of his winnings. 'I'm going to The Shakespeare to meet a girl.'

'Your hundredth and seventh but this one is quite different, is she? Yaah.'

'She is, as it happens. She'd be so pleased to see you, Mick. A definite fan. Come and have a drink.'

'Wish I could, but I have to get on with the job. Sir Lew's been quoting Keats at me: "Does not the Fool by his very levity give the finishing-touch to the pathos; making what without him would be within our heart-reach nearly unfathomable?" That's enough to unnerve anybody. Talking of the horrors of work, you don't happen to want some, do you?'

Charles looked at him enquiringly and Mick Gould thought: how did you actually fight a war – and in Burma, of all god-awful campaigns? There was something indolent about the man. Not when they played poker, though. Then he looked clever. It takes all sorts, thought Gould, filing Charles away in his actor's reference library of characters and habits, mannerisms, ways of walking, pitches of voice.

156

I'm not so tall and not a tenth as handsome, he thought, but I could use a piece of him sometime.

He walked beside Charles, smiling to himself. The idea of suggesting the job had only just occurred to him and he knew Charles would refuse. What interested Mick was how he would say no. The actor wasn't averse to seeing people behave badly, and looked forward to his companion flatly, or gracefully, turning down a chance to work. Mick himself was a dedicated slave to acting, the only profession in which you begged to be worked to death.

'Richard Pensamonn, who is designing the two *Henrys*, was talking to me today,' Mick said. 'He's a clever guy, brilliant at his job. He's got a notion for doing an exhibition at the theatre. Shakespeare, past, present and future, that sort of thing. He wants to feature Sir Barry's two years – as you know they've been a big success – and to add some stuff for this year – although a lot of it isn't ready yet. Then there's the past. Helen Faucit and so on.'

'Yes,' said Charles, who hadn't an idea what he was talking about.

'There'll be designs. Photographs. Paintings from the gallery if Richard can persuade them to lend one or two. Costumes . . . Philip Ashmore, the general manager – do you know him? He's ex-Navy and looks it – is enthusiastic about the whole thing. Well . . . what do you say?'

'About what?' said Charles, quite bemused.

Mick, not for the first time, wondered at people who weren't actors being so slow in the uptake. 'About helping with the exhibition. Richard says he'll need a couple of people to set it up in the morning, strike it in the evening and so on. Philip Ashmore's in charge. He'd give you the gen.'

'But I don't know a blind thing about the theatre,' protested Charles. Mick seemed to be going rather fast.

'It's Richard Pensamonn who *knows*, Charles. All you'd be is a strong man. Carrying things, arranging them . . . sounds dead easy to earn a few quid. I'd do it myself, but I'm in all the plays but one and won't be able to manage it.'

Charles hesitated. He was suddenly aware of the actor's mocking expression as Mick waited, apparently, to hear that his friend couldn't quite manage so taxing an employment. Beyond Mick, neatly parked outside The Shakespeare, was Jenny's little pre-war car, coachwork shining. Money, thought Charles. To spend on that sweet girl. Well. Why not?

'It's very good of you to think of me, Mick. I'd like to have a go. Who do I go and see?'

When the two men parted, Mick Gould walked back to the theatre grinning to himself. It was fun to be proved wrong.

Jenny was sitting in a quiet nook in one of the inner rooms. She and Charles had chosen it for previous, sometimes hasty, meetings, after she'd confessed that she was afraid of being seen. 'My father's friends come here quite often.'

'I'm sorry to keep you waiting,' Charles said. He was less than five minutes late.

The girl's face flowered.

'Mick Gould was talking to me,' Charles continued, 'and I couldn't get away. Unfortunately he had to go. He would have been glad to join us.'

'I wish I could have met him!'

'I promise to introduce you later,' he said, amused at her universal admiration for any and every actor. He took her hand which was pale with youth.

'Well, Beauty. Are you ready to smuggle me back to your house?'

Jenny giggled, a childish conspirator. She had never done such a thing before; it felt rather wicked. Her adult experience of young men had been confined to the usual tennis parties, dances, or the occasional grander occasion dignified by the name of "Ball" where she was danced with, held too tight, hugged too close, and kissed chastely in cars before being driven home. Charles had taught her to kiss in a very different way, opening her mouth, letting his large tongue lick her teeth; she found the kisses upsetting. He sometimes

158

lifted her on to his lap when they were in her car in the dark of Chestnut Walk. He stroked her legs. Their love-making went only up to a certain point . . . Jenny was sure the point would be leaped over, as she put it in her own mind, this evening. She was nervous.

They drove up to Whitefriars and she unlocked the door. Dogs surged towards them in a mass of brown and russet and black and white, wagging, barking. They accepted Charles because he was with their mistress, which was a distinct relief to Charles who found the drama of dogs, that essential of country life, tedious. When they had calmed down everything was very quiet.

He and Jenny stood in the hall, taking off their coats and throwing them on to a large, carved chest. Charles looked about. He'd scarcely taken in Whitefriars on the night he had come here with Lisa and it was years since his visits of the 1930s.

'What a jewel of a place, Jenny. I don't think I've ever realized what a magnificent house this is.'

'It is rather nice. Shall I take you on a tour?'

They went up the staircase, along a passage with many doors open to beautifully appointed bedrooms. Everything was in perfect order. Embroidered bedcovers. Rich-looking carpets. Paintings. Jenny pointed at one door and said, 'This is my room, I have the best view', and tugged him past. Charles showed no sign of noticing the gesture.

He was interested in everything. In the oak furniture, the plasterwork in the gables of a long room once a gallery, showing the figure of a woman with a spinning-wheel, in the bulging ceilings, the linenfold panelling, her father's bathroom which had been an early eighteenth-century closet where ladies and gentlemen stood to have their wigs smothered in powder. Many of the beams, three hundred and fifty years old, were as crooked as rheumatic limbs. The spirit of the house was ancient. And so silent. They finished the tour downstairs in an enormous, stone-floored kitchen.

'It really is wonderful, Jenny. What a place to live. Roundwood was nothing like this.'

159

'I don't remember your house, Charles. Not one bit. Of course Father and I often drive past the house and he always says "that's where Alec Whitfield used to live". But I can't recall what it was like inside or ever having been there.'

'You don't remember it because you probably never got invited,' he said. 'I love your nose. It's so serious. Not like you.'

She grinned.

'And the reason you weren't invited was because Lisa and I couldn't stick you. You were a spoiled stuck-up little brat.'

'Was I?' She was enchanted.

'You certainly were. A conceited, indulged little prig,' he said caressingly. 'Your father used to call you Jenny-Penny.'

'He still does sometimes,' she said, laughing.

'You had spots.'

'Beast! I never had a single one!'

'Spots. All over that face. You were a horrid, fat little beast primping about in smart clothes like a doll. We detested you.'

He picked her up. Jenny was quite heavy, built like her father on sturdy Anglo-Saxon lines, but Charles liked picking up women and he was strong. The Rubens painting *The Rape of the Sabines*, where the men were bearing away enormous, luscious women, had always attracted him.

'Charles, what are you doing?' said Jenny, one arm round his neck as he bore her away from the kitchen. 'We haven't eaten yet.'

'I intend to eat you,' he said and carried her into the drawing-room. The air smelled of woodsmoke, the room was warm. Dogs lay prone. Arriving with his burden, Charles pushed one dog aside with his foot.

'Cruel man. You'll hurt Binker.'

'I wouldn't hurt a fly, but he's in the way. Do shove off,' he said to another dog, stirring him so that the dog yelped and abandoned the rug in front of the fire.

Charles put his burden tenderly down and lay beside her. They rolled together and wrapped their arms around each other. Lust for her filled him, his body grew hard, he wanted

160

her so intensely that his head throbbed. But years of seduction had given Charles the self-control, the capacity to decide when sex surged through him whether he would take a woman or not. In almost every case he did, and she wanted it. But on the rare occasions when he had made a form of love to young girls, he hadn't done so. Now looking down at this virgin lying trustfully in his arms, he had a curious feeling in his heart, a dim idea that he loved her – a little. She moved him, innocent, abandoned little creature. He rolled on top of her and felt her open her legs, something she'd never done in her life. But he did not touch her there nor try to put his hand into the gap of lace-edged knickers, but continued to lie on her so heavily that she was breathless. He began to give her long, long kisses, and now and then move on her, with a rising, aching want.

At last when she was gasping and her kisses wilder, he said in a choked voice, 'Jenny – will you –' and rolling off her soft young body, began to undo his clothes. She had never seen a man naked. She had seen pictures and drawings, had had a form of sex education but not much. The sight of Charles's body erect was fascinating and slightly horrifying. She'd never imagined anything like it, and when he took her hand and wrapped it round him she trembled like a terrified horse.

'Oh Charles, Charles . . .'

She began to hold him more strongly. His eyes were shut and his face was twisted into a spasm which to the wondering girl looked like suffering. He began to thrust inside her hand. She forced herself to stare down at the curved, enlarged thing she held; it fascinated and frightened her. She watched him move and move, up and down. Suddenly there was a crash. A door was thrown open so violently that it hit the wall.

Her father . . . in the doorway.

There was no sofa to hide the couple stretched on the floor, no blanket to make a modest covering for sex. In a moment of incredulity followed by revulsion, Guy Bowden saw Charles Whitfield, his clothes undone, Jenny's hand holding him and the full horror of what was happening. He couldn't speak.

161

Charles did up his fly buttons and Jenny, one breast exposed in its rose-tipped beauty, shoved it back into her brassiere and pulled her dress together. She was shaking too much to manage the fastenings. They scrambled to their feet and stood like murderers.

Seeing their master the dogs set up a wild din of welcome, surging towards him, barking and frisking. Finding his voice Guy shouted at them, ordering them from the room.

'Out! Out! Get out!' They slunk away and he slammed the door.

By now Jenny had managed to do up her dress. When she looked at Charles she showed the whites of her eyes and he squeezed her hand – he saw she was terrified.

'Don't look like that, darling. I'll go right away. Please don't look like that.'

Guy was still by the closed door. He used the words he had used to the dogs.

'Get out.'

'I'm very sorry, Sir – I –'

'Out!' shouted Guy, whose face was grey. 'You're disgusting. I wish I could kill you. Get out of my house and if you as much as speak to my daughter again – ever – I'll give you a beating you'll never forget. Out! Out!'

He flung open the drawing-room door, marched to the front door and flung that open too. Absurdly the dogs had become part of the drama. They came rushing into the hall, mistakenly imagining when they saw the open door that their master was shouting for them to come for a night walk. They belted up to him with joyous barks.

In the hall Charles picked up his coat in silence. Guy's rage did not alarm him; he rather respected it, but he was worried about Jenny who had remained as if turned to stone. He turned round and returned to the drawing-room.

'See you soon, Jenny.'

With an oath – he never swore – Guy advanced towards the young man, looking literally as if he would kill him.

Charles faced him calmly. 'Don't try and hit me, Sir. I don't want to hit you back. I'm twenty-five years younger than you are and if I did I might hurt you. I'd very much prefer not to do that. I'm sorry I upset you.'

Again Guy couldn't speak but stood glaring, impotent, while Charles went out into the dark, waded through frolicking dogs and walked the four miles back to Stratford.

He found his sister at home in the flat, eating a sausage-roll and listening to a play on the wireless. She looked up, surprised, as he came into the room and turned the wireless off.

'Hello, Charles. What have you been up to? I bet you've had no supper.'

The shock of what had happened had somewhat faded; the bitterly cold night walk, the solitude, had cooled him down.

'What's the time?' he vaguely asked. Time seemed to have stopped.

'Quarter to ten. I say, you look freezing. Let me feel your hand. Where have you been? Up to no good, I'll be bound.'

'I was with Jenny Bowden,' he said, sitting down. He felt horribly tired and flat. How late it was. Had they lain so long by the fire?

'*Jenny Bowden!* You're joking.'

'No. I've been seeing her quite a lot lately.'

Lisa looked at him open-mouthed. 'But she isn't your kind at all. What on earth do you see in –'

'She's extremely pretty and extremely sweet and if you're going to be rude about her, shut up.'

'Sorry I spoke,' said Lisa, offended. 'I'll get you some food. You look exhausted.'

She went out into the poky kitchen which always smelled of Mrs Ellerton's cooked sprouts, made an omelette and some tea and found some stale bread for toast. When she returned her brother had fallen into one of his reveries. She detested it when he was in that mood; she dumped the tray on the table beside him and returned to her own seat and the sausage-roll.

'Go on. Eat, since I've been kind enough to cook for you.

163

And tell me about Jenny Bowden, you might just as well. I shall get it out of you in the end.'

Lisa's manner, familiar, easy, sisterly, sarcastic, was what he needed. He sat down and began to eat, realizing that he was hungry as well as depressed.

He eventually told her the entire story. He described how he had first met Jenny, how much he had liked her, their meetings at The Shakespeare and out riding. He only omitted details of what he called 'the rude bit' of what happened tonight.

When he finished the story Lisa looked horrified.

'How embarrassing. Golly. How embarrassing. I can't think of anything worse than being in the middle of a love scene and one's infuriated father marching in. Poor Jenny. You were fools, Charles. Surely you both knew when he was expected home.'

'She said when he went to London he never got back until midnight,' said Charles gloomily.

Lisa regarded him. 'It sounds a bit like an Aldwych farce. You with your pants down . . .'

He managed to smile. 'Yes. They were. He practically threatened to shoot me.'

'Of course. She's the apple of his eye.'

'I hated leaving her to be shouted at. I can't bear to think about it.'

'Chivalrous Charles. You couldn't exactly stay, could you? After he threw you out.'

'I think he would have liked to fight me, but I refused.'

'Quite right,' said Lisa. She was sorry for him but not very; the person she pitied of the three was Jenny. But Charles must have been in such situations before. He seemed more upset than she would have imagined. Was he falling in love with that girl? It wouldn't do. It wouldn't do at all.

'I hope you're not going to hurt her, Charles?'

'What on earth do you mean by that?' He looked annoyed. 'Are you asking if I'm going to seduce her?'

'I suppose I am.'

'The answer is of course not. I could have done it weeks ago.' Male vanity had appeared.

164

Lisa still looked at her brother dubiously. In her imagination the love scene was milder and less crude than it had actually been. But somebody had taken some clothes off.

'If you aren't going to seduce the unfortunate girl – and you're certainly not a guy to go fiddling on without any sex – you'd better say goodbye to her. Now's as good a time as any.'

He gave a long yawn. Sex and its collapse and the long ice-cold walk after the Aldwych farce had worn him out.

Lisa washed up – Charles never did – and he went to bed and fell asleep at once.

Four miles away across the dark countryside Guy had slammed the door on his daughter's near-seducer, then remembered that the dogs had rushed out with Whitfield. He had to go into the grounds and yell for them which took some time; they had gone padding off into the shrubbery and he whistled over and over again. Furious with the animals, Guy eventually herded them together and shoved them into the kitchen.

When he went into the drawing-room Jenny had gone.

He sat down and leaned back, shutting his eyes. His face was a mask. But inwardly, like a volcano which rarely erupts, he seethed. He couldn't forget the sight of that man lying there with his unfastened clothes, all the shame of exposed sex, his daughter's young hand grasping him. It was the worst moment of Guy Bowden's life, far far worse than the night when his wife had insulted and left him. He knew Jenny must marry eventually. The young girl he loved with a terrible, sexless, protective, helpless love would one day cease to belong to him. That was only right. But he honoured the virgin in her now, which was stainless and soon would be gone.

There would be another man whom she would love differently from the confident, spoiled affection she had for him. That man would take the responsibility and Guy would be able to enjoy her company, and that of her children, with a sigh of liberty. Love was such a heavy weight. There were times when he felt it scarring his shoulders and his heart.

Tonight had been degrading. How dared they do such a thing in his house? For some reason he did not examine, the fact that Jenny had been half naked (one breast exposed was half naked to Guy) made it worse. Jenny had been nearly debauched and the man lying there in his shame was a debaucher.

He'd never liked Charles Whitfield when he was young and now the memory that Alec had disliked his own son came back to him. No wonder Alec had got rid of him. Charles Whitfield was no good. He'd wasted his youth, run into debt and disgraced his father. It did not suit Guy to remember that Alec Whitfield had done something far worse by his irresponsibility, his coldness, by selling the very house where his children had been born. They'd come back after fighting a war to find they hadn't a farthing.

Guy Bowden ignored that now. Charles Whitfield, he decided, was a kind of criminal who must be cut out of Jenny's life at once.

In the dispassionate way that he looked at paintings, he could see the man was attractive. He was tall and personable, he had manners and a practised, a disgustingly practised, charm. All the more reason for preventing him from ever appearing here again.

He gave a deep sigh. The house was very still in the icy night; the silence seemed to ring. He felt drained and sad as he walked slowly up the stairs, switching off the lights in the upstairs corridor. Then he had a terrible thought. He suddenly wondered if Jenny had inherited her mother's wanton nature. He had not allowed Frances to come into his mind for years and now he remembered her in bed. She'd been voracious, lascivious, more highly sexed than he was, frequently unsatisfied. He recoiled at the thought that the girl upstairs might be the same. He stood hesitating.

Instinct told him to let Jenny alone. Affection could not bear to. Anger and love wrestled in him; he did not know which was going to win. But he felt softened as he walked slowly down the passage to her door. He tried the handle knowing it would be locked. The passage was in darkness and he could see the band of light beneath the door.

166

He spoke quietly. 'Jenny.'

There was no sound.

He spoke again, not very much louder. 'Jenny.'

There was still no reply and his feelings hardened.

'I am speaking to you,' he called loudly. 'Answer me at once.'

Jenny, sitting up in bed in her nightdress, looked across at the door in plain fear. She did not know what to do. She'd been lying curled up in bed, longing for Charles, crying over Charles, and trying and trying to forget the awful thing that had happened. She knew she was never going to be allowed to see him again. She hated her father. For coming into the room and ruining her life, she wildly thought. That moment, when Charles had been half naked, when her hand – she couldn't think about it. Hearing the threatening voice she climbed trembling from her bed, went to the door and unlocked it.

She was wearing a satin nightdress which clung to every curve of her body; the material was so thin that it was slightly transparent and her patch of hair showed dark through the satin.

'Put on a dressing-gown,' her father snapped. He was like a shouting sergeant-major. It was ridiculous but Jenny didn't think so and, sobbing, rushed over to a chair and pulled on her dressing-gown. With shaking hands she tied the belt so tightly that she discovered later it had made a crimson weal around her waist.

Guy walked into the room, pushing the door behind him which closed with a bang. It was a night of slammed doors.

Continuing to behave as if he were in the Army and Jenny a private caught trying to desert, he sat down and pointed to the chair facing him. She obeyed.

'Now listen to me. I shall not speak about this again. And I forbid you to do so. I was disgusted by what I saw tonight. Disgusted. I couldn't imagine in my wildest dreams that you would behave in that – that way. I was unaware that you even knew Charles Whitfield except as an acquaintance when you were a child, and that single time when he turned up here last month. I presume you've been meeting him in secret. Or did you pick him up tonight?'

'What a filthy thing to say!' She welcomed the chance to be angry and burst out, 'I've known him for weeks. We meet every day. We go riding together.'

'Indeed.'

'Yes, "indeed",' she mimicked viciously. 'I like him and I asked you if I could take him to the Hunt Ball instead of that stupid Howard Bonville. I *told* you I'd met him. I was perfectly frank,' she ended, believing the fabrication.

'You told me no such thing.'

'I did! I did!' cried the girl wildly. 'And why do you think it so disgusting, all we were doing . . .'

Her voice trailed off. He was looking at her so dangerously that she dared not finish whatever insane excuse she might have invented. Could she say sex was natural? Impossible to speak of such a thing to her father. She began to cry in earnest. From shame and anger and despair because she'd lost the man she loved. She sobbed until her eyes were narrow, reddened slits in her poor, swollen face. Every time she'd wept since she had been a motherless scrap of four years old he had comforted her. He didn't now.

'Finished?' All the separation between them was in that single word.

She continued to sniffle and draw sobbing intakes of breath.

'You are never to see that man again,' he said. 'If you do I shall confine you to the house. Don't think that's an idle threat. It is for your own good and that is exactly what I shall do. I will then send you abroad where you'll be safe from that man. He won't follow you. He hasn't two farthings to rub together.'

She said nothing, but looked at the floor.

'If you attempt to disobey me,' he continued, 'I shall keep you here in the house until I arrange for you to go to my cousins in Malta. Do you understand?'

She nodded dumbly. She thought, despite suffocating misery, I'll get round him. I'll tell lies. But she was worn out.

'Very well,' he said. He stood looking at the forlorn figure. 'I've been cruel to you, I suppose,' he said, and bent to kiss the wet cheek. 'You'll thank me one day. Believe me.'

He left the room and Jenny crawled back into bed without bothering to lock the door.

# PART TWO

# 9

Between father and daughter at Whitefriars a silence fell which was not a truce. Jenny avoided any chance of meeting him. She appeared at no meals, stayed in her room and when her father was out of the house, went for lonely walks.

Driving home from Stratford, he caught sight of her walking round the other path of the garden in the thin rain. He'd never seen so desolate a figure.

Twenty-four hours later she appeared at luncheon.

Guy had previously questioned the housekeeper – who was secretly burning with curiosity – and been told that Jenny had eaten nothing the whole of the previous day.

'Not a bite or sup, Sir. She'd no breakfast this morning either. Do you want me to phone the doctor?'

'No thank you, Mrs Dickens.' He made no comment about what she had told him, and the housekeeper left the room unsatisfied.

When Jenny finally appeared in the dining-room at one o'clock, it was raining and blowing hard. The grounds outside were soggy, the leafless trees bounced in a wild wind, sudden gusts beat against the diamond panes of the windows. Guy was eating his usual sparse luncheon when his daughter entered the room. He felt a great wave of relief at seeing her, but waited, getting to his feet, until she took her place beside him.

Then he said, very quietly, 'Well done.'

She ate little but drank some tea, and by the end of the

meal a kind of conversation had wavered into life. They remarked on the unpleasant weather which had prevented him from riding. Guy talked about a painting he had bought yesterday in London. The mention of his visit there had a certain dull resonance but they ignored it.

'They're crating the picture and sending it by carrier,' he said. 'It's a watercolour.'

'Who by?' She was making an effort.

'Charles Rennie Mackintosh.'

'You've got one in your room by him, haven't you? Of the South of France.'

'That's right,' he was pleased and eager to reply. 'A painting of the Pyrenees. The new one is of a place called Collioure in the same district. He painted it about 1924.'

'You love watercolours, don't you?'

The colour was returning to her cheeks. His conscience hurt him. He'd been hard on her, poor innocent. What did Jenny know about thirty-year-old men back from the war with a sexual history of concupiscence? In his thoughts Guy used the words of priests. When he saw the unmarked roses-and-cream of her face, the girlish face he'd seen change from babyhood to young womanhood, his rage against her would-be seducer came back like a flood of poison. What kind of a brute was he? Debauched by God knew what vices, learned God knew where. Guy had been reared to a near medieval reverence for untouched young women. Virgins had, by their purity, a magical power. His youth had been a time of promiscuity among the rich, married upper classes; many aristocrats had not fathered the children that bore their names. Perhaps because of that very looseness the young virgins were defended like jewels in a tower. Guy, at White-friars, was the guardian.

His laws were steel hoops which enclosed both his nature and his actions. Care of the young. Honour to country and to friends. Unbreakable reserve about himself. One of the thickest of the steel bands which was bound round him was never to show emotion. He had shown it the night before last and bitterly regretted it.

The day went by, wild and cold, the wind hammering against the old house, rattling doors and, where window fastenings were loose, making a noise like a ship's distant siren, a sound which always frightened the dogs. Before the day was over, Guy had done everything he could to indicate that Jenny was forgiven. She responded. The strain eased, and they began to be natural again. But there existed a chasm between them created by Charles as if by an earthquake. They still spoke across the divide.

'Goodnight, sweetheart.' He gave her the usual peck and Jenny, putting her hands on his shoulders, suddenly convulsively hugged him. He loosened her arms, patted her and repeated his odd benediction, 'Well done.'

Jenny went up to her room, had a bath and stood staring at her naked body in the long glass in the bathroom. She twisted and turned, admiring her flat stomach, rounded but not fat buttocks, her breasts which really did stick out into points, she thought, turning to look at them sideways, and her nipples which were such a pretty pink. She looked down at the patch of hair which wasn't lint-fair like the hair on her head, but reddish and wiry. She dipped a comb into the bath and combed the curly hair so that it was a tidy, dark triangle. She opened her mouth, licked her lips. Charles. Charles. She utterly forgot her father. To be madly in love and in a way a prisoner excited her.

The next day the storm had blown itself out. There was a pale sun and at breakfast she remarked, with the right air of vagueness, that it might be a good day for riding. She let the sentence end in a question mark, a request.

Guy put down his newspaper and said without preliminaries, 'Do you give me your word?' It was the first time since peace had been made that he owned to the existence of the gulf between them.

She blushed. He misread the bright colour.

'Yes,' she said, and repeated, 'yes.'

He nodded, satisfied, and when she left at the end of the meal gave her a most beautiful smile.

Driving to Stratford, Jenny went to the stables. Her

175

favourite pony Midge had been sold, and Miss Corbett now offered her a friendly, handsome horse called Blackberry whom Jenny decided was just her style. She trotted slowly away from the stables, smiling to herself. She had never realized before what a favour her father had done her when he refused to buy her a horse. It was the perfect alibi. Invented dates with girlfriends were always dangerous, thought Jenny, reared on Hollywood dramas. She had inherited a Bowden caution, and as she rode quietly into the town had worked out her strategy as efficiently as her grandfather, a General, had done in the Boer War.

She and Charles had always met at The Shakespeare or the stables. She hadn't paid much attention to the fact that he'd never invited her to his flat. Thinking about it now she decided it must be because 'the sister', as she called Lisa in her mind, would be there. She and Charles needed to be alone. Now that same sister was going to prove useful.

She ambled down the street towards The Treasure Box. Since the day she had driven Lisa to the shop, she had never called there. The stuff Perdita Smith sold did not interest Jenny, who liked the new and the shiny, not the old and dusty. When Charles talked about Lisa's job, she privately decided that it proved his sister was what she'd first thought – peculiar.

Old and dusty were the words for the shop window which Lisa had incompetently cleaned. Through the smeared glass Jenny saw a row of pewter mugs, a sewing-box, a china greyhound with a dead squirrel drooping from its jaws, and a basket of rubbishy beads.

She dismounted and took Blackberry across the pavement; there was nowhere to tie him up and she kept the reins in one hand while pushing open the door of the shop. The bells rang musically.

Lisa glanced up to be faced in the open door by a horse as well as a customer.

'Hello,' called Jenny unnecessarily.

And I know why *you're* here, thought Lisa, returning the greeting.

176

'I'm afraid I can't leave Blackberry in the street,' explained Jenny, fiddling with the reins. 'I wanted a word, actually.' She pronounced it 'aksherlly'.

'And I can't leave the shop,' said Lisa smiling. 'So we're in a difficulty.'

Jenny made a face. There was something comic about her standing with her pony practically in the shop. Something pathetic too.

'You want to know where Charles is, I expect?' said Lisa, doing justice to Jenny's anxious face. 'Did you call at the flat?'

'No. I – that is – I don't know your address.' Jenny looked helpless.

Because he doesn't want you to see the dreary place, thought Lisa and agreed with her brother. Jenny was like an heiress in one of those symbolically proud paintings, a beautiful house behind her emphasizing wealth and position.

'Charles might not be in if you rang,' said Lisa kindly. 'I'm sure he's told you he likes playing poker. He goes quite often to the Wilton. Would it help, perhaps, if you suggested to me somewhere that you and he could meet?' She knew the reason for Jenny's pale face and slight air of desperation. The girl was in love.

Jenny twisted the reins round her fingers again. The horse stood first on one leg and then on the other. He's very patient, thought Lisa. She had a moment of wondering what horses thought about . . .

'It isn't exactly easy,' said Jenny.

A woman walked by, casting a look of outrage at a horse on the pavement.

Lisa found it difficult to keep a natural, almost uninterested expression on her face. The last thing she wanted was for Jenny to suspect that she knew what had happened at White-friars.

'I could meet him now,' said Jenny with a silly laugh. 'I mean – I'm aksherlly here, aren't I?'

It was already eleven in the morning and Charles would either be at the flat, taking hours to get dressed in lodgings he would detest the girl to see, or would have walked down the road to the Wilton Club. He would be sitting down playing cards. At present, his sister guessed, games of poker were the equivalent – for Charles – of taking to the bottle. He'd been more affected by what had happened at White-friars than he would admit.

Lisa could scarcely suggest Jenny barged into the Wilton, supposing he was there. Women weren't admitted as members, Charles had once told her, to which his sister coldly replied 'Who'd want to be?' The Wilton's gaming-rooms, in any case, were on the second floor, thought Lisa. We are not in a Western movie so – what could one do with the horse?

'Couldn't you meet him tomorrow?' she suggested. Jenny looked as if she were trying not to cry. 'I'm sure he could be wherever you suggest. We could make an arrangement now, couldn't we?' encouraged Lisa. 'Do you go riding every day?'

'Nearly.'

'Well then. Charles rides out with you sometimes, doesn't he? Shall I tell him to meet you at the stables tomorrow morning?'

What a child she is, thought Lisa, seeing the agonized disappointment. Does Charles know what he's doing? Jenny stared fiercely at her boots for some time, finally saying yes, she could meet him at the stables tomorrow at half past ten.

She turned to go, leading the horse back into the road, this time encountering a man who gave a bark of laughter. Then she clip-clopped back across the pavement, opened the glass door and called 'I say, thanks' over the jangling bells.

Jenny spent the rest of the day moping and wondering how she could drag herself through the next twenty hours. Charles was scarcely in better shape. He didn't like himself at present, a sensation to which he was not accustomed. Jenny's closeness to her father had been damaged, and so had Charles's self-esteem. Imagine being caught with one's pants down, he thought with disgust. As Lisa had said, it resembled a stage farce. But there wasn't a laugh in it. All day long he played poker and the changing fortune of the game threw him up and down, giving him a sharp thrill or slaps of muddy depression. He ended the afternoon having lost ten pounds, which was a financial disaster. Mick Gould hadn't appeared either; Charles missed him.

Thoroughly at odds with himself and the world he walked back to Crocker Road. The flat was empty. My God, he thought, what a hole. He looked at the drabness with revulsion. How *could* Lisa remain cheerful, how could she stand the place? He stood at the window and outside was a dreary line of houses, one after the other exactly like this one, trailing up towards the outskirts of the town . . .

His thoughts returned to Mick Gould. He recalled the actor walking with him towards The Shakespeare when Charles was on his way to meet Jenny, and the suggestion Mick had made about possible work at the theatre. Wasn't it something about an exhibition?

Work didn't interest Charles. Nothing interested him at present, not even the glaring problem of the ten pounds he had just lost. But he couldn't stay here. The flat made him feel degraded, less than himself, just as his treatment of Jenny gave him an unfamiliar self-dislike. When he opened the front door, the staircase smelled of cooking. What a hole.

He left the house, walking fast, and made his way towards the theatre. The moment he'd decided to try for the job, he became convinced that he had missed the boat: somebody else would have been given it by now. He found he wanted it. There was even a faint whiff of glamour about the idea.

At the Stage Door, which faced a patch of lawn on the right of the building, were rows of bicycles stacked against the wall. It might have been a college in Oxford in pre-war days. The only car – it looked disgracefully rich – was Lewis Lockton's sports car, open, white, parked under the archway of all that was left of the old burned-out theatre of the past.

A laconic man with a cigarette in his mouth was in the little office of the Stage Door, reading the local paper.

'Yes, Sir?'

'I wonder if I might see Mr Ashmore?'

'I daresay you might,' said the doorkeeper waggishly. 'Got an appointment, have you?'

179

'Mr Gould suggested I should come and see him,' said Charles, beginning to wonder if this was a mistake.

'Aha. If it's Mick,' said the doorkeeper. 'Let's see if we can track Mr Ashmore down.' He picked up the telephone and asked for the General Manager, waited a while, humming to himself, then said, 'Mr Ashmore? Gentleman to see you, name of –'

'Whitfield. Charles Whitfield.'

'Whitfield. Says Mr Gould spoke to you about him. Right, Sir. I'll send him up.' The doorkeeper rang off and nodded to Charles as if he were about to be given an audition. 'Up to the first floor, turn left, first room on the left,' he said, picking up his newspaper. 'Door's usually open and you can't miss the room, there's a big cupboard in the corner. That's where he keeps the sherry.' He gave Charles a wink and returned to the sports page.

Charles followed the directions, found himself in a long corridor, saw the open door and a glimpse of a tall, mahogany bookcase. A stocky man, black hair streaked with grey, was sitting at a desk smoking a cigar. He stood up.

'Come in. You're a friend of Mick's, is that right? Charles Whitfield. A good Warwickshire name. May I give you a sherry?'

The sherry, thought Charles, thanking him, seemed to be a theatre tradition.

Philip Ashmore looked exactly as Mick Gould had described: ex-Navy. The Services had done things to men during the war. The signs, the effects, were with them permanently. They had an aura, a style, even a way of speaking. In Ashmore's case he looked tough like a sailor and tough like a commander. He wasn't somebody to tangle with. Charles recognized the look.

'Mick Gould said you might be interested in helping with our exhibition,' said Ashmore. 'Did he give you the details? No. Well, let me outline the plan.'

Ashmore began to talk with enthusiasm about an exhibition on which the designer had already started work and which they hoped would be ready to open at the start of the season to run for a month or two. The idea was Shakespeare productions, past, present, and what was envisaged for the future, 'but that will be the teaser'. He spoke about the theatre's history and Charles listened and nodded as if he, too, were an expert, all the time wondering when the stevedore's job which Mick had suggested was going to be mentioned.

'Richard Pensamonn has come up with the most ingenious way of solving the problem of having an exhibition in the theatre,' said Ashmore. He took Charles over to a table on which a plan was spread. 'You see this? It's the Dress Circle foyer. The difficulty, of course, is that we can't mount an exhibition inside the theatre which will be open before and during performances. If we did, who'd pay the entrance fee?' He chuckled. 'So what Pensamonn proposes is to fix a track, here, which will run right round the perimeter of the Circle foyer forming a great oval. On this there'll be an enormous photograph, a montage of productions, beginning right back with the Globe, then on to Drury Lane, Garrick, Irving, the Lyceum and so forth. Then, the main feature, our own productions at the SMT. The photograph will be enormous – Kodak have agreed to make it for us. A hundred and forty feet long.'

Even Charles, to whom theatre history was so much Greek, was interested.

His own duties, Philip Ashmore eventually explained, would consist of helping to set up the exhibition every morning, which would include unrolling and fixing the great screen, arranging the model sets, the costumes and so on. In the evening, 'well before the audience arrives', the exhibition would be struck. Charles did know enough theatre vocabulary to realize this meant stowing the stuff away again.

'You'll have a companion to help you. Martin Morris. A good lad, with a pair of broad shoulders. Strong as an ox,' said Philip Ashmore. 'Now. Richard has given me the date he wants you to start.' He looked through his diary.

He did not ask Charles if he had any experience of the theatre, of exhibitions, of Shakespeare or of any damned thing. He wanted somebody strong, and Charles, for all his negligence, looked healthy and big enough. Ashmore also wanted to hire somebody pleasant, and had decided to like this man whose surname was good Warwickshire. Ashmore had a sentimental heart about Warwickshire; he'd been born and reared in Purley.

Charles agreed to everything. To the work. To the hours, 'morning and evening, say a good hour both times, and then there are matinees, of course'. To the salary. £7 a week.

They drank their sherry. Then Philip Ashmore was called over the intercom. He sprang up.

'Good, good, that's settled,' he said, extending a well-kept hand. Charles felt he ought to salute. 'Why not go and take a look at the Circle foyer and get the feel of the thing?' suggested Ashmore. 'Straight down the passage, through that door at the end, turn right, through another door. Glad to have you on board.'

Charles thanked him and left the office.

Like Prospero's island, the theatre was full of noises. Voices laughed or called. Doors slammed. And when he went through the first door, he heard a long bar of music played on an instrument that sounded like a flute. It was dark between the two doors, and Charles pushed the second one and found himself in the Circle foyer.

He had never been a regular theatre-goer when he was young and lived in Stratford. He was surprised by the size of the foyer, its big windows overlooking the Bancroft gardens, its acres of space and walls of polished marble. He wandered over to look out at the two bridges, the slowly flowing river, the pale sky. A few cars had begun to draw up, their lights cutting into the dusk. It was the D'Oyly Carte Opera tonight and people began to walk towards the theatre or to arrive in the Circle early, to sit in window-seats and talk. The atmosphere was sociable and quiet.

As he stood idly looking out, he smelled scent. Woman-conscious, perfume-conscious, Charles turned round, meeting a wave as strong as the smell of tobacco plants on summer nights.

182

A woman was walking past him on her way to the door from which he had come. She was tall, with a luminous paleness, a straight nose which gave her lily face a regal look. Her black dress clung round large breasts and flared in the fashionable Parisian skirts which swung about a seductive figure. Her hair was an extraordinary burnished red-gold, twisted in a knot at the back of her head and curling round her face. He looked at her and she returned his gaze.

Like an actor who becomes more himself merely by standing upon a stage flooded with light and facing an audience, Charles became more himself when stared at by a woman. He was more sexually fascinating, more challenging. He seemed to say a good many things in silence. After a thoughtful glance the woman went through the door to the theatre offices. It swung closed.

Walking back to Crocker Road, Charles thought about her. An actress. A beauty. He smiled to himself. Life was full of possibilities.

He was right, for Lisa was waiting for him, and before he had time to announce that he was now one of the world's workers and demand her admiration, she exclaimed, 'There you are!'

'So I am. Why? Has anything happened?' enquired Charles, throwing off his coat, clapping his pockets for cigarettes and realizing he had none.

Lisa had been feeling responsible. The job of a go-between was one to avoid.

'What happened was that Jenny Bowden turned up at the shop,' she said. 'She was looking for you.'

Charles's idle, somewhat sexy reverie about the red-headed woman at the theatre evaporated. He was conscious and surprised.

'Is she all right? Why did she come to The Treasure Box?'

'Because she doesn't know where you live, of course. Not that I blame you for concealing Crocker Road.'

'What did she want?'

'Don't be stupid! She wanted you. She says can you met her at the Corbett Riding Stables tomorrow at ten. Is that all right?'

183

'Fine. Thanks.'

'Charles!' exclaimed Lisa. 'Don't sit there looking so pleased with yourself. That girl's in a state. By her manner I should guess she's in bad trouble at home and from what she didn't say – you know what a monosyllabic creature she is –'

'Not with me.'

'Do shut up and take off that smirk. I'm pretty sure she can't get away from Whitefriars much and is trying to think of some way to dodge Guy Bowden. If she gets caught, I can imagine dire results.'

'Come on. This isn't a Victorian melodrama.'

Her brother's face and voice, the tickled vanity, the pursuer pursued, roused her indignation. Is he accustomed to outraged parents? My God, how little I know about Charles's sexual adventures. I've seen him make a bee-line for pretty women – I suppose he expects a big reaction. But what happens to the girls who fall in love with him? What about them? She swallowed her annoyance, knowing that if she got angry he'd only say she was like Donald Duck in the cartoons, putting out her fist and quacking. She tried to sound reasonable.

'You're not going to hurt that girl, are you? She's hideously young.'

Stretching out his arms he pulled her to him and made her sit on his knee the way he used to do when she was a child. She sat there ridiculously perched, thinking how bony men's knees were. She couldn't help laughing.

'Don't be self-righteous, Lou. I won't hurt her. How could you imagine such a thing? And I'll see Bowden doesn't frighten her either. In any case, she's his ewe lamb. She's sure to win.'

'You sound too sure.'

'And you sound superstitious. Anyway, I've some news. Nothing to do with Jenny. I've got a job.'

'What!'

'A job. Seven quid a week. How's that?'

'It's – it's wonderful! But doing what? Where? How?'

Pleased at the reaction, warming to his subject, he described his visit to the SMT. He was going to help build an exhibition. His would only be a workman's kind of job but it might be fun, the hours were odd, he hadn't yet met the designer but he liked the manager.

'He was a commander in the Navy.'

'Did he know you were an Army Captain?'

'No, he didn't, you partisan. And I don't intend to tell him.'

'He might make it ten quid if you do.'

The next morning, having enjoyed breakfast flavoured with Lisa's approval, Charles set off for the Corbett stables. They lay in a narrow, overgrown lane beyond Holy Trinity Church. Yesterday's sunshine had slightly dried the mud, and Charles's wellington boots – his riding boots had been lost somewhere in Burma – did not get as plastered with mud as they would have been earlier in the week. He wore old cord trousers, an Army sweater too thin for the English February, a white, open-necked shirt. The clothes were shabby but well cut; they suited his dark looks, the thick column of his neck, his haggard face. Like the actors in Stratford, unlike every other man in Britain, he wore no hat.

The gates to the stables were open. There was the sound of hooves on paving-stones, and when he entered a straw-covered yard, around which were stables from which horses mildly peered, Jenny saw him. Aware of the two stable lads and the owner, Charles and Jenny bade each other good morning.

Jenny walked over – it took self-control not to run to him – and said in a low voice, 'Don't forget, Miss Corbett knows Daddy.' She gave an imitation of a smile.

Charles did the same. 'Would she tell him we're meeting here?'

'Unlikely. They don't see each other for months'. Then more loudly, 'Miss Corbett says you can have Prince.'

'My favourite.'

They were saying quite different things.

'Shall we go?' said Charles.

As they rode out, the stable owner paused in her work of

185

sweeping the yard to watch them. Jenny Bowden has a crush on that man, she thought. He seems a bit old for the lass. Miss Corbett knew nothing about Charles, but saw he was over thirty. She could also see in his face that it was none too easy for him to fork out ten shillings an hour.

Jenny led the way down the lane, with Charles riding behind her. They took the country roads, crossed a field which was used by the hunt and finally entered a beech wood. A path led under the trees – it was squelching with mud from the week of rain. Above them the branches met and interlocked; there was a scent of leaf mould in the air. The winter was all round them. They began to trot side by side as the woody path grew wider. Now and then they looked at each other and smiled for the pleasure of riding in the cold, sweet day.

At last the woods petered out and they took another lane with high hawthorn hedges. No sign of farm or barn, nothing but a single thread of smoke in the distance, rising up straight in the still air.

They dismounted and stood for a moment, carefully looping their horses' reins over the post of a field-gate.

Jenny turned to look at Charles, as a mortal might at a god.


Affected by the fine weather and the distant but unmistakeable call of spring, Perdita Smith informed Lisa they should start cleaning.

'We ought to begin by taking a look round the flat,' she said when Lisa arrived at the shop. Perdita had already been busy for some time; her face was red from exertion and her coarse, bobbed hair stuck out. She reminded Lisa of the White Queen.

Perdita lived in a flat above The Treasure Box. Lisa was often sent up the narrow stair with boxes and parcels which couldn't be fitted into the shop. Lisa was never invited into the flat for a sociable coffee or a drink; employer and helper shared cubby-hole tea, and Lisa only went upstairs to carry the overflow. Perdita lived as it were in the middle of her three seventeenth-century rooms. All round the edges, stacked, stored, arranged and disarranged, was the superfluity of her stock; lately it had begun creeping into bathroom and kitchen. Lisa, whose battle on the ground floor had in a small way begun to show results, averted her eyes from the glorious and disgraceful mess upstairs.

Not today, however.

'Put the "closed" sign up, my child. It's a lovely morning and we must get a move on,' said Perdita. 'We must arrange. Catalogue. We need a clean-out and a clear-out.'

Was her employer serious? thought Lisa. She had never indicated the need of order until now. Lisa turned the card in the window from 'Open' to 'Closed', and meekly followed Perdita upstairs.

'So,' cried Perdita as they entered the sitting-room. She attacked a brown paper parcel on the window-sill and, ripping off the coverings, produced a venerable, black marble clock. On either side of the face were thin gilt pillars. A Palladian clock unmistakeably made in the reign of Victoria.

'Look,' said Perdita, 'it has a brass plate. "To William Collins, respected member of the band of H. M. Royal Engineers. A friend, a colleague and a fine clarinettist." Isn't that good? Will you present me with a clock when I retire? Gentle heaven, is it *going*?' She looked at the clock, at her wristwatch, at two other clocks on the mantelpiece. 'Yes, it is. Half past. I'm due at Kinleigh Manor in twenty minutes. The preview is today and I hear the house is chock-full of stuff.' Perdita sounded hungry. 'Chock-full. I must dash. Down you go,' shooing Lisa out. 'Start in the shop, my child. Organize, organize and organize.'

She hurried down behind Lisa, turned the card back to 'OPEN', dashed out to her waiting van and drove away.

Lisa looked dubiously round The Treasure Box, wondering where to start. On the toppling books, placed along shelves too high to reach without a step-ladder borrowed – rarely – from the shop next door? On the silver turned black with time? She toyed with the idea of fetching William Collins's clock and putting it in the window, but Perdita,

187

being a woman of whim, might well have decided to keep the thing.

She was washing a glass rolling-pin in the sink behind the cubby-hole curtain when the shop doorbells chimed. She recognized the voice calling her name and came out.

Polly came bustling in wearing emerald green and carrying a paper bag.

'Is she out of the way?' asked Polly in a thrilling whisper, looking towards the cubby-hole into which Perdita would most certainly have not fitted in company with Lisa herself.

'She's gone to Kinleigh Manor,' replied Lisa in a normal voice.

'Goody. Don't think I don't like your boss, Lisa,' said Polly in a tone quite maternal, 'but I do get rather frightened of her when she's nice to me. She has a way of making me put my hand in my purse.'

'Perhaps I ought to learn the same trick.'

Polly gave a pitying smile. 'That's something you'll never learn. You are not tough enough, darling. One often suspects a heart of butter.'

Lisa let that go, but she was not exactly pleased to see her friend who had arrived to waste her time. The giant task which Perdita had set was a welcome burden; it was certainly better than worrying. She did not feel in the mood to give the actress her concentrated attention. Polly's society had its own demands. Lisa thought of it as another form of work and wondered, without much hope, whether the visit was to be a short one.

But Polly sat on the high stool meant for customers with the air of somebody who is going to stay. She tore open the paper bag.

'Doughnuts. Four. They make them fresh every morning at the ABC and as I've lost pounds since we started rehearsing *Henry IV* – there's nothing like nerves for making you thin – I thought we'd make pigs of ourselves. If Perdita had been in, I fear I would have eaten all four. Disgusting, isn't it? I haven't seen you since the party, and I've something to tell. I've developed an admirer. Guess who.'

188

Lisa made tea and accepted the task of listener. She ate the sugary cakes while Polly told her story.

'The man,' said Polly, 'is the star. Lewis Lockton. Sir Lew, as we call him. I do, even to his face. You saw him at the party. That reporter you brought – rather attractive, I thought – did tell you Sir Lew actually threw the party, didn't he?'

'Yes. We thanked him. It was so generous.'

'He's like that. I mean, he's *profligate*.'

'And how much of an admirer is he?' asked Lisa. She wondered if Polly was talking about sex.

'That's what's intriguing so far.'

She described her first meeting with Lewis Lockton at Avoncliffe when she'd followed the sound of the piano. She had been fascinated then, she said. Everybody was. Lisa did realize he was a Big Star? Polly spoke in capital letters as for the Deity. Lockton had been a famous Shakespearean actor for years, since back in the 1920s, and he was in movies as well. He'd been to Hollywood in 1938 and made a film with Carole Lombard.

'Imagine! It was called *Kiss and Tell*. Did you see it?'

'We didn't go to films in Burma.'

'Poor you. We did in London all the time.'

He had been nice to Polly at his party, and had asked her to dance.

'He dances like a dream. Have you noticed how gracefully he moves?'

The story dived into theatre. Of course Polly had met Sir Lew that time at Avoncliffe. But the following day he'd been introduced to the entire Company by Anthony Quayle. The actors had lined up, and Quayle and Sir Lew walked along while the introductions were being made.

'It was like reviewing the troops. Or being presented to the Royal Family. I felt I ought to curtsey,' giggled Polly. When it came to her turn to be introduced, Lewis Lockton had smiled at her, looking amused, and said, 'Ah, now we know each other.' He'd wrung Polly's hand so hard that she was sure every bone was cracked.

'Then after the intros we all hung about and guess what.

189

He spoke to me,' said Polly, sounding as if she were still at school. 'I do adore him.'

Polly was adoring the universe today. She loved the play *Henry IV* in which she had her only important part, and she thought Anthony Quayle who played Hotspur was 'enthralling'; and she was, she said, enchanted by Mick Gould. Finally she adored the fact that now she was in Stratford she could see a lot of her parents. The last point was one Lisa didn't for a moment believe.

Listening to Polly, smiling at her, well aware Polly was wasting time, Lisa could not help envying her friend's life. Polly didn't sit alone in a dusty shop, or struggle against memories of a lost love. She didn't work only for money. She belonged to a magical make-believe world where she and her companions banded together, playing rôles written by the greatest dramatist since the Greeks. And the actors worked *here*, where Shakespeare had been born. No wonder Polly twinkled like the sunshine. She was as green as a grasshopper in her vivid dress and, like that insect, restless, giving the impression that she was about to jump into the air.

She chattered about her role as Doll Tearsheet for a while – 'I'm good at playing whores' – then returned to Lewis Lockton.

'We became instant friends.' He had invited her out to dine at The Bear at Woodstock. Polly described the meal.

'He eats like a bird. I was hungry, and I ploughed through roast beef and mash and apple pie and wished I hadn't. *He* had a grilled sole and a dry martini. Why can't I be sophisticated like that?'

During dinner, however, she had made him laugh. 'I don't know why, am I funny?' Refusing to pander, Lisa merely said 'Go on', and Polly, relinquishing for once the tacit demand for a compliment, said a famous producer had come over to speak to Lewis Lockton, who had introduced her as 'the girl of the future'.

Polly then returned to Doll Tearsheet. She'd counted the lines. 'There are twenty-two!'

'Is that a lot?' inquired naive Lisa.

Polly, whose attitude towards the number of her lines changed with her mood, scoffed. Twenty-two lines was huge. Nobody on her level, said Polly as if speaking of an ascending stair, had as many. She finished a second doughnut and brushed the sugar from her fingers. Wearing a half smile at some thought or other, she looked invulnerable. Suddenly the smile vanished.

'I talk too much. I'm a bitch. All this time you've been listening to me boring on and your eyes aren't happy.'

Her intuition was new to Lisa – Polly certainly hadn't noticed such things when they were at school.

'Oh, it's nothing,' Lisa said, not sure she wanted to talk about Charles to this lively, heartless audience.

'It must be. You're bothered. What's wrong, Lisa? It's always better to speak out, you know.'

'Are you quite sure?'

'You sound like Charles sometimes. Yes. I'm positive.'

Polly's face no longer twinkled; the triumph, the self-satisfaction, had for a moment been discarded. And for Lisa the temptation to talk about the thing was strong ... She told her what had happened at Whitefriars.

Polly was enthralled. Her eyes grew enormous as she heard as much as decency – and the euphemisms Charles had used to his sister – could describe.

'Coitus interruptus!' cried Polly.

Lisa looked embarrassed and not pleased. 'I don't think it went as far as that.'

'You mean they didn't? I bet they did. I *say*, Lisa!' She reflected for a moment and then said, 'Of course she's a virgin. You're worried that he'll seduce her.'

'I suppose I am.'

'How old?'

'Under eighteen.'

Polly scratched her short nose. 'Not all that young. I did it at seventeen with a local boy. I've no idea where he is now. It was a boiling hot afternoon, we'd been playing tennis and the parents were out. He was one of those gymnasts. Kept on and on. Very strange, I thought.'

'Really.'

'Don't look prim. I bet you have.'

'Polly, I am twenty-seven.'

Polly gave a violent start. 'Don't mention how old we are, for God's sake! I'm twenty-four. I became just twenty-four when I got this job, you will remember, won't you? Swear? Sir Lew thinks it ever so young. "A mere child," he said in that velvet voice. Well, Lisa,' she returned to the subject in hand. 'What's to be done about your brother and this virgin? Nothing. You're not the angel with the flaming sword at the gates of Eden, are you? You can't defend her virtue and she wouldn't thank you if you tried. I saw Charles at The Duck the other morning and I can imagine the girl would find him irresistible. So it isn't really any of your —' She stopped tactfully.

'Business. I know. So why do I feel that it is?'

'Because of that soft heart. The only thing for you to do, my friend, is to put Charles and his seducing ways right out of your mind. One can't do anything about other people going to bed with each other. As King Lear said, "The wren goes to 't, and the small gilded fly does lecher in my sight. Let copulation thrive."'

There seemed no answer to that.

Lisa said after a moment or two, 'Lear was mad.'

'When he was at his maddest, he was at his most inspired,' said Polly and fell to quoting again. '"A disclosure to the inward eye of vistas undreamed and but fitfully understood . . ." That's from a man called Wilson Knight. I adore him.' She looked dreamily into space. '*You've* been in love, madness and all. I can feel it. And it's finished. That's what makes you sad. Tell me about it.'

Lisa was silent and Polly reflected that her friend was attractive, in a way. But didn't do a thing to make herself more so. She had those large eyes, and a big mouth — actors admired that in players — and Polly liked her inky black hair. She was interested in her. She liked mysteries.

'It's over. It has been for a long time,' Lisa said at last.

'Was it in India?'

'Oh yes. Wartime stuff. We swore it would last, that we'd see each other again. You know those promises one makes.'

'Don't I just?'

Lisa looked into space. 'I was so sure. Certain. I was certain of him – not that he'd survive but that he loved me. But after his squadron was moved he never answered any of my letters. Not one. Not once.'

'Perhaps he's dead.'

'No, Polly. I checked through the RAF list after the war. He isn't.'

Polly reflected, then said, 'What a bastard.'

'Not really. I suppose his love wore out and mine didn't. That's my bad luck.'

Polly still looked sympathetic. She was a great hand at giving advice to the lovelorn. During her years in the theatre – as a nurse, too, during the war – she couldn't count the number of sobbing girls who had confided in her. No sobs from Lisa, though.

'If it was me I'd definitely prefer him to be dead,' she pronounced. 'However, as he isn't, shove him out of your mind. You haven't and you must.'

*She* wanted people and things to come flooding her way. Love and admiration, success, and money to buy glamour. She couldn't bear anything which hit below the golden belt of self-confidence.

'Ruthless Rhymes for Heartless Homes,' said Lisa. It had been the book, by Harry Graham, which used to make Charles laugh when they were very young.

'Yes, and a jolly good thing too,' approved Polly. 'Cripes, is that the time?' She sounded like Perdita. She looked at her tiny wristwatch. 'I'm supposed to be meeting Sir Lew at The Cobweb and he's never late. Lettuce sandwiches. The girls in the company disapprove when they see me with my star. They're green with envy,' said emerald-coloured Polly. 'Still on the vital subject of men, I've forgotten the name of that fair guy who brought you to the party.'

'Peter Lang. He's a reporter on the *Echo*. He writes about the theatre, among a lot of other stuff.'

'Does he? Do let's have a drink with him. Actresses with sense always like journalists. I must fly, darling.'

Polly jumped down from the stool and went out of the shop. Lisa saw her walking jauntily away, carrying with her the wonderful secret of how not to be hurt by love.

# 10

---

Charles had already begun to work at his part-time job at the theatre, although the actual exhibition was not due to open until the day after the first night of the season.

He had called in at the Stage Door one spring morning to ask when he would be wanted. The door-keeper recognized him.

'Mr Whitfield, isn't it? I'll give Richard Pensamonn a buzz.'

A moment later a young man with a mop of curly hair, wearing an old-fashioned, paint-splashed smock, came hurrying over the road to greet him.

'Pensamonn,' he said, shaking Charles's hand energetically. 'You're Charles Whitfield, aren't you? A godsend.'

He took Charles back across the road and into the workshops, talking nineteen to the dozen. Pensamonn looked twenty-two but was in fact older than Charles, had left his theatre design work during the war to be what was called a camouflage artist, and had returned to the theatre like a homing pigeon. He could draw and paint, make model sets in which every miniature piece of furniture was perfect, design everything from a mountain-top to a sixteenth-century inn with costumes to match. He had been asked by Sir Barry Jackson to design this season's *Twelfth Night*, and although he'd begun rough sketches, the play wasn't due to open for some time. The exhibition was his idea, and for the

195

present his passionately absorbing task. Pensamonn loved Shakespeare and knew the plays well. He wanted to show audiences something of Shakespeare that they perhaps did not know, had never thought about; to trace the history of the productions from the time Shakespeare's own players had performed at the Globe open to the sky, right up to the present and beyond. He was an enthusiast and took Charles at once into his confidence.

'Come and see the tables we're going to use for the model sets . . . This' – indicating a dazzling jewel-encrusted costume – 'will be one of the exhibits. Do you like it?' and then: 'My *pièce de résistance* . . . the track for the screen.'

Pensamonn's enthusiasm was contagious as he showed Charles the long track which would run right round the perimeter of the Dress Circle foyer, forming a great oval, to be used for fixing the gigantic photographed montage of theatre productions.

Charles was of use that morning, and other mornings. He carried tables. He helped to haul the photograph which was rolled into a tube eight feet wide and thick as the trunk of an oak tree. He carried model boxes and the models on which the costumes would be displayed. He did a navvy's work and enjoyed it, absorbed by what was being created. It was an emotion which in Stratford had only been stirred in Charles by games of poker or the pursuit of women.

It was Philip Ashmore who had decided that the Shakespeare exhibition wouldn't start until the day after the opening night. Until then there was far too much activity in the theatre. Adding another ingredient, particularly one a hundred and forty feet long, would be unwise. In consequence Pensamonn had time to play and work out the way his exhibits should be set. Nothing was hurried or scamped. The only other helper apart from Charles was a taciturn walk-on – he literally carried spears – called Martin Morris. Neither Charles nor the volatile Richard Pensamonn made any kind of headway with Morris, a big laconic man with a broken nose which was a godsend to directors. Martin Morris was invariably in the forefront of groups of soldiers, peasants, rebels, servants. He had a face which spoke of violent action. He was born to rush across a stage with sword and banner. He was also as strong as Hercules or a man in a circus, and for all Charles's willing arms, the weightiest objects were effortlessly borne by the actor. Richard Pensamonn once remarked to Charles, seeing Morris at a distance with a table in one hand, 'He's on his way to build the Pyramids.'

Lisa had little time to spend on her patently cheerful brother. Perdita's desire to spring-clean hadn't lasted, for spring came suddenly and so did both buyers and customers. Perdita worked Lisa hard, sent her on errands and now and again to house sales. Mean about Lisa's salary, she was generous with her own knowledge and whenever they were alone taught her about the objects for sale, their origins, their histories. Every day Lisa learned something strange, unlikely and at times grotesque. Perdita's Catholicism was at its most evident when Lisa confessed to any kind of ignorance. One afternoon when Perdita had bought some Victorian dolls she sat at the counter, while Lisa mended the dolls' petticoats, and gave her a short lecture. It began when Lisa unwisely remarked that she thought dolls were of recent origin and had come from America.

'Holy St Joseph!' cried Perdita and launched out. She told Lisa there had been walking and talking dolls when Queen Victoria had been a child. There had been a doll – Perdita warmed to her subject – which had a small bellows under its arm. It made a 'Papa, Mama' noise. The dolls could shut their eyes, too; the eyes were of enamelled glass and were usually brown.

'You won't find blue eyes until the 1840s. Remember all this, child! Sometimes at sales there are ignorant country buyers who don't know dolls are valuable.'

In her spare time during her evenings and at weekends Lisa was constantly with Peter. She hadn't quite made up her mind about him. Her feelings for him were not intense, but she had an idea he was falling in love with her. He never said so, but he was very affectionate and considerate, and went out of his way to do things to please her.

Lisa was longing to go to the theatre's opening night, and Peter arrived one evening with the news that he had managed to get two seats, 'the best in the house'. Lisa hugged him, and he gave her his satisfied, serious smile.

Being with him constantly, she saw less of her brother. One morning when she and Charles were having breakfast – now he had a job he got up early – Lisa asked about Jenny. She hadn't forgotten his anxiety and poor Jenny's desperate face. Charles was very casual.

'Oh, she's fine. She's fine.'

Lisa stared. 'Truly? What about the trouble with her father?'

'It's blowing over, Lou. There's nothing to fuss about.'

'To ask, Charles, is not to fuss.'

'Sorry,' he said absently. 'She's perfectly all right and so am I.'

Now he was working on the exhibition, he was in good spirits. It might only be a porter's job, but Charles could sense the excitement of a theatre, could almost hear it. Yet the place had a cosy atmosphere and he felt he had become part of a family. A good many people still working there had been with the Memorial Theatre before and during the war. The elderly ladies in the box office, the usherettes with white hair and sweet faces and soft Warwickshire accents were old employees and old friends. The theatre was doing thrilling new productions of Shakespeare, but it had retained its past.

Charles often worked late now, and one bright evening when Peter called at Crocker Road to take Lisa and Charles for a drive, she said he wouldn't be back until midnight.

'He's working like a dog at present.'

'I'm glad to hear it,' said Peter. He did not add – but thought – that he could have her to himself.

He wanted to take her to see an Elizabethan manor, a beauty, which Lisa scarcely remembered. It was Charlecote, where the Lucy family had lived for eight hundred years. The Lucy tombs were in the church; those were fascinating too. Lisa's lack of knowledge about the county where she had been born and bred shocked Peter in very much the same way that it shocked Perdita that she didn't know the history of nineteenth-century dolls. It seemed to Peter astounding that you could grow up in Warwickshire and forget – or never actually be aware of – anything as remarkable as Charlecote.

'I don't believe you ever learned anything when you were young, Lisa.'

'I remember Shakespeare got caught poaching in Charlecote's grounds.'

'That story has been rejected by many scholars. They maintain there were no deer in the woods when Shakespeare was alive.'

She laughed at his pedantry and said she was going to continue believing the story.

At Charlecote they called into the church and then stood admiring the manor. It was very beautiful: turreted, gabled, the entrance shaped like the letter 'E' of Elizabeth. Across the fields under a group of trees Lisa saw a herd of deer and said triumphantly, 'See?'

They returned to the car and drove off into the evening country, Peter still on the subject of the Lucys. Very old English families interested him deeply. Lisa was listening and asking questions and scarcely noticed the road. Quite suddenly she gave a groan.

He slammed on the brakes. 'What is it? What's happened? Are you ill?'

'No, no, it's just – stop the car. Look. That's where we used to live, Peter! That's Roundwood.'

She hadn't set eyes on her old home and nor had Charles since they'd arrived. They had talked about it and agreed they didn't want to see the house again. What was the point? Neither admitted they couldn't bear to look at a place where they had been young and wealthy. It wasn't sentiment which made them feel like that – it was Crocker Road.

But it was impossible not to look now.

Peter stopped the car, and they sat in silence.

You forget, thought Lisa. You forget everything. The

pale, barred wood of a front door; the group of trees to the left, one an acacia which would drop white flowers in late summer; the brick path edged with low, clipped box. The yew hedges which had grown very high.

There were the windows from which her child-self had gazed out; she was gazing still. There was the lawn across which her mother had raced when Lisa, aged five, had fallen over and screamed because she'd cut her knee on a stone.

Roundwood was a solid, unremarkable house built in 1925 and typical of its period; it had a prosperous, comfortable air like that of a well-off stockbroker. Lisa hadn't realized how little it suited the aristocratic shade of her dead father. The present owners must be proud of it, the windows cleanly shone, the garden was cared for. There were stubby daffodils under the trees.

Lisa had accepted Crocker Road – until now.

'It is nice, of course,' said Peter breaking the silence.

'Yes.'

'And you were a little girl here. That is nice too.'

'Is it?'

He turned to study her. 'You wish you hadn't seen it. You're right. Shall we forget that house?'

'I'd like to.'

'You wrestle with ghosts,' he said in an odd voice. 'I understand that. I –' he stopped speaking, took her hand and kissed it. He started the car.

'We will push it away, Lisa. The past must be escaped from. It can only hurt us.'

He drove away fast and Lisa only remembered what he'd said a long time afterwards.

Later she told Charles she had seen Roundwood and he listened, nodded and was perfectly disinterested. He's managed to forget it, she thought, and envied him. Why must I share everything with Charles? I ought to be grateful that he's so busy and so cheerful.

It was blind of Lisa to accept Charles's vague reference to Jenny Bowden as 'fine' as if he only saw her occasionally and had rather forgotten the Whitefriars drama. The truth was they were up to their necks in a passionate flirtation. They met whenever she could get to Stratford to ride or on other ingenious excuses. They were happy to spend as little as twenty minute in each other's company.

Jenny charmed him. He was attracted to her slim but rounded figure, childlike fair hair, the English rose skin, the upper-class, half-swallowed sentences. He began to love her a little, and to help plot their difficult meetings. It became a nonsensical secret: a game. One that he played well, as he played all games of love and chance.

As for Jenny, she was fathoms deep in love and when she was with Charles being chastely kissed, she was so happy she thought her heart would burst.

Her father, seeing the radiant change in his daughter, was moved and glad. He believed it was because her good resolves were being honourably kept and that, away from sexual dangers, she was carefree, reunited with himself.

'We must go out to dine tonight, Jenny,' he said to please her. They went to an expensive restaurant in Warwick.

'Your clothes bills are very modest,' he remarked on another occasion. 'I think you should have some of my coupons, and buy something pretty.'

One morning after breakfast he stood, hands in his pockets, looking from the window at her tiny Morris car, mud-splashed from many visits to the woods with Charles. I'd like a daughter of mine to have something better than that to drive, he reflected.

Jenny had never been more charming. She hung on his arm, she teased him. When they played ping-pong, he won – did she let him win? She giggled at his jokes. She was critical of his ties.

'They're all so elderly, Daddy. I shall choose your next.'

Father and daughter were constantly together, and Mrs Dickens, sharper than her employer, looked dour. She had worked at Whitefriars for years and knew the family as well as her own. She'd trust that young Miss, she said to her husband, just about as far as she could throw her.

'She's up to something, any fool can see that. Can't think why *he* doesn't.'

'You could be wrong, Vi,' said her husband who was fat and liked a quiet life.

'And when have you ever known me wrong?'

Spring had definitely come. It was no longer a whisper or a promise – it was everywhere. The trees were in bud, the air was soft. The London theatre critics, eating toasted tea-cakes on the train, were talkative and pleased to be coming to see the opening of a new season on such a fresh, green day. Arriving at Stratford station, most of them decided it would be pleasant to walk through the town to their various hotels. One or two of the journalists reflected that it might be amusing to mention the spring in the introduction to their notices. Why not?

On the morning of the opening, before the critics had arrived and while telegrams were being delivered in sheaves at the Stage Door, Jenny had arranged to meet Charles at lunchtime and go for a short drive to Armscote and Dar-lingscott, small places with quiet roads where they were safe, she said. They had been to one particular lane between the villages a number of times. There was a lonely stretch, a coppice of hazels; Jenny parked her car under the trees and, safely screened from passers-by, they sat and kissed. They talked the nonsense lovers talk, discussing the angle of Jenny's nose and the length of Charles's eyelashes. They laughed like children.

Charles was curiously content with this strange love affair, this gentle arousal. He no longer went to London to throw Claire on a bed. Charles needed sex and gambling, both of which made him feel, and feel intensely. Yet at present he seemed to have reached a kind of demi-paradise.

Did the sensualist in him really believe it would last? Did the worldly, knowing man persuade himself it would do? He asked himself no questions; the very innocence of the affair was satisfying. There was something exquisite and pathetic about being adored by this lovely, ignorant girl. When he saw her waiting for him, young as the March weather, his spirit expanded. A flood of happiness went through him.

At noon, when Charles could get away from his work,

202

they drove away in contented silence. Neither paid any attention to the pastoral country, the fields divided by neat thorn hedges, deep lanes, high elms. Here and there they drove past a Saxon church, a few cottages. Once they glimpsed the canal which wound past the meadows where all Shakespeare's wildflowers would grow when summer came. Jenny sang. Her success at fooling her father, her influence over this fascinating man beside her, her assurance of being loved by both men, bathed her in golden confidence.

Charles reached for her hand.

'Jenny. I wish *I* was taking you to the opening tonight.'

'Me too. It would be wonderful.'

'Imagine seeing you a few rows away and us not being able to say a word to each other,' said Charles, sounding as young as she.

'I shall turn round and give you a wink.'

'Don't! Your father might see.'

Jenny giggled. The idea that she and Charles were both going to the play, separated not only by a few rows of stalls but by the watchdog presence of her father, tickled her. It was exciting, as these secret meetings were. It gave her a sense of danger and Charles a flavour of rare emotion.

When they stopped the car in the usual place, on a wide verge of grass hidden by trees, he took her in his arms and gave her one of his exploring, sexually demanding kisses. Her eyes swam; she could scarcely see him. He longed for everything he refused to allow himself to do – to put his hand up her skirt, to feel about for the moist place between her legs, to undo her shirt and suck the pink nipples he remembered and hadn't seen for weeks. He did none of these things.

'Oh darling!' muttered Jenny – thinking why, *why* doesn't he ask me? Why doesn't he say we will get married? He loves me just as much as I do him. We must be married, we must! It's so hard to wait. Too soon it was time for Charles to return to work and Jenny to go home. It would take her, she said, 'hours and hours' to dress for the opening night. 'It's always fun, you know. Putting on the style.' She turned the car and drove back towards Stratford, steering with one hand. The other was held by Charles who nibbled the tips of her fingers.

'They say that falling in love is wonderful,' she sang.

'You're off-key.'

'Don't be nasty, I have a very good ear. My singing mistress at school said I had perfect pitch, so there.'

As she slowed at a crossroads, they were both laughing. They did not notice a car passing on the other side of the road. Neither looked towards it and the car accelerated and vanished round a corner.

Charles and Jenny continued to sing.

When she turned into the drive of Whitefriars she was very surprised to see her father's car parked in front of the house. Blow, she thought, switching off the engine and scrambling out. He's back hours before he said. Where shall I say I've been? Oh, I know, I went to take my jodhpurs to the cleaners. He's always going on about my not looking tatty when I'm riding.

She went through the front door. Mrs Dickens had gone home and the house smelled of polish. There was a surge of dogs, always a sign her father had arrived home. They followed him around and never settled in their baskets in the scullery. Jenny had her foot on the stair, about to go up to her room and get herself tidy – she knew she looked a mess – when Guy appeared.

For a moment she didn't understand the extraordinary look on his face. It was like a mask. A white mask with two holes for eyes. He walked over to her and for one unbelievable moment lifted his hand as if he was about to smack her across the face. She started back with a gasp. But Guy's hand remained frozen in the air. With a shudder, he brought it down again.

'You've been seeing that man.'

How does he know, she thought, how has he found out? It was too late to lie and she said recklessly, 'What if I have?'

He looked as if he didn't know her, didn't believe what he had heard. 'You gave me your word.'

Jenny gave a furious laugh. 'Yes I did and I don't care! Why should you make me promise not to see Charles – I love him! Yes, *love* him and it's no good glaring like that because I shall see him if I want to. I'm not a silly child, I shall do as I like –' Seeing his face, her false courage failed as her voice did.

'I forbade you to see that man and you disobeyed me. You've proved yourself a liar,' he said in a terrible voice, 'and proved I can't trust you. Get out of my sight. Go up to your room. I'll speak to you later. I'm disgusted with you.'

'I hate you. You're cruel and horrible and I hate you!' shouted the girl hysterically and rushed from the room and up the stairs, sobbing loudly as she ran.

Guy Bowden stood for a long time without moving. His head felt as if it was going to burst. He had never been so angry in his life. Not when his wife left him. Not when he had discovered Charles Whitfield lying half dressed and about to seduce his only child. Anger made a mist in front of his eyes. His heart pounded, he could not see properly.

The intense emotion subsided at last and he shuddered.

He walked up the stairs and down the passage to Jenny's room. He knew the door would be locked, but tried it just the same.

'Jenny.'

On the other side of the door, shivering, she tried to hold her breath like a child playing hide-and-seek. She didn't and couldn't answer.

'Listen to me,' he shouted loudly. 'Don't dare to try and see that man again. Don't dare to telephone him. You are never to see him. If you disobey me I shall lock you in. I mean it. It is for your own good and if I have to do it I shall. Do you hear me?'

Still there was no reply.

In a sudden, unreasoning and awful return of rage he kicked the door, then turned and went downstairs.

Next morning when Jenny came out of her room she saw the scarred paint at the base of the door where her father had kicked it.

\*

205

As it grew dark and street lamps lit up, the Stratford streets began to echo to an unusual sound. It wasn't the low-heeled footsteps of workers from offices and shops, nor the heavy tread of farm boots – it was the light tap-tap of high heels. Girls were walking by on their way to the theatre. They were accompanied by men in dinner-jackets.

The effect was curious, glamorous and out of keeping with the times. Ministers made speeches against the 'unhealthy' fashions arriving from Paris. The Government preached self-denial and doing without. The old wartime virtues ought to have been in everybody's minds. But backs could not remain against the wall for ever. The dinner-jackets might be pre-war and borrowed from fathers and uncles, but the girls had embraced the criticized, exaggerated, luxurious and unpatriotic New Look. Their dresses were small-waisted, full-skirted, worn with panache, enormous skirts swinging. Dior was responsible. He called his design 'a picture of the Belle Époque, a time full of happiness, exuberance, peace, everything directed towards the art of living'. Girls were transformed as they walked through Stratford, some with little wreaths of jonquils in their hair.

Lisa couldn't afford a New Look dress. She only had two old wartime party frocks, as they used to be called, both of Burmese silk. She was resigned to wearing one of these when Perdita Smith said, 'Having a new dress for the first night, Lisa?'

'I'm afraid not.'

'Economizing. Quite right. Don't worry, I shall lend you something pretty. Just wait and see what I've got up my sleeve. Well, it'll be your sleeve, won't it?'

Smiling politely, Lisa was filled with alarm. What fusty velvet garment from Perdita's wardrobe was going to be offered to her? And how on earth could she avoid her employer's kindness? Perdita always went to the opening nights, she had been on a VIP first-night list for years, so how could Lisa escape wearing whatever she had in mind for her? The prospect was so embarrassing that she could think of nothing to say and remained panic-stricken and silent.

'Come along now, we'll open Pandora's box,' said Perdita with unfortunate accuracy, and waddled into the cubby-hole to a particular trunk which was used as a table for the tin tray and the tea. She put the tray on the floor, opened the trunk and dived into it, grey head down, tweed bottom up.

Oh help, thought Lisa.

'What do you think of that?' said Perdita, returning with a sort of sausage of black tissue paper which she slowly unrolled on to the counter. It contained a white satin dress. She shook it out. The satin was very thick, the colour of mother-of-pearl and in a thousand creases.

'Pre-war débutante's dress – bought it for ten bob during the war. Try it on,' said Perdita, handing Lisa the dress. Lisa went obediently into the cubby-hole, pulled off her skirt and jersey and wriggled into the dress. It was heavy. It smelled of a far-off scent like dried rose petals. There were little fans of satin at the top of each shoulder, and the same fans all along the hem of the ample skirt.

'Here are her three feathers, whoever she was,' said Perdita, unwrapping three small, crushed plumes, of which two were broken. There was a veil too, but the moths had eaten most of it.

'Wants a touch of the iron but you'll pass muster,' said Perdita, regarding the girl. Lisa looked at half of herself in half a looking-glass. In wonder.

The older woman was satisfied. She'd been right about the dress, which actually made Lisa good-looking. How transforming clothes were, thought Perdita, who considered that if *she* had been living a hundred years ago she would have been known as a fine figure of a woman.

'Bring it back tomorrow. And don't spill anything on it: it brings down its value,' she said.

Charles and Lisa took their time getting ready for the opening night. For once Stratford felt as it used to do. Crocker Road was still a hole, but even these dingy rooms looked better when a handsome couple in evening dress stood drinking a pre-performance sherry. 'There's Peter,' said Lisa, hearing the bell.

207

'I'll go. Wait here and surprise him.'

Charles was pleased with the way his sister looked and fond of her for being beautiful for once. He preferred to admire her and often didn't. He was in an excellent mood. The exhibition was ready for tomorrow's opening. The enormous photographic montage was rolled against the wall of the Circle foyer, ready to be unrolled and to form a great panorama round the walls, showing the theatre of yesterday, today and perhaps – as Richard Pensamonn said – tomorrow. Glittering costumes on stands were stored away in an empty office. So were model sets, blown-up photographs, designs, props. Everything waiting for tomorrow. Charles, the silent Martin Morris and the designer had all worked hard and Charles felt almost as if *he'd* created something. The national press were coming to the opening, and he decided to ask Peter to write about the exhibition as well.

It amused him to think Jenny would be at tonight's play and unable to talk to him. They had arranged to exchange glances when it was safe. Putting on the dinner-jacket made for him in 1936, Charles saw he hadn't put on a pound in weight since then. He went down to open the door to Peter; the two young men chatted as they climbed the stairs.

'Come in for a celebration drink,' called Lisa.

'What are we celebrating?' was Peter's logical question. He went through the door, saw Lisa, and stopped. He said stiffly, 'You look very fine.'

'Do you like it?' She swished to and fro, telling him the story of the dress.

He nodded. He did not want to show that the sight of her hurt him just then.

Lisa, in unaccustomed heavy skirts almost brushing the ground, walked to the theatre between the two men. She was very conscious of her own changed appearance; it felt strange to know people stared at her. 'Don't forget to doll yourself up for the opening,' Polly had instructed, and seeing her friend's expression, Lisa's long-dormant vanity had awoken. It had been Polly as well as Perdita Smith who had affected her.

The foyer of the theatre was crowded with people and

filled with voices. The scene was colourful and busy and now and again there was the flash of a camera. Charles stood looking about. Lisa knew he must be searching for Jenny. Even if he spots her, they won't be able to speak to each other, she thought. I wish he'd give her up.

Peter had taken Lisa's elbow and was steering her through the foyer, murmuring quietly now and then as he recognized a celebrity. That slender girl over there was the ballerina, Margot Fonteyn. There was Aneurin Bevan and his vivacious wife. He indicated a thin, aristocratic figure – John Gielgud.

'You are clever at recognizing people,' said Lisa, stealing brief, unsatisfying looks at the famous.

'I should be, Lisa. It's my job.'

The trio entered the stalls and went down the gangway. Their seats were within five rows of the stage.

'We're very close,' remarked Lisa, surprised.

'Oh, but that is the best,' he said. 'I was glad to be given such seats. I was talking to Polly Holt and she says theatre people always prefer to be as near as possible. She asked us particularly to notice her performance.'

'But isn't she only playing a waiting-woman?' said Lisa, smiling and looking at her programme.

'People can make their mark in the smallest parts, Lisa. Surely you know that?'

The auditorium was filling up now, minute by minute. Peter still looked about, to pick out well-known faces for Lisa's interest. There was an atmosphere of expectancy, a kind of rustle, as people sat down and opened their programmes and talked to each other. A small haggard-looking man went by. Peter murmured that he was a famous critic.

'Let's hope *he* particularly notices Polly,' said Lisa. Peter was unamused. She wondered how her friend was feeling, dressed in costume somewhere behind those great closed curtains. If Polly was to be believed, the entire cast trembled with nerves . . .

Charles kept turning around to look behind him at the stalls. He wasn't still for more than a few moments before he turned round again. He finally said, 'Lisa. She isn't here.'

'I expect she and her father have been held up.'

'But there are only a few minutes left . . .'

'You're not worried about her, are you? She has her father to look after her,' said Lisa, aware of irony.

He gave an annoyed shrug, and the lights slowly went down. There was a moment's pause, a roll of loud, fierce drums, and the curtains swept up.

Across the stage, walking swiftly, came a group of nobles in heavy, dark clothes, furred and clasped with gold.

There was the King, a tall, broad man with the face of a warrior.

'So shaken as we are, so wan with care . . .'

The play had begun.

Charles watched. The scene ended and a second scene, with Prince Hal and Falstaff, began. He couldn't concentrate. Now and again at Falstaff's quips the audience burst into a roar of laughter. But Charles missed the point and once when Lisa, still smiling, looked round at him, she saw his face was perfectly straight. He had not heard a word.

When there was some stage business and a flurry of movement, she squeezed his arm and whispered very low, 'Don't be so worried.'

'She hasn't come.'

'They may be standing at the back of the stalls waiting to slip in.'

'They're not. I've looked.'

Peter frowned and Lisa hastily fixed her attention back to the King, Northumberland and Hotspur. She had caught her brother's anxiety. It seemed to come from the arm which touched hers on the armrest. She began to share his feelings and during the whole of the first Act, with Falstaff at his most bewitching, never tired, never bored, full of energy and comedy and devotion to Hal 'the lovely bully', Lisa was conscious of her brother and his steadily growing alarm.

The Act ended with strong applause. Charles stood up, gave a glance to where Guy Bowden and his daughter should have been sitting – he knew the numbers – and saw empty seats.

'Sorry, Lou. I won't have a drink. I'd rather be by myself.'

'Surely there's an explanation. Perhaps her father's ill'.

'Yeah,' he said, not listening. 'I'll be back before the bell.'

He hurried off, threading his way to the front of the stalls, and vanished through an exit.

Peter was waiting impatiently.

'We must hurry, Lisa, or there will be no time to get a drink. I'm sure you'd like one. That was a long Act. Where is Charles?'

'He's gone for a quick walk.'

'A *walk*?'

'He says he'll be back before it starts but he'd rather not join us. To tell you the truth, I think he wants to be on his own.'

Peter frowned in non-comprehension, accompanied her to the noisy bar, found her a seat, disappeared and returned rather sooner than she expected. She told him very briefly about Jenny and Charles.

Peter was puzzled. 'But didn't you once tell me your father and Mr Bowden were close friends? I do not understand this thing.'

There were times when the words he used sounded strange, as if he were speaking in a foreign tongue. But she didn't notice that now, she was too concerned.

'Yes, my father and Jenny's were friends, but Mr Bowden never liked Charles and doesn't want him going around with his daughter. He forbade her to see him.'

'So Charles thinks there has been trouble, then?'

'He doesn't know. It could be an accident.'

'Or an illness. Bowden is quite old.'

'Is he?' said Lisa, laughing in spite of herself. 'He doesn't seem so. But it's beastly when somebody doesn't turn up. You imagine horrors.'

She looked at him with her charming eyes. How beautiful she is, he thought. And sweet. And good.

They had left the bar and walked out of the foyer into a cold, clear night. They wandered up and down the Bancroft lawns. He said after a moment or two, 'I could perhaps help.'

'Peter! You couldn't!'

He quite misunderstood. 'I would not say so if it was impossible. Mr Bowden is a JP, isn't he? And a governor of the theatre. As a reporter on the *Echo* I could ring and ask for an interview. Suppose his daughter is ill or *he* is, they would explain that when they refused me, wouldn't they?'

'You're a genius!'

She took hold of his arm tightly. He was filled with determination.

'Anything for your brother or for you, Lisa.'

They made their way back to the theatre, a great dim shape glowing with light. Soon they would watch again the story of an old king and a young prince. And the most alluring man of all, Falstaff, Shakespeare's vision of human frailty.

When the performance ended, Charles said he would prefer not to go to The Falcon with Lisa and Peter for a drink. He walked home to Crocker Road alone. He simply didn't know what to do. He couldn't telephone Whitefriars or go to the house and find out what had happened. What a scene there would be if he turned up; Bowden would treat him like dirt. He felt an impotent fury against the prejudiced, old-fashioned, jealous father for interfering. He felt violent against the man for defending Jenny's virginity.

Charles's anxiety banished the detachment of a man who was usually impartial and open-minded. He was too worried to see the way his thoughts were leading. Arriving back at his detested lodgings, he couldn't sleep for longing to know that Jenny was safe. And that she was his.

The exhibition opened the following morning and Charles helped to set it up. It looked magnificent and was received with enthusiasm, even by the hard-bitten London critics. A large number of people crowded in after the private view, to admire the gigantic panorama, the tiny models with spidery chairs and miniature thrones, the costumes, the paintings. Charles, his job done – he wasn't due back until six – congratulated Richard Pensamonn, and left.

There was no word from Jenny the next day. Charles went to the theatre in a filthy temper. Martin Morris, who rarely spoke, actually asked him a question.

'So what did you think of *Henry IV*?'

'It was okay.'

Morris glowered. 'The notices were raves.'

'I know. I saw some of them,' said Charles, who hadn't.

'Don't you like Shakespeare?'

'Of course I do.'

'Doesn't show, does it?' said Martin Morris.

Charles walked back to Crocker Road in a worse temper than before. He was helpless. Bowden had tied his wrists with ropes.

His sister was home from work, and seeing his expression immediately told him what Peter had suggested.

Charles listened, still with a gloomy expression. All he said was, 'It won't work.'

'He is willing to try. I think it's very nice of him. Your muddles are nothing to do with Peter, and it's quite a bother for him to do it at all.' Charles didn't answer. Lisa continued coldly, 'You're disgustingly ungrateful.'

'Okay. So I'm ungrateful.'

She made a face of exaggerated sarcasm. He ignored her.

When Lisa met Peter the following day he said he had telephoned Whitefriars, and Bowden had agreed to see him, but not for two or three weeks.

'At any rate we know *he's* in the land of the living,' he said. 'And he didn't sound like a father with a sick daughter. Very businesslike and quick. Is Charles upset?'

'Miserable and angry. You'd think it was a tragedy. I've never seen him take anything so badly. I simply don't understand it.'

Peter reflected. Then said, 'It is the obstacle, of course.'

'Of course there's an obstacle. Charles is in a mess and he's miserable and he's told us to mind our own business.'

'Then we have to respect his wishes. But what I meant, Lisa,' he continued in the exact voice which she found attractive or annoying, according to her own mood, 'is that

213

what is driving Charles crazy is an obstacle which has come between him and the woman. He is not used to this. He is never, I should judge, eluded by women.'

'Jenny Bowden isn't eluding him, as you put it.'

'Of course she is not. I am sure she *wants* to be with him,' said Peter in a psychiatrist's voice. 'I mean that whatever the reason he cannot see her, he is now like a dog when you take away a bone. He is growling. And nobody has taken away the bone before so he is not used to it. Some of us have lost many bones.'

'What a ghoulish simile,' said Lisa and because she grew more fond of him every day and it was a relief to share, and his hands and his mouth were nicely shaped, she burst out laughing.

Charles went punctually to the theatre to set up, and later to strike the exhibition. He became skilful, far more so than Martin Morris, at unrolling the panorama's giant curtain and arranging the costumes and sets. People in the theatre knew him now; he was hailed by actors, talked to by actresses. It was the only thing which comforted his sore heart.

*Henry IV Part One* had excellent notices. Polly came racing into the shop to see Lisa, only to be faced with Perdita from whom she was forced to buy a small, rose-patterned china box before she was given permission to take her friend out for coffee.

'Why did you come in when you saw she was there?' asked Lisa, amused at the memory of Polly's flabbergasted face when she had paid for the box.

'I wanted to see you. Why didn't you come to the wardrobe party? It's always okay to come. Nobody has an invite.'

'We'd love to come on another first night,' said Lisa. 'How did the party go? Peter and I thought you were so good in the play.'

Polly hadn't spoken a line as a waiting-woman at the Court. She had been dressed in brown, a white veil round her throat, and all she'd done was stand still. But Lisa and Peter found themselves watching her, not because she was Polly but because of the trancelike immobility and the striking expression on her face.

214

'Was I?' said Polly. 'It's difficult doing it like that. Sir Lew wasn't at the party either. I missed him a lot.'

'How's that campaign going?'

'Not sure. We're lunching at The Cobweb again. I'll ask him.'

'Perhaps you shouldn't ask,' said Lisa, wondering what a famous, elderly star would make of the question.

'He adores being taken by surprise,' said Polly with assumed confidence. She had no idea what Lewis Lockton thought of her or what she would do if anything happened – Polly's phrase for sex . . .

Charles was setting up the exhibition when there was a message that he was wanted on the telephone at the Stage Door.

'Hello, Charles, lady for you,' said the door-keeper with a wink.

'Lou?' said Charles, picking up the telephone.

A small, faint voice said, 'Charles . . . it's me.'

'*Jenny!* What's happened? Where are you? I've been desperate.'

'So have I, it's so awful. Oh Charles . . .' She was crying.

'*What's happened?*'

The sobs continued for a moment longer, then she said in a choked voice, 'I'm being sent to Malta. Next Monday.'

'What!'

'Daddy saw us. He went by when we were in the car and saw us together. He's not here now, he's gone to get the tickets and collect my passport. Oh Charles, isn't it awful?'

'Is he taking you to stay in Malta?'

'No, no, he's only going so as to leave me there. I've got to stay with his cousin, my Aunt Lilian. He said he hasn't decided when he'll come and bring me home. It may be months. He's sent Aunt Lilian two telegrams . . Oh, isn't it awful, Charles?'

'I've got to see you.' It was the only thing he could take in.

'I know, I know, we must say goodbye,' said the poor, tearful little voice. 'That's why I rang. I knew you'd be

215

worried. Everything's fixed now and he isn't *watching* so much. I've got to come to Stratford to get some dresses from Jaeger's . . . could you be there? At four? Oh, do say yes.'

At five to four Charles was walking up and down the street outside the pretty shop, which was full of Jenny-esque clothes. He kept looking at the corner where her little car would appear. But when it did draw up and she climbed out and rushed towards him he was looking in the opposite direction – he didn't see her until she clutched his arm. Charles swung round and gathered her in an embrace so fierce that two women who were passing were genuinely shocked.

'Disgusting,' said one of them loudly. 'I thought all that stopped when the Americans went.'

Charles, noticed Lisa, was more cheerful when she arrived home that evening. He put down his book and said in a pleasant voice, 'I'm sorry to be a nuisance, Lou, but what's happened to my two shirts?'

'I haven't ironed them yet. Poor old boy, do you need them? You only have three. I wish you could get some more now you're earning a bit.'

'Could I iron them?'

The suggestion made her laugh. 'Since when have you been able to iron? Anyway, I like doing them for you.'

She was pleased he was better and pulled out the ironing-board which, as usual, almost fell on her feet; it dated from the 1930s and was as heavy as lead. She ironed the shirts and Charles made tea. He even whistled.

He's getting over the Bowden girl, she thought. Possibly Jenny's been spirited off somewhere; it would be like Guy Bowden to do that. And Charles has cheered up and begun another flirtation. Stratford, with all those actresses, must be a perfect hunting ground, thought Lisa, whose morality did not extend to her brother.

The next morning when she was getting ready to leave for work, Charles kissed her goodbye.

'What's that for?' she enquired.

216

'For the shirts, of course.'

'I see you're wearing your favourite.'

It was of blue and white check and the tie, which Lisa had bought in India, was dull pinkish satin and suited his swarthy good looks.

'Off you go,' he said. 'Give my love to Perdita Smith. Tell her the best treasure in that box is you.'

Lisa's day at the shop was busy. Perdita had instructed her from the first week she'd begun her work on the problems arising from people calling in with something they wished to sell. Lisa was not allowed to give a price, nor was she permitted to refuse anything offered to The Treasure Box. 'If they're willing to leave whatever it is for me to take a look at, always give them a receipt,' said Perdita.

Three people called at the shop during the day when Perdita was absent. The private sellers, different from the buyers, were almost always women. Owners of country manors who were on their beam-ends. Nervous girls with gold bracelets inherited from godmothers. Married women selling keepsakes, jewellery. One woman who was miserably thin offered her wedding ring. Many of them did not really want to sell at all and when Perdita offered a price too low, would look relieved at being able to refuse.

Writing receipts, storing away valuables, arranging for the sellers to return tomorrow, Lisa kept thinking about Charles. The kiss made her slightly uneasy. It wasn't like him. He never made her graceful speeches, usually hugged instead of kissing her; he wasn't demonstrative. His way hadn't changed since she was ten years old. It was as if sentiment, any embraces but the throttling hug, would be a kind of denial of their bond. Charles and she were as close as twins. As thieves. As two sides of the same coin.

Perdita came back in the afternoon to meet a customer she was angling for, a handsome, middle-aged American called Arnold who, Perdita told Lisa earlier, was 'rolling in dollars'. She planned to sell him an 1835 earthenware bowl painted in blue, of a girl feeding some ducks. She'd had the bowl for ten years and had at last found a customer who deserved it.

217

'So you can go home early,' said Perdita. 'I don't want to catch your beady eye when I close the deal.'

'My eye isn't beady.'

'It's as beady as those necklaces you fiddle with. Go home. Have some tea and read up about Victorian inkstands. Here's a book with a chapter on them.'

When Lisa let herself into Crocker Road there was no sound from the ground floor flat: Mrs Ellerton must be out visiting her married daughter in Tiddington. The house was silent and Lisa could feel, like an animal sensing solitude, that Charles was not there.

Going upstairs, she wondered why she still felt unsettled. He was probably at that beastly club. Even at the theatre with Michael Gould. Yet the kiss kept coming back to her; nowadays many things he did seemed out of character.

The sitting-room door was ajar, the windows shut, the room smelled smoky and the first thing she saw was the ash-tray and at least half a dozen cigarette stubs. Even those gave her a feeling of foreboding. Why had he smoked so much? I'm being like some stage detective, she thought, and just then heard his step on the landing.

She swung round, smiling.

'There you are! I thought you'd gone out. This room looks remarkably tidy. Where are your books? Did you have a blitz . . .' Her voice trailed away as she looked at him.

'Sit down, Lou.'

She thought: something terrible has happened. Has he been to the doctor? Is he ill? She gripped her hands tightly together.

'I've got a shock for you,' he said quietly. 'Jenny and I are going to get married. By special licence.'

'*What?*'

'Hear me out, Lou, please. I wish I could've told you sooner but Jenny was in a state and made me promise. The fact is we're leaving now. By the 6.10,' he added, in the way of local people who always mentioned the time of trains. 'We won't be back.'

'I don't understand!' shouted Lisa. 'You can't afford to

218

marry anybody! You have no money and no home apart from this –'

'I'm sorry. There it is.'

'There *what* is? You can't do it, you must stop, take back the licence, tell her it's impossible. I won't let you do this, *you're mad*!'

'I shall do my best to make her happy.'

It wasn't Charles speaking. The unaccustomed gravity, the utter indifference to her fury told Lisa everything. She determined to make him see sense.

'Christ, Charles, how old is that girl, sixteen?'

'You know perfectly well she's seventeen.'

'Seventeen, then. What do you imagine you're doing, saddling yourself with a child? What will you live on? Where will you live?'

'We'll manage something. We'll be together.'

'Sentimental tripe. How can she be happy when her husband's down and out?'

'Oh thanks,' said Charles with a momentary return to himself. 'That's very polite.'

'Shut up!' Lisa was beside herself. 'Even supposing you had some money –'

'Jenny has a little.'

'Then that makes it worse. Do you intend Jenny to keep you? Are you expecting to wring money out of her father? You know what he's like, he can't stick you. Charles,' her voice altered, softened, beseeched, '*I beg you*. What you're going to do will be a disaster. *I beg you*.'

'I'm sorry, Lou. Sorry it's like this . . . Look, I must go. She'll be at the station in five minutes.' He stood up and came to her to kiss her for the second time that day but Lisa backed away. He grimaced. 'I shan't tell you where we're going – Bowden might try to get it out of you.' He went to the door and then turned as if unable to leave her. 'I do love her,' he said. 'Very much. I swear it. I'll be in touch soon, I promise. *Don't worry*,' he added, looking at her for the last time. She heard him go into his room, apparently to pick up his luggage. He clattered down the stairs. The front door slammed.

219

Lisa couldn't bear to go to the window and watch him walk away; she didn't know he looked up twice to see if she was there.

She walked up and down the room, too angry and miserable to shed a tear. What in God's name had made him decide to do this? How could he imagine it would have the slightest chance of success? Charles was impossible. Incurable. Her love and respect for him, the blood tie, the loyalty, burned to a cinder. The girl was going to suffer and so was he.

Why did I mention money to him? she thought. She understood now why it was called filthy. It was money, its lack, their need, their helplessness without it which would wreck Jenny Bowden and her brother.

I can't cope, thought Lisa, and for the first time in her life thought: the only answer is to get drunk. She wouldn't, of course.

Wandering through the flat, she found everything of his was gone. His clothes, packed, she presumed, in the battered suitcase they'd brought from Burma. His few favourite books. His underclothes and shoes. Those ironed shirts. For an untidy man he had made a thoroughly clean sweep; there wasn't a thing belonging to him in his room but the newspaper Peter had brought from him yesterday, folded in the way Charles folded newspapers, in a narrow band.

She sat down on his bed, and then she did begin to cry.

Peter was working late at the newspaper, Polly was in the performance of *Henry IV* . . . Lisa had nobody to talk to. She didn't know what to do with herself. It was as if her very body was difficult to inhabit.

She went into the kitchen and tried to cook an omelette but the smell sickened her. She went to the landing, wondering if Mrs Ellerton had come home. She'd have to tell her. All Mrs Ellerton would be concerned about was how it affected the weekly rent.

Yes, how does it? Lisa thought. After the misery, she began to realize that her brother's flight had landed her in trouble too. Without his small contributions, she'd be hard put to it to manage the rent and eat as well. She thought: I must do some sums.

Sitting at the table she began to make a list of what her life at its most meagre was going to cost. She did the painful calculations only the poor know about. Whatever she tried to omit, the total finished by being too large. She must cut out more. Could she manage on less food? No milk? No dry-cleaning? There were shoes to be mended ... She was interrupted in writing yet another list by a ring of the bell. She rushed down the stairs – thank God, that's Peter. She opened the door. It was Guy Bowden.

'I wish to speak to you.'

'Yes. Please come in. We live upstairs,' said Lisa. She did not notice that she'd said 'we'.

The ceiling-light shone down on the table covered by a red chenille cloth, her writing-case and the erased and scribbled sums.

'Do sit down,' Lisa began but he had no time for politeness and said, as if speaking to a man, and a servant at that, 'Where is she?'

'I have no idea.'

'You know what's happened.'

'Yes. He told me.'

He clenched his teeth and, as she'd done, walked up and down the room. He suddenly swung round and said accusingly, 'You do know where she is.'

'Mr Bowden, I *don't*. Please sit down and stop marching about, you're making me giddy. I repeat, I don't know where your daughter's gone or Charles either. He came here two hours ago, told me he was getting married and then left. Didn't *she* tell *you*?'

Her manner was as fierce as his; he could see she looked much as he felt. He did sit down.

'He said he had a special licence,' said Lisa.

Bowden said contemptuously, 'She left me a letter saying the same.' He didn't offer to show her the letter.

They sat staring at each other. For a split second it was as if they confessed to being wounded by the same knife. They

221

bled in the same way and might try to staunch each other's wounds. The next moment he changed.

'Of course you know where he's taken her. I demand to be told. I shall go and get her. It is not too late. Yes, I'll go now –'

'*Mr Bowden, I don't know.*'

'You're lying. *She* lied. You're in it with them.'

'Oh God,' shouted Lisa, at the end of her tether. 'What must I do to make you believe me? I'm as horrified as you are. Charles is mad. He can't support your daughter, he has no proper job, he's walked out of the one they gave him at the theatre, he hasn't a bean and nor have I. Just look round you,' she added with a bitter face. 'We're broke. This is where my father's stupidity landed us. He's to blame, as you very well know. But that's all over. Do you suppose I want my brother to be saddled with a wife? I tell you, he is mad, and I don't know where they are. *I don't know, I don't know.*'

He listened in grim silence, thinking that even a child could see she was speaking the truth. He knew he shouldn't have bullied her.

And he was appalled at the poverty of her home.

'I am sorry. I was unjust. I accept that you know nothing.'

'Good.'

He sighed and got to his feet. Lisa remained in the chair where Charles used to lounge, legs outstretched, waiting for her to come home.

'It is too late,' Guy Bowden said aloud, speaking to himself.

'To stop them? I'm afraid it is.' There was a pause as if the whole drama hung fire until Lisa managed very gravely, 'Mr Bowden, you won't – I mean you won't –' She didn't finish.

'Won't what?'

'Be too unkind to her when they come back. Of course they will come back eventually, there's nothing else for them. Don't be too unkind. She is so young.'

He gave a strange smile. She surprised him. 'Unkind? No, I shan't be unkind. I shall never see her again. Goodnight.'

As if it were a fact to make him escape, he left the room.

# 11

There was no word from Charles and no sign from Guy Bowden either. Thinking it over more coolly as the days went by, Lisa realized it was naïve of her to imagine Jenny's father would get in touch with her again. Why should he? Sharing a misfortune did not make a friend. She began to pity Bowden, and to imagine what his life must be like without the girl he'd doted on since she was born. Lisa's own life was painfully empty without Charles. She missed him constantly. She was convinced she had lost him.

Four weeks after he left Stratford, two things happened. The first was the arrival of a postcard with the postmark 'Roma'. It was from Charles:

> We're not here, Lou, so don't send out the search parties! I bought this card when we were staying a night or two. It's lovely and hot (Jenny not mad on the heat but I'd forgotten how I like it). Otherwise fine. Jenny's learned some Italian. Hope all is well with you. Regards to Peter.
>
> Charles.

His signature was followed by a line of kisses, and the letter 'J'.

Lisa telephoned Peter at the newspaper and read him the card. 'Do you think I should ring Mr Bowden?'

There was one of the longish silences Peter went in for. He was thinking things over. 'Perhaps not,' he finally said.

'But he ought to know they're all right, surely?'

'Maybe she has sent him a card at the same time.'

Somehow Lisa didn't think so. 'Are you sure I shouldn't ring, Peter? Poor man, he must be worried.'

'Didn't you tell me he said he would never see her again?'

Lisa was not convinced. She had asked advice and decided not to take it, and when Perdita was safely out of the shop, she picked up the telephone and rang Whitefriars. She got through at once. Apparently Guy answered the telephone in person.

'Mr Bowden?'

'Yes?' The voice was so abrupt that she knew he'd recognized her.

'I rang to ask if you'd heard from Jenny . . .' said Lisa. She found herself wishing very much that he had, despite his sharp voice.

'No,' was the reply.

'Oh,' said Lisa and then quickly, 'It's just that I had a postcard from my brother. Shall I read it to you?'

There was a silence even longer than Peter's.

Lisa had half expected questions, a change of voice, a slight warmth. She didn't know, when he said nothing again, what more there was for her to add.

At length he spoke. 'I rather think not.'

'You mean you don't want to know where it's from or how they are?' said Lisa, her good intentions drying up. He affected her like that. 'The postmark was Rome but Charles said they're not there now.'

'I'm not interested. Thank you for ringing but I am not interested.' He rang off.

Lisa put down the receiver, positively spitting. Cold fish. Rude pig. So he was still as angry with Jenny as he'd been when he stormed into Crocker Road. Anger was supposed to feed a certain kind of character: Guy Bowden had been eating platefuls. I must stop feeling sorry for him, she thought. I must remember it's not my duty to let him know if Charles writes again. I shall put him out of my mind.

She didn't.

Peter was coming to take her out to dinner that night.

He'd been extraordinarily kind since Charles had gone. He almost behaved as if Charles were his brother too. Knowing Peter had been fond of Charles was comforting.

As far as money was concerned, she had used up almost all her share of the silver sale. On rent in advance. On a warm coat and a few sensible clothes. She had enough to last a few more weeks. But when that money was gone it would be necessary to try and get extra work in the evenings. Her salary at The Treasure Box wasn't sufficient to keep her without Charles helping a little. I could work in the bar at The Duck, perhaps, thought Lisa with some courage. She was nervous in pubs and until recently had only visited them on rare occasions with Peter or Charles.

Peter arrived at Crocker Road that evening, gave her a kiss, and took her down the road to The White Swan, one of the Tudor hotels which had been inns in Shakespeare's time. It was a cold March and when they went into the beamed, whitewashed lounge, there was the usual log fire and a waiter in the corner somewhere.

In the restaurant Peter ordered steak and a bottle of Algerian wine.

'You're being very lavish,' said Lisa who was hungry. But she always was nowadays.

'You need hot food. And a glass of something to cheer you up.'

'Do I need cheering? I thought I was quite recovered.'

'I don't think so.'

They drank the wine and Lisa, indeed, did feel brighter. It's like drinking at a funeral, she thought. It doesn't last long. Thoughts of her brother were never far from her mind and she said, 'You are lucky. Not having a family.'

He had told her when they first met that his parents had been killed in the Blitz; he had no brothers or sisters.

'One worries anyway, Lisa.'

'What about?'

'I worry about you.'

'Why should you do that?' she said, the sour wine warming her. She smiled brightly. Her head was beginning to swim.

He reflected for a moment or two. She thought: I do like the way you look. She liked his eyes which were unusually blue and short-sighted so that the spectacles enlarged them slightly. Glasses gave him a studious air which suited him. He was so clean. As if he bathed and shaved three times a day.

He leaned across the table and took one of her hands, turned it over and spread it flat, regarding it fixedly. Without looking up he said, 'Now your brother has gone you can't afford to live at Crocker Road, can you? Don't say anything, please. Not yet. I'm not a fool, Lisa. You told me some time ago that makings ends meet was difficult. That was before Charles left you. And I saw, that night when I came to the flat after he'd gone, what you were writing. Don't be angry, I only caught a glimpse but you were trying to work out how it was possible to live, weren't you?'

'Peter, please.' He ignored that.

'I have an idea,' he continued. 'I want you to let me give you an allowance. Don't interrupt! I want you to be quiet while I tell you what I've been thinking. Is that much to ask?' He sounded quite foreign, he was very agitated. 'I'm not well paid, but I have a little private money, and I don't spend much . . . You must let me *lend* you some money. Just what Charles gave towards the flat, you see? If you like, we can keep an account, and enter the amount every week –'

When he said that she couldn't help smiling. The smile encouraged him.

'When you earn more from Mrs Smith or perhaps something else good happens, you can pay me back.'

She was so touched that she didn't know what to say. She burst impulsively into thanks and refusals. She protested. She argued. She couldn't possibly accept such a thing. But in the end he made her admit that she could no longer manage to live and they both knew that at present Perdita wouldn't help her.

'Did you ask for a rise?'

'There's no reason for her to give me one. I've only worked a short time and that's what she'd say.'

'She would also say that your brother disappearing is no reason for her to put her hand in her pocket,' agreed Peter.

'Nor you either,' Lisa couldn't help adding.

He looked at her again, and Lisa suddenly blushed.

When they walked home, and he stayed for a moment on the doorstep, giving her a chaste goodnight kiss, Lisa asked him if he'd like to come into the flat for some coffee. The euphemism was plain.

'Very much,' he said.

They climbed the stairs to the empty flat which was so quiet and dreary now. Charles's bedroom door stood open as it always did and Lisa never looked in that direction without a spasm in her heart.

When he had closed the front door, Peter put his arms around her. They began to kiss. Without saying anything, they went into her bedroom and took off their clothes. The dimness of the bedroom was lit by a street lamp at some distance away and Lisa could see him naked, his skin so pale that it was almost opalescent. He looked wonderful, with broad shoulders, a flat belly, straight strong legs: an Apollo. When he took off his glasses she made out a face which had the innocence of somebody blind. She undressed with a feeling of relief, of liberty. To make love with Peter would change everything and she longed for that. It would be the end of the life she'd led as Charles's sister, when caring for him, worrying about him, had occupied her mind and the tender part of her heart. More, much more, Peter must free her from the ghost of her former lover. Here was a man whose opalescent body was waiting to give her pleasure, here was a companion who loved her. She put her arms round his bare shoulders and he said in a low voice, 'Lisa. Little love.'

They went over to the bed and lay down, and she opened her legs, waiting to receive him and feeling so strange, so strange, because this time it had no bliss and ecstasy and desperation. As he entered her she felt him trembling. He thrust lightly, then more deeply and the pleasure of sex, forgotten since Tom had been inside her, came back, not in the same exquisite pain, not in the same wet delirious bliss,

227

but a pleasure just the same. She put her hands on his buttocks and pushed him into her and after they had made love for a short, silent, almost entirely selfish time, he said in a strangled voice 'I – I can't wait –' and came, groaning and shuddering.

He made her come later with his hands, vibrating his fingers until her climax came too.

They were silent as they separated.

'I'm sorry. Sorry.'

'Don't be stupid, dear Peter.'

'It's terrible.'

'Peter, *don't*. It's all right. It's lovely to be with you like this.'

'It won't be like that tomorrow. It was because – so long – so – because it was the first time with you.'

'I know,' she said, and rumpling his hair which he always wore tidily combed, added mischievously, 'Is there going to be a tomorrow?'

He had been tensed in misery. He relaxed and managed a smile.

'Tomorrow and the next day and the next. I shall make love to you until the stars fall. What are you doing every night this week?'

When he left her she turned on her face and cried.

Polly had been much in Lisa's life since Charles's disappearance. She was a friend in need; she was also burning with interest and foretold, much more strongly than Lisa, the disasters of the marriage. 'It'll be the most god-awful flop' was Polly's elegant way of putting it. She appeared at The Treasure Box too often, disapproved of by Perdita. Somehow Polly wheedled the Old Monster, as the actress privately called her, to let Lisa have time out for coffee. 'I do bring hundreds of customers to your wonderful shop,' said Polly boldly.

The day after Peter and Lisa first made love, Lisa was glad to sit with her friend at The Cobweb, in the lazy silence which is the aftermath of sex. Polly eyed her.

228

'You're rather serene for a change.'

'Have I been so gloomy, then?'

'Not exactly bursting with joy, darling. I think . . . I think it's that boyfriend of yours. He's jolly attractive. Don't look smug. He is and you think so too. I feel quite jealous. All I've got are men who look at themselves over my shoulder if there happens to be a mirror in the room.'

'Does Sir Lew do that?'

'Oh no. He's gone beyond that. I daresay he did in his twenties. But now, you see, he *knows* he's all right.'

'And how is he with you?'

'Devoted, of course,' said Polly, who had lately avoided talking of her middle-aged admirer and star. She rolled her eyes expressively upwards, which was Polly's way of indicating volumes and saying nothing on the subject, and then launched into a long story about the problems of being an understudy. Lisa saw this was why she'd been dragged out for a coffee.

That evening she was not meeting Peter until late, he had a long article to write, and she returned to the Crocker Road flat thinking about sex. It would be different tonight. Better tonight. It excited her, and she felt light-hearted as she let herself into the house with her latchkey.

Mrs Ellerton came out from her own kitchen the moment she heard Lisa's key. She had been on the look-out, and Lisa felt a wave of gratitude to Peter. Without his help the sight of her landlady watching for her would have been alarming.

Mrs Ellerton's dislike for Lisa was rooted only in antagonism for a young woman who was Charles Whitfield's sister. She had been secretly upset at his departure. His sister had given the unlikely explanation that Charles had a job in London, but Mrs Ellerton didn't believe it. She accepted Lisa's rent with scarcely a thank you. She missed the fascinating lodger. In her bosom there still lived a woman longing for romance and Charles had unconsciously known that and spoken to that woman. She used to smile when she saw him. Once she'd made him some scones.

She thought his sister prissy and didn't miss the fact that

her boyfriend kept coming in and out of the house. He was polite enough, but Miss Whitfield was no better than she ought to be. However, she supposed the girl was an improvement on an actor or actress. She'd heard terrible stories from fellow landladies.

'Got a minute?' she said as Lisa entered the house.

'Of course,' said Lisa who did not like her either and knew it would be foolish to show it.

'Something came for you.'

They went into Mrs Ellerton's untidy kitchen and the landlady pointed at the floor. A smallish, battered suitcase was lying by the table. The moment Lisa set eyes on it she recognized it – it had belonged to her father. It had been kept with the rest of the family's luggage in a cupboard under the stairs; when Lisa was a child playing hide-and-seek, she used to stand on that case. The lid was springy and covered with bright ships' labels. Now the labels had been torn away, although here and there were ghostly rings or squares or fragments of once-coloured paper.

Seeing the suitcase again was like watching a ghost rise up out of the ground. It was as familiar as her father's voice. The case was stoutly tied with rope, heavily knotted. It was knocked about, the leather peeling, plastered with newer labels, some glued on, some fixed to the half-broken handle.

'Come for your brother by Carter Paterson. I signed for it.'

'Thanks, Mrs Ellerton.' Lisa continued to stare at it.

'Want to get it upstairs, I daresay. I'd better give you a hand.'

'Is it heavy?'

'As lead. I got the man to fetch it in here. Better let me help,' said the landlady. She was filled with curiosity, but wasn't going to give her lodger the satisfaction of showing it.

Together, Mrs Ellerton sighing and puffing a good deal, they staggered up the stairs. In Lisa's sitting-room they let the case fall rather than placing it. It crashed down on the floor.

The landlady did not ask Lisa what was in it. She had seen the foreign labels, and was sure it was full of valuables.

Those Whitfields used to have a bob or two, one of her Stratford friends had informed her. She stood looking first at Lisa and then at the booty. Silver? thought Mrs Ellerton. Clothes? Too heavy for those. Whatever was in it had taken a long time on its journey. Looked as if it had been halfway round the world. She hoped it did not contain bananas . . . she had vaguely read of tarantulas.

'You'll be letting your brother know it come for him,' said Mrs Ellerton after a pause.

'Of course.' Lisa nodded absently, but offered no explanations.

'Well, I'll leave you, then,' said Mrs Ellerton lingering at the door. Lisa appeared not to hear, and the landlady, disappointed, returned to her ground-floor flat. She made herself some baked beans on toast, and settled down to read a historical novel from Boots library. Now and again during the evening, she remembered the suitcase.

When she was alone, Lisa knelt down and looked at the case. She vaguely recalled something about it. Her father had changed his solicitor three times, and after his death, with Charles still fighting in Burma, Lisa had written to all three from India. She had hoped that somehow, somewhere, her father had bequeathed Charles and herself a little money. The three firms briefly replied, all in the negative. But one, Lisa faintly remembered, had mentioned 'a valise of Mr Whitfield's old papers etc. which is lodged with us. A member of our firm did suggest to Mr Whitfield some years ago that the contents were no longer relevant, but Mr Whitfield particularly requested us to retain it. We are dispatching it to you as soon as it becomes possible to send it overseas. There appears to be nothing of importance or present use among the documents.'

Papers. My father's old papers, thought Lisa. She went to fetch the bread-knife.

Fortunately the case was not locked but the ropes were thick and it took some time to saw through them. There was sealing wax too; she cracked that off with the heel of her shoe. Finally she opened the lid.

231

A strong smell of musty old paper rose up. The case was filled to the brim with documents. It was clearly not airtight and somewhere in its journeyings by land and sea had been slopped over by water in the hold of a ship or left on a platform during the monsoon. The first layers of paper were covered and spotted with mildew. Lisa took them out. As she delved deeper and deeper – there was no mildew in the lower documents – she felt she was pulling out the whole of her father's tragedy. The papers lay like maps charting his journey into disaster. There were insurance policies long since expired, and share certificates for companies long ago collapsed. Lisa would not have known any of this if across elaborately decorated certificates tied in bundles her father hadn't fixed labels or scraps of paper. 'This firm went into liquidation, 7/8/32.' 'No longer in existence.' 'I ceased to pay the premium.' 'Cancelled.' She forgot the time, forgot where she was. She sat cross-legged, taking out more and more papers. At first the sight of her father's foolishness hurt her. She could feel his misery. His bitter disappointments, even desperation. 'Poor Daddy,' she said once aloud. But later the very scale of his idiocies with money filled her with a kind of dull resentment. She peered into the trunk. At least four more layers.

'Nothing of importance or present use.' All this stuff was fit for was to light the fire . . .

Glancing up for the first time at her watch, she gave a start, realizing she'd arranged to meet Peter at The Dirty Duck and was already slightly late. She stood up, looking at the mess all over the floor. She wouldn't keep it to show Charles supposing – when? when? – he turned up again.

'I'll burn the lot in Mrs Ellerton's boiler,' she said aloud. 'And good riddance.'

She pushed a comb through her hair, snatched up a jacket and clattered out of the house, not bothering to lock her door. What was there to steal?

The Dirty Duck was a pub facing the gardens which in their turn bordered the banks of the Avon, five minutes from the theatre. The pub was a pleasant stone house built high up above the road and approached by two flights of stone steps. In summer the steps were lined with people sitting as if on a staircase at a débutante's ball. The wall high above the road was also a place to squat, drinking beer and talking in the Stratford sunlight. The pub's real name was The Black Swan and that rare bird flew on one side of the inn-sign. On the reverse a mud-splashed duck flapped with less grace. Rumour said the pub had been rechristened by actors years ago. True or not, it was now simply The Duck and everybody from the theatre went there at one time or another. Visitors might see a world-famous actor or a walk-on, a Prince or a Prologue leaning against the bar.

Lisa jog-trotted most of the way, arriving breathless. She raced up the steps into the crowded interior, certain of finding Peter who was never late. The place was crammed, the talk as loud as at a cocktail party. The sound of practised voices and a good many belly laughs indicated that most of the people were actors. They had a strong, aggressive gaiety.

One plumpish, dark man wearing an enormous fisherman's sweater was telling a story and when he arrived at its climax the laugh he received would have gladdened the heart of a world-famous comedian. Lisa tried not to watch, but the crowd fascinated her. She felt a sort of envy for people who belonged to so united an assembly.

She did not elbow her way through the group to buy herself a drink. She never went to pubs by herself; it was in fact the first time she'd found herself at The Duck unaccompanied. Charles had brought her once or twice, but never asked her to meet him here when he had been working at the theatre. Old prejudices were in Charles as well as Lisa. In the 1930s women did not go into pubs alone, and preferably not at all.

She went to a far corner and sat in a window-seat out of range of the noisy actors. She began to think about her father's papers. Her despisal of him had faded. All the shares and insurances, carefully preserved in their uselessness, moved her somehow. Alec Whitfield had thrown nothing away. Except his children. She felt a touch on her arm and

233

looked up to see Peter. He was concerned and apologetic for having kept her waiting. There had been a fire at a furniture factory in Leamington.

'The blaze was fifteen feet high, such crowds – why do people enjoy fires?' He'd tried to telephone The Duck but the line was permanently engaged. 'An actor, probably,' he said. In the end he'd thought it better to drive as fast as possible to get here.

'I'm so very sorry,' he repeated, his eyes on her face.

'I was rather late too, Peter. It's very nice of you to be so bothered at keeping me waiting.'

'Of course I bother. How could I not?'

They sat talking about the fire. Then they left The Duck and walked slowly up Chapel Lane and the high street towards Crocker Road. On a corner when there was nobody in sight, he kissed her. She clung, looking at him almost joyfully. She particularly wanted to make love tonight, not only because yesterday's sex had been imperfect but because she was determined to make Peter a real part of her life. To take him into her heart. It was the way to do what Peter had said she must, to escape the past. She wanted to forget her girlhood, her father, the brother who had left without giving her a thought, the house which existed without them – it too had cast them off. Most of all she wanted to rid herself of Tom Westbury. The only way to destroy his ghost was for another man to possess her fully. When Peter did so, she'd know a different kind of joy.

As they went into the house she was thinking about the sex to come, and had literally forgotten the state in which she'd left the sitting-room. Peter opened the door and recoiled.

'My God, what's happened?'

'It's nothing. I mean, an old suitcase of my father's turned up. A lot of muck, really.'

'But surely some of it could be important.' Astounded, he took in the litter of documents spread all over the carpet.

'Nothing's important, Peter. It's ancient out-of-date rubbish. I'll pack it all up and Mrs Ellerton can shove it into her boiler in the morning.'

Lisa was fretful. The sight of the dingy room knee-deep in papers had apparently put sex right out of her lover's mind for the moment. He did not answer, but knelt down in exactly the same place she'd been for long, tedious hours. He picked up a sheaf of documents and began to study them.

'Some of these are interesting,' he said. 'I remember the reports on Albion Chemicals. Yes, I recall a lot of this . . .'

'Peter, do leave them! You're not going to expect me to spend another three hours reading them. They're just a lot of old *stuff*. It was dreary enough earlier this evening, we aren't going to go through them all again, are we?'

She expected him to put them down; Peter always did what she wanted. This time he put up his hand in a gesture Lisa wasn't accustomed to, a 'stop, I am thinking' wave of the hand. Taking no more notice of her, he began to sift through the documents one by one, reading each in turn, now and then murmuring to himself.

Lisa marched ostentatiously out to the kitchen, made some coffee, offered him a cup which was refused and threw herself into a chair.

Peter suddenly said, 'Ah.'

'Ah what?' She'd given up trying to stop him in his self-appointed task.

'This is an old life insurance policy your father took out years ago. He let the payments lapse.'

'Of course he did.'

'That's not what I'm talking about,' he said patiently. 'The policy has a surrender value, as they call it.'

'No!'

'Certainly. I'd judge about £20.'

'Peter, you are clever!' Delighted and ashamed she knelt down on the floor beside him to look at the piece of paper he offered her.

'No, no, Lisa, don't kneel on those, I haven't looked through them yet. You see this policy? Paragraph at the bottom. Surrender value, clearly set out. I'm not such a fool after all.'

'As if I'd ever think you were that.'

235

'What I mean is,' he said, picking up another sheaf of papers which seemed to draw him as a pack of cards drew Charles, 'I am not the fool you thought for wasting your time just now. Shall we see what else there may be to discover?' He looked at her with a smile of pleasure, like a man giving her a present.

Under his instructions Lisa helped to arrange the documents in neat piles, sorting out the mess she had left. They were separated under headings. Insurance policies. Share certificates. Reports to shareholders. Letters. Poor Alec's letters must have been legion; the replies were long and always in the negative. Squatting down beside him, Lisa was as obliging as she could be, inspired by the merry news of £20. Sex flew out of the window.

At last they unearthed the final layers remaining in the suitcase, placing them on now toppling piles of paper. No more delightful surprises emerged, but Lisa didn't expect one. That discovery of Peter's would pay the rent for five weeks. Peter was leafing through a last fistful. Suddenly he jumped.

*'Gott in Himmel!'*

'Why the German?' she said with a burst of laughter. 'What's happened now – bad news? What has God in Heaven got to do with it?'

'What?' Peter looked at her as if he'd just woken up. 'What did you say?' He was holding a thick packet of elaborately decorated share certificates. They were fastened with a rubber band and as he went through them it broke into fragments: it had gone rotten. 'These are shares in the Lennox Aero Company. An old company started up around 1931. Your father bought two thousand.'

'What a ridiculous amount to buy.'

'He paid sixpence a share.'

'Goodness,' said Lisa flippantly, 'poor Father and his sixpenny shares. How could he waste his money like that?'

'They cost him £50.'

'Yes, Peter, I can work that out for myself. I agree. An utter waste.' Something in his voice made her brighten.

'Don't say you've thought of a way we could get the fifty quid back?'

He did not join in the smile or the cheerfulness. He was still fingering the packet of papers.

'I've read about Lennox Aero,' he said, after a moment. 'It was in the *Birmingham News*. De Havilland have been making moves to buy them up. Apparently Lennox is worth having, but De Havilland want control.'

'So I might get more than fifty quid? How marvellous!'

He looked up at her. His voice was hoarse.

'I can't be accurate. But I think they're worth over twenty thousand pounds.'

# 12

---

It had never entered Charles's head that he would marry. When women in love with him wanted to know why, he kissed them fondly and said it must be because he'd make a dreadful husband. The answer wasn't popular but it was the only one Charles's lovers were given.

The taxi halted at Caxton Hall, a serious red building enhanced by statues – the place where Charles was destined to give up his liberty. Jenny, in a fine tweed suit, her lapel pinned with some small pink orchids he had bought, looked nervous. The couple were shown into what was called The Wedding Room and which reminded Charles of a reception room in a fusty, old hotel. It matched London's air of dispirited shabbiness.

The Superintendent Registrar received them cordially, shook hands and introduced them to two strangers.

'Your witnesses, Mr Whitfield. Mr and Mrs Marchant.' They were cleaners at Caxton Hall and glad to earn a few extra shillings. The woman was small and prim, the man portly and good-natured.

'Well, now, stand here, if you please. Miss Bowden? Welcome,' said the Registrar to the silent girl. He was being kind; perhaps he put on his manner with his grey suit which was the same colour as his hair brushed back like Henry Irving's. Charles and his girl-bride stood among a positive throng of empty chairs.

Charles thought: do people actually come here to celebrate?

brate? He missed a real wedding, the atmosphere of an ancient church, its solemnity, even the smell of stone, leather, lilies. He missed the presence of a religion to which he scarcely gave a thought.

They were told to sit down. The Registrar picked up a much-worn book and began to drone paltry words.

'I must start by telling you that this room has been sanctioned by law for the ceremony of marriage . . . a union entered into for life . . .'

Charles turned to the girl at his side and when she looked back, her shyness pierced his heart.

They both repeated the words said to them, 'I do solemnly declare . . .' The Registrar enquired 'Is there a ring?' and Jenny anxiously held out her hand. Charles slipped on the ring he usually wore on his little finger. It was his mother's wedding ring.

Then the ceremony was over and the Registrar gave the signed document to Jenny, making his usual joke which always went down well. 'We like to give the marriage lines to the bride. In our experience, the young ladies take the best care of them.'

The bridal couple laughed, and the witnesses, who'd heard the joke fifty times before, both managed a cheerful smile which turned into a beam when Charles gave them two pound notes each. There followed congratulations from three strangers. Charles and Jenny went out into a clouded morning.

They travelled second-class to Rome. Sleepers were out of the question on the little money they possessed, which consisted of Charles's theatre salary, some recent winnings from the Wilton Club, and the sale of Jenny's two diamond clips at the pawn shop in Wardour Street. The princely total happened to be more than the travel allowance set by the Government: £35 for each Britisher going abroad. But Mick Gould, not saying how, had found Charles some extra lire, and Jenny had twenty pounds smuggled in the toe of her shoe.

Their wedding night was spent in the train as it roared

and rattled across France into the mountains. A dim blue light near the ceiling shone down on figures swathed in coats and rugs against the bitter cold of the Apennines. The train heating had gone wrong.

They arrived in Rome early in the morning, dirty and white-faced. A blessed sun was brightly shining as they emerged from the station to be set upon as if by wolves. Packs of eager, jabbering, dark-faced men were shouting, smiling and waving small packets of notes. Charles had seen all this before. Jackals looking for foreign prey could be of any nationality but all behaved in the same way. He put his arm round Jenny's waist and pushed her straight through the crowd, shouting 'No, No, No!' Outside the station, still being waved at, he bundled her into a taxi. But not before, in broken Italian, he had fixed the price with the driver. He asked to be taken to The Bristol Hotel.

'Bristol,' agreed the driver, and set off as if competing in the Monte Carlo rally.

'Charles, you are wonderful,' said Jenny. 'All those men – '

'They were nothing to be frightened of. All they were doing was offering millions of lire for ten English quid. It was the same at Port Said.'

'But how do you know about the hotel?'

He squeezed her arm and looked omniscient, deciding not to spoil it by telling her there was generally a Bristol Hotel in all large cities on the Continent. He kissed her, saying her face was dirty. Jenny smiled in stupefied rapture.

The hotel's full name was The Royal Bristol & Gray, and it turned out to be as sombre and dark as Caxton Hall, but larger than Crocker Road. It was an enormous, half-closed building in a street of other palaces of peeling paint and boarded-up windows. In the war it had been used relentlessly. By Italian staff in their exaggerated uniforms. By Nazi commandants in theirs. Finally by the Americans, wearing the roses of a Victory drive through cheering mobs.

Now the place had settled down to dust and emptiness. The carpet was so worn that Jenny caught her heel in one of the holes, and the woman at the desk, who had a moustache, demanded their passports as if she were going to arrest them.

Jenny didn't care. In a room with windows large enough for a museum and ceilings as high as a church, Jenny washed her face, kissed her husband, and lay down on the bed to fall into the sleep of the innocent.

Charles sat and watched her for a while, then went to have a shower – the water was cold and rusty – and put on a dressing-gown. He returned to sit on the vast bed with the girl lying there, her pretty mouth half open, deep, deep asleep. He lit a cigarette and continued staring at her. In all his years of sexual experience, from the Claires of the world to little Burmese girls with skins the colour of copper and polished black hair dressed in cylinders on top of their graceful heads, Charles had never made love to a virgin. To seduce the innocent had not been to his taste. Subconsciously he'd never intended to break Jenny's virgin knot, and had been content to lie beside her, to be caressed by her inexperienced hand, to teach her to kiss, to drive them both to a pitch of frustration and that was all. He'd chosen the way both of them had behaved during their many passages of love in Stratford.

Jenny had happened at time when he was unhappy and humiliated. Poverty was biting him like an adder and his pursuit of her had been another kind of game. Some people could wear poverty with grace. Lisa did. But Charles felt debased by want and to escape from England to a place where the sunshine and beauty of Italy might make things bearable, even enjoyable, had strongly appealed to him.

There she lay. So sound asleep that he could not contemplate waking her. She slept for four hours as the Roman day went slowly by and sunshine moved across the polished floor. In the unaccustomed Italian heat she sweated, her babyish yellow hair damp on a forehead the colour of a magnolia. She looked about twelve. Yet it was this innocent, who might have climbed down from the clouds on a painted church ceiling, small wings attached to her shoulders, who

241

had somehow managed to do what no other girl had done. She was his wife. His senses stirred as he sat looking at her. There was something thrilling, sinful, about deflowering this schoolgirl. He put out his hand and softly ran a finger down the bridge of her nose. She stirred and made a blind dab as if to brush away a fly. Charles caught the hand and chuckled.

'Wake up.'

'Mmmm,' murmured Jenny, snuggling deeper into oblivion.

'Wake up, little girl.'

'Oh –' a huge yawn. She opened her eyes. 'Have I been asleep?'

'Nearly four hours.'

'It can't be as long as that.'

She widened her eyes, yawning again. Blue eyes looked black in the light filtered through the venetian blinds. 'Perhaps I'll sleep again.'

'No, you won't. You have something else to do now.'

He put his arm under her and leaned over and kissed her for a long time. She responded almost automatically, then more eagerly, then with passion. He rolled over on top of her. She had gone to sleep wearing only a satin slip, and he pulled it up, expertly getting it over her head. He'd undressed many girls. She lay passive while he undid the small lace brassiere and leaned down to suck her pointed breasts. All she could see was the dark, bent head with its thick, curling hair. She was frightened of the strangeness and lay like a sacrifice while he pressed his face between her breasts, then took them and pushed them, small and perfect, together to make a crevice which he licked. She was afraid but roused. She was here with a man she worshipped and did not know, her husband in title, and in a few minutes to be her despoiler.

She could no longer return his embraces, it was too strange and too alarming, as if he were taking away her self, the self she'd lived with since she was born. He put both large hands on the thin elastic of her knickers and pulled them off and then she was naked beneath him. He pushed her legs apart with his own and penetrated her with one painful, terrifying plunge. His body inside her seemed to the girl enormous, and as he moved she automatically resisted as if she would push out the thing which had entered her. But she was pinned and helpless. He paused. He waited inside her, looking down at the child's face. He smiled. He was never not in control of his body, never unconscious of his partner, always the man whose pleasure came from giving pleasure. So now, at her involuntary and pathetic resistance, he stopped thrusting and said, 'Try to move, my darling.'

'I can't –' said poor Jenny, her face anguished.

'Yes you can. Move just a little. Kiss me and move a little. That's right. Again. That's good. Now. Kiss me and move some more.'

Suddenly she began to understand, and he, by embraces, by his hands on her buttocks, his open mouth against hers, felt her growing wet.

When his climax came Jenny hadn't yet learned to follow. But she was excited and far gone and he finished her love-making with his hands while she groaned.

During the three days they spent in the huge, empty hotel, lying in a carved black bed on sheets which were so coarse that they scraped her skin, love-making absorbed both of them. They spent a good part of every day, the long Roman afternoons as well as the hot nights, locked together. Jenny learned quickly. She had inherited her passionate sexual nature from her vanished mother, and a grandfather who had been active in his wife's bed and the beds of his female servants. He had been infamous among his staff who never said no to him; he was far too exciting. Jenny did not know and nor did her father that there were illegitimate aunts and uncles of hers all over Warwickshire.

Guy Bowden had none of his father's ardour and never once suspected the sexual hunger that flowed in Jenny's veins. All Charles did was wake her up. She learned to come, to reach her climax quickly or slowly and, later, in harmony with his own. She was in that state of sexual pleasure when she couldn't have enough, was ready day or night, and

243

Charles took her over and over again. The more they made love, as all sensualists know, the more they wanted to.

They left The Royal Bristol – Jenny felt sentimental about the enormous funereal bed – and took a train, third-class this time, sitting on slatted, wooden seats. They were bound for Naples. Jenny looked like a rose which had opened in the Italian heat; Charles more haggard than usual. In the looking-glass when he was shaving he grimaced. He knew that drained look. It was a paradox that women in sex burgeoned and men looked so played out. Even Charles thought a night without sex would be a relief.

They arrived in a Naples blinding in sun and beauty, and walked, leaving their suitcases at the station, down to the long white promenade and the cornflower sea. They sat on a bench and simply gazed. Jenny, of course, uttered the inevitable.

'See Naples and die.' Charles, head back and letting the sun skewer him to the seat, gave a groan. 'Haven't you ever heard that, Charles? It means –'

'Yes, I know. The Italians also made a joke about it when Naples was riddled with cholera and typhoid. Now stop chatting, my darling, it's like being married to a myna bird.'

'I've never heard of those.'

'They're talking starlings. The girls keep them in cages in Burma. The birds imitate every sound one makes. One of them used to say "Charles, Charles!" to me like some elderly aunt.'

'Girls in Burma! Did you –'

'Of course not. Pipe down and enjoy the sun. I'm thinking.'

'Okay. I'll think too.'

She lay back and shut her eyes. But she didn't think. She could only feel.

'What time is the boat?' he finally asked.

'Two o'clock.'

'We'd better buy some cheese.'

Jenny agreed. Since arriving in Italy, their lunch had consisted of bread, slices of Bel Paese, swigs of bottled water

244

and now and again a peach in a paper bag. Jenny always wished there was more cheese, but it was expensive and she filled up with the long loaf of bread, tearing pieces off as if she were starving. They found some shops and returned with their picnic, to sit and stare at the bay which had entranced the world since Grecian days. There was no happier girl in Italy.

Charles, sated with sex, embraced by the sun, was thoughtful. Like Englishmen in Italy for the last two hundred years, including Shelley and Keats, Charles had been doing sums on the backs of envelopes. He had scribbled on menus and the margin of the *Corriere della Sera*. He calculated that his Stratford winnings and the money from the diamond clips would last if he was clever and careful for a good month. After that, who knew? He believed religiously in luck. Perhaps Guy Bowden would telegraph Jenny some cash. He'd have to be told where she was, of course, but Charles could persuade her to do that. Another possibility was that Charles might win some money. At present he felt no inclination to gamble, his child-wife absorbed him. Making love to her was delicious, her response exciting. And he'd never been to Italy before.

Mick Gould had been posted to Southern Italy at the end of the war after adventurous times in India. He'd told Charles about Capri.

'We both know the East and all that, but Capri really *is* paradise.' The whole of this Italian trip had come about because of Mick Gould's description of the island. 'Tiberius got up to all kinds of terrible things in Capri. Delights and debauches,' Mick Gould had said. 'When you go there – if you go there – you'll never forget the place.'

The steamer they boarded for Capri, a *vaporetto*, belched black smoke and looked as if it had been battered in the North Sea for the entire duration of the war. It was the most dilapidated-looking craft that Charles had ever seen; there wasn't an inch of its surface which was painted or decently repaired. It smelled overpoweringly of oil, and Charles and Jenny sat on deck, carefully out of the lee of the wind and consequent stink, on seats of the similarly excruciating kind they'd suffered on the train from Rome. Jenny cared not at all, snuggling up to him, winding her thin arm under his, exclaiming at the blueness of the sea, the towering shape of Vesuvius – Jenny had once seen a film called *The Last Days of Pompeii* – 'Did you know there's a *dog* all in lava, Charles?' It was like Jenny, English to her fingertips, to mention the dog and not the people.

The boat bucketed across a sea which was surprisingly rough for the Bay of Naples. The wind was sportive. As the island came gradually close they saw it was much larger than they had imagined, its mountains climbing to the sky, grey rocks like pointing fingers scattered in the sea. The houses were balanced on the mountain sides, even on what must be the most precipitous slopes.

The small crowd which always gathers when a boat comes into harbour was hanging about as they came to land. Charles wondered how on earth he was going to find the *pensione* recommended by Mick Gould as 'really cheap. And if you roll up your sleeves and bargain, you'll get it cheaper.'

As Charles, with Jenny still hanging on his arm, walked down the gangplank, they heard a raised voice chanting: 'Pensione Williams! Pensione Williams!' A man in uniform of musical-comedy style, with gold braid and gold buttons, continued to call: 'Pensione Williams!'

'That's the one Mick told me about,' said Charles. 'Good, we're going to get a lift.'

To Jenny's delight the uniformed man picked up their luggage and handed them into an open, horse-drawn carriage. He gave his horse a flick of the whip, and set off up a winding road which climbed a mountain.

While his wife exclaimed over flowers, houses, glimpses of blue sea and steep falls of land, Charles was wondering whether the driver was a porter or the owner, and whether, as Mick Gould had said, there was no human being in Italy from waiter to prince who wasn't glad of a tip. When they arrived it turned out that their driver was the owner and that Mick Gould was perfectly right.

Pensione Williams, named after a Welsh owner long forgotten, was a white house set in a garden of palms and bougainvillaea; modest, clean, unexceptional and destined to be Jenny Bowden's idea of paradise.

She was in a state bordering on bliss during the entire time she and Charles spent there. With seventeen-year-old recklessness, she looked at the panorama of an endless future and accepted joy as a right. Glorious happiness was something every girl, thought Jenny, achieved sooner or later: she was just lucky that it was sooner. She resembled the roses which spilled from windows, opened in gardens, hung down from walls; she flowered. She was sorry for every woman in the world because they were not married to Charles. Beautiful and unheeding, spoiled from birth, she was religiously certain that she must always have her own way, and that having it would of course make her happy. Nothing could stop this inevitable process. Her little craft, shoved on by Charles, had sailed on to an ocean of delight. She had only known unhappiness once since she was born – she did not remember her mother leaving her – and that was when her father had separated her from Charles. Now like a woman after childbirth wondering why she is hoarse from groaning an hour ago, Jenny forgot her father, her anger and her suffering.

The three weeks they stayed at Pensione Williams – she had no idea that that was all it was going to be – were Jenny's crown of joy. She was never out of the company of an alluring and enigmatic man who was, she was certain, as madly in love as she was. She was learning, day by day, all kinds of new sexual joys. Every afternoon when they returned from lying on the tiny beach picnicking on bread and cheese under the shade of a rock, they climbed the high mountain to the hotel, lay in their room with the venetian blinds drawn and made love. What she enjoyed most was to lie on her side so that Charles could penetrate her from the back; she liked the sensation of being in a way attacked, the feeling of helplessness, the moist joys and the knowledge that as he grasped her with large hands and pressed into her with his seemingly huge self, she could not escape.

247

The Italian weather was scorchingly hot. They lay in the striped shade from the shutters, absorbed in pleasures of the flesh and – on Jenny's part only – a helpless surrender of the heart.

In the evenings she changed into one of the costly white dresses her father had bought her. She had a New Look dress of fine lawn, with huge skirts and a tiny laced-in waist – she looked like a Monet painting. They walked arm in arm to the piazza and ordered a drink each, which they had to make last for an hour. The evening was still hot, the stones of the walls of the old church were radiant from the day's heat. Old women in black went to pray, a bell rang out from the campanile. Charles and Jenny sat idling.

Then he took her down narrow streets which smelled of coffee or roasting veal to the restaurant where, at Mick Gould's suggestion, they had arranged with the owner to eat every night. 'You'll get a set price and save a fortune,' said Mick. 'Always bargain in Italy. They think you're a fool if you don't.'

Every night Charles and Jenny had the same meal: escalope of veal, pasta, thin, white, almost waterish wine. They finished with pistachio ice-cream. People danced in a space the size of a pocket handkerchief, but Charles refused to.

'I've never been able to dance,' he said, listening to a record playing a treacly Italian song.

'Of course you can. *All* men can.'

'Not this one.' Almost, but not quite, he added there was no need. For Charles, dancing was only useful as a step towards a seduction.

Jenny nibbled at the biscuit which had been on the top of his ice-cream. She had eaten her own and was trying to make this one last. She was still hungry. Charles watched her when she was not aware of it; he knew most of the Italian men in Capri looked at Jenny every time she walked by. English girls were a rarity and her radiant Anglo-Saxonness glowed. He knew that particular aura; it came from sexual delight.

He gestured for more coffee and said with a certain vagueness, 'Have you thought about your father at all?'

248

'Of course not.'

'Isn't that a very hard-hearted reply, my love?'

'No, it isn't. It's natural.'

'Nature's pretty hard-hearted too. Why haven't you thought about him? I have.'

'I don't see why. He doesn't like you.' That made him laugh.

'Do you only think about the people who like you? That must limit your range.'

'Most people like me,' was the flippant reply. 'And anyway, we're talking about Daddy. No, I don't think about him. I think about *you* all the time.'

She was unaware that there were certain times for speeches like that. She was wonderfully ignorant of how men's minds worked. It was clear that she had never studied her father and was totally ignorant of masculine psychology.

'Yes, my love, I know,' he said kindly. 'But we've hurt your father a great deal. I am sure I have made an enemy of him. However, he still loves you, and I begin to think you must write and tell him where you are. He must be worried sick.'

'You've never said that before,' said Jenny, pouting. She had put her father out of her mind. She refused to have a bad conscience about him. He had done the unforgivable thing, tried to rob her of the wonderful man beside her; it did not give her a single pang of guilt to think of what she may or may not have done to Guy Bowden. He deserved it. When they did return home, whenever that impossible day came, she could always get him back . . .

'Write to him tomorrow,' said Charles, fixing her with a look which meant what he said.

'I don't want to. And I wouldn't know what to say.'

He laughed again. She often made him laugh when she did not mean to do so and she always looked annoyed when that happened, which pleased him more. He loved to see her cross. Everything about her, her looks, her short-syllabled upper-class voice, her reactions, her worship, pleased him in a patronizing, fond, indulgent, doting way. His reaction to her was not unlike her father's.

'If you don't write, I shall, and you can imagine how a letter from me would go down. You must do as I say, Jenny.'

She obeyed him. The following morning she spent an hour sitting on the bed in her bathing dress – they always walked down to the beach with bathing things under their clothes so that it was easy to go into the water at once. She sat, wearing a cotton two-piece bathing dress bought in Stratford, brown and white and with far skimpier lines than she'd ever worn before, and sighed over the letter. She tore up several versions and finally came up with something which Charles said wouldn't really do.

'It's very brusque.'

'He doesn't want a lot of mush,' said Jenny and didn't see her husband raise his eyebrows.

He took the letter, which was about as bald and childish as it could be, and rewrote it but kept enough of her style for it to be believable. He added a few sentences which Jenny grumbled over. Things like, 'I'm thinking of you.' And 'I hope you are not too angry with me.' And 'When we see each other, you will forgive me, Daddy, because I never meant to hurt you.' Things like that.

Somehow she couldn't argue when Charles made her sit down in their room before going out to dinner and painstakingly write out the letter, giving their Capri address and ending more affectionately than Jenny had planned.

'All you've put is "Love". I think you should say "With much love".'

*'Oh all right.'*

Jenny finished off the letter. It was sealed and stamped and posted that evening. After some time had passed and no answer came, all she said was: 'I don't know why you made me write. It was an abs'l'te waste of time.'

Days went by. They swam, and each day they grew browner, like slowly toasting bread, losing the pale look of English skins. Charles's swarthy skin and its sun-tanned surface from his years in the East protected him, and he grew dark as an Indian. But Jenny's skin burned an angry scarlet, and only after the first week did it settle down to begin turning a honey colour. They scraped together enough money to go for a boat ride into what was called the Blue Cave under the rocks, where the water shone as if it were made of ground-up sapphires. The island was almost too beautiful, with mountains of changing colours – pink, lavender, silver, yellowish grey. The sea was so brilliant that it looked as if the light came from under the surface. They swam ten times a day, and when Jenny licked her fingers during their beach picnics, her skin tasted salty.

It was a long, slow climb after lunch to get back to the *pensione*. They were dazed by hours on the beach, by the long swims out to the jutting rocks and back, and by the cheap wine which they drank to wash down the monotonous diet of cheese and bread. They climbed in silence, the Caprisi sun beating on their backs as if with rods, and Jenny sweated and counted the steps cut into the mountain and inefficiently paved with strips of flaking wood. She longed to be back in their shaded bedroom where they would make love.

At last they came to the top of the cliff, and stood looking down at the blinding blue of the sea. It was very calm that day, the cicadas thrummed like machines, the air smelled of herbs.

'Look at that little boat, darling,' murmured Jenny in a sun-drenched voice. Across the sea, coming slowly towards the beach, was a craft still the size of a child's toy; they watched as it came nearer. They saw the rise and fall of four oars, and saw, too, that the sides of the boat were painted in blue and brown and white. Ulysses had sailed in boats like that.

'Come along, my love. You'll get sunstroke.'

She sighed. 'Do you think we could live here for ever?'

As they went into the hotel cooled by marble floors and dark green blinds, the owner was leaning on the desk, talking on the telephone in Italian. Giving them a smile which flashed with gold teeth, he passed them a telegram.

Jenny gave a sort of gasp after Charles had torn it open and shown it to her:

251

Essential you return at once.

Lisa.

*

It was one thing to run off and marry in the flamingly romantic tradition of Gretna Green, another to trail home to England without a penny. Charles hadn't mentioned their money troubles when they left Capri; it wasn't until they were on the train from Dover to London that he told her they couldn't afford a proper breakfast. Jenny had the unaccustomed experience of sitting facing two people eating bacon and eggs, toast and marmalade, and resenting every mouthful they took. All Charles could afford was a pot of tea.

For the first time, he got on her nerves. Lack of food did not worry him; he drank his tea, glanced meaningfully at the two people opposite them and winked at Jenny. But she starvingly watched two stout middle-aged travellers leaving half their breakfast, and resented him. He wasn't looking after her. He could at least have kept a few shillings to feed her this morning.

Ahead of her there wasn't a thing to look forward to.

No longer drugged by sex and sun and salt, Jenny's thoughts turned dispassionately towards her father. It was boring to realize how cross he was going to be, even though there was nothing he could do any more. She was a married woman and he'd just have to get used to it. She would have to see him and smooth things over. The point is, thought Jenny with unconscious cruelty, I need my allowance.

When the telegram arrived Jenny had been frightened at first – perhaps it meant her father was ill. What had most alarmed her had been the idea that if he was she'd have to look after him, which would take her away from Charles. She didn't say so. It was not the kind of thought Charles would approve of. She had begun to discover he was not always the passionate and indulgent lover; now and again he disliked something she said or did. He had told her once that she was selfish.

'But I'm always thinking of *you*!' cried Jenny.

'That is not what I am talking about.'

When Charles had seen the sheer fright in her face as she read the telegram, he comforted her; he was sure it wasn't bad news.

'I suppose your sister got our address from Daddy,' said Jenny, cheering up at once. 'I put it on my letter to him, didn't I? Do you think he made her send it to get me back?'

'People don't "make" Lisa do anything.'

'My father's a very determined man,' said Jenny, who was jealous.

Charles didn't argue. He was not telling the truth when he reassured her about the telegram. He saw no point in having a hysterical girl on his hands before it was absolutely necessary, but it was very probable that Guy Bowden *was* ill. Jenny's father was the only person who'd been insulted and wounded by the marriage. Lisa had been furious but she was a hardy young woman and knew very well he'd turn up again, not only because he would run out of money but because he was fond of her.

It had not occurred to Charles that he'd left his sister without enough to live on, or that her feelings for him might cool. He was as sure of her as of his life.

Is Bowden dangerously ill? thought Charles. Or planning some move against me? He did not underestimate his father's tough-minded friend, his own considerable enemy. Guy was capable of some eccentric belief that Charles had eloped with the girl against her will. After all, Jenny was a minor. He remembered Bowden's murderous face at Whitefriars. He could well use clever lawyers and be willing to spend a lot of money to break up the marriage; what he'd try to do was impossible, but, damn it, Jenny would get very upset.

At Victoria they squeezed into a telephone booth together and Charles rang The Treasure Box. Lisa answered.

'Oh. You're back.'

'We're at Victoria Station.'

'How's Jenny?'

'Very brown,' said Charles, looking at his wife whose radiance had disappeared when Capri faded across the bay of Naples.

'What's happened, Lou?' He waited for the worst.

'I can't tell you on the telephone. Are you catching the 9.10?' Lisa had become very Stratfordian.

'Yes, but surely you can –'

'No, Charles. See you both at Crocker Road around twelve. I must go. 'Bye.'

Charles rang off, mystified. He reported the conversation and saw by Jenny's sulky face that she still believed his assurances about her father's health. All she was thinking was that she loathed returning home. Supposing the man's dead, thought Charles, as they boarded yet another uncomfortable train. Would she feel guilty? It was hard to know what Jenny would feel. She had fallen into a cross sleep and looked more childlike than usual.

The train hurried through the Oxfordshire countryside, while Charles asked himself with growing concern how this girl would take tragedy. Until now all she'd known had been indulgent love. It would be terrible, a crime, if by marrying her he had killed her father. People did die of anger and heartbreak, it was perfectly possible. God, he thought, I should have left her alone. He loved her well enough . . . but that was never enough. He stared out of the smutty window, then looked at his watch, thinking how slowly time crawled when you were afraid.

He tried to put his mind to practical things. Work, for instance. Would Philip Ashmore take him back? Unlikely. He'd behaved badly, although he'd written to Richard Pensamonn and to Ashmore and apologized. Work, he thought for a second time. Mick Gould had once suggested Charles might serve behind the bar at The Duck; young actors did sometimes. I'm nearly thirty-three, he thought. It wouldn't suit my style, whatever that is.

Jenny grew steadily more disagreeable as the diesel made its rural way towards Stratford. She had no idea that in Charles's mind her father was either in Warwick Hospital having suffered a paralyzing stroke, or dead and buried. All Jenny thought was that having to go and see him was a beastly idea. He'd be angry and nasty, she knew he would.

He'd be horrible about Charles; she dreaded and guessed what he might say. She never doubted she could smooth things over and get her father back to his previous state of devotion.

It was only when Charles was walking with her away from the station towards the flat that it suddenly hit him – Jenny had never been to the Crocker Road flat in her life. Even when they had eloped he'd arranged to meet her in the town out of reach of his and Lisa's poverty. For a moment he forgot the image in his mind of Guy Bowden huddled in a hospital bed and unable to speak. He nerved himself up to see the look on Jenny's face when they turned into the long road with its lines of workmen's cottages.

He expected a look of shocked disbelief as he halted at Number 27, saying heartily, 'This is it.'

But Jenny was beyond caring where they were going or how dismal it was. She followed him up the steps of the house and Charles opened the front door. South American music flowed down the stairs to greet them.

'Your sister must be home,' she said.

'Or the landlady. She likes Edmundo Ros. We're on the first floor.'

They climbed the stairs to the throbbing rhythm of dark, graceful dancers wearing white, stiffened frills. The door of the sitting-room flew open.

Lisa saw two strangers coming towards her. In this England of white faces, their suntan was a shock – a disturbing reminder of hot Burmese nights, of scented, quickly-dead flowers, of the exotic, the unobtainable. Charles, throwing down the suitcase, put out his arms and Lisa sprang into them; brother and sister hugged each other. When he released her she greeted Jenny who was standing beside them looking foolish.

'I'm sorry, I should have kissed you first,' said Lisa with a slight laugh, bending towards her. Jenny, who never kissed anybody but her father in the past and her husband in bed, awkwardly offered a nut-brown cheek.

Lisa accompanied the travellers into the sitting-room

which struck Charles as very much worse than he re-membered: his eyes were still looking for the brightness of Italy. Standing on the fumed oak table was a large unsuitable vase of red roses. Lisa took Jenny's coat which was crushed with travelling, and remarked that Charles's hair was too long. She went into the kitchen to make some tea. He sat down, pulling Jenny beside him on to the rock-hard divan. His sister, he thought, seemed quite cool for somebody about to announce fatal news. I suppose she doesn't like to blurt it out at once.

When she returned with the tray he waited until she sat down and then said, 'Well? What's happened? It is Jenny's father, isn't it?'

Jenny gave a gasp, realizing what he'd been thinking all along and cried in a loud trembling tone, *'Why did you say he was all right?'*

Lisa looked from one to the other.

'Is *that* what you thought? I'm so sorry! Of course Mr Bowden's not ill. When I rang to get your address he sounded perfectly all right.' That wasn't true. He'd been as rude as a well-bred man could be to the daughter of an old friend.

'You rang Daddy!'

'I thought he may have heard from you. It was a possi-bility, although I hadn't heard a word except for that two-line card from Rome,' said Lisa not without edge.

'What did my father say?'

'He gave me your address.'

'I suppose he's still furious.'

'Yes.'

Jenny scowled. How dreary everything had become; this awful flat, the sister who had a tinge of Charles at his most schoolmasterish, the prospect of seeing her enraged father, the frightening prospect of being poor.

'What on earth did you bring us back here for?' asked Charles. He did not say 'we'd have had to come back anyway, the money was running out.' He did not even think it, since somewhere in Charles the goddess of luck was whispering that she might, she just might, have smiled on him in Capri.

'Well, I'll tell you,' said his sister looking straight at him. 'I rather think you and I are going to be rich.'

Perdita Smith was glueing minute Victorian figures, crimson, navy blue, cinnamon yellow, to matchstick-sized wooden bases. She had what she called fiddley fingers; nobody would know this looking at them, they were as thick as chipolata sausages. But it was pleasant to watch her find an antique key and fit it into an ancient lock, or clean scrolls of brass on a box for eighteenth-century letters, or in this case place a soldier, flourishing a sword no thicker than a thread of cotton, on to his steadying base. She glanced up to see her employee coming into the shop.

'That was a long lunch hour.'

'I'm sorry. I'll work an extra hour this evening.'

'Good.'

Perdita never refused Lisa's amends. She watched the girl hanging her coat and hat on a peg in the cubby-hole. Lisa came meekly over to join her.

'Mrs Smith —' she began.

'Mm?' Perdita was no longer paying her any attention. She had picked up a tiny figure of a woman with voluminous skirts, a shouting face and extended arm.

'She's lost a hand, poor bitch,' she remarked.

Lisa looked at the figure. 'Is there anything we can do about it?'

'You use the editorial or royal "we". I take it that means yourself? Well, why not? What about making the lady a nice, new hand before one of our customers hoves into view?'

Lisa had done such repairs to toy theatre performers once or twice in the past. She went off to fetch her paint-box, scissors, some fine cardboard and a tube of glue. Perdita put the shouting woman down in front of her.

'The most enjoyable part of the toy theatres, I always think, was the lighting. That was where the fun came in. See that tin torch? All we need is a wick floating in oil and these

257

little windows' – she reached over and demonstrated – 'would flash blue or red or green. Later, with any luck, the entire performance would go up in smoke. Toy theatres were always catching fire. That provided some drama in the nursery.'

'How horribly dangerous.'

'Not at all. The parents or the nursemaid poured a jug of water over the flames and that was that. The only pity of it was a lot of the characters were burnt to a cinder.'

She picked a turbaned sultan from a medley of tiny objects which lay inside a carved, up-ended proscenium arch. She examined the sultan and returned him to his friends, selecting in his place a handsome elephant.

'And he,' said Perdita who never called animals 'it', 'has lost his tusk.'

'It looks as if I'm going to be busy.'

'You don't appear displeased.'

'I like this kind of work.'

'You're not bad at it.'

Perdita was seated on the high stool over which her stout person bulged; fat thighs, thick legs, and the concealments of voluminous woollen skirts and, beneath them, ancient petticoats. Lisa admired her employer's way of dressing which was as uncompromising as that of Queen Mary.

'I have some news,' said Lisa. She began to draw a tiny hand on her drawing-block, and then measured it against the left hand of the shouting woman. Her drawing was too large.

'Don't tell me. That scallywag of a brother has turned up again?' Like every other woman, Perdita liked Charles.

'As a matter of fact he's just arrived back from Italy.'

'Oh he has, has he?' said Perdita with a guffaw. 'Bringing Bowden's gal in tow.'

'Of course. She's his wife.'

Another louder guffaw. Perdita was not uncharitable but she couldn't help being amused. She could well imagine Guy Bowden's rage. She could also picture Lisa, the good-for-nothing brother and the debby Bowden daughter all crammed into that hole-in-the-corner at Crocker Road.

'You'll be asking for a rise in salary, I suppose?'

'No, I won't.'

'Oho, you talk big but you're soft over that young man. Doting sisters aren't good for big brothers, you know.'

She lined up the cast of the play. A raggedy lot. Half a dozen players at least were missing from the production of *Aladdin and his Wonderful Lamp*. The genie, typically, had vanished into thin air. But where were the smugglers and some of the sultan's harem? What *did* people do with their possessions? wondered Perdita. They did not respect them. She often brooded over who had owned a broken toy or jewel, where it had once been treasured, what child or eager girl, long dead or now very old, had handled it and loved it. The past moved her. Now and again she became attached to something she'd bought, and took it upstairs to her flat where it was once again beloved.

Not the toy theatre, however. She intended Lisa to put it in order, then she would place it in the window, dead-centre. Londoners bought things like this and they were streaming down to Stratford, thank heaven. Lisa continued to draw the little hand and after a while was satisfied with the results. She went to fetch an egg-cup filled with water, pulled up her stool to begin to paint, leaning over intently, her face hidden by her hair.

'Mrs Smith . . .' she said for the second time that morning.

'Isn't it time you called me Perdita? Silly name but it's my own.'

'I'd like to.'

'Go on, then,' encouraged Lisa's employer, blowing dust off young Aladdin, lamp in hand.

'I have some news.'

'Yes, yes, so you said. Your brother's home.'

'Something else. Something very –' Lisa looked up from her painting – 'something surprising.' And she told Perdita about her father's suitcase. Perdita whistled like a schoolboy.

'Have I got this right? A piece of luggage appeared from somewhere east of Suez and you found some share certificates which may turn out to be valuable?'

'They *are*. Peter recognized them, he'd read about Lennox Aero recently, and he knew De Havilland's want to buy the company. We rang a broker Peter knows and Peter drove into Warwick and gave him the shares and – and it looks as if Charles and I may be quite well off.'

'De Havilland! You certainly will be. How many shares did your father own?'

'Two thousand.'

'Holy St Patrick! And you say it was Peter Lang who knew what they were?'

'Entirely Peter. I was for throwing everything away. Honestly, Perdita, the stuff was all so old and dusty and depressing. A muddle and a mess. But Peter insisted on going through every bit of paper, I thought he was being so boring. And he found them! He's so clever.'

'Wouldn't say that. He's thorough. Exact. He has a good memory which passes for brains. Well, well, well, you're the sly one. Why didn't you spiflicate me just now when I ticked you off for being late?'

Lisa looked ingenuous. 'But I *was* late.'

'If that had been me come into a fortune, I'd have been bellowing through the door. Aren't you excited?'

'I can't take it in.'

'Oh,' said Perdita, looking her up and down. 'You will. This calls for a cup of tea.'

Lisa regretfully put down her paint-brush and went out to make the fourth of Perdita's seven daily pots of tea.

Yes, she thought, it is exciting. But she felt cautious. She had lived for months in Crocker Road and before that in a borrowed flat and before that again had travelled across Burma with Charles. The habit of poverty was strong. Now and then she was alarmed by the thought that Charles would lose his share of the money by gambling. Would having a young girl as his responsibility change his ways? She returned with the tea-tray.

With the toy figures now standing in line in front of her, Perdita looked like a big grey bird perched and waiting to be fed. Her hands were on her lap, her necklaces of pearl, jet and amber almost brushing her knees. She watched Lisa pouring out the tea just as she liked.

'So,' she said, taking the cup, 'you're giving me notice. I trust you will be civilized enough to give me two or three weeks before you go and buy a mink coat. Until you came along I managed alone. But now I've got used to having somebody to run about after me.'

'Why should I leave, Perdita?'

'Don't be naïve. Rich women don't work.'

'I like it here.'

'Kind of you but that won't wash. How will your mind be on your work with all that cash pumping into the bank? You will be' – Perdita savoured the phrase – 'deafened by the sound of falling coins.'

'Mrs Smith. Perdita. I don't *want* to stop working. It's a rotten idea. Why must I?'

Perdita folded her arms on her stomach. She pointed out that the whole impetus of work was the pay envelope on Saturday morning. Surely Lisa knew that by now? When your circumstances changed, and Lisa's had positively exploded, *you* changed. Impossible not to.

'Take this job, now. There is going to be no reason for you to get up at the crack of dawn and be here to open up before I come downstairs. No reason for swallowing a sandwich sitting at the counter, or running – I've seen you haring down Sheep Street to get back on time. Why should you work on Saturdays? Go to sales and return at all hours? Get your clothes filthy unpacking old boxes or sit for hours through tedious house sales because the item we're interested in comes up as Number 365? Why should you work when you don't need to?'

The shop was quiet. Somebody clopped by outside on a pony; it was not Jenny.

'*You* don't work because of the money,' Lisa finally said.

'Of course I do! That's what it's all about, shoving cash into the bank. Making a good profit. Pulling off a tricky deal and using my wits to do it. Do you think profit doesn't interest me, my child? You can't be as naïve as that?'

'I know it's what amuses you. You love to win, to judge what will sell, to snap up bargains. Now and then I've seen you make a lot of money –'

'Merely the usual margin.'

'A lot of money. And I've felt as exhilarated as I think you are. We're both a bit like my brother when he wins at poker. You're pleased when the cash comes in, but that's not the real thrill. The real bug. I've caught it too. It's buying things, risking that *your* taste is the same as other people's. It's knowing, of course, but it's gambling too. Winning now and then. I feel exactly the same.'

Perdita picked up a horseman who brandished his cotton-thread sword at her. She balanced him on the palm of her hand.

'Are you saying you really want to stay? There's a turn-up for the book.'

When Lisa went into the flat that evening she found her sister-in-law had already created a staggering untidiness. The sitting-room was littered. The kitchen piled with dirty plates. Jenny was sitting on her bed among half-unpacked bags doing her fingernails. She wore a turquoise-coloured woollen dress and had just washed her hair which was the colour of pale butter. There was a scent of Elizabeth Arden floating in the air.

'Hello,' she said, with an embarrassed smile. 'Charles has gone out. Wouldn't say where. Only that it was to be a surprise.'

Lisa looked dubious. He must be spending money already. She went into the sitting-room, put down her coat and shopping-basket and wondered what he was up to. She didn't need to wonder long, for almost at once she heard his step taking the linoleum-covered stairs two at a time.

'Lisa, Jenny. I want you.' The voice had an imperious tone. 'Come into the sitting-room. I've got news.'

He pushed his sister and his wife ahead of him in a bustling manner. They exchanged looks.

'You'd better pack,' he said.

Lisa frowned and Jenny wailed.

'But I've only just begun to *un*pack!'

'Charles,' said Lisa, 'what have you done?' He had the winning face, the extra dimension. It was worse than she'd thought.

'Merely arranged for us to live elsewhere. Until we buy a house, that is.'

'To live where?'

'Aha. That's the surprise. Now let's get started. How quickly can you girls throw a few things into a case?'

'You're not suggesting we go now!' Lisa glared.

Jenny only gasped, 'But Charles!'

It was to his sister and not to his wife that he spoke. 'Lou. I am not staying here one more hour. As far as I'm concerned, Crocker Road never happened. Thanks to you and Peter and a million to one chance, we have money. So just pack a toothbrush. We'll come back and get the rest of the stuff to-morrow.'

'But *where* are we going?' repeated Lisa, fascinated and exasperated. Her brother's face still wore the winning half-smile but the lines in his cheeks were deeper as if from suffering. When had he suffered? From his father's rejection? From the terrible war in Burma about which he used to speak with casual references and now never mentioned? From detested poverty?

'Until we get a decent home, I've taken us a suite of rooms at The Shakespeare.'

# 13

'That's crazy,' said Lisa.

'Marvellous,' breathed Jenny.

Charles, looking complacent, said he had spoken to the manager, seen the rooms and made the bookings. The rooms were attractive and the price wasn't too bad. He again addressed his remarks to Lisa and although she hadn't replied he behaved as if she had.

'No. We are not going to take things slowly, Lou. Get it all on paper, hang about here and finally move out when everything's organized. The broker is just about to sell our shares. That's right, isn't it?'

'Yes – but –'

'But nothing. We are not going to be civilized about clearing out because I don't feel civilized.'

She looked about. At the table covered with whitened rings from plates which were too hot and had marked it years before. At a sideboard where two moulded bottles in a tarnished holder were supposed to hold oil and vinegar and contained only a sediment she'd never been able to remove. At green, pre-war curtains which time and penury had turned to streaked yellowish grey. At the gas fire with broken burners like the stumps of decaying teeth.

'I'll fetch a nightdress,' she said.

Lisa had already informed the landlady that Charles was due back from a holiday abroad and 'was bringing his wife'. Mrs Ellerton hadn't known that her favourite was married, was offended by being given no information and was dying to ask more. She was quite excited at the thought of seeing Charles again but did not show it, as it would give his sister satisfaction. At the news of his coming return all she'd said, in a not particularly pleasant intonation, was 'Oh yes?'

When Charles went downstairs he found her at the kitchen table, some potatoes in front of her, reading the newspaper on which she'd begun to spread the peelings. She stood up and held out her hand.

'Nice to have you back,' she said, in a very different voice to her usual one. 'My, you're brown. Been getting a bit of sun, that's obvious. Your sister says your wife's here too. I'm looking forward to meeting her. Anything I can do for you?'

She thought how handsome he was. In the months since the Whitfields had lived in her house they had never asked for a thing. She wouldn't have put herself out to lend a safety pin to Lisa, but Charles was another matter. She'd always hoped he'd ask her for what she called a cup of sugar.

'I'm afraid I have some rather sad news,' Charles said. He could no more give notice brusquely to the middle-aged woman whose house he loathed than he could have been unkind to a child. He treated the slatternly landlady as if she were young and beautiful. He was not aware that he deepened his voice and that its tone caressed; such things were part of Charles like his dark hair and dark eyes. They were the essence of the man. He explained that his wife, his sister and he himself were leaving tonight. They'd pay two months' rent instead of giving notice. He was very sorry they had to do so unexpectedly. He didn't say why, and again Mrs Ellerton didn't ask any questions, this time from a kind of shyness.

'I want to thank you for all you've done for us,' he said, pressing her hand. She'd done nothing, but they both thought she had. When she said goodbye, her eyes brimmed.

He waited by the front door for his wife and sister. Jenny's expression, when she came up to her husband and he took her little suitcase, reminded Lisa of a spaniel she'd had as a girl. That look of hers must be a trial, thought Lisa.

The trio set off down Crocker Road for the last time.

At the hotel they were shown luxurious rooms, white walls branched with beams. Every bedroom in the hotel was named after a Shakespearian play. Charles had a good deal of fun over his and Jenny's room, which was *As You Like It*. Lisa's was *The Winter's Tale*, and a neighbouring bathroom was called *King Lear*.

Dinner was festive – it should have been baked beans on toast and stewed apples. Lisa had left the food on the table in the flat. She wondered if Mrs Ellerton would eat their supper and spared a thought for the landlady's doleful face when Charles had said goodbye.

Peter joined them at the end of the meal, full of news. The broker had telephoned and wanted to see Charles and Lisa tomorrow. He had the official price they had been offered for their shares.

'Of course he wouldn't tell me exactly how much – he said it was confidential – but it looks as if it will be very good. You have to settle things tomorrow, there is no time to lose,' said Peter.

Charles ordered more wine. Jenny and Lisa were lively, and Peter attentive and informative. It was Charles who grew quiet. The glorious subject had begun to lose its novelty. And although he liked Peter Lang, Lisa's friend couldn't make a joke to save his life. Charles wanted to be on his own, to sort out his feelings, to have a respite of solitude. He hadn't been out of Jenny's company since the day before they married. Saying he wanted a breath of air and refusing, kindly enough, to let Jenny come with him, he left the hotel.

Rain was falling. It spangled his bare head and made the pavements shine black. He walked past the Guild Chapel and down Chapel Lane, passing the New Place Gardens. He made his way without thinking towards the theatre. It was only half past nine. The play wasn't yet over, it would continue for an hour more, and as he approached the building it glowed with interior life. There was an audience crowded in there. Backstage, actors waited in the wings or stepped

266

forward to take their places on a dazzling stage. But Charles wasn't thinking of the drama, of the hypnotic power that one man born in this small town held upon the soul of the world. He was thinking about money, which since his schooldays had been his teasing companion, as coy in its appearings and vanishings as Luck herself. Money was for comfort, style, for never walking again up the stairs of Crocker Road, for freedom, gambling, women.

It made him smile to remember that his father was responsible for this change of fortune. He imagined Alec Whitfield listening gravely, years back, while one of those solicitors talked to him about Lennox Aero. 'Air transport is going to be the coming thing, Mr Whitfield, mark my words.' His father must have been impressed, and followed the suggestion. He had bought the shares, a great many of them. Later they had been pushed to the bottom of a drawer along with all the other misjudged investments. Those thick papers had been destined to change the lives of Alec Whitfield's two children. I daresay he would be pleased to know that, thought Charles, striding along. No, on reflection he wouldn't be pleased at all. It would annoy him.

Crossing the Bancroft, the lawns beginning to squelch under fine, steady rain, he turned into the theatre on an impulse. He knew the exhibition would have been stacked away before tonight's performance, but thought he'd go up to the Circle to look at where it would be displayed tomorrow. Maybe peer into a cupboard at the costumes. In a moment of nostalgia for the fun of working in a theatre, he went up the stairs to the Circle foyer.

It was a shock to see that the familiar track running below the ceiling had vanished. The Circle was empty, to Charles doubly so because he realized the exhibition was gone. For a moment it emphasized the very nature of theatre: impermanent, quick-fading. He knew it was absurd to feel disappointed.

The elderly usherette known in the theatre as Aunty Babs went by, smiling at him and clearly thinking he still worked here.

'What's happened to the exhibition, Aunty?'

'It finished last week, Mr Whitfield. Weren't you here?' said the woman with her innocent, old smile. She walked off with her armful of programmes.

Charles hesitated. Through the closed doors to the auditorium he heard the unmistakeable raised and ringing voices of actors. Back in this familiar place, he realized he had missed it and wondered if he should have a word with the general manager. He'd sent a letter to Philip Ashmore, with apologies for his sudden leaving 'owing to a family crisis' and thanking him for the opportunity of working for the Memorial Theatre. He'd written another, warmer letter to Richard Pensamonn. He'd liked Richard and was sorry he had probably offended and inconvenienced him. Charles felt a twinge of conscience; a desire to re-establish himself in his own eyes if not in theirs. His new circumstances demanded that.

He went through the pass door. The corridor was dark but Philip Ashmore's office at the far end on the right had a door open and a square of light shone out.

Standing there was an apparition. It was a woman in Renaissance costume with masses of curled russet hair, her throat and brow shining with pearls. She stood so still and looked so extraordinary that she could have been a fifteenth-century ghost. The light enhanced the monstrous, billowing skirts, pearls, gleaming gold, silver and pink. Not moving, she watched Charles walking towards her.

He had never seen an actress in costume offstage and when he approached, her appearance was a shock. What at a distance had been magical was coarse and false, her eyes edged with thick black streaks to represent lashes, her cheeks white and crimson, her fingers covered with giant rings of gilded cardboard.

'Hello.' Her voice had a curious timbre, a sort of break in it. 'Are you calling on Phil as well?'

'I thought I might.'

'Let's call together. I know where he keeps the sherry.'

Charles and the apparition entered the office which was furnished like a Victorian drawing-room.

'I've seen you before. Didn't you work on Richard's exhibition?'

'I helped with it. I remember you too.'

'Don't lie. You haven't an idea who I am. Actors hate not to be recognized, haven't you learned that yet?'

'You're the first one I've seen in costume. Close to, that is.'

'Yes. You did gawp.'

'You must be used to that,' said Charles.

Walking across the room, she rustled and crackled. Her costume was of stiffened satin with many petticoats which made noises like dried twigs freshly thrown on a fire. Going to the cupboard she took out a decanter and two glasses, handed Charles a sherry with a ringed, white-painted hand and told him to sit down. She leaned against a chair.

'Won't you sit?' he said, half rising.

'I daren't. My underskirts are treated with double-strength starch. Worse still, Jacky's added an extra fabric which would disintegrate if I put my bottom on a chair. This is my costume for the Warkworth Castle scene. Only to be worn standing up.'

'It's very beautiful.'

'Yes,' she said, vaguely looking down gleaming expanses and crackling some more. 'It isn't bad. You've worked me out by now, have you? I am Gemma Lambert. What's your name?'

'Charles Whitfield.'

'How do you do, Charles Whitfield. If it wasn't for the underskirts I'd give you one hell of a curtsey.'

'I should like that.'

His glance went from her green-lidded, black-rayed eyes to the flush painted on her cheek-bones, up to the crown of reddish gold hair twined with pearls. She returned his look with a lazy smile. To Charles in his superstitious mood, half excited, half disturbed, she was the epitome of fortune. A figure all in gold. Sensual, scented, monstrous. An apparition indeed.

*

269

Spring had come and so, too, the journalists from London for another opening – *King Lear*, with Lewis Lockton playing the mad king for the first time. Hard-bitten newspaper writers were affected by Stratford: they wrote lyrical, moody pieces about tulips and wallflowers. Any morning a passer-by walking down Southern Lane leading to Waterside might see a press photographer conferring with a group of actors. Then he would crouch down and the players walk towards him, carefree, laughing and talking together against a background of theatre and trees.

There were a good many features in the papers about the forthcoming production, including a long interview with Lewis Lockton who talked of the last of Shakespeare's great tragedies, 'the most haunting in English literature'. It was a mountain, he said, that he felt he had to scale. 'But I may break my neck.' There were photographic studies of the star in costume, noble and tragic. And news-pictures of him in tweeds, handsome and dashing. There was also a particularly large and telling photograph of Gemma Lambert who was to play Regan. The photographer had taken a fancy to Gemma who had beguiled him for a well-spent half-hour.

April the 23rd was the traditional date of Shakespeare's birthday and also, handily, St George's Day. It was a big celebration in the town, beginning with the unfurling of the flags of the nations by their respective ambassadors. The road by the Bancroft was lined with flagpoles and at a given signal, each ambassador, sober in formal suit, tugged the cord and out fluttered his country's bright flag. This was followed by a procession through the town to Holy Trinity Church; ambassadors, actors and townsfolk all carried flowers.

Lisa and Peter were in the procession; she carried a little bunch of vivid blue scillas. At the church they lined up to wait their turn and lay the flowers at the altar steps. Daffodils, scented freesias, jonquils, out-of-season roses, bunches of quick-fading violets. Shakespeare, holding his quill pen, gazed down impassively. Lisa looked about for Polly. No sign.

If Lisa was busy with the complexities of inherited money,

Polly was absorbed by her non-existent role in *King Lear*. She was a waiting-woman again, this time to Regan. When she and Lisa happened to meet, Polly was white-faced and irritable, talked of nothing but the boredom of not having a speaking part, of long hours of rehearsal, and of the actress Gemma Lambert whom she had to 'attend', which meant standing beside her taking her cloak and on another occasion her embroidered gloves.

'A real bitch and you needn't look so holy,' said Polly. 'I grant you she can act. She's exciting as Lady Percy. But she's one of those females who loathes her own sex, particularly somebody younger than her who stands onstage at her elbow. I just wish she'd catch the 'flu with a temperature of 103° on the opening night. The rotten thing is she'd play if she was dying, and all of us would catch her filthy germs.'

'She can't be as bad as all that,' murmured Lisa. They were at The Cobweb and she thought Polly's trained voice too loud.

Much Polly cared. Her comic face was pinched. She was not sleeping well and was far too self-absorbed to share Lisa's recent good fortune.

'You're not a pro, you don't understand a word I say.'

She felt hard done by, and had only agreed to meet Lisa so that she could talk about the horror of Gemma Lambert. Her theatre friends were unamused by Polly on that subject, and she needed a new audience. Polly was also on a ferocious diet which explained her thinness, pallor and ill-temper.

Their chat over, Lisa walked with her disagreeable friend as far as the Stage Door, through which Polly ran as if either to or away from a fire. Lisa returned slowly to the shop.

Since she had told Perdita about her inheritance and said she would like to continue to work, Perdita's actions had been unmistakeable. She began to pile jobs on her one after the other with a sort of relish. She sent Lisa to a number of house sales not, as was previously her custom, for Lisa to keep an eye open for anything of interest, but with a list of specific items.

'Now. What I want are the following: some jugs and

basins, but attractively patterned, I don't like damn great roses. Look for some with geometric patterns and so on. I'd like a Garniture' – seeing Lisa's puzzled face she explained with her usual assumed patience – 'a Garniture, my child, is a clock with two matching vases. They are usually Continental, nineteenth century, and are just beginning to catch on. They can be porcelain or some kind of bronze . . . I also want some Staffordshire figures. Generals. Kings. Animals are getting popular, particularly those pairs of spaniels or pug dogs for putting on either side of the fireplace . . .'

Lisa attended four house sales and returned with one jug and basin which Perdita detested and a Staffordshire pug with a broken ear.

'There wasn't a sign of the things you asked for,' said Lisa, when Perdita registered exaggerated surprise.

'What? No chests of china?'

'I asked at the Wellesbourne sale, and they told me the family had withdrawn the china.'

Perdita looked glum. 'I begin to think I've over-estimated your talent.'

Critical and miserly, exacting and unreasonable, difficult and demanding, Perdita was never tedious. She had become rather fond of Lisa and was deeply interested in the girl's finances and the difficulties of getting things satisfactorily settled. It was Perdita who advised her to take her business to John Denham, a first-rate solicitor who had helped Perdita over such problems as buying The Treasure Box, and being sued for libel. 'The man who sued me was a hysterical actor, years ago, and we had a bit of an up-and-downer in The Falcon. All settled out of court,' said Perdita, 'thanks to Denham. Go and tell him what you want. Tell him, mind. Solicitors must do as they're told.'

John Denham had an office in Warwick in an old stone house overlooking the castle. He was small and fussy, with a slightly high voice, a long upper lip, thinning hair and a taste for grey suits. He was delighted to accept Lisa as a client and became, at once, as interested in her difficulties as Perdita. He welcomed her to his office like sun in wet weather.

'You'll see we are facing one of the thunder towers,' he said, indicating the castle's looming shape on the other side of the road. 'False perjured Clarence was connected with the family, you know. There have been many violent deaths there,' he added. 'Its history is bloodstained, Miss Whitfield. Bloodstained.'

'Isn't all history?'

'Of course. Men don't change. Or do you think they get worse?' He smiled through his spectacles. 'Talking of more cheerful things, shall we take a look at your situation vis-à-vis these shares that have just been sold?

Denham was what Lisa needed. He was intelligent and cautious; he was thorough. He liked his new client and when he saw her, his pale yellowish cheeks went slightly red. His secretary, who was very fond of him, was jealous. She was a devoted worker, had been in Denham's office for ten years, felt possessive about him and was a great snob. Even a Countess was kept waiting once when Lisa was in her boss's office.

'There is one little point, Miss Whitfield,' said Denham on her third visit, when her affairs were looking in better shape. 'I have only met your brother once, when the relevant documents had to be signed and witnessed.'

'Do you really need to see him again, Mr Denham? He does leave things to me.'

'Let us say it would be preferable,' was the reply. Lisa groaned inwardly. It wasn't easy to get Charles to do what she wanted these days. She promised to bring him the next time, and mentioned that at present her brother was house-hunting.

Jenny had been enchanted at the prospect of looking for a home of their own. When they had talked about it she told Charles that there was only one thing he must remember. 'Abs'l't'ly vital,' Jenny said. She didn't care where they lived or what kind of a house he found – provided it was far away from Whitefriars.

Charles looked down his nose. He was in the mood for mending fences, putting things right. He didn't like Jenny's

273

father, who certainly disliked him. Charles thought Bowden unpleasant and old-fashioned. But he'd taken Bowden's only child and that had been wrong. At the time Charles had found it exciting; idleness and poverty and boredom combined with Jenny's virginal charm had made it an adventure. But things had startlingly changed and he realized Bowden might now accept him as a son-in-law.

Jenny and Charles were sitting in the lounge of the hotel, having morning coffee and studying an estate agent's list of properties for sale. It was the day after the celebrations and bunting still flapped along the High Street. The sun was out, the latticed windows open. Charles chose his moment.

'We'll have to make it up with your father sooner or later, you know.'

'I wrote to him from Capri, *if* you remember,' Jenny said, martyred.

Sometimes her youth astounded him. In any case it was he who had written the letter; all Jenny had done was to copy it out in her illegible upper-class hand.

'So you did,' he said. 'And perhaps now we've broken the ice a little you could telephone. You might even go to Whitefriars to see him.'

'Charles, you are extraordinary.' She swallowed part of the long word. 'Why should I make the move? It's Daddy's turn. I wrote, didn't I? If he wants to see me he can jolly well ring *me*.'

'It isn't a game of tag.' He received no reply but a sulky face. 'He may still be very hurt, Jenny. About the way we ran off.'

She raised her eyebrows as far as her hairline. He was used to her adoring and biddable. Now she wore an expression he hadn't seen before.

'I might remind you, I might remind you that he forbade me to leave the house. He practically locked me in. That first night after he'd seen us in the car he *would* have locked my bedroom door, only I locked myself in instead.'

He tried to keep a straight face.

She continued to smoulder. 'I don't forgive Daddy for

274

being so horrible, and it's extraordinary,' she repeated the word, 'that you can. Anyway I don't want to live anywhere near Whitefriars and what's more I won't.'

Charles scratched the bridge of his nose and picked up the list of houses.

She agreed later, with her old eagerness, to see 'any house anywhere provided it isn't – well, you know'.

The local estate agent, Adrian Latimer, bespectacled and sanguine, told them he was sure he could find 'a pleasant property which would suit Mr and Mrs Whitfield'. But the fact was there was no property, pleasant or otherwise. The aching shortage of houses since the war hadn't improved, there were no new houses being built and it wasn't unusual for newly-married couples to take a year or more to find anywhere to live. The shortage was serious. The Labour Party had said they had turned their backs on the 'economics of scarcity', but their boast had been absurd. Now there was more money than goods in the shops and more money than houses, which were sorely needed. The Government was using the wartime machinery of controls, but planning meant rationing. Nothing, thought Charles, was easy even when you had money in the bank.

Leaving their hotel each morning with a picnic provided by The Shakespeare's kitchen, Charles and Jenny set off in a hired car to drive through a country joyful with spring. Day after day they travelled for miles to see perhaps two houses or only one. Nothing was within the faintest reach of the unpretentious place they'd imagined. They were shown a dreary terraced house at the back of Stratford: 'Crocker Road,' said Charles. They saw an enormous flat in Coventry with seven bedrooms, a poky bathroom with a geyser and a lumbering cockroach in the kitchen.

One rainy morning they set off, determined to remain cheerful, to visit Alderman Manor. This 'spacious period Family Residence' turned out to be a Victorian Gothic manor at the other end of nowhere. As they drove up, the house loomed out of the heavy rain like a vision in one of the

275

horror films so popular during the war. It only needed frightening music. The place was enormous, with turrets and cupolas, red and yellow pseudo-Byzantine brick similar to that used for Westminster Cathedral, and gargoyles from whose gaping mouths the rain poured. The garden was a wilderness. Jenny clutched Charles's hand when he'd stopped the car.

'Don't let's go inside.'

'How can we possibly tell what it's like if we don't go and look?' said Charles. 'It may be just our cup of tea. Huge ballrooms, billiard rooms and a minstrel's gallery thrown in. Come on, Jenny, cheer up.' House-hunting had begun to entertain him. The inside of any building, palace or cottage, was never what one expected and was always engrossing. He climbed from the car, gave her his hand, and they ran towards the Gothic entrance, heads bent against the rain.

Latimer had given them the key.

'What I like is to know my clients are able to view in peace,' he'd said, meaning what he preferred was to remain comfortable in his own office. What he did not like was to listen to complaints from houseless optimists turned into pessimists.

Charles unlocked the door and they entered an enormous, vaulted hall straight from a horror movie. He peered into the dining-room which had broken stained-glass windows. He laughed at a carved staircase and an outsized spider's web. Emerging from the house he noticed a further building surrounded by the withered remains of last year's weeds. He went over to look in through a dusty window – Jenny was too small to see – and reported: 'Four sarcophagi. It must be a private chapel. I say! I wonder who they were. We must ask. Nobility? Midland grocers? Whoever they were, they're still hanging about keeping an eye on their house. Do look at the table and the candlestick, Jenny! I'll lift you up.'

But she had run through the rain. Perplexed, he followed her. She was already inside the car.

'What is it, darling?'

'I'm cold.' Her teeth were chattering. He reached for her hand.

'Poor girl, you're like ice. You hate all this tagging around, don't you?'

'It isn't that, it's the house. It's haunted. Don't laugh at me, I tell you, it *is*.'

Charles did not laugh at all, asked her no questions and drove away from the grotesque building, leaving it to the rain and the foxes. Nobody who had lived in Burma could disbelieve in the presence of ghosts; that country was possessed by them. By the 'nats', as spirits were called, of murdered women, of forests, of rivers where they dragged travellers and horses to their death. Once Charles had woken suddenly to see a huge tree outside his uncle's bungalow shaking and shivering while all the trees around it were perfectly still. No wind blew. Nobody had climbed the tree, its branches were empty. His uncle, Lisa and the servants came out to watch the strange happening and the cook, terrified, said there was a nat in the tree. While they all stood in awed silence, quite suddenly the tree became still. Charles had known a dark bungalow too. Haunted by sorrow.

The Gothic manor dispirited Jenny, and after more house-hunting without seeing anything they liked, she nearly burst into tears in the estate agent's office. It was such a rare occurrence that Charles decided they would give up the search for a while.

*King Lear* had made its mark at the theatre, but had not been the tremendous success people had expected. Lewis Lockton was impressive, but something was missing in his performance. The critics were kind but one sensed, thought Lisa, their disappointment. The next production was about to open swiftly on the mad king's heels: a comedy everybody loved and looked forward to – *Twelfth Night*. On the afternoon of the opening night Lisa finally persuaded Charles to go to Warwick and see the solicitor.

'Would you like to come too, darling?' Charles asked Jenny. The respectful way he consulted his wife surprised Lisa. It was not like him. Jenny said airily thank you very much, what an abs'l't'ly awful idea, she was going to meet Angela.

'Quite right,' agreed Charles, guessing Jenny and her friend would go to The Cobweb and hang about hoping to see some actors.

For the first time since his return from Italy, Lisa was alone with her brother. When she went to Warwick she always travelled on the diesel, but Charles now had some petrol coupons, and said he would drive them in the funereal car he'd recently bought. It was comfortable but middle-aged, with pre-war ash trays.

They set off together into the country. They were quiet when the journey began. He glanced at his sister now and then, thinking that in repose her face was melancholy. His thoughts ran on Peter Lang. Isn't he much of a lover, then? thought Charles to whom sex was as easy and necessary as bread and gambling. If Lang knew how to please her physically, she wouldn't have that strange little sadness about her. He felt tender towards her. She was pretty and brave. He understood her as he'd never completely understand his child of a wife.

Lisa looked at her watch. 'You can drive as slowly as you like, Charles. We're early and Mr Denham will only leave us hanging about in his waiting-room. His secretary is a dragon, she never offers me a cup of tea.'

'Perhaps she's jealous.'

'Oh you! Sex as the explanation of everything.'

He put out a hand and took hers and Lisa's hand reacted and pressed his back.

'Let's keep our eyes open for a house,' she said.

'Not much point, Lou. If anything is up for sale, Latimer would have offered it to us by now.'

'Not necessarily. Perdita told me there are people who prefer to sell privately. They don't want to give the agent a whacking percentage.'

'You're getting very businesslike in your old age.'

'Somebody has to.'

'A hit. A palpable hit. And do you disapprove of your brother more than ever nowadays?'

'Of course not. But you do let things happen. Instead of making them happen.'

278

'Not so with Jenny, was it?'

'True. You made that happen,' agreed Lisa, trying to sound approving.

She hoped he did not know what she thought about his marriage. She was particularly nice to Jenny, who never responded but had her own offhand way of taking people for granted while offering little in return. Lisa was more, not less, pessimistic about the marriage than when he'd originally broken the news. What had her brother and Jenny in common but sex? And how long before he began to look elsewhere? Marrying Jenny had simply been another form of gambling.

They fell into silence again. It was that time of year, that time of day. Springtime. The road straightened out and as they were still early, Charles took a side road leafier than the rest. He slowed the car to a walking pace, Lisa wound down the window, and they heard the shrill sound of a chiff-chaff, monotonously repeating his two notes.

Then they saw it. A small, weatherbeaten sign on a post beside a rusty wrought-iron gate: 'For Sale'.

'Charles!'

He slammed on the brakes so suddenly that Lisa was thrown against the windscreen and bumped her head.

'Sorry. Sorry. Are you okay?'

'I'll have a lump like an egg,' she said, rubbing her forehead, 'but perhaps it'll be worth it. Shall we have a look?'

'If you like. It'll be hopeless.'

They left the car and began to walk up the drive, which was edged with young cherry trees showing signs of white blossom. The drive was in a bad way, cracked and bursting; in one place the asphalt had disintegrated into broken gravel. They passed discarded and forgotten allotments and a huddle of Army huts, now boarded up. A bicycle leaned against one wall. It had only one wheel and must have been there so long that weeds had grown round it, smothering the remaining wheel and winding round the handlebars. It could have been a painting by Magritte. In the distance they saw a house of weatherbeaten stone spotted with lichen.

'Do you think anybody lives there?'

'Doesn't look like it.'

They walked round, looking into windows, exclaiming over stone doorways. The Army huts told the house's history and from what they could make out through smeared windows, the place was empty, unkempt, dirty and in bad repair.

'It's falling to pieces,' said Lisa. Her brother was trying yet another locked door, this time at the back of the house. 'Come on, Charles, or we'll be late instead of early.'

'Lisa, do look at that oven! You could cook a whole ox in it.'

'What do you suppose they cooked during the war?'

'Army scully. A sort of pretty revolting stew.'

'What a wreck,' said Lisa, as they hurried down the drive, again passing the bicycle. 'Somebody will pull it down one day.'

She thought no more about the house but remembered later to tell Jenny when she and Charles had returned from Warwick.

'It sounds awful,' said Jenny. 'I'm glad I wasn't with you.'

'Why?'

Jenny shrugged and answered it would only depress her. Lisa noticed that her sister-in-law had an obsession about avoiding such an emotion.

Jenny was already in her first night finery, and there was scarcely half an hour for Lisa to get ready. She ran upstairs to have a hasty bath before getting dressed. Since receiving her inheritance, Lisa had bought a few clothes, the most daring of which was a New Look dress. It was of dark green net, with Dior skirts of white under the green. The result was a floating, misty costume, like that of a ballerina. The dress was strapless, the bodice boned, with a spray of green and white lilac at the bosom. Lisa did her hair, made up her face, rubbed scent along her arms and, looking at herself in the glass, thought: I'll do. She wasn't used to seeing herself like that.

When she came downstairs again Peter was waiting. He

had already ordered her a drink and put it into her hands. He said in a low voice, 'You look wonderful. I wish . . .'

'What?' she said, amused at his face.

'That we could make love now before the play.'

'Do you? Why before?'

He was her practised lover now and they made love a great deal. He grew more skilled, knew how to make her want him, plunged into her until she pushed her nails in pleasure into his back. Lisa loved being made love to by Peter, did not love him at all and did not know why.

'Why *before* the play?' she repeated. He took off his glasses, looking helpless, polished and replaced them and immediately looked himself again.

'Because then I could relax and pay attention to the words.'

There were the usual brightly-dressed, festive crowds already walking through Stratford towards the theatre. Lisa thought they could have been guests going to a party at Government House in Calcutta before the war. They had the same air and style. One or two of the girls began to hurry, their full-skirted dresses swinging like the bells of flowers.

When Peter and Lisa were swept into the foyer of the theatre it smelled of scent and of that particular theatral smell which Polly had told Lisa was scene paint and a whiff of size that was used on scenery. 'I love it. It's the best smell in the world,' Polly had said. Men looked at Lisa as she came in and Peter felt proud and possessive, taking her through the crowds as carefully as if she might break. They had been given the same seats as on the first night of the season, close to the stage.

Peter turned and looked about. 'There's Ralph Richardson with his wife,' he murmured. 'The pretty girl in grey. The shortish, trim man with straight hair is A. V. Cookman. Critic of *The Times*. Very influential.'

'How do you know it's him when the notices are never signed?'

'I've met him once or twice. He's very nice, but reserved. Perhaps that's best for a critic.'

281

He liked to show off, and Lisa smiled. She took off her stole and sat bare-shouldered, turning round to see if she, too, could spot a celebrity. She twisted right round in her seat and found herself staring straight at a man sitting in the row behind her.

For a sickening moment she felt she'd been hit in the stomach.

It was Tom Westbury.

# 14

He looked at her intently. He did not seem shattered as she was. He said with a slight note of humour, 'Hello, stranger.'

'Tom,' was all Lisa said. She turned her back on him.

But Peter heard the exchange, twisted round and spoke to him with a pleasant smile. 'Mr Westbury, we've met before, I think. At the Press party the other evening. My name's Lang, I write for the *Echo*. Are you feeling slightly nervous tonight? Or do you take these things calmly?'

'Not calmly at all. I'm always terrified and wish I didn't have to be here.'

*What are they talking about?* she thought.

'Your wife is playing Olivia,' said Peter easily, '"the honourable lady of the house". One of my favourites.'

'She's rather more nervous than I am,' said Tom. 'She won't admit it, but I think she's haunted by a good many previous Olivias. Lisa, have you seen *Twelfth Night* often before?' Deliberately forcing her to turn round again, he sounded as natural as Charles.

Lisa did turn, answering coolly that she hadn't seen the play for years and was looking forward to tonight. She turned back as soon as she could. Married man, she thought. I can't bear to look at you.

The house lights went down and the curtain rose on a dazzling vision of Renaissance Italy. A vast, looped awning, transparent sky, an arcade of delicate columns. There was the music of a flute and the bearded Duke, in a rich, gleaming costume, began to speak . . .

Lisa hadn't seen the play since she was a schoolgirl and the change in design and pace was extraordinary. The scene was lit with the golden Italian sun; it shimmered. The actors spoke the verse as effortlessly as birds flying. Lisa stared at the bright stage, forcing herself to concentrate. I will. I will. But she was frightened. By shock. By seeing in physical reality the phantom who had possessed her in dreams, whose body had entered hers in dreams, for whom she had woken sobbing. Sometimes during the first Act she heard the rat-tat-tat of Tom's laugh, particularly at Anthony Quayle's Malvolio.

When Olivia, veiled, made her entrance Peter whispered, 'That's Gemma Lambert, Tom Westbury's wife. Have you seen her before?'

'Never.'

'But you know him?'

'From ages ago.'

He is married to you, she thought, staring with painful attention at the actress speaking Olivia's lines. That was why he was in Stratford. She wondered how she could bear the rest of this evening, knowing he was a few feet away. What a cool look he had given her. Guilty. He feels guilty. I don't want him to, I would hate that. Lisa – *listen to the play*.

It was Shakespeare's last comedy and a fairy story. Of a brother and sister separated at sea, of girls disguised as boys, of fools who were wise and wise men who were fools. It was full of tricks and mockery and cruel jokes. But the under-current was melancholy when Mick Gould as Feste the clown sang 'What is love? 'Tis not hereafter.'

It was impossible for Lisa not to keep her eyes on the woman who had stolen her lover. Gemma Lambert was beautiful and she could act. But that wasn't all that Lisa saw. Here was a woman with an aura of sensual allure, whose lower lip seemed ready for kisses, whose thick russet hair tumbled down white shoulders, whose bosom thrusting out of the Renaissance dress showed the shadows between full

284

breasts. She did not only flirt with Viola disguised as a page, she flirted with the whole audience . . .

Lisa did manage to concentrate on the play, on the character of Olivia who falls in love like the Sleeping Beauty waking up. But a thrill of nerves went through her as the curtain fell at the close of the Act. She dreaded Tom speaking to them again. It did not happen. When she and Peter left their seats, Tom remained in his and a man had come over to talk to him.

The play ended with a kind of sigh as Feste sang 'the rain it raineth every day'. As the applause burst out, with some cheers, and the actors bowed and curtseyed, Lisa had tears in her eyes. The players stood in costume, but turned back into real people, half arrogant, half vulnerable, bathed in the pleasure of pleasing. This time Lisa did not look at Gemma Lambert.

'Wasn't it good!' cried Charles, when he and Jenny joined them and they made their way up the staircase to the restaurant. The audience of over a thousand people was rapidly disappearing out into the dark, still talking of the play.

They sat down at the table and Charles ordered champagne. Lisa drank hers rather fast. The first shock had faded. What had come back was an ache she had thought was gone for ever.

During the meal Polly appeared, glowing with the excitement of her performance and accompanied by a young actor with the face of a youth painted by Botticelli. Polly had the air of a girl who very well knew the advantage of having such a handsome partner. Seeing her, Lisa suddenly realized she had scarcely noticed her friend onstage, playing one of Olivia's ladies-in-waiting.

'Well?' cried Polly standing by their table. 'Did you all enjoy it? Did you like me? Was I any good?' The shameless demand resulted in compliments to which she listened with hands clasped on her breast. 'I know I had absolutely nothing to do,' she said, modesty returning. 'This is Alex, by the way. We hope we're seeing you at the Wardrobe party.'

285

Alex laughed. Everything about him was perfect. His thick hair. His smile. His white teeth. His way of standing.

'Polly, I have no invitation for the party,' began Peter.

'Who needs an invitation? It isn't that kind of thing at all. Everybody just wanders in, which is what's fun about it. To my certain knowledge some people don't even see the performance, they come down from London just for the Wardrobe party. Disgusting of them. Alex and I will expect you, won't we, Alex? You *can't* all go home and drink Ovaltine when you can be with us. Now, kids, I must go to the old folk and give them a chance to say what a brilliant daughter they've got. See you in the Wardrobe. Through the courtyard, the big doors will be wide open. You can't miss them.'

There was a lull when she had left.

'Shall we go?' said Charles.

'It sounds fun,' sighed Jenny.

'What do you think, Lisa?' from Peter.

Lisa said calmly that of course she would go if everybody else wanted to.

Charles who never missed implications said, 'Does that mean that you don't?'

She found herself denying this and agreeing that the party sounded just the thing to end an evening after a wonderful play. She knew she couldn't get out of it. She knew Tom was certain to be there. What does it matter after all, thought poor Lisa, I shall meet him sooner or later. I shall have to get used to it. She remembered Polly's appalling declaration, with which in her heart she'd agreed: 'If it was me, I'd prefer him to be dead.' The pain that had come back was like earache returning all over again, an ache which she had staved off with too much aspirin. Peter had been the drug and for tonight at least it didn't seem to work.

When they left the restaurant the quartet crossed the road, went under an arch which looked as if it might have been the entrance to some stables. Beyond was a yard and a jumble of buildings, some with iron stairs leading to higher floors. Two huge, battered doors were ajar, and there was that unmistakeable noise, steady yet fractured, strong and

286

now and again broken by laughter and what could be drowned music: a party in progress. Peter pushed the door wider open.

They found themselves in what appeared to be an enormous cavern lit by rows of candles in bottles, ranged on trestle tables. From high ceilings swathes of fish-net had been draped, pinned here and there with objects which shone in the candlelight. Lisa made out a crown, a Mayor's chain, a pair of steel gauntlets and a dagger. The place was crammed with people and as they came into the room more people came crowding behind them. A little man like a gnome darted up to Jenny who had asked if she could carry the champagne Charles had brought as their offering. She held it as a talisman against shyness.

'You're from heaven. An angel in person!' cried the gnome, taking the champagne and putting his arm round her shoulders. 'You are quite enchanting and I love that shade of blue. We used it once in *Hamlet* for the Court scene. It showed up his black, do you see? It really suits you, dear. Come along and we'll both drink the champagne and I shall introduce you to everybody. I'm Jacky Grimsdyke, in charge of the Wardrobe, so you happen to be with your host.' He marched an excited Jenny away.

Lisa and Peter were given some fruit-cup which, when he'd tasted it, Peter whispered was of 'remarkable weakness'. Mick Gould came over to talk to them, and he and Peter discussed the performance while Lisa tried not to look round. Without Jenny, Charles merely stood alone among crowds of vivacious people.

The rooms – there were three leading one from the other – were arranged with comic flair. Costumed figures like those used in the exhibition were dressed not as elegant examples of the art but as surrealist jokes. Their cloaks were scattered with goldfish; they held tridents or scimitars. On the walls among the fish-net were crowns, coronets, tall hats, bracelets, necklaces. Spotlights were trained here and there to make things glitter. As Charles looked about, the double doors were pushed open for the umpteenth time. A woman came

287

in. She wore a dark yellow dress from which her rounded shoulders rose soft and creamy, and like Charles she seemed untroubled by being alone in a host of people glued together by talk. She glanced in a leisurely fashion around the room and her eye finally fell on Charles who hadn't moved. She smiled slowly and came across the room, weaving between people, some of whom stretched out their hands to her – one man kissed her – until she reached Charles.

'Hello,' she said.

'Hello again.'

'Last time we met, I stole some sherry for us.'

'I remember.' In a roomful of unmeant compliments, he paid her a real one. 'You were wonderful tonight.'

'One does one's best.'

'Such an enchanting best.'

'Was it?'

'I've seen nothing more bewitching on stage.'

She looked at him thoughtfully. There was an odd resemblance between them of which neither was conscious, yet a stranger could have taken them for siblings. Both had faces which nature had formed in heavy moulds and which youth made beautiful. Both had strong noses, a sign of character often disproved. Both had a manner of relaxed, self-conscious stillness; they knew it was not necessary to appear eager. In fact it was better not to. Most similar was the shape of their mouths with the thick under-lip.

She took her eyes away from him and surveyed the crowd. 'Can I come back?' she said, as if at the end of a conversation.

'Must you go?'

'I have to make my curtseys to various people. I can't concentrate until I have.'

'You mean you must talk to the big stars and later you may have time for me.'

'How nasty I sound,' she said with complacence. 'But it's true. I mean, I did want you to say what you did just now, but compliments for us only count if they are from pros.'

'A good thing the public doesn't know that.'

288

'Ah, we can't do without *them*,' she said, her face becoming solemn.

'What about critics? They don't count either, I suppose?' Charles liked to tease.

A very tall man was walking past them. He turned and said pleasantly, 'Wonderful, Miss Lambert. First rate.' He had an avuncular, humorous manner.

She replied with a radiant smile and whispered thanks and when he'd gone muttered, 'God, I hope he didn't hear about the critics not counting! That's George Bishop on the *Telegraph* – he writes about theatre. I'm terrified of journalists.'

'You poor thing.'

'Don't laugh at me.'

'Off you go and make your curtseys or whatever you call them. Come back later.'

'How do I know you will still be here?'

'You don't.'

She made a coquettish face at him, and walked away towards the stars. He saw her talking to Anthony Quayle and a regal woman he recognized as Diana Wynyard. Gemma was kissed and welcomed and all three began to talk with the eagerness of players. When Gemma Lambert looked back later, Charles had gone.

In an inner room where more costumed figures on stands stood in mute witness, Lisa and Peter danced. Peter danced well and she enjoyed moving in his arms. The spell of the party, the feeling that the night would never end, had taken hold of them. Peter led her between other dancers, many of them moving on the same spot on the splintery floor, for the excuse of being in each other's arms. The music came from an old upright piano in a corner, candle-brackets holding real candles which burned, making a fearful mess on gilt holders. Beside the piano was a costumed figure in Victorian mourning: a bonnet on a faceless head, a thick veil hanging down, stuffed calico hands clasping a white prayer-book.

The pianist, comic face absorbed and serious, was Mick Gould. He played, slipping from one dance tune to the next. There was a glass of wine on the top of the piano and when he drank it he went on playing with his left hand. At last he finished a familiar tune and stopped with a loud chord. The dancers halted. Somebody shouted 'More!' but Mick shook his head and stood up.

Peter released Lisa.

'Let's go and talk to Tom Westbury.'

'Must we?' said Lisa with a fixed smile.

'Don't you like him? I thought you used to know him years ago.'

'Charles knew him at Oxford. They played cricket or something. I met him a couple of times.' She had an idiotic desire to run.

Peter was apologetic. 'It would be good to have a word with him. He's quite a coming writer, you know. His play *Somersault* is running in London. You must have read about it. It's a big success.'

A dramatist? Lisa was astounded; she couldn't fit it into her remembrance of her lover. It was like hearing about a stranger. She remembered he'd been a journalist and had talked sometimes about newspapers. But a playwright?

'I've heard he's already working on something new,' continued Peter, wanting to interest her. '*Somersault* is a comedy but one of the London critics told me that the next play isn't going to be. My editor would be pleased if I managed to get something from him. It would be a scoop.' The old-fashioned Hollywood slang came out with perfect seriousness.

'All right, Peter, off you go and get your scoop. I must find the Ladies if there is one in this odd place. If there isn't, I shall pop back to the hotel.'

'On your peril do you walk home in the dark alone. If you can't find a Ladies, come and get me and I'll take you back to The Shakespeare.'

'You're so chivalrous,' she said, teasing him, and made her escape. She found Polly on the stairs examining a bare foot.

'I know there's a splinter. Why did I think I could dance barefoot? I'm dotty.'

She obligingly took Lisa up a flight of wooden stairs

resembling the ladder in a hayloft to a lavatory under the roof. It was the size of a broom-cupboard and the door had no lock.

'I'll mount guard,' said Polly, pulling up a moth-eaten plush and gilt chair and sitting down. She continued to prod her foot. When Lisa reappeared Polly was fastening on her sandal again. She said sweetly, 'Can I ask the tiniest favour? Would you kill me if I had a dance with your guy?'

'Who?' said Lisa stupidly. She was wondering how soon she could leave.

'Come on, Lisa, use your brains. Are you a little drunk, darling? If so I don't know how you've managed it on Jacky's fruit-cup. I mean can I dance with your Peter Lang? I'm drawn to him. He's attractive and besides he might write something about me in his column.'

'So he might. Of course, dance with him. He isn't my property.'

'Yes he is, but thanks. Come on. Don't let's miss anything.'

They made their way down the rickety stairs.

It was very late. Time seemed to have no end. People no longer stood in groups, attentively listening as if the speaker, always an actor, were saying something of desperate importance. They had begun to sit on trestles, on chairs, on the floor and on the stairs; Lisa and Polly had to pick their way over couples roosting like hens on perches. Lisa gave a nervous glance across the room. No sign of Tom, thank God. If he'd come to the party, he must have left, and she had missed him. There was no sign of Charles either. Jenny was sitting on a trestle table laughing with the Botticellian Alex.

'Goody, there's Peter,' said Polly and tripped across the room.

Lisa hesitated. She thought with longing of her quiet room in The Shakespeare, of being alone, of being able to sleep and forget tonight. She only had a walk of five minutes to solitude. She drifted towards the doors of the Wardrobe and tugged her stole out from under a heap of shawls, minks, scarves and raincoats. Wrapping it around her naked shoulders, she went into the dark. It was bitterly cold and after three in the morning. The icy air struck her arms and throat and seemed to pierce the flimsy dress. She shivered. Looking ahead, dazzled by the lights indoors, she was conscious of a figure standing in the dark. She had a sudden thrill of fear followed by contempt at herself – this wasn't an Edgar Allen Poe tale, she was two feet away from crowds of people. She saw the glow of a cigarette.

'Is that Lisa?' It was Tom. 'What are you doing out here alone?'

'Going home. It's just down the road. What are *you* doing?' Her voice was strained. She scarcely recognized it.

'Waiting for Gemma. Heaven knows where she's got to. She always disappears at dos like this. Probably to some actor's flat to talk shop. You know these parties.'

'She'll be back soon, I expect.' She found she couldn't move.

'Lisa,' he said after a moment, 'I had no idea you were in Stratford.'

'Didn't you? This was Charles's and my home town, you know.'

'So it was. It was a surprise seeing you tonight. A great surprise.'

'Yes.'

'Are you working in Stratford?' He actually seemed to want to talk, to want her to stay. She wished he'd stop.

She said brightly that she was working at The Treasure Box, perhaps he knew it? 'We sell pretty things.'

'I must come round and take a look.'

What are we doing here in the dark talking rubbish? she thought.

'Are you staying in Stratford?' She forced herself to continue the charade. She didn't care where in hell he lived as long as it was not near her.

'Gemma and I have a flat in Avoncliffe. We're lucky. You must meet her. You saw her tonight, of course.'

'Yes. She's very good.'

292

'Isn't she, though?' he said and chuckled.

She felt a wave of anguish. To be at arm's length away from the only man she had ever loved, the only body she had longed for, the only creature who had utterly owned and then thrown her away. She both hated and wanted him.

'I must go. Goodnight, Tom,' she said and vanished through the archway into the dark before he could speak.

Gemma Lambert eventually located Charles. She came back from talking at length to the people who mattered and it took her a good half-hour to find him. He wasn't in any of the places where guests were sitting or eating, dancing or sprawling, kissing or telling secrets. She eventually saw him perched on the top of a stepladder, smoking and watching the dancers. He looked perfectly content.

'There you are,' she said, standing at the base of the ladder and looking up.

'You sound surprised.'

'You're a difficult man to find.'

'Want to come and sit with me? I'm not sure the stepladder will hold two but we could find out,' he said, half shifting and patting a small space beside him.

'I don't think so. Actors say "break a leg" for luck but suppose I actually did. I came to ask if you'd like to see the picture gallery with me?'

The gallery was in the old Victorian part of the previous theatre. There was a tower that survived the fire of 1926 which had been built into the new theatre and remained now a Gothic fantasy side by side with 1930s realism.

'I know a way in,' she said. 'I managed it the other night. I was there a good hour and nobody caught me. It was lovely having her to myself.'

'Who?' enquired Charles, still looking at her from his high perch. She was charming with her face upturned.

'Ellen Terry, of course.'

He climbed down and they went through the Wardrobe, unnoticed by people absorbed in their own companions. There was no sign of Charles's wife or Gemma's husband when they went out of a back door into the dark, crossed to the theatre and Gemma led him through a smaller door and up polished stairs into a gallery. High windows reflected the night sky. It was dark and very cold and smelled of oil paint as galleries are apt to do.

They stood alone with many theatre ghosts looking down at them. They turned and embraced.

It was the first kiss they had exchanged and it happened in a kind of mutual suddenness. Their mouths opened, their tongues touched, they pressed close, they gasped a little, they forgot everything but the sensualist's embrace. Neither Gemma nor Charles felt anything but violent lust, a sensation that must be made worse before it is assuaged, a kind of struggle as if they were not kissing but fighting to the death. They sank – still locked together – to the ground and Charles pulled up her satin skirts and penetrated her at once – to find her slippery with desire. Lying on the hard floor in a silence broken by gasps and grunts, they made love. It was not quickly over, as was often so with new lovers. It was fierce and yet languorous, hard yet soft. They lay intent only on pleasure, their own.

'I must come. Now.'

'I will too.'

They finished making love exactly together, shuddering, embracing, and separating to roll apart on the parquet floor, still looked down on by the painted faces. They lay without speaking for a few minutes. There was no tenderness in his voice when he said, 'Ought you to go?'

'Oh yes. And you?'

'I daresay.'

A pause. How dark it was, he thought, doing up his clothes. He felt a swimming satisfaction, a sensation that topped all the sexual congress he'd ever known. A feeling of repleteness, of goodwill.

'What am I going to do about you?' he asked the glimmering shape at a distance from him. He saw in the shadows that she was sitting up. The half-light caught the pearls in her hair. She was vaguely pinning up a russet tress.

'What do you want to do?'

'The same. Again and again.'

'You do, don't you?'

'So do you, my love.'

She slid on her bottom across the floor without grace. She leaned over and pulled his hair. 'Oh, I shall want you a lot. More than you can imagine. More than you will manage.'

'Don't be too sure about that,' he said and bit the edge of her fleshy hand.

# 15

Lisa did not mean to confide in Charles. She was never sure
of his reactions when she told him something which concerned or hurt her. His sympathy could not be relied upon.
There were times when he was wonderfully understanding
and perceptive, would help with imaginative thoughts and
solutions and, making soothing sounds when she described
some trouble or other, would give her a hug. At other times
he was different – matter-of-fact or critical, refusing to see
or dismissing her problems.

Charles had not been sympathetic in India when she had
first told him about her love affair. They had met again after
he had come from Burma. It was the time when they still
believed their future might be back in Taunggyi. Everything
in a peacetime which was another form of chaos had been
uncertain and dangerous. On an endless train journey
through India, when they were too hot to sleep, she told him
about herself and Tom.

He had been lying, arms behind his head, on the wooden
plank which was all that counted as a bed. The two other
occupants of the so-called sleeper compartment had left
hours ago – he and Lisa were alone. The train thundered
across thousands of miles of parched land and Lisa sat
upright on the facing bunk, bare-legged, talking, talking.
She told him how she'd met Tom in the Chowringhee flat,
of their passion, their promises, of when they had said
goodbye. She described his early letters – followed by utter

silence. She'd written and written. No answer. Nothing. When she thought about it later, she knew she'd talked for too long and her brother must have been bored by her selfish sorrow. Talking about it had made her cry, the stifling heat mingling sweat with tears.

'Wasn't it sad, Charles, oh wasn't it sad?'

'A bit.'

'Only a bit?' she said, wiping her face with the back of her hand.

Charles had listened attentively, but his eyes wandered now and then. He said after a while, 'You'll fall in love again. We always do.'

She couldn't bear to hear that. 'But *why* hasn't he written any more? What's happened?' When he didn't answer but merely sat looking at her she added, 'Perhaps he's dead.'

He shook his head. 'You said you'd made a lot of enquiries, and he was posted at one stage.'

'Months ago. He may have been killed –'

'Lou,' he interrupted, 'the last letter you received from him was after V J Day. How can he possibly be dead?'

He didn't say he would try to help find him. He didn't offer her a crumb of comfort. He remained looking at her, his eyebrows slightly raised, which gave his face a quizzical air as if he were waiting for her to make up her own mind. Lisa saw he believed Tom had deliberately not answered her letters. He'd thrown her over. Charles understands that because he's done it himself, she thought.

If her brother pitied her he certainly didn't show it and after pouring out her heart, pride stopped her from speaking about Tom again. But she longed and longed for him. He came into her mind all the time. It hurt her so. But what was the use of talking about it to Charles?

As the memory of her love affair grew cold, she never again mentioned Tom. She needed Charles's good opinion and he would only think her sentimental. In London when she scolded him for gambling Charles couldn't point out that she was as lacking in will-power as he; he listened with the

297

air of a man who hasn't a leg to stand on and has to put up with the little woman nagging again.

But it was different now. Seeing Tom had been a hideous shock – she had to confide in somebody. She walked back to The Shakespeare after work, hoping for the chance to talk to Charles alone. If Jenny's with him, I can't say anything, she thought. She could imagine Jenny's reaction, her upper-class embarrassment at Lisa showing her feelings. Perhaps a dash of pity at somebody as elderly as twenty-eight having troubles of the heart.

Lisa went into the hotel and up the stairs towards the door of *As You Like It*. She hesitated, listening for voices, screwed up her courage and knocked. She heard Charles's voice.

'Come in.'

He was seated at a table drawn up to the window, dealing himself out poker hands – five cards which he dealt, picked up, looked and considered.

'Where's Jenny?' asked Lisa, interrupting.

'Out with Angie enjoying girls' jokes and trying on each other's clothes. A favourite pastime.'

He continued to shuffle and deal in an effortless, practised way. She always liked to watch him handling cards. It reminded her of the dancers called Minthamis or princesses, whom she and Charles and their uncle used to see performing in Burma. The faces of the dancers were smeared with white paste, they wore brilliant clothes, and essential parts of the dance were the graceful hand and arm movements which resembled the shaking of the stems of flowers.

'I suppose I mustn't talk,' she remarked, after time had passed. She was strung up. It was difficult.

He picked up another poker hand. 'That's a funny one. Queen, jack, ten of spades and two eights, one of them is spades . . . okay, talk on. What's the news?'

Prepared to shock and shatter him she burst out, 'Tom Westbury's in Stratford. He was at *Twelfth Night*.' She expected a start.

'I know.'

'*You know?*'

'Of course, Lou. He's married to Gemma Lambert who plays Olivia.'

'Then why the hell –'

'Didn't I tell you? I decided it might be better if you found out later by chance. Not from me.'

'It wasn't better. It was horrible.'

'I don't know why you're looking so tragic. People have a habit of turning up out of the past. Look at Ingoldsby.'

'What's he got to do with it?' She might have known she wasn't going to get a breath of sympathy. She was more annoyed with herself than with him.

'It's an interesting point, isn't it? I owed Ingoldsby money which left us in a pretty mess. (Though it's worked out rather well thanks to you and Peter being so clever, and our sainted father, of course.) Weil, Lou, Westbury owed *you* something. An explanation. A decent kind of goodbye. But I take it that unlike Ingoldsby you don't intend to march into his Avoncliffe flat and demand your due.'

She gave a sort of shrug, looking at the ground. Sometimes, thought Charles, inwardly sighing, I wish Lou wasn't so little. If she was tall, now, like Gemma, one could cope. But there are times when – damn it, I won't be sorry for her. She's strong enough, for God's sake. But she sat like somebody in pain. She fidgeted as if that might relieve it.

'Do have a sense of proportion,' he said, more irritably than he meant because she touched him. He looked at the cards in front of him again. 'Anyone with any sense would chuck those spades and try and get another eight. But what *I'm* going to do is chuck the eight.' He paused, picked up the top card of the pack and held it face downwards. 'If this game was at the Wilton, and this card the nine of spades, it could be worth seven hundred pounds. On the other hand it could be rubbish.' He flicked the card on to the table. It was a six of clubs. 'You see, Lou? Everything's luck. Chance. Meeting guys. Losing them. They walk out on women all the time. Women do the same thing, as I should know, having been at the receiving end.' It wasn't true but he wanted her to believe it. 'Chance brought you both to the same town. Shouldn't you simply accept it?'

299

'I never said I wouldn't.'

He laughed at that. 'You won't need to see much of him – you're scarcely likely to call at Avoncliffe now you know he lives there. Your friend Polly will have to meet you somewhere else. Of course, there is one risk.'

'What's that?'

'He might find it hard to resist coming to the shop.'

'What on earth do you mean, Charles?' She positively stared.

'It's one of the unpleasant traits in the male. Men do like buzzing round their old flames. Just to see if they still have the same devastating effect.'

The tone, the advice, the perfect coolness of the expert in sexual games affected her. He was right and to hell with him. She could never accept that her brother loved her when he treated her so. How could he be so hard? Where was sympathy or a shoulder to cry on? Brother and sister both thought the other like iron sometimes.

'I'll go and change for dinner.'

'Wear your yellow. It suits you. Now I think I'll play Dark Thirteen.' It was the name of a particular and difficult form of Patience and Lisa thought it ominous. As she left him he was dealing the cards. The Minthamis hand-dance again.

To the horror of his wife and the incredulity of his sister, Charles turned up one evening at The Shakespeare to announce that he'd bought a house. Yes, he had agreed to the purchase. No, he wasn't going to change his mind. They'd like the house and in any case Lisa had seen it.

She knew at once he was referring to the manor they'd discovered on the way to Warwick. It was, he told them, called Lyndhurst and the price was three thousand pounds.

'That includes a big garden, admittedly overgrown, and some fields. And some delightful Army huts,' said Charles.

Lisa refused to laugh.

Jenny had the look of somebody who'd been struck on the head. She wasn't used to instant decisions. Her father had never made one during her entire life: except to try and keep her from Charles.

The two girls were driven over to see Lyndhurst. Lisa tried to see the house differently, knowing her brother had a vision which at present she had not. He looked positively triumphant, ignoring Jenny's wails. They'd fix up two rooms to start with and live in those, he said. They'd camp out. The repairs would be done bit by bit and the house would slowly return to itself and be what it actually was, a gem.

For the next few weeks the sale trundled through its tedious stages. The survey made on a place used until recently as a small barracks was no worse than Lisa and Peter imagined. There was damp and dry rot, but who thought there wouldn't be? There were also wedding-cake ceilings, a carved oak fireplace burned with cigarette stubs, magnificent but damaged floors and obscene messages in any room which had been occupied by the licentious soldiery.

Perdita came down strongly on Charles's side.

'It's a wreck but your brother has an eye,' she said. 'I suppose his wife would prefer a ready-made nest decorated by Selfridges.'

She had driven over to Lyndhurst in the van to meet Lisa and stood studying the house keenly, hands on her hips. She reminded Lisa of a nurse looking over an elderly patient who is on the mend.

'I remember the owner and his wife. He was a little puffing man like a train, she was all vague draperies. I used to come here to tea – they collected blue and white china. Well, well, it looks in poor shape but it's worth the whistle. The great trick when you buy something in bad repair is to start by living in the kitchen.'

'That's right, Mrs Smith,' said Charles who came out of the house to greet her. He talked to Perdita for a minute or two, then excused himself and wandered away, hands in his pockets. He did not go into the house but across the unkempt garden. Jenny had remained in Stratford declaring somewhat shrewdly, 'I can't be very useful.'

When Charles left them, Perdita looked at Lisa and raised her eyebrows.

'He seems rather vague for a man I thought was showing signs of gumption. Why isn't he inside measuring everything in sight? I hope he's going to put his shoulder to the wheel.'

'All he's done so far is admire cornices.'

'I can imagine. However, he's taken a fancy to Lyndhurst and wants to make it come alive. That's admirable. There is another little point. A nice big house in disrepair is bound to keep his wife busy.'

'Perdita. What can you mean?'

'Nothing. Nothing.'

Charles did put his shoulder to whatever wheels were necessary in the next few weeks. When the damp and dry rot people finally departed, leaving a house pervaded with intense smells, Charles drove Jenny to Broadway and Birmingham in search of furniture. Jenny cheered up. They even went by train to London but returned saying it was so run down and shabby they couldn't wait to get back to Stratford.

Much of the practical work on the house was left to Lisa. Perdita, who didn't want her employee's time swallowed, found a good builder, an electrician, and a couple of actors to do the whitewashing and the hacking of the wilderness which had once been a garden.

Meeting two actors, one of whom was the Botticellian Alex, had an inspiring effect on Jenny who began to help with the work. In June, in a patch of ground outside the kitchen an enormous spread of green spears produced buds and turned out to be madonna lilies which filled the air with scent. One morning Lisa saw Jenny standing among them, looking just like a girl in a sentimental Pre-Raphaelite painting.

It is possible to live closely to a person, know him as well as you know yourself and have no idea what is in his head. It was like that with Lisa and her brother. She saw him every day. They discussed Lyndhurst. They drove over to the house. They made plans. Charles, Lisa and Jenny had meals together. But what Lisa could not know, what Jenny did not know and what at least two members of the theatre company

302

knew very well was that Charles Whitfield had fallen in love.

Theatre people have eyes. They are observant egotists who study the faces and gestures of their friends, their acquaintances, their enemies and total strangers. They can use anything. The position of a girl slumped in a chair, the quality of a laugh dirty with double meanings, a sniff, a cough, a walk, a groan. They use physical attributes: thrust-out chins, squashed noses, a high colour, a pair of stooped shoulders. One famous actor during a Stratford season spotted a man in the audience who had curiously-coloured hair. Playing to perfection, the actor was still aware of everybody in the stalls. He often picked out a friend at the back or a relative who'd come to the performance un-announced. After the play he caught sight of the man crossing the Bancroft and hurried up to him.

'Do forgive me. Might I have the smallest smidgin of your hair?'

The man, astonished and flattered, scarcely had time to agree when the actor produced a pair of nail-scissors and snipped off a tiny strand.

The actor reverently placed it in his wallet. 'So kind of you. The perfect colour for my beard in *Timon*.'

Lisa wasn't an actress. She didn't stand on a stage and have eyes so sharp that she could spot a stranger who might be useful to her. She didn't study manners and mannerisms, character, human nature. She was with Charles, talked to Charles, laughed and joked with him and didn't see a thing.

Mick Gould had a different pair of eyes. He was sitting with Polly on the wall of The Dirty Duck and making her laugh. Polly had chosen the wall to give her a commanding position from which she could look down and passers-by look up. She hoped they would know she was Polly Holt who played Doll Tearsheet. Dressed in a new white Horrocks cotton, the acme of fashion now that Princess Marina chose the same manufacturer, Polly looked her best. And the sun was bleaching her hair. She and her fellow actor talked shop, discussing *Twelfth Night* and its difficulties. They spoke of Sir Lew and *King Lear*.

'He doesn't seem to care a jot that he's only in one production,' said Mick. 'Amazing. Rumour has it, by the by, that he took you to dinner again at The Spread Eagle.'

'Yes. We swam by moonlight in the swimming-pool afterwards.'

'How frantically romantic.'

'Don't be rude and anyway it wasn't. Sir Lew said I can't swim for toffee. I've never managed the crawl.'

'Isn't he rather elderly to swim at all?'

She was shocked. 'He swims like a champion. Dives without a ripple and – well – is altogether marvellous.'

'Don't be a bore, darling.'

'Sorry.'

Seeing her expression he set out to amuse her. He was a natural comic, which contrasted with his look of melancholy; he was perfectly cast as Feste in *Twelfth Night*. Polly was fond of him and – more importantly – admired his work. He was clever and funny and sad. She envied him for knowing how to speak verse. She as yet hadn't got to the heart of it. She hadn't the rhythm or the breath control. It wasn't until you mastered the technique that you could give colour to the words, show what imagination was doing in your eyes and the tone of your voice . . . all that came only after you'd learned the craft. With Doll Tearsheet she'd got away with it. It wasn't enough.

'Your friend Charles Whitfield is up to no good,' remarked Mick when he had weaved his way through the Saturday morning crowd and returned with two glasses of cider. Actors spent their money on things that mattered: books, clothes, lotions for their skins, more books. For drinks, cider was all they could afford.

'Charles is *your* friend. Lisa is mine, we were babies together,' declared Polly. 'I suppose Charles still plays poker with you and loses money in that smelly old club.'

'He's a reformed character as far as gambling is concerned.'

She shrieked with laughter. She knew Charles's history from long before the time when he'd been banished by his father to the Far East. She had always admired Lisa's brother, his womanizing was titillating, she liked his looks, admired his dash. His marriage to a local virgin, however, Polly did not admire.

'You're not saying that debby girl with a voice like a character in *Raffles* has reformed him!'

'He doesn't play poker as much as he used to ... How women do dislike a man, any man, getting married. You don't happen to be after him yourself, do you, Polly?'

'After Charles! You must be mad.'

'You sound as if you were once upon a time.'

'At sixteen who wasn't? The girls at school used to go puce when Charles was around. When he came to collect Lisa on Sundays to drive her home, we congregated in the recreation-room and peered out of the window. He never let on that he'd seen us but Lisa said he did.'

'Men don't miss things like that.'

'Conceited lot. Anyway, that's old history. Charles leaves me cold now. Of course I like him, one couldn't help it, and he's attractive, but he isn't for me. Why do you ask?'

'No reason.'

'I don't believe you. What's been happening?'

'This and that.'

'Don't be annoying, Mick Gould. I can see you're going to tell.'

'I was sounding you out first in case you'd be hurt,' he said. 'Okay. Listen to my tale. To begin with, have you noticed anything about Gemma Lambert lately?'

Polly groaned and said you couldn't help noticing her, considering she prowled about devouring audiences.

'She's eating more than audiences.'

'She makes passes at anybody,' said Polly with contempt. 'She sort of ogles. She's got that good-looking husband too. Perhaps he beats her.'

'You hope.'

'I do, rather.'

'The husband isn't the burden of my song, darling. Gemma is. Or was last night to be precise.'

Mick Gould had lodgings in a house in Old Town facing the small, elegant William & Mary Hotel. The house was owned by Jack Lacey, a retired farmer whose family had lived in Stratford for generations. Local people said the Laceys were descendants of Shakespeare's. Jack Lacey had had red hair as a boy, and a certain broad-faced look which resembled the bust in Holy Trinity Church. There was a local tradition that Shakespeare had been a redhead.

During the season the Laceys took one or two lodgers from the theatre, to eke out a smallish income. Jack went to the Farmers' Union on most evenings, while Mary enjoyed fussing over her actors. She liked to wait up for Mick with cocoa and chat, and also spoiled her other actor, an ambitious walk-on called David, with home-made gingerbread.

It had been Mary's rare absence the previous night which disappointed Mick when he returned home after the performance. The play had gone particularly well; he could still hear the audience's laughter and applause when he let himself into the quiet house. Finding the place empty, no Mary, Jack or David, he was depressed. He went up to his attic room feeling thoroughly flat.

'Where's this tale leading?' Polly interrupted.

'Wait a bit. It improves.'

He had the artist's desire to give his best, to paint in backgrounds, to enhance effects before arriving at the climax. He continued to describe his boredom, adding praise for Mary Lacey, such a dear . . . must have been so pretty when she was young.

'So I went to my room, wondering how the hell to get through the next hour or two hours. Of course one needs one's sleep but I was excited after the show.'

'I know the feeling.'

'So I went into my room,' repeated Mick. 'And there, large as life and twice as natural, was Eileen Bird stark naked on the bed.'

They roared with laughter. Eileen Bird was Stratford's most notorious barmaid, in winter an amateur actress, who had affairs with anybody who was interested; she was sizzling in bed and according to Mick who had sampled her delights, her legs were covered with black hair like wire.

'No such luck. Empty bed. Midnight tolling from Holy Trinity, and scarcely a light in The William & Mary. My room was hot as an oven, too. It's those low ceilings.'

'Do get a move on.'

'Impatient. Well . . . I went to the window and opened it as wide as possible; Mary *will* shut it, she says it's cooler and she's quite wrong. I looked up and down the road. Nothing doing there. Then I turned and stared into the room wondering what the hell to read – my books are a dead loss, nothing new and nothing rude. And then, Polly, I began to look at the thingumajig which Jack Lacey had screwed to the wall.'

'What thingumajig?'

'It's one of those fire-escape things. He's very serious about fire in his house, the staircase is so narrow. This contraption is a sling made of canvas with a long canvas band wound round and round a wheel. When you sit in the sling your weight releases the band, it runs free. So you can go over to the window and let yourself down, see? Hilarious. I can't tell how often I've been in bed and stared at it, it's so enormous, and thought I'd like to try it out. I'm good at heights, I played Jim Hawkins in *Treasure Island* at Hammersmith and had to shin up a fifteen-foot mast . . . Anyway, I just looked at that fire-escape, Polly, and I thought why not? I went over and climbed on a chair and sort of wriggled myself into the sling. It wasn't too uncomfortable. Then, don't laugh, the weight released the band and I sort of dragged across the room with the band behind me and went to the window.'

He had her attention at last.

'Oh, oh!' cried Polly.

'I made sure everything was okay. I tugged at the band. Firm as a rock.'

'Firm as a rock,' repeated Polly.

'I climbed up on to the window-sill.'

'I *wish* I'd been there.'

'I looked like Dracula. Well, I would have but he flies and I would only be sitting hovering. Then –'

307

'Then what?'

'Then, just as I got both legs over the window-sill, and was preparing to descend into the night . . . I heard voices. Guess whose?'

'Mick, you are a *bore*.'

'Okay, okay, I'll put you out of your misery. It was Gemma. And who do you suppose was with her? Charles Whitfield.'

Seeing Polly's eyes were like saucers he went straight on with the story. He had recognized Gemma's voice at first and then 'looking down through my legs', saw the man with her was Charles. They had apparently come from walking by the river. They stood together whispering while Mick hung idiotically overhead scarcely daring to breathe. They began to kiss: 'I mean, *really* kiss.'

Suspended three storeys above them, Mick could see the way they threw themselves into each other's arms, how long the embrace lasted. He heard broken words. 'Darling, darling.' 'My beautiful.' And from Gemma, 'Charles, Charles, Charles.'

'I couldn't move a muscle,' said Mick. 'I was clutching on to my sling for grim death and had the feeling that if I didn't it would start to descend right on top of them. Imagine their faces.'

'Serve them right.'

'True. Anyway I hung on until at last they separated and went round the corner with their arms twined. Then I fell back through the window practically on my head. My hands were crimson. I've smothered them with Germolene but it hasn't done much good – do you think they're infected?' He spread them out to show a red weal on each palm. Polly didn't bother to look.

'Imagine a leading actress kissing in the High Street. She's the limit.'

'What about him? He only married that young girl the other day.'

Polly still mulled over the story. Despite disliking Gemma, she admired her. And every woman thought Charles Whitfield sexy. 'Imagine Gemma,' repeated Polly. 'I mean, she *is* a leading member of the company. Kissing like that in public in the street. Anybody might have seen them.'

'Somebody did.'

Unaware that a human bird had been perched above their heads at midnight, Charles and Gemma Lambert were trying to behave well and to embrace only where they would not be seen.

It was a new sensation for Charles to be an unfaithful husband. Up until now he hadn't considered he owed fidelity to any girl. He never promised it. Like the Earl of Rochester, Charles was faithful while he embraced a woman: that was just about all he could manage. Now he found himself in a different game and it was his lover who was the practised player.

It pricked his conscience to realize that the woman he was obsessed with was the wife of Lisa's lost love. If his sister knew that, it would hurt and disgust her. It was bad enough to discover that Tom Westbury was living in Stratford. Poor Lisa, thought Charles. But the new complication didn't bear looking at too closely, and he decided to ignore it. What mattered was Gemma. She mattered too much.

When he woke in the summer mornings in the same bed as his youthful, sweet-smelling wife, Jenny would mutter in her dreams and snuggle closer, pushing her nose against his neck. Charles liked making love to her when she was half asleep. It stirred him to take the half-conscious girl in his arms. In any case he could no more resist a beautiful naked woman beside him than he could fly. These mornings he took Jenny before the poor girl had time to gather her wits and her sensations. He made love suddenly, quickly, rolling on top of her, separating her legs and almost before Jenny could begin to respond and move with him he had finished. He rolled off her and went back to sleep.

But he woke again too soon. Sex had not banished the pain in him, as it had always done until now. When he was sad. When life was empty. Now the girl he'd enjoyed was forgotten as soon as he'd taken her. He lay with his eyes shut and did not understand why it was his heart which was hurting.

One fine Saturday morning he, Jenny and Lisa were due to drive out to Lyndhurst where work was now in full swing. It looked as if they would soon be able to move into three repaired and repainted rooms. But at the last moment Charles made an excuse and said he would join them later, taking a station taxi. He accompanied them to the car and gave Lisa the keys. They drove away, with Charles waving cheerfully as if they were leaving for days.

Lisa had decided he was going to the Wilton instead of helping with the work at Lyndhurst; she felt resentful. What was more the ancient car was difficult to handle, the gears were sluggish and the steering unresponsive. She was occupied with disliking it when Jenny said in a thin voice, 'He didn't say where he was going.'

'He's bloody-minded. He knew we wanted him to come so he simply did the opposite. He'll only go for a stroll through the town and buy himself a tie.'

'He bought one yesterday.'

Lisa laughed in spite of herself. 'Don't worry. The thing with Charles is to let him stew in his own juice.'

The advice was as sensible as it was bad.

They drove into the country, passing the long white building of Avoncliffe among its trees. Lisa knew exactly at which point of the road they would drive by the gate and kept her eyes ahead. She never looked in that direction.

Mr Matthews the builder had already arrived at Lyndhurst, his van was in the drive, and as they came up to the house he appeared on the front steps, pleased to see them and full of builder's news of this which was going right and that which was all wrong. In the distance the two actors were scything the tall grass. Lisa went into the house with Mr Matthews, Jenny into the field to the actors. Time took wing.

Charles had walked to the theatre's Stage Door and asked for Gemma Lambert.

'Not in the theatre just now, Mr Whitfield,' said the doorkeeper, tearing himself away from the sports pages.

Charles stood irresolute in the sun. He wandered back to the High Street, bought *The Spectator*, and read an article about the Stratford season which mentioned *Twelfth Night* in glowing terms, and *King Lear* with tetchy reservations. Gemma was called 'flamboyant'. It was the first time Charles had ever read a notice about an actor he knew, and he was sure she would be pleased with it.

As he left the shop with the magazine under his arm, he saw her, walking hand in hand with a small boy who must be the son Charles had heard about from someone in the theatre. Gemma wore a full-skirted dress of coffee brown, her bright hair escaping from tortoiseshell combs. She stopped when she saw Charles, and waited for him to come to her. She smiled.

The little boy, dressed in a sailor's suit, took no notice of Charles. He was absorbed in a red matchbox bus which he clutched in the hand not grasped by Gemma.

'Hello, Charles . . . you don't know Bobbie, do you? My son Bobbie. Say how do you do to a friend of mine, my darling.'

The child greeted him shyly and looked away.

Charles and Gemma lingered, talking like acquaintances. Now and then she laughed, showing her pretty teeth. Her voice had a sweet cadence, she was all generous charm. People looked at her covertly as they walked by; it was always like that for actors in the streets at Stratford.

Charles told her he had just read *The Spectator*. 'You have seen it, haven't you,' he said, lifting the magazine enquiringly, 'because if not –'

Gemma gave a little scream. 'I never read them! Well, not for weeks and weeks until it doesn't matter any more.'

'Why should it matter, providing they are good?'

'It throws me off balance. I keep thinking the critic saw something I didn't see, or imagined I was trying for an effect when I did that bit by mistake.' She seemed the pure soul of honesty, and exquisitely vulnerable.

311

'*The Spectator* calls you alluring.'

'Stop, stop!'

Bobbie looked up, still shy. He was not a romping, cheeky, confident, bold child. He was dignified and timid. The moment Charles smiled at him he looked away.

'I called at the Stage Door,' remarked Charles to Gemma.

'I thought you would.'

'When may I see you?'

'Do you want to?'

Even Charles in his weakened state wasn't falling for that. He merely grinned.

'Come to Avoncliffe tomorrow afternoon and have tea. You can meet Tom again – you used to be great friends, didn't you?'

'Did we?' he said.

She looked at him, her head slightly back. She parted her lips and licked them a little.

'I'd like to have tea with you,' Charles said.

Gemma bent down, pushed the child's cap straight, gave the upturned face a kiss and said she would see Charles at four.

In a mood of exaltation which he did not question, Charles walked to the station to find a taxi. He even managed a glance of indifference at Crocker Road. Climbing into the lumbering cab he asked the driver to take him to Lyndhurst.

There was a picnic going on at Lyndhurst. Lisa had bought some food and set up packing cases under the trees. The two actors and Jenny were cutting sandwiches, Lisa arranging plates and Mr Matthews opening bottles of ginger beer. When Jenny saw her husband she came running over to him, full of news about Lyndhurst and its possiblities. It was all 'tr'mendous fun' pronounced Jenny, the house would soon be 'abs'l't'ly marvellous'. Even the stables were possible.

'Do you know, Charles, somebody looked after them.'

'In a way,' said Lisa, who'd been whitewashing off the obscenities.

'Perfect for a horse. Two, actually. You will come and look, won't you, darling?' said Jenny.

The afternoon following the picnic hurried by. Mr Matthews and a helper were busy, so were the actors who enjoyed hard work, and so was Lisa. Charles did not exactly do anything but was very encouraging. When the day was over there was an exodus. Charles and Jenny were having a cup of tea in the kitchen when Lisa appeared, yawning.

'Progress,' she said, and sat down on a pile of bricks. 'I've been all round the house looking at everything, and I've selfishly decided which bit I'd like to live in if you two approve.'

'You can live in any bit you want, Lou.'

'What about the dining-room and the big bedroom and bathroom? And we could make you a kitchen if you like those rooms. Or anywhere else of course,' said Jenny, 'if you want to be separate from us.' Not in the least attached to her sister-in-law, she'd named the best rooms in the house. Charles, less generous, twisted an eyebrow but said nothing.

'Jenny, that's very kind of you and I do want to be on my own. I've found three perfect rooms. Up the back staircase.'

'The back?' repeated Charles.

'Yes, you know, the outside entrance to them is on the right. I've worked it out and they'll do beautifully.'

'You're talking about the servants' wing. You don't expect to live there and us to live in the main house.'

'I don't see why not.'

'The house is half yours,' he said, thoroughly annoyed. 'Don't be so bloody noble.'

Jenny looked worried. She wasn't fond of Lisa but she was impressed by her. Jenny's friends spoke the same clipped language and looked at things in the same way. Lisa was twenty-eight, which was quite old. Jenny never felt at home with her; ten years and a war lay between them.

'Don't you like the rooms I suggested?'

'Of course I do, Jenny, they're lovely,' said Lisa with an exasperated laugh. 'They're by far the nicest in the house. But what I want are the rooms I've just mentioned. They have their own front door and they *suit* me. My mind's made up, there's really no point in us arguing about it.'

Charles scowled. 'Out of the question.'

'Why?' said Lisa sweetly.

'You know perfectly well. I won't have it.'

Lisa rubbed her hands together. They were filthy with dried paint and dust and made a rasping sound. She wondered if they would ever be clean again. Oh, my poor fingernails.

'There's more news,' she said. 'Mr Matthews came up with me to have a dekko and he says work needed on the rooms is going to cost a bomb. The roof at the back is leaking in three different places and some of the floorboards in the front room are practically rotten. Then there's a bathroom to install. Things like that. Goodness, I'm afraid it's going to cost a lot of money.' Charles's face, as Jenny watched, cleared like a sky when the clouds roll away. 'When the flat is ready I shall be able to have Peter round every night,' added Lisa.

'Damn you, lewd minx,' said Charles, laughing. He'd been reading *Othello*, lent to him by Gemma.

Lisa, trying not to look as if she had won, left the kitchen to go and clear away the remains of the picnic. Charles took Jenny to see the rooms his sister had chosen. They were smallish and the windows looked over the garden. They were certainly in bad repair and much knocked about. But there was some panelling and an alcove and an old-fashioned set of bookshelves.

'How dingy it all is, Charles darling. Are you cross with her for wanting to spend a lot of money on this when she could easily –'

'Jenny, don't be a noodle.'

Avoncliffe was a pleasant house in summertime or any time. It was spacious but unpretentious; it lay back from the road, protected by trees, giving it a privacy which is the grace of many English houses. A kind of secret air. The river ran through the back of the gardens, and the lawns were wide enough for someone sooner or later to suggest croquet.

Tom Westbury and his actress wife had been allotted a

flat in one of the stable blocks adjoining the big house. Their flat overlooked a cobbled yard. A honeysuckle had grown up by the front door and was in full bee-heavy bloom.

Bobbie had settled down happily in his new home. He was Gemma's son by a previous and disastrous marriage to an actor, was not yet four years old and was Gemma's heel of Achilles. By luck, of which Gemma had large slices, there was another married actress with children living in a neighbouring Avoncliffe flat, which meant Bobbie had companions. The actress was not playing this year, she was keeping house for her husband and children and was glad to add Bobbie to the gang. She drove him with her three to school every day, and collected them in the afternoon. Afterwards they romped in the gardens.

Gemma was not a woman's woman, she didn't much like her own sex, but she was genuinely warm to anybody who did her a kindness. Patsy, the actress-mother, a thin-faced young woman with ambitions for her family but no longer for herself, was a godsend. Gemma showered her with thanks, and an occasional bottle of champagne.

Bobbie had just come back from school and was playing alone under the beech tree. The other children had gone in to tea, and although he'd been invited to join them he'd said a polite 'no thanks'. He was having one of his periodic fits of shyness. He sat on the grass, pushing his matchbox bus to and fro and taking no notice of anybody.

His mother had prepared an alfresco meal and brought it out on a tray – tea and ineptly cut doorsteps which were supposed to be sandwiches. After spreading a checked cloth, she sat down, placing an enormous straw hat beside her. Tom emerged from the stable flat and walked across the grass.

'Hurry up,' called Gemma, 'or the wasps will discover the honey.'

'It could only take you, darling, to make honey sandwiches on the hottest day of the year.'

'Bobbie loves them.'

'So do the wasps,' said Tom, picking up the hat and waving away excited wasps.

'Don't use my hat, you'll bend the brim. Use your hand.'

'They'll sting me.'

'Not if you're quick.'

He put down the hat which Gemma now decided to wear, pinning it on to her thick hair with a hatpin and tying black velvet ribbons under her chin.

'By the way,' she said, 'we have a visitor for tea.'

'And who may that be?' said Tom without enthusiasm.

She smiled, unsurprised. Tom had not been in a good mood for days. He hadn't wanted to come and live in Stratford; he would have preferred to remain in his Hampstead flat and work in peace. But Gemma had been offered a very good line of parts in the Stratford season, and to be a leading player here was much sought after. She made such a flattering fuss about Tom coming with her that he relented.

The Memorial Theatre gave them the pleasant, smallish flat and Tom had now met most of the Company, including all the various people living in Avoncliffe. He and Gemma had been entertained by the hospitable and glamorous Quayles. They'd met young girls and young men, some players, some in stage management. He liked them, and because he was a dramatist was given a certain respect. But he wasn't part of this life.

They were easy and friendly and bitchy and above all they were sociable. At any time of day you would hear shouts of laughter. Tom was a writer and needed solitude. He was also inhospitable which was something Gemma couldn't get used to. Her previous husband had been petulant and selfish, none too generous with money and a hypochondriac. He'd often been unkind to her and for all his actor's charm was cold and withdrawn when they were alone. But he had welcomed anybody who came to their poorish flat. He was always pleased when she invited people, took trouble to look after them and to entertain them too. He was a show-off, and his guests enjoyed that and competed. Among his many faults, thought Gemma, you could never say Adam was anything but the soul of hospitality. When the front doorbell rang anytime from morning until night, he beamed. It was not like that with Tom. He differed in every way from her previous husband. He was thoughtful, unselfish, clever with her and never indulgent. He loved Bobbie deeply and Bobbie's own father had been jealous of the child. On the subject of her acting, he was Gemma's most loyal yet perceptive critic whereas all Adam had given her was praise as hollow as the voice of a speak-your-weight machine. But you couldn't deny his warmth with visitors.

Now Tom looked martyred, waiting to hear who was coming to tea.

'I've asked Charles Whitfield to drop by. He isn't a stranger, apparently you knew him in the dim and distant.'

Tom was suddenly still. She did not notice. 'I knew them both.'

'The sister as well? I haven't met her ... someone said she works at The Treasure Box. Anybody working for Perdita Smith must be a hardy girl. Did you know Charles had bought Lyndhurst, that old stone house we noticed when we were driving to Warwick? Anyway, that's who we're expecting and stop looking the picture of gloom.'

'Did you invite his wife?'

'Should I have done? He and I were chatting at the Wardrobe party and then I met him in the town. No sign of the wife, though,' said Gemma. 'I think I shall count the sandwiches,' smacking Tom's hand stretched out for one.

She fidgeted with the becoming hat and looked half a dozen times towards the turn in the drive. Finally, while Tom leaned on his elbow watching Bobbie making a garage with twigs for the matchbox bus, Charles came into view. He was walking with the unhurried pace of the long, hot afternoon. He wore tennis flannels and a white shirt with rolled-up sleeves. At a distance, the tall, white-clad figure could have been an actor. But as he came nearer, Gemma thought: you can see he isn't. No actor is as casual as that. Or as unselfconscious.

The group beneath the trees, a woman in a pale dress and shady hat, a man sprawling beside her, a child playing nearby, resembled a group in a Victorian painting. So did the summer afternoon, the big house dozing. Gemma stretched out a freckled hand.

'How nice. You know Tom, of course. An old friend from centuries ago.'

The men smiled and shook hands. They made the usual remarks about the gap of time between Oxford and the 1930s and now. Each summed up the other, each thought the other much older and much changed. Tom was struck, as people always were, by Charles's haggard good looks, and Charles by the solidity and loss of youth in his one-time university friend. Tom, thought Charles, looked considerable. He banished from his mind the fact that he'd made this man a cuckold.

'Sit down, sit down, I've made tea and cut sandwiches,' said Gemma, announcing it as an achievement.

If Tom was inhospitable, Gemma was an engaging hostess. She couldn't cook for toffee, but if she offered you a cake bought at the tea-shop, she did it with the air of somebody who had selected it particularly because she knew it was your favourite. She was attentive, fluttery. She passed tea-cups.

The conversation was of Lincoln College, names and places almost forgotten, a time and a world away. It had no substance to renew a friendship between the two men. Gemma called Bobbie to her, cut little squares of bread and honey as if he were two years old and arranged them in a ring on the plate.

'Careful. You nearly bit a wasp.' The little boy practically choked.

Gemma sipped her tea and looked from one man to the other and then back again. For once she had no desire to demand attention.

Her nature was essentially competitive; she sprang into action when she was with anybody of any age. She would arrange the lights and switch them on to herself. She played with a grace akin to music whichever rôle was handy – wife, enchantress, good friend, mother. Sometimes the rôles happened to be genuine, and had she ripped away the veil, reality would have lain underneath. She was real as a wife because she was confident with Tom. She was more than real, artlessly so, when she was a mother loving her son as a lioness does her cub. But real or play-acting she needed floods of light.

Except this afternoon, when she leaned her back against the tree and listened idly to two men talking rubbish about a past they had scarcely shared. It was the kind of conversation Gemma sometimes overheard when she was travelling. It always filled her with wonder. Men without women, she decided, were truly boring. She sat contentedly studying the men, both of whose bodies had penetrated her own within a day. It was impossible not to compare them, and her sensual self enjoyed doing so.

Charles's features were heavier and his cheeks more lined than Tom's. He had a sardonic, lazy look. That amused her when she remembered how he'd thrown her down in the picture gallery, and the violent way he'd made love to her. She thought he looked slightly debauched. Drink? Too much sex? She liked that exhausted look.

There was nothing exhausted about Tom who was big and curly-haired, with an aquiline nose and brilliant grey eyes which blazed with mirth and sometimes with anger, but were never tired. He had a more powerful frame than Charles; Gemma judged that although the two men were of a height Tom probably weighed a stone more. She had lain under both of them. Their voices were different too, she thought as she listened. Tom's had an incisive quality. Charles drawled. For a man who looked considerable, Tom was modest about his own gifts whereas Charles, who probably had no talent but sex, was casually satisfied with himself.

'What do you think of our house, Charles?' said Gemma, when there was a pause in the talk. She waved towards Avon-cliffe.

'Gemma, it is not out house. To be precise, Charles, we've rented a flat over there in the stables.'

He's always shooting me down in flames, thought Gemma in defunct wartime vernacular.

319

'My husband likes to make things sound small. I prefer them enlarged,' said Gemma, conscious of the *sous-entendu*. 'You can't deny the garden at present belongs to *us all*, Tom. During the season we can use it any time we want.'

'It is very good of Tony and Dot Quayle,' said Tom.

'Yes, yes,' said Gemma impatiently. 'The point I'm making is we look on it as ours during the season. We give tea parties –' she gestured at the picnic. 'Will you come again, Charles?' She was innocent and artless. She imposed on Charles the necessity to smile and smile and be a villian.

He glanced at Tom Westbury lolling under the tree. How could he be so complaisant? Had he any idea of exactly what he'd married?

Bobbie came over to sit on Tom's knee, winding thin arms round his stepfather's neck. Tom kissed him.

'Didn't you tell me you're going to play with Sally and Joe Aston?'

'Yes, we're going to dig in the kitchen garden. Sally says we can plant love-in-the mist and it'll grow and there'll be flowers in a few weeks, definitely.'

'Then off you go. I saw the kids coming out of the house.'

Bobbie sprang up and left them, running, so as not to miss the fun. He forgot to say goodbye.

'He has a crush on Sally Aston,' said Gemma. 'She's eight. He likes the older woman.'

It was Tom's turn to leave. He must, he said, put in another three hours' work, or the first Act would never be right.

Charles made the predictable remark. 'I don't know how you chaps think of it all.'

Tom and Gemma laughed, and Tom, saying goodbye, wandered off towards the stables.

Gemma chewed a stem of grass. 'See that wall over there? It's the limit of our property.'

'What's on the other side?'

'A field of cowpats. Horseflies are beastly. I got stung the other day. My leg went crimson and swelled up all horribly. I was sure I was destined to be a second Sarah Bernhardt.'

320

'Did a horsefly sting her too?'

'Of course not. When she was playing in South America there was a scene where she had to throw herself over a wall – to commit suicide, you see? Sarah always landed on a mattress behind the wall quite safely. One night somebody forgot it – wasn't that dreadful? She threw herself over and fell on the ground and damaged her knee so badly she fainted with pain. Years later the leg had to be amputated. They gave her a wooden one.'

'Good heavens. I can't imagine an actress with a wooden leg,' said Charles, trying not to laugh.

'You don't know a thing about theatre, do you? My mother actually saw Sarah playing L'Aiglon, that's Napoleon's fifteen-year-old son. Sarah was past sixty and because of the wooden leg, couldn't budge. Ma said she was very bad. I don't believe it . . . Does theatre talk bore you?'

'On the contrary,' he said. 'But as you say, I'm very ignorant. Do you mind?'

She rested her wonderful eyes on him. They were strangely coloured, like the topaz of some cats' eyes. 'I like it. It's restful . . . See that swing under the trees? Tom put it up for Bobbie. Tom's good at knots so it's quite safe. The other kids use it, but when Bobbie's alone, he sometimes swings himself into a dream, funny fellow.'

'You have a very handsome son.'

'Don't I? Not Tom's. Did I tell you I've been married before?'

They stood up and began to walk away from the house, turning towards the river. The lawn descended into a mass of laurel and privet bushes and there – greyish, blueish, sparkling, flowing fast – was the Avon.

'You've told me nothing about yourself,' he murmured.

'I will. I promise.' She met his look with an unconcealed one of her own. They could scarcely tear their eyes away from each other.

'I don't think,' she said in a low voice, 'we can make love in the punt, do you? Suppose it tipped over?' He had known when he had her the first time that she was as promiscuous, as sensually aware, as desirous and perhaps as experienced as he. She melted as he watched. 'The river curves along by the willows. We'd be out of sight. We could kiss. It would be something.'

'Yes,' he said, laughing at her. 'It would be something.'

The punt was old and rickety, the rope beginning to fray. Charles unknotted it from the branch around which it was tied, and Gemma stepped into the craft, taking its centre so that it scarcely bobbed. Charles had punted in Oxford, and they set off, spinning along the surface as he thrust the pole down and lifted it, dripping, to run it through his hands.

They reached the trees away from the eyes of the house. He caught a branch of a low-growing willow and tied up, then lay down beside her, the punt slowly swinging out and staying in the current. He began to embrace her. He was lost at once in the pleasure of her response, her moist mouth, her ardour, the smell and feel of her. He did not know, and nor did she, that this was more than sex.

# PART THREE

# 16

Lisa and her sister-in-law were together a good deal during the high summer of 1948. They spent the weekends at Lyndhurst doing not very competent house decorating, and overseeing the work of Mr Matthews and a carpenter. The house was progressing and by the end of August the trio were able to leave the expensive kingdom of The Shakespeare Hotel and say goodbye to the *King Lear* bathroom.

Charles continued to go off on his own and leave the girls to do the work; neither of them complained, Jenny because she loved him too much, and Lisa because she decided her responsibility over her brother was at an end.

Mr Matthews admired Lisa, and it was not an accident that the large jobs of repairing her flat, seeing to the roof and reflooring her sitting-room were done ahead of the work in the main house. Lisa's sitting-room and bedroom were quickly ready, painted white. Her parquet floors were relaid and polished. Finally she and Perdita went to Broadway, a Cotswold village where under Perdita's direction Lisa bought some Persian rugs. She also bought one or two restful paintings, mostly the work of English artists of the 1900s.

She and Charles paid off Drury's Depository, and the boxes arrived. The poppy-patterned plates, the photographs in silver frames, everything was fairly divided between brother and sister. Rory belonged to Lisa and was carried up to her sitting-room where he stood in a corner, vainly hoping for a rider.

Lisa was enchanted with her new home. She had the luxury of a bathroom – it had once been a room with shelves and a sink where maids in the past had fetched cans of hot water for the gentry. In the sitting-room Lisa had an open fire and Charles promised he would carry up her logs; 'just ask any time'.

Queen of a domain at last, Lisa roosted there like a bird in a new-built nest. It was here that she would entertain Charles and Jenny or old friends – there were a few at Stratford. Polly, of course. Most important of all, here she and Peter could be alone together.

When Lisa had first heard Charles say he had bought the house, she'd had a pang of real alarm because it was close to Avoncliffe where Tom lived. Yet she never saw him. The road to Stratford, and consequently to The Treasure Box, went past Avoncliffe and every morning, driving the cheap second-hand Morris car she had now bought, Lisa was forced to go past the big house, its familiar white gate propped open as if in welcome. She saw actors on their way to morning rehearsals; they walked in couples or set out on bicycles. Once two cyclists came through the gate as Lisa drove by; she caught a glint of russet hair and was sure it was Gemma Lambert with a companion. She averted her eyes. She did not want to look at the woman who had stolen Tom away.

Days turned to weeks and she didn't meet him once. The miserable first shock became a bruise, painful if touched. She turned in relief, affection, with something like a sigh of gratitude to Peter.

She had grown fond of him, as a woman does who knows how much she is desired and admired. She liked him very much. In bed he satisfied her craving for sexual love. His love-making was intense and intent, he always made love to her naked, never wanted to take her when she was dressed, never asked for anything but that she should lie down with him. He loved her strongly, simply, and never said tender things when it was over. Her climax came with a certain melting relief and that was all.

Waking beside him, sharing meals, a social as well as a

326

sexual life, talking of everything from her work to her worries about Charles, Lisa was always aware that there was something mystifying about Peter. Why was he content with that small job on a small newspaper, reporting council meetings and summer fêtes? He was clever and well-informed, thirty-eight years old, a mature man and not a young reporter on his first job training for larger things. He apparently had no ambition. She couldn't understand it. When she was alone in her flat where she had taken up her life and felt comfortably at home, she often thought about Peter and tried to make sense of his life.

She had noticed, as any girl would, that he hadn't asked her to marry him. It surprised her, for men were inclined to want to marry Lisa. In Burma before the war she'd had at least four proposals of marriage; officers in India had tentatively suggested it – and there had been Tom. 'We will spend our life together,' he'd said. 'If we still have one.'

She swerved away from remembering that and returned to Peter. She knew him very well. He was reliable and thoughtful, generous with money although he did not have much. He had little sense of humour but he liked to laugh and when he did his blue eyes shone. She could never forget how he had offered to lend her money when Charles left her. It was one of the kindest things anyone had done in her life. He was a good-looking, serious, hardworking enigma. When they made love he never spoke. Tom had whispered things in her ears which had been so exciting and which afterwards she could not remember. Peter was a good lover, intense, passionate, considerate, and he smelled so clean. But who *was* he? Where had he sprung from? She did not quite believe some of the things he said when she had questioned him about himself. He told her he had fought in France. Yes, said Lisa, where? Oh, the Normandy landings, Peter answered vaguely. He had nothing interesting to say about the great drama of liberated Europe. During all the time Lisa had known him, he never mentioned meeting a single erstwhile regimental friend. When she asked questions about the Invasion, he looked bored.

327

Of course, the memory of war was receding. Soon it would vanish like a burnt-out comet from many people's minds. Three years had gone by since VJ Day, and the peace which stared people in the face was called Austerity. The country was shabby and shoddy, rationing was severe. Now was scarcely the time for reminiscences. Yet people enjoyed them. The most dangerous, heightened or ludicrous things had happened during the war. Everybody still talked about it except Peter.

There were many favourite stories. Charles talked about Burmese ghosts, about realigning a river using bamboo mat screens, swimming ponies across streams, and riding tough little horses called Burmese tats. Mick Gould, who had been stationed in India, had tales which were a delight. One night when Lisa and Charles were with him at The Shakespeare, and Jenny out with her friend Angela, Mick told them of the day he'd had his shoes repaired in Trincomalee.

He'd been leaving the army headquarters one morning when he saw a sort of small tent erected by the side of the road and festooned with pairs of mended shoes. The owner sat busily soling and heeling some Army boots. Mick, delighted, asked how long it would take for a pair of his own shoes to be done.

'Do it by tonight, Sir. Without fail. Tonight.'

Mick fetched not one but three pairs and arranged to call for them by sundown.

'So I did,' said Mick.

'And?' prompted Charles.

'The booth was gone. Into thin air. I couldn't believe it. I rampaged up and down the camp, I looked along all the road, there wasn't a sign. Finally I spoke to a sergeant-major. He looked at me more in sorrow than in anger.

'"You'll never clap eyes on them boots of yours again, Sir."

'"What?" I cried. "But that man had at least fifty hanging all round waiting to be mended or collected!"

'"I'm sure he did. All of 'em got from Englishmen. He'll be in China Bay or Uppveli by now, setting up another booth. Good British boots and shoes for sale."'

328

People told stories like that. They talked of the times when war had thrown them to the four corners of the earth. They had dropped into the ocean from the sky, they had hidden in ditches, worked on bomb sites, been captured, escaped. Not Peter.

Lisa didn't give up trying to get him to tell her at least something which would make the war's effect upon him seem real, create a picture of him in her own mind long before she had known him.

'Being in India we missed D-Day and the tremendous excitement. What was it like when you landed in France?' she asked one evening when they were having supper in the flat.

'Lisa, you've seen the newsreels of lines of troops marching through the French villages. I was among them.'

'Being given swigs of wine and bunches of flowers?'

'You're a very romantic woman.'

'Am I? They did give you flowers, didn't they? Did you have lots of army friends?'

'Not really. I'm not what is called clubbable.'

'I'll tell you what you *are*,' she said, bending forward to kiss him. 'A solemn old owl.'

He looked embarrassed.

He came to visit her or stay the night, and was with her almost every evening. She looked forward to seeing his car, and ran to the window for a sight of his ash-blond head as he walked towards her front door. He behaved like a husband. He brought food and flowers, books sometimes. He changed electric plugs and repaired the broken leg of a chair. He discussed domestic things – the way her rooms were arranged, the choice of new curtains.

But he never mentioned marriage.

Stratford was full during the summer. The streets were busy and American voices, which hadn't been heard since the troops went home in 1945, were a familiar sound again. The transatlantic visitors were interested in everything the town had to offer. In the timbered inns and prim knot gardens, the ancient mulberry trees, the oak cradle in the Birthplace which might have belonged to the baby who was William Shakespeare. In Holy Trinity they looked at his bust in limestone, asking each other – everybody always did – if he'd really looked like that. They read the blessing and the curse he'd written. And in the theatre at night they greeted him with their full-hearted applause.

Perdita watched the Americans, Londoners and Scandinavians with a bright eye and remarked that now was the time to do some real business.

'Everybody wants to take home a present, and people on holiday have time to browse. We'll put some tempting things in the window. The Treasure Box is just the place for them to find something at a most reasonable price.'

'Of course.'

'Don't laugh at me, Miss. I only mark up when it is absolutely necessary.'

Perdita had taken a fancy to Lisa. She still ignored her if a customer was about, or ordered her to make cups of tea as if Lisa were a skivvy. Alone, she treated Lisa like a daughter. She was never too tired to teach. Lisa grew knowledgeable about vinaigrettes, which Perdita called 'the toys of the upper crust'. The vinegars they once contained had been sweetened with perfumed oils, rosemary, sage, mace, lemon, cloves or the fragrant juniper. Once Perdita bought a vinaigrette which they sold to a lady from Texas, and when she sniffed it the scent, a hundred and fifty years old, was still there. Lisa learned also about coral, not only the Mediterranean red, but the black, the yellow and the blue. She began to know such unlikely facts as the dates of coffee-pots by their curved spouts and double-twist handles.

Perdita watched her progress.

'It's time you came to more sales with me. I've stopped wearing my specs, you know. When I do I look too interested. Somebody said I was like a bird of prey. Charming. My sight,' she continued not without vanity, 'is that of an eighteen-year-old but only close to. And it would be foolish to pick up something, a menu card, a snuffbox, and hold it to

330

my nose. How much chance would I have of getting it with some smart London cookies watching me?'

Perdita was in an expansive mood after she and Lisa had gone to a house sale in Chipping Norton where Lisa, running up some steep stairs her employer baulked at, discovered a basketful of Victorian china which Perdita later bought for a song.

She decided to celebrate in a local pub, and asked Lisa to fetch them sandwiches and drinks. Looking reflective, Perdita sat down on a window-seat and stared at the floor. Lisa, returning, wondered if her employer was already deciding on the prices she would put on her booty.

'There is nothing, absolutely nothing, like a gin and Italian,' said Perdita, as they drank to success. She regarded the girl for a moment. 'You did well today,' she said. 'Very well. You used your eyes and I like that. I wish you did the same in other directions. But you don't.'

'Did I miss something else? I thought I'd been careful . . . In the room upstairs there was only –'

'I'm not talking about the sale. Or about business either, as it happens. For a young woman I have been teaching to use her eyes, you don't seem able to see what's staring you in the face.'

'Perdita,' said Lisa, thinking it some sort of tiresome game, 'I really have no idea what you're talking about.'

'Charles.'

Lisa looked startled. Then reflected. And sighed. 'Don't tell me. He's begun to gamble again.'

'Of course he's gambling. He goes to the Wilton twice a week. David Murdoch owns the place and he tells me so. Once a gambler always a gambler. They need excitement and not only in cards. Jenny Bowden isn't exactly the Du Barry, is she?' Perdita sipped her drink. 'Getting there yet?' she enquired. 'I'm referring to Charles's affair with that writer's wife. What's his name? Tom Westbury.' The intense momentary stab that accompanies fear went through Lisa. 'Westbury came into The Treasure Box the other day when you were out, did I tell you? I sold him an inkwell reputed to have belonged to Henry Irving. I told him it definitely was Irving's. Of course I could have been right.' Lisa, looking straight at her, said nothing. Perdita had been expecting a bad reaction but ploughed on. 'What I am trying to tell you, my child, is that your brother is taking Westbury's wife to bed. Not sure he's cottoned on yet, history doesn't relate, but everybody else seems to know. Except you, that is.'

'I don't believe it.'

'Because you don't want to. It's true, I'm afraid. You're quite fond of young Jenny Bowden, aren't you? I'm told she's fretting.'

'What did you mean when you said everybody else knows?' said Lisa. She looked so shocked that the older woman had a moment of remorse.

'Because Polly Holt mentioned it to me yesterday. I saw her in The Falcon where she was waiting for Lewis Lockton and she was full of gossip. Now, Lisa', with severity, 'if an actress in the company knows what's going on, you can bet your boots all fifty-five of them do. What price the blind sister?' Lisa's face was so stricken that Perdita's uneasy feeling of contrition grew. She said impatiently, 'You needn't look as if I'd hit you on the jaw. Didn't you once say Charles had a string of women? So he hasn't changed, has he?'

'There's Jenny.'

'I know, I know. Why do you suppose I took on the unpleasant job of telling you?'

When she drove back to Lyndhurst, Lisa left the car in the shade. The evening was hot and heavy and there was a scent of cut grass from the only part of the garden as yet reclaimed.

She went to the open front door of the main house and called out, 'Jenny?'

No reply.

'Charles?'

Silence.

She turned back and walked into the garden. There was one enclosed piece of lawn with a paved walk and a wall on which an espaliered pearl bush grew in long, flat branches.

It was there that the grass had been cut and left to dry in the sun. Jenny was lying under a crab-apple tree in the deepening shade.

Lisa came up and stood looking down at her. Jenny lay still but she was not asleep. Her arms were behind her head. She said without moving, 'Looking for Charles?'

'For you.'

'Oh really? What for?'

The clipped words, the brusque voice, recalled the girl Lisa had first met whose coldness had been marked, almost offensive. Damn Charles, thought Lisa. And damn Tom for not keeping that actress wife. She sat down on the grass. 'How dry it is. Little cracks.'

'And ants. I was watching them carrying their eggs. They shove each other out of the way.'

'I'm not keen on ants. I hate the flying ones.'

'Daddy said they don't sting.'

'I don't agree with him,' said Lisa, smiling slightly.

Jenny still lay flat. She looked as if she had been knocked down. What had she been doing here all day along? Had Charles gone out this morning to keep some appointment, some tryst, and forgotten about her? Was that the reason for the sudden mention of her father? She hadn't once spoken of him to Lisa since she and Charles had returned from Italy.

'Where's Charles?' Lisa said.

'Out somewhere. I don't know.'

'Perhaps he's playing poker in that dreary old Wilton Club.'

'I expect so.'

She isn't going to say a thing, thought Lisa. She intends to be miserable alone or tell herself lies. But Jenny didn't look capable of such self-protection.

'Shall I go and get us some tea?' said Lisa, rallying her. 'I'm dying of thirst.'

The girl still lay staring up at the tree on which the crab-apples were green knobs, far off from the yellow and scarlet fruit of the autumn.

'Okay, if you want. I don't mind.'

Lisa was suddenly exasperated by the flattened voice and the flattened girl. 'I did not ask if you minded, Jenny, I asked if you'd like some tea. If you don't, just say so and I will make it only for myself. I wish you'd sit up. You look –'

'Look what?'

'Oh, I don't know, as if you were dead,' said Lisa, laughing crossly. Her sister-in-law got on her nerves.

'Perhaps it'd be better if I was.'

'What *are* you talking about?'

'Don't you know? Everybody else does.'

'For goodness sake, sit up. I can't have a sensible conversation with somebody looking like a tree that's just been felled. Everybody know what?' The shock tactics worked and Jenny came to the surface, sitting up and vaguely brushing away a dead leaf from her hair. How long had she been lying there? It must have been for hours. She had caught the sun; her delicate skin was uncomfortably red on cheeks and forehead. 'You need some sun cream. You ought to wear a hat.'

Jenny did not answer. She said, refastening her watch-strap, 'Charles is with Gemma Lambert.'

'At Avoncliffe, you mean. Having tea with her and her husband. Charles knew him years ago at Oxford.'

In this instance it was easy to mention Tom. She looked casually at her sister-in-law who muttered, 'He doesn't see her husband. He picks *her* up and they go off together.'

Lisa reacted loudly. 'How on earth can you possibly say that! Charles scarcely knows her any more than you or I do.'

'He knows her very well. Since *Twelfth Night*. It must have started then.'

'What started?' said Lisa, deliberately cruel.

She was too successful for the girl's eyes slowly filled with tears which rolled down the poor, reddened cheeks. She didn't wipe them away. Her nose was red too. 'He's in love with her. They go to bed together.'

'What is all this? It's your imagination. He never told you any such thing.'

'No, he didn't. That's not Charles, is it?'

'What do you mean?' asked Lisa, who knew.

'He never tells women when he's unfaithful to them. He just does it. He's doing it now.'

'Jenny, this has got to stop! You're torturing yourself and I'm sure it's all in your imagination.'

'It isn't,' Jenny said and felt in the pocket of her cotton dress. She produced a handkerchief as dirty as that of a schoolboy, scrubbed her eyes and said in a matter of fact voice, 'I suppose it's inventible.'

The misuse of the word, even more than the woebegone red face and childish eyes, tore at Lisa's heart. She was furious with Charles.

'I realize I'm not being sympathetic but you can't *know* if he hasn't told you. I expect you've been lonely and he's a selfish so-and-so, he always was, and you've been too much on your own. Why don't you see your friend Angela? You shouldn't stay here alone all day, imagining things.'

'I don't imagine them. Polly Holt told me.'

'*She what?*'

'She came round this morning looking for you, and I was quite pleased to see her because she talks about the Company and she is an actress and it's lovely to hear about backstage. And – and – she said it.'

'I can't believe you.'

'Oh, she didn't say "your husband is having an affair",' said Jenny listlessly. 'She didn't say anything outright. She was just sort of smiling and nudging about him. She said what a flirt he'd always been and if she was me she wouldn't invite Gemma Lambert here – as if I would – and that she didn't like her. Things like that. She thought she was warning me.'

Instead of which she was breaking your heart, thought Lisa. My God, don't actors understand ordinary people at all? Don't they care about their effect except onstage? She detested Polly.

'I daresay Polly's seen Gemma Lambert making a dead set at Charles. She's probably that sort of woman. Maybe Polly saw them at The Duck. Charles does pop in there for a drink sometimes.' That was Lisa's line. Her flag, as it were, with which she ran on to the stage, sticking it into the ground and standing beside it. 'Now listen to me, please. Don't lie about, upsetting yourself. Come indoors, you've had hours too much sun, and we'll have some tea and decide what you should say to my boring brother.'

'I daren't say anything.'

'Oh rubbish!' Lisa put out her hand, which Jenny unwillingly took, and tugged her to her feet. 'All you've got to do,' continued Lisa in a reasonable voice as the girl walked with her back to the house, 'is to indicate without saying it outright that you miss him. He rather likes people missing him, I think he finds it flattering. Ask him to take you to a film, you'd both enjoy that. Say I want you both for supper. Be natural and ordinary. Make plans. Come on. Didn't Charles tell me he wants to buy you a horse?'

Like the game of Hunt-the-Thimble in which the thimble is magically invisible until it is spotted, and then looks perfectly obvious, an unnoticed fact once pointed out begins to glare. After hearing the rumour from Perdita and after Jenny's pathetic performance at Lyndhurst, over the next few days Lisa saw her brother on two separate occasions with Gemma Lambert. Once, looking out of the window of the shop, she saw the couple walking down Wood Street on the other side of the road, arm in arm. The second time, her brother's car drove past The Treasure Box and she recognized two heads, one dark, one with a russet crown of curls. He isn't even trying to hide the affair, thought Lisa. She felt dully angry with him, more so when she left for work one morning and found Jenny on her knees by a flower-bed, planting Candytuft and Virginia Stock seeds.

'Angie says it isn't too late to plant these and they'll look gorgeous in weeks.'

'You're up bright and early.'

'I know. Charles teases me about it. When I get my horse –'

'You asked him?'

'Last night. He says we can go and look at some ponies Miss Corbett has for sale.'

Her fixed cheerfulness had a ghastly quality and when Lisa said goodbye she was uncharitably relieved to leave the poor girl digging in the unweeded garden.

Work claimed Lisa all day long. She went to a Stratford house sale in the afternoon to bid for an opaline casket. It was of fine milky glass, made in France about 1890 and very beautiful, no bigger than an ostrich egg, with a crazed tourmaline on its domed lid. It was exactly the kind of useless treasure she and Perdita preferred, and Lisa bought it for only £10, which surprised her. She was carrying it away when a buyer whom she did not like hurried up with a smile which was all teeth.

'I'm green with envy. Would you take a profit on it?' she said, pointing at the shining egg in Lisa's hands.

Lisa's instinct as a seller was strong. She scarcely hesitated before saying, 'What are you offering?'

'Ah. What would you take?' Another effusive smile.

'£40,' said Lisa almost at random.

The woman laughed. 'That *is* expensive . . . but, well, I simply must have it! Shall we arrange things right away?' She plumped down on a chair by the wall and opened a worn handbag, producing a roll of pound notes.

Lisa returned to the shop. She kept thinking about the opaline casket, the tourmaline, the sheen on the glass. Perdita was in the shop, listened to the story, and locked the money into the cash box.

'I keep wishing I hadn't sold it,' Lisa said. 'After she'd gone, I was furious with myself. What I'd wanted was to bring it back here, set it out on our counter, see what kind of person bought it . . .'

'I know, I know. Profit isn't what it's all about, is it?' said Perdita.

The day with its frustrated success was over. After saying goodnight, Lisa went out into the warm street. She didn't feel like going home. She needed to think . . .

Along the river bank by the Bancroft, children were feeding the swans. There was the usual queue for punts, the usual shouts from youths lucky enough to be on the river, ineptly

337

rowing or punting under Clopton Bridge. The river sparkled and flowed, reflecting the theatre. Lisa sat down on the wall. She thought of Charles and Gemma Lambert. When they'd walked down Wood Street they had been laughing together. There was something unmistakeable about lovers, a kind of dreadful, excluding joy. Did Tom and I look like that? She was sure Charles had fallen in love. How could he be so cruel? To run off with that vulnerable girl, steal her away from her father and her home and make her his wife, only to dive into love with somebody else a few months later. Where was Tom in all this? *He* had proved as faithless as Charles now was. Tom is getting his come-uppance, thought Lisa stonily. He deserted me and the same thing is happening to him.

A voice in her head spoke just then. It was an inner voice which she often tried to ignore or shout down when it said things she hated to hear. It told her she must see Tom. I can't, she thought. You must, said the voice.

Hell, thought Lisa. She stood up and walked over to the theatre where the posters displayed the repertory. It was *Twelfth Night* this evening. Gemma would be playing. And Tom would be alone.

What could she say to him? How could she face the man who had deserted her? By not thinking about that, she told herself, and by thinking only about Jenny. He'll be angry and embarrassed, and so will I. Why do I imagine I ought to do this?

Jenny came straight into her mind again.

When they had been lovers, Lisa had known Tom was brave. She had loved that in him, it was a quality everybody worshipped in those times of death. He'd flown planes into the thick of the Burma war, he'd saved lives, he was a man to admire as well as to adore. Will he fight for his marriage? she wondered. And am *I* the one to tell him to do that?

She sat in the noisy solitude of the open air, a breeze of evening fanning her hot cheeks, and when it was time to go she almost ran back to the car. I must get it over, she thought. She set off on the most courageous journey of her life.

Avoncliffe lay dozing in the last rays of the sunshine when Lisa, for the first time since that long-ago party of Lewis Lockton's, drove through the open white gates. She looked at the house. There wasn't a soul about. The windows, like the front gates, were open but there seemed to be nobody in the gardens which spread further than Lisa had realized. A shabby car was parked in the stable yard on the right.

She stopped her car at the end of the drive and sat hesitating. Then she walked up to the main house and rang the bell. She heard footsteps and a fair-haired woman with a face like a flower opened the door. She gave Lisa a radiant smile which reached her eyes. When she spoke her voice had an odd quality, like laughter.

'Hello. Are you looking for us?'

Lisa recognized her; it was Dorothy Hyson, the actress married to Anthony Quayle. 'I'm sorry to be a bother. I was looking for Tom Westbury and I don't exactly know where he lives.'

'Avoncliffe is a rabbit warren, isn't it? A beehive. Something like that. You'll find Tom over in the stable flat – you can't miss it because of the honeysuckle outside. He's typing. Follow the rat-tat-tat.'

Dorothy Hyson looked very slightly amused, very slightly curious when the young woman thanked her and said goodbye.

The stables were built round a yard and as Lisa approached she could hear the woodpecker noise of a typewriter. There was the honeysuckle climbing up the side of a stable, a pillar of flowers with scent as sweet as the honey of its name. She pressed the bell. The woodpecker immediately stopped tapping.

She waited. The door opened. And there was Tom.

There was a moment – to Lisa – of a quite awful pause. He stared at her as if she were the last person in the world he expected to see. She wore a dress with a frill on the shoulder which, the evening being hot, she had pulled down, showing her thin brown shoulders. Her hair fell across her face, her eyes looked enormous. He did not know they were enlarged from sheer alarm.

339

'Hello, Tom. I want a word. Is that all right?'

'Of course. Come in.' He showed no surprise, nothing but polite hospitality. They might have met once at a party. 'We live upstairs,' he said. 'Shall I lead the way?'

He began to ascend a steep stair not unlike her own at Lyndhurst, the kind of creaking staircase which belonged to very old humble buildings. It was narrow and seemed to exaggerate the burly figure and looming strength of his back. He wore a thin Air Force shirt of worn blue cotton, the rolled-up sleeves exposing his brawny arms.

They went into a low-ceilinged room. The typewriter was on a table facing the trees that edged the river. There were books on the chairs and a child's toy car on the floor.

He took some books off an easy chair. 'Do sit down. May I get you a drink?'

'No, thank you. I apologize for disturbing you when you're working. I shan't be long.'

She was nervous, her voice didn't sound like her own. But when Tom, sitting down nearby, looked at her enquiringly *he* was perfectly natural. Lisa had not been alone with him, except for the meeting in the dark outside the Wardrobe, for three long years. In the split second when she braced herself to look, she saw those years and what they had done to Tom. He looked older and tougher, less humorous, not approachable. The greatest change of all was the way he was looking at her. He was putting up with her out of courtesy.

'I'm afraid,' he said in a low voice, 'we'll have to speak quietly. Bobbie went to bed early and he's a rotten sleeper. We always creep about. He's my stepson, by the way.'

'Yes. I know.'

'He's a dear little chap.'

His tone suddenly infuriated her. She was bitterly jealous. 'I have something to say,' she began.

Tom interjected extraordinarily, 'Don't you think, Lisa, it would be better not?'

'No, I don't!' she exclaimed very loudly and immediately remembered and put her hand in front of her mouth like a caught-out child, continuing in a furious whisper. 'I'm sorry,

I didn't mean to shout, but no, I do *not* think I should shut up and it astonishes me that you do.'

Listening to the intense whisper, he sat still, his mouth thinly closed, the aquiline nose making the face very hard. Many things they hadn't spoken seemed to pass between them.

'I didn't ask you to come here –'

'You certainly didn't,' hissed Lisa.

'Let me speak, please. I did not ask you to come and now you are here you seem determined to open up a subject we should both forget. It's dead, Lisa. It's over. Please don't try to revive it.'

Lisa went crimson. She realized he had utterly mis-understood her: he actually believed she was here to reproach him for deserting her. For a moment the blush seemed to impair her very eyesight; she unconsciously put her hands against her cheeks and shut her eyes. She regained her self-possession and said contemptuously, 'Did you think I'd come to talk about the past? Did you think me capable of that?'

He looked in bewilderment at her burning face. 'I'm sorry, I must have misunderstood.'

'Like hell you have. Don't you *know* why I'm here? It's about my brother and your wife.'

It was out. Whatever she had expected didn't happen; Tom's expression changed and grew merely thoughtful. He turned to the window-sill and picked up a cigarette-box, opened it and offered it to her. She refused after which, saying 'May I?' he lit a cigarette and snapped his lighter shut, the noise like a small pistol shot.

'You don't look very shocked.'

He gave a somewhat meaningless smile. 'It's a flirtation. Nothing to make a song and dance about,' he said, drawing on the cigarette.

'That isn't true.'

'You probably don't know much about actors, Lisa.'

'No. I don't know about actors,' she said. Mercifully she was now cool. 'Why should I? What your wife does or

341

doesn't do isn't my business. What *is* my business is my sister-in-law's unhappiness, and it's only because of her that I'm here.'

Tom listened to this in silence, smoking, then looked at the tip of his cigarette. 'I'm afraid our morality is not as clear cut as yours.'

'*Our!* Are you one of them, then?'

'One sees things in a different light nowadays. Nothing is straightforward, Lisa. Nothing.'

No, she thought, it isn't, is it? You loved me and I worshipped you and you said you'd come and find me but you threw me over and married that woman. Here you sit telling me your morality and mine are not the same. She hated him and hated more the fact that he looked invulnerable. He was a cuckolded husband. Why wasn't he shamed and guilty?

'What are you going to do about it?' she said after a moment.

'Are *you* going to talk to your brother?'

'Naturally. Tonight.'

'Your sister-in-law has a brave champion,' he said dryly. 'I'll do what I can.'

'How weak you sound,' she burst out before she could stop herself.

It was Tom Westbury's turn to enlarge his eyes. For the first time since he'd opened the door to her he looked angry. 'That's very good of you,' he said and Lisa, jumping up with something like a sob, rushed from the room and down the stairs and out into the yard. A moment later he followed but she was already in the car.

She cried painful tears as she drove home.

# 17

She supposed he had changed completely. It gave her a spiteful pleasure to believe his attitudes, beliefs, morals even, had become messy and despicable. Then her opinion veered the other way and she wondered if his indifference about Gemma and Charles had been assumed. What she tried to forget was the moment when he believed that she'd come to see him to revive their old romance. He could never have known me, she thought, to imagine I could do anything so humiliating. But her brother had told her men were vain.

The meddling job of speaking to Charles proved not to be necessary after all. The day after Lisa went to Avoncliffe she met Jenny in the garden, looking entirely different. The strain, the falseness, were gone, Jenny had pink cheeks and a merry grin. So Tom had done something after all. Charles was at Lyndhurst that morning, and later in the evening when Lisa drove home from Stratford she saw him with Jenny, talking contentedly under the crab-apple tree.

When the week was almost over, Charles was still much in evidence and Lisa had decided she could relax. Polly appeared at The Treasure Box in a brand new dress, of Boucher blue and full-skirted *à la française*, her blonde hair tied with a bow. She looked a good ten years younger than twenty-seven going on twenty-eight. Lisa was not pleased to see her.

'Hi,' said Polly. 'No sign of Perdita, good-oh. I'm here to waste the treasure of your time. *As You Like It.*'

'Perhaps I'd rather you didn't.'

'What does that cross face mean?'

'Nothing.'

'Come on, Lisa, you're annoyed and I can't imagine why,' said Polly, looking at her perkily.

Lisa, immune to the charm, said, 'You did something the other day for which I don't forgive you.'

'Me? What could I possibly?'

'Don't you know? I thought actors always worked out their effect on other people. Isn't that their job?'

'Lisa! What a horrible voice. What *are* you talking about?'

'About you telling my sister-in-law that Charles and Gemma Lambert are sleeping together. It was a disgusting thing to do and I shan't forgive you.'

Polly sank on to a boxful of books at a distance from Lisa and gave a loud groan. 'Oh cripes. I'm so sorry. I thought – well –'

'What *did* you think?'

'Golly, you are angry. I've never seen you like this. Look, Lisa, I didn't mean to be a bitch, truly, I just thought it was a damned shame she didn't know. I'd prefer to be warned if it happened to me – as a matter of fact it has once or twice and when somebody tipped me off I was grateful. Did I hurt her? How awful. I never meant to.' The actress's beseeching voice was almost real. Or as real, thought Lisa, as anything could be with these strange people. She supposed she must accept Polly for what she was. 'Do you believe me?' continued Polly, woebegone.

'I suppose so. Yes, I believe you didn't do it from malice – '

'Lisa!'

'Okay. Polly, yes, I believe you. Perhaps it was for the best. Charles, at any rate, seems to be behaving better.'

'I'm glad. What he sees in the Lambert woman – God knows. It's good of you not to be angry any more. After all, you are my one friend.'

Harmony was restored. Lisa was amused in spite of herself at the swiftness of Polly's recovery. She came over to perch on the stool facing Lisa and asked what was new in the antique world.

'I don't think we can exactly call what we sell by the grand name of antiques, although Perdita sometimes does.'

'I've heard her. I suppose it *is* a lot of junk,' agreed Polly, looking about, 'but ancient just the same.

> O good old man; how well in thee appears
> The constant service of the antique world,
> When service sweat for duty, not for meed!

That's also *As You*. Is it relevant, darling? Do you happen to sweat for duty not for meed?'

'I like selling things to people who want and perhaps understand them. I don't think about the percentage Perdita gives me, I suppose. Just about the people and the things.'

'I believe you do. Ah well. I haven't come to make you happy by buying something, though I do like that rock with the amethysts poking out of it. Is it expensive? Don't answer that. I came to tell you something rather nice. Sir Lew mentioned you. I was telling him about us both at school, and when I described you he said did I mean the girl with the eyes? I thought that was rather sweet. One more thing. Do you think Mick and I could buy you and your boyfriend a drink one night?'

'We'd love that.'

'Would you? Mick has met Peter, and I danced with him at the Wardrobe once. He's fun,' said Polly. It was an overall description for any man who paid her attention – which embraced, thought Lisa, the entire male sex. 'Lisa,' continued Polly, looking thoughtful, 'I've been wondering one thing about that affair we're not mentioning. Is it possible your brother and La Lambert have called it a day?'

'You know more than I do.'

'Don't have digs. I've said I'm sorry. It's just that Lambert has been looking down in the mouth, and now and then has been so disagreeable. Even to Mick. She's usually all gooey

345

with him. What's more, not a sign of your brother in the Green Room.'

'Did he go there? I thought only actors –'

'Yeah. Only actors. But people connected with us hang around and Charles positively haunted the place. Not recently though. A good sign?'

'It might be. Honestly, I don't know what's happened between them.'

'He's the sort who loves them and leaves them,' persisted Polly who wanted Gemma Lambert to suffer. 'But how can one be sure anything is over? Sex is such a nuisance. So peculiar. All this blazing and cooling and then blazing up all over again. There's also the corny question about who loves who. One or other always loves more, you know. Take you and Peter Lang.'

'Are you collecting material for a new rôle, Polly? Because if you are asking about us the answer is we both do. In a way.'

'My God, you're English. Like one of those Galsworthy heroines who never utters. I suppose Galsworthy admired that sexy reserve, but I don't. You won't gossip, will you? "Thou art not of the fashion of these times." Sorry, *As You* again! And I see I'm getting unpopular a second time. Shall we meet with Mick and your guy at The Duck on Sunday morning?'

Lisa was going to a house sale again on the following day and Peter had arranged that he would come with her.

'The family who owned the house are Warwick people. I'll do a short piece about it. Are you sure you wish me to come?'

Peter often used 'wish' instead of 'want', and Lisa never heard it without wondering if it was his pernickety use of the English language, something he'd considered and weighed, or whether for Peter the use of 'wish' meant he was only considering her and not himself. He was like that.

Perdita was interested in the coming sale and annoyed that an appointment made weeks ago prevented her from going in person. There would be some bird prints which would be of interest to The Treasure Box, she said. 'From what the catalogue says, there'll be a damned great set of them. As a nation, we have always been aware of bird life,' remarked Perdita. She was in her informative mood and Lisa was glad to listen, while the older woman talked on one of the myriad subjects about which she had so much knowledge stored away under her grey fringe. For the last two hundred years or more, Perdita expanded, the British had been engraving pictures of birds, drawing them in pencil, painting them in oils (Perdita did not like those, they were too heavy, she said) and in watercolours. They had lithographed bird prints. In Victorian times there were photographs of English birds, coloured by hand. All these were to be found in fine books. 'Take Edward Lear. He painted some likely ones . . .' said Perdita. 'Do you know I could have bought some of his books during the war for ten bob each? Why didn't I? I must have been off my head.' At the sale there would probably be a good many old prints torn out of books. Those would suit her very well. 'Look at the bottom on the left where there'll be an abbreviation. *Del* or *delin*. That indicates which artist drew the original.'

'What do *del* and *delin* mean?'

'*Delineavit*. "Did it". I'll give you a list of the artists who are too hot for our blood,' said Perdita.

Lisa and Peter were going to take a picnic and set off early on Friday morning. Peter stayed the night at the flat, and when they came out to the car, they met Jenny mounted on her new pony. She looked embarrassed, hastily waved her crop and trotted away. Lisa made a face. She knew Jenny disapproved of her affair and thought it blatant of Lisa to let Peter stay and leave the house quite openly. Moral attitudes were changing . . . had already changed. Jenny belonged to a new generation. Lisa's own attitudes came from a time when death, the queen of spades, was the most powerful card in the pack. If you loved, you made love. Things were violent and simple. It wasn't like that any more. People disapproved of girls having any sexual experience before marriage. Even little Jenny Bowden thought that, as she went riding hastily away from Charles's sinful sister.

347

The sale was to be held at a Victorian vicarage and when Peter and Lisa arrived there were already a good many cars and vans parked in the drive. The front door was open, and people were busily walking about inside. The house had been the home of a rector, his wife and six children. It was shabby and hadn't seen a lick of paint for years. During the war it had been a reception centre for evacuees. The invaders had left their marks on kicked furniture, grubby walls, and a set of blackboards, one of which still retained a half-erased column of sums. When the sale was over, the house was to be turned into a school. 'The blackboards will be useful,' said Peter, making his nearest attempt at a joke. The contents of the house, set out on tables, trestles, in piles and in laundry-baskets, were many, varied, dusty, cluttered. Too many books. Incomplete sets of glasses. Oil paintings. A hammock. Though on a very large scale, it reminded Lisa of the miscellany her father had left Charles and her in Drury's Depository.

Lisa had a tenderness for things. She disliked seeing them ill used. When the cases had arrived at Lyndhurst, she had carried her share up to her flat and set to. She'd washed every single item; she repaired, re-glued, reframed. Now she used all the glasses and poppy-patterned plates. Old photographs of her parents stood on the window-sill. Rory, the rocking-horse, was in her sitting-room. She dusted him regularly and polished his wooden face. But his tail was very thin.

Lisa had been taught by Perdita not to seem interested in things she wanted to bid for. She saw with dismay a large group of buyers clustered around a table where the bird prints were displayed. She and Peter took their turn. Some of the coloured engravings were old, dating from the 1750s, and some even earlier. One that Lisa particularly liked was of two long-beaked, unfamiliar birds, looking proud and absurd as they balanced on a stylized tree.

'Albin,' said Peter. 'Out of his book *Song Birds*, 1736.'

'Don't sound so fascinated,' she whispered. He looked mortified and she touched his hand. 'I didn't mean to snap. We can't afford them anyway.'

Taking his arm Lisa wandered through the house deciding against this and noting that. A glass teapot. Jewellery made of shells. An iron picture-tray of Anne Hathaway's cottage. She and Peter went into the drawing-room and took their places as the room began to fill up.

It was an exciting sale. Lisa bought a variety of articles and not a single bird print. She bought eight silhouettes of an Edwardian family, two china inkstands, a brass coal-bucket, some tiles patterned with pansies and four vinaigrettes – Perdita specialized in those. Lisa opened a lid set with pearls and sniffed the withered sponge once soaked in scented vinegar.

'Used for ladies who fainted, is that correct?' said Peter, sniffing in his turn.

'Girls keeled over in those days. I expect Perdita will when she sees how much I have bought.'

'Why should she? You are sure to sell everything.'

'I'm never sure of anything,' said Lisa, as they joined the people leaving the house.

'Ah Lisa . . . you can be sure of me.'

She looked up at him, making a kiss in the air with her mouth and smiling. Over his shoulder she caught the eyes of a man looking straight at her. It was Guy Bowden. He raised his flat tweed cap. She nodded in reply.

'Shall we hurry,' she muttered to Peter who was walking slowly down the path. 'I've seen someone I want to avoid.'

When they were driving home she told him who it had been. Peter was interested. 'Why did you want to get away? It would have been sensible to wait and talk to him. Mightn't you, perhaps, have done something to heal the breach?'

'Peter, that's absurd. What can I do? It's his business and Jenny's if they don't speak to each other any more. I'm surprised he raised his hat to me, I should have thought he would cut me dead.'

'It wasn't your fault your brother took away his daughter, Lisa.'

'He blames us all. I should think he misses her horribly.' Guy Bowden had been alone. Was he always? Lisa wondered.

'Why the deuce doesn't he ring her and come and see her?' she said.

'Does he know,' said Peter, always logical, 'where she is?'

'He could scarcely miss knowing, since everybody in Stratford knows everybody else's business, unfortunately. He must certainly have heard we'd bought Lyndhurst. He probably has spies checking up on Jenny.'

'Why do you say that?'

'What?'

'About the spies.'

She was surprised. 'It was a joke, Peter. Nobody with a nosey housekeeper, and that woman at Whitefriars is one I'm certain, needs a private detective. He'll be told all the local news whether he likes it or not. Anyway, I think it's crazy that he won't see his own daughter. He's like my father. A parent who expects the children to toe the line, and when they don't, washes his hands of them. All the same . . .' she paused, 'he did look lonely.'

Peter watched her. He liked her to drive because he could see her in profile. She had such a pretty nose. 'Some parents love their children with all their hearts and are wounded because it is the children who will not come home,' he said.

The sentence brought Lisa up short. What did he mean? Or rather, she knew what he meant. He was talking about himself. Why, why doesn't he tell me about his family and his past? He's a sphinx.

On Monday morning when she showed Perdita what she had bought at the Rectory sale, her employer was very sarcastic. She was derisive about the silhouettes, she'd always hated the things. One of the china inkstands had been mended with seccotine and the coal-bucket was too small – no wonder Lisa had only paid eight shillings for it. And who the devil was going to spend money on a set of pansy-patterned Edwardian tiles? 'Nowadays, and clearly you haven't noticed, they *paint* over them. I think they're off their heads but that's the fashion. Everybody who has an open fireplace boxes it in. One young woman I know has turned hers into a drinks-cupboard. You really should move with the times.'

350

Thoroughly disagreeable, Perdita left for lunch with some actors. She always knew most of the Company by midsummer and liked to hear of disasters and scandals. Lisa, depressed, was cleaning some silver when the telephone rang.

'The Treasure Box,' she answered in a businesslike voice.

'Is that Miss Whitfield?'

'Yes. Who is speaking, please?'

'Guy Bowden.'

'Oh. Good morning. Can I help you?' said Lisa who knew he hadn't telephoned to buy anything.

'I wonder if we might meet. Could you come to Whitefriars?'

Lisa had a sudden picture of a self she disliked. Wellmeaning. Officiously minding other people's business.

'Are you sure it's me you want to see?'

'Certainly I am. Would this evening at six-thirty be convenient?'

She did not know why she said yes. After she rang off she felt annoyed. It's time I led my own life and let them all go hang, she thought.

When it was time to leave the shop she looked at herself dubiously in Perdita's old, clouded mirror. As she put on her little hat, her eye fell on the pansy-patterned tiles. If Perdita doesn't want them I'll buy them myself, that'll shut her up, she thought.

When she turned into the drive leading down to Whitefriars, she saw the difference between Guy Bowden's house and her own. She and Charles had money now – some, anyway – but it would take a long time and half a fortune to make Lyndhurst look even half cared-for. Whitefriars breathed respected wealth. There was not a sixteenth-century brick which hadn't been repointed, a beam which had not been sized or painted. The house stood in its gardens like a man among courtiers.

She rang the bell. The housekeeper whom she'd seen on that distant winter visit did not come to the door. Guy Bowden opened it, accompanied by the regiment of dogs.

He gave her a brief smile and his expression was kindly, as

351

if he knew the favour she was doing him. He was more hospitable than she remembered; it occurred to Lisa that he was a man best met alone. 'Thank you for coming,' he said. The dogs eddied round them like rough water as they walked through the house to the drawing-room she knew from girlhood and those two winter visits. First, when she and Charles had appeared out of the snow. Then, when she and Jenny had unpacked the silver. Now the beautiful room was altered by the presence of summer, the latticed windows were wide open to the bird-whistling garden, the silky stone floors were cool.

'May I offer you a drink?'

'No, thank you,' she said, as if to say, 'shall we get on?'

He took his place opposite her, crossing thin legs. For a man who was going to woo an intermediary, he did not look tentative. The strongly-hewn face was as uncompromising as on the day he had come to Crocker Road and shouted at her. He paused, choosing his words.

'You wonder, of course, why I have asked you here.'

'To talk about Jenny.'

'No. I don't wish to discuss my daughter, Miss Whitfield.'

Did I imagine he was going to be friendly? she thought. He's simply ridiculous, calling me 'Miss' when he's known me since I was born. It was part of the upper-class arm's-length attitude. He warded off her least attempt to intrude, to be familiar, to take him for granted because of a shared past. He rejected being human.

She leaned forward. 'You must want to discuss her. It would be unnatural if you didn't. Surely it's time you and Jenny buried the hatchet? How many months is it since she married and since you've seen each other? Ages. She misses you,' added Lisa. She remembered Jenny had mentioned her father. Once.

'I am sure she does not.'

Lisa had the uncomfortable vision of a girl lying under a tree. 'But she does. She misses and needs you. People do need their parents. Some of us who have none realize it only when it is too late.'

352

It was a handsome attempt at an *amende*, based on a desire to help him and not on the truth; all he gave her in return was a cool, 'Indeed.'

Lisa's good intentions withered. I might as well be talking to a block of ice on a fishmonger's slab, she thought. She persevered. 'I know what Charles did, rushing off with her like that without telling you, was horribly unkind and –'

'Unforgiveable,' he said, handing her another adjective.

'But it's in the past,' Lisa persisted. 'The point is Jenny is married, and her life is different now. She's not the same.'

'Exactly.'

'What do you mean?' she said, struck and chilled.

'I agree with you. She's changed. Or, shall I say, she must have done. I haven't seen her so I can only judge on previous knowledge.' He frowned, looking at Lisa, and said suddenly, 'I wish you'd let me get you a glass of sherry.'

'I'd rather not. Thank you.'

He studied the girl facing him, noticing her thinness. His daughter had been – he thought of her in the past – a rounded lass. The Whitfield girl sat anyhow; young people nowadays had no grace or physical poise. She ought to ride, it would give her a straight back.

'Surely it's time you forgot about Jenny running off in that stupid manner,' said Lisa returning to the point.

'You think it stupid, then?'

'Really, Mr Bowden, you do take me for a fool. I told you when you came to Crocker Road that I thought they were ridiculous, and cruel into the bargain. I was furious with Charles. Much good that did. The thing now is to accept that they're married. I have. Why can't you?'

'Oh, I accept it, for what that is worth.'

'But you still won't see her?'

'I'm afraid not. And if I know her, she feels the same.'

Lisa did not answer and he gave an imitation of a smile. The dogs lay about like so many discarded fur coats, and one of them sighed loudly. Guy put out his hand and patted a furry rump. The dog turned to look slavishly at him, thumping a tail as feathery as an ostrich-feather fan.

'I think we should clear the air,' he said. 'I didn't ask you to come here on Jenny's account, and I'd prefer, if you don't mind, not to talk about her.'

'She needs you.'

'So you said. If so, it's a pity.'

Lisa fairly gaped. What am I doing, she thought, messing about with other people's business? Trying to fight battles that aren't mine? I'm interfering and self-righteous, I make myself sick. Last week it was betrayed husbands – she shuddered inwardly to remember that – now it's deserted parents. The sooner I leave this house the better. She made a movement as if to stand up. He held out his hand and to her surprise she obeyed him and sat down again.

'Now,' he said, seeing that he'd got his own way, 'as I've just explained, I didn't invite you here to talk about Jenny. Things are best left as they are. I know you don't agree with me, and I'm sure you have the best of motives but aren't those often' – he was making a sort of joke – 'the ones which end in the worst results? I wanted to see you to say something which I'm afraid you won't like. I wouldn't have dreamed of doing so if your father hadn't been a close friend of mine. As it is, and you have no older relatives, it's my duty to speak.'

Lisa wondered what he was talking about. The only person, the only subject she and this man had in common was Jenny.

'I'm afraid,' he said, 'that I must warn you.'

'Warn me?' she repeated stupidly.

'Yes. It's only fair to you. I think you should consider very seriously about associating with a person whom you appear to have made into a friend.'

'Mr Bowden, what are you saying?'

'I thought I was making myself perfectly clear.'

'Of course you aren't! I don't understand a word. Who's this person I am supposed to be 'associating' with, as you call it?'

'I saw you with him at the Rectory sale.'

'*Peter Lang!*'

'Yes.'

She was outraged. 'What on earth do you mean? What's wrong with him? He's a nice man, and a great friend of mine.'

'So I gathered.'

'What have you got against him?'

'I am not in a position to reveal that.'

'My God!' exclaimed Lisa. 'Are you serious? Do you expect me to listen to you? You tell me my closest friend – yes, I am very fond of Peter and see him all the time –'

'I am aware of that –'

'*What*? Are you having me watched?'

'Now, now, Lisa,' he said, calling her by her name for the first time. 'Don't be melodramatic. Of course I have heard you were friendly with him and in any case the man writes for a local paper, doesn't he? I've seen his name a number of times. I'm sorry I can't tell you why I feel you should try to see less of him. I wish I could. You must believe that I'm speaking for your good.'

'I won't listen to another word!' exclaimed Lisa, springing up and almost running towards the door. But he hurried after her. Dignity and stand-offishness were gone; he looked genuinely concerned. Before she got to the door he had opened it for her, and somehow stopped her in mid-flight.

'Please don't rush away believing me the villian of the piece,' he said. 'Just think for a moment. Why should I take the trouble to speak to you about this if there wasn't a grave reason for doing so?'

If Lisa had been seventeen she would have ranted at him, using the virulence and near-hatred of the young against the old when they meet head-on. But such an emotion had left her years ago. She was indignant, but she saw what he said was true. She looked up at him with a fixed earnestness, her large eyes filled with feeling, and he thought: I've never noticed it before but she is like her dead mother. He remembered with a moment of aching wonder that he had almost loved Bernadette Whitfield, and how merry she'd been, and how teasing and uncomplicated. Even – that old, old word – how good.

355

'Answer me something before you go,' he said. 'How much do you know about Peter Lang?'

'I've told you. He is a close friend.'

'That doesn't answer my question. Have you met his family?'

'He has nobody. They were all killed in the Blitz.'

'Indeed. What of his own history?'

'He was in the Army during the war and fought in the Normandy invasion.'

'I'm afraid not, Lisa.' They were walking towards the front door. She felt strangely disturbed, but not angry now. 'I don't ask you to stop seeing him. I know I suggested it, but I wasn't right. I can see you'd never do that and I respect you for it. For your loyalty, your affection.' He was almost solemn. 'All I'm saying is, don't get too close. Ask yourself, ask *him* who and what he really is.'

They had left the house and were in the drive. The dogs had surged joyfully out after them, trotting busily back and forth, giving the evening a festive air. Guy accompanied her to the car. Not knowing what to say, she climbed in. The window was down, and she sat for a moment staring ahead at the windscreen which was a grave of summer insects. Guy stood by the car.

'Goodbye, Mr Bowden.' She gave no indication that she had accepted anything he'd said.

'I'm sorry,' was all he answered.

As Lisa drove away, he stood solitary and upright among his canine companions, with the old house behind him like a tapestry.

Half a dozen times during the following week she wished she'd never been to Whitefriars. It was mean-spirited to become suspicious of a dear friend merely because somebody had sown a doubt in your mind. Guy Bowden was prejudiced. Why should she listen to him?

Yet she couldn't deny Peter was secretive. Perhaps he'd done something disreputable in the past, something he wanted to hide and forget. Perhaps he'd been unhappy. It

356

might be something as undramatic as a divorce. In 1948 divorce wasn't looked on with favour by many people ... maybe that's it, thought Lisa. My father would have disapproved – and so does Guy Bowden. He seems to know everything so I suppose he's found out we're living together. What has it to do with him? She ignored the fact that it was kind of him to be anxious over her. She tried to get rid of her doubts. But the things Guy had said to her had stuck. She had never quite believed Peter had been in the Normandy invasion; Guy had categorically told her he hadn't. How was Guy so certain? The thing was full of uncomfortable questions. Peter was important to her. She was sure he loved her and although she'd never loved him, her fondness trembled on the verge of love. Yet he was as enigmatic about himself as when they'd first met. Another curious thing was his lack of ambition. She often teased him about it.

'I can't understand why you don't try for a bigger paper. You're good at journalism. You might get a job on the *Birmingham Post*. That would be far more exciting than your old Council meetings and flower-shows.'

'I like flowers-shows, particularly the dahlias.'

'You're changing the subject. I mean it. You're too clever to be doing such a small job.'

'Thank you. Not clever. Merely hardworking.'

He had closed the subject and she was offended. He warded off questions that acquaintances might ask, let alone his lover.

When Lisa arrived at the shop the morning after seeing Guy Bowden, Perdita was already downstairs, instead of lingering over breakfast in her own flat. She was wearing a voluminous red and white patterned dress and was bent over a thick exercise book which she called her Stock Book. In this she or Lisa recorded all the things presently contained in the shop, plus what was bought, what they paid for it and what price it was later sold for. She looked up with an exaggerated start as the Eastern bells rang their musical chime.

'I wish you wouldn't make such a racket. Come in *quietly*.

It is far too early in the day for noise or for one's nerves, come to that.'

'Sorry. It's a beautiful morning.'

'Is it? I haven't had time to notice. What I have noticed is that we are shockingly low on stock. I have Mr Eysham coming in tomorrow' – Lisa knew Eysham, a dealer who bought greedily – 'and that American, what's his name?'

'Langton Walford.'

'Yes, that's the man. He is supposed to be calling in the afternoon. He wants to look round for a present for his daughter. What do I find? You appear to have sold everything in sight.'

'It's been a good week so far.'

'Apparently. There is only one thing to do in these unfortunate circumstances, and that is to work.

> Work apace, apace, apace, apace;
> Honest labour bears a lovely face.

That's from a poem by Thomas Dekker, in case you didn't recognize it. A Jacobean poet.'

Lisa nodded politely, hung up her straw hat and bent to look in the mirror to comb her hair.

'No good wasting your time on your appearance. What *you* have to do now, my girl, is drive to Warwick. There is a jumble sale at the Town Hall, aid of charity, and you may pick up something if you're quick about it. There's also Wellby's shop behind the Castle. Worth a visit. I rely on you to find something to replace all you have sold so *fast* this week. We can't sit twiddling our thumbs and I can't go, I have to do my clerking.'

It was the only part of her work that Perdita disliked and put off from month to month. She insisted on doing her accounts sitting at the counter and never took her papers up to the flat. Once Lisa had gone as far as suggesting this and Perdita had irritably said, 'I've got no intention of taking my work home.' Her home, thought Lisa, was so crammed with things they couldn't fit into The Treasure Box that it was a miracle Perdita didn't fall flat on her face when walking from sitting-room to kitchen. When the clerking was eventually completed Perdita always declared she was running at a loss.

Lisa made a noise between a 'pooh' and a sigh. She knew those Town Hall jumble sales, and she also knew Wellby's poky little shop. People who thought The Treasure Box sold junk had not seen what junk was really like. It consisted of crumbling books smelling of mildew, many in tiny eighteenth-century print, their covers missing. There would be chipped enamel mugs, mended china candlesticks with lumps of grease sticking to their unattractive pink or blue stems. Hideous flyblown pictures of *The Last Judgement* or *Hide-and-Seek with Grandpapa*. Most depressing were the clothes, dirty, old, torn, returning in the strange way of ancient fabrics to the colour of the earth. And the heart-breaking sight of misshapen shoes.

'Off you go, off you go,' said Perdita, shooing her back into the street. 'I see you have already sold the excellent stuff you bought at the Rectory sale.'

Lisa spent a frustrating day. She did not find anything she wanted to buy except a brass hob for a kettle, and another dealer got it two minutes before she did. She was tired and rather hot and cross when she decided, as she was in Warwick, to call on Peter at his digs. He was usually home by half past six. They might have a drink at a pub on the river before driving home for supper at Lyndhurst.

Peter had lodgings in an old house in a back street of Warwick. He liked the town which he said was 'still medieval enough', and knew more of its history than Lisa or Charles had ever done growing up a few miles away. He liked telling Lisa curious stories of Warwick's past. In the seventeenth century the floor of a magnificent chapel had fallen in, and the body of an Earl of Warwick buried there two hundred years earlier was found to be perfect. 'He looked as if he were still alive,' said Peter. The air had destroyed the marvel almost at once, but Warwick women had time to snip off some of his curls and later had made them into rings.

The house where Peter had lodgings was hundreds of years old, and had once been the home of a mayor infamous for bribery. Its wicked grandeur quite gone, it was now a boarding-house for students. Lisa called to see Peter sometimes in Blacklock Street and this evening when she rang, the door was opened by a ginger-haired girl with her arms full of books. She and Lisa had met before.

'He isn't back yet. When you see him, please tell him I'm desperate, will you? Joanna is desperate,' said the girl. 'He's helping me with my English. He's a born teacher. A walking library. One can ask him *anything*.'

Except about himself, thought Lisa, promising to give the message. She went upstairs to his room. As she opened the door she knew precisely what she would find. Peter's sense of order was the only poetry she had discovered in his nature. The room was plainly furnished. Peter had added no pictures or photographs, not even one of herself. His books were lined up like soldiers on the floor under the window. Everything in the room was spotless and symmetrical. The bed was made, the cover pulled taut and without a crease. On a table with his ancient typewriter, dusted, a pile of typing-paper, a decorated papier mâché dish – one sign of herself at least for she had given it to him – holding pen and pencils, a rubber and a pencil-sharpener. The dressing-table was covered with a lace-edged linen mat as clean as everything else, though yellowed with age. There was his brush and comb, leather travelling-clock, a small saucer for collar stiffeners – slivers of white bone for slotting into the edge of collars to make them set – and various studs. Peter never ran out of studs. In one corner was a cupboard where his suits were hung and his clean shoes lined up with shoe-trees in them.

She admired the way his room was kept: it showed a respect in his nature both for himself and the way he wished to live. She thought everybody must benefit from that respect – she certainly did. He kept his love for her, if that's what it was, in its own careful cared-for place. It was the same with inanimate objects, they had a kind of sheen because he treated them well. Like Lisa, he didn't allow the things he owned to be broken or dirty. He did not forget them.

Taking off her hat, she sat down at his desk. She never had the heart when she visited him to plump herself down on that perfectly-made bed. They had never made love on it either. She leaned back – the chair was uncomfortable – and thought about him. Now she was in his room, breathing his air, the threads of suspicion that had spread across her thoughts began to loosen and melt away. What will become of us, she wondered, will we marry? Do I want to marry Peter? Somehow I don't think I want to marry anybody. She wished she was in love. She remembered the state as a man in an arid land might imagine rushing water. Did I really think I'd faint with happiness? Did Tom and I really lie together in that Indian garden, swearing to love each other until we died?

She looked at the desk, wondering what Peter was working on at present. Even the simplest story, if Peter wrote it, had style. On the right of the typewriter was a pile of papers anchored with the only other present she had given him, a ruby-coloured glass paperweight she'd bought at The Treasure Box – Perdita had allowed her 5 per cent off its sale price. Lifting the paperweight, she idly picked up the letters.

There was an invitation which he'd taken out of its envelope for an exhibition of 'Warwickshire Watercolours'. One or two bills, including the bill for her kitchen curtains which he insisted on paying. At the bottom of the small pile was a letter in pale ink, the handwriting all curlicues, and Warwickshire was misspelt. It had a German stamp; she turned it over and saw a Berlin address without the name of the sender.

Lisa was fascinated. Who did Peter know in Germany? The moment she saw it she thought – is this the answer? Is this what Guy Bowden was warning me about? Peter had never said so, but he must have been stationed in Germany after VE day; this letter was from a girlfriend or an ex-mistress. Even from a wife. Perhaps he married a German girl when he was out there. Perhaps. Perhaps.

She heard a step outside – she'd left the door ajar – and Peter came in. He carried his jacket over one shoulder, it being hot that afternoon, and broke into a smile when he saw her.

'Lisa! You didn't tell me you were coming to Warwick. Have you been waiting a long time? Why didn't you telephone the paper?' He came over, took her hands and kissed her on both cheeks, a habit of his. She pressed her cheek against his lips, feeling tenderly glad to see him.

'I didn't know I was actually coming. Perdita got it into her head to send me packing. I've had the stupidest day. Are you free now? I thought it would be nice to go to The Crown and sit by the river and have a drink?' She suggested it with the certainty that he'd be pleased. He always wanted to be with her.

To her surprise he said, 'It sounds wonderful. I only wish I could.'

Lisa pouted a little. 'Don't tell me you're going to desert me when I need you most!' She smiled at him charmingly, expecting him to give in, to explain and capitulate. A muscle tightened in his cheek.

'I wish I could,' he repeated. 'But I have a job to do, a difficult one. I shan't be able to get to Lyndhurst until nine or even ten. Would that be too late for you?'

'Of course not. Is the story you're working on an interesting one?'

He had turned to his desk and hung his jacket on the back of the chair on which Lisa had been sitting. He draped the jacket so that it hung without being creased. 'What is that?' he said.

She laughed. 'I asked you what piece you have to write tonight.'

'Oh. That. Yes, it's –' It was blazingly clear that he was searching in his mind for something to tell her. It was the first time she'd seen him literally preparing to lie. 'It's an idea they have at The Castle for opening during the winter. And they may enlarge the museum.'

'Okay, get to work,' she said, picking up her hat and

clamping it on her head. She mentioned Joanna and he nodded absently. When Lisa looked at him, his eyes weren't candid any more. In a voice as light as a feather she said, 'Nosey me, I've been looking at your letters. Don't scowl like that, I only read the envelopes! Who do you know in Berlin, Peter? I didn't know you were stationed in Germany.'

'In Germany?' he echoed blankly. 'Oh, you mean that letter. It's from the friend of a friend. A woman who got my address from somebody in my regiment; she's looking for a man she used to know.'

'Poor her. A deserted female.'

'More or less. I think she would like help. There have been food riots in Berlin and other places. Queues everywhere and people hungry.'

She felt guilty, as if the suffering were her fault. 'I'm sorry,' she feebly said. 'Can you find out where the man has gone?'

'Yes. Yes, of course, he works in London. I shall send her the address.'

It was time for her to go. They arranged for him to come late to Lyndhurst. Putting his arm round her, he gave her a long kiss. Her body responded. She let him hold her, pressing his open mouth to hers; she had always liked the way he tasted, it reminded her of the scent of chestnut flowers.

'See you, then,' she said. 'Don't forget to write to the poor deserted female.'

She drove home. Wishing and wishing she had never been to Whitefriars.

# 18

---

Like the gambling impulse, sexual adventures were necessary
to Charles. He could not do without them. He sometimes
marvelled to remember that for three years in Burma during
the fighting, he had only once had a woman. He was too
fastidious in sex to go with the whores the soldiers sometimes
found in ruined villages. How had he existed without it? He
supposed it was due to the curious fact that if you didn't
have sex you began not to need it. A just and comforting
present of Nature. He and his friends had talked obscenely
enough, had suffered danger and terrible privations, yet the
lack of women had not haunted them after the first few
weeks of celibacy.

When he returned to Stratford in peacetime, he found no
girl who excited him, which explained his London visits to
the sexy and smouldering Claire. He had not managed to
make love to her as often as he needed; when he telephoned
her, Claire, sounding as provocative and available as always,
was usually leaving for yet another aristocratic country weekend.

'You will ring again, won't you, Charles? Don't forget
me!'

But it had been the chase and capture of the young deer
Jenny Bowden which had occupied and excited Charles
during the months of poverty in Crocker Road. The excitement left him when the hunt was over; he was like a man
freed from being possessed by a dybbuk. To be husband to a

loving innocent girl, to make love to her constantly, meant little to Charles; he never intended to be faithful, only to treat her well.

He found it laughable, he thought it ludicrous, that he'd fallen in love. He had truly believed himself incapable of the lunacy. Like a man vain of his perfect health and living among the sick, Charles had thought how painful it was for the poor diseased creatures and how fortunate that he never caught the infection. Now he was the sickest of them all. He was pierced through with love. Jenny's tender eyes scarcely made him feel guilty; his mind and body were obsessed with desire for Gemma.

There were ironies. His own astonishment that he should fall so deeply in love. His resentment at being at passion's mercy. And the fact that his taste for gambling was now the perfect alibi.

His wife had been astounded, excitedly shocked and finally complacent when she learned that Charles had gambled since he was a boy. While they were in Capri he pointed out that it was the gambler who had married her. What reliable man, what man with common sense and practicality would have been so reckless? This romantic argument was completely accepted by Jenny. She never again thought of the hazards of gaming, but came to regard Charles's love of play as an intriguing oddity. When he returned home sometimes from the Wilton Club and described a game that he had won, she listened enthralled. It was so brave to take risks. She saw him like some man in the Regency, some spendthrift lord. Byron, for instance. How unlike her father he was, thought Jenny; it made Charles all the more fascinating.

From the start of their marriage he never promised not to play and used this as an excuse for getting away from her from time to time. He was devoted to Jenny but like most men he needed a breath of air. When they came back to Stratford he began to pay court to any attractive women if she took his fancy. He did not do so in front of Jenny but managed to flirt, though not to go to bed, with a number of women, not one of whom would have resisted had the opportunity come their way.

Never sought for, Gemma had appeared. She snatched away everything that belonged to his separate self. His liberty. His lazy attraction to any pretty woman. His easy seducing ways. He couldn't get free of her, something in Gemma glued him to the ground. It did not seem possible when she told him that she was as hard hit.

During the immediate weeks after they first made love they met – for sex – anywhere that could be managed. At night in her car after the performance. In midnight fields flooded with moonlight. On the river bank. In her car again. Once she had to go to Leamington to collect some clothes and Charles travelled with her in a train with no corridor. They made love in the compartment, full length on cushions smelling of dust, half undressed, their thrusts matching the motions of the train.

These desperate meetings and matings, the sexual congress repeated over and over again, had to end when Gemma met him one evening outside the theatre, her face brilliant with anger. They walked along Waterside towards The Duck.

'Tom knows.'

'You mean he has an inkling. Nothing to worry about, love-bird.'

'Don't be a fool, Charles.' She was walking close to him; scent, sharp and resinous, came from her russet hair. She had been at a rehearsal and some of the excitement clung to her. 'Don't be a fool. We've got to stop.'

'Stop making love?'

She turned in the glaring sun and said contemptuously, 'You could stop, could you?'

'You know I couldn't. Can't.'

'Well, then. What I mean is we'll have to be far cleverer than we've been till now. It's a nuisance. I'll make some plans and you use your brains as well. Tom has got to believe we've given each other up.'

'I don't know Tom all that well –'

'Of course you do.'

'Gemma, we were never close friends in Oxford and that was years ago. I don't *know* him.' It had often struck him as strange that he and his sister should be entangled with people closely united and so dissimilar. What Lisa had loved in Tom was nowhere in Gemma.

'You're wondering why I bother about what Tom thinks, I suppose,' said Gemma almost artlessly. They had walked past The Duck, making for the gardens running by the side of the river.

'Whom do you love?' Charles good-humouredly asked. 'As a matter of interest.'

Gemma paused. 'Tom's fine. Tom's a good man. You're not.'

'True.'

'I need him.'

'I was under the impression you needed me.'

'Yes,' said Gemma.

They entered the gardens. It was midday and midweek and there were few people about. They wandered over to a seat which was under a tree with drooping, thick-leaved branches. Nobody went by, and Gemma put her hand on that part of him where desire lay. She stroked him, feeling the strong arch, pressing it, satisfied it was there. She took away her hand.

'Yes. I do need you. Want you. Sometimes I wish to hell I didn't. But Tom has Bobbie and if I misbehave he might get custody. I wouldn't be a "suitable person" to bring up a child, he said.' Her thoughts made her shiver.

He was silent longer than she expected and when she looked at him with the same trouble in her face all he said was, 'I see.'

'You do, don't you? Sometimes I think you yourself quite love Bobbie.'

'I know nothing about children. It sounds absurd but I've never actually known one until now. I'm not sure why it is that I sometimes feel Bobbie will break my heart.'

She gave a long sigh. 'That's it. That's in Bobbie. Tom says it's because of the divorce. Bobbie doesn't feel quite safe.'

Although she was tense and troubled, she was too vain to

tell Charles how much her husband had scared her. What had been most alarming was how calm he was. Earlier in their marriage he'd discovered her infidelities, had been very angry and once, discovering her embracing a young actor when he returned home unexpectedly, had shoved the man out of the flat, then hit her so hard that she'd fallen against the edge of a door and cut her head. She'd deserved it, bore no malice and made the most of his consequent concern. After being furious, shouting at her, reproaching her for things she denied as loudly as he accused, he was penitent and particularly kind. He never said he was in the wrong – he was not – he simply behaved well and Gemma enjoyed that. It wasn't so this time. The threat to take Bobbie away 'if you go on proving you're simply no good' thoroughly frightened her, as did the idea of a second divorce. She determined to make him believe in her again.

So the lovers changed their ways. They met, of course, in public, sometimes at The Duck when Gemma arrived with a phalanx of actors. Sometimes Charles came to tea at Avoncliffe and sat in the garden with her and Bobbie; Tom was always working and rarely joined them. Charles looked forward to seeing the little boy, whose large eyes were so like his mother's, and who broke into an intimate grin when Charles appeared. But it wasn't possible for the lovers to make love in the old snatching, rutting way. It was Gemma who found the solution.

A fat comic actress, specializing in roles of countrywomen, whose accent from Devonian grandparents was invaluable to her as well as to theatre directors, suggested it. Olive Greenaway had a dressing room next to Gemma's and came in during the matinee interval one afternoon – the performance was *Twelfth Night*. Gemma was sitting at her dressing-table staring into space.

'I've come to cheer you up, pal,' said Olive, handing her a key. 'As you know, I've rented a cottage on the Kineton Road. It's called Victoria Cottage. Rather sweet. I'm never there at lunchtime.' Gemma threw her arms round the actress's neck.

368

When she told Charles he looked dubious. 'So your friend knows about us, does she?'

'Of course she does. Has from the beginning,' said Gemma, who often thought her lover missed the obvious.

'You said you were afraid Tom would hear something. The best-kept secrets are known to nobody.'

'Rubbish. You don't know actors. We're a gossipy, catty lot, but we stick together. Olive would no more give me away than cut my throat. We starved together in rep. Well, I starved. Olive ate Turkish Delight. Come on, Charles. We have' – she looked at her tiny gold watch – 'just half an hour.'

Sex. All sex. Nothing but the promise, the lure, the beginning, the rise, the fierce climax, the aftermath, sleep, unison. Sex.

'I never knew I could feel like this,' he once said as they lay on the rumpled bed in the cottage miles outside Stratford, with nothing but the baa-ing of sheep in the distance and the breezes of summer blowing through an open window. They were stark naked.

'You sound like Angelo.' She lay with her white legs stretched out; rounded and fleshy, tired and pale. Her shoulders were freckled and her hair fell across her face.

'Who's he?'

'You're an ignorant bastard. He's in *Measure for Measure*. The villain of the piece.'

'That's odd. I thought,' he said, sniffing her scent and the scent of sex, 'I was the hero.'

'There is no hero in our story, only a brilliant heroine. Anyway, I shall tell you about *Measure*. I played the chaste Isabella once and don't you laugh like that. Angelo is not like you one bit. He's ice cold, a man of rigid virtue. But. There's a "but". He falls in love. He can't believe it has happened to him. There's a line of his which is you, Charles:

Ever till then, when men were fond
I smiled and wondered why.'

369

'And wondered why,' echoed Charles. 'And what do *you* feel?'

'The same. Alas.'

He learned to know Gemma better than any woman he'd had in his life. Generous and greedy, sexually voracious, promiscuous, passionate, tiresome. She liked presents. She wheedled a string of cultured pearls from him, and Schiaparelli scent and black-market nylons and silk camiknickers. He bought clothes for Bobbie and paid for the little boy to learn to ride. When he asked her what Tom would think of such arrangements Gemma laughed. 'He imagines I earn more than I do, bless him.'

It flattered Charles, amused and often bored him to find Gemma was jealous. She resented every woman he knew. She was jealous of his sister, and showed her claws when Charles spoke of her. She was worse about his wife, and since he only laughed when she made spiteful remarks, she grew more confident. Meeting Jenny one day at The Duck where Charles had taken his wife for a drink on the terrace, Gemma was rude to her. Charles looked like thunder.

The next time Gemma saw him was the following evening at a party. He did not speak to her or acknowledge she was in the room, and she was forced to walk over and eventually get him to herself, which took a good deal of considerable social skill. She knew she was looking what she called to herself 'my most beautiful'.

'When are we going to the cottage? she asked in a low voice.

'I don't want to go there.'

Gemma went pale. Her freckles stood out. 'But when?' she managed to repeat.

'I'll tell you if I want to see you.'

She turned on her heel, returned to Tom, and five minutes later was flirting with one of the leading actors. But Charles had left.

It was not Gemma who capitulated. It was Charles. He telephoned and came to Avoncliffe. He suggested their next meeting at the cottage.

Safe in the knowledge that he couldn't escape her, astride him when they made love so that she stared down at his face twisted as if in pain, she claimed him. She knew that what held them together was not only sex but herself, the thing in her that held audiences, that she felt when she went onstage, the flood of emotion coming from her. She used it pitilessly on Charles.

Sometimes he was weary of her strong presence. She was nagging, exorbitant, unreasonable and often absurd. Why must he take his wife here or there? He had promised, hadn't he, to drive Bobbie and herself to Chipping Norton Fair. There was the garden party she'd been invited to. There was a boating party, a concert, anything, anywhere in the county that would mean Charles was with her and prevented from being with Jenny.

She was tiresome and funny, lustful and exhausting, hard as a diamond, soft and golden as a potful of honey. Wishing to be free of her, he sank deeper into love. It was due to Gemma that their affair was now discreet. Her care, her meticulous lies, were because of Bobbie. Tom would never allow her to hurt the little boy a second time.

The oddity was her unlimited capacity to surprise. Just when he found her excessive, she would change to become a comedian. When he thought her mean-spirited, she showed a profligate generosity. Her way with money was awesome. She despised it. Then there was another side to that extravagance. '*You* give it to me, Charles. You're filthy rich.' He was never sure when she begged and demanded for him to buy or pay whether she did this because she was acquisitive and greedy, or simply to prove her power. For whatever reason he denied her nothing.

Her attitude to her husband was a contradiction. She betrayed him every day and yet held him in respect, even slightly in awe. Charles was not sure if it was the man's character or his talent: he thought it a bit of both. Tom's first play, a wartime comedy, had been put on in the provinces. His second, *Somersault*, on the subject of post-war Britain and its moralities, was now running with success in

371

the West End. It had interested the critics and the notices had been good. 'Unusually well written', 'full of surprises', 'excellently and humorously observed', 'this is a voice for the 1950s', they had commented.

Charles considered a writer's life was dire, and marvelled that anybody could spend his time bent over a typewriter. On one of the hot afternoons that he enjoyed out of doors, he was sprawling in the Avoncliffe gardens playing with Bobbie under the trees. The child produced a much-thumbed pack of Happy Families, and they played for nearly an hour. Tom eventually came from the stable flat and joined them.

Charles's attitude to any husband whom he deceived was benevolent. He never felt he was making a fool of the man. He never reflected on that tender subject of whether the husband also did what Shakespeare called the deed of dark-ness with the woman Charles enjoyed. He always supposed his mistresses slept with their husbands. He'd never been physically jealous and he wasn't now. Charles thought sex the least of sins. He liked Tom Westbury, yet continued to steal, almost daily, the soft jewel of Gemma's body.

When Tom sat down under the trees, talking of this and that, there wasn't a shadow between the two men. Tom drew Bobbie on to his lap. Bobbie liked Charles, but had a different way with his stepfather, clinging like a monkey, putting stick-like arms on either side of Tom's big shoulders, pressing hard with hands, legs, heels. Tom kissed him absently.

'What have you been up to, Bob?'

'Me and Uncle Charles have been playing Happy Families.'

'Who won?'

'He lets me win.'

'And Bobbie cheats so that I will,' said Charles.

'That sounds a somewhat dubious game,' said Tom. He stared across the lawns, which were turning yellow in the summer heat, at two figures sitting in deck-chairs under a further group of trees.

'There's Tony Quayle with Dot. Rare for him to manage an hour off. He deserves it.'

'You admire him,' said Charles, following Tom's eyes and seeing the tall actor, looking relaxed, talking to a pretty woman in a pale dress.

'Yes. He's strong and imaginative. A leader. The theatre needs men like that.'

'Gemma's impressed with him,' said Charles, who had listened to a deal of talk about Quayle.

'She is, isn't she?' Tom's unemphatic voice indicated that Gemma was apt to repeat herself.

'What a curious life it is, being an actor,' remarked Charles. 'I've never understood it.'

'Haven't you? They're interpreters. Musical instruments. They speak the thoughts of other people and add their own imagination, and when they're good, they can't touch anything without enhancing it. They're artists. Children.'

'You don't sound as if you rate them highly.'

'That isn't true. I worship good acting. At best they can be geniuses. Even when they're not very good, they can make me cry. They show off so,' he added and smiled.

'Your wife does.'

'True. Limelight is what Gemma needs. Buckets of it.'

'Doesn't it,' said Charles idly, 'get on your nerves sometimes?'

Tom was dry. 'Yes. As I do on hers. And *you* do on hers, I daresay.'

There didn't seem to be a *sous-entendu* in sight.

In a pause which followed they heard Dot Hyson break into an infectious laugh and her husband joined her.

'I'm glad to have this chance of a private word,' said Tom, watching Bobbie who had run off towards his friends in the kitchen garden. 'Would you mind, Charles, if I broach a difficult subject?'

Charles drove back to Lyndhurst at the time of evening when birds whistle loudly and the shadows are as long as church spires. When he turned into the drive he saw his sister's car parked outside the house. There was the sound of voices in the open air, the ping of tennis balls. He stood at

373

the top of a rise in the grass below the ill-shaved tennis lawn which spread out like a yellow oblong of linen. Jenny was playing with Angela, her schoolfriend and now a constant visitor.

The girls, flushed with exercise, greeted him noisily.

'Do come and play, Charles! Your wife is winning and I want to take her down a peg or two.'

'No, no, be my partner, Charles, and we'll beat her into the ground,' from Jenny.

Charles said he might join them later. He went in search of Lisa, hoping to find her alone.

She was. She had just had a bath, was wearing a dressing-gown, her wet hair plastered to her head, and was doing her nails. He knocked at her open door and she called, 'Hi, Peter. You're early.'

'It's me.'

'Oh, hello.' When she glanced at him she saw he looked serious. Not a Charles face at all. I refuse to worry about him, thought Lisa, I've done it for too long. Her brother sat down on the bed. Unlike Peter's chaste couch at his lodgings, Lisa's bedcover was awry and there were a couple of dresses flung across it. He pushed them aside.

'Come for a chat? It would be better if I got dressed. My hair's dripping.'

'I noticed.'

'I can't curl it up and dry it with you staring at me, brother dear. You'll only make jokes and I have my dignity.'

'You look rather sweet.'

'Of course I don't. Anyway I suppose you want something,' she said, bright and slightly nervous, sensing a kind of danger. 'What is it?'

'How suspicious you are.'

'You never call for nothing.'

'I call from fondness. We don't see enough of you.'

'You see too much. At least, Jenny does. I hope you're treating her properly.' It was a feather touch of accusation. One it would be easy enough to ignore, to misunderstand or, more likely, to miss.

374

'She looks very well on my treatment, whatever it is.'

'She does. Quite blossoming. So what am I supposed to do for you both?'

'Nothing. Something for yourself, though.'

'Oh lor, you're going to start suggesting I do something different with my share of our money. I'm not going to, Charles, and you'll be a fool if *you* do.'

'I'm not discussing money, Lou. Or Jenny either. Do stop chattering like a little monkey. I may as well come out with it and not beat about the bush. I think you're seeing too much of Peter.'

Her reaction was violent. She almost shouted. '*What* did you say?'

He was cool. 'You see him all the time, and unless you intend to marry him, which God forbid, I believe it's a mistake.'

'Why shouldn't I marry him, pray?'

'Are you thinking of it?' he said sharply.

Lisa was dumbfounded. First Guy Bowden. Now her brother. What on earth had they got against poor Peter and what business – 'I'm not thinking of marrying anybody. I doubt if I'll ever marry, I don't fancy the state. I like my freedom and I've got it, thank heaven. I also like Peter. We've never mentioned it but you know he's my lover, don't you?' The phrase was quaint and old-fashioned. It made Charles smile.

'You mean you go to bed with him.'

'What's the difference?'

'A very great deal. Are you saying you love him?'

Lisa hadn't had a conversation about herself with Charles since the long night of the Indian journey, and the short, rather chilling little talk when she'd told him Tom was here in Stratford. What had got into him? He sprawled on her bed, having pulled off the bedcover and made himself more comfortable, putting her pillows under his head. His way with her was still that of an elder, stronger, wiser person who wanted to see her happy. She was thoroughly unnerved. What made things sillier was that here he was asking about her affair when she should be speaking about his.

375

She fiddled with her wet hair.

Charles was silent a little, then spoke with a seriousness that sounded weighty. 'I said do you love Peter Lang by any unfortunate chance?'

'No I don't, and what on earth has it to do with you? I am very fond of him indeed, and we suit each other. Please stop this.'

'I'm afraid I can't. I don't like saying it ...' He was uncannily echoing his father-in-law and even, thought Lisa, amazed, seemed to have the same look about him, as if he disliked what he was doing. 'I am not asking you to break off with Peter completely. Don't make that face, just listen and be sensible. I know you wouldn't break up with him, it is out of the question. What I *do* ask is for you not to feel –' He paused, looking for the words. 'Not to feel you can't do without him. To surrender yourself. Yes, I think that's what I mean.'

She stared at him. She thought: you look old for thirty-three. She had never noticed before, but there were threads of silver in his abundant curling hair. His face was too lined, she had often thought it. Isn't the affair finished, then? she wondered. Is that what he is speaking about? What has that to do with my poor Peter? I suppose he is warning me because he himself is ensnared. But I'm not.

She still looked at him, but without indignation. 'What have you against Peter? I thought you liked him.'

'I do. I – well – I just think you shouldn't –'

'Feel I can't do without him,' quoted Lisa. 'Charles. Thank you for bothering about me, but I won't go on with this. My love affair – my friendship,' she corrected herself when he enlarged his eyes, 'is absolutely nothing to do with anybody but Peter and me. I'm sure you think you're being brotherly. But I'm perfectly capable of looking after myself. Corny but true. What about when I was alone in Calcutta all that time? I can cope. I'm not sure,' she added, 'that *you* can. I'm not going to stop seeing Peter. Nor stop going to bed with him either, since I am not allowed to use the word "love affair". So that's that.'

'Not really. The police have been calling on him.' She was speechless. 'I'm sorry. I'm sorry. I don't like telling you, and yes, I have always liked him, he's a nice guy. But it's true about the police. Somebody at the theatre heard it from one of the students who live in his house.'

'I don't believe it.'

'Then ask him.'

'What? Oh, hello, Peter, I hear the police have been coming round to your house. Are you under arrest yet? Dear oh dear, what can you have been up to? You'd better make a clean breast of it because what we ask ourselves is should a nice little girl like me be seen with a man like you.'

'I knew you'd be furious.'

'Then why didn't you hold your tongue?'

They had never quarrelled. When they had been young, the gap of years between them was too large. If Lisa tried to annoy him, buzzing round him like a mosquito, he simply laughed and picked her up and stood her on a table. It made her furious. Once he put her right on the top of a high bookcase where she screamed down at him while he sat laughing helplessly. Another time when she was being a pest, he picked her up, marched out into the garden and put her, too high, on to the branches of a tree. How easy it used to be, thought Charles, when one was young. He believed it just then.

He saw despite her closed face that she was still angry. His task had been impossible from the start. If Lisa herself had come to him with a story about someone he was fond of, he would have grinned and told her to pipe down. But his sister was unlike him in almost every way. She was not sexually confident. She had not been happy and Peter Lang had given her what she sorely needed.

Charles had done his duty, something which did not appeal to him, and all he had achieved was to annoy her. He hoped to God he hadn't hurt her as well.

'Sorry, Lou.' He left the room.

Lisa stared after him. What am I to do? she thought. Charles must have been listening to gossip in the Green

377

Room. From Mick Gould. Mischievous Polly. Even Gemma Lambert whom he might run into occasionally. Lisa herself had been at The Duck with Polly once and been introduced to Gemma. The actress appeared to dislike her. She'd thought Gemma alluring and hard, and had wondered if Tom's wife by some instinct sensed that she and Tom had once been lovers. It was not impossible . . . so much of sex was made of intuition. But that was old history. What mattered now was Peter.

There were always places in a person's heart that you cannot know, she thought, and I suppose you shouldn't try to unlock them. But in Peter's case this wasn't a small private place, a secret garden, but his whole life. Having angrily denied what Charles had told her she believed it. There *was* a mystery about Peter. Something he was ashamed of or feared. Was it so sacred or so terrible that nobody must know? And had the police – incredible thought – discovered it?

Peter's reserves and enigmas had added to the interest she had in him; what was forbidden always had an extra power. He was stronger because he was more than he seemed – for better or probably for worse. But things had gone too far now. Two men had separately warned her about him. She couldn't pretend not to be affected. Because of Guy Bowden and then Charles she did look at Peter differently.

He was coming to the flat tonight as usual. They were going for a late walk after supper. I'll ask him then, she thought. They loved their evening walks; it would be the right and peaceful time.

He arrived punctually, running up the stairs to kiss her and present her with a big bunch of roses. He looked as if he'd just had a bath and when she returned the kiss she smelled soap on his fresh skin.

'Not shop flowers,' she said. 'Much too special.'

'Lady Branksome gave them to me.'

'Goodness, how grand.'

He smiled but did not laugh. 'I went to see her this afternoon. I'm writing a piece about her garden, and she

378

showed me all round. While we were walking in the rose garden, she cut these for me. She knew the name of every one.'

'You sound impressed.'

'By her knowledge, yes.'

'What is she like apart from knowing the names of roses?' Lisa was amused.

'Well . . .' he reflected, 'very patronizing. Very English.'

'Are the English patronizing?' enquired Lisa, sniffing the heavy-headed flowers.

'You know they are.'

'You mean the upper-crust. Not you and me?'

'What nonsense you talk! As if you could be like that!' He put his arms round her. She knew he wanted her but was too disturbed to respond.

'Peter. Shall we sit down and talk a little? There's something I want to ask you.'

'What a pity. I thought first we might –'

He looked serious even when he smiled, even when – as now – his senses longed for her. His expression struck her to the heart. If only he had a little of Charles's self-mockery, Charles's you-can't-fool-me nature. It would be too easy to hurt this unreadable man who, disappointed in desire, still did just as she asked and sat down waiting for her to speak.

She pushed one of the roses, a dark rich red, into a vase and a thorn went into her finger. She sucked the blood away. She had meant to speak of what was in her thoughts when they would be walking in the lane and everything was peaceful and quiet, but instead heard herself say feebly, 'There's something I want to ask you. You mustn't be offended.'

'How could I be?'

'You haven't heard what it is yet,' she said hurriedly. 'I wouldn't ask at all except that I feel bothered. You will forgive me, won't you?' It was an impossible request yet she believed she could ask it, just as Peter believed nothing she could say or do would need that grace from him.

He looked at her, his brows raised quizzically, waiting for her to ask some favour he would be glad to do for her.

Lisa ploughed on. 'I've just been told, please don't ask me by whom, that the police came round to see you. Are you in trouble?'

He did not react at all. Yet the tenderness in his eyes seemed to drain away. 'That's an odd question.'

'Of course it's not. If the police turned up asking for Charles do you suppose I wouldn't be worried?'

'It is not the same. He is your brother.'

'Oh,' she cried, forgetting caution, 'so it's natural to be worried about him but not about you. It's you who say odd things – I simply don't understand you.'

'Perhaps it's better that you don't.'

All her anxiety and frustration, her need to know because without it she could not trust, flew into her face and she cried loudly, 'You drive me mad!' With a sudden flinging gesture she knocked over the roses, scattering them and spilling water all over the carpet.

'I'll do it.' He sprang up and hurried to the kitchen to get a cloth. They went down on their knees while Peter mopped and rubbed and Lisa retrieved the scattered flowers, bunching them in her hands and pricking her fingers again.

There was a lull. She refilled the vase and began to put the flowers into it one by one. He said nothing. When she sat down again she was calmer.

'I'm sorry if you don't like me asking questions,' she said carefully. 'You think I am intruding. Surely you must see I need to know what's happening to you.'

He gave no sign of taking this up. 'I'm perfectly all right.'

She looked at him hard. She was not going to let him off. 'You don't get it, do you?'

'I don't understand you, Lisa.'

'Aren't you supposed to –'

'To what?'

'Well, to love me, actually.'

'Maybe I do.'

'Maybe?' she repeated, laughing and angry. 'I'll say it again. I am sorry if I am trespassing and you don't want to talk about it, but it is perfectly natural for me to ask. I'm

380

sure it's nothing important, the police can be so officious and perhaps you're too proud to admit what happened. But you must tell me. Otherwise –' She paused and finished with unconscious bitterness, 'Otherwise I can't feel comfortable with you.'

'Yes,' he said, seeing the point fairly, 'I understand that.'

She wanted to shout at him. To yell 'don't be so bloody reasonable!' Didn't he realize what he was doing by his stubborn secrecy? He was killing their affection. He was not even annoyed. This was not Bluebeard, murderous because she had discovered his room of hanged wives. It was Peter, fresh and grave, responsible and honest, coolly refusing her. She had an uncomfortable feeling that he had expected this scene; had rehearsed it in his mind and was word and performance perfect. She hammered her fists against his nature, not against circumstance.

'I am sorry about what you heard,' he said at last.

'And . . .' she just faltered.

'And the fact is I cannot tell you what it's about.'

'Won't, you mean.'

He was silent, but only for a moment. 'I suppose that's true.'

Lisa paused a long while. Here it was at last, she thought, that desert in him. A parched land you could never cross without dying of thirst. Whatever it is he won't tell me is something to do with his past. The few things he has said I've never believed and now – who is he? What awful thing is he determined to hide even from the woman closest to him? Then she knew she wasn't close at all.

'You won't be satisfied until you know, will you?'

She answered with another question. 'Do you think it natural to have secrets?'

'Yes. If they are necessary,' was all he said. He was looking at her then with a painful attention. She was so thin, so dark, so familiar. Her slender body and his knew each other. The very tones of her voice wrenched at his heart. 'I see you will not feel the same about me now.'

Lisa stared back. 'You've made up your mind. You won't explain.'

381

'No, Lisa.'

How long a minute can be.

'Yes,' he said, almost as if he were speaking to himself, 'So. There will always be questions in your mind. You will think things, untrue things maybe, and since I do not deny them, they will get worse.'

'Are you saying we must part because of your silly mysteries?' She laughed because he was hurting her.

He walked over, bent down and put his hand to her face. There was something strangely familiar about the gesture, the look. He gave a long sigh. And she remembered Hamlet giving up Ophelia. Raising a sigh so piteous and profound that it did seem to shatter all his bulk and end his being. No, no, that's not right, she thought. I certainly shan't go mad.

'I am sorry, Lisa. So very, very sorry.'

She heard his step on the stair, and the coughing noise of his old car starting up. When she ran to the window it was already disappearing down the drive.

# 19

In Stratford, people talked of the end of the season as if on some appointed day autumn suddenly stopped and winter came marching into the streets, wearing furs and turning the ground into hardened frost. What they meant was the end of the Shakespeare season, the last night of the final play and the disappearance of the actors from the town and from The Dirty Duck.

Charles and Gemma met almost every day at the cottage, even for an hour, a half-hour. Love-making now had a desperate quality; it tasted of goodbye. They asked each other how it would be possible to meet in London, and each looked blank and neither could answer the question. They could only live in the present while Victoria Cottage was still theirs, while they could open its door, and go into the bedroom, and fall into the delight which seemed, said Gemma, to get 'worse'.

They met one September day which was chilled after unremitting rain, and lay, after a long, breathless, seemingly desperate struggle of pleasure, on the rumpled bed in a small room festooned with Olive Greenaway's clothes. The windows were shut. Summer days, open windows and naked-ness were gone. Gemma snuggled under the eiderdown. Charles, emerging from possessing her, noticed that she was smiling. Yesterday there had been tears and dramatic – over-dramatic – cries that they were soon to be separated. Today she was in good spirits.

'It looks as if Tom's new play is going to be accepted,' she said in a proud voice. 'It's exciting for him.'

'I thought you said he was writing a part for you,' said Charles, thinking Gemma playing in London is Gemma lost.

She pulled the eiderdown up to her nose, regarding him with heavy-lidded eyes. She looked different today. He'd often noticed how she seemed to change physically; at present she looked like a golden-skinned fruit, a luscious peach anyone could bite into.

'I haven't told you my news, Charles. What a thick neck you have. You'd make an actor with that pillar of a neck. It means the voice has the right timbre. Comes from the diaphragm.'

'I take it this isn't your news.' He submitted to being tenderly throttled.

Her flattery was automatic; she flattered men from habit and then waited, mouth open, for her share. It wasn't Gemma's words which enslaved him, it never had been.

'You do taste nice. Sort of like grapefruit,' she said, licking the lobe of his ear.

'I wish you'd stick to the point.'

'How cross you are. You soon won't be, though. Tony Quayle is to be crowned, did you know? Yes, he's next season's director. Prince Hal is turned King, except that I don't think Tony would ever go off and get plastered with Falstaff, do you? Anyway, Barry Jackson is going and Tony steps on to the throne and – here's my news – he's offered me a line of parts for next season.'

He digested this while she waited expectantly. 'That means you'll be back.'

'Back, back, back with you, my darling! At the end of Jan or the first week in Feb. So stop brooding about how you are going to lose me. Think of it. In around three months we'll start all over again. Well, of course, we'll have to meet somehow in London but Stratford is what counts. Charles . . . I've been wondering since Tony told me . . .' The voice altered. 'Do you think *you* could take this cottage next season? Olive's not coming back, she's going to Nottingham.

If you took it, it would really be ours.' It was the voice she used when coaxing money out of him and it made him grin.

He agreed. Of course he'd take on the cottage. Satisfied, Gemma threw aside the eiderdown and lay in a certain inviting way. He wasn't in the mood and seeing her ruse was a failure she sat up good-naturedly, reaching for pillows.

Charles enquired about her meetings with Anthony Quayle and the parts she had been offered for the 1949 season. She settled down to describe the interview. As usual, she interspersed any story about her acting or plans for her career with descriptions of blind terror. 'I was shaking in my shoes.' 'I was feeling *so* sick.' 'I scarcely knew what I was saying and my voice came out sounding like a crow's.' Quayle had offered her a second season as Olivia in *Twelfth Night*; the French Princess in *Love's Labour's Lost* – she would be the female lead; and a 'wicked, incestuous princess' in the rarest of the plays chosen, *Pericles*. 'Tony's playing the title rôle. Won't he be good? He's a kind of hero, I always think. Adventurous. Daring. And the play is an epic, a journey. Unfortunately my character disappears after the first Act, but Tony got over that,' she added, laughing, 'by describing what a challenge the part would be. I've never actually played anyone evil before.'

Charles was so glad to think they would be together that he scarcely spoke. He simply looked at her. Of course, he said as they dressed and tidied the room, and repeated again as they locked the cottage door, of course he would pay for this house. It was a perfect idea.

'Our own little home,' cried Gemma who always grew sentimental when she got her own way.

All tickets for the last night of the season were sold weeks beforehand. The play was *The Comedy of Errors*, and the atmosphere would be festive yet sad, a time of thanks and speeches and farewells. There would be the Wardrobe party, of course.

Charles, Lisa and Jenny were going to the play together, but then disaster struck. Jenny caught an autumn dose of 'flu and ran a high temperature. She lay in bed, scarlet-cheeked and doleful, disappointed as a child.

385

'Mrs Welstead says she'll come in and look after me and make me glycerine and honey,' croaked Jenny when Charles and Lisa came to the sickroom. Jenny had the upper-class gift of finding people to serve her. Her new housekeeper, who lived ten minutes from Lyndhurst, cleaned and shopped and had become a kind of nanny, not unlike Mrs Dickens at Whitefriars except that she was fond of her young mistress instead of being jealous of her. 'How lucky you are,' wailed Jenny. 'I so love the last performance and you'll both go to the party.'

'We won't stay long,' said Charles. Picking up her hand he practically recoiled. 'My dear girl, you're on fire!'

'I always burn like that,' said Jenny in weak satisfaction. 'Mrs Welstead says when people are young and run high temperatures it's good. It burns all the bugs. Go on, you two, or you'll be late.'

Brother and sister were quiet as they drove towards Stratford.

'Poor Jenny,' said Lisa at last. 'I feel such a pig.'

'So do I.'

A further silence.

'Nothing we can do about it. So we might as well enjoy ourselves,' from Charles. 'By the way, Lou, are you okay? About Peter, I mean.'

'Of course I am,' said Lisa who did not want to talk about him. She had recently told Charles, when Jenny was not in the room, that the affair was finished. Charles had, perversely, thought Lisa, been rather horrified. It was all his fault, he said, he should never have repeated the story, there was probably a simple explanation, should he go and speak to Peter? Charles's reaction did not surprise her. He'd always been contrary. She told him he must leave things as they were and he wasn't to blame in the least. She and Peter had simply called it a day. Charles had questioned her and Lisa admitted that, yes, she had asked him about the police. And yes, that had led to an argument. 'Well, Peter doesn't exactly argue, does he? But anyway, we decided to part and that,' said Lisa brightly, 'is that.'

Charles was annoyingly concerned. He kept coming round to her flat to invite her to a meal or take her out for a drink with Jenny. He persuaded her to play tennis with them 'before summer's over'. He took her with Jenny to the cinema. His solicitude was both comical and touching, and Lisa thought that he looked at her like a doctor searching for symptoms of heart trouble.

Lisa did miss Peter. She missed him all the time. Missed his companionship, their conversation, their walks. She missed the sex which had given her pleasure but not bliss. She had had a man who – she thought – had loved her. She'd shared with him her interests and problems and fun. Even, in a way, her home. She'd never been alone until now. It struck her as quite strange to realize this. As a child and a girl she'd been at home in Roundwood. Then in Burma with Uncle Rod and Charles. In Calcutta there had been two friends and the crowded apartment and the intriguing life with its unending cavalcade of men. When the war ended she and Charles had travelled together, and then just when she needed him, she had met Peter. Now she had nobody.

Peter's absence made a little hollow in her life, not an active pain. She wondered if that meant she was getting rather cold-natured and selfish, but began to realize that when she thought about Peter, she unwittingly compared him with Tom. I must grow out of making comparisons: they're pathetic. She did not yearn for Peter. But now in the early autumn evenings she never went down the green lane where they had walked. And she was lonely.

Charles slowed down as they reached Clopton Bridge and joined other cars, headlights cutting into the misty dark as they drove towards the theatre. The great building on the river bank shone, its lights like those of a big ship reflected in the water. On the roof the gold and black flag flapped in the night wind.

Both brother and sister were in evening dress. Lisa had bought a new black and white satin which had a domino effect. She had a white orchid – those flowers she used to buy in India for threepence – pinned on the top of her head. Charles glanced at her, thinking she looked fetching – his

387

word for a pretty woman. He hoped Peter wasn't going to be in the audience, it might upset her. Or if he was, that he'd be sitting a good distance away. Then, because he never stopped thinking about her for long, he savoured the idea of Gemma. He would see her tonight, romping and glittering across the enormous stage.

*The Comedy of Errors* was the perfect choice for the final play. Two pairs of twins. Endless opportunities for misunderstandings. Shakespeare was young, under thirty, when he wrote the play which was full of high spirits in a crazy, magical Ephesus, where men refound their brothers and themselves, and women refound their husbands and their own hearts. There was the final dance, drenching applause, speeches and deep curtseys. Lisa laughed at the play. She enjoyed it more because there wasn't a sign of Tom in the theatre, and knowing he was not there gave her a sense of liberty.

'Wasn't that lovely!' exclaimed Lisa, her face still lit with laughter as the curtain fell at last and the audience began to stand up and make their way along the stalls.

'Terrific,' agreed Charles, smiling back at her.

It had been a shared delight. And yet . . . there upon the stage Gemma Lambert had played with swiftness and wit, looking beautiful and making the audience laugh and love her. Neither Charles nor Lisa had mentioned her once. The affair's over, thought Lisa. I'm sure of it. She recalled Jenny's burning cheeks and the dying-duck look she often gave her husband. It was an expression Lisa couldn't get used to. Jenny's subservience to Charles told on her nerves. All lovers are mad, she thought. I wish I were.

Love was still in her thoughts when she and Charles joined the crowds leaving the theatre after the play and the speeches; she was doubly glad that there was no sign of Peter. Both my ex-lovers are out of the way, she thought. I can stop looking round in case I see them.

'What about popping into the Wardrobe just for half an hour?' said Charles. 'Going straight home would be an anticlimax, don't you think?'

I'm tempting fate, she thought. Damn it, why not?

She waited while Charles hurried back to the restaurant to buy some wine. As they then crossed the road they saw the barn doors hospitably wide, rows of candles burning with dim radiance, stuck into wine bottles. The actors had not yet arrived at the party but there were already a number of people noisily talking and greeting each other. Back in the theatre, the actors were in their dressing rooms changing out of costume. They were kissed. Congratulated. They ran down corridors or hastened through the ghostly set of the play now over and silent. It's the end of an era, they thought. It never was, but they were too superstitious to look forward.

As Charles and Lisa came into the glowing dark, they were welcomed by Jacky Grimsdyke, his domain already crammed with visiting players and journalists.

'Nice to see you!' cried Jacky. He wore a Russian shirt and baggy green trousers. 'Do you like my get-up? *Cherry Orchard* Act One, Scene One. Yepihodov. "There's a frost outside, three degrees of it, and the cherry trees are covered in bloom".' He took Lisa's hand and kissed it but his bright eyes like a sparrow's were fixed on the two bottles Charles had brought.

'Just a small offering from my sister and me,' said Charles, presenting them.

'My dear, you are a wonder. Most people arrive empty-handed. I don't know how they dare. Heaven knows I drop hints until I'm exhausted. Why isn't everybody like you? As for *you*,' to Lisa, 'I worship the domino dress, black and white is so à la mode, but the orchid is not quite right. May one?' He stood on tiptoe. Lisa was small but Jacky was even shorter. He fiddled with the flower in her hair. 'What a fearful kirby-grip, it needs bending. That's better.' He stood back critically.

'Jacky's right,' said Charles. 'Now it looks perfect.'

'Of course it does. Ah, there's Dot. I must go.' He trotted across the room to the door where a slender figure dressed in drifting white tulle stood against the dark.

The Wardrobe, as usual, was ingeniously decorated. There were swags of crimson hanging from the rafters, a huge peacock feather fan, purple and gold turbans skewered to the walls. Here and there were the figures used in dressmaking, headless and stiff in paint-encrusted jewel-hung costumes. A girl wearing a wreath of leaves came over to pour out glasses of weak punch bobbing with slices of apple. Lisa saw with a smile that Jacky was lavishly offering his guests Charles's champagne.

Now at last the actors from tonight's performance began to pour into the Wardrobe, tired and eager. They clustered together talking energetically, or darted here and there like fishes thrown into a pool, joyous at being in their own element. The long hours of the party were around them, translucent as blue water. The party was filled with goodbyes, kisses, laughter. People held each other at arm's length, then kissed as if they would never see each other again. Charles, holding the undrinkable punch in one hand, wandered off into the throng. Lisa knew he would. When she was a shy seventeen in Burma, he had never stayed with her at parties; he made sure she had a partner or somebody to talk to and then walked away. A man had come over to speak to her and at that moment, off went Charles.

'Hello,' said the young man sociably. 'My name's David Morris. I do a column in the *Evening News*. I always tell people at once that I'm a journalist. They prefer it. How do you do?'

Lisa smiled, and gave her name.

'Surely you're not in the Company?' he said, giving her an interested look. 'I pride myself on remembering all the actors in a show and I'd scarcely miss *you*.' He was fattish and flirtatious, practised at talking to strangers.

Lisa said she wasn't an actress. She worked at The Treasure Box. That also interested him; he had been to the shop last season, he said. He had bought a nice little piece of Straffordshire, a teapot, but the spout had been slightly cracked.

'Of course Perdita gave me a bob or two off the price, but

when I enquired later in London, I found I still had a bargain.' He launched into the subject of nineteenth-century teapots. Lisa, perched on the trestle-table, leaned back, pleased to talk her own kind of shop. They discussed Rockingham and Spode, salt-glazed stoneware and the lustre-decorated teapots which Perdita loved but couldn't afford; they were, Perdita said, 'too old and too beautiful'.

David Morris was describing his own collection – 'I live in Islington, when you come to town you must pop in and see it' – when suddenly Lisa was hit violently on the back. She was seized in somebody's arms – she didn't understand what was happening – and again beaten violently on the back while a man shouted, 'It's okay, it's all right', giving her a series of blows which almost knocked her down. There was a hideous burning smell. People close by gasped and – half stunned – Lisa found she was in Tom Westbury's arms. David Morris had begun to pour a jug of water over her.

'Don't drench her, for heaven's sake, I've put it out,' said Tom, and swivelled her round, then pulled her back to face him again. 'Yes, not a smoulder left. Poor Lisa. I hurt you.'

'Wh-what happened?' Her teeth were chattering.

'Your dress caught fire, you leaned against that candle.' A bottle lay on the table; the candle, its wick blackened and extinguished, had made burn marks on the cloth. 'Poor Lisa, I'm so sorry. You'll be covered in bruises tomorrow.'

'*My dear girl!*' Jacky Grimsdyke came rushing through the crowd to Lisa, who stood trembling. 'My dear girl, come with me at once. That poor dress. We'll see what can be done. I can't have beautiful guests singed to a crisp.'

She had no time to thank Tom. Her wrist was seized by a surprisingly strong grip and Jacky dragged her through the crowds and out of a side door into a tiny room scarcely bigger than a potting shed. He switched on some lights.'We must treat you for shock, dear,' he said, going to a shelf ranged with hats. Feathered, buckled, beribboned, there was even a hat circled with a golden crown. He picked up the crowned hat and produced a bottle.

'Have a swig. That's right, down it goes. My best brandy.

That playwright moved fast, didn't he? I saw him positively beating out the flames! Dress ruined but not its wearer. Take it off. No, no, dear, finish the brandy first. Now, let me. Buttons, well I never. Don't you like zips, then?'

He unfastened the dress while Lisa swallowed a second mouthful of coarse brandy which caught at her throat and made her cough. Jacky expertly took off her dress and stiffened petticoats. She stood meekly in her camiknickers. Jacky ignored her, spread the dress on a table and surveyed an enormous hole in the black and white satin and the under-slip, the fabric singed, blackened and jagged.

'Goners,' he said. 'A pity; you did look such a dear little domino. Well, well, better the dress than the girl. Let's see what we can find you? Helen of Troy? Not really. Queen Katherine? Much too stout and ponderous, all those black beads. Bianca in *The Shrew*? Too insipid, you aren't a pink and white kind of girl. Ah . . . here's the one. Cressida. She's just your style and Janet who played her is a pocket Venus like you.' He unhooked a costume from a packed rail of various trailing dresses, and came over cradling it in his arms. 'Not still suffering from shock, are you? Put it on, now. There's nothing to look upset about when you have one of my glorious frocks to wear instead. Need another slug of brandy?'

His voice was hard, his fingers too. He was businesslike as he slipped the heavy costume over her head and pulled it down, slightly scratching her nose as he did so. Lisa was still somewhat dazed, although her back miraculously was only slightly stinging and that may have been from Tom's battering. Jacky was busy fastening the dress. She couldn't help; she had never worn a real theatre costume before. Ordinary dresses slipped over the head and were fastened with buttons or zips. This creation was unbelievably complicated: a robe of bands and folds, segments and double skirts and draped sashes. Jacky fastened it in moments, then stood back to look at his handiwork.

'The orchid's no good,' he said and took it off her hair. He went to a cardboard box, rummaged about and produced a thin golden band. 'This, dear, is a fillet. You wear it across your forehead. Bend down.' The band had a spring and held firmly on either side of her head. 'Now you can look,' he said, pushing her to a mirror which ran along the wall of the little room.

She saw a stranger. A Greek stranger robed in gold. When she moved, the dress shimmered like falling water.

'Now we'd best get back or all the booze will be gone.'

'Jacky . . .'

'What now?' He was switching off the lights.

'How can I thank you?'

'By not setting fire to my party again, please, dear. Come along. Isn't it nice to know all the girls are now going to be green with jealousy?'

When they returned to the party, people turned round to look at them with interest. David Morris hurried up, exclaiming 'What an escape!' and 'Are you really all right?' and how dangerous candles were and how he wished he'd been the one to put out the flames.

'I feel dreadful. What an idiot looking for water when that guy did the right thing and just rushed up and hit you! Are you really all right?'

Lisa assured him she was. She could scarcely listen to what he was saying. There was only one person she wanted. He came through the crowds.

'Here's your rescuer,' said David Morris.

Lisa did not reply, she was looking at Tom. Offended at being ignored, conscious of not having played the hero, Morris left. Lisa's eyes rested on the man coming towards her. He drew a breath.

'You gave me a fright.'

'I gave myself one, rather.'

'You should be more careful.'

'I have always been a fool.'

He gave her a strange look. They stood in silence. Then he said, 'I hit you very hard. Did I hurt you?'

She shifted her shoulders and wriggled a little. 'I expect so,' she said and smiled. She thought her heart was slowly

393

splitting into two. How could she have told those contemptible lies to herself about not loving?

'You bruise easily.'

'I always have.'

'I damned near knocked you down. But your dress caught fire so quickly . . .' Only then did he realize she was no longer wearing the same clothes. He looked at the golden figure, the Grecian folds outlining her breasts and thighs. 'You look amazing. Where did you get that extraordinary dress?'

'It's a costume. Cressida's, Jacky said. This too.' She indicated the band of gold across her forehead.

'You look very beautiful. I don't think I see you as Cressida, though.'

Faithless? thought Lisa and went no further with the image. 'I haven't thanked you,' she said. 'How does one? Thank a person for saving one's life?'

'That's too dramatic. I daresay I was in time to stop a nasty burn on your back. It isn't burnt, is it?'

'A little red, Jacky said. But nothing.'

'You see. It wasn't so dramatic, Lisa.'

'But there's shock,' she said perversely. 'People can die of it. Birds do. If you pick one up, the poor thing can be so frightened it dies in your hand.'

'I have heard of that.'

They looked at each other and she knew, because her body answered his, that he wanted her. That he still, if only just this moment because of emotion and fear, cared for her in some way. She thought: I must stop this. For him and for me. It is dangerous and it can never do us good. But she stayed, a little figure in mysterious Greek clothes, thin and pale, golden and unobtainable.

'I ought to find Charles. I'm a little tired.'

'It is shock, after all.' He spoke with an effort. 'You must go home. Shall I drive you?'

'Oh no, no,' said Lisa very suddenly.

He gave a smile which had in it something of a grimace. 'I'll find your brother,' he said.

394

# 20

Lisa's mishap was much discussed by Charles and the recovering Jenny. The reddened back turned into a blister. Charles, who behaved nowadays as if Lisa were his responsibility, applied a cream for which he drove into Stratford to consult a chemist.

The season was over. No actors laughed in The Duck, or strode the streets with the innocent air of knowing they were being looked at. It was curious to see outside the theatre big posters for the Amateur Operatic Company in *Lilac Time*, instead of *Henry IV Parts One and Two*. Save for market days, the town was quiet. There wasn't a sign of Polly.

Business at The Treasure Box took a dive and Perdita actually decided to spend a day in her flat 'sorting things out', which meant reading *Bleak House* with her feet up on a chaise-longue. Every year at this time she became depressed by sitting in the shop without a soul coming in to buy.

Lisa was given instructions not to disturb her. On a dull autumn afternoon, again untangling necklaces, Lisa looked up when the temple bells rang, and saw with pleasure the enormous figure of Harry Buckley.

He was her favourite buyer, a big, broad-faced Cockney, whose weatherbeaten face looked as if he'd worked on the Thames as a bargeman all his life. He had a larkish manner and was given to meaningful winks. When he laughed the glasses on the shelves reverberated, and when he bought anything from the shop he paid from a thick, dirty roll of notes which filled his mighty fist. She had once enquired where his shop was in London and he'd given a shout of laughter.

'I gotter stall, Miss. Portobello Road. Big stall it is, and getting bigger. I work with a mate of mine, sharp old geezer called Nick Nicholas.'

This afternoon Harry bustled in, took a look round, bought some china, some glass and a bead cushion embroidered with 'Bless you, dear Uncle', and unrolled some of his usual thumbed notes pulled from his trouser pocket. He busied himself stacking his purchases in a cardboard box, and when Lisa offered him tea, beamed all over his face.

'I call that handsome, Miss W. Really handsome. Where's Her Highness? Out at a sale?'

'Upstairs sorting out things.'

'Is she, then?' said Harry, not believing a word of it. He sat down gingerly – he was far too large for the stool by the counter – and noisily drank his tea. He was in wonderful spirits, but Lisa had never seen him otherwise.

'I got a bit of news,' he said. 'Nick and I have started on something that'll interest you. Bound to. Tell Her Highness about it when she makes her appearance. She'll envy me. See this, then?' He fished in an inner pocket and produced a map of the British Isles that was beginning to tear at the folds. He put it on the counter and anchored it with Lisa's cup of tea. 'Nick and I divided England in half, right down the middle.' He traced with a forefinger. 'Last Monday we set off in our vans (not big, don't eat petrol) and drove up our respective halves of the country as far as the Border. We stopped at every town on the road. Bought anything that took our fancy. Back we came on Friday night, three hundred miles each way, give or take a bit. Showed each other what we'd got on our travels. A real treat.'

'Are you going to do it again, Mr Buckley?' asked Lisa, deeply interested.

'Bless you, we're going to do it every fortnight. Sell in Portobello. Then off again. Only next time we swap sides, see? Nick takes the right and I take the left. It's a big joke to see if we do better or worse, getting to the same towns.' He gave his explosion of a laugh.

When he had gone, his prizefighter's arms loaded with two cardboard boxes, also containing some photograph frames and a case of medals – Harry was a romantic at heart – Lisa envied him. She imagined those journeys. Sagas, she thought. The thrill of entering an antique shop for the first time, with your pocket full of money; searching through ancient cities like Chester and Durham never knowing what you might find. It was a quest, like being in the ship setting out to find Treasure Island. And Harry was Long John Silver.

Harry put the idea of travelling into her head, and on the following day, when Perdita decided to come downstairs and sit, none too willingly, at her own counter, Lisa asked if she could take a day off and go to London.

'What for?' enquired Perdita, looking about the shop for something to criticize.

'I'd like to go to a play, as a matter of fact.'

For some reason, the fact that Lisa did not mention business appeared to satisfy Perdita who said yes, she could go and waste her time if she wanted to. 'I bet a pound to a penny you'll be wasting your father's money as well.'

Lisa had been to London during the summer once or twice, allowed her freedom by a grumbling Perdita. She'd bought some clothes, including the ill-fated domino dress. Now when she arrived in Paddington, still fired by Harry Buckley, she decided to look at some antique shops. As Polly Holt had remarked about going to the theatre, it was necessary to study the competition. She took a bus which landed her up in Kensington Church Street, and she walked slowly, first up one side of the street as far as Notting Hill Gate, then retraced her steps on the other side. She looked in windows, and examined the contents of tables set out on the pavement. One or two shops were entirely different to The Treasure Box – they sold amber, or Victorian jewellery, lockets, real diamonds. But there were other shops not dissimilar to Perdita's. It pleased Lisa to see their stock was

397

not more varied and the prices were higher. She bought a silver elephant with a howdah of red plush for pins. She also bought a pair of tortoiseshell combs scattered with little points of gold, and a porcelain pot which had contained Gentleman's Relish and had a view of Scarborough on its lid. She was amused and interested and hadn't realized to what an extent her work was central to her life.

There was another reason for her London visit: to see *Somersault*, Tom's play running at the Globe.

With the knowledge she had picked up from Polly, and from Peter who had talked a good deal about the theatre, Lisa knew it would be safe now the play had been running for some time to go and see it without the risk of bumping into the author or his wife. They had probably seen it a dozen times. Now it had settled into its West End run.

It was odd to walk up to a theatre and read Tom's name on the poster. Odder still to sit for two and a half hours listening to his voice. The play, set in the present, took place in a provincial newspaper office. It was a comedy, very much post-war. The chief character was a reporter home from fighting in France and Germany and taking up civilian life again. He epitomized the returning soldier, bringing home ideas of an England which didn't exist any more. It showed how people had changed. The play was funny, quick-fire, sharp. Now and then in scenes between the girl and the hero, there was a certain melancholy. But the strongest theme was the discovery of a town scandal, and what happens when the reporter determines that those who were implicated should be exposed. In the end his own nature stops him from doing that because of the wider harm it will cause. If the play had a moral, thought Lisa, it was about our values then and our values now. It was a comedy on a serious subject, the strongest points made when the writer forced the audience to laugh. It was Tom's voice speaking and she could hear, again and again, the years that separated them. On the late train and on her drive back to Lyndhurst, she thought about him. Untroubled by hope.

The following evening she had been invited by Jenny and Charles to dinner. Her sister-in-law proudly served a meal cooked entirely by Mrs Welstead: Jenny was often the little girl playing house. During the meal, Charles said he'd seen in the papers that the 1949 season's plans at the theatre had been announced.

'Want to hear what's being offered, girls?'

'Yes, yes, what about our tickets for all the opening nights?' asked an excited Jenny.

'Mick Gould says he'll be able to fix those,' put in Lisa.

'Goody. I can't wait.'

'Now,' said Charles, 'for the plays.'

'Lewis Lockton? I love him,' said Jenny.

'Not this year. He's going into a new Rattigan in London. What have we then? *Hamlet*. *Love's Labour's*. *Pericles* – that's a rare one. *Henry V* – Anthony Quayle is playing the King – and a repeat of *Twelfth Night*. One or two stars . . .' He read out famous names. 'Mick Gould, whom I know Jenny admires. Gemma Lambert and our own dear Polly, who is in *Henry V* as the Princess of France, I see.'

Is he too light? thought Lisa. She wondered if it was the voice of the gambler swearing he hasn't touched a card for weeks. Jenny chatted about the plays, interspersing uncritical admiration with the demand that Charles should share her opinion of Shakespeare's work.

'Don't you always blub at *Hamlet*, Charles?'

'*Henry V* is one of my favourites, I just *love* the bit when he flirts with the French princess, don't you?'

She sighed with advance delight. Certainly the girl was happy.

But after her London visit Lisa's own life was dull again. Perdita went off on expeditions and returned having bought nothing; her temper was shorter than ever. She was out one morning when the telephone in the shop rang. It was Polly.

'Got you at last. I rang last week and Perdita Smith said you'd gone to town. Beast, why didn't you ask me to come?'

'I didn't know you were still at Avoncliffe,' said Lisa, who had decided that Polly had upped sticks and gone to look for work in London until the next season began, when she was again to be part of it.

399

'I'm not in Avoncliffe, darling. Most of it's shut and they're covering everything with dust sheets. It stinks of paint. I'm with the parents, worse luck. Mick's gone to town. He's got a radio play, lucky bastard. I say, Lisa, what about you going up in flames! I was livid to have missed it. Jacky told me it reminded him of the last Act of *Faust*, and that Gemma Lambert's husband rushed to the rescue like a commando. Jacky was dead impressed. He said Tom West-bury saved your life. Funny, when you came to think of it.'

'He was rather quick and brave.'

'I wish I was. I rang to say come to supper. Do say yes. The old folk are in London doing some Christmas shopping. They asked me to go but they stay at the most awful hotel in Bayswater. I suppose it was okay when they were young. Mummy says it used to be chic, as she calls it. Not now. Mushrooms in the wardrobe.'

'Why should your mother buy –'

'No, no!' interrupted Polly, laughing. 'Mushrooms *grow* in cupboards when things are *damp*. It's a certain sign, and you can tell the smell the minute you open the bedroom door. When I was in digs at Sheffield you should have seen the mushrooms, they were pale mauve and enormous. They only needed pixies sitting on them. I will tell you all about them, and you can tell me about catching fire. By the way, will eggs do? You don't know how to scramble them, by any happy chance? Oh, excellent. You will come, won't you?'

'I'd like to very much.'

'Good. Good. Lots of talk and Daddy has some filthy wine which he said comes from Yugoslavia. How did it get to England? We'll drink it all.'

Perdita came back from her sale and was on the telephone to some customer exclusively her own. She put her hand over the mouthpiece in case Lisa recognized the voice. She seemed relieved when Lisa whispered that she'd like to go early.

Lisa drove through Stratford passing Crocker Road, and turning into a richer part of the town, to the steep road where the Holts had lived for years. Polly's father, now

400

retired, had been a successful Birmingham businessman who had made money. He had married late, in his forties, a pretty, snobbish young woman he had met at the tennis club. She was no longer a girl, and Polly's arrival had been a kind of miracle to both of them. Polly's mother remained a snob but a hospitable one. She spent her husband's money freely on their rich over-furnished house. It stood up well to wartime shortages, since every piece of furniture, square of carpet and cup and saucer were of the best quality. In pre-war days she'd also spent money like water on the charming child of her middle age. No little girl had prettier clothes or more expensive toys. Polly was given enormous children's parties, taken to circuses, petted and made a fool of. During the war when she was a VAD she was showered with black market clothing coupons and black market gin. They were dotingly proud of her as an actress, and there were large photographs of her in all her rôles – leads when she was in rep, vignettes now she was at Stratford – about the house.

When Lisa drew up at Broadoaks, Polly dashed out into the foggy evening. She'd been on the lookout for her.

'Stranger, I've missed you. Come in. God, it's freezing, I've lit the hugest fire. Mustn't mention fires, must I?'

She dragged Lisa indoors, into the drawing-room furnished with Mrs Holt's particular taste. It was all pale blue and silver, the furniture balloon-like and covered in brocade, the cushions so filled with down that they looked pregnant. Piles of extra cushions were heaped here and there – they were pregnant too. There were tables for Polly's silver-framed photographs, a grand piano, white fur rugs. The girls went to the crackling fire; Polly fetched gin and tonic and they sat, arms round their knees, as they'd done at school.

'Mick Gould said you caught fire on purpose to brighten up the party. He says he wished he'd thought of that,' said Polly. A rain of questions followed. She relished the drama and mocked the victim. It would just take Lisa, she declared, to sit on a table and lean into a naked flame.

'What do you mean? Anybody could have done the same!'

'Not an actor. When we sit we know where and how. We know exactly how our bodies will be placed before we make a move to a chair or a sofa. Take that table you sat on. If that had been me, I'd have measured the space with my eye, I'd have known how much room there was to sit and I'd have moved the bloody candle. There isn't an actor in the world who'd lean against a naked flame. That's why we all talked about it so much, darling. People kept saying "but how did she *do* it?" It is rather like you, you know. You throw yourself about. Don't think,' Polly added kindly, 'you don't look rather good when you sprawl. You're nice and thin and quite graceful in a way. But no art. No art at all.'

Lisa had told her friend, months ago, about Tom Westbury. It had been when Tom and Gemma Lambert were living at Avoncliffe and she'd judged it was necessary. Polly had been engrossed, sympathetic, and rude about Gemma. She rarely mentioned Tom to Lisa afterwards. Surprisingly for an egotist and a gossip, she occasionally displayed a certain tact. Now she was full of admiration.

'Imagine your ex being the one to save your life. What did it feel like when you realized it was him bashing out the flames?'

'It was rather a surprise,' said Lisa dryly.

Polly laughed. 'I wonder how *he* felt when he saw that the girl who'd caught fire was *you*. What a story.' Lisa wondered not for the first time if Polly were in search of material; actors were such magpies. 'I suppose you went to London to see his play,' added Polly. 'I wish we'd gone together.'

'Haven't you seen it?'

'Of course. It's my job. There's also the fact that your ex's wife happens to be coming back to Stratford next season. One never knows . . .'

'You mean he might write a part for you.'

Faced with what she had been implying, Polly denied it. 'Too far-fetched. He never would. Will. But I still have to know about Tom Westbury's work. It's awful, Lisa, how much one has to know. Particularly about rivals who are better actors than oneself.'

'At school we called that fishing. The expected answer being "Oh my dear, nobody's better than you".'

'I don't remember that,' said Polly with dignity. 'Pour us another G and T. I need it.'

'You haven't said what you think of Tom's play,' prompted Lisa, handing her the refilled glass. Like a lover, she wanted to hear him talked about. Polly gulped down most of her second drink, licking her lips like a cat.

'I love gin,' she said. 'Did I ever tell you my mother's mother, Granny Lucy, now fortunately dead, was an alcoholic? Mother keeps it very quiet, but she was. Drunk as a lord, darling, at ten in the morning. I've inherited Granny Lucy's vice. I love drink. Gin. Scotch. Rum. Liqueurs, the stickier the better. Wine, even the vinegarish ones from Yugoslavia. Not beer, it smells. Ugh. Yes, there's a Granny Lucy in me somewhere but I have an iron will. I control it. Now. Tom's play . . .' She launched into a shrewd dissection. They talked about the play in detail. Lisa liked the way actors spoke of imaginary characters. 'I don't think the reporter would have thrown that girl over. It was the only false note in the play. He truly loved her.' Polly hugged her knees. 'I bet you're hungry.'

'Not particularly.'

'Shall we do the eggs?'

'Any time you like,' said Lisa, sensing Polly had a reason for lingering.

'You know Sir Lew won't be back next season. I daresay you noticed that among the new plans in the paper?'

'I did notice. You must be sorry.'

'I *was*.'

'Not any more?'

'Things change. People too. Sir Lew changed, come to that.'

Polly began to talk about the star and herself. She described things she'd never told Lisa before and did so with a certain brilliance, evoking the atmosphere of the season now dead and beginning to be forgotten. All Lisa had heard from actors until now had been gossip and jokes; but while her

403

friend talked she began to see unrolling in front of her a painting, a tapestry of the actor's life in this 'glamorous village' as Polly called it. Stratford was so special, so small, it was like a university town and when you belonged to it you were happy. Actors went about on bicycles, their scripts in their baskets. They sat in groups on the grass by the river, saw each other for work and for play. At parties 'you knew every single person there', and they crowded round the piano as Mick Gould played Feste's ditty:

> When that I was and a little tiny boy,
> With hey, ho, the wind and the rain;
> A foolish thing was but a toy,
> For the rain it raineth every day.

All the actors sang it together, it ran through the Company like a love song. Walking with his particular grace through the months had been Lewis Lockton. He had singled Polly out, taken her to dinner, sat with her in the wings during performances of *Lear*. 'We didn't say a word.' When they'd dined in Woodstock, they had met Noel Coward. There wasn't anybody grand Sir Lew didn't know, he was so famous. Polly spoke the way Jenny did, like a fan. Yet now and then it was clear she had been conscious of holding the strongest card in the pack: her youth. 'He often said did I remember this actor or that production and then I'd say "but I wasn't born then". It used to make him laugh.'

Lisa wanted to ask if Polly and the star had been to bed. Listening to the long story, she saw something was omitted from the tale of great actor and little understudy. It was not complete. Like Peter's tales of his non-war, Lisa heard the missing bits without being able to make out the words.

'Do you love him, Polly?'

'It isn't in the present tense any more. But the answer during the season was yes.'

'You were in love?'

'I hate that phrase. It's so sentimental.'

'Tripe.'

'Well, I think it is anyway. Let's say we were loving friends. That's what we were.'

'How did he feel about you?'

'The same,' said Polly looking as if Lisa were an idiot.

Oh fine, thought Lisa. Why are you bothering to tell me this rigmarole when all we're getting are euphemisms? She wondered if the distinguished, elderly, handsome and exceptional man, old enough to have been Polly's father, had fallen for this restless, selfish comedienne. Or had Polly been the one to love, a rash thing to do when you must jump with closed eyes over the wall of thirty-five years of a man's life.

Lisa's silence worked on Polly, as questions would never have done. When the actress saw that her audience was no longer attentive, she finished the story, making confessions. The fact was she had become proprietorial over Sir Lew. It was natural, wasn't it? She'd been his 'loving friend' – she firmly repeated the phrase – for the whole season and she supposed she had taken him for granted or taken his affection for granted, which came to the same thing. She had imagined they would continue to meet when the season ended, but in London instead of Stratford. He invited her to a dinner party he was giving on his last Sunday at the Spread Eagle Hotel. He had given his final *Lear* performance on Saturday night and was only staying one day afterwards, having no intention to remain until the whole season ended. 'He's like that. He loves 'em and leaves 'em,' said Polly. She had a new dress which Jacky Grimsdyke had made for her, green satin, down to her toes. 'I looked stunning.' She had been excited. It was going to be a big occasion, and Lewis Lockton said he was going to invite somebody to meet her: Brian Sulgrave of J. Arthur Rank's. He was casting director and was on the look-out for promising young actresses. 'I thought – fame at last. Then – would you believe it – the dinner was a non-stop disaster. Sulgrave never showed up. A good many London people drove down specially and they were all as old as God. And who do you suppose was the *pièce de résistance*? Sonia Bell, who only happens to be the wife he separated from.' Polly looked dark. 'I suppose she's good-looking if you like that kind of thing. She's got that half-starved look of people who slim all the time. Her hair's dyed, rather a nice colour, and she was just back from Hollywood and letting us know it.' Lewis Lockton had put Polly on his left at dinner, but the ex-wife had been on his right. He'd introduced Polly to a number of celebrated people. Lisa imagined a brilliant gathering, but Polly said it had been deadly and she'd decided to leave early. 'He saw me to his car. His chauffeur was driving me back to Avoncliffe. Sir Lew took my hand and kissed it. It was like being in a play by Barrie. Do you know what he said? "Goodbye, my dear child. I shall never see you again. And I shall never forget you."' A pause. Polly eyed Lisa.

'He sounds rather marvellous,' murmured Lisa.

'He is. I mean, was. Anyway I was perfectly furious, wouldn't you have been? I cried all the way back in his beastly car. It's all entirely to do with his being sixty-two, you know. Men get very odd at sixty-two. Shall we eat?' finished Polly, jumping up.

In Mrs Holt's late 1930s kitchen, the boiler glowed and a cat large enough to make a second rug for the drawing-room was lying stretched in tortoiseshell luxury on a coconut mat. Lisa cooked and Polly laid the kitchen table with formality, spreading a cloth edged with lace, fetching real silver knives and forks, a set of Georgian silver salt and pepper pots, and cut glasses for the Yugoslavian wine. The table was a poem. They sat down to scrambled eggs, khaki-coloured bread and two raw tomatoes.

During the meal Polly talked about the coming season. She had only been offered one real part: Katharine, the princess of France, who marries Henry V.

'"Your majesty shall mock at me, I cannot speak your England",' quoted Polly with a perfect French accent. 'I wanted to refuse, actually, because that's all I've got except waiting-women again, and understudying horrible Gemma Lambert. But Daddy said his motto was "Play Safe". Mad, isn't it, for an actress? I don't know why I said yes . . . except that Tony Quayle was nice about me and said Doll Tearsheet

406

was good, and went on about how I was suited to Katharine. Oh well. You really know how to scramble eggs, darling, they're delicious.' She said this in such a way that Lisa knew Polly preferred the role of being helpless in the kitchen. The actress picked up a tomato, sniffed it, said it smelled like scent and put it down again. 'I still think I'm a fool to take the measly parts Tony offered me. Katharine only has twenty-nine lines.'

'You accepted because you want to be here in Shake-speare.'

'Of course I don't. Well, yes, who wouldn't want to play Shakespeare in decent parts, but not ladies-in-waiting. That's just what I am in more ways than one. But it isn't why I agreed, although my father nagged rather a lot.'

Lisa's face had a certain irony about it; she looked like Charles just then. Now, she thought, I'm going to be told why I was asked. It wasn't to hear the story about Sir Lew, which I'm sure she's told half a dozen times before. It's something more important. I wonder what. Polly had a very faint air of embarrassment, surely an emotion foreign to an actor.

'Promise you won't be offended by what I'm going to say.'

The irony in Lisa's face grew more noticeable. How often she'd heard and said that. Guy. Charles. She herself speaking to Peter Lang. The warning sentence which is usually per-fectly useless.

'How can I answer that, Polly? I daresay I shall be livid and leave in a rage.'

'You wouldn't, would you? I'd feel ghastly.'

'I wish you'd tell me what you're talking about.'

Polly began to play the piano on the tablecloth. 'The fact is – God, it's difficult to say. The fact is . . . Peter Lang.'

'Peter Lang what?' asked Lisa stupidly.

'That's what I want to know. Peter Lang what? I told you about Sir Lew because I thought you might imagine there'd been something between us and as I said, we were loving friends,' reiterated Polly. 'But – well – I've been seeing Peter since you and he split up. We were at the Wardrobe party but in another room which was why we missed your fire, darling. Peter was avoiding you. I think at that time he was still upset over you. Anyway, since then . . . that's all I can say, really.' Her face was solemn. She waited for Lisa to speak.

Lisa realized that at that moment Polly was at her mercy. It was interesting and unexpected. She didn't choose her words but spoke the blunt truth. 'I don't mind, Polly, if you go around with him. It doesn't hurt me. I promise.'

Polly, who had been painfully waiting, gave a little significant sigh. 'I suppose it would be more flattering to Peter and to me if it did hurt. I minded about *you* when Peter and I first started going around. I was sure he was hankering and I was so jealous. That's why I didn't come to The Treasure Box. He told me you and he separated "mutually". He does use peculiar words. I do like him, Lisa. In fact, it is more than that.' She looked as tragic as her comic nose would allow.

Lisa was unaffected by this new turn of fate. A few months ago the idea of losing Peter would have wounded her. She would certainly have been jealous, especially as she thought Polly infinitely more attractive than she was. Lisa belittled her own attractions, saw other women as sexually fatal beauties with whom in a war of love she would always be defeated. She had felt it when she first saw Gemma Lambert appear upon the stage. She would have felt the same with Polly. But she and Peter were lovers no longer. Since they had parted, what had replaced him were her thoughts of Tom and the past.

'How does Peter feel about you?' she asked in a gentle voice.

'He never says.'

'Could you get him to say?'

'You know Peter. He's incapable of uttering a word,' said Polly, and gave a wild sort of laugh. 'That maddens me because theatre people are just the opposite. We talk. We explain and describe. We tell.'

Not about Lewis Lockton, thought Lisa, and wondered if even Polly removed from her impulsive stories the things that did not flatter or please. After all, the drama of Lockton's farewell had not been unflattering. But perhaps the 'loving friendship' had . . .

Polly was warming to her subject. 'You know, Lisa, reserve truly is death to us. If we clammed up, how could we act? Look, would you mind if I talked about something *you* never do? About sex, I mean?' She peered at Lisa as if expecting disapproval.

Lisa did not answer. It was true she didn't talk about sex, but it fascinated her just the same.

'You see,' said Polly, having seen nothing to alarm or chill in her friend's face, 'we made love that very night during the party. It was exciting in an awful kind of way because I felt a thief. I thought I was stealing him from you – no, don't interrupt. He'd said you and he had parted, but I still had an idea I was doing something wrong, cruel even, and it made the sex more thrilling, and oh, Lisa, I did want him so. He is gorgeous to look at, isn't he? So pale and fair and he isn't young. I mean, I think he's over forty, I really do. He says thirty-eight but I'm sure it's a lie. Since then we've continued meeting and I've always been astonished that you haven't seen us together. I suppose that's because he takes such trouble to call for me here and won't take me to The Duck – a big bore as I love it – and he drives down different roads so as not to pass your house. By the way he goes on you'd think he was a spy. That's what I wanted to talk to you about. Lisa, do you know *anything* about Peter?'

'Of course. What do you want to know?'

'Don't give me the line about fighting in France and parents killed in the Blitz. I don't believe any of it and I'm sure you didn't either when he told you. He's a mystery. It drives me mad being in love with a mystery. Another thing. Why did you and he part? May I ask you that?'

Lisa had had enough time to be prepared for the question. She took refuge in saying something which could have been true and wasn't. 'It wore itself out, really. We both felt it.'

409

Polly went on with her own more troubled thought. 'I wondered if it could be the stuff about him being called on by the police in Warwick?'

'Oh. What was that?' said Lisa coolly. She thought: why am I lying? Because she looks as if she's going to cry.

'It was all a lot of talk about nothing,' Polly said. 'The police were asking about his car licence. Anyway, I'd heard about it as who hadn't? When we made love at the Wardrobe party, Lisa, we went up the iron stair, there's a sort of attic up there and a huge pile of costumes and we did it lying on those. It was wonderful. He is, isn't he? Oh, sorry. Anyway, that very night while he was in my arms I said it, I said how everybody in the theatre knew about him and the police, and was he a criminal on the run, and I'd hide him and what a thrill, and do you know, I managed to make him laugh. He doesn't usually at my jokes. Then he told me about the car licence being expired and he was sure I knew how keen the police are on you not driving unless you've paid up. So . . .' She gave a sigh and stood up. 'Shall we go back to the drawing-room?'

'Okay.'

The fire was almost out. The enormous cat had padded after them and Polly picked it up; she looked like an Edwardian actress carrying a fur muff. Its vast striped stomach, its long legs, hung from her arms. It began to purr like an engine.

'Stupid animal. It thinks I like it. Mummy feeds it too much and it's called Tiger. What a name,' she said, plumping the cat down on the blue brocade sofa where it lay not bothering to budge.

They sat on the mat again and Polly put a log on the fire but it didn't catch. The room grew colder.

'You know, I was the one who told everybody at the theatre about the police. I never keep my mouth shut. I didn't actually mention it to you, darling, that really would have been unkind, but I told other people and we were all fascinated. It's the sort of thing you discuss and make up theories about. Agatha Christie, third Act. Some people

410

invented really funny explanations. Of course the chat didn't last and we started talking about someone else. Incidentally, I heard about the police hovering into view – they came twice – from Joanna, a student who lives in Peter's digs. Her parents are friends of my mother's. I've known her ages.'

Lisa remembered Joanna, who seemed to have played the part of destiny in her own life.

Her friend continued to talk, her face troubled. 'Joanna told me something else yesterday. It was much worse than about the car licence.'

'Polly, what's this all about?' said Lisa, beginning to catch her friend's anxiety; up until now she had only listened and felt more or less easy about her.

'Joanna told me a woman turned up at their digs. A blonde. She appeared three days ago and Joanna has seen her with Peter lots of times. Lisa. Tell me the worst. Did you know he has somebody else? Is that why you parted?'

'Of course he hasn't. I told you, we agreed quite amicably. Who is this woman? She is probably connected with his work on the paper. He's always interviewing people.'

'She's staying with him. In his room. She's still there and I can't bear it.'

Lisa exclaimed, denied, tried to laugh it off but Polly scarcely bothered to listen. She gouged at the carpet, looking young and sad. She seemed truly in love, and Lisa wondered if she should tell her to ask Peter no questions. But who wants advice? All Polly wanted was to talk. To talk on and on. To wallow, even. Looking at her friend's bent head, Lisa felt helpless. She was in an impossible position. How could she tell Polly it had been Peter's secrets which ended their love affair? Polly must somehow get herself out of the tangle of loving such a man, either by accepting him or cutting herself free as Lisa had done. What was Peter? Lisa still didn't know. When she finally said goodnight, and Polly walked to the door to see her off, Lisa left a girl still full of suspicion.

Lisa was selfishly relieved when a few days later her friend telephoned, sounding very brisk indeed, and said she was going to London to stay with Mick Gould.

411

'He's got rooms in Long Acre and we can walk to any theatre anywhere. Don't you envy me?'

December went by, and Stratford smelled of woodsmoke again. At Christmas the Whitfields spent their first feast-day at Lyndhurst; Charles bought both girls expensive presents – out-of-season white lilac and champagne and angora sweaters. Jenny cooked the Christmas dinner for the first time in her life. Charles made a great fuss about that. His manner to his wife was positively deferential.

In February when the fifteen-foot-high holly tree at the gates of Lyndhurst was still shining with red berries and there was frost like cold sugar beneath it every morning, quite suddenly, like a flock of birds from tropic climes, the actors reappeared. The Duck was noisy with voices. Lisa called at W. H. Smith's to buy Temple editions of the six plays to be seen during the season, and Polly met Lisa at The Cobweb, bringing Mick Gould. There was no sign of heartbreak on Polly's impudent face. She was very vivacious.

# 21

Certain lovers have something in common with experienced criminals: well-laid plans. Gemma had laid hers while she was in London during the winter. Charles had met her seldom; it was too difficult and living with Tom in their Hampstead flat, taken up with his success – which impressed her – Gemma could only meet her lover at rare intervals when he came to London and took a room at The Dorchester. Gemma managed to come to Park Lane for a short hour. They scarcely bothered to talk but went to his room and made love in a feverish silence. Afterwards Charles thought of it as if they had run through a forest fire.

Charles let things happen. He wanted Gemma and he had her. He knew that in February she would be coming to live in Stratford again and in the meantime – apart from their few violent sexual encounters – he called once at the Hampstead flat and took Gemma and the little boy to a pantomime. Again and again the thought returned to him that he had never believed he would fall in love. The lunatic state had never had anything to do with the kind of sex he enjoyed. He'd been so certain he would never become mad. But he was.

There was another unexpected thing: Charles had not thought himself capable of loving a child. He'd thought the children of his friends very tedious. Slowly, without his knowing it, a love for Bobbie crept across the indifference of his heart, just as his mother stretched out her hand and gripped his soul.

What is there, he thought, driving back from London to Stratford one winter's night, about that woman and her child which affects me so? He didn't know. But every time he saw Gemma he felt as if he would tremble and every time he kissed the child there was a funny feeling in his heart, like pain. What would it be like to have a child of his own? He began to wish, knowing it made no sense, that Jenny would get pregnant. Did she know that thought of his?

One night after they had made love, she lay in his arms and whispered, 'I wish we could have a baby.'

'Yes. It would be nice,' he said, kissing her.

'But why can't I?' she said and sounded hideously young. 'I don't do anything to stop it. Nor do you.'

'Some women can take quite a long time,' said Charles, who'd never talked about the matter before in his life, but faintly remembered it was something he'd heard his mother say. Getting pregnant was scarcely a subject that a seducer would discuss with his women. 'I expect it will happen soon,' he comforted her. She clung.

Jenny had become intuitive about him. The opposite sex, as Charles knew to his cost, could be uncannily perceptive at times. In love affairs he had learned to cope with those intuitions whilst marvelling at them. Now he was faced with the same thing in his youthful and unthinking wife. Jenny, seeming so uncomplicated, interested only in riding her pony Paintbox, giggling with old schoolfriends or throwing herself into his arms. She'd recently had her nineteenth birthday, she was virtually still a schoolgirl. Why should she suddenly want a child?

Concern about Jenny vanished like the frost which melted in the thin February sunshine. Red japonica buds were opening on a wall in Lyndhurst's erstwhile orchard. Gemma telephoned.

'Tom isn't in Stratford yet. He's wildly busy,' said Gemma complacently. 'Come round to Avoncliffe. We've got the same flat and Bobbie wants to see you.'

When he arrived at the house there were half a dozen bicycles leaning against the stable walls and one or two cars parked. The door of the stable flat was wide open, there were suitcases piled in the tiny hall, and a voice from upstairs shouted, 'I'm here!'

He found Gemma kneeling in front of an old school trunk, pulling out dresses and underclothes. She turned a radiant face to him and made a *moue* with her lips. Bobbie was sitting on the bed, dressed in a thick brown sweater, swinging his legs; he, too, gave Charles a grin of welcome. The sun slanted into the white-painted room and when Charles saw the beautiful figure of his lover, her whole body seeming to glow, he was filled with joy.

'Mummy says you're going to take me riding,' said Bobbie. 'Would you really, Charles?' Gemma had now taught him to call adults by their first names. She had decided the old-fashioned 'Uncle' and 'Aunt' had begun to sound absurd.

'Am I?' said Charles, laughing.

'Yes, you must ride with him, darling. Tony Quayle says one should start riding when one's really young, it's so good for the back. I want Bobbie to grow up like a warrior.' The word was very like Gemma and most unlike the timid boy.

Charles agreed to the riding. He would have agreed to anything his greedy lover asked. Throwing satin clothes on the bed in shiny heaps, she was in the asking mood. Would he take Bobbie and her to tea at The Spread Eagle? Would he buy her some cultured pearl earrings, 'big ones'? Would he drive her to the theatre now, and come back later to pick her up?

'The Astons are minding Bobbie,' said Gemma. 'Or perhaps while I'm at the theatre, he'd prefer you.'

Charles and Bobbie looked at each other in a friendly way and Charles thought, I'm to be saddled with my small conqueror, am I?

'I'll take him back to Lyndhurst,' he suggested. 'Shall you be long?'

'I don't want him going to Lyndhurst. He's better with the Astons.'

It flattered him to see her jealous.

When Bobbie had clattered off to a neighbouring flat, he

415

and Gemma walked out into the Avoncliffe garden to look, she said, for snowdrops. 'White and green are my colours.' She bent to look under trees.

'I believe Bobbie likes me,' said Charles after a while.

'Of course he adores you,' Gemma replied. She had found a large clump of snowdrops.

'What about Tom?'

'What about him?' her voice had a tinny ring.

Charles liked it when she sounded like that. He liked her hardness which matched her passion. He liked her greed which went into her sex. He liked her hungry maternal love which affected her sensual love. He wouldn't change a vice in her.

'Does Bobbie like Tom very much?'

A silly question. Why had he asked it? 'Bobbie likes everybody.'

'How indiscriminate. I was under the impression that he had grown quite fond of me.'

Gemma knelt down on the wet grass and picked one of the thin winter flowers. Standing up again she shook it as if expecting it to ring like a bell.

'Some people are full of love. Bobbie's like that. He's nervous and he needs to be safe but he also needs to love and that's what happens.'

He raised his eyebrows. 'I suppose I shall have to make do with that.'

Gemma looked him up and down. 'I sometimes think,' she said, 'that you're as hungry as me.'

Being a successful dramatist had altered Tom's life. He was interviewed and written about. People wanted his opinions on things as disparate as sport, women's fashions or the changing Labour party. He was sought after, admired or envied by friends, and he was considerably richer. During the early spring he had to drive to London two or three times a week, staying in their Hampstead flat, while Gemma was on her own at Stratford. She was taken up with rehearsals for her role as the French Princess in *Love's Labour's Lost*.

The person at a loose end was Charles. He saw a good deal of Bobbie, collecting him from the Aston family. When Charles drove into Avoncliffe's gardens, he usually found the children playing ball, or digging in the vegetable garden, or collecting caterpillars which they fed on a certain kind of leaf. 'He just loves them!' said Bobbie, studying a matchbox in which the caterpillar was busily munching.

Tom was in London again, and Gemma arranged for the Astons to look after her little boy. Gemma, thought Charles, had a never-failing gift for getting people to do things for her; it was another version of Jenny's talent with her daily help. Both women repaid their devoted retainers with loud gratitude.

Almost every night when Gemma was back from rehearsal, Charles drove her to the bitterly cold cottage which this year had been let 'to a local gentleman'. When the lovers, shuddering in the chill night, let themselves into the cottage where nobody lived now, they went round lighting gas fires, lighting the cooker to let it roar the kitchen into faint warmth. They trembled – but only with cold – when they took off their clothes. And then they were back in the sexual bliss which never failed or palled. She was the most thrilling lover he'd ever had, the most practised. She had many ways of exciting him, surprising him. 'Why don't we . . .?' she would say. She made their sex together different every time they lay down in the damp room in the silent winter country.

When he met her after the long hours of rehearsal she was always strained and pale; as they entered the cottage her voice was scratchy. And then she turned, like a tulip opening in a hot room, into thrilling beauty. He never tired of her, never ceased to desire her. She engaged his thrusting body and his aching imagination. It was a terrible slavery and he often wondered, when their mating was finished, if she was as helpless as he.

Perdita Smith and Lisa were working at the not very accurate accounts of The Treasure Box on a winter's afternoon a month after the Company had arrived at Stratford. Perdita had decided to give Lisa 8 per cent of any sales in the future, a rise of 1 per cent.

'Not that you need a farthing with all your father's money.'

'It isn't as much as you think, Perdita.'

'You look rich enough,' said Perdita, regarding Lisa's dark dress with a little muslin collar and the pearl earrings shining on either side of her face. 'However. As my mother used to say, there's no taste in nothing, so it is 8 per cent. Not back-dated,' she added, reading Lisa's enquiring face. 'We start from today. That is if you make a sale, of course. If I am out or away then the sale is yours. But not if I'm here – as now –' she added. The temple bells rang musically, and the glass front door swung open.

Lisa went slightly pink when she saw who had entered the shop. It was Guy Bowden. He came in briskly, raised his cap, gave them a formal 'good morning' and inquired how they were.

'Do you mean our health or the business, Guy?' said Perdita. She changed her manner with a man, any man, and Guy was a favourite acquaintance whom she rarely saw, grumbling that he hadn't spent a farthing in her shop for five years.

'Of course I meant both,' said Guy Bowden with his frosty smile. He looked trim, handsome, as tough and seasoned as ever Lisa had seen him. How well he wore his rough tweeds and the flat cap like a stable lad's which he now removed and kept folded in his hand.

'You're not here to pay compliments, I suppose,' said Perdita, descending from her stool. 'What can I tempt you with? How about a pretty little Georgian candlestick? Makes the mouth water.' She reached for the candlestick, which Lisa had recently cleaned so well that it shone.

He picked it up. It was very old and Lisa had noticed that the silver did not seem solid but soft, as if you could press it into folds like silk. It stood sturdily where he placed it in front of him on the counter; by the way he handled it, she thought it pleased him. He lifted it up

418

again, looked at the base and began to discuss silver marks.

'George III by the duty mark, but it seems different from some of mine.'

'The King's head was altered in 1786 from facing left to facing right. Can't think why,' said Perdita.

He nodded, still fingering the candlestick. 'I'd like to talk to you about hallmarks sometime,' he said. 'They can be confusing, particularly in the provinces. Towns seemed to have authorized assay offices at one time but only for quite short periods. They're very inconsistent. You must also tell me something about the leopard uncrowned.'

Perdita was very glib. '1821. Yes, we'll talk about it. A favourite subject of mine.' Favourite subjects were anything to do with Perdita's encyclopedic knowledge connected with her stock.

The two continued to discuss silver. The talk was above Lisa's head, being of balusters, cartouches, strapwork and reeding. She scarcely listened. She was thinking that it was unnatural for a man to be so untouched by his loss. How could you love a daughter with such devotion, such indulgence, and cut her off like a diseased branch of a tree? Guy Bowden stood straight. He looked healthy, in command. Was there a loving bone left in that trim fifty-year-old body? She admired him without wanting to do so, and began to see why her weak father had needed him.

'As a matter of fact,' said Guy, when the subject of silver marks, at least for the present, had been satisfactorily dealt with, 'I've come to ask a favour.'

'Shall we get this matter settled first?' Perdita was stroking the candlestick. 'Tell you what. Take it home and see how it looks at Whitefriars. Put it on a bookcase or your Sheraton sideboard. Or your desk.' Perdita had an elephant's memory for people's houses and furniture. 'Live with my candlestick for a bit and then if it doesn't please you, bring it back. I'll always be glad to have it again.'

Guy Bowden turned the idea over in his mind. Lisa had never known this move of her employer's to fail.

419

'Very well. If you insist.'

'Oh, but I don't. I merely thought you might like to see how it fits in.'

'Yes. Well. Could you wrap it for me?'

'Lisa,' said Perdita, in the voice reserved for her minion in the presence of customers.

Lisa took the candlestick into the tea-making cubby-hole from which she heard Guy ask Perdita if she could come round sometime and 'be good enough to take a look at my grandfather clock. It isn't going as well as it should. Perhaps you know something about it, since you originally bought it for me.'

'Tomkins and Allen, 1787. I daresay it needs oiling. All those magnificent old mechanisms need is a touch of almond oil on the brass wheels behind the face. I use a goose's feather. Would tonight be convenient, after we close?'

'That would be first rate.'

'I shall expect a good strong gin and ginger.'

'It will be ready for you. Many thanks, Perdita.' Lisa came out with the neatly packed parcel. Guy added his thanks to her and then to her startled surprise addressed Perdita again. 'Might I have a word with your colleague?'

'Fire away.'

'I'm afraid I meant in private. We could just run along to The White Swan.'

Perdita, looking keenly interested, picked up her pen and opened her account book. 'Very well, if you must. But don't keep her too long, there's a mort of work to do before six.'

Lisa took her hat, pulled on her thick winter coat and went into the street, preceding Guy who stepped back to wait for her.

'Shall we have a cup of tea at The White Swan? Or we might go to The Falcon?'

'I mustn't be very long,' she said.

'I don't intend to let Perdita browbeat us. She managed the shop for years alone. It was I who found you for her and she is fortunate to have you. Let's go to The Falcon.'

They walked in a not very comfortable silence along

420

Chapel Street to The Falcon, close to The Shakespeare where Lisa with Jenny and her brother had lived for that unlikely three months. It was getting dark and the street lights were shining. It was slightly foggy and smelled of winter. Her companion didn't say a word and she didn't either. She was certain she knew what this was about. At last and about time, she thought.

The Falcon, like Whitefriars, was unspoiled Tudor, wearing the burden of the years with lopsided grace. It had been an inn, as many of the oldest Stratford buildings had been. It had known rough times, loud voices, the ring of hooves in the courtyard, the terror of civil wars, the lean faces of hunger. Now it had a hush of luxury and the inglenook could seat four people.

The room was deserted except for one old gentleman in a far corner, asleep over a newspaper. Places like this, vibrant with people and movement in spring and summer, slept as he did in wintertime. What looked like half a tree was gently smouldering in the fireplace.

Guy ordered tea. She expected him to sit down and begin to talk at once. She was interested to know how he would approach the painful subject. Lisa had forgiven him for his part in the Peter Lang affair. She had come to like him. But Guy did not mention Jenny at all. He talked sociably about Perdita, about grandfather clocks, and a new interest he had lately developed in old pewter. 'Do you know what the craftsman in George II's time used to call it? Tin and temper,' he said. 'It was difficult to make and took so much time.' He had bought some old pewter and asked Lisa if she and Perdita could keep an eye open for any of particular interest. Did Lisa know, by the way, that they used to clean it with sand and rushes? Clearly, he had no intention of telling her why she was here until the tea arrived. Sure enough, when the waiter had put it down, and Lisa had poured out, he finally said, 'Good of you to see me like this.'

'Nice of you to ask me.' Once again, as in the past, she caught his way of speaking.

'Your father was my oldest friend,' he said.

This claim, this statement of implicit affection for her, wouldn't wash. But all she did was smile. He looked at her thoughtfully, his masculine vanity gratified because she was elegant, something he called presentable. She had a piquant gentle air.

'You've guessed what I want to talk about.'

'Jenny.'

'Last time we met –'

'Was about something different. Should I thank you for that?'

'Good God, no!' he exclaimed. 'I didn't want you to be hurt. Were you? Are you?'

'A bit. Not very much.'

'Good.'

She saw in his face that he knew she had separated from Peter. How did he know?

'The last time I saw you, when you wanted to speak about her, I said I preferred not to do so. I was wrong. I should have talked to you. I believe you're fond of her.'

'She's a dear girl. It's good to see her happy, Mr Bowden,' said Lisa, eager now she thought she saw a chance of reconciliation. 'If you'd only agree to meet them, and accept Charles and clear the air it would be wonder . . .' Her voice trailed to a halt. He was shaking his head decidedly. He hasn't changed after all, she thought. I was mad to think I could do any good with a man like this.

'She isn't happy,' he said abruptly.

Lisa's feeling of friendliness had turned to indignation. Was he saying he was going to continue that miserable old vendetta? How could he say Jenny wasn't happy after all Charles was doing to make her so?

'Of course she's happy!' she exclaimed, slightly blushing because she was angry. 'My brother and Jenny are devoted. You've only got to see her.'

'Do you?'

She didn't understand him.

'Do you see her?' he repeated.

'Of course. Every day.'

422

'Surely not. Just think for a moment.'

She looked at him, and then she realized she hadn't seen Jenny for days. She'd been busy at the shop, and often came home quite late. She couldn't remember having talked to Jenny for – for she didn't know how long. When you lived in part of the same house with people, you had an impression of seeing them regularly. But days went by and all she glimpsed was one or the other in the distance. She'd heard Jenny riding out on two or three frosty mornings and looking from her own window had seen the girl's straight back, the swishing tail of Paintbox, as horse and rider disappeared down the drive. Once, driving to work, she'd passed them and waved. Jenny and Charles had been asked to have supper with her at the flat. But the date had been cancelled.

The pause was too long. She said reluctantly, 'I'm afraid I haven't seen her lately. Well, in the distance. Not to talk to. Why?' She was nervous.

'I was riding yesterday morning well before eight. I went to the woods where she and I used to ride together and I saw her. She'd dismounted. She was standing leaning against a gate.' Guy Bowden turned his head and looked out of the window. 'She was crying.'

'Mr Bowden. Are you sure?'

'Oh yes,' he said. 'I am sure.'

Everything Lisa had feared, everything she'd believed was ended, rushed into her mind. It was Gemma Lambert again. Charles hadn't given her up. He had just pretended to.

Guy sat watching her changing face. 'What am I to do, Lisa? Your brother must be the reason she was weeping. He is committing adultery.' He made the word sound like the seven deadly sins.

'We can't know that.'

'Of course we can. Women don't stand in a field alone and weep for no reason.' He stopped speaking for a moment. 'Jenny always tries not to cry. There's no other reason why she is suffering. And I can't help her.'

'No. You can't.'

'It's my fault. I should have mended the breach. I should

have asked her to see me months ago.' He gave a long, slightly shuddering sigh.

She hated to see his strength leave him. She wanted him to hang on to his certainties. There was no victory for anybody in this.

She poured him more tea, and when he spoke again his voice had its usual matter-of-fact tone.

'You're fond of your brother.'

'Very.'

'Then isn't it up to you to do something for her?'

She thought: yes I will. For a moment she quite hated Charles, who loathed cruelty and was himself so cruel.

'I'll try. I promise. I will try.'

Guy insisted on walking back to the shop with her. They talked of indifferent things and when he said goodbye, raising his flat cap, he gave her his odd, slight smile. Lisa didn't go into the shop at once, although she could see Perdita waiting for her. She watched him get into his car. As he drove away, he waved as if they were old friends.

'Well?' said Perdita as Lisa came in to the sound of bells.

'It wasn't anything. A muddle over an old desk of my father's which is still at Whitefriars. It had gone clean out of his mind.'

'What period? Edwardian?' said Perdita.

Lisa sat by the fire trying to read. She couldn't. What Guy had told her wouldn't go out of her head. She thought bitterly of Tom. She could not respect him, any more than in the past she had been able to forgive him. He married a promiscuous actress, could not keep her faithful and apparently let her behave like a bitch on heat.

Guy expected Lisa to confront Charles. How could she? She had never spoken to him, except jokingly, about sex, and had rarely known any of his women, although now and then she had seen his technique in wooing. He paid exaggerated attention to a girl when he was attracted to her, and the girl reacted with an eagerness which Lisa thought too keen and too soon. Her brother's affairs were part of his privacy.

424

His mystery. In any case, she had promised the impossible. Who could help in another person's troubled marriage?

As for Jenny, Lisa's heart went out to her. She had ridden off to cry in solitude, poor child. She was keeping the stiff upper lip of her class, and if anybody asked how she was she would doubtless say 'abs'l't'ly fine'. It was true she had – once – shown Lisa she was unhappy. But that made it all the more difficult; Jenny's pride would stop her from admitting it a second time.

Lisa went round and round the problem as if she were in a cage. She was too worried to sleep and was lying in bed, the unread book in front of her, when the telephone rang. It startled her. She looked at the clock: after eleven.

'Lisa?'

'Jenny. Hello.'

'Did I wake you? I'm sorry.'

'Of course you didn't. Are you all right? You're not ill again, are you?'

'Abs'l't'ly fine,' said Jenny echoing Lisa's thought. 'I just wondered . . .'

'Yes?'

'If you'd do something for me, actually.'

'Of course,' said Lisa, alarmed.

'You couldn't come over, could you? No, of course you couldn't if you're in bed.'

'I'm not,' lied Lisa.

'Oh. Good. That is, if you *could* . . .'

Lisa pulled on her clothes, wrapped herself in an old fur coat she'd had when she was seventeen and which had been unearthed from her father's packing cases, and went out into the night. The frost almost crackled, it was so cold. The moon was full and floated in a clear sky without a cloud. A million stars.

The door of the main house was wide open and Jenny's figure stood against the light.

'Come in quickly, it's freezing.'

Lisa followed her into the sitting-room where every light was blazing, the fire made up, and the gramophone was

425

playing Irving Berlin. The record ended and Jenny switched it off. She said in a quick self-conscious voice, 'I know you'll think me a fool, but Charles is not home.'

Lisa felt a slight thrill of fear. She said easily, 'He must be at the Wilton Club. He still goes there to waste his money. Charles has been gambling since he was at prep school, you ought to try and get him to stop. You'd probably have much more success than I did.'

'I don't mind his gambling,' Jenny said.

She looked terrible. She wore no make-up, her hair was stringy and lifeless as if it hadn't been washed, there were black rings under her eyes. Lisa had the unbelievable thought that she might have been drinking, for her young face had become old. But sorrow could make you look like that.

'I haven't the guts to ring the club,' Jenny blurted out. She sat down at a distance from Lisa, picked up a cushion and pressed it to her stomach. 'He'd be furious with me if I did.'

'Why? It's perfectly natural to want to know where he is if he didn't say.'

'The nagging wife. It's a joke.'

'I used to ring places when he didn't come home. I got bloody furious,' said Lisa in the kind of head-girl, hearty voice Jenny must have heard at school.

But Jenny heard nothing but her own thoughts. She said timidly, 'I can't. I daren't. It's – it's humiliating.'

'My dear girl, you're making a mountain out of a mole-hill.'

'I know,' said Jenny meaning no such thing. 'But – but he's started going out every night at about nine. I don't like to ask where, he hates it if I do. He's usually back in an hour and tonight seems so long. I keep looking at the clock. Idiotic.'

'Oh, he gets involved in gambling. It was like that at Crocker Road.'

A faint kind of life had come into Jenny's face. She spoke as if it were an effort. 'I hate to ask. I'm a fool. But would you ring the club?'

426

Lisa's heart plunged. 'Of course, I'll do it right away. You don't happen to know the number, do you?

'No. I've never rung,' said Jenny, not offering to fetch the telephone book, and still hugging the cushion

Lisa looked up the number, found it and pretended that she had not. She wanted time. Finally, saying 'here it is', she dialled the number, put her hand over the receiver and said it was ringing. Jenny sat looking at the telephone as if it were an instrument of torture: red-hot irons or the rack.

'Is that the Wilton Club?' asked Lisa, when a man's voice answered.

'Yes, Madam. This is the Wilton,' was the cautious reply. It was the tone of somebody none too keen on calls from the opposite sex. Lisa had a vision of indignant wives.

'My name is Whitfield. Charles Whitfield's sister. I was just wondering,' Lisa spoke with cheer, reassuring the girl who was watching her, 'if I might have a quick word with my brother. You can tell him I won't keep him long.'

Jenny was mercifully too far off, thought Lisa, to hear the reply. She was conscious of the girl's staring attention. There was a long pause.

'I'm afraid Mr Whitfield isn't in the club, Madam,' said the voice. 'He did call in earlier and I thought he might still be in the Smoking Room. But it seems he left here at ten o'clock.' The voice spoke with more assurance. A sister was not a wife.

'Oh, I quite understand. Many thanks,' said Lisa and rang off.

'He's not there,' said Jenny quickly.

'Of course he is, silly! The guy said Charles was sorry but didn't want to be disturbed, he was right in the middle of a game. I'm sure he was busy skinning some poor actor of a week's pay. That's why he wouldn't take the call. He sent me his love. So,' finished Lisa, 'you needn't imagine Charles is going to be cross when he gets home.'

Jenny sprang up. She looked young again. 'Oh thank you. Thank you.' Jenny never kissed, but she did then.

Lisa slept badly and woke early. Lies gave your fingers, and everything you touched, a coating like rancid jam. What was Charles going to make of her performance last night? He'd be certain to come and see her. He was like Lancelot: his honour rooted in dishonour stood.

When she heard the clip–clop of Paintbox's hooves during breakfast and went to the window to see Jenny trotting down the drive, she knew who was going to appear. Jenny's back in the well–cut riding-jacket looked debonair. Well, that was something.

Within ten minutes there was a hasty step on the stair. She was having nothing but appropriately bitter coffee for breakfast, not being hungry, and when he came in she said, 'I hope you got the point.'

He made a grimace.

I seem to spend my time gaping at the appearance of my relations, thought Lisa. Jenny last night. Charles this morning. If ever a man looked as if he'd had so much sex that he could scarcely totter, that man was Charles. Angry with him though she was, she couldn't help being half amused. She'd never seen such bags under his eyes in all the years she had been with her profligate sibling.

'I didn't let you down,' he said.

'Oh, thanks.'

'Don't sound like that. I'm in a mess.'

'You can say that again.'

'I see you're going to be nasty.'

'Someone's got to be.'

'I'm very grateful. For what you did.'

'I didn't do it for you.'

He more or less collapsed on to a chair opposite her. Lisa looked at him and gave an involuntary groan. She couldn't be angry with him. She wanted to be, but couldn't be. What was there in Charles that made you helpless? Something in his face, his voice, his manner with its humorous, tired, sardonic knowingness, his heavy-lidded eyes. It was as if Charles were a victim of his nature and shared with you the whole inextricable knot. What are we both going to do? he seemed to say. She remembered how it had been in the past when he'd gambled their money away. It was the same now.

'It's Gemma Lambert, of course.'

'Yes. Gemma.'

'Are you in love with her by any horrible chance?'

'Horrible chance is right. I'm mad about her. I wish I wasn't. But I am.'

'I thought you'd given her up.'

He looked surprised. 'Never. She just decided to play it more carefully.'

Lisa remembered Tom. 'Why?' she said blankly.

'You don't care about Tom Westbury any more, do you, Lou?'

'Of course I don't. What's that –'

'Got to do with it? A lot. He told her if she misbehaved he'd divorce her and keep the boy. He said somehow or other he'd get custody, he wouldn't have Bobbie exposed to more misery. Apparently –' He stopped.

'Go on,' said Lisa, more wounded than she could possibly have guessed.

'Apparently Bobbie had a rough time during her divorce. He was so unhappy, only a mite, of course, just two, and he wouldn't eat for weeks. Gemma was out of her mind with worry until Tom came along. He loves the little boy. It isn't surprising. Bobbie's sweet.'

She heard the tone of his voice and thought: where have we got to?

'Charles. We're not talking about that child, but about Jenny. What are you going to do?'

'What *can* I do?'

'For Christ sake! Give the woman up. After all, *you* ran away with Jenny, *you* took her away from her father and became responsible for her. You're stuck with her, Charles. She loves you.'

He nodded absently.

How accustomed he is to hearing people say that, thought Lisa. How often he must have been told by women that they love him. He almost expects it. It is not the extraordinary thing it is to other men. The undeserved delight. She knew she'd lost Jenny's battle before a second shot had been fired.

'So Jenny just has to sit at home imagining you're at the Wilton, does she? And what happens next time, when she makes the telephone call herself?'

'I don't know, Lou. Gemma will think of something.'

Lisa clenched her fist, feeling violent. Gemma. Did he actually mean *she* was in charge of Jenny's fate from now on? She longed to hit him.

'Thanks, anyway,' he said. He came over and touched her shoulder, pressing down his hand in the way he used to do when she was a child and it was she, not he, who was unhappy. He gave her a rueful, half-helpless look and went out.

No further troubles rained down over Lyndhurst and when Lisa saw her sister-in-law, Jenny was usually playing with the new arrival at the house, a retriever pup Charles brought home for her. The dog was soft, creamy blonde, its coat matching Jenny's hair; its enormous paws indicated that it would eventually grow, Jenny told Lisa, to be 'the size of a pony'. She named the dog Honey. She was constantly occupied with Honey, carrying him about in her arms like a baby, teaching him to walk, then to sit, scolding him for making puddles in the house. When she wasn't riding Paintbox, Honey absorbed Jenny's attention. Charles knew his wife.

Lisa wondered now and then if she ought to telephone Guy Bowden. But to say what? She could scarcely give him any news, bad or good.

She called in at the main house on a fine March evening to discuss the coming first night. *Hamlet* was the opening play of the season, with a brilliant, new young actor in the lead and Mick Gould as Tybalt. Lisa had booked the seats and wanted to discuss arrangements. She found her brother and his wife looking comfortable in the sitting-room, Jenny on the fireside mat playing with her dog, Charles reading *Country Life*. Looking up, he gave his sister a smile with a question in it; she rarely called for no reason.

'I thought we'd fix up about *Hamlet*,' Lisa said.

'Lovely,' sighed Jenny, holding the puppy, whose legs dangled. 'Honey, don't wriggle. You're a pest.' She sat him down and he rushed at Charles's shoelaces.

'I collected our seats. Fourth row slap in the middle,' said Lisa.

'Perfect. I love being close, don't you, Charles? One can see the make-up. And the voices are so exciting when you're really near,' said Jenny.

'Yes. I know you like to sit practically on the stage, darling,' said Charles. 'But look, both of you, I'm sorry as can be but I had no idea, Lou, that you'd be so quick about collecting the tickets. The fact is I can't come.'

'*Can't come!*' chorused the girls in disbelief.

Everybody in Stratford thirsted to go to the opening night of the season. To have tickets was to be envied by all the people who had tried and failed to buy or wheedle some from Stratford VIPs. Apart from Shakespeare's birthday procession to Holy Trinity, the opening night at the theatre was the most important event of the town's year.

Charles was very apologetic. He was as disappointed as they were. He had first thought the date at Stratford was not going to clash with something in London, but had discovered yesterday that unfortunately it did.

'Frankly, I've been dreading having to tell you. I knew you'd be annoyed.'

'We're not annoyed, Charles, we're surprised,' said Lisa.

Jenny burst into persuasions. Whatever Charles had promised to do, it couldn't, simply couldn't be as important as coming to the opening night. He must put the London date off!

He shook his head. He explained that there was a regimental reunion in London on the same night. It was the most appalling luck and of course he'd see *Hamlet* later. Jenny would come a second time, wouldn't she? The point was the regiment hadn't collected together since peace broke out. He found it impossible not to be there.

'All the chaps are coming, it's going to be a really big thing. The Colonel, the adjutant, about half a dozen officers, including Jerry Paxton. Do you remember I told you about Jerry, Lou?' It was a pitiful attempt at changing the subject. Neither girl said anything, and he continued. 'It'd amuse

431

you too, Jenny. We called him Daffodil. We had to take tablets of yellow mepacrine to suppress malaria and everybody went yellow, but Jerry was positively jaundiced. Looked like it for weeks. Fun to see him again . . .' His voice trailed off.

Lisa said, 'Shut up, Charles.'

Jenny was staring fiercely down at her dog. She looked up and said, 'I shan't go either.'

She had bought a new dress for the occasion and had shown it delightedly to Lisa yesterday. It was very fine white lawn embroidered with pink daisies.

Charles's expression changed. 'That is just damned silly. Of course you must go to the first night. Or are you saying I have to cancel the regimental thing? Is that what you want?' His voice was so harsh and unpleasant that they stared – he never spoke or looked like that.

Jenny burst into a torrent of words. She didn't want him to cancel anything! It was obviously an important evening and he must go and meet all his friends. She'd go with Lisa if that was all right? She looked desperately in Lisa's direction.

Despite making the expected answer, Lisa was genuinely shocked. What a climb-down! Why, Jenny was no different from the puppy now sprawling on his back, soft and helpless and waiting for Charles to scratch its stomach. Lisa wasn't sure she believed her brother's story either. It could be true. Possibly it was true. She certainly hoped so.

Lisa had been invited to have a glass of champagne with Jacky Grimsdyke at The Shakespeare before the opening night. After transforming her from blackened wreck to Grecian Cressida, Jacky had taken a fancy to her. He had called to see her at The Treasure Box, had a knowledgeable conversation with Perdita, took an hour examining everything and bought a vase of Poole pottery which Perdita had under-priced.

'He is not to be encouraged,' said Perdita to Lisa when he had left the shop carrying the vase like a trophy.

Lisa had tried to get out of the invitation, which he gave

432

her just before leaving. She had planned to go home and have a bath before changing her clothes.

'It's really kind of you, Jacky, I do wish I could come . . .' she unwisely began.

Jacky looked astounded. It was obvious that he had never in his life had an invitation refused. 'Of course you are coming, dear. It is my birthday. Just a few friends. I am expecting you.' His voice had the sting of a wasp. Perdita listened to the exchange, pretending she wasn't as she entered the sale in her stock book. 'You can bring your finery to the shop, can't she, Perdita? Change over there in the corner. The curtain goes up at seven, so be at The Shakespeare at quarter to six. Plenty of time for a slice of cake. Don't be a minute late.'

Perdita, as usual, was going to the opening night with a distinguished actor from London. She had grand friends, none of whom she introduced to Lisa. She left The Treasure Box early and Lisa had the stuffy little shop to herself. She went behind the plush curtains into the tea-making cubbyhole to strip off her day clothes, wash in the sink – cold water was horrid – and wriggle into her dress. She did her face and hair in Perdita's sphinx-decorated Regency lookingglass. When her own face was reflected in the clouded mirror, she wondered, as she had often done, what other faces, long-dead, beautiful, perhaps sad, had once stared into its surface at themselves. She felt a wave of unexplained sorrow. For the past and its silences. For the helpless yearning of unrequited love, that longing like thirst; and for the nights when she had lain with Tom, drenched in the scent from the lily tree.

Her melancholy did not last. When she emerged from the shop and locked the door and rustled down the street, she was busy with the difficulty of walking. Her full-length, heavy satin dress had a motion of its own, swinging backwards and forwards like a bell in a tower.

One of the smaller rooms in The Shakespeare had been taken for Jacky's party. There was a table laid with a dazzling cloth, champagne and a cake, also dazzling, which sported a

433

single candle with a satin bow. Jacky, wearing a dinner-jacket with a velvet collar and an exaggeratedly frilled shirt, bustled about. There were the boys and girls who worked in the Wardrobe, friendly, gossipy and pleased to see anybody who was a particular friend of Jacky's. There were also a number of actors not in tonight's performance.

Just after Lisa came into the room, Polly made an entrance. She wore a dress of magnificent simplicity, with huge sweeping skirts. It was black and she wore no jewellery except her sparkling face.

Jacky kissed Lisa first, and held her at arm's length. 'Very nice. Dior copy, isn't it? Quite pretty, but my costume suited you better.'

'You're a beast,' said Polly, floating up to him, having already collected a glass of champagne. 'You mustn't be unkind to my one friend. She won't answer back, and it isn't fair.'

He patted Lisa's cheek. His old eyes were clever and wise like those of a monkey, which he greatly resembled. 'She's got the gumption to answer back, but she isn't one of us and doesn't believe in upsetting her friends. She has a soft heart which is very silly of her. Come and talk to my actors, Lisa, and don't waste your time on Miss Holt.'

The talk was spirited and there was a lavish amount of champagne. Jacky was well-known for his generous heart and sharp tongue. The single candle was lit, cake cut, toasts drunk, all exactly in an hour. By ten minutes to seven Jacky had called the waiter and told him to start clearing away. He then rapped the table and said in a loud clear voice, 'The party's over, my dears. We must hurry. We don't want to miss the opening scene, and Barnardo's wig is a master-piece.'

Polly took Lisa's arm. 'Shall we walk together?'

They went out into the street, looking in their full-skirted dresses like figures from another century.

'I keep ringing you, Polly, I never seem to have any luck.'

'Oh, that's kind!' cried Polly who liked to be sought after. 'I'm rehearsing *Twelfth Night*. And then it'll be *Love's*

*Labour's*. I've grown out of being waiting-women. I'm no good at them any more. Why, oh why did I think I could be an actress?'

Lisa was not a pro, but she recognized a question not worth a reply.

Polly wasn't expecting one. She said, 'That women hasn't appeared at Peter's digs again.'

'Good. I told you it was nothing to worry about.'

'And you were right. I didn't say a word about her to Peter. He's been sweet lately. He's so strong. I usually fall for actors and they're tough – we all have to be – but they are not like him. Not for *me*, if you see what I mean. It's too bad of me talking about your ex, but you don't imind, do you?'

Lisa murmured a suitable reply. I always seem to be saying what is expected of me, she thought. Jacky Grims-dyke's damned right. Why can't I tell her straight out that I wish she'd be quiet?

The fact was that Lisa did mind, not because she loved Peter – she never had – but because he had been her dear friend, her physical lover, her companion; he had been strong for *her* then. Now he had gone to the beguiling creature tripping beside her.

The theatre was brilliant with lights, crowds pouring through the doors. There was the same feeling of occasion that Lisa remembered from last year. She was looking forward to the play and thought: I'm probably the only person in this entire audience who's never seen *Hamlet* before. She had lived in Stratford as a girl, had been dragged with her class to one or two plays, but had never been excited or interested. It made this evening the more intense to think what was in store.

Directly they entered the foyer Polly left her. Lisa glanced around for Jenny, always punctual; she was certain her sister-in-law had already arrived. There was as yet no sign of her. Lisa walked to the staircase where a marble fountain trickled, and went up to book a table in the restaurant for supper, thinking ruefully that Charles ought to have been with them. She and Jenny had decided they wouldn't go to the Wardrobe party. Jenny hadn't admitted it, but did not want to go without her husband. Lisa did not say so, but preferred to avoid either Peter or Tom.

On her way down the stairs again, Lisa passed many girls sweeping by in their New Look dresses, their escorts in dinner-jackets. It was all very grand. She crossed the foyer again, still positive that she would see Jenny, who was never late. Lisa used to have the same sureness about Peter. It had been a kind of blessing in him. Her eye travelled from one group of people to another, looking for a fair-haired girl in a white dress.

After a few minutes the crowds began to thin, and people started drifting into the auditorium. There was still no sign of Jenny.

The first bell rang.

In the ensuing four minutes Lisa grew steadily more annoyed – how stupid Jenny was sometimes! Had she found a dirty mark on her new dress and was scrubbing it with petrol? Was she fussing with that blasted dog? Had her car broken down – no, that was unlikely, Charles always kept it in good condition. From annoyance, Lisa's mood began to turn into alarm.

At the very last minute when the final bell loudly rang and the only person apart from herself in the foyer was a man dashing up to leave his coat in the cloakroom, she surrendered her ticket. She had already given Jenny hers this morning. Lisa went down the gangway and took her seat.

Within a minute, the house lights had gone down. The curtains rose on a bleak castle rampart lit with icy moonlight. Two cloaked figures approached. 'Who's there?' shouted the first. The reply came ringingly, 'Nay, answer me: stand, and unfold yourself.'

Lisa stared unseeingly at the stage. The play continued. The ghost in silver armour floated in front of the horrified soldiers ... the scene changed to the Court at Elsinore where Hamlet stood, black-clad, among the crimson and gold. Lisa could take in nothing. All she kept thinking

436

was: *where is she?* Simple explanations died; she was plainly frightened. Now and then there was a pause in the action and Lisa half turned, hoping to see a figure in a white dress at the back of the stalls waiting for a quiet moment to creep down to her seat. There was nobody.

In miserable anxiety, Lisa sat trying to watch the greatest play in the world. She couldn't. The words did not enter her numbed mind. Then she began to have a strange sensation of familiarity. She realized that exactly the same thing had happened once before. Charles had been sitting here, waiting to see Jenny with her father. They had never appeared either. Lisa recalled him turning round every now and then just as she was doing. His whispered 'Where *is* she?' repeated itself in her own mind. Like Charles, Lisa was utterly unable to concentrate.

The play continued its thrilling way. The ghost appeared to Hamlet. 'Mark me!' said the ghost, in a voice from the dead. The actors' voices spoke the verse, the drums rolled, the tragedy moved onwards and Lisa took in nothing. Anger was said to bring a mist in front of the eyes. Fear did the same. All she did was wait until the long Act ended and the lights went up. And she could escape.

She was almost the first person to hurry up the aisle ahead of the crowd. She emerged into the foyer and gazed around. Without hope. There was an elderly usher standing near by; Lisa asked her if there was a telephone in the theatre.

The old woman, dressed in black with a lace apron like a maid in a 1920s comedy, said there wasn't. 'But there's a box on the corner by the tobacconist's, Miss. Have you got some coppers?' She put her hand into her apron pocket and produced twopence.

Thanking her gratefully, Lisa went out of the theatre and ran across the grass. She saw the telephone box. Its light was on. It was as empty as the street and the lawns and the cold night. She went into the box and dialled Jenny's number. She heard it ring. It went on ringing and Lisa waited, but there was no answer. No welcome girlish voice replied to apologize and explain. There was nothing but the burr-burr

437

of a telephone ringing in what must be an empty house. At last she rang off and stood still for a moment. She wondered if she should telephone the police. But that really was too extreme. She'd probably make Jenny look as much of a fool as she would look herself. The first thing to do was to go home.

With a spasm of dismay she realized she had not driven her car to the theatre but had walked to The Shakespeare, leaving the car outside the shop. She began to run. The stiffened petticoats and skirts of the long dress impeded her progress, getting between her legs, and she had to tug them away every few minutes. Running through the streets she nearly collided with two men coming out of a corner pub who looked at her in astonishment as she panted 'Sorry', and pelted past with satin skirts swinging.

Arriving at her car she jumped in and switched on the engine. But the night was cold, the car would not start. Lisa said aloud to nobody 'Oh please' and tried the ignition again and again. At last the engine stuttered into life. She drove the three miles fast, turned into the drive and as she approached the house she saw the lights.

The front door was unlocked and Honey came tumbling to meet her, making small noises between a bark and a cough. She picked up the puppy automatically and stood at the foot of the stairs.

'*Jenny!*'

There wasn't a sound but the snuffle of the little dog.

# PART FOUR

# 22

'Jenny!'

Lisa went into the drawing-room. The lights were on, the cushions, crushed, there was a newspaper on the floor. The fire was out.

'Jenny!'

Calling at the top of her voice, Lisa ran out of the room back into the hall and stood at the bottom of the stairs again. She was suddenly terrified. Horrible thoughts came into her mind. Murder. Rape. She started up the stairs and as she had once dreamed in the unhappy past, stumbled and fell upwards in her hurry. She had put the puppy down and he began to yelp from the bottom of the staircase. He was too little to climb the steep risers.

*'Jenny!'*

She ran along the broad landing – Charles and Jenny's bedroom door was ajar – and rushed into the room.

She froze.

Jenny, wearing her long white evening dress, lay half on and half off the bed, face downwards. Shrieking her name, Lisa rushed to the bed and turned the girl over onto her back. She was unconscious, heavy for so light a body, and breathing with a terrible stentorian sound like a long grunt, her mouth hung open. She was the colour of paper, and lay more like an object than a human. Only the grunting, gargling breath showed she was alive.

Lisa thought: she's had some kind of seizure, an epileptic

441

fit, she looks as if she's dying, oh God! She rushed to the telephone, but when she had picked up the receiver realized she did not know the number. She looked wildly round. There was no address book or telephone book and almost sobbing, with another look at the body on the bed, Lisa ran down the stairs again. The dog came moaning up to her but Lisa did not hear or see him. She found a telephone book and dialled the number.

'St Elizabeth's Hospital,' said a voice.

'Emergency.'

'What kind of emergency, please?'

Lisa babbled her name and the Lyndhurst address and said she had found her sister-in-law unconscious. Would they send an ambulance? At once. An ambulance.

'A moment please.' There was a pause which was scarcely more than a minute but seemed an hour.

'This is Doctor Matheson,' said a man's voice. 'Would you describe to me what has happened.'

'I told your nurse –'

'Yes, but it is important that you tell me. Speak slowly. When did you find her?'

'Just now.'

He asked questions and she answered them. He said when she had finished speaking, 'And the pills? There is an empty bottle by her bed?'

Lisa answered stupidly that she hadn't seen one. She didn't understand what the doctor was talking about, her mind was running on an epileptic fit.

'Miss Whitfield, it sounds very like an overdose of barbiturates. No, not a fit,' he added when she interrupted. 'Go up at once and try to shake her awake if you can. Do your utmost to get her back to consciousness before the ambulance arrives. Yes, yes, I shall order it at once, but where did you say you lived?' He seemed to be consulting some notes. 'It will take over ten minutes to arrive. Now, please listen to me. You must get salt and water down her somehow and the stronger it is the better. Hurry, please, there's not a moment to lose. You must make her sick.'

442

Lisa ran to the kitchen for salt and back up the stairs. For the next few nightmarish minutes she tried and tried to wake the unconscious girl and force the saline solution into her mouth. She propped her up. Jenny collapsed like a sawdust-filled doll. Lisa shook her, slapped her face. Still Jenny slept on, if one could call the awful insensibility a form of sleep.

'I must get help,' Lisa said aloud. 'Oh God, why doesn't the ambulance come?'

Leaving Jenny who fell back like a corpse on the bed, Lisa went to the telephone. She rang a number she knew by the bitter trick of memory and had used only once, to fetch Charles. It was burnt on her mind.

A voice answered.

'Tom.'

'Lisa? Hello, what can I –'

'Can you come? Jenny's tried – I think she's tried to kill herself. I've sent for the ambulance but I can't wake her.'

'At once,' he said and rang off immediately.

She returned to her hideous, useless task and suddenly heard footsteps. Tom came into the room.

'Don't let go of her. Here, I'll stand her upright. Hold on.'

He was perfectly practical. He picked Jenny up, her legs buckled, he propped her up again. Together he and Lisa began to drag her up and down the room like a life-sized doll.

'Oh Tom. I was too late.'

'No, no,' he said, as they struggled with the dead weight between them. 'It's going to work. Try and get those legs to function while I keep her upright.' A breathless minute went by while they half supported, half pulled her with them. 'Ah. It's beginning to happen. She's trying to use her legs and she's – yes – she's opening her eyes.' As he spoke, they heard the ambulance bell outside in the drive and voices. Tom shouted loudly, 'We're up here!'

When the two men in uniform, carrying a stretcher and blankets, came into the room, the older man, weathered and grizzled, took one look at the figure between Tom and Lisa. 'Taken the salt and water, has she?'

443

'We've only just got her to come to,' answered Tom.

'Then we'd best get it down double quick. Will you do it? Better if it's the family, it doesn't frighten them.'

He spoke as if what was happening was a nightly event. Lisa said the bathroom was down the passage, and Tom picked Jenny up in his arms again. She hung like an armful of clothes. Lisa carried the glass and the jar of salt. The grizzled man began roaming round the bedroom, opening and shutting drawers. She heard him say, 'Ah, there it is. Can I use the phone, Miss?' As Tom and Lisa went down the corridor his voice followed them. 'Doctor Matheson? Sidney here. Yes, I found the bottle. Nembutal. No, nothing left. No, not yet . . . they're doing it now.'

With Lisa supporting her, Tom began to pour the drink into Jenny's mouth. Eyes shut, dribbling and collapsing, forced upright, she finally opened her mouth automatically as children sometimes do and Tom poured the scalding stuff into her mouth, making her splutter and choke. The salt and water had the effect of getting her to open her eyes. She looked at them dazedly.

'Drink it. Drink some more. *Drink it*!' shouted Lisa, as if the girl were a great distance away. Jenny's eyes had begun to close and Lisa shook her arm violently. The eyes, heavy as lead, half opened, then shut. Tom put an arm round the girl's shoulders and Lisa shouted, 'Wake up, Jenny! Do you hear us! Wake up!'

Tom put the glass to her lips again, making her drink. She turned her head away and began to weep, except that there was no sound, only tears flowing from eyes which wouldn't stay open. Tom somehow forced some of the saline down her. More. Then, miraculously to Lisa, Jenny began to vomit. Tom held her head and she was violently and continuously sick. 'That's it. Good. That's better,' said Tom. Lisa turned on the tap to wash away the vomit and Jenny, reeling, supported by strong arms, vomited again.

'Good work,' said the ambulance driver peering in. 'That's what we want to hear.' He meant the sound of retching.

After a while it stopped and Tom, leaving Jenny more or

less conscious and balanced on the edge of the bath with Lisa supporting her, went down to ask the ambulance man if the patient had taken enough. Yes, was the reply. Now they must get her to hospital and look sharp about it. They wrapped her like a parcel, in scarlet blankets that reminded Lisa of the war. They laid her down on the stretcher, and asked Lisa and Tom to accompany them.

'Need you to sign, that sort of thing,' said Sidney.

There was not room in the ambulance for both Tom and Lisa and Sidney suggested that she should sit on Tom's lap. He put his arm round her shoulders and she sat, her skirts splattered with salt and water as though with tears.

In the hospital the nurses were waiting and the doors of the hospital opened the moment the ambulance drove up. Jenny was wheeled away into an inner room, at a run. Tom and Lisa stood for a moment in silence. A charge nurse appeared, asking them to sign a paper.

'The husband has to sign, please,' she said, passing it to Tom.

He looked surprised. 'Oh, did you think . . . I'm just a neighbour. Miss Whitfield telephoned me. She is the patient's sister-in-law.'

The nurse, who was dark and handsome, gave a frown. 'Where is the patient's husband?'

'He's in London,' said Lisa quickly. 'He won't be back until tomorrow morning.'

'You must telephone him right away, Miss Whitfield.'

Without realizing it, Lisa clutched at Tom's hand. It was he who said quietly, 'Is Mrs Whitfield in danger, Nurse?'

'You must speak to the doctor about that. But it is necessary for next of kin to be informed at once.'

'When can we see the doctor?' asked Tom. Lisa still said nothing. She held his hand.

'You will have to wait.' She left them and went through some double doors.

Lisa and Tom sat down on a bench in the glaring light. Neither spoke a word and after a while Lisa took her hand away. At last a doctor, with the face of a frog and a smile which did not reach his eyes, came out of the ward. He wore a white coat, his hands deep in his pockets.

'Charge Nurse informs me you are not the patient's next of kin,' he breezily said, addressing Tom. 'But you brought the patient in. Good work. Must get in touch with the husband, though. We don't want this to be a police case, do we?'

'I don't understand you,' said Tom coldly.

The doctor's breeziness continued to blow. 'Attempts of this kind ... awkward in every way. Suicide, curiously enough, is a crime.'

'But how do we possibly know –' It was Lisa, her voice faint.

The doctor looked at her with the impassive air of a man who has coped with relatives in the middle of the night and knows their simple ways. 'Miss Whitfield isn't it? Sidney, our ambulance man, found the bottle. Here.' He held up an empty pill bottle which he had extracted from his pocket. 'This is nothing new. In fact these shows are pretty straight-forward if you get the emetic down in good time which –' to Tom – 'apparently you did with some success. I'm afraid I must get back. Staff and I have the merry task of keeping the patient awake for the rest of the night. By morning she'll be tired out. So will we, but it's all in a night's –'

'Is she still in danger?' said Tom, showing his dislike of the doctor by his voice.

'I scarcely think so. She's brought up her boots, and now she has to walk as far as John O'Groats and back. I take it you'll both call round in the morning? Good. Be sure to get hold of that husband, please.'

It was only when they walked out of the hospital that Tom and Lisa realized they had no coats against the bitter night and no car either. They stood in the hospital drive.

'I'll go back and get them to ring for a cab,' Tom said.

Lisa looked at her watch. 'It's after ten. The garage will be shut.'

'You're right. I'm a fool. I should have remembered my car –'

446

'We'll think of something.'

He stood irresolute, looking as if for inspiration up and down the empty drive. Somewhere inside the hospital, with its dim lights and its disinfectant smells, its low voices and quiet hands, people were getting Jenny back to life.

'We could walk to the theatre and cadge a lift,' he said. 'The curtain's not down yet.'

She did not reply.

He looked at her. 'You couldn't bear to talk to anybody, could you? Okay. We'll walk. It'll only take us three quarters of an hour. Wear this.' He took of his jacket and forced her, protesting, to put it on. It was warm from his body. He made her link arms with him, 'for our circulation' he said, and they began to walk as fast as Lisa's thin-soled satin shoes would allow. The night was frosty, it seemed to crackle and so did the stars. They simply walked and did not talk, bracing themselves against the cold and hastening under the starry heavens along a road which cut through the outskirts of the town, avoiding the theatre, and a shorter distance to Avoncliffe. In Stratford people went to bed early if they weren't theatre people; every house slept, curtains drawn, as Tom and Lisa walked, their steps ringing on the empty road. Once or twice a car went by but Tom did not flag it down or try to get a lift. They were half frozen when they passed Avoncliffe.

'Don't you want to go into your own flat? It's been so good of you –'

'Don't be an idiot, Lisa. You don't imagine I'd allow you to walk the rest of the way to Lyndhurst alone?'

'What about your little boy?'

'He's sleeping next door with his friend David. I'd planned to stay up late and my typewriter makes a row.'

They walked on. Down the curving road, under the bare trees which had not yet started to bud, past the farm and at last to Lyndhurst. All the lights still blazed but Tom had remembered to lock the front door. They went into the main house in silence.

'What we need is a drink,' he said. 'Where's the kitchen?'

447

'Over there.'

They went across the hall and into the kitchen where the jar of kitchen salt stood on the table. And the glass. 'Sidney must have brought it down from the bathroom,' said Tom. 'He has a tidy mind.'

His voice was rallying and Lisa gave a pale smile as she took some milk out of the refrigerator. The puppy who had been dolefully sleeping in his basket began to trot round Tom's feet making noises of relief. Tom bent to pick him up, kissing the creamy head. 'Poor scrap,' he said, and for the life of her she did not know if he meant the dog or the girl.

It was Tom's idea to find the whisky, which he discovered in a cut-glass decanter in the dining-room. He poured it into the milk, and drew two kitchen chairs close to the boiler which glowed gratefully. The drink was warm and very strong.

'Better?' he said, after a while.

'I'm okay.'

'Of course you're not and neither am I.' He paused, reflecting. 'Do you know where Charles is?'

'In London. At a regimental do. A reunion or something.'

'Did he say where he was staying?'

'At the regimental club. It's at the back of Pall Mall.' She said as if in self-defence, 'I must ring him. I should have done five minutes ago.'

'Five minutes makes no difference, but he's got to be told. As that not very pleasant doctor said.'

'Charles will have to leave London at once.'

'Yes. I'm sure they expect to see him.'

She climbed down from the stool and went into the hall, followed by the little dog. She looked at the telephone book – the London telephone book – and after a moment made a choking noise. Tom came out from the kitchen.

'I can't find the number.' She was crying.

He took the book from her, asked her the name of the club and found the number. He rang and a few moments later got through. Lisa remembered another telephone call. Jenny's simple joy. And then she knew what the answer was going to be.

'I see. The Regimental reunion is next month. Yes, silly of me to get the date wrong. Many thanks.' He replaced the receiver. 'I think,' he said, 'we need a slug more of that whisky.'

Going back into the kitchen, they resumed their seats. Tom poured out more milk and whisky. A coal in the boiler fell noisily. Lisa started.

'You're very nervous,' he said, sipping his drink.

'*You* aren't.'

'Am I not? You misjudge me. Your brother and my wife are off somewhere, Lisa. That child in the hospital found out, Christ knows how, and tried to put an end to herself. I'm nervous all right.'

'How do you know –'

'Don't pretend. Not to me. We both know it's been going on for months. Since before you came to see me that time.'

She was suddenly, painfully, ashamed for him. Poor Jenny's ghastly face and figure disappeared from her mind because of whom she was with. She was ashamed for his rôle in the hideous affair.

'Why didn't you stop it?' she drearily said.

'Oh, I tried. I used the only good weapon I have, God help me, which is my little stepson. Gemma loves that child like a tigress. I told her I'd get custody if she didn't stop whatever it is she's doing.'

'She didn't stop.'

'No. But I thought she had. She got clever. She does. She is.'

'How can you talk of her like that?' burst out Lisa, weak and grief-stricken. 'How can you speak about the woman you love, your wife, your whole life, in that horrible way?'

He wiped his face with his hand in a gesture of exhaustion. 'Yes. I love Gemma. One can't help it, she has a trick of making you love her. She's so spoilt and beautiful and ridiculous. But I'm not in love with her. How could I be? I never –'

'*Don't say that!*' She jumped up and went to the other side of the table, putting it between them. 'Don't dare say

449

you were not in love with her because I know it's a lie. I've heard nothing but lies for weeks. Months. From Charles. From poor Jenny thinking she spoke the truth. Now you. Of course you were in love with her, you threw me over because of her. You swore we'd be together, we said we'd marry if we survived the war. You stopped answering my letters deliberately, and you married her. I won't have you say you're not in love with her.'

Springing up, he came over to her and she turned away, refusing to look at him. He took hold of her wrist and pulled her round to face him, holding her so tightly that there was a mark on her wrist at once, a burning bracelet.

'What are you talking about? A fantasy. It was *you* who did not answer *me*. You threw *me* over. I couldn't believe it at first. I wrote and wrote, but then I finally realized you were never going to answer and wanted nothing more to do with me.'

They stood, not like one-time lovers who had embraced until they wanted to die of rapture. They stood like enemies. He finally let go of her wrist.

'Oh God.'

'I don't understand.'

'Nor do I. Sit down, for Christ's sake, you look as if you're going to faint. Are you saying you wrote to me after I left Calcutta?'

'What do you mean? Don't you *believe* me?'

'How often?'

'Three times a week – more. I don't know . . . I just wrote and wrote.'

'So did I.'

All her sorrow possessed her. 'But what happened?'

He said heavily, 'I don't know. I don't know. Did you write to my squadron?'

'To the address you gave me.'

'And the next, when we were moved?'

'I never got it.'

They stared at each other without words, seeing the ruin of the vows they had made. The bright hopes which had

450

lived in both of them had crashed to the ground like a plane in terrible, devouring flames. They saw their last night together, the union of their bodies and their souls, their love, their hope and the hope that had been betrayed for both of them. All the East where they had loved was in their faces just then, with its smell of jasmine and sandalwood, and the sacred rivers where the dead floated by, and the wondrous shapes of jewelled temples and the forests and jungles and giant lizards and snakes and butterflies. They saw themselves distanced and futile, little victims of the gods.

'So you never gave me up,' she said at last.

'Nor you me.'

'What happened to our letters?'

'Lost in the monsoon. Destroyed. Mislaid. Perhaps even now lying in some mildewed mail-bag in India or Burma. I wrote to you in Taunggyi a dozen times.'

'To my uncle's house? It doesn't exist. When Charles and I got there, there was nothing.'

'Did the enemy bomb Taunggyi?'

'It wasn't the enemy. It was our own planes. His house and land and all the buildings in the jungle for his forest staff, everything had been destroyed. Burnt and overgrown. There was no sign of where my uncle's bungalow had been.'

He shook his head. 'Our love was doomed, my darling,' he said quite dryly. 'Like Romeo and Juliet's. We're a bit older, of course,' he added with something like a smile, 'but it doesn't make it less sad.'

She sat down, crossing her arms and hugging her shoulders. He remembered that way she had of sitting, looking hunched and thin. A coal fell in the boiler again, glowing a fierce orange. She was thinking: he loved me after all. He never threw me away. It wasn't how I believed. Then, her heart running, she came to the barrier. 'But you married Gemma,' she said.

He had taken a chair on the other side of the table and sat, his legs stretched out, large and strong and real in a world of yesterday. He wasn't quite within her reach and she looked across at him bravely enough.

'Yes. I married her. I was in a bad way. Do you know what I thought? Still do, come to that. That the kind of love we had for each other, Lisa, so intense and passionate, in a war where both of us could soon be dead, was the most powerful emotion we'd ever know. I was haunted when I lost you. Everything was pale. Mattered so little. I was very unhappy, and so was she after a painful divorce. Bobbie was the problem, the child wouldn't eat and it looked as if he would be seriously ill. Gemma wanted us to marry. She's very captivating,' he said as if speaking of a stranger, 'and always gets what she wants . . .' He stopped short and exclaimed suddenly, 'Don't look like that. You'll break my heart.'

He went to her, pulled her to her feet and laced his arms round her waist. Bending down, he kissed her. Lisa stood pinned against the man whose body she had longed for and known, whose heart she had claimed and lost. She pressed against him in an ecstasy of sadness, thinking: I have come home. With a smothered sound like a sob he picked her up in his arms, carried her through into the sitting-room, and laid her down on the carpet by the cold ashes of the fire.

They made love in a frenzy which said everything their hearts and souls needed to say. They embraced and joined their bodies, their lips, their cheeks, their bared breasts. They were too intent, too desperate, to sustain the love-making for long, and too soon their climaxes came together. They lay still, joined by their bodies' fluids, quite still as if dead. She slowly put up her hands and laced her fingers into his thick curls. She pushed her hands into them as she did with the knotted necklaces at The Treasure Box. Slowly she separated from him, first her body and then her arms. He let her go, and they sat up in the dark and began to dress.

When they stood up he opened his arms without a word and she ran into them.

'We never meant to,' was all she said.

'No. We didn't.'

'I love you horribly much.'

'And I you, my darling girl.'

452

'It's no good, is it?'

'No. It's no good.'

She left his arms and found she belonged to herself again. She could scarcely make him out in the dim room, and she said with a strange, soft sigh, 'I must go.'

'Yes. Go to bed. There's tomorrow to face and it'll be rough. When is Charles due back?'

'He said in the morning.'

'So did Gemma.'

He walked with her to the front door and waited while she locked it. She had taken the puppy with her and was carrying the little thing in her arms from where it tried with contorted movements to lick her. Tom waited again while she opened her own door. They didn't speak. They did not touch either until just before he left her he put his hand on her face, like a blind person, trying to memorize it.

Alone in her flat Lisa pulled off her ruined dress, put the puppy on the end of her bed and fell into an exhausted sleep.

She woke suddenly to the sound of loud knocking and was immediately, alarmedly awake. It was broad day, the dog was trying to bark, and the knock thundered at her bedroom door. She called, 'Who is it?'

Charles came striding into the room. He looked aghast. 'What's happened? There's been an accident. Where's Jenny?'

She saw how late it was – after midday – and that he was frightened. Sisterly love drained away. 'Jenny's in St Elizabeth's Hospital. She tried to kill herself last night.'

'*What did you say?*'

She climbed out of bed and put on a dressing-gown. She was nearly naked. Then, knotting her belt, she told him without any kind of pity exactly what had happened. She described how she'd come back to the house to look for Jenny – and what she'd seen there. She told him that Tom had come to help her, how they'd forced Jenny to be sick, how the ambulance had driven them to the hospital. Charles listened in horror.

453

'They said at the hospital you had to be found. You're next of kin. Tom and I wouldn't do. I told them I'd ring at once so you could come back. But when we rang, of course, what you'd said had all been rubbish and the reunion isn't until next month.'

'*I'm so sorry* – how was I to know –'

'Don't husbands know what their wives are thinking? Anyway, I've done all I can. Now it's up to you.'

Charles paused and then said, 'Why did you send for Tom Westbury?'

'You wish I hadn't because he's Gemma's husband. He was the one who pushed the salt and water down your wife's throat and saved her life. Do you resent that? Do you think because he was here it makes things worse?'

'I don't recognize you,' said Charles, staring.

'I don't recognize *you*. I thought you were kind. Loving. In my stupidity I thought you had a sort of heart. You're responsible for Jenny and you'd better see her before the police do. I don't want to talk to you any more. I'm going to have a bath.'

For once he did not think of Gemma. Men returned from the war brought back a knowledge that would stay with them for the rest of their lives. Charles had done. He'd seen death many times. Death of friends in the jungle, the loss of a man beside him, hit by a sniper's bullet, death from fever, from machine-gunning when planes swooped down on soldiers too exhausted to run. But this wasn't the meaningless, bloodstained, inescapable slaughter of a war. It was the near-death of a young girl who had wanted to destroy herself because of him.

He wondered confusedly how long Jenny had known of his affair with Gemma, and how many or how few of his lies she had believed. He was filled with a passion of pity and guilt when he drove up to the hospital. Terror went through him as he went through the doors. Perhaps she had died in the night.

At the reception desk he asked for Mrs Whitfield. The

man didn't look grave or send for a nurse. He examined a register and said, 'Room ten, on your left. Can't miss it.'

Down a corridor smelling of Dettol Charles passed closed doors until he saw the room-number. The door was half open. Jenny lay in a narrow bed, her eyes shut. She was so white that he actually did believe she was dead, until he saw a tiny strand of hair across her haggard face blowing gently up and down with her breath. The bed was so rigorously well made that it seemed as if she'd never be able to get out of it. The coarse sheet was as tightly stretched as the skin of a drum, the red blankets tucked in symmetrically. She wore a linen gown like a garment worn by the insane in asylums.

He drew a chair across the floor. It juddered and the sound woke her up. She slowly opened her eyes and saw him. She did not move.

'Jenny. Dear Jenny.'

She looked at him with a piteous face, ill and pale. Two tears rolled from her eyes and ran down her cheeks. He leaned over to wipe them away.

'How could you, Jenny? How could you?'

'What's the use when you don't love me,' she whispered. Then licked her dry lips. 'I'm thirsty. Thirsty.'

'They'll bring you something.'

'They won't. They hate me.'

'What do you mean?'

'They think what I did was wicked.'

'So it was.'

'If I ring for a drink they'll never come. I'm thirsty,' she repeated and shut her wet eyes.

He found a nurse at the end of the corridor, busy with a dressing-trolley: packed bandages and lint, scissors and rolls of cotton wool in perfect order.

'Mrs Whitfield needs a drink. Can you give me something? Water or orangeade.' She continued to arrange the trolley. 'The poor girl is dying of thirst!' he said angrily, not aware of the word he'd used.

'It doesn't do them any harm to wait.'

'*Them?*'

'Attempted suicides. You're the husband, I take it?'

'Yes, I am the husband, and I don't think I understand you. I was under the impression that the hospital's job was to care for the sick.'

It was the same nurse who had received Lisa and Tom the night before, a charge nurse with a good deal of responsibility. She finished laying the trolley and glanced at a blue enamel-edged watch pinned to the breast of her starched apron. She slowly picked up a water-jug.

'Yes, we care for the sick,' she said with more sarcasm than he. She filled a tumbler. 'If it interests you, and of course I have no idea if you are interested or not, four of us in relays kept your wife awake for the entire night. We talked to her, asked her about her childhood, walked her up and down the corridor until she begged for mercy; we even succeeded once in making her laugh. It took seven hours until the doctor was satisfied she was out of danger. Then we were able to put her to bed and leave her. We now feel, Mr Whitfield, none too friendly towards her. She wasted our time which should be spent on the truly sick. She committed the – to us – unforgivable crime of trying to destroy the life God gave her. I'm afraid I'm old-fashioned but that's what I believe. *She* apparently thinks what happened is your fault. For myself and my colleagues, we think the fault is her own. We resent, Mr Whitfield,' she added, handing him the tumbler and the jug, 'we resent time spent on such capers. We do everything we can when it happens. We're with them. Helping them. We laugh and joke and by some miracle we keep them awake. Finally we save them. After that we can't wait for them to get the hell out of our hospital.'

When he went back into Jenny's room she didn't look at him but at the water. He lent over to support her head while she drank and drank.

'You're spilling it, darling. Wait a little.'

'I want some more.'

'Not yet. Wait a moment or two.' He put the glass out of reach and sat down. Then let her drink again. At last she'd had enough and lay back, her eyes on his face.

456

'Lisa found me.'

'I know.'

'I wish she hadn't. I wish she hadn't.' She turned her poor head away and cried with the weak tears of the very sick. He bent forward in pain and made her turn back. Taking her hand he pressed it to his face.

'Do you know why –' she faltered, but Charles couldn't bear any more.

'We won't talk about it. Let me take you home. Let me take you home.'

# 23

---

Charles was not allowed to bring his wife back from hospital for the next twenty-four hours. The staff continued to treat her with matter-of-fact coldness, scarcely speaking to her unless it was unavoidable. Jenny was miserable and silent. It was clearly a matter of policy, thought Charles, returning with some things the Charge Nurse told him Jenny needed. As he himself slowly recovered from the first shock, he saw the fairness of the medical people. While suffering for the shrunken girl, while suffering from searing guilt, he saw they had a strong if self-righteous moral point of view. It was true Jenny had taken hours of their time through an entire night. They had been forced to work at snatching her away from a death *she* had sought. He couldn't blame them for being angry.

In the afternoon he was told the doctor wished to see him. He was left in a corridor for an hour and a half, so deeply occupied with his thoughts that he scarcely noticed the time. He was finally directed to a bare office where the doctor was sitting at a desk; this was not the froglike, breezy physician who had spoken to Tom and Lisa last night, but his senior. John Favell was thin-lipped and greying, and wore the expression of a man dealing with a prisoner.

'Sit down, please.' A pause. 'You are of course aware that this is a police matter?'

'I beg your pardon.'

'Come, Mr Whitfield. Your wife must have told you that

when she regained consciousness there was a plainclothes policeman by her bed.'

'She told me no such thing.' Charles spoke quietly. His mind was racing. He hadn't thought of this. Terrified at what had happened, he'd never thought of this.

'Attempted suicide is an indictable offence.'

A noticeable pause. 'Has she told you, or anybody else, that she tried to kill herself?' asked Charles.

'Mr Whitfield.'

'You don't answer my question, doctor.'

'Your wife swallowed an entire bottle of sleeping pills.'

'Did she leave a letter? If so, it has not been shown to me.'

'No. Nothing was found.'

'Did she speak to this policeman by her bed? Did he question the poor creature?'

'He did. Apparently she did not reply.'

'Then it could have been an accident. My wife,' Charles heard himself say, 'has blinding headaches. She is also extremely clumsy.'

The doctor reflected. Both men knew what the conversation was really about.

'Yes. Well. You will consult your solicitor about this.'

'Naturally.'

'I gather you have been asking when the patient may leave hospital,' said the doctor, plainly choosing a different turn to the conversation.

'Surely you'd prefer her to go home?' said Charles without emphasis.

'She should remain here until tomorrow noon. She may leave then. Of course,' added the doctor, 'you are perfectly entitled to take her home now if you so wish. She could discharge herself. Patients take it into their heads to do that occasionally.'

'You've just said you think she should stay.'

'Yes. She's recovering well, but I prefer it. She should be under observation for another twenty-four hours. She will also need care while convalescing. You know that, I presume?'

John Favell examined his fountain pen. Something about the patient's husband got on his nerves. This man, clearly responsible for the young woman's near-death, whatever story they intended to cook up, was a sensualist. The doctor's experience of men told him so. By Whitfield's bearing, the self-indulgent face, the betraying, thick-lipped mouth; even by the eyes. It is perfectly just, thought Favell, that a man's vices should show. It is a warning. But not to girls scarcely nineteen years old.

'I've known a number of cases like this one,' he continued, still a prison official. 'I have also talked to colleagues. Let us say, for argument, that it was attempted suicide. Yes, yes, I heard what you said, but let us discuss the other version for a moment. People who try to take their lives often do the same thing again. Possibly two or three times. Their relatives persuade themselves after the first time that it was a sudden aberration, but it is rarely thus. A person wanting to do away with himself thinks it over, sometimes over a long period, sometimes for no more than half an hour. He – or she – looks at the idea quite dispassionately and decides it is a very clever way out. Then empties the pills into a glass. Were you aware, incidentally, that your wife was taking Nembutal? She told you your doctor prescribed the pills for her?'

'Of course he didn't.'

'Mr Whitfield, she consulted him a week ago and said she was sleeping badly and he prescribed them. Clearly, she omitted to tell you deliberately. People with even the slightest propensity towards self-destruction – again this is hypothetical in Mrs Whitfield's case – are most ingenious.'

Charles had nothing to say. The doctor's manner was as accusing as that of a policeman to a murderer caught with the blood-stained knife in his hand. Charles's story, of headaches and accident, might hold. But the doctor had had his say and stood up to end the interview. Charles went out into the corridor again and a nurse finally appeared to say he might see Jenny.

During the second time he was with her, Jenny told him in a whisper that she had known about him and Gemma for

460

a long time, had felt it and later on been certain. When he left for London and before she left for the theatre she had telephoned the regimental headquarters and discovered the reunion was not for a month.

He held her hand in a tight grasp, cursing himself for a fool. When you lie, you must do it well if – the cant words trotted into his mind – if you aren't going to hurt people. Gemma lay in his imagination like Bathsheba, golden, sexual, wanted, known and never to be relinquished. But the woman lying on the bed looked up at him with the face of an animal in a trap of metal teeth. It was up to him to release the stricken deer.

He asked her carefully about the policeman who had questioned her. She looked aghast. The man had frightened her. He'd been quite kind but she couldn't talk. She hadn't said a word.

Charles kissed her when he said goodbye and she cried again.

At Lyndhurst, his sister was in the main house cooking supper. She gave him a slight smile and asked about Jenny.

'Will she be home in the morning? Did you give her my love?' After his wife's haggard face, and many more stony ones, Lisa was a balm to a bruised heart.

'I'm allowed to bring her home tomorrow.'

'I'm so glad.'

'Lou. When she regained consciousness the police were there.'

Lisa stared, then grasped his meaning and put a hand to her throat. 'I'd forgotten that!'

'So had I. I told the doctor I was sure it was an accident, that Jenny had splitting headaches and is very clumsy ... Lou ... *did* she leave me a letter?'

'No,' said Lisa, alarmed and tense. 'Nothing. Nothing. I'm sure of it.

'Thank God for that.'

'Do you think they'll believe you? And poor Jenny too?'

'I don't know. Perhaps. They can't *want* to prosecute a kid of nineteen with a husband to care for her, can they?' He

461

seemed unaware of what he had said. He sighed. 'I wish I'd been allowed to bring her home today.'

'I expect she needs rest.'

'They had to keep her awake. All during the night, walking her up and down. Well, you did that too, didn't you? Apparently they talked and talked to her and wouldn't let her shut her eyes. What torture. Horrible.'

'Did they let her sleep today?'

'Oh yes. Most of the time. It's safe now.'

'Did you sit with her?'

'A bit. Much longer in the corridor waiting for the doctor.'

'Poor Charles.'

'Aren't you going to accuse and despise me too?'

'The hospital people did, then?'

'Yes. They were rather worse with Jenny, I gather. I thought,' he said, 'you'd be very angry.'

'No need. You've told yourself worse things than I ever could. I was wrong to turn on you this morning. Let me give you a drink. Dinner won't be long.' She added involuntarily, 'You do look awful, Charles.'

'You don't look too hot yourself.'

'Oh, lack of sleep,' she said, shrugging.

'And shock.'

'That wears off quickly when things aren't as bad as one thought,' said Lisa, deliberately using lame words.

'Does it, Lou? Does it wear off? I feel it never will.'

She waited upon him. She made him eat, and then later they went to the drawing-room and sat by the fire. The puppy hung about, looking at the giant humans and wondering why nobody picked him up. Lisa saw the little creature lying forlornly on the mat, and dumped the soft body in her brother's lap. He stroked Honey automatically without looking down at the dog.

She was tender with Charles, treating him the way a person does when binding up a wound, trying to avoid the slightest pressure. She saw him begin to relax and after a while they stopped talking and he leaned back and shut his

462

eyes. He was asleep. She had given him ease and was glad. She looked at his sleeping face and thought of what might have been if she hadn't left the theatre at the interval and driven here – to what might have been waiting for her.

She wondered fearfully if the police matter could be smoothed over, if Charles's weak story would hold. She wondered with a greater fear what Charles would do next. He had been shattered by the act of despair which had faced him with his own nature. Looking at the lined and beloved face, its sensual indulgence not banished by the erasing hand of sleep, she thought the future ominous.

She began to think, then, of the extraordinary fact that Tom loved her. Would she ever have discovered it if it had not been for poor Jenny? And wouldn't it have been better never to know than to have needed a tragedy to bring her back into Tom's arms? There was no sense in what happened. Yet she was full of wonder that he hadn't thrown her away. He had believed, as she did when war ended and the ruined world began to stagger to its feet, that their love was dead. It had died with millions of soldiers and civilians. Part of the carnage of war. Polly had said to her, 'If it was me, I'd rather he was dead.' The implacable egotism of rejected love had spoken then, and Lisa had almost agreed with her. How could she have done?

Last night's love-making, too fast and violent, reaching its climax in what seemed moments, was not what stayed with her now. It was his words and voice. The fact that he loved her, not the rapture of their naked bodies. She hugged it to her in all its weight and lay beneath it like a lover.

She looked across at her brother still in an exhausted sleep. She remembered other times. Once in Roundwood she'd come to look for him and found him at his desk, his head on the book he was supposed to be studying for his tutorial, deep, deep asleep. She had been fifteen and had thought – it was a day of rich September – that her brother was Keats's figure of autumn: '. . . on a half-reaped furrow fast asleep, drowsed with the fume of poppies . . .' She remembered a night journey in Burma before the war when

463

Charles had sat with her in the back of the car, and slept all the way to the bungalow, his head so heavy on her shoulder that she had pins and needles. She thought of journeys across India, and sometimes she was the one who slept, and sometimes he did, on cold platforms and in filthy trains. Now she looked at the sleeping man whose actions, whose nature had so nearly caused a death, and felt a protective and helpless love. I don't know why women love you, she thought, including me. It's so bad for you. It's incurable.

She stood up and went over to kiss his cheek. The puppy on his lap woke and almost fell off his knee. Charles opened heavy eyes. 'So tired . . .' he said.

'Yes. I must leave you and go to bed.'

'I will too,' he said and fell asleep again.

When Jenny was safely home and resting, Charles went to see John Denham, the Warwick solicitor, who was immensely practical. A statement from Jenny was prepared and given to the police. It contained – in Jenny's handwriting – Charles's version of the accident due to a blinding headache . . . pills upset into a glass, scarcely knew what she was doing . . . and ended with a sentence written for her by John Denham. It regretted the great trouble and anxiety her stupidity had caused the hospital and the authorities.

Within a few days Charles was informed that the matter was closed. He guessed that unsuccessful suicide bids smoothed over by concerned relatives were crimes the law was willing to ignore if offered an explanation, even one which was far-fetched.

Free from the near-incredible shadow of being prosecuted, Jenny slowly recovered.

With joyous heartlessness crowned with green leaves, spring was breaking across Warwickshire. The notices for *Hamlet* were universally good, crowds thronged into the theatre. Stratford was beginning to fill up, and when people went to The Duck in the feeblest gleam of sunshine, actors were sitting on the damp stone wall or against the backs of wooden seats, glad to drink out of doors.

Matching the bright season, Lisa made promises to herself. She saw Jenny every day, calling in the morning or evening or both times. Whenever she went into the house, or found Jenny in the garden or the stable, Charles was with her. From the day he'd brought Jenny home muffled in a rug like an old woman, he looked after her. What had happened was never spoken about, but between the three was a close unity. They were like people who had been in a bombardment.

Jenny's attempt at suicide changed a good many things. It brought her husband back. It strengthened Lisa's feelings for her sister-in-law and made her love the girl. And without realizing it Jenny had solved the miserable past for Lisa and for Tom. Lisa made up her mind not to see him alone again. When she had been fourteen and hungry for books, any books, she had bought a tattered copy of *The Story of the Operas* for threepence in Warwick one afternoon. She had read every word and it had been *The Valkyrie* which had gripped her imagination. That had been long before Wagner and his hauting music and legends were hated in wartime England. She remembered *The Valkyrie* now. Thrust deep into the tree that grew in Sieglinde's house was the sword named *Votung* – Needful – which only one hand was strong enough to extract. Lisa's *Votung* was there when she wanted it. She loved Tom with all her heart; she had no intention of throwing herself into infidelity.

In the lives of all three, at Lyndhurst there still glimmered, like a ghost that people grow accustomed to seeing in broad daylight, the figure of Gemma. Lisa wondered if Tom had told Gemma what had happened. Would he? Would she care if he did? Perhaps Charles had done so. Had he broken with his mistress for good? Lisa had no idea.

She couldn't fault her brother's behaviour. He was genuinely affectionate and cheerful with Jenny; Lisa often heard them laughing in the garden or walking towards the stables. Above all he was natural, there wasn't a shade of nervousness, over-protectiveness, self-consciousness, of anything but a lively presence without a care in the world.

Charles took Jenny to the next opening night at the

theatre and they actually went to the Wardrobe party afterwards. Lisa did not accompany them to either. Gemma had a leading role in the current play, *Love's Labour's Lost*, and when Jenny talked to Lisa later, prattling about actors and performances, Lisa hid her astonishment. Charles, she thought, is a miracle worker.

Lisa continued to see her brother and his wife more than she used to do, and was always welcomed with pleasure. 'Hello!' 'Hi!' 'Come and have a drink – we haven't seen you since yesterday.' She perceived in them the particular, slightly patronizing kindness of lovers to a woman with no man of her own.

Approving of Charles, tender to Jenny who with the resilience of nineteen fairly flowered with the Stratford spring and the lakes of forget-me-nots in Lyndhurst's unkempt orchard, Lisa held one thing against both of them. Not a small thing either. It was their attitude or lack of it, towards Jenny's father. His name never came into the conversation: Jenny could have been orphaned years ago. Lisa disapproved, and once when she was alone with Jenny purposely mentioned the separation.

Jenny shrugged. 'He's still sulking, I suppose. He's like that.'

'It seems a very long time to sulk.'

Another shrug.

Lisa did not give up and waited until the occasion arose when she found herself alone with her brother.

'Isn't it time you cleared things up with Jenny's father, Charles? It really is monstrous to let it go on like this.'

He was comfortable. 'The break-up was his idea, Lou. I can't dig all that trouble up again, it would only upset her. Besides, if the old chap' – Lisa did not recognize this as a description of the man she knew – 'if the old chap hankers to see her, he'll just have to eat humble pie, get in touch and come round.'

'You don't think he ought to know what happened?' It was the first time she had broken their tacit silence on the subject, and his face changed.

466

'Good God, no.'

Alone in her flat, Lisa thought about the situation. She found their behaviour repellent. Not to tell Guy Bowden about his daughter was a crime against nature. Charles and Jenny's intensified clutching at one another, their mutual denial of anybody's claims but their own, was cruel and selfish. They discounted or despised the rights of a father. They were set only on recovery; on healing and then discounting their own shock and guilt. The woman who had tried to lose her life, the man who had, so to speak, nearly killed her, clung close. Nobody, nobody mattered but themselves.

Lisa thought of Guy. She remembered his soldierly bearing, the abrupt voice so like his daughter's, the moving love that used to light his face when he looked at Jenny. Lisa could not forget him.

On an evening lovelier than the rest, Charles and Jenny were in the garden making a tour of the so-called lawns, examining trees and suggesting grandiose plans for planting. Jenny ran ahead, chasing the puppy and imitating his lopsided run. Charles stood laughing. Lisa came out into the drive. He saw her and shouted, 'Come and have a drink.'

'Sorry, friends to see,' called Lisa.

As she drove away, Jenny galloped back to her husband. 'Friends, mm? That's promising, Charlesie.' She had taken to the diminutive.

'You want her to find a new boyfriend?'

'Oh yes. I was sorry she and Peter separated. Did she ever explain why?'

Charles, remembering his own part in that – he often wished he'd held his tongue over the futile matter of the police calling on Peter Lang – said breezily, 'I haven't an idea. When Lisa wants to be, she can be silent as the tomb.'

The mention of death which would have affected another kind of woman in these circumstances passed Jenny by. She snatched up the puppy to kiss him. 'I *do* want her to have somebody. It's abs'l't'ly wonderful to be happy, isn't it, Charlesie?'

How the birds sang. They seemed louder than usual, and

467

given to separate solos like actors advancing to the front of the stage for a soliloquy. The Warwickshire countryside was putting on every jewel, it was too beautiful for comfort, and when Lisa finally turned into the drive of Whitefariars, she saw beds of multi-coloured polyanthuses in the dark earth and rows of red tulips, and the vine which climbed the front of the house was sprouting. It was all too much. There were times when winter was a relief.

Would he be at home? She knew nothing about his life, his routine. She knew none of his friends although there had been a time, long ago, when her father had spent almost every day in this old house. Lisa's own acquaintances and friends from the long past had dwindled to a few middle-aged people who kindly invited her to middle-aged suppers: and Polly, the only schoolfriend Lisa still knew.

She rang the bell.

There was a step on the gravel and Guy Bowden appeared from round the side of the house. He wore tweeds but was hatless, his thick, once fair hair the colour of silvery, over-ripe barley. He gave her a real smile.

'My dear Lisa. How very nice.'

'I do apologize –'

'What on earth for?'

'Calling unexpectedly.'

'That's what I like,' he said. 'Come in, come in. It is far too long since I saw you.' He pushed open the great barred front door and they went indoors. There was no sign of the usual mass of dogs. 'Come into my study. There's a fire in there. Are you looking for the dogs?' He saw her glancing round. 'My stable girl takes them for long walks to tire them out, I'm glad to say. Two of them have been hunting lately which is not so good. They killed a cat.'

'Oh, poor thing.'

'Yes. Not pretty. But the instinct's there,' he said, asking her to 'sit down, sit down' and fetching her a sherry. His manner, his welcome, were both so marked that Lisa felt anxious. She was suddenly aware that this man admired her, was somewhat attracted to her. Might even be fond of her. It

468

wasn't vanity which told her so, she had never been a girl to imagine a kind of universal admiration in men's eyes. But it was there in Guy, and it moved her.

They talked about anything but the reason she had come; she was sure he believed the call was a social one. They talked about the plays at the theatre, about the fine weather – 'it won't last, it never does!' She told him about her flat and he remembered that she had had some new floors laid and asked about those. He did not once mention his daughter and for the moment Lisa didn't either. He talked about the Birthplace Trust; had Lisa heard about the decision to buy Hall's Croft?

'It really is one of the best Tudor houses we've got,' he said. 'A beauty. And as for the mulberry trees, you should just see them.'

'I'd very much like to.'

'I shall make sure you do,' he said pleasantly.

The study, with its shelves of old books – it did not look as if Guy ever bought a new one – was comfortable and welcoming and rather too warm. Sunlight shining through the latticed windows seemed to extinguish the flames of the log fire. The room smelled of cigars and leather and a tang from Lisa's scent.

Guy looked across at his visitor. She wore simple clothes, a pretty, dark suit fashionably cut, a blouse of creamy silk. He liked the shape of her long neck.

'Now tell me why you're here,' he said.

'It's about Jenny.'

'Of course.'

'It's difficult, Mr Bowden.'

'Guy, surely?'

'Thank you. You won't like it, Guy, and nor do I. I'm not at all sure I should have come. I expect you'll be angry and then I shall have done more harm than good.'

He waited for a moment and then said quietly, 'I think you'd better stop beating about the bush.'

'It's –' She paused and repeated, 'it's difficult.' Did he think she was being cowardly? Prudish? Merely affected?

469

He actually smiled and said, as if humouring her, 'Try me. Would it help if I promise not to react to whatever it is you find hard to say?'

How could he promise any such thing? She leaned forward, and leaned, too, on his old-fashioned courtesy and the outmoded chivalry of men towards women. 'You will hear me out?'

'Yes, but I would be glad, I really would, if you'd get to the point, Lisa.'

She didn't know how to wrap it up, how to spare his feelings, and realized that she couldn't. There was nothing to do but to be plain. 'I hate to tell you this, it sounds very terrible, and it was. Jenny tried to kill herself last month. She took an overdose of sleeping pills. She'd been to the doctor, told him she was sleeping badly, and two days later took the lot. Thirty, I think. She was found unconscious, rushed to hospital, and they saved her life.'

He was very still. She thought: have I done wrong? She felt unreasonably cruel.

He said at last, 'And now?'

'She was brought home,' said Lisa. 'Charles is being so good to her and she's fine. Better than before,' she foolishly ended. Guy Bowden looked old. 'You don't ask why she did it and of course you've guessed that Charles had been unfaithful to her. She found out. A miserable business, messy and sordid, and I hate it. My brother is entirely to blame. He knows it. He was so horrified. He's making all the amends he can and she does look remarkably better. They seem very happy now.'

Again she thought how inept and empty were the words she used, how whatever she said would hurt this man more and that he'd never show it except by that ageing face. He did not speak. She couldn't let the silence continue.

'I think you should see her.'

'You told me that before,' he said, making an effort.

'Yes, I did. But much more strongly now. You must see her again, Guy. You love her.'

Guy gave her a momentary look which she couldn't

470

interpret. She found it difficult to stare him in the eyes. Her own gaze dropped.

'I'm not sure I do "love her", as you call it. Not any more. When people change towards you, you know, you find you've changed as well. How can one go on caring for somebody who's thrown you on the scrap-heap? Jenny detested me when she ran away and I don't doubt she is now perfectly indifferent to me. I see by your face that you think I'm right. Why are you playing the peacemaker? I'm deeply shocked by what you've told me, but you assure me she is now safe and well. What more do you want?'

He's all of a piece, she thought, and wished passionately that this time he'd taken her by surprise, done the opposite of what she expected, behaved senselessly, wildly, exclaimed, wept. Not he.

'I suppose you think it was despicable of her to try and take her life. *You'd* never do such a thing.'

He gave an imitation of a smile. 'True. I can't imagine that. But she's a woman and I don't pretend to understand your sex. What more do you want of me?' It sounded as if she had some rights over him.

'I want you to mend it between you.'

'Can't be done.'

'It can. It *must*.'

He sat, legs crossed, neat and trim as an engraving of a Victorian soldier. The desolate look that had come into his face when she first told him about Jenny was gone. He was himself again. He looked at his fingernails.

Lisa had a curious feeling. She knew she attracted him and because of that had a certain power over him. She felt it strongly and realized she didn't need to say any more. She waited with curiosity to see what would happen next. What did happen was unexpected.

'Who found her after she'd taken the overdose? Who got her to hospital? You did not say it was your brother.'

'He was away at the time,' she parried. 'In London.'

'I see. He was in London. She discovered something which proved his adultery and decided to do away with

471

herself.' He spoke without feeling, like a lawyer. 'One hears of such violent acts but somehow I can't connect them with my little girl. Who found her? A servant?'

'She hasn't got one. Only a woman who comes in from the village.'

'So who found her?'

'You know very well.'

'You.'

'Yes, me.'

'Don't you think,' he said carefully, 'you should tell me exactly what happened?'

She had overlooked what the man was. How could she think she could come here and break such news and not be forced to explain all its sad details? She told him the story from the time she'd missed Jenny at the theatre until the moment she and Tom had seen Jenny wheeled away into safety. But she left out the most harrowing things.

'That's how it was,' Lisa finished. 'We were in time.'

'*You* were.'

'Well, yes, I did find her. But it was Tom Westbury who got her to stand up and forced her to walk and brought her to, thank God.'

She had a sudden thought which came in miserable self-reproach. In Jenny's extremity, Lisa had treated Guy just as his daughter had done. Cruelly excluding him. She'd never for a second thought of telephoning *him*, begging *his* help. At least I'm here now, she thought. My job's done. He isn't being kept away from Jenny and lied to by omission.

He was silent and Lisa began to be sure that he wanted her to let him off. He knew the worst. He could now return to the impasse which apparently suited both the Bowdens. I shan't let you off, she thought. I'll force you to give in.

He was staring out of the window, his face in profile. A rough-hewn sort of face, the nose oddly shaped as if, possibly as a boy, he'd been in a fight and some small bone or other had been broken. The face lacked symmetry, which suited him very well; she liked it. She liked his clear eyes and thin cheeks and the barley-coloured hair.

'So you'll see Jenny?' Lisa cruelly said.

He stirred and made a grimace. 'It might be managed.'

'I'm certain it can.'

He gave a mirthless grin. 'Jenny's stubborn. I wonder where she gets that from? Yes, I could go and see her, I suppose. I would very much prefer not to see him.'

'Because you hate him?'

'My dear child, I don't hate him in the least. I simply prefer not to know him. Surely that's reasonable enough?'

'Nothing about parents and children makes any sense to me,' said Lisa, and her voice, not the words, made him laugh. He got to his feet.

'I'd like to ask you to dine but I have an idea you'd refuse. Perhaps I'll ask you another time . . . if things get patched up between Jenny and myself. Would you accept?'

'Oh yes.'

They walked together out of the house. At the top of the drive a gang of dogs appeared, their tails high as those of hunting hounds. They rushed pell-mell towards Guy, accompanied more slowly by a thin blonde woman who waved at him.

'Five miles, probably six. I'm a wee bit frazzled but of course they aren't. Rufus and Rex discovered something disgusting, a dead rabbit or a weasel in the ditch, and they're plastered with mud. They set off hunting afterwards, but I got them back with this.' She flourished a leather whip.

'You couldn't take them to the stables and clean them up a bit, could you, Marion?'

'Sure thing.' The woman whistled and disappeared in a forest of furry heads and wagging tails.

Guy waited for Lisa to get into her car, which looked dirty and shabby parked near his own spotless pre-war Alvis. She was sure he noticed. He noticed everything. He took off the cap he'd just formally put on, leaned through the window and pressed his lips to her cheek.

'I'll do as you ask,' he said.

As Lisa drove home she knew it hadn't been a sense of justice which had taken her to Whitefriars. It had been fear.

She didn't trust her brother. She didn't believe in the golden age reigning at Lyndhurst. What was he really doing? Thinking? He was still an enigma to his sister, she did not understand him. She wouldn't put it past him, despite this new sober existence, to do something crazy. The gambler was in him still and gambling wasn't like alcohol. Too much did not make you ill or mad, what it gave you was a thrill, an intensity to life. Lisa knew that because he had told her so. The lull now surrounding him could send him back to play against the gods of chance . . .

Where was Tom in all this? Now she knew it was her whom he loved, how much did he care to save his marriage? She knew he was determined to protect the little boy, but was that the only reason? Lisa didn't believe it. The world was filled with questions, and she couldn't answer one of them. But she did know something. Guy would do as he promised. You could tell when a man was honest.

From boyhood Charles had never been in any woman's power. When he saw other men go under, as he called it, he despised them. He also despised women who turned their men into puppets, who interrupted them, talked them down in public, showed off to the detriment of their husbands or admirers, who seemed to revenge themselves on the opposite sex like Furies. Charles's love affairs had lasted just as long as he was sexually interested: then he ended them gracefully. He couldn't bear to see a woman cry. His whole way with women had been skilful, amoral, enjoyable. With Gemma he capitulated. There were times when the virago in her got on his nerves. She was excessive, boring, enveloping, yet he couldn't leave. All during their year-long affair he was imprisoned and had encouraged his gaoler. It was Gemma who drove the engine of their lust, made the dishonest arrangements and told most of the lies. She commanded. Or had done until now.

On the day Jenny was due to come home from the hospital he telephoned the Stage Door of the theatre and left a message asking Gemma to ring him without fail before one o'clock. He said nothing of what had happened – he was due at the hospital at two. He knew Gemma was at rehearsal and that they broke at half past twelve. Gemma would certainly get the message. He waited at home for her call.

She did not telephone. Charles, on his way to the hospital, left a brusque note at the Stage Door:

Don't ring or get in touch. Will explain later.

C.

Gemma came back to the theatre after having a drink at The Spread Eagle Hotel with Lewis Lockton and some of his notable London friends down to see a performance of *Hamlet*. She liked the company of fame, and when she was given Charles's message at the Stage Door had ignored it. Now, when she was handed the note, she tore it open with the casual smile of a reigning queen. She could scarcely believe what she read. 'Don't ring'. Was she somebody to be given orders? How dared he? She was filled with rage and during a long, difficult rehearsal that afternoon was alternately morose and sharp. She rudely refused Mick Gould's invitation to go to The Duck, and drove home.

Tom was back from London and sitting at his desk by the window at work. She could hear the typewriter. Bobbie was in a neighbouring flat with the Aston children. Gemma found herself without anybody to quarrel with, alone and still angry. From the sitting-room she saw Anthony Quayle's car driving up to the house, and his tall, vigorous figure jump out. She had the sudden, lunatic idea of confiding in him. What would he say? Something uncomfortably direct that she didn't want to hear. His devotion to his beautiful wife was a legend; how could he possibly want to know about Gemma's messy affairs?

Gemma, quick, grasping, ingenious and possessive, could see no way out at present. She picked up her script which was rolled and difficult to flatten and looked at the lines marked in red, her part as the Daughter of Antiochus in *Pericles*, the 'short and challenging role' she'd been given.

475

Inches in front of the page she saw Charles's inescapable face.

The noise of the typewriter stopped and a moment later Tom came into the room, wearing the old velvet trousers and RAF shirt which he called his working clothes. He stood in the doorway.

'I thought I heard you. You didn't go to The Duck as usual?'

'I didn't feel like it.'

'Charles telephoned,' he said casually. It took all her training, her self-command which held an audience, not to jump to her feet.

'What did *he* want?' she said with wonderful indifference.

'He believes he promised to come and have tea with you and Bobbie, but his wife's ill. Which is perhaps a time to say, Gemma, that you must see less of Charles Whitfield.'

'Must?'

'You heard me.' He walked out. Gemma's enormous golden eyes filled with furious tears. She mopped them and picked up her script.

She did not see Charles for more than a month. She was needed for rehearsals, for fittings, for voice training: all the actors went to an expert in that difficult art, just as they were trained by a ballet mistress to dance. Gemma was noticeably disagreeable, a state of mind accepted by actors to whom temperament was part of life. She was rude to Polly who, said Gemma sarcastically to the stage manager, 'is the worst understudy I've had the ill fortune to be saddled with. Why have they decided that *insect* could play my part if I was ill?'

Gemma wasn't the only one to think the choice of her understudy was, at the least, eccentric. Polly was short. Gemma tall. Polly pert and mischevious. Gemma sexually smouldering. Gemma had a low, caressing voice, Polly's was sharp and bright and could be tinny. The mysterious reason for choosing understudies was something actors never solved. It was unfortunately necessary for the two to stand close together onstage, as Polly played a maid-in-waiting, both in *Twelfth Night* and *Love's Labour's Lost*. Mick Gould said

476

that seeing them together before the curtain went up was like watching two cats on a roof. Their fur stood on end.

Polly cordially loathed Gemma. With the myopia of bitchiness she refused even to concede that Gemma was attractive. 'All that hair and that bee-stung mouth and her bosom wobbles.' As for Gemma, if she could have succeeded in getting Polly sacked, she'd have jumped at the chance.

The month went by crammed with work, including long fittings in the Wardrobe, a place where Gemma did not misbehave because she was frightened of Jacky Grimsdyke. She was sure that if she was difficult and threw her weight about he would do something, invisible to others and appalling to herself, to make her costume less of a success. People said Jacky was a dangerous enemy. He could make an underdress of itching material, or leave your costume damp; he might even leave a long pin inside it. One unbelievable story was that he had revenged himself on a certain conceited actor by sewing up the pockets of his satin coat, into which the player had to place a letter vital to the action. Jacky ruled his Wardrobe like a king and Gemma was never more charming than when she stood, putting up with hour-long fittings, in his domain.

At last, one early summer evening after rehearsals a few days before the opening of *Pericles*, she was called to the telephone at the Stage Door.

'You,' said Gemma with venom, hearing Charles's voice.

'It's my first chance to speak to you.'

'What a lie.'

He was alone at Lyndhurst. Jenny was out riding. The sunny afternoon spread outside the windows. He was idle in a world of action. Jenny's absence brought a certain relief, and the thrilling voice affected him.

'Don't waste time reproaching me. There is a great deal to say. When can we meet?'

'I don't know.' Gemma used her wiles as automatically as a woman of the last century fluttered a fan. But he was not his usual self.

'I could come to Avoncliffe. For an hour or so.'

477

'What an honour.'

'Don't be foolish. Do you wish me to come or not? I won't if it is inconvenient.'

She had a moment's disbelief, horror even, that her silk net had developed a gaping rent through which he had escaped.

'Of course it's convenient, it's fine. Nobody's there except Bobbie and me.'

'Bobbie? Oh, I'm glad.' That was the voice she knew, filled with love. Not for her, though. He said he would be at Avoncliffe in twenty minutes and rang off.

The puppy was hanging round him hoping for attention, a walk or some food. Honey wagged her small tail and Charles picked up the bundle of soft fur and plumped the dog beside him in the car.

Avoncliffe's gate was wide open and – she moved fast when she wanted to – Gemma was already under the beech tree. Bobbie came dancing up to the car shouting, 'Charles! Charles!'

Charles caught him in his arms and swung him round. The child squeaked with pleasure. Then, setting him on his feet, he returned to the car and scooped out the puppy, too small and scared to make the large jump from seat to ground. Honey's welcome from Bobbie was vociferous. Boy and dog ran off across the grass, tumbling over in the pleasure of each other's company. Gemma leaned on one elbow and waited for him to come to her.

Sun and shade made a chiaroscuro, dappling, embracing, enhancing and hiding her. When you have not seen a lover for a month, for thirty days, for over seven hundred hours, she has a quality of newness about her. Gemma had. She seemed to have put on an extra beauty, to be what he could only describe as more so. Plumper, more rounded, more golden. Certainly harder. She made no effort with her lovely voice; to listen to it, nobody would believe it could move an audience to tears.

'I suppose I am expected to say "At last, at last!"'

'It is I who should say that,' he said, sitting down beside her. 'I've missed you every hour since we were in London.'

478

'How amazing.'

'Gemma, don't play games. Something happened. I couldn't see you or tell you about it either. Until now there has been no chance.'

'Pooh. Tom told me.'

His expression immediately altered. 'What do you know? Who told you?' he said. Lisa had been certain Tom would say nothing.

'Tom told me your wife's been ill. Nothing trivial, I hope?' said Gemma, quoting Winston Churchill's cruel joke.

So Lisa had been right. He saw, then, that Gemma's mood came not from vanity, but from passion. He saw it in the very way she lay upon the grass. Everything about her, her shape and scent, the colour of her skin, the abundance of her hair, her jealous eyes, stirred him. And he was here to renounce them.

He told her what Jenny had done, expecting her to be distressed, even horrified. He was quite wide of the mark. She took it as something that happened occasionally, raising her eyebrows and giving a nod as if to say 'we might have expected that'. Gemma was no stranger to suicide. Two actors who had been friends of hers had taken their lives. They had killed themselves from despair. Not she. Life throbbed in her, beating as strongly as her sexual thoughts. She knew he had come to say they must part. Could he actually sit beside her, wanting her as she knew perfectly well he did, and be willing to give her up?

'I've decided to take Jenny away,' he said after a pause.

'To London?'

'Italy.'

'Not,' said Gemma in derision, 'back to Capri?'

He ignored the jibe. 'It seems a good idea,' he merely replied.

'But you said she's recovered now.'

How could he tell this woman that he was haunted by something the doctor had said? Would-be suicides didn't give up: they often tried again. All Charles knew was that he had not purged away the guilt he felt. He made love to Jenny

479

now every day, but it remained the easy, almost automatic sex of a sensualist with a pretty girl. It had nothing to do with his emotion for *this* woman. If he was strong now, it was not for Jenny's sake but his own.

She leaned against the beech tree and did not stretch out her hand or touch him at all. She knew by doing this she affected him more. She began to argue. She did not beg – Gemma had no idea how that was done – but she did her bewitching best to stop him from taking the path of virtue. Charles listened. He laughed occasionally, for Gemma at her crudest was unconsciously funny. He didn't budge from his decision.

To his mother's annoyance – twice she had to tell him peremptorily to go and leave them in peace – Bobbie kept running up. He sat on Charles's lap and chattered about the dog. Was Honey Charles's very own? Where had he bought him? Perhaps Mummy would buy *him* a dog exactly like Honey. He was a clever dog, Bobbie was certain he'd be able to teach him tricks. Charles paid the child a lot of loving attention and Gemma smouldered. At last Bobbie and the puppy ran off again.

Charles said, 'I have told the agent I shan't be needing the cottage.'

'Charming.' She dug her nails viciously into the grass.

'Darling –'

'Don't call me that.'

'Very well. Gemma, then. You'll scarcely want the place if I am going to be away, will you?'

She gazed at him, making her eyes very large, a trick she called popping them. 'Oh, I might. I might.'

'Do you mean what I think you mean?'

'Guess.'

'If you are going to use the place with another man, Gemma, you can pay for it yourself.'

'I intend to.'

He stood up. The puppy and the child came tumbling back to them, and he bent to kiss Bobbie's sun-flushed cheek. He picked up the dog. Bobbie stroked the folds of fat round the puppy's neck.

'You're the dearest, darlingest thing, the stupidest, fun-
niest, cleverest, the silliest old dog, that's what you are.' The
puppy put out a pinkish mauve tongue and licked his face
and Bobbie gave a delighted shriek.

'Goodbye, Gemma,' said Charles.

Just when he expected the spoilt scowl, the angry rejection,
she gave a wonderful smile.

'Goodbye, Charles,' she said, stretching out her hand.

# 24

Jenny was fully recovered but she was very nervous, and any other girl but Guy Bowden's daughter would have cried a good deal. When Charles suggested he should take her for a holiday to Italy, she thought it was the most important thing that had happened since she returned from hospital. She no longer felt the deceived wife. She was suffering from a different, painful emotion: she felt a fool. She tried to forget the treatment she'd been given at the hospital, and when she managed to face what she had done, was overwhelmed at her own idiocy and courage. How had she actually managed to swallow down those pills? She remembered the exact moment when she'd drained the glass, cloudy with melted tablets, and had gone over to the mirror to look at herself with deadly curiosity, seeing her face and the funny look in her eyes. She had reeled to the bed into sleep. But woke what seemed only a moment later, her heart thudding like a satanic engine. She would have screamed with fright if she had not lost consciousness a second time.

She thought of Capri. It was so beautiful and so far away, the sea shimmering, the misty island of Ischia floating away in the distance. She thought of the flowers, the wine, of the blue grotto and the tiny beach, the sound of church bells, the soporific heat. Of lovely sex in the afternoons and lazy supper in the scented night. She was being taken to Capri again. She felt safe. She was certain Charles had parted from 'that woman', as she called Gemma Lambert in her mind.

Jenny was not original. Charles was real again, she thought. He was sexy and kind and indulgent and he was *there*. He went gambling sometimes, but always telephoned from the Wilton Club to tell her at what time he would be home.

English summer was its usual perverse self, and when the visitors to Stratford in thin clothes began to queue early in the morning outside the theatre, eager to buy standing tickets for the evening performances, the skies usually opened and rain soaked them to the skin.

Charles had to drive to Birmingham to fetch the tickets for Italy on a day which was wetter and darker than most. Jenny decided not to go with him and remained at home, idly playing with Honey. Mrs Welstead came into the drawing-room at eleven o'clock, wiping her hands on her apron.

'Gentleman to see you, Madam.'

'Who is it, Mrs Welstead?' Jenny rolled the puppy on his back and pulled the hair under his throat. He pretended to bite her with his little teeth.

Mrs Welstead, Warwickshire born and bred, knew exactly who the caller was. Everybody knew Mr Bowden of White-friars, just as everybody knew that he and his daughter were estranged.

The housekeeper had been taken aback when he appeared at the front door and gave her his card. It was now wet and somewhat soapy when she handed it to her mistress. Jenny jumped as if she'd been given a snake.

'The poor kid's voice was that hoarse,' said Mrs Welstead later to her husband. 'She could scarcely croak the words telling me to show him in.'

'Mr Bowden, Madam.' Mrs Welstead stepped back for Guy to enter, then reverently shut the door.

Jenny had been crouched on the sofa. She tried to get up and couldn't. She had gone scarlet even to her ears; she positively flamed. Guy saw the blush, the familiar, unfamiliar and beloved face under its swathe of hair. He recognized the awkward way she'd tucked her legs under her. Jove, she was thin. She made a noise like a dry sob and held out her arms.

He went to her in a moment and pulled her to him. She

half tumbled off the sofa as he kissed the scalding cheeks. For a little while they clung, then they gave embarrassed laughs and he let her go.

'I'm sorry –'

They said the same words at the same time and laughed in the same way. There was a moment's pause.

'Let me speak first, my darling.' How long it was, over a year and a half since he'd used the endearment, the devalued love-word of the theatre. 'I want you to say you forgive me. I should never have stayed away.'

'Nor I. Nor I.' She leaned towards him, certain of him as she hadn't been about a man since the day she left White-friars. 'But Daddy, you don't know –'

He put his finger to her lips. 'Yes, Jenny, I do know and we won't talk about it. It's in the past. Let me look at you. You've become very skinny. Is that by mistake or have you been wasting?' It was the jockey's word he always used.

Jenny denied it, saying she ate all the right things. 'Cream and butter and lots of cakes,' she said vaguely, adding with a serious face, 'It must be my age. I'm nineteen now.'

'I do recall that important fact.'

They laughed again.

The rain poured down over the drowned countryside, and Guy stayed all the morning, talking – as the Bowdens did talk – of prosaic things. Jenny told him about her horse.

'Paintbox has such good manners. He's not too boisterous but he's got lots of spirit. I really trust him.'

Guy in his turn told her about the new trees which would be planted in the autumn at Whitefriars, and his plans for repaving the terrace. They exchanged news and half jokes. They sat looking at each other, blissfully at home. In each there was a country which the other intimately knew and rode over, checking fences and woodlands. They loved and never said so.

At last he stood up and said it was time to go. Privately he was shocked to see how much the strain of seeing him was showing in her face. She was so happy yet so drained. No longer the sturdy daughter who had lived at home with him.

Before they said goodbye he asked if she and Charles would like to come to the opening night of *Henry V* and have supper after the play.

'Daddy, we'd love to! And can we bring Lisa? You don't know her well, but I'm sure you'll like her.' Guy let that pass and said he would be very glad for her to join them.

They walked to the front door. And then he took her in his arms again and called her by the rare, worn-out name. For a moment she hugged him, and what Shakespeare called all her love and duty flooded back into her heart.

Guy duly invited Jenny, her husband and Lisa to the opening night of *Henry V*, the final play of the season. Anthony Quayle was 'the blazing comet . . . the mirror of Christendom and glory of his country'. Polly was his French princess. Like all actors' friends, Lisa was nervous for Polly; she had no need to be. In the last scenes of the play when Polly appeared, she was beguiling, comic yet oddly moving. No wonder, thought Lisa, as the actors bowed and the applause rang out and Polly curseyed low, no wonder Polly agonized over her career. She was a true actress.

After the play Guy took them to a grand restaurant outside Warwick where he was very hospitable and ordered champagne. Nobody, thought Lisa as they all sat talking and laughing, would have guessed this was a historic meeting between two men who couldn't abide each other. Guy did his duty manfully and Charles was at his courteous, somewhat ironic best. Lisa knew that her own presence helped.

The following morning Charles came to see her before she left for Stratford.

'Only popped round to say thank you.'

'What for?' asked Lisa, looking at him amusedly.

'If it hadn't been for you, that would have been one of the worst evenings of my life.'

'I thought it went rather well. He isn't so bad, now, is he?'

'Lou, *you* may like him, I have an idea you do. But he and I haven't changed as regards each other. We simply pretend we have.'

485

The ice was broken, the reconciliation effected and Guy Bowden accepted his son-in-law rather as a man accepts that he has rheumatism or gets migraine. Nothing to be done about it. He had taken his daughter back into his love, and so must put up with her husband. But he did not approve of him and could not like him. Somewhere deep in Guy were worse thoughts, the creatures which swim fathoms deep. He did his best to be civilized and it was only Lisa who noticed that when they were all together, Guy never looked in Charles's direction.

Jenny's father rarely came to Lyndhurst and Jenny dropped into the habit of going over to Whitefriars, where she asked his advice or teased him or sat on the arm of his chair, demanding attention. They went riding a good deal. The first time that Lisa heard the welcome sound of horses' hooves outside, she ran in her nightdress to look from the sitting-room window. Surely, she thought, Charles is not so transformed that he is willing to get up and go riding with her at half past seven in the morning. There instead was the soldierly figure of Guy, cap as flat as a pancake, and there was Jenny in jodhpurs and silk shirt, mounted on Paintbox. What idiots people are, thought Lisa; why didn't they do this months and months ago? She watched two straight backs elegantly balanced on two handsome horses.

Jenny's approaching visit to Italy with her husband gave her two headaches – her horse and her puppy. Guy agreed to look after them both.

'You won't let Rex or Rufus bite Honey or frighten him, will you, Daddy? He's so little.'

'I'll look after him as if he were a baby,' said Guy with resignation, as his daughter dumped the furry little creature in his arms.

Charles and Jenny drove away one fine morning, bound for the Rome Express and what Jenny sentimentally called – in private to Charles – her second honeymoon. They left Lisa in her small flat attached to a very large and very empty house.

Lyndhurst became, from the moment the sound of their

car died in the air, eerily quiet. There was nobody playing tennis. No slammed doors or music from the windows. No puppy on the steps or horses in the stables. At night the main house lay in total darkness. Lisa pretended to herself that she did not mind.

Polly appeared at the shop the day after they left, arriving to the sound of bells and carrying a basketful of garden roses. She gave a Cockney thumb-sign in the direction of the cubby-hole and raised her eyebrows enquiringly.

'All clear. She's at a big sale in Tiddington,' said Lisa.

'Thank gawd for that. I'm in no mood to fend her off if she tries to force me to buy a teapot. I brought these for you' – handing Lisa the roses. 'Mummy cut them specially.'

'How very kind of her. Will you thank her for me?'

Lisa did not for a moment believe that Polly's battleship of a mother, who respected only the notable and the wealthy, would send her flowers. But the roses, yellow and red and white, both in bud and bloom, were glorious.

'To be honest, she cut them for *me*, but I'm presenting them to you because Peter gave me a big bunch of white daisies – wasn't it sweet of him? I don't want to put his flowers' noses out of joint, do I? You're not to give them to your sister-in-law or I'll be offended.'

'Couldn't if I tried. They've gone to Italy.'

'No!'

'You seem surprised.'

'I wouldn't have thought . . . oh, forget I spoke. My tongue is always running away from me.'

'You wouldn't have thought Gemma Lambert would let him go anywhere. Well, *she's* out of the picture, I'm glad to say. Charles is back with Jenny and, Polly, they're both so happy. A treat to see them.'

Polly's expression was a mute 'tell that to the Marines' and Lisa steeled herself for blunt questions, none of which she intended to answer . . . or answer to herself, come to that. Surprisingly the actress let the subject drop.

'So you're all on your ownsome, darling, at Lyndhurst. Come and stay with me. There's a sort of divan thing.'

'At Avoncliffe?'

'Hell, I forgot your ex is there. Oh, love, love. "Here come a pair of very strange beasts, which in all tongues are called fools." That's *As You Like It*, Lisa, as I'm sure you know . . . It's just the same with one's life. Love is complicated. Mick, for instance. He's got rather interested in me . . . The other night at a party he dragged me on to the theatre balcony in the dark and gave me great wet French kisses and thundered against me saying "you know you want it". Of course I didn't. Then he was simply livid,' finished Polly, pleased. 'Can I come round to your flat one night when I'm not playing? I'd love a gossip. Or is there a new man taking all your time?'

'Alas, no.'

Polly took her favourite perch, climbing up on a stool, her fashionably long skirts forming a circle around her. She sniffed her mother's roses.

'Can I talk about Peter?' she winsomely asked.

Now what? thought Lisa. Her brother and his wife and Guy Bowden between them were enough to last her for a year. Was Polly going to produce further problems? Love, love. A pair of strange beasts was the right description.

Yet Lisa no longer minded the idea of Peter with her friend. She'd become accustomed to them, and Peter must have done the same, for he sometimes saw her at a distance in the town and waved. Lisa wasn't affected when, walking along Waterside, she saw him sitting with Polly in The Duck. Her own love, her real love, had run without her knowledge like a subterranean river under her life; now it had emerged into the daylight and flowed at full spate. Perhaps there really are people, and I am one, she thought, who love only once.

She pulled over the basket of beads and began to disentangle a string of badly worn artificial pearls.

'I wish you'd stop messing about with those old necklaces,' complained Polly. 'Haven't you finished them yet?'

'These are a new lot. Well, a new old lot. We sold all the others.'

488

'Fascinating,' said Polly coldly. 'Actors do like some attention, Lisa. Now your brother has taken his wife abroad it's
time you concentrated on me, I do think.'

'Is it?'

'You're laughing at me and it isn't at all funny. I need
advice.'

'About Peter.'

'Yes. I know you can help me. After all, you and he were
together for absolutely ages.'

'About a year.'

'As long as that?' cried Polly, very put out. 'I thought it
was four months. Anyway, you remember the woman my
friend Joanna saw at his digs?'

'Of course. Did you ask him who she was?' said Lisa,
hoping that she hadn't.

'No. I wanted to and couldn't. You know how he sometimes closes up like a clam? He was like that at the time I'd
heard about her. I just felt miserable and sort of baffled . . .
I'm afraid I'm in love with the bastard.'

'How can you be sure about that?'

'You sound like a doctor. What are your symptoms, Miss
Holt? What makes you sure it is whooping cough, apart from
that horrible noise you are making? Okay, I'll tell you.
Firstly, he's on my mind all the time. I don't seem able to
stop thinking about him except when I'm working. Secondly,
if I see him across the street my stomach drops. It happened
yesterday and I had to stop in my tracks. Thirdly, if we
don't meet for a couple of days because of my work or his
and so we haven't made love, I can't sleep. I lie awake for
hours, or drop off and then wake at four and make tea and
try and think about my lines. I'm worn out. Love's awful.
We lose our wits.'

'But do we want to get them back?'

'No. Oh Lisa, the worst thing about loving Peter is this
longing to know. To know everything. I want to know what
his parents were like and where he was born and what he
looked like as a little boy and where he grew up and whether
he's loved other women – apart from you, darling. I want to

489

know why he is what he is. He's so clever. So well educated. It's beautiful to listen to him. Lots of actors like me are pig-ignorant, but think how much Peter knows! He can quote Shakespeare and Marlowe and Goethe and Schiller and Chekhov. He's got a phenomenal memory. He's wonderful in bed – hell, sorry.'

Lisa met the apology calmly. 'You're not hurting me, Polly. You must know that.'

'Still . . . he was yours.'

'He never was. I swear it.'

Polly folded her hands across her breast. 'Wasn't he? Wasn't he? I am so glad.'

'That's what you came to ask me, is it?'

'No, but it's comforting.'

Polly leaned over and pulled the basket of necklaces away from Lisa and towards herself, rather like a Catholic borrow-ing a rosary. Many of the previous beads had been untangled by Lisa. Perdita, uninterested in them when they were mere fistfuls of colour, had hung the strings in the window. Amber and green, red and blue. All had been sold. Just when Lisa's self-inflicted task was finished, Perdita bought a boxful of jet, pearl chokers tied with frayed ribbons, and funereal black crystals. Watching Polly's long fingernails trying to unknot a chain, Lisa thought that Freud – or was it Jung? – would have something to say.

'I came to ask a favour.' Polly paused. Lisa said nothing. When no question was forthcoming Polly said with less *élan*, 'I bet you'll never agree.'

It was the old technique they had used at school. The dare. 'I bet you'd never shin up the drainpipe past Miss Benjamin's bedroom.' 'I bet you'd never ask Miss Adams how old she is.'

'Ask away and you'll find out,' said Lisa.

Polly paused, then more excited than distressed burst out, 'That woman's turned up at Peter's digs again. This time I'm determined to find out who she is.'

Lisa raised her eyebrows. 'How can you possibly do that when you know he'll never say?'

490

'I've thought of a way. Suppose, just suppose you and I called at his digs by-mistake-on-purpose.'

There was an interested silence. 'Why do I have to go with you. *If* you go?'

'More friendly with two. And more likely. We could be spending an afternoon in Warwick and thought we'd look in on the offchance.'

Lisa mulled this over. 'He'd hate it. He might never forgive you for intruding. It's the way he is. The way he wants to be.'

'You sound as if you dislike it in him. Well, I'll tell you, Lisa, *I* hate it. I won't be had for a fool. I'm in love with him, damn it and damn him. I won't be two-timed. If he's got another woman and is having both of us on different nights, to hell with him. I shall break it off.' She didn't believe that she would. But she wanted to. 'Bloody love.'

'Polly, do be careful with that necklace, the string's quite old, I don't want it broken. One has to be fiddley to do things like that. Do leave it alone.'

'Okay, okay.'

Polly pushed the basket crossly towards Lisa, adding, 'I knew you'd never come with me.'

Lisa rubbed her chin. Well, why not? Wasn't it fair enough? She'd left Peter because of his secretiveness and the certainty that he had lied to her. Here was Polly, not just a companion who shared sex with him, but genuinely in love. If what Polly suspected was true, wasn't she better without him? If it was not true it might stop him behaving in a way that must alienate any girl foolish enough to love him.

'Very well. I will come with you.'

Polly burst into actressy thanks. She informed Lisa that Joanna, who'd met her in the town yesterday, said the woman had arrived again at Peter's digs four days ago 'and doesn't show any sign of leaving'.

'It's obviously because of her that he told me he was covering a charity cricket match in Priors Marston, and before that was being taken up on the church roof to see how the stone's crumbling round the parapet or something.

491

Couldn't meet me until the weekend. A lot of alibis to keep me out of the way. If we go this evening at about the time he usually gets back from the paper, we'll catch them together.'

The mask of tragedy with doleful mouth and gaping eyes had turned into a merry grin. Polly looked lively and began to discuss what she should wear for the occasion.

'My black cotton is pretty dramatic. I'd be Donna Anna in *Don Giovanni* "in all the wrath of a betrayed woman". What do you think, Lisa? Or there's my new pink cotton, it has a plunge neckline.'

Lisa had been with her friend once before in a moment of Polly's high emotion. Polly had fallen in love with a romantic-looking actor at the Memorial Theatre when she and Lisa were still at school. She had carried his signed photograph about with her, much battered. One afternoon after the matinee Polly had asked Lisa to go to the Stage Door with her to leave some flowers and a fan letter. 'If he comes out and I *see* him, I know I shall faint.' At the last minute she had run all the way home to change into a more becoming straw hat.

'Shall we meet at The Falcon at six, Lisa?' she now said. 'Be on time, won't you? We must have a drink. Two drinks. We're going to need them. It's all very well for you to giggle, you're not in love.'

Punctually at six Lisa arrived at The Falcon for the adventure about which she was growing more and more dubious. She found Polly, not dressed as a betrayed Spanish grandee, but in a full skirt and white blouse. She looked extrordinarily young, her hair tied up in a pony tail like an American bobby-soxer. She wasn't wearing a scrap of make-up.

It intrigued Lisa, who believed she was being drawn into something foolish and probably cruel, to see Polly creating the character she thought suitable to the drama ahead. Here was the girl she wanted to portray and had begun to believe. The mask and what lay behind it were identical.

Polly ordered them both a gin and Italian with a cherry; she insisted on buying a second round. Then another.

'Polly, we don't want to be smashed.'

492

'I do,' said Polly quaffing down her third cocktail. Lisa left hers but Polly was too self-absorbed to notice.

It was nearly seven o'clock, by which time Peter would certainly have returned to his digs, when the two girls set off in Lisa's car. Polly talked loudly on the drive to Warwick, her manner hectic, her unpainted face flushed. Lisa touched her hand.

'We don't have to do this, you know. Let's change our minds.'

'No, no. I need to. I must. I *will*.' Comedy had disappeared; the voice was desperate.

Twice more during the drive Lisa tried to dissuade her, wishing she herself had never agreed to come.

The streets behind the castle were very quiet when Lisa arrived in front of the house she hadn't seen for months. Polly sprang out first, tapping her foot with agitation while Lisa locked the car. The front door, as usual, was slightly ajar and they entered the house.

They walked in silence up to the first floor. It gave Lisa a sharp twinge of guilt to look at Peter's closed door. He would be there in his ordered room, his jealously guarded privacy. And she and Polly had come to smash it to bits. We should not be here, she thought. Suddenly she caught hold of Polly's arm, gesturing for them to go back down the stairs.

Polly whispered 'Sh!' She was listening tensely to the muffled sound of voices. She drew a deep breath, braced herself for her entrance, opened the door and called out gaily, 'Surprise, surprise! Look who's come to call!'

The room was filled with pungent cigarette smoke. Sitting on the bed, leaning against the wall and smoking was a heavy-faced woman with hair as blonde as a Scandinavian. She wore an old-fashioned wartime-styled dress with a lace collar. Her face was thickly powdered and made up, her eyebrows pencilled, her lips painted dark red. Peter was sitting nearby, legs crossed, also smoking. When the door opened he sprang up as if he had heard a revolver shot.

Polly stared at the woman, then turned to him with a starry smile. 'A friend of yours, oh do introduce me!'

The colour had drained away from his face, he had gone yellowish white. When he spoke his voice was choked.

'I did not invite you, Polly. I am sorry. It is not convenient.'

'No, it isn't, is it?' Polly's performance crumbled to pieces, her face was anguished. 'I hate you, Peter Lang, I hate you and I wish you were dead!' She burst into hysterical tears, throwing herself into Lisa's arms. 'Take me away. Take me out of here. I'll never see that man again.'

As Lisa put her arm around her she looked across the weeping girl towards Peter. He did not look at either Polly or her. He might have been a block of ice, a lump of wood. He didn't move. The woman on the bed gave a long, loud sigh.

Lisa dragged Polly down the stairs and out into the street, pushing her back into the car. All the way to Avoncliffe, Polly sobbed.

'Poor girl, I am so sorry. We shouldn't have gone,' said Lisa, patting her hand.

'I'm glad we did, I'm glad we did,' Polly sniffed and wiped her eyes. 'What a pig. What a bastard.'

'But we still don't know who she is.'

'He didn't say because he couldn't. It's obvious the sort she is.'

'What sort is that?'

'A fat, middle-aged tart.'

Lisa delivered Polly to the gates of Avoncliffe and watched her walk down the drive towards the house. She wondered what explanation Polly would give to her theatre friends for her red eyes and swollen face. She'd never tell them the truth, thought Lisa. It makes her look intrusive and betrayed at the same time.

It must be easy to be an actress. Alibis lie round you like fruit in autumn, waiting to be picked up. You can say you are ill, and look it too. You can say you're worried about your next part and the director is dissatisfied with you. You can say anything because you are the master of pretence, and as you begin to speak you already believe the fantasy and that's the best lie of the lot.

The days were shorter now and already as she drove home to Lyndhurst it was almost dark. In the drive, caught for a moment in the straight beams of her headlights, she saw a fox. He dashed right in front of the car and vanished into the trees. For an instant the animal, supple, russet-coloured, reminded her of Gemma Lambert.

Perdita had gone to Broadway the next morning, and Lisa had a quiet time at The Treasure Box. She unkindly hoped Polly wouldn't call. She didn't want to hear that the woman in Peter's room had been a whore. Fortunately Polly did not appear and Lisa remembered she was rehearsing.

She was locking the shop at lunchtime, having hung the card 'Closed until 2.00 p.m.' on the glass-fronted door, when a taxi drew up. A woman descended and paid the driver. Lisa stood hesitating. She had the same instincts as Perdita and was incapable of leaving if a customer appeared and wanted to look round. The woman crossed the pavement very deliberately and walked towards the shop; it was the stranger who had been in Peter's room.

'Miss Whitfield, isn't it? Could I speak with you please?' Lisa positively goggled. 'We could go into your shop, maybe?' said the woman in a pronounced Dutch-sounding accent. In the strong autumn sun she looked more painted than ever, with the particularly thick make-up which actors called slap.

'Why, yes, we could,' said Lisa, wishing Polly at the bottom of the sea. What idiot became involved in other people's love affairs?

'But somebody might come and you would wish then to speak with them. We would be interrupted. Also you would not have had your rest-time without work. Could we maybe drink a cup of coffee?'

Something in the serious voice, the formality, touched Lisa and she suggested that they should go across the road to the hotel for luncheon. The woman brightened up at the prospect of a meal.

The restaurant was not full and a waiter hurried up to give them a corner table.

'I must introduce youself. I am Hildegarde Altmann,' said Lisa's visitor, stretching out a work-worn, capable hand.

'How do you do. My name is Lisa Whitfield.'

'Of course. You were a friend of Peter's one time, is it not so?'

'I hope we are still friends,' said Lisa politely.

When the waiter reappeared they ordered a meal. Lisa chose a salad, Hildegarde Altmann a full four-course meal. Soup, fried plaice, roast beef and apple pie. Lisa had a moment of inhospitable dismay, first at the cost and then at how long it would take. I shall have to explain that I open up again at a quarter past two at the latest. Will she have got to the apple pie by then? I wish she'd come to the point. She's quite old . . . perhaps he likes the older woman. Or liked her once and she's a bit of unwelcome past . . .

Hildegarde Altmann exchanged a few touristic remarks about Stratford until the soup arrived. She drank a spoonful and said it needed salt, then covered the soup with pepper. Having tasted a little more, she put down her spoon.

'I am sorry,' she said. 'I have not told you why I am here invading your time. It is good and kind of you to spend this hour with me. I am sure you have work responsibilities. But Peter's friend Miss Holt was very unhappy last night. And argue and argue I have done but he refuses to explain to her.'

'I'm sure she got the picture. I mean, I think she understood,' translated Lisa tactfully.

'Understood? She understands nothing. She thinks I am a person in Peter's life of the body. I am something different. I am his sister.'

Lisa was staggered. 'But that's impossible! He has no family, his sister and brother and parents were all killed in the Blitz.'

'That is his story,' agreed Hildegarde Altmann, looking at the soup. The pepper had spoiled it but she finished it just the same. 'Peter is my brother, Miss Whitfield. His true name is Dieter but that he has changed. My younger brother – I am older by seven years. Also two other sisters, younger than he, and a brother dead in the war. Our parents and family live in Berlin. We are German. Does that explain why he told you the fairy tales?'

'*German!*'

'That shocks you. It is natural.'

'But how can Peter possibly be German! No, that really is too much. I don't believe you. Why, he speaks English as well as I do!'

'Yes, at languages always brilliant. At university it was so. No, he is not of your country. But of one which until four years ago was your enemy. As *your* country was his enemy and mine also. He is a German officer who commanded an *Unterseeboot*, U-boat you call them. That is what I come to tell you.'

Hildegarde Altmann ate the rest of her meal hungrily, while telling her enthralled listener the story of Dieter – or Peter – Lang. He had joined the navy before the war and had been raised to the rank of commander. He had done well. In the war his submarine had been in the Mediterranean, then in the Atlantic. The submarine was cruising round the Highlands of Scotland on the look-out for convoys when it was spotted from the air, depth-charged, badly damaged and forced to the surface. Many of the crew were killed. Peter and two survivors were taken prisoner. He spent the war, 'long long years until 1946 – a big time in the life of a man', on the isle of Skye. He had used the time, being studious, to learn both English and French. 'He was respected by his teacher – that pleased him.' After the war he managed to get work, first in a Glasgow library and later, as he wanted to come further south, on the *Echo*. Here he avoided any form of promotion, always fearing his nationality would be discovered. It was no longer illegal for 'we Germans' to work in England, but it was different for Peter. He wished for a new life. 'There is more,' said Hildegarde Altmann, nodding to the waiter for a second helping of roast potatoes. 'We had an uncle, Heinrich, brother to our father, very high in the National Socialist party. He is fortunately dead. Dieter was very disgraced –'

497

'Disgusted?'

'Yes. So. Uncle Heinrich was a cruel man. Your police know about him, of course, and sometimes come to speak to Dieter. He finds it humbling. Dieter does not wish to return to Berlin. Last winter many people dead of cold. There is no fuel, women have no stockings, one man shot for stealing food. No, he will not return. He obtained permissions for me to come here – a little.'

Lisa looked at the painted, good-natured face of Peter's sister; Hildegarde had returned to the business of eating, now and again remarking on the goodness of the food.

'I still don't understand about Peter,' Lisa finally said. '*Why?*'

'Must you ask this thing?'

'Of course I must. Why all the lies to me and then to Polly Holt? The war's been over for years, Miss –'

'Frau. I am Mrs. That is Frau.'

'Why the deceptions, Frau Altmann? Surely there is a blessing – a blessedness – in the truth?'

Lisa had looked at the woman with curiosity. Now the position was reversed. These English women are naïve, she thought. *Mädchen*, as I was in the spring of life when I too believed in simpleton's words. Hildegarde Altmann thought of Berlin, burned, ruined, shamed and by many still hated. How could this well-dressed young foreigner believe such *Torheit* – what was the English? Such rubbish. It was necessary to lie if you were to live.

'Some of the British are willing to forgive. To be friends, even. I hear this from those I know in Germany. But the officers in the U-boats, that is another story. They killed many, they were much feared. In Scotland once he was attacked and beaten by a farmer who had lost his boy in the Atlantic. Dieter says he cannot forget the look on the man's face. *Hass*, that is hating . . . hating. I must tell you why I have come to you,' she continued, as Lisa took this in. 'The young lady you were with, Dieter's friend, would not be glad to speak to me. I think she would not listen maybe. Dieter told me last night you were with her from schooldays.'

'You want me to tell her.'

'I suppose it is best,' said Hildegarde Altmann, after a moment. 'Best would have been had she never come last evening. But that is now done. He was very sad it happened, more than you can think. That after all his care she saw somebody from his other life. He thinks she will wish now to break off her *Liebeshandel*.'

'What a beautiful word.'

'Like Tristan and Isolt, is that so? Some things German then you like.'

'Of course! Does Peter truly think she won't want him because of his nationality? That's crazy. He's mad.'

'No, he is not mad,' was the sober reply. She sounded exactly like her brother.

When Lisa paid for the meal Frau Altmann was embarrassingly grateful. Lisa wished she would stop thanking her. They crossed the road and Lisa unlocked the shop. Frau Altmann peered through the window and paid her some compliment about a colourful porcelain inkstand.

'Ah, that is our Dresden. So pretty.'

'Unfortunately not. Made in Birmingham in 1870. A copy.'

They shook hands formally when they said goodbye.

'You will speak to the young lady? I will tell Dieter what I have done. He will be angry but that cannot be helped. He is a good man. Very good. Do not expect, my dear Miss,' continued Frau Altmann kindly, 'that your friend will be full of forgetfulness of the past like you. I feel she will not wish for my brother now. Goodbye.' She walked away briskly as if the meal had given her renewed energy.

Lisa telephoned the Stage Door. Polly was at an understudy rehearsal.

'Could you tell her to call Lisa Whitfield at the shop, please? Urgently.'

'Righty-ho.'

Each time the telephone rang during the long afternoon Lisa sprang up, but was disappointed. The customers who came into the shop were of the kind who took hours to choose something very inexpensive. At teatime a Scottish dealer appeared to share Lisa's tea and biscuits and to offer her a trayful of worn silver thimbles. Mr McBride was balding, well-informed and rather proud. He knew the history of every thimble. 'Flower patterns were popular in the 1880s. You see the daisy design? Very charming . . . This one here came from Whithead House in Inverness. I always like the thistle motif.' There were thimbles so worn that a needle might have pressed a hole in their wafer-thin tops. 'Would you like to choose two or three?' he finally said, accepting more tea.

'I'm afraid we haven't yet sold the six Mrs Smith bought from you, Mr McBride.'

'Now that is a surprise. They go down so well in Canterbury and Chester. Glasgow too . . .'

He suggested fetching from his van some table napkin rings which were 'pretty as a picture'. He was a rogue but Lisa bought two; she hadn't the heart to refuse every single thing he produced. She imagined Perdita's scorn.

At last, when Mr McBride had gone, Polly rang.

'Yes?' She sounded like flint.

'I have something important to tell you. Can we meet?'

'I don't expect so. I'm going to Hall's Croft.'

'Must you?'

'Yes, I must. What's important? Has Peter Lang turned up and told you some cock-and-bull story? I suppose that female was the chairwoman of the Townswomen's Guild.'

'Don't be silly. I must see you, and if you insist I'll come to Hall's Croft. But I'd far prefer you to come to Lyndhurst.'

'No chance.'

'You'll be with a crowd of people at Hall's Croft.'

'Yes I will and a good thing too. You can come there if you want.' Polly, who could be very rude when unhappy, slammed down the receiver.

Before she left The Treasure Box, Lisa put a card on the inside of the door to show through the glass:

Closed until 6.30. Then open until 7.30 p.m.
*The Treasure Box.*

She was half expecting a visit from an American customer who had shown an interest in an inlaid mother-of-pearl Victorian sewing-box. Lisa wanted to sell it to him. Perdita said she wouldn't succeed.

She walked through streets busy in the sunny evening, passed Old Town where Mick Gould lodged, and arrived finally at Hall's Croft. The house, beautifully Tudor, had been the home of Shakespeare's daughter Judith and her doctor husband. The mulberry trees in the garden were so old – had Shakespeare sat under them perhaps? In autumn the soft, dark fruit fell off the trees, staining the grass. Lisa saw Polly at once, sitting under the ancient trees with a group of actors. It was just as Lisa had expected: laughter and talk with Polly slap in the middle of it. Her friend waved.

'Yoo hoo,' she shouted.

When Lisa walked over to them, Mick Gould sprang up and took her hand.

'You look very pretty. Can I get you some tea? A cider?'

Lisa thanked him, but said unfortunately she couldn't stay, she just needed a word with Polly.

'Have a bookful,' said Polly who wore the glistening brightness of the unhappy.

The actors were all talking shop, Shakespeare shop, Marlowe shop. Polly showed no signs of leaving them. Half kneeling beside her Lisa said in a low voice, 'There's something I want to tell you.' Her friend shrugged. 'If you don't come and talk somewhere quiet, you'll miss what could affect the rest of your life.'

'Coo,' said Polly.

In an even lower voice Lisa said, 'Don't be a silly bitch.' Polly threw her eyes up in mock horror, sniggered and began ostentatiously listening to the talk. 'Oh, go to hell,' said Lisa loudly and stood up.

From sheer perversity Polly did the same and when Lisa walked away, she followed her.

'You are in a stew, aren't you? I suppose Peter's been moaning to you all the afternoon.'

'I haven't seen him. Go back to your friends, they interest you far more than hearing what I came to say. In any case you don't deserve to hear it. I can't imagine why I bothered.'

Polly, looking at her with curiosity, followed her across the gardens to the high brick wall. The sun glared down, there wasn't a patch of shade.

'Golly, it's hot,' said Polly, fanning herself. 'I don't know what this is all about, but it's obviously about him, and frankly, I don't want to discuss him. I am going to forget the whole boring business and if you had any imagination at all –' she spoke as artist to clod – 'you'd understand.'

'The woman we saw at his flat had lunch with me today.'

'She did *what*? Of all the bloody – why didn't you refuse to speak to her? You call yourself my friend –'

'Oh Polly, do pipe down and stop emoting. Her name is Frau Altmann and she happens to be Peter's sister.'

The effect of this piece of news on Polly was similar to Lisa's own, but a hundred times stronger. She laughed out loud. She gave a diatribe about Lisa's credulity. How could Lisa believe such rot? It was pathetic. Lisa, at the end of her tether, actually had to shout her down. She had had hours in which to think about Hildegarde and Peter, and she caught hold of Polly's hands and yelled, 'Will you shut up?' She repeated her conversation with Hildegarde. She spoke of Peter's family, his career, his imprisonment, giving every detail she had been told. After her dramatics Polly listened in total silence. Lisa ended with Hildegarde's words, 'So he thinks she will wish to break off their *Liebeshandel*.'

'Love affair,' said Polly.

They looked at each other.

'Now we know,' finished Lisa, 'his mysteries. The things unexplained. The things he invented, poor Peter, about the Normandy invasion. It's ancient history about Peter and me and you know I was never in love, but it was that which split us up. You remember the police came to see him? Well, it was because of his connection with that detested Nazi uncle.

502

I suppose they know things like that. Naturally I couldn't tell you why we parted and anyway I never understood it – but Jenny's father warned me against being friends with Peter. Of course it was because of all this. Guy Bowden was in MI5 or something during the war. When I asked Peter about the police he refused to explain and I told him I hated secrets . . . You and I both came up against what he wasn't going to tell. Peter. Dieter.'

Polly heaved a great sigh. 'No crimes. No Jekyll and Hyde. No middle-aged mistress. Just being a German.'

'He's got into the habit of thinking nobody would want him because of being in U-boats. How do *you* feel about what he is?'

Polly was transfixed. 'Does he imagine I'd see him as an enemy? He's Peter still. He hasn't changed. Oh, I know there are people who still feel terrible about the war, they suffered and lost people they adored, but I'm selfish, I don't think like that. Nobody I loved was killed and – and I always think the poor things have suffered too. They're like us, we're the same. What a fool he is, how could he think – I must see him . . .'

She sprang up and began to rush away, stopped and swerved round, running back to give Lisa a hug. Then she ran off very fast, flying across the garden, ignoring the shouts of her friends.

Lisa returned to the shop with the sensation of a job well done. Little Miss Scattergood, Charles had once jeeringly called her. That had been when she'd tried to make peace between him and Uncle Rod in Burma, after Charles had been gambling or womanizing. 'But not, Lou,' he had patiently explained, 'at the same time.'

The last person in the world she expected to see as she walked down Wood Street was Peter. He was waiting for her.

'Your notice said you would be here at six-thirty. It is quarter to seven.'

'You could start by saying hello,' said Lisa.

He did not answer that, but stood by as she unlocked the

503

door, followed her in and burst out at once, 'My sister has told me everything!'

'She told me everything too.'

'I am very angry with her. She had no right –'

'Peter, do stop. Of course she had a right since Polly and I invaded your room and drew all kinds of wrong conclusions. It was very brave and good of her and I am grateful.'

'It was wrong. I have told her so. How dared she!'

'I do wish you would stop being melodramatic,' said Lisa who, after coping with Polly, felt quite tired.

She tried not to smile at the way he threw back his head and stood as if to attention. Something in him exaggerated his outrage; he was different from the man she'd known. If he weren't such a solemn owl, she thought, he might have laughed at how well he had taken us all in. But he saw nothing comic, only tragic, and she could see that for two pins he might burst into tears. He was fairly letting rip and his face, despite the melodrama, was agonized. When she touched him, he shied away.

'It is over. I will go back to Germany.'

'Do you want that?'

'No, but she will never care for me now.'

'Oh, don't be so extreme!' said Lisa. 'Are we still carrying on the war? Are we still enemies? Come on . . .'

'There are things we can never forget. My uncle was in the Party.'

Lisa wouldn't listen any more. She raised her voice just as she'd done with Polly and shouted, '*Peter*. Get it into your thick head that Polly doesn't care fourpence, nor do I for that matter, that you're German. *We don't care.* It was brilliant of you to get us believing you were English, but it's exciting to know who you really are.'

She had no effect at all. He said in sombre tones, using his favourite first two words, 'Of course it is not possible.'

'If you don't believe me, believe her. I just told her what Hildegarde told me, and she's gone haring off to Warwick to find you.'

'*Oh God!*'

Without a goodbye he rushed out of the shop. The sacred bells set up a racket as he slammed the door. She saw him running as fast as Polly had done.

The jangling bells took a long time to settle down as Lisa sat thinking of the *Liebeshandel* and Peter's real life. She had never known a submariner. Among all the scores of men she'd met in Calcutta there had been nobody in that Service; there were few sea battles in the Indian Ocean. Now she tried to conjure a life of peril in vessels lurking like deep-sea creatures far down in the darkest parts of the ocean where light could not reach, never far from an icy death. It must have been a life as hidden as the subconscious and in a way as fearful. It had none of the false glamour the poets had given to soldiering or to the world of great ships. It had none of the heartbreaking romance which still clung to the young men who died in the heavens, the Johnny heads-in-air.

Would Polly ever hear or want to hear about that part of his life? There had followed that other life on a Scottish island where he had learned to speak – oh, so well – his enemy's language with all its beauty and subtlety, and had decided, perhaps from shame, to give up his own country. Polly has taken on a world of past suffering, thought Lisa. How will she deal with that?

# 25

The weeks of summer and early autumn were a coloured ribbon which had seemed endless, but the ribbon grew shorter and the amount left on the reel was almost gone. The sweet colours too. The brilliant green and sage of the leaves, the crimson of roses and the white of girls' dresses began to change to tan and yellow, brown and cinnamon. Autumn was here, the season was almost over, and you could smell burning leaves.

Charles and Jenny finally returned in September. They had managed to remain abroad far longer than was legally possible on the meagre amount of foreign currency allowed by a Government set on austerity. They'd smuggled out a good deal of sterling when they left England, and when that store was used up Charles had made friends with a laconic, grey Northcountryman staying in Capri after doing some business in Rome. He cashed them a good-sized English cheque.

When Lisa collected them at Leamington she scarcely recognized them.

'Good grief. Two Red Indians.'

'Lisa!' called Jenny running to her and – Jenny was no kisser – offering her a sunburnt cheek. 'Good to see you. Did you get our cards? I've bought a rubber bone for Honey, he *is* all right, isn't he? I kept being afraid he was ill. You didn't mention him the last time you wrote.'

'She's been going on about that blessed dog right across

Europe,' said Charles, bending to give his sister a real kiss. He looked wonderful: the exaggerated suntan suited him, his skin was swarthy, his black hair slightly bleached on his forehead. He seemed lazily glad to be home.

On the drive back to Lyndhurst Lisa asked for news of their time away. There was none. All they had done was swim and lie about, eat Italian food – 'Am I fatter, Lisa?' – and swim again. Now and again they had gone dancing.

The *Pensione* Williams was the same pleasant hotel where they had stayed previously but the great change was being able to afford a large bedroom, their own bathroom, and the luxury of dining out at different restaurants. Previously they'd been so poor they had eaten cheese and dry bread in their room at lunchtime, and been forced to go to the same cheap restaurant every night. 'We really went the pace this time,' said Jenny. 'Charles took me to the Tiberio, it's the best hotel of all. I mean –' Words failed her. They told their interested audience the usual travellers' tales. They had drunk ice-cold wine in Pepinella's cave, literally a cave turned into a restaurant, the floor made of earth. They had climbed to the ruined lighthouse, and dined one night in a cellar where they'd seen Capri's most celebrated dancer do the tarantella. 'It's called that because people danced it in *agony* after being bitten by that huge spider,' explained Jenny. They had driven to Anacapri to see Axel Munthe's house. The writer had died a few months ago, and in the village they had met his housekeeper who invited them to visit the house. 'It's haunted. Every room was icy cold,' said Jenny. Charles put his arm round his wife's shoulders and laughed, saying the trouble with Jenny was that she was under the impression she was psychic: it came from seeing too many horror films when she was fifteen.

He had reasons for discouraging her superstitious dreads, some of which alarmed him. At times she was uncanny, and had once told him of a vision of himself – and Death – which she'd seen before losing consciousness the night of her attempted suicide: 'It was me with you. I know it.'

When Lisa brought them home and Mrs Welstead opened

507

the door the first thing Jenny saw was the stout little figure of her dog. She screamed with delight, threw herself on her knees, shovelled him into her arms and kissed him over and over again. Jenny kissed dogs and horses, not people.

'Honey, you're a pig. A beast. How dare you grow so much bigger when I wasn't here to see,' she cried.

It was her father who had brought back both her pony and the little dog that morning, arriving hours before they were due. He and Lisa walked round the main house which was looking its country best. She pressed him to wait for Jenny, but he refused. No, he said, he'd come back tomorrow and would telephone to arrange a convenient time. When he said goodbye to Lisa he pressed her hand.

'Thank you.'

'For what, Guy?'

'The fact that you don't know is the best of all.'

Now Jenny, cradling her dog, asked, 'Is Daddy coming round?' Honey was licking her fervently; like Browning's Last Duchess, he loved everybody. Lisa explained that Guy had come earlier to deliver the pony and the dog and would see her the next day. Lisa waited for Jenny to jump up and rush to the telephone; Jenny didn't.

Leaving his wife and sister chatting, Charles went upstairs to unpack his clothes. He had bought a good many new things in Italy. Fine shirts and handmade shoes, a silky leather jacket which a Capri tailor had made for him in a day. He'd spent too much money both on Jenny and himself and wasn't too happy about his bank balance. The dividends from his investments were not a bottomless well of gold. I might go to the club and play tonight, he thought. Maybe I shall be on a winning streak. But it was too soon. The reformed gambler, like the reformed drunk, should keep away from what tempted him. Now with a hunger near to needing sex, he wanted to sit at a table and pick up the cards again.

Week by week in Italy in the company of his wife, the guilt had slowly healed in his soul, and at last even the thick scab had fallen off leaving only a long, jagged scar. During

508

their love-making every afternoon in the shuttered dimness of their room which smelled of flowers and dust, while they made love for a longer and longer time as she learned the finer arts of sex, he wanted her to become pregnant. He thought of it and then of Gemma and her little son, whose large brown eyes and little dignified presence came often into his mind when he saw the beautiful Italian children playing in the piazza.

He had told Gemma it was over and he had meant it. He was set on one thing only: nursing Jenny back to safety. But as he and Jenny travelled in the rocking train and he lay awake while the kilometres steamed away into the night, taking him further and further from his love, he remembered her smile. She had sat under the tree at Avoncliffe, held out her hand and smiled. He closed his mind against her but he was a man locking up his treasure to visit it later and sit running gold coins through his fingers.

She wrote to him in Capri. How on earth had she found out where he was? She could never have obtained the address from Lisa who would have given her a very dusty answer, and nobody at the theatre would know or care where he'd gone. But she had found out because Gemma was like that.

The letter could not be faulted, although he hid it from Jenny with the resentment of a man whom women had chased since his puberty. 'My dear Charles,' the letter blandly began. Gemma wrote in her strong, over-large hand which covered an entire page with four sentences, enquiring how he was, how was Italy, was his wife well and other meaningless politenesses. There was a fish hook in the end of the letter sharp enough to make the fingers bleed.

'Hope you're back before *Love's Labour's* final perfs. You missed me in it, didn't you? Anyway, shall see you on your return as Tom wants to finish his play in peace and we're going to hang on at Avoncliffe a bit. Bobbie sends big kisses.'

Bobbie had drawn a house, a curly-haired figure at the door

with a balloon coming out of its mouth saying, 'Hello!' Underneath he'd written: 'Mummy at Avoncriff'. There was a row of kisses from one side of the page to the other.

Charles tore the letter into small pieces, put them in his pocket and threw them into a rubbish bin in the piazza later that day. It was like effacing fingerprints after you had committed a crime. He did not reply to the letter and tried to forget it, but some days later she wrote again.

This time Jenny asked who his letter was from. He said, 'Oh, nothing, darling. A boring note from the solicitor.' Jenny nodded without interest; she was, in her sunny happiness, only too easy to deceive. Gemma's second letter contained a folded piece of pink paper on which Bobbie had drawn a car containing two figures; the balloon said: 'Me and Tom going to see Mummy in her play.'

She has not given me up, thought Charles. He had a revulsion at the idea. He wanted and did not want her. He thought of her lying naked in the cottage, her legs open, her eyes heavy. He had sworn to himself he wouldn't see her again. But there she lay in his mind.

The return of her brother and Jenny, brown from Italian suns and relaxed from weeks untroubled by the dangers in his nature, had a decided effect on Lisa. The big, empty house had been forlorn. Lisa was not the only one who had known it was empty. The fox had come back – she'd seen him at least three times – and pheasants walked in a stately way across the grass. Once in her headlights she'd seen a hare. The wild creatures had known they were safe and the grounds were their own. She supposed that now, peering with enlarged eyes in the dark, they knew all about Charles and Jenny coming back. She didn't see them any more.

The return of her brother and Jenny, much missed, made Lisa sharply conscious of her own busy but empty life. The world was full of lovers: she noticed it time and again when she drove or walked through Stratford. Two people with their arms round each other. A couple kissing. Two figures hurrying towards each other. It was in Shakespeare's plays, reverberating, thrilling. Orlando and Rosalind. Romeo and

Juliet. Orsino and Viola. Posthumus and Imogen in *Cymbeline* – she thought of the heart-stopping words when the lovers embraced:

> Hang there like fruit, my soul,
> Till the tree die!

It was in nature. The fox she had once seen with his vixen, the beautifully-coloured pheasants. It was the secret of the world.

The most blissful couple at present were Peter and Polly who were inseparable. Perdita watched them through the window of The Treasure Box.

'There they go again. Gentle heaven, they're holding hands. Lisa, have you noticed that there are no people more excessively tedious than a couple in love?' Lisa did not reply and Perdita gave her an incredulous look. 'You can't sit there and tell me you enjoy their company?'

'I'm fond of both of them.'

'Considering that he was *your* admirer first, I simply don't understand you. Where are your healthy female claws?'

Peter, looking very smart in navy blue with a new spotted tie, called into the shop one afternoon and after greeting them without the old ease, asked Perdita if he might take Lisa out for tea.

'Hey,' exclaimed Lisa, 'what about asking me first?'

'He's asking my permission which is perfectly proper and the answer's yes but only for half an hour,' said Perdita.

Lisa kept a serious face while he accompanied her to The Cobweb, exchanging banalities. When they were sitting down and he had ordered tea – 'I know you like gingerbread' being his only sign of humanity so far – he said, 'I have to apologize for the other evening, Lisa. I was not myself.'

'It was very understandable.'

'No, it wasn't, I was rude. I must thank you for everything you've done.'

'It was your sister who made things happen.'

'Of course,' he said, meaning something different. 'She is back in Berlin now and we are reconciled.'

'So I should jolly well think.'

He courteously offered her the plate of sticky gingerbread and when Lisa was enjoying it, said, 'We are friends now, aren't we?'

She was touched and wanted to laugh as she used to do when he was at his most humourless. She saw why she had been so fond of him: his dignity had a positive pathos. She knew, too, that he was hoping she wouldn't speak about his deceptions, his true identity, that she wouldn't say a word to open up so vast a subject. She read his thoughts and agreed with him. What claim on him had she now, even for a single question?

'Lisa, I want you to be the first to know. Polly says she'll marry me.'

'Oh, that's perfect!' cried Lisa, so surprised and pleased that she leaned forward to kiss his cheek. He looked shy. A U-boat commander shy, marvelled Lisa.

Polly herself was so radiant that Perdita became bored when she had been in the shop for sixty seconds, and Lisa hastily suggested she should call at Lyndhurst one evening. Yes, cried Polly, would tonight do? When she arrived at the flat, her happiness filled the rooms like scent.

'Isn't it ridiculous that he wants to marry me? I've told him only a crazy man marries an actress.'

'Quoting his sister, I'd say crazy is exactly what Peter isn't.'

'Don't disillusion me. I think he is quite off his head and taking me on is the proof.' She described what had happened after Lisa had told her Peter's secret. 'I knew there'd be trouble and the only thing to do was to go at it like a bull at a gate. After I left you at Hall's Croft I drove to his newspaper office and hung about outside. Well, of course, he didn't come out but one of the girls did, and said he wasn't around, and just when I was talking to her I saw his car. He got out and came marching up to me looking so stiff and sort of intense that I thought my heart would break. We started walking. I should think we walked all round Warwick twenty times, and I said something about how stupid it had all been

512

just because he was a German, and then he interrupted and wouldn't let me finish and said 'You hate it, you must. And my uncle –'. Well, then I barged in and began to be very rude about the Nazis and used some juicy swear words and he forgot to be riven with guilt and got shocked. He hates women swearing.'

'But all you theatre people do.'

'Now you sound like him. Yes, of course we do, the f's and c's burst out of dressing-rooms like fire-crackers. I've got to stop when I'm with him, though, because he says it's "unwomanly". Isn't he sweet? I'm dotty about him, Lisa. I love him so much I feel quite weak. When we're married, do you realize I shall be Frau Lang? I'll tell you something. Nobody in the UK would hire an actress called Frau Lang.'

Polly was like the water boatmen insects on the Avon in summertime. She skidded merrily on the surface at top speed. The depths in Peter, the angst, did not affect her. She recognized them in Shakespeare. When Anthony Quayle talked to her about her part in *Henry V* when as a princess she accepts the hand of her enemy, he described the hero-king's ambivalence between the vision of glory, the horrors of war, and the golden princess, symbol of the France he'd loved and defeated, and Polly was rapt. This was the world she lived in. But when Peter was in a dark mood she sat on his lap. His German gravity needed what Polly lavishly gave him.

It was the end of the season, there was just a week to go. The leaves spun down from the poplar trees and floated on the river. They fell in showers on the country roads. The wind blew them into little heaps or set them dancing, and when the day was still, they lay so thick that to walk on them was like feeling a carpet under your feet. It turned hot again. It was the weekend and everybody was busy. Leading members of the Company decided to give a party, following the pattern set last year by Lewis Lockton. Both Polly and Peter had been invited. Charles and Jenny left Lyndhurst early to spend the day with friends and play tennis.

513

It was hot and quiet that afternoon. Loneliness, which Lisa kept at bay with work, or seeking out the company of family and friends, came suddenly back. The garden looked so empty. Tom was less than three miles away, but she could never meet him to talk now and then. I suppose Gemma's with him today, she thought. And then she realized that Avoncliffe, like Lyndhurst, would be empty. Tom and Gemma and everybody from the big house would be at the party. Polly had told Lisa it was starting at lunchtime and continuing right on into the evening.

Suppose, thought Lisa, I walk as far as Avoncliffe. They won't be there, it will be quite safe. I can look at the house, it will be something to do. The idea had a sort of doleful interest about it. She set off, a small figure in a pale dress, on a journey no different from the lover in the ballad who comes at night to look at a lighted window.

The gate was open and she stood in the drive, looking at the empty lawns now turned the colour of straw. How silent the afternoon was. Even the birds did not seem to be singing now that summer was ending. The windows of the big house were open. There was a pram by a wall, and some bicycles. In the stableyard a child's tricycle. Signs of people and not a sound.

She walked slowly into the courtyard where she had come one night a long time ago to confront Tom with his wife's infidelity. Her mood was subdued and she thought: there's his front door – and foolishly put out her hand to touch the sun-warmed surface.

A sudden noise above her head made her jump. A window was pushed wider, a tanned, enquiring face looked down. Tom.

'Why, it's Lisa!'

She looked and felt ridiculous but before she could stammer a word she heard his steps clattering down the stairs. All he said as he came out of the house was, 'How good to see you,' and took both her hands.

'I didn't think you'd be here,' she said and he burst out laughing, did not ask her to explain but suggested they should go into the garden.

514

In the humming silence they crossed the grass to the beech tree under which her brother had sprawled with Gemma in the spring.

Tom glanced at her. She was thin and quiet, her hair like the feathers of a blackbird. There was something invisible and pervasive between this girl and himself. He wrote of her in his plays. Never present, she was never absent. They sat down in the shade.

'I suppose I shouldn't have come,' she suggested.

'I suppose you shouldn't, too.'

'Was it wrong, then?' she asked, looking as if it might have been.

'Very,' he said, smiling.

'I truly didn't know you would be here.'

'My darling. I know that.'

They sat close enough to embrace, both conscious of the other in a pause which gave them too much and too little. Lisa waited, surrendering herself to the moment and then pulled herself out of it. She knew one of them had to do so and was certain that he would not.

'Why don't we talk about your work?' she suddenly said and he gave a laugh which showed that her effort was both admirable and funny. 'Oh, there are all kinds of things I want to know,' continued Lisa, gaining confidence. 'You never once said when we were in India that you wanted to become a dramatist. I do wonder why I never knew.'

Tom took her lead: the spell was broken. He said that writing a play had been an unformed notion in his mind while he was in the RAF. But to be a flyer and look into the future was tempting the Fates. All the pilots had felt like that. After he had come out of the Service and begun to write, he'd found the play was the form he preferred. It was concentrated. It was an intense way of communicating ideas; you could use tragedy, humour, anything you liked and if you pulled it off you had the actors and their imagination to add immensely to your work.

'But it is a tough assignment. The fact is a bad play is so very much worse than a bad book. At least, I think so.'

515

Lisa told him she had seen *Somersault* in London and how much she had loved it, yet found it an enigma. Talking together, at ease now, they didn't speak of Gemma or Charles or the night of Jenny's desperation. All they did was to sit as they used to do on the roof of the Chowringhee flat at sunset and talk idly and smile sometimes. Silences said more.

Shadows began to creep across the grass. Nobody returned to the great, sleeping house and they stayed talking or falling silent.

At last she said, 'I suppose I ought to go.'

'So soon?'

'What's the time?' He lifted his wrist, and she saw he wasn't wearing a watch. There was a white circle on his tanned forearm. 'That's the best way to know the time this afternoon.'

When she stood up, he did not dissuade her and they walked idly down the drive under the trees. They came to the gate.

'Let me come with you as far as your house.'

'I'd rather you didn't.'

'Dear heart,' was all he said.


After she came home from Italy, Jenny fell into the habit of seeing her father almost every day. They rode in the mornings. She drove to Whitefriars when Charles was out, and sometimes when he was not, to spend time in her old home. She only realized now how much she had missed her father. She had denied it in her head and told herself lie after lie. She had forced herself to believe that nothing and nobody mattered but Charles.

Now her father had taken her back and loved her more than ever. She saw how much he differed from her husband and worried about it. He listened so kindly, he noticed her more than Charles ever did. She felt confident with him, and safe. She was more herself with Guy than she was with Charles. She respected him and looked up to him but he did not oppress her. Jenny knew her father admired her; she returned the admiration and they were comfortable together. She felt none of the slavery of her sexual life with Charles.

Whatever she wanted to talk about interested Guy. She never bored him and he never gave her an incredulous or sarcastic smile. Because she didn't disappoint him she felt cleverer and prettier. She had forgotten how much she loved him.

The Indian summer lingered. It was the last day of the season and Jenny decided to spend it at Whitefriars. She'd be back before six, she told Charles, in good time to change for the play. Guy suggested she should bring Honey with her, but Jenny said it was too hot and shut the puppy in the sitting-room to bark and scratch at the door until Charles, who had risen late, came yawning down to release him.

Charles took his coffee into the garden, escaping Mrs Welstead's domesticity. He collapsed into a deck-chair which he'd forgotten to put away the night before. It was still drawn up to another chair in which Jenny had sat with him watching the moon.

'The moonlight's quite warm,' she had cried, stretching out her arms. 'Do you think one can get moonburn?'

He sat wondering what to do with the day. In a world pulling itself up by its boot-straps, ruined and poor, exhausted by trying to make ends meet, in a country where Government posters cried 'We Work or Want', Charles was the only idle fellow.

What in blazes shall I do this afternoon? he wondered. I've scarcely touched a card since we came back from Capri. I'm reformed. A reformed rake. A reformed gambler and advancing into middle age, Lord help us.

His thoughts bored him. He was often bored nowadays, it had become his demon. Leaving the garden he went down the drive and made his way into the lane where Peter and Lisa used to walk at night. The weeds of autumn were high and there was the steady, leafy, hot scent of hedges which no pruning hook has touched. Walking slowly, thinking about nothing, he finally arrived at the place where a plank, so blackened and split with age that a heel might go through it, had been laid across a small, foaming weir. There had been a mill here once but now the building was neglected

517

and had fallen into decay. The water bubbled, in places pure white, in places turning over in a dark green curve. The river was deep and the noise was loud. He stood staring.

Somebody touched his arm. He spun round, startled.

Gemma was standing beside him.

Like the moment when he'd seen her at the end of the passage in the theatre, she seemed to him an apparition. The dress she wore was the very colour of the autumn, her freckled shoulders were bare and although she had pinned up her hair it trailed down as if its weight was too heavy to stay in place – one auburn tress fell down her back. She was sun-tanned, but pale compared to the dark man facing her. Raising her voice against the noise of the water she shouted, 'Charles!' She was shaking with laughter. She pointed to a grass space in front of the deserted mill. It was smothered with yellow nasturtiums which would go on flowering with nobody to look at them until the first frosts came.

They walked away from the roar of the water and sat down at a distance from each other.

'What are you doing here, Gemma?'

'What are *you*?'

'Wandering about.'

'Typical. I happen to be working.'

'How can you possibly be doing that?'

'*Hamlet*, of course.'

'I still don't get it.' How beautiful and tiresome she was.

Gemma looked at him pityingly. '*Hamlet*, Charles. Tony Quayle's reviving it next season.'

'You don't mean you're going to play Ophelia?'

'You're very rude sometimes. No, I'm not going to play Ophelia, I've never liked the part. 'Re-enter Ophelia, fantastically dressed with straws and flowers.' Her mad scene is hell to pull off without being tedious.'

'Janet Field does it well,' he said, naming the actress at present playing the rôle.

'Oh, do you think so? Anyway the rumour is, nothing definite, that Tony might offer me Gertrude next year. Which is why I'm here to look at the water and the trees.

There is a willow grows aslant a brook.
That shows his hoar leaves in the glassy stream.

There's one over there.' She gestured to a tree washing its hair in the water. 'I see you don't recognize the big speech. I thought I'd educated you. Gertrude tells Laertes that Ophelia's dead, remember?

Her clothes spread wide,
And, mermaid-like, awhile they bore her up;

Then the poor creature drowns.'

'Oh. That.'

'Don't be so –' She paused.

'So what?' he asked.

'Philistine. It is not like you. *You* aren't like you either. You're as dark as Othello.'

'You hate that, I expect.'

'Now how could I hate it? You must know you look astonishing. The people who hate you will be the men in Stratford when all the women drool. How are you? I haven't enquired. Are you well? There's a silly question that doesn't deserve an answer. Did you get my letters, Charles?'

She surveyed him quizzically, her eyes very slightly closed which emphasized their heavy lids. They gave her face a look of exhaustion belied by those blazing brown eyes. Oh yes, Gemma blazed. He felt his whole self taken by her. By her voice, her even white teeth, her thick tumbling hair, her laughing face.

'I don't believe you liked my letters. You weren't supposed to. I wrote to annoy you. Did your wife read them? I do trust so.'

'No, she didn't. I threw them away.'

'I'm surprised you could ̀bear to part with them.' She held out a dimpled hand. Round her wrist was a gold chain bracelet unsuitably hung with a locket in the shape of a heart. 'After all, I'd touched the paper, did you think of that? I might have kissed it too. Girls during the war often

519

did. They marked their letters with lipsticked kisses, pressing the paper to their mouths with open lips. Very sexy.'

'You used to do it, did you?'

'Of course. I was quite an artist. I thought I'd use my old technique when I wrote to you but decided it was rather risky.'

'Cautious of you.' He spoke in his old sardonic tones. For some masculine reason he had begun to elude her. Her strength had, for a moment, ebbed. She fidgeted with the ribbon which tied a frill round her bare shoulders. 'You remember I told you Jenny tried to kill herself.'

Now he's really escaped, thought Gemma. She waited for the noise of the water to wash the sentence away.

'I bet she isn't the first girl who's done that because of you.'

'Don't be flip, Gemma. It's very unattractive.'

She raised russet eyebrows. 'I mean it. I don't feel guilty because of what your wife did. In my profession it can happen for all sorts of reasons, not only sex. Last year a sweet boy I used to know in rep killed himself because he wasn't any good and theatre meant everything to him. The poor love preferred to be dead than to fail. People,' went on Gemma with a large gesture, 'jumped out of windows in New York when the Big Crash came. People do kill themselves. Others try but get snatched back to life. I can't feel the least responsibility because I happen to be in love with you.'

Sounding miles away he said, 'That is simply not true.'

Then she knew she'd got him again, had him as strongly as if she'd gripped his hand and forced him to come with her to drown in the foaming water, sinking together without a struggle. She turned slowly to him, possible, possessable, as moist as the centre of a yellow rose after the rain. She pulled at the knot on her shoulders and let the dress fall to her waist, exposing breasts as pink-tipped and full as those of women in sexual dreams. She took one of her breasts between finger and thumb and waited for him to suck it.

*

520

It poured with rain later in the day. There was a thunder storm and the lightning scattered the Stratford crowds. Guy and Jenny, Lisa and Charles went to the final performance of *Love's Labour's Lost*; they were dining in the theatre restaurant after the play.

Outside, the river was beaten by the rain, windows rattled in the storm. The meal was not much of a success. Guy was pleasant and hospitable, talking more than he usually did. Lisa knew he felt it necessary. Charles was morose, only rousing himself when spoken to. For most of the time he sat twirling the stem of his wine glass and staring into space. Jenny caught his mood.

When the dinner ended, they had to run out into the rain to their cars. Behind them at the Wardrobe, Lisa knew there would be gaiety and end-of-season goodbyes. She was sorry not to be there to see Jacky Grimsdyke, and talk to Polly and Peter. But Charles's mood seemed to have affected all of them. Guy said goodbye hastily, and went off in the wet to find his car. Lisa ran to hers and drove behind Charles and Jenny. Their red light shone ahead of her through the rain until they arrived at Lyndhurst.

She shouted goodnight, and ran up to her own flat, feeling tired and inexplicably sad.

She slept late – it was Sunday – and woke to hear the rain still falling steadily. When she pulled the curtains in the sitting-room there was a dreary prospect of sodden grass and two forgotten deck-chairs on the lawn, turning black in the rain.

Yawning and only half awake, she noticed how cold the air had become as she wandered into the passage. There was a letter lying on the mat. She picked it up and stared at it myopically, noticing it was unstamped. Then a sensation of terror went through her.

It was from Charles.

> Lou,
> By the time you get this Gemma and I will be gone. Jenny sleeps so soundly, I know she won't wake and I

521

packed when she was out yesterday. Gemma and I are leaving at four and taking Bobbie with us.

Tom's in London. He doesn't know anything.

You're going to be angry all over again, as you were when I married, but it isn't any good, Lou. What's happened is stronger than I am. I suppose you'd call it love which looks pretty damned stupid written down like that. But I worship her and she, like me, feels it's impossible to stay apart any more. We've got to be together come hell or high water.

For Christ's sake look after Jenny. When she gets over the first shock she'll see that she can't want a man who wants somebody else the way I want Gemma. I'm certain she won't try a second time to do what she did. It frightened her too much and now, thank God, she's got her father. Jenny must get a divorce. That will tidy things up.

I wish I could say I'm sorry, but I can't.

God bless you, Lou.

    Always,
      Charles.


Lisa began to tremble as she went to the telephone, tried to look up a number and couldn't find it because her eyes didn't seem to function. At last she made it out.

'Stratford 0766.'

'Guy. It's Lisa.'

'My dear girl –' he began, but she cut in.

'Charles has left Jenny. He's gone with Gemma Lambert.'

The pause was scarcely an intake of breath. 'Does Jenny know? Did he tell her?'

'No. I just found a letter on my doormat. I think she must be still asleep.'

'Get dressed and go and see. If she is not awake, leave her. I'll be round in a few minutes,' snapped Guy.

Last time, thought Lisa as she pulled on her clothes, I sent for Tom. Charles, I really hate you.

She went quietly into the main house, crept up the stairs

and slowly, fearfully, opened her brother's bedroom door. She stood motionless. She could hear the gentle sound of breathing, as soft as a child's. Closing the door again silently, she went back down the stairs. She scarcely realized what she was doing as she went out into the rain and waited. The car came slowly up the drive, its headlights bright in the dark, wet morning. Guy jumped out.

'What are you thinking of, you're drenched! Come inside.'

He led her dripping into the porch and then into the hall where she left pools of water on the carpet. He took off his macintosh and cap and Lisa passed him the letter. The ink had begun to run. He read it with a face of iron.

'Did you check if she's awake?'

'She's asleep. I heard her breathing.'

'Did you notice a letter anywhere in her room?'

'Oh, I forgot.'

'It's probably on the dressing-table. I'll go and look. Are you all right?'

Lisa nodded, unconscious of wet, clinging clothes. He went up, taking two stairs at a time, as softly as a cat, and disappeared down the passage.

What seemed like an hour went by.

His square-shouldered figure reappeared, silhouetted against the landing window. He held up his hand and she saw he'd found the letter. Leaning over the banisters he whispered, 'I'm going to wake her up. Go back to your flat at once and change into dry clothes. I'll see you here in the kitchen in a while. Hurry.' He might have been her commanding officer.

Lisa went back through the heavy rain, up to her flat and stripped off. She noticed with surprise that she was almost wet to the skin. Drying her hair, she kept wondering what terrible scene was being enacted at this moment. She thought of her brother, but could not bear to. Gemma stood in her mind like a symbolic figure of the Plague. Kali, the destroyer. When she was dressed she pulled on a raincoat and ran back into the storm.

In the kitchen there was no sign of Guy.

To give herself something to do she put a kettle on the gas and made tea. The little dog was asleep in his basket near the boiler. He woke and came lolloping over to her. Picking him up Lisa kissed the soft head and shut her eyes. Charles is lost to me. It is a tragedy for Jenny, he has been so cruel to her. But I've lost him too.

She had left the kitchen door half open and it banged noisily against the wall. Guy came in.

'Dry now?'

'Quite,' said Lisa in his vernacular.

'Good.' He drew up a chair and sat down. Lisa waited for a verdict, but not about Charles. 'She seems determined to remain in the land of the living this time,' he said after a moment.

'Are you quite sure?'

'You're afraid, are you? Well, I understand that. You were the one who found her. Set your mind at rest, I assure you she is quite safe.'

'I'm sorry. I'm so sorry –'

'What can *you* possibly be sorry for?'

'Everything. Coming to Stratford. Coming to Whitefriars with my brother. Bringing him into your lives. Everything.'

'Don't be a fool,' he said without anger. 'Do you imagine anybody can have control of anyone else, when it comes down to it? I damned nearly locked her up to keep her away from him. What good did that do? Simply made him more attractive and excited her to defy me. It drove me on to separate from her, the worst thing I could have done. We're not the masters of our destinies, let alone of other people's. What's happened has nothing to do with you except that you saved her life.'

'And you believe –'

'That she won't try again. I'm certain. There's no chance of a repeat performance.' She did not believe him. She poured him some tea and he drank it thirstily. Rubbing his chin with his hand he said, 'I need a shave. I apologize for looking like an ape at the zoo. You have no need to worry over her. Of course, she's in a bad way. Bawling her heart out. But she'll pull through. Haven't you noticed a change in her? I did last night. Hard to put one's finger on it, but she was somehow detached. Jenny's pregnant. *He* doesn't know it and I intend to see that he never will.'

# 26

It was Lisa's job to break the news to Tom. Guy didn't spell it out, but he made it clear that nothing interested him except Jenny. He said in a businesslike voice that he would take Jenny to Whitefriars 'the moment she's up and dressed'. He would keep her there and look after her. 'As I told you, you can set your mind at rest about her.' His only mention of Tom was that 'the husband will have to be told', and since he said nothing more it was obvious who was expected to take on the unpleasant task.

He remained in the kitchen, turning things over in his mind, and suddenly asked, 'Did she take that child with her?'

'Yes. It was in Charles's letter.'

'Of course. I remember now.' He nodded as if to imply that that made things tidy.

He hadn't said a word against Charles. He wasn't angry, he was simply matter-of-fact, making plans with an expressionless face. She hadn't seen Guy in action before. When he had thundered into her life that day at Crocker Road he had been out of himself with shock and fury, impotent because the girl was gone. Now it was different. Lisa scarcely recognized in the man sitting opposite her the approachable, almost affectionate friend she had grown to like. He stood up and marched about, his hands behind his back. He spoke brusquely. His interest was totally concentrated on Jenny and Lisa knew *she* scarcely existed. When

526

she said, 'Charles mentioned in his letter that Tom Westbury's in London', he replied vaguely, 'Is he?', thinking about something else.

'I must telephone him.'

'Yes. Do that. I'll go up to her.'

He left the kitchen. Jenny's first heartrending disbelief, the awful grief that must follow, were to be none of Lisa's business.

She went back to her own flat, supposing Guy would prefer her out of the way. In the corner of her sitting-room stood the rocking-horse, a mute companion reminding her of her lost Charles. She went over and set the horse creaking to and fro. He creaked away the past, the Roundwood days, the time when her brother had been her whole existence. He creaked her back to the present and to Tom.

Sitting at the telephone, Lisa spent a disjointed two hours trying to find him. The theatre was adamant about not giving her an address or a telephone number.

'Sorry, Miss. Matter of policy.'

'But it is very urgent –'

'Sorry. Wish I could help but there it is.'

She could not even remember the name of the family at Avoncliffe who, Charles had once mentioned, sometimes looked after Bobbie. She telephoned Polly, whose mother told her Polly was 'out for the day, I'm afraid. With her fiancé.' A note of triumph there.

Putting down the telephone again, Lisa sat trying to concentrate, to find a lead which could indicate where Tom lived in London. She remembered he had said he and Gemma lived in Hampstead. She telephoned London directory enquiries and was told there were four T. Westburys in the Hampstead district. The girl at the exchange gave her all four numbers.

Lisa painstakingly telephoned. The first was a lady called Teresa. The second a Trevor Westbury, old and quavery. The third a brisk young lady – 'No! He's not me!' – who put down the receiver before Lisa had finished speaking. This left the last number to which there was no reply. I suppose this must be Tom's, she thought.

She telephoned at intervals throughout the morning and into the early afternoon, persuading herself that Tom would return home, and suddenly, while she sat listening to the monotonous ringing in his empty flat, it would stop and she would hear his voice. Nothing seemed to matter now, except that Tom should know. While she was for the twentieth time on the telephone she heard the sound of a car, rang off and went to the window.

It was Guy's car driving slowly away. She glimpsed a fair head beside him. Jenny. Lisa had not spoken to her once since Charles had gone.

The hours went by in a sort of trance. She left the exhausting telephone calls, had a bath and changed into different clothes. How quiet everything was. She supposed Guy and Jenny had taken the dog, and when she went downstairs to the stables, she found that Paintbox, too, had disappeared. Somebody must have come for him while she was in the bath. She recognized Guy's touch. He had organized for the horse to be taken to Whitefriars in the same way that he had spirited Jenny off into the rain. He had not asked for help. Nor had he come to find out how Lisa was, how she felt. And he had no interest in the other player in the drama, Gemma's husband. He had driven away, taking with him the only love of his life.

It was getting dark when Lisa left the house and stopped on the Oxford Road for petrol. The rain was over and the fields, already harvested, were shorn close the way men's hair used to be cropped in the Services. She did not drive fast. There was no reason to hurry, her journey was one of chance unlikely to succeed. She passed the pompous gates of Blenheim Palace, and The Bear, where Polly had queened it with Lewis Lockton. She went through Oxford. The undergraduates had not returned, the colleges were empty, no carefree figures slopped along the wet pavements on their way to waste their time or fall in love. There wasn't a bicycle.

It was quite dark when she drove down the Western Avenue on the edges of London, passed the Aladdin Company's tower in the shape of a magical lamp and the gaping holes which had been small houses, destroyed by bombs and landmines and untouched since nights of fire and death. The ruins remained next to suburban houses with net curtains and neat gates.

London did not look neat at all. She thought it drab and depressing; there were bombed and derelict sites everywhere. The city was dirty and shabby after the green country and graces of Oxford.

Hampstead proved difficult to negotiate, an ancient town-village with twisted, hilly streets, and many unexpected alleyways. She asked half a dozen times before she found Glenbrook Grove; it was a narrow thoroughfare behind a road of big houses.

At its far end, just by a single street-lamp, she came to an odd-looking house with a tumbledown studio look about it. A flight of steps ran from the ground floor to what was presumably an upstairs flat. When she left her car and went to the gate, she saw a nearly defaced notice: 'Flat 2. Up steps.'

She supposed this was Tom and Gemma's home. Or perhaps it wasn't? At any rate it was the address the exchange had given her, after much persuasion on Lisa's part, the place she'd been telephoning all day. She had already written a note which enclosed her brother's letter:

> Have been trying to get you all day. Please ring when you get this.
>
> Lisa.

She climbed the steps on to the balcony. What looked like a front door opened on to it. The street-lamp was rather dim, but she couldn't see any lights in the flat. Before putting her letter into the box she paused for a moment, realizing it was possible that it would be found by a perfect stranger. She pressed the doorbell and waited.

She noticed for the first time that she was aching with tiredness, and thought: I haven't eaten all day, how stupid of me.

Tom opened the door.

He saw her face and said at once, 'Something's happened.'

'Charles has gone. With Gemma. They've gone.'

'When? Where? How do you know? We can't stand here, come in.'

The floor of the room into which he took her was covered in papers, not thrown about but arranged in bundles weighed down by books. The window overlooking a garden at the back of the house was open. Lisa handed him Charles's letter. What a message to bring, she thought. There is only one which is worse.

Tom stood reading the letter for what seemed an age, then carefully read her note which accompanied it. He said nothing. They shared the trouble, but it didn't feel as if they did. How could she know what he felt? When he read Charles's letter a second time, she thought she saw him shut his eyes as people do in pain. He put the letters down on a desk, and only then seemed aware that she was still standing.

'Do sit down.'

She picked her way to a chair like a woman crossing a brook on stepping stones. Tom remained on his feet.

'Have you been expecting anything like this?'

'*Of course not*! How could I?'

'I don't know. I just thought you might have done.'

'Surely *you* guessed?' she said in counter-accusation.

'I wish to God I had.'

Then you could have stopped it, she thought. So you do love her. What I believed was an illusion. All the worse for me.

'Lisa, I would like you to tell me exactly what happened.'

She did as he asked, thinking drearily, what good will that do? She described finding her brother's letter this morning outside her door when she got up at about eight o'clock.

He interrupted. 'Let me get this right. You didn't hear a car at all? You didn't hear it even dimly when you were half asleep and wonder who on earth was driving off in the middle of the night?'

530

'I heard nothing.'

'Very well. Go on.'

He interrupted again, questioning what she'd said and wanting to know every detail. When she spoke about Guy he said, 'Surely you saw your sister-in-law?'

'Not once. He –' she stopped, realizing she must get it right, 'didn't seem to want me to.' Tom nodded as if he would have behaved in the same way.

My God, thought Lisa, I don't understand men. All Guy did this morning was behave as if there was an air raid and he must get Jenny to a shelter. Now Tom's going on as if he's the police and I'm a witness. Do men feel things at all? I don't understand them and I never shall. Not Charles. Not Guy. Not Peter. Most particularly not Tom.

She wanted somebody – the deserted wife she hadn't set eyes on, the outraged father, the betrayed husband – to break down. To sob, to call Charles and Gemma filthy names. It would be natural to curse them. It ought to be like a Shakespeare play, made bearable by intensity and rage and poetry and sorrow. She felt so tired. I've done what I came to do, now he knows and that's all there is to do, she thought. Where am I going to sleep? I couldn't drive another mile.

He had not sat down since Lisa had arrived, but continued to walk about, sometimes standing in front of her when he asked her a question, sometimes at his desk where he picked up a paper-knife, once with his back to her, contemplating the tree outside.

He wheeled round. 'You didn't go to Avoncliffe?' he suddenly asked.

It was the last straw.

'No, I didn't,' she shouted. 'I didn't go to your flat to check if they had gone *because of course they have*. Do you imagine my brother would leave me that letter, creep out of his house and simply drive along the road to Avoncliffe? Don't be bloody silly.'

'That's not why I asked. I merely wondered –'

'If I'd made sure she hadn't left your stepson behind?' She was still furious.

'No,' he said queerly, 'I didn't wonder that. It would be impossible.'

'I should have thought anything your wife did was possible.' Her stinging answer, her angry eyes, did not appear to reach him. He was looking at his own thoughts.

'I always know what she'll do as far as Bobbie is concerned. She's taken him with her.' There was a pause. He said, as if annoyed with himself, 'I asked about Avoncliffe for no reason at all. Automatically. I'm not used to people disappearing, Lisa. It feels very odd.'

He said nothing else and stood deep in thought. She felt the loneliness of the messenger when the job is done. Her journey had been momentous, her news had brought a whole revolution to his life, and now she wasn't needed any more. He struck her as being hundreds of miles away with Gemma and the little boy wherever they might be. It was curious to realize they were probably in London.

When Lisa got to her feet he looked up.

'What is it?' he said and frowned. 'Are you all right?' Guy had said the same thing. They spoke as if she were ill.

'Perfectly. But it's time I went. I only came to leave the letter since I couldn't get through on the telephone.'

'I was at the theatre.'

'I didn't know that. Just as I didn't know your address. It was difficult to find you.'

'I'm sorry,' he said with a politeness which wasn't polite at all.

'I suppose you'll come to Stratford when you're less busy, and see Jenny's father. Or don't you think there's any point in that?' She did not speak kindly and he was not listening. He returned to something she'd said earlier and was looking at her in hard perplexity.

'What did you mean, you ought to go? You're not proposing to drive back to Stratford tonight?'

'I suppose I could. Or . . .'

'Or what?'

'Stay at a hotel, I suppose.'

'Lisa, don't be ridiculous.'

532

The impatient, unloving exclamation, after all that had happened, affected her unexpectedly; it was as if, tired as she was, he'd put out his foot and deliberately tripped her up. She sat down again and began to cry. He watched her with a look of sympathy, but nothing more, and at last the sobs quietened and she dried her eyes.

'Does that make it better?'

'Nothing makes it better. I was crying about Charles.'

'I know you were crying over your brother, my poor love.'

'Don't call me that. I'll go.'

She stood up again, unsteady with tiredness, and this time he came towards her. She stiffened as he took her in his arms. He kissed her not with passion but as one would kiss a poor, hurt child, over and over again. Her eyes were still full of tears and the kisses weren't wet from their mouths but from salt.

'Let me go.'

'Why, for Christ's sake? Don't you love me? I know very well you do.' He put his hand under her chin and tipped up her face and looked at her. She stared back. He understood now. 'Lisa! You don't imagine what's happened has changed how I feel about you? How could it possibly do that?'

'You love her. I saw it in your face when I told you!' she said almost in a scream.

He looked bewildered. 'What in hell is all this? Of course I'm shocked at them running off in that craven way. It's disgusting and it makes everything I tried to do a farce. Why did I bother? She used to make such a carry-on when she came back after some affair or other. Oh yes, she slept with other men, she's naturally promiscuous and it's easy to have casual affairs in the theatre. Besides, she's vain. When men made passes it fed her vanity. But I never imagined she'd go, never. Certainly I was shattered when you told me, not about Gemma, about her I was *surprised*. Did you really not know what upset me?'

He looked at her accusingly and she muttered, 'Bobbie.'

'Of course. Bobbie. What a peculiar girl you are. You don't understand a thing about my marriage, do you? And

533

don't start yelling that you don't want to. I don't expect you to understand it and I sometimes don't either. But I thought you'd know it was all mixed up with duty and what I thought was right for Bobbie. Only for him.' She knew he was telling her something she was supposed to have known through instinctive love, and that he thought less of her for not doing so. 'I love that little boy with all my heart. How often I've wished he was my own son. I think of him as mine and forget for months on end that he is not. Until I'm brought up against her, and her rights over him. Then I'm helpless. Gemma worships him. Too much, too greedily. Whatever happens to her she hugs him to her. She married me for Bobbie and she allowed me to love him but she's jealous and any time would snatch him away. Now he's gone. If you've lost your brother, I have lost my little boy. When you told me I thought my heart would crack.'

He stared at her with his sorrow and she said timidly, 'Do you think they will come back?'

'Probably.'

'Then you haven't lost him,' she said in a thin voice.

He gave a kind of shrug. 'I can't tell. He won't be mine again.' He had loosened his hold of her some minutes ago and now, looking at her intently, he said, 'You look dreadful, Lisa.'

'I'm a bit tired.'

'And on the verge of tears again. Take that hat off, it must make your head ache. I'll get you something to drink. We won't have any more nonsense about hotels. You must have my bed. I'll sleep on the sofa.'

He spoke of their separating as the obvious arrangement. He reminded her of Guy. He had said nothing between them had changed but it was not true. Gemma's bright ghost hung with pearls, wearing one of Jacky's elaborate costumes, rustled into the room. The little boy too. They were in his mind and they were stronger than she was.

She awoke the next morning in an unfamiliar place, facing a line of low windows against which the autumn-touched branches of a tree outside uncomfortably leaned. Tom must have opened the curtains, she had not heard him come in. He had pulled them close the night before, saying the light would wake her. With a practical concern he'd turned down the bed and plumped up her pillows. She had gone to bed in the strange room and, worn out, fallen at once into an exhausted sleep.

Now she lay thinking about Charles. The thought of him was heavy, as if a lump of iron was inside her. She had been angry when he had run off and married Jenny in that sudden, selfish way, but she had never believed he would cast *her* off. She was still his only family, his only sister. She had never thought he didn't love her. Now she felt discarded. Where had he gone? He had confided in her recently that he had spent too much money in Italy and had stayed away too long. A pang of sisterly anxiety now went through her. Old concerns died hard.

What a tangle Charles had made of his life. Gambling had estranged his father and been the cause of him leaving England. Gambling might have ruined him, but Charles had a kind of devil's luck. It was the same with women – they couldn't resist him and *he* couldn't leave them alone, he did what he wanted with them. Even with Jenny. I'm the only one who tried to help him against himself. Perhaps that's why I lost him.

There was a scent of coffee and Tom, his curly hair tousled, came in with a tray and sat down on the bed which creaked under his weight. He wore white pyjamas, much creased.

'How did you sleep?'

'Very well. I never thought I would.'

'I spiked your hot milk with brandy.'

'I know. I tasted it.'

He poured out her coffee and watched her drink it. He buttered small squares of toast and spread them with marmalade. He treated her as an invalid, and was concerned and fatherly. He said nothing about what had happened.

While she was having a bath in a bathroom which must be too small for the large man who lived here, Lisa decided that

Tom was convinced the runaways would come back. Sooner or later they'd be forced to do so, because Charles wasn't rich enough to range the world. In any case, if they had now gone abroad they'd have to get foreign currency from somewhere. That couldn't last for ever.

Was Gemma willing to give up her fascinating career for love? Might she try to work in America if that was possible and earn enough to keep all three of them? But Charles wouldn't allow such a thing. He was lazy and self-indulgent but he was also an arrogant male; he'd never agree to be kept by a woman.

Tom will take Gemma back, Lisa thought. Not only because of Bobbie but because he is bound to her. And Lisa knew then that the lump of iron was not only her mourning for her brother, it was because she no longer believed in Tom's love. He's still attracted to me. We made love once. He cares for me in a way. But he belongs to Gemma and the boy.

She sat down to do her hair at an old-fashioned skirted dressing-table covered with bottles of scent and expensive pots of skin cream. The door was half open and she heard Tom on the telephone and the name 'Mr Bowden'. She put down her comb and listened.

Tom's side of the conversation consisted solely of agreeing with whatever Guy was saying.

'Yes.' 'Of course.' 'I'm afraid you're right.' Once he did say 'It's good of you, but I don't think I want to do that.' There were more words in a lower voice. Eventually he rang off and looked round Lisa's door.

'May I come in?'

'Of course.' Formality had arrived. What could she do about that?

'I've just been speaking to Guy Bowden. He said there is no more news, no telephone calls. Nothing. He's not expecting to hear from them, and neither am I. But I keep thinking about Jenny. A second shock, a worse one, after that last time ... I asked about her. He said she's fine. Which I doubt.'

536

'Poor girl,' murmured Lisa, but added, 'At least this time she has her father.'

He nodded absently. Then he said, 'Bowden asked me an odd thing. He said if I wanted to try and trace them, it wouldn't be too difficult. He could help find out where they are.'

Lisa stared. 'Did he mean hiring a detective?' She remembered Guy and Peter Lang.

'I'm not sure. He's a curious man. Do you know him well?'

'Yes and no.'

'Elucidate,' he said, half smiling.

'When I was young I thought him a dry old stick but my father was devoted to him. I think Father admired him tremendously and he was his only friend, really. I never liked him. I felt the same when we first got back to England. But recently I've seen him alone once or twice, and I began to look on him differently. Or did until yesterday.'

'He sounds strictly practical.' So do you, thought Lisa. 'Very much in charge,' continued Tom, pouring more coffee which she refused. 'May I, then?' He finished it with a gulp. 'Anyway, about tracing them, I said I didn't want that. Then, of course, I asked if Jenny did – want to find out where they had gone, I mean – since apparently it would be quite easy. Bowden said that was out of the question, and would I tell you she was fine. He said it twice.'

'I don't believe him.'

'Some women have great recuperative powers,' he said with considerable irony.

She disliked him just then and said rather angrily, 'You're very unsympathetic to a girl who's expecting a baby.'

'*What did you say?*' The voice was so rough that she stared.

'Jenny's pregnant. I told you last night.'

'You did no such thing.'

'I'm sorry. I thought I had.'

'Does your brother know?' he demanded.

'Apparently not. She told her father yesterday and *he* told

537

me. I don't know anything but that. I haven't seen or spoken to Jenny.'

He still glared. 'How could you possibly have forgotten to tell me last night?' She waited, confessing her own selfishness in silence. Suffering was selfish. She had lost her brother and lost Tom's love. It had pushed Jenny out of her thoughts. 'This changes everything,' he said.

'You mean they must come back. Be brought back.'

'I mean it changes everything,' he repeated impatiently. Lisa hadn't the courage to ask again.

The rest of the morning entailed the practicalities of two people coping with a sudden death. Lisa telephoned Perdita to explain that she couldn't be at work and her employer, full of interest said, 'Charles is a mutt. Don't hurry back. Tomorrow will do perfectly well.'

Tom spent some time on his knees in the sitting-room, collecting and collating the stepping stones of manuscripts on the floor. He was also on the telephone for half an hour, first to a director, then to somebody else – it sounded as if he were speaking to an actor. Lisa felt out of place, at a loose end and longed to get away. When between telephone calls she said so, he looked put out and said, 'I shall not be five minutes.' Half an hour dragged by. Finally she went into the bedroom, put on her hat, and fished her car keys from her handbag. She returned to the sitting-room. He was still on the telephone but he put out his hand, caught her arm and mouthed with his hand over the mouthpiece, 'Wait, darling!'

The telephone call continued. It must be the same actor who had rung before; Lisa remembered in the previous conversation Tom had called him 'Jonathan'. By Tom's replies she gathered the actor was asking how some of the words in the text of the play could be interpreted. The make-believe struck her, listening to Tom speaking of a character in his play with the same intensity he'd used last night when she'd told him Gemma was gone. Do they know what is real and what is make-believe? she wondered. Does he?

All *she* knew was that she was unhappy and wanted to get away. He affected her. She had been through too much, and to be here listening to his voice with its familiar cadences was like hearing a language she used to speak perfectly and which now eluded her.

He rang off at last.

'I'm sorry. I expect you think that I shouldn't have bothered with all that?'

'Of course I don't. It is part of your work.'

He rubbed his chin. 'Writing's a peculiar job at the best of times. I sometimes wish I did something more satisfying. Carpentry, for instance.' He looked at her with a hint of comedy.

In India he had told her that he loved carpentry and had been good at it as a boy at school. They had watched a woodcarver dexterously working in teak and Tom said how satisfying the work was. You used your hands, made things which were useful as well as decorative. Metal was hard and needed heat. Clay had to be baked. But wood was a pleasure when you handled it, and it smelled so good.

'Aren't dramatists like actors?' said Lisa, setting aside the idea of Tom at a lathe. 'Holding a mirror up to nature?'

'I wish the mirror wasn't clouded. It always, always is. Now. Will you drive ahead or shall I? I admit I prefer to be leader.'

She was very surprised. 'I didn't know you were coming back to Stratford.'

'Of course I am. I must pack up the Avoncliffe flat. More important, we must go and see Guy Bowden and your sister-in-law. I had an impression he did not intend to let us see her. We can but try.'

Lisa had wanted to leave him and to drive home alone, but found instead that she was following his car on the road to Warwickshire. It was a very different journey from last night because Tom, after all, shared the burden. He drove better and faster than she did. Now and again she lost sight of him, only to see him waiting at the side of the road giving an ironic thumbs-up sign. He seemed in good spirits. He's sure Gemma will come back and bring the little boy, Lisa thought. He hasn't lost Bobbie as I've lost Charles.

When she drove into Woodstock, she saw that Tom had stopped again. He'd already parked and was standing on the pavement by a row of little shops, waving energetically. She drew to a stop.

'Lunch?' he asked.

'That would be nice.'

'I think we need a meal. Did you have anything to eat last night? I thought not. And I never gave you a bite –'

'Hot milk and brandy.'

'Not enough to keep body and soul together. We need a good meal if we're going to cope with Guy Bowden. What do you say to The Bear?'

The old inn, comfortable and intimate on the dark autumn day, glowed with open fires as The Shakespeare had done when she, Charles and Jenny had lived there.

'This is the first hot meal I've eaten at lunchtime since Hildegarde Altmann appeared at the shop,' she said.

Tom asked her, of course, who she was speaking about. Lisa had already made up her mind to tell him the story, for Polly had recently mentioned to her that Peter was no longer set on keeping his nationality a secret.

'He thinks, if we do it casually, people will get used to the idea,' Polly had said.

Tom was deeply interested, and when she had finished the tale said thoughtfully, 'So your friend couldn't believe anybody in this country would accept a man who had been in U-boats?'

'That's what he thought. He wasn't right, was he? People only talk about the war now to tell adventure stories. Look at Perdita. I think *she* looks on the war as a sort of interlude . . . Of course I don't know how strong anti-German feelings are in Britain. I suppose there are people who can't forgive Germany, just as in their country . . . but it was different in India. We were never bombed in spite of those endless air raid warnings. In any case "the enemy" we talked about were the Japanese.'

'Yes, they were the enemy,' he said dryly.

She went on with her thought. 'Peter's a very serious

man,' she said. 'He must be sure there is still anti-German feeling about. He went to such trouble covering his tracks. Apparently he was quite a hero in the war, he won the Iron Cross. I didn't know that. Polly found it hidden under his socks.'

He said abruptly, 'Peter Lang used to be very fond of you.'

'Who told you so?'

'Stratford's a small place. People know about each other. Besides, I saw you with him once or twice.'

'I didn't see you!'

'No, you were with a companion and enjoying yourself.'

'He's a nice man.' She fended it off.

'Yet you gave him up.'

He did not ask why and she had a sensation of freedom which she didn't want.

Without a sound, gradually, almost indiscernibly, winter was creeping towards the countryside. When they left The Bear it was already almost dusk, and by the time they drew up outside Whitefriars there were lights shining out through latticed windows.

'What a superb place,' Tom said as they walked to the front door. 'I've noticed it occasionally when driving past.'

Guy opened the front door before Tom had time to ring the bell. He had been watching for them.

'You're early.' He was all practical hospitality. 'You had a good drive from town?'

He took them into the great ordered room which had the quality of matching any and every kind of English weather. The silky stone floors were cool in summer. Now the room, sparkling with a log fire, looked warm, intimate. The usual mass of dogs jostled each other on the rug.

'No news, I take it?' said Guy, immediately after asking them to sit down. He did not look at Lisa but at Tom. She'd become, as she had been long ago, a 'mere' woman again. One of the dogs, a wolfhound, remembered Lisa and came padding over to lay a long, pointed head on her knee. *He*

541

liked women. When she put her hand on his rough head, he shut his eyes.

'My wife may decide to write to me from wherever they have gone or she may not. I simply don't know,' said Tom with no particular emphasis.

Faintly, distantly, Lisa remembered that Guy Bowden's wife had left him. Hadn't she also run away, and was that why he was regarding Tom in a friendly manner? The housekeeper appeared with tea which Guy poured out. As he handed Lisa a cup he went so far as to address a remark to her.

'Jenny will be down directly. She's been having a nap.' Lisa nodded and said nothing.

Guy was dressed in his usual fine tweeds, a woven tie the colour of love-in-the-mist, greenish and blueish, tied in a broad knot. The colour reflected his clear eyes. He looked soldierly. Were you really in Military Intelligence? she mused. I wish I'd asked when things were different between us. You wouldn't have told me much, but it would have been fun to provoke you. I could have teased you about Peter. She hadn't known until now, when it was too late, how much she'd liked his regard for her. Now he wasn't interested and treated her with courtesy and a mind elsewhere.

'There's something I must say, Mr Westbury,' he said, after studying his fingernails for a moment. 'To Lisa as well, of course. It is about my daughter's pregnancy. Lisa told you Jenny is expecting a child next spring?'

'Yes. Apparently Charles doesn't know. Perhaps if he'd been told –'

'No, no,' interrupted Guy. 'You're going to say if he'd known he wouldn't have left her. All I can say to that is that I'm glad she didn't tell him. This desertion was bound to happen. I am sorry if I offend you. But better to let it rip. Get it over. I was never comfortable about the marriage. Lisa can bear me out.' He acknowledged her, but scarcely looked at her as he went on. 'Charles Whitfield may be – I suppose I must admit he *is* attractive to the opposite sex.

542

Women run after him as he does after them. My daughter tumbled down like a heap of child's bricks. I know Lisa has a soft spot for him –'

'I love him,' Lisa cut in, smashing up the English euphemisms.

'I daresay you do,' he said. 'But what I want to say is this. If they come back,' again he was addressing Tom, 'and from what you said to me on the telephone this morning I gather you think that's possible?'

'Probable.'

'All the worse. *When* they return, Jenny doesn't wish to have anything to do with him. She will refuse to see him. Since this is the situation, we prefer, if and when you hear from either of them, that her pregnancy isn't mentioned.'

Tom faced this with consideration and finally made a cool enquiry: 'Do you think that decision is right?'

'I most certainly do. He has no claim on her or the child now he's abandoned her.'

'Those are rules we don't keep as rigorously as we used to do.' Tom's voice was mild.

Guy appeared to turn the point over in his mind and having fairly looked at it, shook his head. Lisa thought: where's Jenny in all this? Where *is* she, come to that? Here they are talking her over like some abstract moral dilemma, and all she does is hide. Does she intend to let her father speak for her from now on? She used to do that when she was a girl. She isn't one any more.

'The only rules which interest me, Mr Westbury, are those which will give my daughter the necessary comfort and peace of mind. And – yes – some protection. You can't deny she would have been in better shape' – Guy didn't seem to realize the ludicrous *double entendre* – 'if she'd never set eyes on Charles Whitfield. If I appear old-fashioned, well, that's what I am. I've told you what she wishes and what I wish too. Ah, here she is.'

He stood up. Tom also got to his feet as the girl entered the room. The scene had some of Guy's middle-aged formality; both men remained standing while Jenny crossed the room.

Lisa looked at her anxiously and eagerly. Jenny wore an unbecoming black velvet dress Lisa had never seen before. It must be something Jenny had dug out of her daughterly wardrobe in Whitefriars. It made her paleness and awkwardness worse. There were rings under her eyes, her hair looked stringy and lifeless.

She pushed a cheek in Lisa's direction. No kiss as usual.

'Hello, Lisa.'

'Jenny.'

Forced to print a kiss on the cheek so meaninglessly offered, Lisa also squeezed Jenny's arm. The girl did not appear to notice. She went over and sat down close to her father, like a dog within its master's radius. She gave Tom a brief nod and that was all. Does she remember, thought Lisa aghast, that this is the man who saved her life? I suppose she's blotted out the whole thing. Perhaps that's best.

Nothing was said about Charles after Jenny appeared. She and her father behaved as if he didn't exist. They ignored his sin against her and treated Tom and Lisa as if they had come to pay a social call. They offended Lisa deeply. Her sympathy dried up. What they were doing was unnatural; she disliked it and disliked them. Jenny, however, did speak about her dog.

'Honey ran away this morning, stupid old thing. He padded off all the way to Lyndhurst.' Jenny didn't call the house 'home'. 'Daddy had to go and get him. He guessed where he'd gone.'

'He was sitting on the doorstep howling,' said Guy jovially.

'Now he's in the kitchen making up to Mrs Dickens, said Jenny with more vivacity than when seeing her sister-in-law. 'Mrs D. spoils him. If I don't watch out, Honey will get fat on kitchen scraps.'

Lisa looked about for something to say in this false atmosphere. She inquired about Paintbox and Jenny, again with life in her voice, talked about the horse.

'He's no trouble. He's still out in the field as the weather's so mild.'

Tom joined in and there was more meaningless chat which appeared to content the Bowdens but filled Lisa with disgust. They were being courageous. She despised their way of showing it.

At last Tom stood up. Lisa followed suit and they made their adieux. Am I supposed to congratulate her on the baby? wondered Lisa. It was impossible. Guy, not Jenny, walked with them to the door and Lisa lingered for a moment.

'Guy.'

'My dear?' A warning note.

'Don't you want me to pack up Jenny's things and see to the house and so on? There's an awful lot to be done.'

'I have already had her clothes and bits and bobs brought here. Many thanks, but there's nothing needed on that score. Good of you.'

'But the house –'

'I scarcely think we can dismantle it,' he said with a slight laugh. 'Particularly if what Mr Westbury guesses proves to be right.'

This time he did not walk with Lisa to her car but stood at the entrance of the house, giving them a sort of civilian salute. Then he disappeared, shutting the door behind him.

Tom and Lisa were alone in the dusk by the parked cars.

'Mm,' said Tom, opening the car door for her. 'Some adversary.'

'My brother's, you mean?'

'And Gemma's. Yours and mine as well, if we don't toe the party line. I'd say he could be a pretty good opponent of actual events if he doesn't like what is hoving into view. Well, Lisa, where to now?'

'I could make us some more tea.'

'Good idea.'

They drove away from Whitefriars into the falling darkness. Lisa felt weighed down in spirit.

By Guy's hard way of receiving her. By Jenny's empty manner and the thrust-out cheek which meant exactly what it was, a lack of warmth to somebody who loved her. She had a recurring sense of loss.

Tom's rear light shone as he drove ahead towards the deserted house. The fox will soon be back, thought Lisa, and the hare and the pheasants.

She unlocked her door and preceded him up the stairs. In the flat she went about switching on lights and an electric fire and, in the kitchen, filling the kettle. While she stood at the sink he came up behind her and put his arms round her waist, as he used to do in India. She did not relax and lean against him. She stayed tense. He kissed the nape of her neck.

'I love that bit of you. It's very touching. It isn't as sure as you are.'

'Let me go, Tom. I must make the tea.'

'So you must. Did you think the Bowden tea was somewhat fierce? That bright red.'

'I expect it is what Guy likes.'

'Very probably. It suits him.'

He released her and went into the sitting-room. She felt shivery as she followed him with the tray and set it down on a low table. After Whitefriars, the floors like grey silk, the painted shields, the medieval spread of dogs, Lisa thought her room as bare as a cell. It had never looked like that to her before and she thought: it isn't the room that's changed. I am less than I was.

Tom sat with his elbows on his knees, leaning forward and watching the girl who knelt by the table. The light from the electric fire shone on her thin cheeks and a crescent of dark hair. Neither of them spoke for a while. They sat drinking their tea, seemingly in separate worlds. In the corner of the room Rory stood motionless and Lisa, looking at his faded wooden face thought: Bobbie ought to have ridden on him. I wish he had.

She made an effort to break the silence which had become oppressive.

'You haven't met Jenny before, have you?'

'No. I've seen her once or twice, usually at Wardrobe parties enjoying herself. I've never spoken to her until today.'

'What did you think?'

'Cowed.'

'Oh, surely not!'

'I would be, wouldn't you?' he somewhat flippantly said.

'Never. There was a time when Guy was quite fond of me. He doesn't scare me. It sounds conceited but I believe I could have managed him very well. If I'd cared for him, that is. He's the kind of man who lets a person do anything with him if he happens to love her.'

'Not with his daughter. Not just now.'

'I wish you hadn't said that about her being cowed. Why did you?'

'Something in her eyes. I believe she's in a bad way. Of course the early months of pregnancy can make a woman feel pretty ill. Sick all the time and a sensation of having a prolonged dose of 'flu. It wears off as the months go by.'

'How experienced you sound.'

'I had a blow by blow account from Gemma. When we first married she was rehearsing for the rôle of a pregnant, unmarried woman. She read every book about pregnancy she could lay hold of in the public library. She hadn't read a word on the subject, she said, when expecting Bobbie. She became a walking expert on pregnancy in its various forms, spent hours on her make-up and argued with the designer about the padding for her stomach. She played the rôle with a very pale face and a lot of lines and shadows. When I walked into her dressing-room I scarcely recognized her. She used to enjoy describing her symptoms in the play to me . . . most dramatic.'

'So you think,' said Lisa, taking this in, 'Jenny feels ill.'

'Ill and sad. Don't be anxious about her, Lisa. Her father may behave like a martinet but he'll look after her almost too well. And you can't take your brother's actions on those little shoulders. The burden's too heavy. Come here. Nearer to me.'

'I'm okay.'

'No, you are not and neither am I. Come close.' She scrambled awkwardly across until she was within his reach.

He put a hand on her arm. 'I've made up my mind about something. I decided it when we were driving to Woodstock, which is why I daresay I seemed cheerful in spite of the shocks that flesh is heir to. I think I can calculate more or less accurately how long they'll be gone.' He took her hand, looking down at it like a man who is holding a bird. She sat uncomfortably, not close enough to relax. 'They'll be away four months. Five at the outside. Just about the time their money will last, unless Gemma works that spell of hers and gets some acquaintance to lend them more. But who does she know except people in England? Yes, I think they'll be back, unless your brother's richer than I imagine.'

'Poorer. He said so to me recently.'

'Then it's four months. Gemma has saved most of her SMT salary and she will now be going through it like a drunken sailor. She's a profligate creature, there isn't a mean bone in her body. They're sure to have gone abroad. She's been dying to go. She loathed being stuck here during the war and she was deadly jealous when Charles took his wife to Italy. She's like a plant needing the sun. Before the war she lived for four months in the South of France, making some twopenny-halfpenny movie and adoring the whole thing. My guess is they'll be back January or February. God knows whether they'll have had enough of each other by then,' he continued. 'How long do such things last? It's on the cards, it's possible that Gemma will want to return to me. She'll have no money, she'll need a safety net, she'll be thirsting to act again, and she'll want somebody for Bobbie. There's another point. Gemma was offered the chance to join Tony Quayle's company next year. Big parts too. She's properly messed that up and she'll need to start getting back into various good books to reinstate her career.'

'You have it all worked out,' Lisa said. She took her hand out of his. Her arm was aching.

'Of course this is all guesswork. As for your brother, Guy Bowden knows the governing force, the absolute in all this is Jenny's baby. Even if Charles is still in my wife's toils, he may feel forced to return to his wife and child. How do you imagine Charles will feel when he eventually hears about the baby?'

'Shattered with guilt all over again.'

'Is he fond of children? He seemed to have a soft spot for Bobbie.'

'Did he? I don't know how he feels about them. He's never said.'

'Men without kids don't,' agreed Tom. 'But Guy Bowden knows, no one better, how a man feels about his own child, and for Charles to resume his marriage is just what he's determined to stop. Who's to say he isn't right?'

'*You* didn't think he was when he said that.'

'At first I didn't. Now I am not sure.'

'If all this happens the way you think it will,' she said, desolation creeping into her, 'and Gemma comes back to you and Guy keeps hold of his daughter, where does that leave Charles?'

'Where he is now.'

She said wearily, 'I don't understand you.'

'It leaves him with Gemma, which is what I want to tell you. What I decided this morning when we drove from London. It's over, Lisa. I intend to divorce her. That will mean losing Bobbie which cracks my heart. But he's Gemma's son, she'd never let me have him. What I *can* do is cut her out of my life before she gets worse. I suppose I was wrong to take her on,' he continued. 'It's true she's beautiful and sexy, but that wasn't why. She was so unhappy, poor thing. Divorced, with no work and a sick child on her hands. Isn't that the most awful reason for marriage? I was sorry for her. Sexually attracted, of course – she's good at that. But never for a minute in love. I was in love with somebody else. A girl I believed had forgotten me, as I could never, never forget her. Well, Lisa?'

He looked intently at her. Between them were suppressed passions, heart-searchings, and only the beginnings of belief.

'Well?' he repeated. 'Will you have me? Will you let me have you?'

\*

The snow fell all night in Champéry but by morning it had stopped. The people who lived in the little mountain town looked with approval from their windows at the thick fresh covering to the familiar whiteness. It shrouded the sloping chalet roofs and the branches of the pines which crowded halfway up the slopes. Above were the pure heights against a sky already pure blue.

When Bobbie woke in the room which adjoined that of his mother and Charles, he saw the frost stars covering the windows and the snow which each morning was thicker on the window-sill, like icing sugar on a rich Christmas cake. He did not climb out of bed and go into the next room. He didn't even knock on the door. His mother slept deeply and late and Bobbie would lie in bed thinking about her and the day soon to start, and waiting until she came.

At last she did. She always did. To embrace him and sit on his bed and give him sweet-smelling kisses and let him plait the russet hair which poured down her back. She liked wrapping him in her arms and hugging him so tight that he could scarcely breathe. She ordered croissants for his breakfast and sat beside him, dipping them into his milk and feeding him like a sucking lamb. She made the croissants horridly soggy and Bobbie meekly ate them, loving her much too much to say he disliked the messy, dripping fragments of bread and preferred them crisp and flaky.

It seemed to the little boy whose entire life consisted of only four years that it was a distant age since he had lived in the stables of a big country house, ridden his tricycle in the gardens and played with Sally Aston. The months since he and the two grown-ups had left England made a great segment of time. They were his 'now'. He accepted the enormous change with nervous philosophy. One autumn morning before it was light he'd been taken out of bed by a mother giggling and crying. She had dressed him, her eyes full of tears. That hadn't frightened him because his mother often cried; she even cried sometimes when she laughed. He was dressed in thick clothes and wrapped in a blanket, and she carried him in her arms downstairs to a car waiting outside. It was dark. There were whispered instructions and more stifled, excited giggling.

'Isn't Tom coming with us?'

'He went to London last night, darling.'

The practical reply satisfied him and when he saw it was Charles driving the car, he felt comfortable and dozed off during the journey to London.

The trio set off on their travels. First to London, where they sold the car, glad of the extra cash, then to a stuffy hotel in northern France and later after a long train journey to another hotel in Provence. To his mother's loud exclamations of disappointment and astonishment – she had been here once before years ago – the weather was bad. Rain fell heavily day after day, it was cold and damp. When, wearing macintoshes, the three walked on the beach it was covered in seaweed and there were branches from trees washed up from an island you could scarcely see through the spray from huge, thundering waves. The sea frightened him, and so did the deserted, desolate beaches.

'Isn't it nasty, Bobbie?' cried Gemma as they trudged back to their hotel. 'Charles, isn't it beastly?'

Just before Christmas they left France. Both Gemma and Bobbie had heavy colds and in any case the hotel was closing until March. They piled all their luggage, trunks, boxes, baskets like those used for taking animals on journeys and filled with Bobbie's toys, and took a train from France through the night to Champéry. When they woke after a night's sleep – there were the Alps. Bobbie had never seen a mountain before and these climbed to the sky.

The very morning they arrived he was given his first lesson in skiing. His mother had learned years ago and liked showing off to Charles who was less of a natural skier than she was. Gemma skimmed down the mountain like a bird, hallooing and making her voice echo round the mountains, the sound following as her shadow did. Bobbie now had his lesson every morning. His teacher was painstaking and the child made progress; he wanted to fly as his mother did.

He enjoyed the great, rich hotel, the Swiss food, the

servants who spoiled the dignified little fellow. In the way of the very young he forgot his stepfather. He was happy.

Charles was happy too. The guilt he'd felt about Jenny, the dreadful sense of having sinned against her, was gone at last. It had oppressed and haunted him and now it grew lighter and lighter and finally blew away. Possessing Gemma, lying in her silken arms, knowing her sexual joys, excited and lustful, burying his face in her bosom, between her legs, in her scented hair, he was more satisfied than ever in his life. Perhaps to fall in love when you are a sensualist means you fall too hard, he thought. You're too used to sex and too confident and that's when you break your neck.

The morning when he'd seen her by the weir he had known a kind of awful inevitability like the tolling of a bell. He knew he couldn't live without her; he would rather be dead. Now she was his and night after night he learned the sharp and seemingly endless mysteries of what lay inside her body. Nothing slaked his returning thirst and nothing diminished it.

This morning when he woke and saw the fresh snowfall through a window misted from the central heating, he thought of her skill when skiing and compared it to her arts in bed. Was there nothing Gemma couldn't do more exquisitely than any other woman? He turned to wake her and found he wanted her again. She stirred and smiled, eyes shut, mouth and legs open to embrace him.

When they finished making love, Charles rang for breakfast. Gemma, untidy and with burning cheeks – she always had a high colour after sex – went into her son's room, her satin gown trailing on the ground.

She kissed and hugged him. They exchanged ridiculous jokes.

'Listen, do you know this one, Mummy?' He whispered something.

'Bobbie! I'm shocked! Who's teaching you such rude things?'

Breakfast arrived. Brown earthenware bowls of coffee, croissants, black cherry jam. Bobbie came into his mother's bedroom, climbed into bed with both of them and had his breakfast, his little body pressed for companionship against Charles. Gemma poured the coffee and discovered an envelope tucked under the basketful of rye toast. She licked her jammy fingers and said scornfully, 'Monsieur Schiller doesn't half drop hints. I've already told him we'll pay. He really must stop nagging during breakfast.'

'The bill?' said Charles, not scornful.

'Of course. Huge, too.'

Charles muttered that he wished to Christ *he* could pay it right away.

Bobbie, deaf when grown-ups talked to each other, arranged the sugar lumps in the basin. They were wrapped in coloured paper, blue, yellow, scarlet and patterned to look like dice.

Gemma said comfortingly, 'Don't be an idiot, Charles. Of course I shall pay the blasted bill. I've still got heaps and you know perfectly well we're going to blow the lot. Then you can win some for me. What's that lovely phrase they use in the Bulldog Drummond books? "His fortune hung on the turn of a card". You'd better start playing again, darling Charles.'

'How do you know I'll win?'

'Because you're a lucky sod,' she said, giving him a pinch. 'Anyway, I'll pay the old miser and put him out of his misery. I made him wait this week to tease him. I like seeing his fat little face when he purses his lips. He's like a vicar. And he does so hate not getting his fat little hands on our cash.'

She trailed into the bathroom to have a bath, then came out wrapped in an enormous white towel to fetch Bobbie and give him his bath, dropping the towel and climbing naked into the water with him. She told him a long, frightening fairy story from Grimm. Charles heard the actress's practised voice with all its colour and drama. 'The witch put the children into a cage and every morning she came to see them and her bony fingers prodded them like *this*.' She told the story so well that Bobbie screamed.

Later Gemma rang for the chambermaid who had become

her slave; Gemma was used to slaves. With a queenly gesture at her son, now dressed in two vests and small long johns to keep his legs warm, she said, 'Finish dressing Master Bobbie for me, Greta *Liebchen*, then he has to go to Herr Edelstein for his lesson. Learning to ski now means he'll be a champion when he's grown up. Children are so bold. It's fun to watch them.'

Greta did not think little English Bobbie was bold at all, but knelt down to dress him in stout boots and quilted coat and woolly hat. He thumped away with her, hand in hand. Gemma was kneeling on the window-sill admiring the landscape.

'Do you know what? This is ideal weather. In fact it's perfect. Sun out. Fresh powder snow which fell last night and a nice solid base underneath all packed down hard. Glorious skiing. Look at the slopes!'

Charles was glad that he was now almost as good a skier as she. He had learned when he was young, his father in a rare spurt of generosity having sent him to stay with a family of wealthy friends at Zermatt. When he came to Champéry he was pleased to discover that he had not lost all his skill.

'It's like riding,' Gemma said on their first day in the mountains. 'Or acting, come to that. I've always thought of it as a confidence trick. It's your confidence that tells you you can go fast, do dramatic turns or stops. You know that if things go wrong you can cope. But if your confidence wavers . . . boy, you can't do anything on skis!'

She had loved skiing since she'd first learned at seventeen. It had been hell during the war to realize one would never set eyes on a mountain, never fix on a pair of skis. She had been to Switzerland before the war as Charles had done, but in very different circumstances.

'Did I ever tell you about it, Charles?'

'I don't think so. What happened?'

Gemma smiled, ready for the story. She was like Scheherazade in *The Arabian Nights*. 'There were three of us, all actresses just starting at Worthing rep, and we had some time off when the theatre went dark before the winter season. We pooled our money and travelled third class and got to Montreux. There was only one hotel open, a vast Victorian edifice, very fancy, all plush and gilt, and we went and bearded the manager. We were all, I might add, good-lookers.'

'Still are.'

'Thank you, darling, I was expecting that. So we were very, very charming to the manager and got round him, and he gave us huge pompous rooms at the teeniest rate. What a time we had. Then we went up to the mountains and stayed in a ski chalet . . . mad affairs with handsome ski-instructors all called Franz. It was a case of *schlafen mit dem Wörterbuch*.' She looked at him, hoping he'd ask for a translation.

'Sleeping with the dictionary?'

'Clever old you. How many teachers have *you* pleasured, and learning what?'

'Eastern women teach only about love.'

'I know, I know. It shows in your technique, Charles. I often feel like one of those bits of rude Indian sculpture with the girl wearing a broad grin and her legs wrapped round the man like pincers.'

They giggled. Their jokes were always to do with sex. If Gemma fascinated him with her stories of theatre love affairs, Charles in turn told her of the East. Before the war in Burma he'd had a sixteen-year-old mistress the colour of copper who believed sex with him gave her magical powers. The more they made love the more she could turn him into her slave. It was she who told him the greatest sexual pleasure was supposed to be had under water. But you had to learn 'certain sounds'.

'Oh, oh, can you remember one?'

'Vaguely. It sounded like this. Honggg . . . honggg.'

Gemma laughed so much she nearly fell out of bed.

Down in the hotel's vast, wide-windowed restaurant decorated in crimson and gold, with a panorama of snowy mountains outside the windows, and heat and the smell of expensive food indoors, everybody was eating breakfast – croissants, black cherry jam, oat cakes, coffee – and staring out at the new-fallen virgin snow.

555

It was well after eleven by the time Charles and Gemma left the hotel. They had changed into heavy canvas jackets, carried skis on their shoulders and went to catch the funicular which would take them up to the highest point of the piste. As they emerged into the dazzling sunshine Charles noticed that a wind had sprung up. The atmosphere was not what he'd expected. It wasn't as cold as it had been yesterday, but was slightly warmer, slightly muggy.

Gemma didn't notice that anything had changed. She was excited at the prospect of the morning's skiing. To be the first down the mountain, to leave her tracks, turning and turning again in perfect curves on the untouched whiteness of the new snow was the goal of all powder skiers. Her eyes behind the smoky glasses shone as they did when she was onstage.

They left the funicular and made their way to a kind of plateau from which they could ski down the still untouched slopes. Charles noticed the wind again. It was stronger here on the heights, blowing steadily and making flurries of the soft powder round their feet. Standing surveying the panorama, the dark spread of pine trees through which Gemma had decided to thread her difficult way, and the more distant bulge of a great bluff, was Hans Ziffer. He was a mountain guide and the leading ski instructor of the region, a tall, narrow-chested man who looked as if he'd never taken part in any form of sport in his life. His nose was long and red at its pointed end like a wooden puppet's. His ears stuck out. He was physically unattractive and Gemma always referred to him to Charles as 'poor Hans'.

But Hans in motion was the most extraordinary of skiers, arrow-swift, effortless, daring, perfection to watch. He bade them a polite good morning, bowing his head and standing very stiff.

'The *Föhn* is blowing, Herr Whitfield,' he said.

Charles knew the name of the wind. Utterly unpredictable, when it blew across the mountains everybody dreaded it. The atmosphere grew muggy, the snow sticky, the temperatures rose and the snow began to break up, turning into leg-breaking slush before nightfall.

Gemma sighed loudly. 'Oh *Hans*. I don't think it's the *Föhn* at all.'

'It is the *Föhn*,' he repeated.

She made the martyred face of a spoilt child. She was poised, gazing down at the untouched whiteness sparkling in the sunshine, imagining the tracks she'd make, the thrill of her speed, the challenge to do something beautifully, to make perfect turns and patterns, to use the terrain and to experience the delight of knowing she could do the impossible and do it superbly.

Hans pointed to the bluff known as the *Brustkorb* – the 'woman's breast' – which shone pure white, the wind just ruffling its rounded surface. 'That must not be taken, Frau Whitfield.' He had seen Gemma skiing from its top, racing down its full steep curves.

'But it's my favourite and nobody's been anywhere near it this morning. Hans, don't be a *Dummkopf*.' She often called him that and he was never offended because she was beautiful.

He said unsmilingly that conditions were 'not satisfactory. It is after eleven o'clock and with the *Föhn* now blowing, it is dangerous in many places to ski for the rest of today.'

'But the snow's perfect.'

'Now, yes. But every minute less so. There' – he pointed from where they were standing to the piste falling away below them – 'there, yes, for another hour, maybe. There' – gesturing at the *Brustkorb* – 'no. Always respect the *Föhn*.'

Gemma turned while he was refastening his glove and gave Charles a music-hall wink. She was in her daring mood. It came on her sometimes when she was at her most actressy; she showed off like a child. It was as if she could conquer not only every man in the world but the world itself. It was this mood that had first brought Charles to her feet and to her mercy, and although *she* was physically in his thrall, it was Gemma, in all her strength, who was the ruler.

They began to move in unison, Charles and she. Their speed grew faster, the powder snow flew up on either side with a hiss, music to the ears of people who love the swift sport. They swerved and turned in graceful movements. Gemma suddenly laughed.

'There, *yes*!'

She shouted aloud, giving Charles an urchin's grin and with a faultless turn of her skis was away towards the *Brustkorb*, skimming like the swallow she was, effortless, airy. She began to make the calling, hallooing noise that skiers use at their most joyful.

As he turned to follow her there was a noise like low thunder – a yell from far above him – and with a speed the eye could not follow, an avalanche came rolling from the icy curve of the mountain, rolling in pursuit of the single figure, hungry to take her in its giant arms.

It took twelve hours. They worked by flares fixed to avalanche poles in the snow. Charles, standing like a statue or a rock, was not allowed to help the guides assembled to dig through the enormous masses of fallen ice and snow in places thirty or forty feet high. They used more avalanche poles pushed into the snow, to see if they could find her. Every time he tried to help they refused, saying in angry German that there was a way to look and a way to find, an amateur could injure a human being and it was possible – yes, yes, it was a thousand to one chance but it had been known – there could be an airlock and the woman would be unconscious but alive.

They were the worst twelve hours of Charles's life. Nothing he'd known in the Burma war, when he'd fought hand to hand in the jungle with half starving enemy soldiers, when he'd lived with fever in the drowning jungle, nothing he'd suffered when poor Jenny tried to kill herself, was like this. The pain was so terrible that afterwards he relived its excruciating agony in dreams and woke shouting.

He stood in the dark on the plateau and watched the flares and the figures moving over the frozen snow. He hadn't told the little boy, who had been deliberately taken by Greta to a party on the other side of the town and kept there to stay the night.

Charles stood freezing and silent until he heard what he waited beyond bearing to hear: the sudden echo of shouts. He skied down towards the tumbled masses of the fallen avalanche, arriving just as they were dragging something out of a kind of icy cave they had made in the snow. The doctor who was in the rescue team threw himself on the ground. He bent over the body. Charles arrived as the man looked up and shook his head.

'She has been dead many hours. The snow smothered her.'

The man got to his feet and stood looking down at Gemma whose cap and glasses and hood were gone. Her thick red hair lay round her ice-white face.

To Charles the days that followed went by with no colour or smell. It was as if he, too, were buried under a mountain of snow. He behaved with a certain automatic grace, remembering to thank every person connected with the tragedy, the guides, the doctor. He wrote cheques – God knew if the bank would meet them. He wrote to the manager of the bank in Birmingham explaining the circumstances and saying he would call to see him on his return to England. In any case the manager knew of his securities.

He did not tell Bobbie his mother was dead, only that she had 'gone away for a while'. The little boy said nothing but did not eat for three days. He pushed away his food, said he was sorry, got down from the table leaving meal after meal, having simply crumbled a bread roll. No coaxing or tender patience had any effect. Bobbie didn't sleep either and when Charles went into his room on the first night after Gemma's death he found the child, his wide-open eyes seeming enormous in the dim light, and carried him back to his own bed. After that Bobbie slept in Gemma's place beside him. No, he didn't sleep. He just lay there conscious of Charles's body next to his.

On the third afternoon Bobbie did fall into a restless slumber after refusing to eat anything at midday. Charles was sitting at the desk in his bedroom writing to Lisa – or trying to – when the chambermaid came into the room.

'Herr Whitfield. I must speak with you.'

'What is it, Greta?'

'Bobbie knows.'

Charles started. 'It's impossible. Nobody has told him.'

'Yes. Little Ursula Strauss did. The morning it happened. She was supposed to have her ski lesson and they said not, and all the guides were speaking of it.' Greta's eyes brimmed. 'Children are so funny. He will never say what he knows. Not to me. Not to you. But you must take him away from here, Herr Whitfield, he hates it.'

'Did he tell you so?'

'Oh yes. This morning. Very polite in that little way of his and said he was grieved to say such a thing.' She gave a sob.

Charles booked the tickets that afternoon.

When the long train journey through the mountains had begun and Charles had tucked Bobbie up in his bunk in the sleeper, it looked as if the boy would sleep at last. Later, in the dim blue lamp of the compartment, Charles climbed from his lower bunk up the velvet-covered ladder to look at him, and found Bobbie, his mouth half open, looking indeed so like his mother that Charles returned to his own bunk and wept.

It seemed to Charles the journey back to England would never end. There were train journeys, interminable waits, the hotel in Paris, the hotel in London. He had brought all Gemma's possessions, trunkfuls of them, and porters fetched trolleys on which to pile the boxes she would never open filled with clothes that smelled of her scent. The anaesthesia which comes from shock, the impossibility of grasping that the woman flying down the snowy slope hallooing to him was dead and buried, that the mistress whose body had stirred him to unbearable joy was gone forever, began to leave Charles. It was as if he began to wake up and sorrow, deadened until now, was the more excruciating.

What was bringing him back to Warwickshire? he thought, as the train went puffing its laborious way through the English countryside. Bobbie had developed the habit since Gemma's death of sitting on his lap and leaning against him.

They watched the stations go by. Bicester. Banbury. At Leamington they left the train and Charles spent time arranging for the huge, unmanageable pile of luggage to be delivered to Lyndhurst by Carter Paterson. Gemma's possessions weighed him down. What was he to do with them?

Holding Bobbie's hand he left the station and found a taxi.

'Where are we going, Charles?'

'Home.'

'I'm glad,' said Bobbie and gave a deep sigh.

Charles didn't known what he himself meant by home. Was the little boy to stay with him or return to Tom – wherever Tom might be? To whom did this small, sensitive scrap of humanity rightly belong? He had sent Lisa a telegram last night to tell her what had happened. He thought: it's like the telegrams people received during the war. He had decided against writing to her after all. A telegram left her no time to respond and in his lacerated misery he couldn't bear sympathy, any sympathy. He gave Lisa the facts and nothing else. He hadn't wired Jenny. How could he?

It was winter in England now. Not the blazing, dazzling mountain winter where the snow literally shone and the sky over the shoulders of the Alps turned mauve and crimson in the sunset. Here the skies hung low and grey, the fields were sodden, the thorny hedges bare. Piles of fallen leaves lay along the edges of the road in blackened pools of water. When the taxi drove up to Lyndhurst, the house looked rain-streaked and shabby. It gave him a shock; he remembered it in summer, warmed by the sun and with life inside it.

He paid the taxi fare and lifted out the little boy. The door of the main house flew open and Lisa and Tom came running out. She threw herself on her knees to kiss Bobbie, then stood up to hug her brother. Tom put out both arms and Bobbie sprang into them. So many kisses.

'Come in, come in.'

Tom went ahead still carrying Bobbie and for the first time since Gemma had been killed Charles heard the boy laugh.

The return was not what Charles had imagined when he'd tried to think what was waiting for him. He came as a visitor to his own house and sat as a stranger in his own, unchanged drawing-room with Lisa beside him and Bobbie on Tom's lap. Lisa and Tom were concerned, delicate. They said nothing of his disappearance, they simply drew him close. While Bobbie was with them they did not talk about Gemma, but about the journey home, and mundane Stratford matters. Lisa told Bobbie about Rory.

'He's our rocking-horse, Charles's and mine. You'll be able to ride him. Nobody has for so long.'

'Poor horse,' said the child.

'Yes. But not any longer.'

Lisa had prepared a meal but the two travellers ate little, and Bobbie began to yawn very soon. Tom said he would put him to bed. As he carried him up the stairs, Charles heard him say, 'We're all staying here in Lyndhurst. Lisa and me, and you and Charles. I'm in the room next door to yours – look! A door between us! I'll leave it open. Isn't your room cosy?' The voice trailed away as they went into the bedroom.

Alone in the drawing-room Lisa looked at her brother.

'Poor Charles. Your wire said nothing about how she died. Mountains are so terrifying. Was it a precipice?'

'No. She was skiing and went down a dangerous slope. They'd told us it was forbidden but Gemma thought that was funny, Lou.' There was a moment's silence. 'I had no time to follow her,' he said as if speaking of a lost golden opportunity. 'The avalanche came rushing out of nowhere. The guides said it travelled at a hundred miles an hour.'

'Poor beautiful woman.'

'Yes. They found her, you know.'

'Oh Charles.'

She didn't know what more to say. When she'd shown Tom the telegram he'd gone ashen with shock and all he'd said was 'Oh God', and then to himself, 'Poor girl, poor girl'. He hadn't wept, had been very silent, and later talked about Bobbie. Now she faced a worse grief.

562

She wondered if she should speak about Jenny and when Charles did not mention her, forced herself to say, 'We haven't told Jenny.'

'Not that I'm back?' He answered as if this was expected of him.

'No, Charles.'

Lisa had only seen Jenny once in all the months since Charles had gone. Her sister-in-law had disappeared as if it had been she who had left England; she had never telephoned or come to Lyndhurst, she'd simply vanished. Once Lisa caught sight of her out riding with her father. She was poised, riding side-saddle, wearing the curious dark habit worn by women of the past. Lisa was sure it was Guy's idea for her to ride in that way; it was more suitable and safer for a pregnant woman. Jenny looked stout and solid, entirely different from the slim girl Charles had married. She'd given Lisa an embarrassed nod and lifted her whip. Guy had raised his cap as if to an enemy.

'Can I get you a drink, Charles?'

Lisa went to a table where Tom had lined up some bottles, poured a gin and tonic and took it to Charles who thanked her and sat without raising the glass to his lips. She looked at him earnestly. The premature lines of the face were no longer fascinating and unexpected. He had grown into those haggard cheeks. What happens to you after such a thing? she wondered.

Tom came back into the room while silence still separated her brother and herself.

'He isn't asleep, is he?' Charles said, looking up.

'As a matter of fact he is. I sat on his bed and he dropped off almost at once. I've left the door open. If he wakes he can see the light on the landing and hear our voices.'

'He hasn't slept at all. Except for a few hours on the train. I didn't tell him. But he found out from a child at the hotel.'

'Did he speak about it to you?'

'No. He's said nothing.'

'He looks worn out,' Tom said. 'A good long sleep will help.'

The two men spoke like fathers.

'Charles,' Tom said, sitting down beside Lisa, 'would you mind if we talked a bit?'

'You mean about Bobbie?'

'Yes. I do.'

'You think he should go back to you?' Lisa saw the look of pity on Tom's face; they both heard the things Charles didn't say.

'I think it would be best. I'm so sorry. But he doesn't look too well,' Tom said.

'I know. I know.' Without being asked, Charles spoke of the child refusing food, the sleepless nights, the silences. 'That was why I came home. For Bobbie.' Not for me, thought Lisa. Not even a little for me. Did he hear his sister's thoughts and see in her face that he had hurt her? He said restlessly, 'I don't seem to know where I am. How I feel. Anything.' He looked from one to the other. 'I particularly don't know where I am with Jenny. I suppose there will be a divorce. It's fair enough.'

Lisa said suddenly, 'Tell him, Tom.' She wanted it said not by the fond sister, the go-between, the sympathetic woman, but from one man to another in the plain language she'd never be able to use. 'Tell him,' she said again.

'Lisa thinks you should know Jenny's expecting a child.'

It was the first time since he'd arrived that they saw life in his face. For a moment he looked as if there was hope somewhere. Lisa watched him, remembering his weakness and Guy's strength. Poor Charles. He loved children, it seemed. He loved the little waif upstairs who was now lost to him, and he was going to be robbed of his own child as well, doing eternal penance for the past. He would say it was worth it. That he'd have done nothing differently and if Gemma came glimmering into the room that moment, he would break his marriage all over again. But would he? In a game between birth and sex she did not know which power would win.

'I'll go and see her,' Charles said and stood up.

'Charles, I'm afraid you can't. She said, or rather her

father said it for her, that they didn't want you to know anything about it. They asked us not to tell you she was pregnant. That wasn't difficult, you were abroad and in any case Lisa never saw Jenny. But Lisa's right. You have to know now.'

'I'll see her,' repeated Charles.

'Guy Bowden won't allow it.'

'Ah. I can but try,' said Charles with a very faint smile.

He asked Lisa if he could borrow her car. They walked with him to the front door and watched him drive away.

Tom shook his head. 'Hell. I don't like to think what will happen. I wish I'd gone with him.'

'Better if he's on his own.'

'Why?'

'I don't know. Instinct,' she said. They returned to the house and sat down in silence. Gemma had not yet lost her power. She was in both their thoughts.

Charles drove the small car with difficulty. The gears were stiff, the engine rough-sounding; he had never driven a car in such bad condition. He wondered why his sister had done nothing about it. The very sound of the engine was enough to set his teeth on edge. He concentrated on the now unfamiliar journey from Lyndhurst to Whitefriars. All he did was drive. He deliberately made his mind go blank about the coming interview and what he was going to say or do. He felt the old sensation which he used to have before gambling, the expectation, tense, tight, that came when he sat down and was dealt a hand of cards. Everything to lose. Everything to win. Except the ice-cold woman in her cave of snow.

When he drew the car to a stop and walked to the door of the house, he thought how rich and ancient and cared-for it looked compared to his own drab, old place. He rang the bell. There was a volley of barks. A man shouted '*Will* you be quiet?' and a girlish voice answer gaily, 'Shout all you like, they won't stop, they never do!'

The door swung open and Jenny stood there.

When she saw him she did not go pale but a deep burning red. She was heavily pregnant, wearing some kind of brown

565

woollen smock with a blue collar and cuffs; the sight of her misshapen body was extraordinary to him. She had become dignified, stately, big, middle-aged. Her fair hair was tied with a girlish ribbon which did not suit the large, slow-moving matron.

Jenny kept her eyes fixed on him as a woman would do when faced with a wild beast, and shouted over her shoulder, 'Daddy.'

'What is it? What's the matter?'

Surrounded by the Whitefriars pack, Guy appeared, saw Charles and pushed Jenny behind him.

'I will not allow you to enter this house.'

Charles was unmoved by Guy's voice and manner which were no longer suave but bullying. He remembered being spoken to by his father's friend in exactly the same way when he was a boy. The effect now gave Charles a kind of vitality. He put his hands in his pockets.

'Jenny,' he called, raising his voice, 'it's you I'm speaking to. Do you want me to go?'

'I repeat, I will not allow you to enter my house,' said Guy, standing four-square. He, too, appeared to be face to face with a wild animal. Charles could see part of his wife, the brown dress, the blonde head hiding behind her father.

'Jenny, if you want me to leave of course I will, and at once. But are you quite sure?'

Guy did not interrupt again but stood guarding her, his mouth tucked into a thin line.

A voice behind him said, 'I am willing to speak to you.'

'My dear child!' exclaimed Guy loudly, wheeling round. It was too late.

She had stepped forward, moving clumsily, and said, 'Come in, Charles. I will see you for a short time. No, Daddy, not with you there. You'll only get angry and that will make me feel ill. I'm sorry but I must see him alone.' She put her hand gently on Guy's arm. Without a word he walked away, followed by the dogs. 'We'll go to my room,' Jenny said.

She led the way up the staircase. Her bulk and weight

made her move slowly and she held on to the banisters. He wanted to help her but dared not. He'd rarely been to the first floor of the house, had seen her room once but never entered it. She opened the door to a spacious chamber fretted with beams, enhanced by long latticed windows, decorated in chintzes patterned with hunting scenes. Horses and hounds galloped across the chairs and curtains. There was every kind of girlish trophy in the room: school photographs, books, a framed photograph of her father, a scatter of china animals. Her father must have kept it untouched from before she married. She motioned him to a chair too small for him and without arms. She sat down on the bed, an elaborately carved four-poster with chintz curtains. She leaned against one of the posts.

Charles scarcely knew the matronly woman calmly regarding him. Where was the slender, adoring girl he had known, the young creature who had wanted to die for love? This woman in her fruitful beauty, with fattened, grave face, seemed cloaked in indifference. A protected stranger. All his sexual power left him when he looked at her. Then unbidden came the memory of a gaping hole in the snow and long, trailing red hair.

'Did you come for a reason, Charles? Have you and Gemma returned to Stratford, then?'

'Gemma is dead. She was killed in an accident in Switzerland.'

Her blue eyes grew large. 'Why didn't you tell us?' He noticed the 'us'.

'It happened five days ago. I've been travelling –' He gave a vague gesture.

'And her little boy?'

'He is going to live with Tom Westbury.'

'Is he his guardian, then?' It was a question his old Jenny would never have thought about.

'I suppose so. Yes. He must be.'

'I see. You've brought him back. What about you?'

'How cold you sound,' he suddenly exclaimed.

She looked faintly surprised. 'Do I? I'm not. Not a bit.

I'm sad for you. You loved her and you must be very unhappy. I would never wish such a thing to happen to you.' She folded her hands across her stomach and said after a moment, 'He moved.'

'What?' he said. He was thinking about Gemma. Her silken figure, jewelled, red–haired, ample, sexual, stood behind him like a ghost in a hideously romantic painting.

'He jumps when I sit down sometimes.'

'Oh. Oh, I see.'

'No, you don't, Charles,' she said, very slightly smiling. 'Wouldn't you like to feel him?' She leaned forward, took his hand in hers and placed it on her belly. Dragged back to the present he waited, nervous, embarrassed, resentful. Suddenly there was a flutter as if a bird were imprisoned there. She let go of his hand. 'Are you interested, at all, in your baby, Charles?' she asked mildly. She raked his face with her eyes, slowly and thoughtfully, with curiosity and in the end with a certain sly amusement. 'I'm not used to you looking –'

'Looking what?' he managed. He had felt a swelling of his heart as if it were expanding after being withered, as if it were growing as her body was.

'At somebody's mercy. It's *him*, isn't it?' She put both hands on her stomach again.

He found it difficult to speak.

'Daddy will be furious,' she said dispassionately. 'But I shall manage him. Do you want to come back, Charles?'

He bent his head and this time she looked at him almost tenderly.

'If I take you back . . . and I could, you know . . . you will have to change. Won't you?'

Charles came home very late that night. Lisa and Tom had already gone to bed, after looking in to see that the little boy still slept.

Alone in the spare room, they undressed and made love in silence. They returned, sighing, blissful, to the country they'd known in India with all its beauty. They made love for a long time and when it ended, Tom wound his arm

568

round her so that whichever way she moved, she could not get free.

'What do you think happened to him, Tom?' she murmured.

'I don't know. I can't guess. She may take him back. You women are beautiful at forgiving.' Then, without knowing he was repeating Jenny's words, he said, 'But if she does, he will have to change.'

Lisa sighed.

'Ah. But will he?'

R2 Smith